Tessa Barclay is a former editor and journalist who has written many successful novels including *A Professional Woman*, the Corvill Weaving series, *A Web of Dreams*, *Broken Threads* and *The Final Pattern* (all available from Headline); the four-part Craigallan saga and the Champagne series. She was born and raised in Edinburgh and is a member of the clan McKenzie. Tessa Barclay now lives and works in south-west London.

Her latest novel, *Gleam of Gold*, is a gripping story of artistic talent, ambition, love and tragedy that moves from Art Deco Paris to the traditionalist Japan of the twenties and the turbulent Pacific of the Second World War.

Gleam of Gold

Tessa Barclay

HEADLINE

First published in 1992
by HEADLINE BOOK PUBLISHING PLC

First published in paperback in 1992
by HEADLINE BOOK PUBLISHING PLC
10 9 8 7 6 5 4 3 2 1

ISBN 0 7472 3862 6

Typeset in 10/10½pt Times by
Falcon Typographic Art Ltd, Fife, Scotland

Printed and bound in Great Britain by
HarperCollins Manufacturing, Glasgow

HEADLINE BOOK PUBLISHING PLC
Headline House
79 Great Titchfield Street
London W1P 7FN

Gleam of
Gold

Chapter One

On the edge of her attention, there was a voice calling her name. But she chose to pay no heed. The spokeshave in her hand was the important thing, that and the wood with which she stroked it so gently.

'Miss Gwen! Miss Gwen!' Harold, the shop foreman, appeared at her elbow. 'Miss Gwen, your father wants you!'

He's not my father, her mind said at once. But she didn't utter the words aloud. Childish to harp on the fact that Wally was her stepfather – and at eighteen she was surely grown up enough to take a dispassionate view of the fact that her mother had married again.

Harold Akers stood watching her make her final caressing movement along the rosewood bar. 'Looks a treat, Miss Gwen,' he remarked. 'How many more you got to do?'

'Eleven. Twelve to each bedhead.'

'Lor, they'll be a masterpiece when you've finished 'em.' He ran a finger over the curved surface of the wooden bar in the vice. 'All the same, Miss Gwen, you'll never get a price for them twin beds as'll reward you for the work you've put in.'

She laughed, laying the spokeshave in its case on the bench. 'Oh yes I will. You said that about the bookcase, and the set of nesting tables. But we did get a good price for them, and now we've adapted them for mass production we'll do well with them.'

Harold grunted in agreement. No gainsaying it, the lass had a head on her shoulders for all her high-falutin'

view of cabinet-making. Pity in a way that Mr Baynes
had taken the firm out of her hands. Still an' all, hardly
suitable now the war was over, was it, a slip of a girl in
charge of a furniture workshop . . .

The design for the bedheads was tacked to a board
propped against the wall near the bench. Harold studied
it. Good, that. Who'd have thought of making a bedhead
out of a row of curved rosewood spokes? Pretty. The
design showed the frame into which the rods would fit –
it extended out at the top corners so that it had a slightly
Oriental look, like the tilt of a pagoda.

Liked Oriental things, did Miss Gwen. Mr Baynes, on
t'other hand, thought them a pain in the neck – though
he had to admit they made money in the end.

'Hi, come on!' Harold said, suddenly recalling his
errand. 'The boss wants you – some foreign bloke's in
the showroom.'

Gwen brushed down the front of her holland-cloth
apron, where tendrils of fine wood had caught. On the
periphery of her vision she could see a shaving tangled
in her hair where it touched her cheek. She waved a
hand at it; a square, capable hand with unpolished nails.
There was no mirror in the workshop – should she go
to the cloakroom to see if she looked respectable?

'Is it somebody important, Harold?'

'Nah, just dropped in on spec, I think – driving by,
you know, some foreign tourist . . .'

So she left her soft, bronze-coloured hair uncombed,
didn't even trouble to take off her apron. She hurried
to the showroom, for a tourist might easily get bored
and drive on. Still, a car . . . that meant he had money.
Even though the war had accustomed people to the idea
of motor transport, cars were costly and everybody was
so poor.

She glimpsed the car as she crossed the yard between
the workshop and the showroom. A Bentley! She felt
a surge of hope. Perhaps he'd noticed her maplewood
bureau – she longed for someone to buy it so as to

justify to her stepfather the hours she'd spent on it.

'Useless thing,' he'd grumbled as he watched her inlay the mother-of-pearl on its drop-flap front. 'Who wants fancy-work on a writing desk?'

'Somebody will want it,' she replied.

Her stepfather was waiting at the door of the showroom as she went in. 'You took your time,' he muttered. 'Left me here trying to talk to this chap – can't understand a word he says, hardly.'

She stepped round him. A tall slender man in a very well-made grey suit was standing before the controversial writing bureau. He turned as she came in.

Surprise washed into his long face. *'Mon dieu, c'est une jeune fille!'* he gasped.

A Frenchman, Gwen thought. And a very well-off Frenchman judging by the suit and the Bentley. Also, at the moment, a very surprised Frenchman. Gwen was used to that. People seemed unable to come to terms with the idea that a girl should be involved in cabinet-making, let alone be a designer of furniture.

'Bonjour, monsieur,' she said, ready to summon her schoolgirl French.

The Frenchman's surprise gave way to pleasure. *Charmante!* Small, rounded, with hair the colour of beech leaves in autumn. Grey-green eyes, studying him out of a face with rose-petal skin, the sprinkle of golden freckles – how *jeune-fille*. Lovely mouth, wide and full lipped – ah, the mouth of a passionate nature!

But the clothes! Dear heaven, the clothes! What was wrong with the British, that they let their lovely young girls present themselves to the world in these lumpy woollen skirts and plain blouses? And knitted worsted stockings, too – when those slender ankles ought to be clad in flesh-coloured silk.

'Bonjour, mademoiselle,' he said, with a little bow. *'C'est vous qui avez dessiné les chaises de Monsieur Groves?'*

3

'I beg your pardon?' said Gwen, taken aback at the sudden flow of French. In school, Miss Collins had always spoken quite slowly, and her pupils even more so. She'd no idea what this stranger had just said.

'Ah, forgive me. I ought not to conclude you can talk about business in my language. Permit me to introduce myself.' He took a gold-edged case out of his breast pocket, extracted a card, and held it out. When she took it, he bowed again, somehow giving her the impression she was conferring a great favour by taking it.

There was a little coat of arms engraved on the card, with below it the name: Jerome, Comte de Labasse. No address – presumably he thought everyone would know where he lived.

'How do you do, sir,' Gwen said, handing the card to her stepfather. With a slight frown she signalled: he's important, let's treat him with care.

'Oh, ah, I see,' Wally said, reading the card and looking at a loss. A French count! What in the name of goodness was a French lordship doing in the showroom of a small furniture-maker in St Albans?

The French lordship began at once to explain. 'I have come down from London with my friend Mr Groves to spend a few days at High Hall. In his apartment in Mayfair he had . . . I think you call it a dining set? A dining table and six matching chairs—'

'Ah, well, now, as to that, sir,' Wally said, with a mixed expression of obsequiousness and triumph on his fleshy features, 'I'm afraid we can't oblige you. Mr Groves made a bargain with us not to repeat those items within two years – "exclusivity", he called it.' And a good price he paid for the privilege, he added to himself.

But the Frenchie was waving that away with a well-manicured hand. 'No, no, *ça ne m'interesse pas* – it is not to have the same table and chairs that I came. I wished to meet the designer, to see what else he—' he broke off, bowed charmingly to Gwen, and resumed, 'she could show me. *Voyez*, I am redecorating my Paris

4

apartment. Very large, very elegant, but my grandfather and grandmother chose the furniture. *Empire* – you know *Empire*? The style of Napoleon?'

Wally did not, but Gwen took it up. 'Certainly, monsieur, all heavy gilt and red plush. Mind you, the Egyptian motifs are rather nice.'

'Oh, certainly, but it becomes weariness to the eye – and so heavy, you comprehend? Your chairs which I saw in Mr Groves' dining-room . . . so light, so elegant . . .'

Gwen thought so too. She had loved those chairs, almost hated to part with them when she had finished making them for Mr Groves. The back had as supports the carved wooden stems of stylised irises, which rose so that the flower petals formed the cresting rail. Inlaid with lacquered repoussé leather and (after Mr Groves had approved the expense) filigree silver, they shone in the candle-light of a dining-room.

The table in her view hadn't been so successful. Palisander was a pretty wood but a large expanse of it was tiresome and the iris motif at the corners had somehow not worked so well.

'Glad you liked them, sir,' Wally was saying with a hearty, proprietorial air. 'My daughter here designed them.'

The Count caught a flash of denial in the daughter's eyes, quickly veiled. What was this? Was she in fact not the designer?

'Could you show me some of your design sketches, perhaps, Miss Baynes?' he inquired.

'My name is Whitchurch, not Baynes,' she returned with instant accuracy.

Ah. So the man should have said 'stepdaughter', not 'daughter'. That was what she had been denying, that he was her father.

'Well, then, Miss Whitchurch, may I see what you have to offer?'

'There's the items here, sir,' Wally put in, moving

his heavy body with surprising alertness to show with a spread of his arms the contents of the showroom. 'That screen, you see – the one in macassar with the sharkskin panels – now that's a one-off piece, not likely ever to see another like that.' And it cost the earth to make, he added mentally. Perhaps he could flog it off to this silly Frenchie.

'Thank you, yes, I already admired that while I was waiting for someone to answer the shop bell. Also I like the cabinet, with the ivory *marqueterie* – how do you say that in English?'

'Inlay – yes, monsieur, the cabinet isn't bad, though I think it's too low. If I made it again, I'd give it another six inches.'

'You made it? I mean, mademoiselle, you literally made it?'

'Yes, sir.'

'But . . . this is unusual? A girl handling woodwork tools?'

Gwen smiled, a dazzle of pleasure that lit up her pale features. 'My father taught me,' she explained. 'I always used to play in the workshop, you know, even from a tiny girl, and I always loved the smell of wood. It has a scent; you can tell which wood is being sawn or planed by the scent. Applewood, rosewood . . . And then when I began to ask to help, he showed me how to . . . you know, handle a chisel, angle a saw . . . And it just grew from that.'

'A good thing! How excellent! You had talent, and he sensed that. Your father is alas dead, I take it?'

She nodded, the light dying from her dark-lashed eyes. 'In Flanders,' she said in a low voice.

'Ah, with so many . . . I am sorry, mademoiselle.' He gave a glance towards Wally Baynes, who was hovering and looking peeved at being excluded. 'I like also the writing bureau, and other things I see here, but nothing seems quite right for my Parisian rooms. You permit that

I see Miss Whitchurch's drawings in search of perhaps an idea?'

'Oh, certainly, mongsieur, a great pleasure. There you are, girl, a chance to show your collection, eh? Off with you to get it.'

Gwen hurried to the far end of the showroom, through a door which gave entry to the house proper. Hearing her flying footsteps Cook put her head out of the kitchen to say, 'If you've come for the elevenses you're too early—'

'No, no, special customer . . .' She darted into the main hall and was half-way up the stairs to her room when her mother's voice halted her.

'Did you say a special customer, Gwen?'

'Yes, Mother, a French gentleman, friend of Mr Groves. I'm just fetching my sketchbooks—'

Her mother came a step or two after her. 'Darling, you're a mess! Brush your hair and take off that apron while you're upstairs—'

Gwen glanced down at herself. 'Too late. He's seen me and knows I'm a mess. Can't stop, Mother, he's waiting.'

Rhoda Baynes sighed to herself. If this was a customer likely to buy some of Gwen's special designs, he was worth offering a cup of coffee and some home-made biscuits. To Rhoda, one of the main reasons God had created woman from Adam's rib was to ensure that menfolk had someone to provide the tea and coffee.

As to why her own daughter should be such an untypical woman, she'd given up wondering. In a way she blamed Edward – dear Edward, in every way a kind and gentle man – but what had possessed him to teach his daughter how to make chairs and tables?

Wally, now . . . Wally was different. A real man's man, was Wally . . . And such a comfort about the business, always so sure he knew what was best, taking all the responsibility from Rhoda's unwilling shoulders.

And from Gwen's too – not but what the child would

have been willing to soldier on as they had done during the last three years. After Edward had joined the army in 1916, Rhoda had tried to keep things going with the help of the foreman Wally Baynes, and somehow it had not seemed wrong when fourteen-year-old Gwennie began to give advice and play a part. Things were simple enough then, in any case – no call for elaborate cabinet-work, only plain desks for Civil Service offices and tables for Army canteens.

But then Edward had been killed and peace came, and the business had to be put back on the rails properly. Gwen had left school so that she could devote herself to running the workshop and designing the beautiful, unique pieces which were earning St Alban Cabinetwork its new reputation.

What was to become of her, Rhoda wondered as she made her way to the kitchen to order the coffee tray. So unsuitable, running about the place in a carpentry apron and with her blouse sleeves rolled up. Really it had been for the best when Rhoda had married Wally and let him take control. People could say what they liked about the foreman waiting to pick up the dead man's tools, but Wally already knew the business and could handle the run-of-the-mill items.

And besides, besides . . . widowhood was lonely, and she needed a bit of human comfort just the same as everyone else . . . Even though Gwennie couldn't come to terms with it. Idolised her father, that child . . . Well, sighed Rhoda, I don't care, I *love* Wally and there's an end of it!

Despite what she'd said to her mother, Gwen Whitchurch paused a moment in front of the dressing-table after she'd picked up her portfolio from the drawing-desk. She did look a mess, no denying it. She grimaced at herself in the mirror. Freckle-face! And her hair was all over the place.

She laid down the portfolio, unrolled her sleeves and fastened the cuffs. She took off the holland apron.

Well, that was no great improvement – a dull cotton blouse with crumpled sleeves. Should she change into a dress?

No, absurd. M. de Labasse had seen her in her work-clothes.

But, on the other hand . . . Her dark blue with the cotton lace collar was just to hand over the back of a chair where she'd left it after sewing on a fastener. And her silk stockings were in the dressing-table drawer.

Almost in anger at herself, she dragged a brush through her tawny hair then, turning her back on the temptations of lace collars and silk stockings, she ran downstairs again.

After all, he'd come to the shop to look at furniture, not at Gwendolen Whitchurch.

Even so, Jerome de Labasse was quite aware that Gwen had tidied herself up for his perusal. Her hair gleamed from the strokes of a brush. Such fine hair, like old gold spun on a fine spinning-wheel. He stood admiring it as she bent her head over the open portfolio.

Coffee was handed in through the door after a whispered colloquy between the bringer and Mr Baynes. Privately, Jerome thought the coffee abysmal – why couldn't the English learn how to make it? But in politeness he sipped it, and as it happened the spice biscuits were surprisingly good, so he was able to be complimentary.

For which he was rewarded. Mr Baynes was needed elsewhere, and Jerome was left tête-à-tête with his charming English rose.

What could be more agreeable than to sit side by side with a pretty eighteen-year-old, looking at furniture designs of charm and originality and considering how they would intrigue his Parisian friends if he bought them?

'This I like – there is something Eastern about the concept. I have the notion to have an Eastern motif in one of the main rooms, I thought perhaps the music room . . .' He pointed to the early version of the bedhead with its pagoda heading.

'Oh, but that's a bedroom design.' She felt herself blushing at saying the word to a man, and a stranger at that.

'*Bien entendu*. But then I have not decided which rooms should have the exotic touch. It could be one of the bedrooms. Ha!' he said, laughing. 'What about the Pasha look, all satin cushions and veiled draperies?'

She knew it was mere mischief, called forth by the blush when she'd said the word 'bedroom'. She assumed a severe expression.

'That would be for your interior decorator to discuss, sir,' she said. 'Have you in fact agreed on a unifying idea, or on fabrics or curtains?'

'No-o. No, I myself am the interior decorator – after all, this is my apartment, I want to express something of myself. You see, my dear young lady, I of course inherit the apartment from my parents, not so long ago. I came back from abroad at the end of the war.'

'Ah, you served overseas?' She was always interested in war experiences. To hear of them brought her closer to her dead father, somehow.

'Served, yes, but in the *Corps Diplomatique*. I was in the Embassy at Tokyo.'

'Tokyo!' She stared at him in wonder. No one she had ever met had travelled so far. Japan was practically the other side of the world. And she knew it was a country of marvels. She had looked at many books of Chinese and Japanese art in search of inspiration for her furniture designs. Their misty landscapes, their exquisitely drawn blossom trees, their cranes leaning over pools of fish . . . .

Jerome studied her. Her face was aglow. His amusement at her naïvety was touched with pleasure. What a charmer, so unspoiled – and so much talent! Yes, the sketches showed a mind stretching out to new ideas, still a little influenced by the William Morris and Rennie

Mackintosh era which was just ending, yet reaching for something new, something striking.

Gwen's view of Jerome was changing too. Until now he had been a rich foreigner, well dressed, well barbered, his sharp dark blue eyes missing nothing and his long thin mouth ready to smile at her simplicity. But to think that he had been to Japan . . .

She longed to have a long talk with him, to hear about the wonders he had seen. She knew, of course, that she ought to be selling him her furniture designs, yet here was a chance to learn almost at first hand about the temples, the sacred gardens, the flowers which played so important a part in Japanese art.

As if he were reading her mind – and perhaps he was – he said, 'Could we perhaps talk about this at more leisure? You have ideas here, basic sketches, which make me think you could understand what I'm trying to do with my new décor. And this is not the most comfortable place—'

'Oh, I'm sorry, we don't usually sit down to mull things over – I know the chairs are rather hard—'

'No, no, not at all, a charming showroom, but after all, you and I are perhaps going to do a lot of business. What if we were to meet for lunch later today?'

Her lips parted in surprise. 'Lunch?'

'Yes. You do eat lunch?' Once again that laughing glance from the dark blue eyes.

'Oh, of course. Only . . .'

'What?'

'No one has ever—'

'I understand. I am a stranger. Quite so. But I have some little sketches of my own in my case at High Hall, showing the dimensions of my rooms and the placement of the windows . . . What if I go there to fetch them, and we meet – where? – there is a good hotel in St Albans?'

'Certainly, the White Hart, you probably passed it—'

11

'I recollect it. Yes, a very elegant entrance, and near the Cathedral. The food is good?'

Gwen was at a loss. Good? What did a Frenchman mean by good? 'It has an excellent reputation,' she said, 'but I've only ever been there for afternoon tea.'

'Well, let us be trustful and imagine that it will serve at least the good *rosbif* for lunch. Shall we say one o'clock?'

'I . . . I should have to ask my mother.'

'Certainly.' He gave his little bow. 'And Papa as well, if you wish.'

She gave a little shrug which said, Oh, him, I wouldn't want to ask *him*.

'Then I shall wait here while you ask Mama, and look through the rest of your portfolio.'

This was more or less a command. She obeyed. Her mother was in the sitting-room, writing out the order for the butcher. 'Well, dear, did you sell him anything?' she asked, setting aside the notepad.

'Mother, he wants to take me to lunch!'

It had come out more dramatically than she intended. After all, it was a business lunch, the kind her step-father had quite frequently and which often resulted in lucrative commissions. She amended the announcement at once.

'He wants to fetch some sketches of his home in Paris – the furniture he wants is for his apartment – we can't come to grips with the problem because I've no idea of the room dimensions.' It all came out rather breathlessly, and she asked herself why she was so excited. After all, it was a *business* lunch.

But Mrs Baynes had got to the heart of the matter when she replied, 'Is it right, that he's a French count? Your da said—'

'Yes, the Count de Labasse, from Paris. He saw some of my work at Mr Grove's Mayfair flat.'

Perhaps if Jerome had been a French grain merchant, or an agent for nails and screws, Rhoda Baynes would have withheld her consent. But she asked, already considering it as settled, 'Where exactly are you lunching?'

'The White Hart, Mother.'

Well then. Nothing bad could happen to her daughter at the White Hart. Besides, the idea of boasting to her friends that her daughter had been invited out by a count was irresistible. Her romantic Welsh heart was caught by the idea of nobility.

'Very well, dear, so long as it's the Hart. And of course you won't stay long, will you – back for afternoon tea at three.'

'Yes, Mother. He's waiting to know if it's all right.'

'I'll just come along and have a word.'

Jerome had expected the mother to put in an appearance. He greeted her with his most charming smile and the little bow that seemed so continental. Moreover, he kissed her hand when Gwen introduced them.

'Enchanté,' he murmured.

Enchanted. It was Rhoda who was enchanted. There's lovely, she said to herself, treasuring it all up to tell Mrs Hutchings and Mary Dwyer.

Jerome pointed out those of Gwen's sketches which interested him, chatted a little about his flat in Paris and the problems of redecoration.

'Your wife leaves it all to you?' Rhoda inquired.

'My wife is dead, madame, from the influenza epidemic.'

'Oh dear, I'm so sorry. Wicked, it was, the influenza.' She felt she couldn't make any further inquiries about his domestic arrangements, and besides, it was only going to be a brief acquaintanceship. Gwen would talk over design ideas, he would order some pieces and leave; in due course the table or the sofa or whatever would be shipped over to him, and all that would remain was the anecdote to tell her friends: my Gwen got this big order from a French nobleman and, what do you think, he kissed my hand when he met me . . .

Already inclined to favour the outing, she was completely won over by Jerome – as he knew she would be. He could always twist women round his little finger, especially at the beginning. Later, they sometimes became fractious – but in this case there would be no 'later'. He too saw himself as ordering a few things and taking his leave.

But in the meantime, the company of the pretty little carpenter was to be enjoyed.

'I look forward, then, to one o'clock,' he said with formality, bowed once more, and took his leave.

'Well,' sighed Rhoda to her daughter, 'who'd have thought it! A French aristocrat! And your Da always saying you shouldn't be wasting your time on those special pieces . . .'

Gwen refrained from replying that her stepfather was often wrong. Her mother idolised her new husband, but a year of his management had convinced Gwen that he could only be successful in run-of-the-mill furniture-making. He had no real eye, no flair, no ability to foresee trends. He was a follower, not a leader, despite his appearance of forcefulness and command.

But it was that air of being the boss that had won Rhoda's heart. She needed someone to lean on. She was frightened of business, whereas Wally seemed to meet problems head on and quell them.

Moreover, he was a strong physical presence. He gave off a sort of animal warmth that Gwen found repellent, although her mother basked in it.

She put all that out of her mind, however, as she raced upstairs to get ready for her appointment. To tell the truth, she too felt there was something thrilling in having lunch with a French aristocrat.

She washed to rid her skin of the fine sawdust that always clung to it when she'd been in the workshop. She brushed her long hair again, then did it up in the soft double chignon which, so her mother said, was her most becoming style. Then she put on the frock of soft,

dark blue wool, fastened the lace collar, and adorned
it with a moonstone brooch which had belonged to her
father's mother.

The precious silk stockings were taken from their
tissue wrapping in the dressing-table drawer. Alas, she
had no matching dark blue shoes, but as it was fine
weather she could wear her thin black kid.

Her winter coat was a serviceable tweed check. How
she longed for something more elegant, but the only
other outer coat thick enough for a day in early February
was her velvet evening wrap – and that was entirely
inappropriate. So she brushed the tweed well, put it
on, then softened its sturdy look with a silk scarf. With
care she put on her new felt hat, bought in Harrods'
January sale.

How did she look?

She surveyed herself as best she could in her dressing-
table mirror. She looked what she was – a country
bumpkin clad in her best clothes.

Well, Jerome de Labasse hadn't asked for high fashion
in clothes, but for talent in furniture design. That, at
least, she could provide, she told her reflection.

With a tilt of her head and a frown of self-admonishment,
she went downstairs. Her mother was hovering in the
hall. 'There's nice you look,' she said, nodding her head
once or twice for emphasis. The brown-button Welsh
eyes gleamed with approval. Then she paused. 'But
you're spoiling it all by carrying that great briefcase
as well as your chain-purse.'

'It's got my sketching things in it—'

'Goodness to gracious, you're not going to the White
Hart to meet a count and spend the time sketching—'

'That's exactly what I am going to do, if you recall,
Mother.'

'I thought it was him that was going to bring the
sketches—'

'Never mind, never mind – I'd better be on my
way.'

15

There was plenty of time, but they both knew it would be better if she left before Wally became aware of the engagement. Not that he could really prevent her from going, because after all it was strictly business, yet they both knew there would be argument and dissension.

'Well, enjoy yourself, Gwennie,' her mother said, giving her a kiss. 'And when it comes to the pudding course, don't forget to try that Sussex Pond Pudding – it's new on the menu and I want to know what on earth it is.'

Gwen laughed as she went out. How like her mother – incurably romantic yet with an odd layer of practicality underlying it.

She sauntered towards the centre of the town. It was a Wednesday, a market day. After a cold and snowy January, people were out in force in this fine weather to stock up on farm butter and fresh vegetables.

She was early at the White Hart, but that gave her the chance to study the menu in the lobby. Roast beef, as M. de Labasse had predicted, also her mother's Pond Pudding. But she felt as if she couldn't eat a morsel. She was too excited.

The inner glow of that excitement charmed Jerome de Labasse as he came to meet her. He had reserved a table by telephone; they were shown straight to it.

Once the food and wine were ordered he produced sketches of the main rooms of his Paris home. Gwen saw that they were very spacious, each with several high, narrow windows.

Dimensions were pencilled in, but alas they were in metres and centimetres. She had to do sums in her head to convert them to the familiar feet and inches.

All through the meal they discussed and compared, pushing aside their plates to draw diagrams or set down outlines of ideas. 'No, no, not flowers – something more architectural in inspiration – my dear Miss Whitchurch, I wish you could see the rooms yourself, it would be so much easier to know what would work and what would not.'

In the end they parted with Gwen promising to work on one or two ideas he had partly approved, one of a sideboard and another for a chaise longue. 'But there ought to be much more. Can we meet again?'

'Certainly. How long are you staying at High Hall, Monsieur?'

'Until Sunday. I know what we ought to do! You shall work on those drawings tomorrow and I will ask Martin to have you to dinner. You could come to dinner, tomorrow?'

Dinner at High Hall! To Gwen, High Hall meant 'the gentry', whereas she was a tradesman's daughter. 'I don't know whether . . .'

'Whether your mama would approve? Oh, I will ask Martin's sister to write a note of invitation. Surely that will reassure?'

What Gwen had meant was that Martin Groves might not want to invite the daughter of a cabinet-maker to dinner. And in fact she expected a note of excuse to arrive – 'So sorry but it proved not to be convenient' or something of that sort.

But not at all. At six-thirty that evening a boy delivered a note to the house, addressed to Mrs Baynes and asking if it would be quite agreeable to her to allow her daughter Gwen to come to dinner next evening at eight o'clock.

'Oh, it's utterly dazzling!' cried Rhoda. 'Dinner with the Groves! What will Mary Dwyer say to that!'

'They'll probably high-hat you, girl,' grunted Wally. But he didn't try to prevent it.

The dinner was an ordeal for Gwen. Miss Groves sought to put her at her ease but the array of knives and forks, the fine china, the scent of the hothouse carnations on the table all bespoke a style of living quite outside

17

her experience. Once again she scarcely ate a morsel, though she took careful mental note of every course so as to report to her mother.

'Now, I know you and Jerome want to talk furniture,' Miss Groves said with a frown at her brother to prevent him from detaining Jerome over the port. 'The fire is lit in the study and I'll send in some coffee in a moment. If I give you an hour without interruption, will that be long enough?'

'Perhaps not. But after all, there are another two days before I leave. Let us hope we can settle one or two things by then.'

Somewhat dazed at the idea of spending more or less the whole of the next two days on M. de Labasse's furnishing requirements, Gwen followed him into the study. It was a masculine, bookish room, with worn leather armchairs and an old turkey carpet. A friendly fire glowed in the grate.

Jerome had made further sketches, but his drawing ability was not up to his own high standards. Gwen was puzzling over them when the coffee was brought in. Then she had to pour – a task which alarmed her but which she managed quite well.

'So, shall you be able to devote yourself to working on my furniture once we have made a choice?' he asked, stirring sugar crystals into the tiny cup.

'Oh, of course, why not?'

'M. Baynes will not object?'

To tell the truth, he might, unless he were brought in to settle the costing. She hesitated. 'I'll show him the sketches, and explain how far we've got, tomorrow morning.'

'Will he understand them?'

'What makes you say that?' she asked, surprised.

'He is not artistic, I think.'

'Well, no, he isn't.'

'And he is not *sympathique*.'

'As a matter of fact, he's a lot too *sympathique*,' Gwen

blurted, her tongue loosened by the wine at dinner, the cosy room, the warmth of the fire.

'*Comment?* I thought his manner towards you was somewhat critical.'

'That's in public. In private it's quite the opposite—' She tried to catch back the words.

Jerome laughed. 'You are a very attractive girl. One can hardly blame him.'

'It isn't funny!'

Jerome wasn't a very imaginative man, but the despair in that cry brought him a moment of illumination. Indeed, it would not be funny to have your mother's husband making advances.

'Have you told your mother?'

'Of course not! You don't understand – she adores him! If she believed me, it would break her heart. But worse still, he'd deny it and she might prefer to believe *him*.'

'Oh, surely not—'

'She might think I was just making trouble. She knows I didn't want her to marry him. And I don't know how she could,' Gwen cried, 'after my father, who was so completely and utterly different . . .'

Jerome had not taken to Wally Baynes, but he could tell there was an earthy attractiveness about him which might appeal to certain women. 'I see that you can't discuss it with her,' he agreed. 'It is a big problem, no?'

'Sometimes I feel I'll go mad.' She shuddered. The other night, sitting dreaming by the dying embers of her bedroom fire, she had heard a shuffle outside and seen the knob of her door silently turning in the red glow.

'Who's there?' she'd cried. 'What is it?'

'Only me, Gwennie,' came her stepfather's voice. 'Just checking.'

Just checking? Checking what?

The moment he had gone she had dashed to the door and turned the key. From that night she had locked herself in, but she knew that one night, weary or sleepy,

19

she would forget – and that might be the very night he would try again.

And then something awful, something unspeakable, would happen. She couldn't quite envisage it, but she dreaded and loathed the idea with all her heart. Already she hated the way he would brush against her needlessly in a doorway, or slip an arm around her when they were discussing something in the workshop. She had taken to keeping one of the other workmen in the room if she could. But things couldn't go on like that.

Strangely, perhaps because he was a stranger and would never let any of it slip to her besotted mother, she was able to talk to Jerome about it. He set down his coffee cup with an emphatic rattle of spoon in saucer.

'You ought to leave home,' he said.

'Don't you think I've thought of that? But I'd have to give some sort of explanation and I'm sure everything would come tumbling out in the argument. And in any case, where could I go?'

'Come to Paris.'

'To Paris!'

'It's the best possible solution. You have a reason to come – you need to see my flat, you want to work directly on site. It's perfectly reasonable. It would take – what – six months, so that would bring us to the end of August. When you come back, you would have made the break and need not return to live with your mother and stepfather. Perhaps you could share a flat with a woman-friend in London – that is done these days, I believe.'

'But . . . but . . .'

'You need to take strong measures,' he urged. 'What would you prefer? To stay waiting at home until there is a disaster? Or to leave home and come to Paris?'

'But Mother would never let me.'

'Ah.' Quite so. The mothers of young girls were apt to say no to this kind of enterprise.

'Then don't tell her,' he said. 'You could leave home

– leave a note, I think that is the done thing – leave a note explaining what you are doing. By the time she reads it you could be on the ferry to Calais.'

'Oh, I couldn't! I really couldn't!'

But already she was feeling that she really could. And in the two days before Jerome was due to leave High Hall, it became not only possible, but the perfect solution.

Anything was preferable to staying on in the same house as her stepfather. And if she must go, where better in the world than that centre of art and design, that shining light of all that was civilised and decorative, Paris?

Chapter Two

Gwen's first sight of Paris was enough to do away with any remorse she might be feeling about her behaviour. The hurt to her mother, the scandal her flight would cause – these were nothing compared with the sense of homecoming as she was driven into *'La Ville Lumière'*.

Her flight had been, in fact, uneventful. Since the family retired early she had tiptoed out of the house at ten-thirty. By midnight she was in London boarding the boat-train at Victoria. Jerome was there waiting for her, having gone to London earlier in the day to make arrangements.

Exhausted by four days of excitement and tension, Gwen slept soundly in her single first-class cabin through a rather rough crossing. A chauffeur-driven Charron-Renault was waiting for them on the docks at Calais. They came into Paris in the late morning of a cold, sunny February day, with the bare trees outlined against an eggshell-blue sky.

'How *beautiful*!' Gwen breathed as they drove in along the Avenue de Neuilly towards L'Étoile.

Jerome smiled. *'C'est mon village,'* he murmured fondly, and though her French was poor she guessed it meant, 'It's my home town.'

He took her to a quiet, plain hotel in the Latin Quarter, the Hotel des Saints-Pères. They were clearly expected, the porter hurrying out to take her luggage – though it was only an overnight bag and her briefcase – and Madame herself appearing to greet them.

There was a fairly long exchange in French. Madame turned to Gwen. ''Ow do you do, I am Mme Garzier, I am own the hotel. M. de Labasse suggests you . . . settle? Settle in. Then ve are to go to buy clothings.'

At once Gwen was in distress. 'But, M. de Labasse, I've only got English money.' And not much of that, either, she thought, her entire savings amounting to something under ten pounds.

'That can be taken care of. Madame will pay for the clothes and I will refund her the money.'

'But that means . . . that means . . .' One of the tenets of Gwen's upbringing was: a lady does not accept gifts of money or of clothing from a man other than a husband, father or brother.

'Don't distress yourself,' Jerome said, with that little smile that half-approved of her naïvety. 'You certainly need some clothes to change into, so we shall keep careful accounts and I shall deduct it from what I pay you for the work on my flat. Yes?'

'Oh. Yes. Thank you.'

Mme Garzier, who was unable to follow this, quite took it for granted M. de Labasse was going to pay for everything on the usual grounds – that the English girl was his new playmate. Yet, it seemed odd. The girl had no style, no presence. Though quite pretty and with splendid hair and attractive grey-green eyes, she made no attempt to use her assets. A French girl would have chosen her clothes to set off her colouring, would have had a little darkener on her lashes, would certainly have had less sensible-looking shoes and stockings, though the English tweed coat had *le gout sportif* about it.

'I leave you now in the hands of Mme Garzier,' Jerome said. 'I must go home to see to a few things. I shall give you a little *coup du téléphone* later – say about five?'

He took Gwen's hand, kissed it in farewell but with gallantry, not with apparent affection. His manner towards her throughout had been just right, she thought to herself – protective and friendly yet respectful. He was really what her mother would call 'a lovely man'.

Madame took her upstairs to show her her room and the amenities. The room was rather heavily furnished in mahogany, but there was a big bed with a feather mattress and plentiful pillows. A washbasin and ewer stood on a marble washstand.

The bathroom was a few doors down the hall. Later Gwen was to learn that the cistern howled when you pulled the chain and the water glugged and gurgled in the pipes for hours if anyone had a bath. But for the moment she was merely charmed by the glazed floral fitments and ornate brass taps.

'If you vould care to unpack, downstairs in a moment I vill serve coffee. Zen ve go out to the *grands magasins* for clothings. Perhaps you make a list of vat you intend?'

'Merci infiniment,' said Gwen, thinking it was time to try out her school French.

It was perhaps a mistake. Mme Garzier beamed, broke into a flow of speech, and took it for granted from then on that Gwen could understand and respond to everything she said. Yet perhaps it was a good thing. Gwen would be forced to speak the language, to try to think in the language.

After coffee and tiny biscuits in Madame's sitting-room, they went out, Gwen still in the English tweed, Madame's formidable figure wrapped in a beaver-fur coat. Her grey hair, elaborately arranged, was topped by a toque of brown velvet. She was not a good-looking woman, but her severe elegance somehow gave the impression of handsomeness, and certainly her small feet – she had the small feet and slender ankles that often go with a burly figure – twinkled delightfully as they walked to the Métro.

Everything was new and wonderful to Gwen. She loved the Métro with its clanging green gates and its frightening ladies who clipped the tickets. They came out at the Chaussée d'Antan, with great department stores all around them.

'*Alors!*' cried Madame, and plunged into the nearest.

They bought skirts and blouses of exquisite cut and fabric, many pairs of stockings both silk and mercerised cotton, three pairs of shoes – though Gwen protested that one would be enough – and a coat of plain, dark green frieze-cloth.

'This colour is good with your hair,' Madame instructed. 'You should wear green often, and also blue and grey, but I think you should avoid brown and beige and amber, and certainly pink and red – with your hair red will make you look feverish. Now, we shall go to the lingerie department.'

'No, no, I've brought underwear with me—'

'Ha! English underwear! We shall go to the lingerie department.'

'No, madame, absolutely not!'

Mme Garzier couldn't understand it. At the outset of an affair one should buy as much as one could at the expense of the lover. Soon enough, heaven knew, he would start complaining about extravagance and the need for economy. More love affairs foundered on the money question, in Madame's opinion, than on any other, except perhaps jealousy.

The shops promised the goods should be delivered that evening. The two women then went for a late lunch in a restaurant on the Avenue de l'Opéra, where Madame ordered the food and wine with such authority that the waiters were practically kowtowing.

As an introduction to Paris it was perhaps one of the best. Gwen had been plunged into the workaday life of the city. She never saw it as if she were simply a tourist, from the very outset it was part of her daily round.

They lingered so long over the meal that they were only just home in time for Jerome's phone call.

'How did it go, the shopping? Did you get what you need?' he asked.

'I got a lot more than I need! Mme Garzier seemed to think we were buying an entire new wardrobe.'

Well, weren't you? Jerome thought to himself. At least the groundwork of a new wardrobe could have been laid. But he left that for the moment.

'Now, about this evening. I thought I would take you out to dinner and then we can go night-clubbing—'

'Night-clubbing? But, M. de Labasse, I don't have an evening frock with me.'

'You didn't buy one?'

'There was no need, monsieur. I have one at home and I'm writing this evening to let Mother know my address and ask her to send on some of my things.'

'You're letting your mother know . . . ?' He was astonished. He had taken it for granted she wouldn't tell her mother her Paris address, at least not for several weeks.

'Of course. Otherwise she'll be awfully worried.'

'But . . . but surely if she knows where you are, she'll come and fetch you home?'

'What, my mother?' Gwen knew how absurd the idea was. Her mother had never been further from home, since her marriage twenty years ago, than Burnham-on-Crouch for the summer holidays. Even a visit to the grandparents in Machynlleth was too much of an undertaking.

'But then perhaps your stepfather—?'

'Wally wouldn't leave the business. No, truly, no one is going to come looking for me. And in any case, I couldn't leave my mother in a state of anxiety.'

'But will she know how to send your clothes to you in a foreign country?' Jerome ventured, still hopeful of never seeing again that awful pink satin dinner dress she had worn at High Hall.

'Certainly. We're quite used to sending furniture abroad, you see.'

Was she fond of those dreadful clothes? Didn't she know they spoiled her lovely shape, failed to do anything for her pale clear skin and striking hair?

But after all, she was here for at least six months. By that time he would have got one of his mature women friends to take her in hand. He was certainly not going to be seen about Paris with a frump.

'Ah . . . Mme Garzier did buy you some nice things, however?'

'Oh yes, a beautiful topcoat – just the kind of thing I've always wanted. And the prettiest blouse—' She stopped short, wondering if it was proper to discuss her clothes with a male. She hadn't yet learnt that Parisian males took a genuine interest in the clothes of their womenfolk. But then, she didn't know yet that Jerome regarded her as one of his womenfolk.

He was relieved to hear she had something decent to wear. He gave up the idea of nightclubs, but envisaged himself with her in a candle-lit restaurant, her russet tresses gleaming . . . 'Well, let us have a quiet *dîner-à-deux*,' he proposed. 'Let's say I pick you up about eight o'clock—'

'It's awfully kind of you, monsieur, but you mustn't feel you've got to take care of me or entertain me. And honestly, I'm dead on my feet in any case. I think my best plan is an early night.' As she said it she was imagining herself with a bowl of hot soup and her sketchbook propped on the table. Then a long hot bath and bed . . .

Jerome de Labasse was baffled. He knew she liked him. He had seen it in her face when she turned to him for guidance during the journey. Why wasn't she eager to come out to dinner with him?

She was tired – yes, of course, so was he. But all the more reason to dine together, to let the food and the wine relax them. Then she would fall into his arms and into his bed.

Not yet, it seemed. Once more he reminded himself

that there was plenty of time. He sighed inwardly but admitted momentary defeat.

'I understand,' he said. 'Well then, let us see each other tomorrow. You will want to come to my apartment to see the rooms. We must make a decision, mustn't we, about which of them you are going to furnish. Shall we say about ten o'clock?'

'That will be fine. But, by the way, you haven't given me your address or directions on how to get there.'

She could hear the shock in his voice when he answered. 'I will send my car for you, naturally.'

'Oh, I see. Thank you.'

'*À demain, alors*. Goodnight, mademoiselle, sleep well.'

It turned out the bowl of soup had to be brought in from a restaurant a few doors down, because there was no restaurant, no kitchen, in the Hotel des Saints-Pères. Madame supplied only breakfast to her guests, and that, as Gwen found out, consisted of coffee freshly made but with too much chicory, croissants warm from the baker, butter in little pots from the dairy, and honey in a jar.

She was ready when the car arrived, clad in a new blouse and skirt and shoes, and with the new coat over her arm ready to put on. Madame and the old porter stood by to admire both her and the limousine. She stepped in, thrilled with the situation, to be whisked off through the busy streets of the Latin Quarter, across to the Right Bank, and by stately, tree-lined roads to the Avenue Foch.

She tried to take note of the names of the Métro stations so that by and by she would be able to make her way to the Count's home by public transport. She had no idea that the Count hoped she would soon have no need of transport to bring her to the Avenue Foch because he intended to instal her there.

Jerome's apartment proved to be one wing of an enormous mansion, standing back in a tree-filled garden behind a wall. There was actually a drive up to the entrance. The chauffeur handed her out to a man in a sort of livery – a lightly quilted black waistcoat with pearl buttons and sateen sleeve-coverings over his shirt. He greeted her with gravity. She learned later that this was the count's valet. He took her coat and hat, tried to take her satchel. She kept hold of it. 'I need this, thank you.'

He insisted on taking it so as to carry it for her. 'This way, mademoiselle.'

She followed him along the hall, up a flight of curving stairs, through a large room handsomely furnished in the style of the last decade and into another, even more handsome, with walls of crimson silk and Empire furniture. Jerome was waiting for her at an ornate desk, with swathes of cloth spread out.

'Good morning, mademoiselle, how are you this morning? Did you sleep well?'

'Yes, thank you, and thank you too for sending the car.'

'That will be all, Tibau.' He waved the servant away. 'Come and sit down. Look, I had Tibau bring out all the samples of cloth that I have selected so far. Perhaps they will give you some idea of my intention.'

The cloths were mostly of heavy silk, and most of them had a decided sheen. The colours were neutral – oyster, champagne, ivory, pearl-grey.

'You want a much lighter appearance than you already have – at least in the rooms I've seen.'

'Exactly. The others are just as heavy. There are eleven of them, not counting the servants' quarters. In a moment I'll take you on a tour, but first let me show you some magazines.' He swept the cloth aside to uncover two or three copies of *L'Illustration*. 'This is a French magazine which uses very good graphic designers—'

'Oh yes, I've seen it—'

'You know of *L'Illustration*?' he said, surprised.

'Oh yes, you can buy it in London in the Charing

Cross Road, so of course any time I was in London I would get it. You see, monsieur—'

'One moment.' He held up a finger, almost in admonition, and she stopped with her lips parted for speech. Looking, he thought, very inviting. 'Can we accept from today that you call me Jerome? We shall be working together over several months. I think we shall be friends – no?'

'Oh *yes*, mons— I mean, Jerome. I feel we're friends already.'

Shall I kiss her now? wondered Jerome. And yet perhaps not. At a quarter past ten in the morning, she would think it a little too early for romance. 'And I may call you Gwen?' he prompted.

'Please, I wish you would.' It was delightful, the way he said her name, softening the opening sound to something that seemed very French.

They sat side by side at the desk, turning over the pages of the magazines, inviting each other to notice originality in the editorial and in the advertising pages.

'You see, when I came home from Japan,' Jerome explained, 'I found that really great artists were interesting themselves in design. Perhaps it began some time ago – Toulouse-Lautrec drew posters for *La Revue Blanche* and Bakst designed costumes for the Russian Ballet. But coming back from abroad, I was struck by how much new and original work was going into things like jewellery or furnishing fabrics or pottery. I was interested because in Japan, you know, the least little thing is made beautiful – ladles for serving soup, the spokes of a water-wheel, headcloths that the peasants wear in the fields – they are all in their way small works of art.'

'How wonderful. It sounds so beautiful.'

'Oh, it is. Japan is a paradise. But my wife didn't think so, she didn't like the climate, and so she went home. And then the war broke out and it would have been foolish for her to attempt to come back. And then, of course, there was the flu epidemic. It was because of her death that I returned home and now, after all, I've decided the diplomatic life isn't for me.'

'So what shall you do instead?' she asked, full of sympathy for him in his loneliness.

'Do?' The truth was, there was no need for him to do anything. But he sensed it wouldn't sound well to her if he said so. 'I'm taking an interest in this new outburst of talent in the decorative arts. You know we have a school – *L'École des Arts Décoratifs* – and in fact that's the slang term that's beginning to be used for it – "Art Deco".'

She nodded. She herself was already being drawn more and more towards the style. It was modern, flowing, was full of movement that seemed to have the rhythm of a dance.

The tour of the house took them up to lunch-time. Tibau then appeared to announce that the meal was served. The dining-room, which faced east, was filled with the cold, clear, noonday light of winter. Bathed in it, the gilding and plum velours seemed funereal.

'What *this* room needs is the warmth of Asia,' Gwen exclaimed. 'Some of that misty silk on the walls, like morning on the shore of the Indian ocean. And tropical flowers, like on a jungle pool – lotuses.'

'Made from mother-of-pearl, with big yellow centres—'

'And furniture of some pale wood to make you think of the trunks of palm trees—'

'Yes, and with touches of soft green like palm-leaves . . .'

'In suede—'

'Yes, for the dining chairs. And curtains of yellow and pale green – I saw some fabric like that at the workshops of Paul Dumas, but it didn't occur to me to take a sample—'

'Could I see it?' Gwen asked eagerly.

'Of course. We'll go this afternoon. Tibau, ring

M. Dumas and say we'll be at his shop about three
o'clock.'

'Very good, monsieur.'

'And have the car brought round.'

'Yes, sir.'

Gwen was clearing a place by her plate to lay out
a sheet from her sketchpad. 'Afrosia wood,' she was
muttering to herself, 'the table ends fronded like palm
leaves but not too much because it would look fussy . . .
No, it ought to be a round table—' She glanced about at
the room. 'No, a round table would look wrong. Oval,
then . . . What about an oval table, Jerome?'

'Why not?'

'In fact, an elongated oval, like a palm frond . . .'
Her pencil was busy. 'And then the chairs, you see,
their backs would be an elongated oval too – something
like this.'

She handed the sketch across the table to him. In
quick lines she had drawn a top and a side view of a table
made in a long leaf-shape, and alongside a simplistic idea
of a dining chair whose 'splat' or back rest consisted of a
thin vertical rail from which others ran off like fronds.

'But that would look sensational!' Jerome cried. 'No
one in Paris would have anything like that!'

'The table legs . . . I don't know about the table
legs . . .'

'There would have to be a sideboard for the servants
to lay out the food—'

'I don't see that yet. I'm still thinking about table
legs. I need to mull it over, make some sketches. I'll
do that this evening. The problem is, once I've got the
design right I'll need to draw out some plans for the
actual making, and there isn't a surface big enough in
my room at the hotel.'

'Oh, but you must work here!' Jerome said at once.
'There are plenty of rooms here—'

'But they're full of furniture, Jerome—'

'I can easily have one cleared. Or there are the attics

– but no, that would be too cold.' He threw up a hand as an idea struck. 'I know! The conservatory! It's all glass, so the light—'

'But the plants would block that . . . ?'

'No, no, it has a grapevine in it and at the moment the vine is dormant. No, for the time being it would be excellent – it has some garden chairs and so forth but I'll have those moved out. A plan table – you'll need a plan table? I'll tell Tibau to order one at once!'

She was too immersed in her designs to think about the way everything was organised without regard to expense. It was only later, when she was back in her own room at the hotel, that she reviewed the day and realised how immensely rich Jerome must be. And he was prepared to use his money to back his interest in art.

He wanted to be a leader, she saw that quite clearly. His remark that 'no one in Paris' would have anything like the furniture she was designing told her a lot. She had heard something like that from Martin Groves and others of the customers who had come to the St Albans works. There was a new following for what Jerome called Art Deco, and there were those who wanted to be in the lead, encouraging new talent, blazing a trail that took them away from the conventional and the traditional.

When they chose the curtain fabric at Dumas' shop, Jerome had insisted on buying every scrap that existed and paid a corresponding price, so that no one else should have it. To her mind there was something wayward, almost childlike, in that. What did it matter if others used the same design? If a design was good, surely the more it was used, the better?

But no, Jerome wanted to be the only one to have the yellow and green fabric from Dumas, just as he wanted to be the only one to have dining chairs and tables inspired by palm leaves. He had carried her off to a lawyer, and dictated a financially generous contract, by which all the designs she made through the next six months were to be his exclusively for a period of two years.

'After that, of course, you can make as many copies as you like, Gwen. If you stay on in Paris, I daresay you'd get plenty of customers. When my friends see my new rooms, they'll be envious, so you'll be in demand.'

'How can you be so sure they'll be envious?' she said, shaking her head. 'They might not like what I do.'

'Don't be silly! Parisians have an eye for talent and originality. Besides, I've something of a reputation for leading the way. It was from me that the rage for Japanese lacquer was caught. You'll see, once you've finished the work on my rooms, you'll be in great demand. You might even be asked to join Ruhlman's studio.'

'Join his studio? I don't know what that means.'

'Well, he has large premises where a team of designers—'

'Do you mean that other people do the designs for him?'

'Oh, yes, Chanaux is one of his men—'

'I've never heard of Chanaux.'

'No, you see, the work comes out as Studio Ruhlman.'

'I shouldn't like that,' Gwen said very firmly. 'What I make has my name on it, no one else's.'

'But to work at a big Paris studio . . .'

'No, thank you. Either I succeed on my own or I go back to St Albans and make my name there.'

It dawned on her as she said it that her ambitions had crystallised today. If anyone had asked her hitherto what she'd wanted out of life she'd have said she was happy simply making sofas and cabinets. But now Jerome had unintentionally opened her eyes. She saw that there was a career in front of her, designing and making furniture for people who had good taste and could afford to indulge it.

Paris was certainly a better place to get her talent

known than St Albans in Hertfordshire. There, a small band of customers had come to hear of her, and perhaps her reputation would have grown. But it would always have been hindered by the British attitude to the young. It would have meant continually explaining that she'd been accustomed to working in a cabinet-making shop since she was ten or eleven years old, that behind her eighteen-year-old appearance there were years of practical experience.

Here in Paris, she guessed, her youth would be a positive advantage. It would be something to talk about – 'so young, extraordinary, and no formal art training, a natural talent . . .'

She went to bed late that night, after spending hours on the designs. She could hardly wait for next day, to get back to the great mansion on Avenue Foch so as to sense the scale on which her pieces must be made for those high-ceilinged, aristocratic rooms.

As he had promised, Jerome had had the conservatory made ready. He was waiting in the hall to lead her there personally. The great trunk of the old vine spread along one whitewashed wall. Otherwise the big glass room had been emptied except for the heating stove in a corner, which made faint burbling sounds as hot water moved through it. The floor was tiled, the framework for the glass was of wrought iron – it would have been a very cold place without the heating for the vine.

In the centre stood a drawing-table with a desk-lamp attached by a clamp, and a padded office chair. A case of instruments lay open on the desk – T-square, protractor, a steel rule.

'I didn't know if you had your own things with you so I provided—'

'Thank you, I do have my own draughtsman's pens and drawing instruments but I couldn't pack a T-square.'

He laughed. 'No, an awkward thing to pack in a hold-all. Anything else you require, simply tell Tibau.'

'Thank you.'

'Now, come and have coffee and you can show me the sketches.'

They went into the house proper and up to the first-floor sitting-room. He pored over the sketches of the table and chairs. 'I love them! They are just what I expected! And as to the lotus blossoms, we need not include them—'

'But I was thinking last night, Jerome – those could be the lamps.'

'The lamps!'

'Yes, wall lamps, the shades shaped like lotus petals.'

'Good, good . . .'

'And I thought, you know – since we want it all to look Asian – how about if, as well as curtains from the Dumas fabric, we had blinds mounted on rattan canes? I've never worked with rattan, but we could slot canes across the blinds and draw them up by cords.'

She produced another sketch showing the blinds made with the rattan visible on the inside, so that somehow the effect was of the sail of an exotic ship.

Jerome was nodding his head over it.

That was how, imperceptibly, Gwen found herself responsible not only for the furniture but for the entire décor of the room. Jerome had intended to make all the choices himself, but he was the kind of man who knew what he wanted when he saw it, rather than being able to initiate it.

After coffee Tibau was called to help her measure the room in a detailed fashion. Tibau shifted furniture so that she could get into corners, climbed step ladders so that she could measure heights. Jerome stood by supervising until about midday, when he confessed he had a lunch engagement.

'However, Tibau will give you lunch in your work-room, or anything else you require. There's a bell by the door, you need only press it for service. And of course, since I know you are going to be busy here for weeks, you must feel free to come and go just as you please, Gwen. The servants will let you in at any time.'

'Thank you, Jerome.'

He took her hand in farewell, kissed it. 'This is turning out quite differently from what I expected,' he said, his gaze resting on her with admiration. 'But I'm so glad we met!'

She thought it a strange remark. Quite differently? But he had brought her here to design the furniture for his apartment, and that was what she was doing, wasn't she?

This conundrum was cleared up about two weeks later. It was about five o'clock, the natural light had gone and she was working under the desk-lamp which she found trying. She decided to call it a day. But the prospect of going home to her room at the Saints-Pères somehow didn't seem attractive.

In general Gwen ate her evening meal at one of the cafés in the same street. They were inexpensive, the food was good, and the atmosphere was cheerful, but although her French was improving greatly, she still didn't feel brave enough to join the lively conversations that seemed to go on all around her.

She was lonely. Once or twice she'd cried herself to sleep from sheer homesickness. Several times young men had smiled at her in a café, and she'd understood she only had to smile back to have a friend, *un ami*, but in Paris that seemed to mean something different. Women as a rule paid her no heed; she guessed she didn't look chic enough to interest them. Dressed mainly in the home-made English clothes her mother had sent on to her, she struck them as dowdy.

She was going through the main hall to fetch her coat when Tibau appeared. 'Mademoiselle, you have finished work for today?'

'Yes, thank you.'

'Monsieur de Labasse asked me to say he would be

glad if you could come upstairs. He has some friends who have dropped in for *le five o'clock*, artists whom he would like you to meet.'

Le five o'clock was the Parisian equivalent of afternoon tea. One of the things Gwen missed most was a good cup of English tea. Besides, here was a chance to meet some French artists. She accepted the invitation eagerly and followed Tibau upstairs to the sitting-room, where a bright chatter of voices could be heard.

'Mademoiselle is here, monsieur.'

. 'Ah, Gwen, splendid. Come, I want to introduce you to some fellow-designers. Everyone, this is my little protégée, Gwen Whitchurch.'

'Veetcha? What manner of name is that?' asked a plump young man, waving both hands in perplexity.

'That one who can't pronounce your name, that's Gaston Arriac – he makes silverware. The girl with him is Sybille Lespançon, who designs dress fabric for Poiret. The blonde next to her, that's Valerie, she does ceramics and garden sculpture. Erik is a graphic designer, and that's Jean-Luc . . .' Jerome reeled off eight names, almost all of them followed by an occupation concerned with decorative design.

Gwen murmured greetings, then tried to answer questions that were at once fired at her. Was she proposing to hire Daum to make the lotus lamps? As to suede for the chair seats, didn't she think it would lose its nap? The blinds she was planning would be difficult to raise and lower, didn't she think?

She tried to cope with all this in her halting French. Tibau brought her a cup of tea and a plate of tiny sandwiches *à l'anglaise*. As soon as she could she took refuge behind these. She found this group intimidating – loud, opinionated, interfering. She wasn't used to arguing the merits of her work – her customer had either liked it or had not, and anything that didn't sell had soon been dropped from the St Albans' display on Wally's orders.

Although she still found it difficult to summon up the words to speak, she was now at the stage where she understood almost all that was said to her in French. The fact that she hesitated so much in responding led others to think her French was minimal.

No doubt it was for this reason that two of the girls – she thought they were Sybille and Toinette – embarked on a discussion about her.

'She's prettier than I expected, *l'anglaise*. Someone told me she was quite plain, but I couldn't believe Jerome would take up with a plain woman, could you?'

'I'm told it's her talent he admires, not her looks.'

'Oh yes, if you believe that you believe the moon is green cheese. But as to talent, she does really have some. Those sketches he showed us are remarkable.'

'He always manages to come back from his trips abroad with some worthwhile little souvenir, Toinette.'

'This is different. You can see he's tremendously taken with her.'

'And she with him? I wouldn't have thought so. Although, with the English, how can you tell? They're so cool.'

'Only cool on the outside, perhaps. And inside, all warmth and emotion. Think of Romeo and Juliet, that was written by an Englishman.'

'Aha,' laughed Toinette, 'I hope this affair doesn't end up like the play with the lovers dead in a tomb. A high price to pay for a few months' pleasure and some good furniture!'

'Ah, Toinette, you are so cynical. Myself, I say good luck to her, the poor little thing. It seems to me she's got no idea of the catch she's landed. Should we tell her?'

'Tell her what? That he's rich? That his family's title only dates back to Napoleon so he's really not much of an aristocrat? That he's almost twice her age?'

'I mean, that he's generous, that he's kind-hearted,

that none of his women friends have regretted being in love with him.'

'Except Estelle.'

'Oh, he only married her for family reasons. Besides, if you want my view, she was incapable of loving anybody. No, no, apart from that wife of his, every woman I've ever heard of has fond thoughts of Jerome.'

'Yourself included.'

'Now, now, Toinette, don't let's discuss my past. Shall we have another of Jerome's delightful cakes?' The conversation ended as she rose to raid the cake-dish. And Gwen, guilty at having eavesdropped, hid her face in her china cup.

What she had heard had cast a sudden light on several puzzling things. Foremost was Jerome's remark the other day, that things had turned out quite different from what he'd expected. So they had, indeed, if he had expected a love affair! She for her part was being so businesslike, so keen not to be a burden to him.

Yet the reason was simple. Although she found him terribly attractive – cultured, handsome, attentive – it had never occurred to her that he would bother with her other than as a furniture-maker. She had a poor opinion of herself as a woman – gingery-haired, freckly, awkward with people . . . Why should the likes of Jerome de Labasse want her?

But these sophisticated, knowing people at his tea-party were saying he was 'taken with her'. What if all the time he had wanted her to respond with more warmth; what if he had been waiting for some sign that she cared for him?

How willingly she would have given it, if only she'd known. Less quickness in withdrawing her hand when he took it, more closeness when they were together in his car . . .

She wasn't skilled in letting a man know she was interested, because in the first place that was utterly forbidden where she came from, and moreover she lacked the ability to pick up the clues. She'd never been good at that. That was one of the reasons she'd let her mother drift into marriage with Wally Baynes – she'd failed to pick up the signs that should have warned her it was on the cards.

She sighed to herself. Toinette and Valerie had said Jerome's marriage had been loveless. They'd implied, too, that there had been several women in his life – well, that was to be expected, why shouldn't he find consolation if he wanted to?

But there was no reason, absolutely no reason, why he should be disappointed in his relationship with Gwen. She owed him so much, not least because he had been so patient and . . . and *noble* over her lack of response. As soon as she could she would let him know . . .

Though how, she couldn't imagine. She had no experience in such matters.

The tea-party went on and on, then transferred to the dining-room to become an impromptu dinner party. Gwen made no move to go. It was so interesting to be with these lively people, there was so much warmth and vivacity compared with the dullness of her hotel.

At about ten o'clock there was some murmuring among the guests. Then Gaston Arriac seemed to emerge as speaker for all of them. 'Thank you, Jerome, for a lovely evening, but we feel it's time we left you two love-birds alone.' He wagged a finger at them, shepherded the others before him, and a moment later they could be heard clattering down to the hall to collect hats and coats from Tibau.

Jerome turned an apologetic glance on Gwen. 'I'm sorry,' he said with a shrug. 'They take things for granted.'

She studied him. 'I've been very obtuse, haven't I?'

'Don't say that. You mustn't feel that—'

'How long would you have gone on handling me with kid gloves, Jerome?'

'As long as necessary,' he replied slowly. They were

standing close, Gwen's head lifted so that she could read his expression. He put one finger under her chin, tilted her face up a little more, and kissed her lightly on the lips.

An exquisite shiver went through her. Some misty wave seemed to sway her forward. He put his arms around her. He murmured little endearments against her lovely hair, which he'd so often longed to unpin and let cascade down her back.

'Jerome, I'm sorry it's taken me so long to wake up,' she whispered, the words half-lost against his shoulder.

'Don't wake up, my darling. This is a dream, let's enjoy it together.'

And when Tibau came up to inquire whether he should have the car brought round to take Mlle Whitchurch home, he found the dining-room empty. But above he could hear footsteps crossing Monsieur's bedroom; two sets of footsteps: the Count's, which he knew well, and another, those of the little English girl.

Tibau smiled to himself. He extinguished the lights in the dining-room, then quietly withdrew to the servants' quarters where he told Cook that there would be breakfast for two in the morning.

Chapter Three

When Gwen awoke next morning she experienced a moment's complete disorientation. An only child, she'd always slept alone. Yet here she was, warm and half-awake, with someone's arms around her.

Memory flooded back. Happiness and gratitude swept through her. She heard Jerome's even breathing, felt his chest rise and fall against her shoulder. And she thought to herself, This is my lover.

She understood that last night had been an initiation. She had begun her lessons in the art of love, and her teacher was a master.

How patient and understanding he'd been of her shyness, her ignorance. 'Don't be afraid, just give yourself to me,' he'd whispered. 'My little English rose . . .'

With gentleness he had helped her undress, carried her to the bed, kissed her as he brought the covers over her nakedness. A moment later he had joined her. For the first time in her life she had felt a man's body against her own, skin against skin, lips against lips.

Little by little she had relaxed under his touch. She had begun to respond, to anticipate what he wanted from her. 'Ah,' he had murmured, 'you are quick to learn, dearest.' But soon there were no more words, only quickened pulses and the moment of no return. She knew pain and bewilderment and then a surge of desire that changed her for ever. She was his and he was hers and nothing else mattered.

They had slept then, and woken to make love anew, and drifted off again in each other's arms.

A wan early-morning light was filtering between the louvres of the outer shutters. She pulled herself up on an elbow to gaze at this man, this other part of herself, this teacher of wonders.

She owed him everything. He had changed the world for her. Until he came into her life she had been a nothing, an ignorant girl. She'd never even had a boy-friend. Attending a girls' school, thought of as 'different' by the girls who might have introduced her to their brothers, a wallflower at the sedate school socials . . . Even if she'd felt the slightest impulse towards romance, the sight of her own mother mooning over her stepfather would have been enough to stifle it.

She thought of herself as very ordinary, rather dull. Why should Jerome have cared for her at all? Oh, she was so lucky! Even if she wasn't head over heels in love – and she sensed somehow that true love, real passionate love, would be something more overwhelming than what she felt for him – gratitude, friendship, and affection seemed enough. She had felt she owed it to Jerome to be his lover. But it had been a debt she was more than willing to pay.

This great mystery into whose secret he had led her might have been thrust on her by someone else – someone clumsy and selfish. But no, the heavens had sent her Jerome, and she had been given the greatest gift of her life.

She could never thank him enough. She must do all she could to please him, be all he wanted her to be . . .

She leaned over to put the gentlest of kisses on his temple. He stirred, made an indeterminate sound. Then he opened his eyes. A smile lit them up.

'*Bonjour, mon amour.*'

She kissed him good morning. He drew her down. 'Well, little English rose, are you well? Are you happy?'

46

'So happy, darling.'

'No regrets?'

'How could I regret something so wonderful?'

'Ah, you know, we French have a saying, that a woman never forgets her first lover and never forgives him.'

'I shall make that something different. I'll say she never forgets and never fails to be grateful.'

He laughed. 'You are such a . . . I don't know . . . there's something so innocent and yet so direct about you, Gwen.'

'I've been a total ignoramus up till now.'

'You think so?' He was still laughing. 'Well, there are other things to learn, *ma chère!*'

And so, this time teasingly and with gaiety, he made love to her again, letting her see that although it was the most important thing in the world it needn't weigh her down or scare her. Delight seemed to shine all around them until the moment of climax, in which everything was washed away in splendour.

When she woke again a clock was chiming eight o'clock outside. To her that was very late, she ought to be getting up. But when she pushed the sheet aside, Jerome caught her back.

'No, no, I'll ring. Tibau will bring coffee—'

'Jerome! Tibau will see me—!'

'Ah, *chut*, why should that trouble you?' But he went to a door, strolled into a wardrobe, and came out with two robes, one of which he tossed to her.

It was a kimono, long and soft, embroidered with a slender branch on which bright-plumaged birds perched. 'This is beautiful, Jerome,' she said as it slid caressingly around her body. 'Did you bring it back from Japan?'

'Yes, pretty, isn't it? Japan's full of things like that.' He sat on the side of the bed, studying the curve of the silk over her breasts. 'When you wear it the local scenery becomes even more beautiful.' He leaned over to put a little kiss on a green and yellow finch. 'Shall I

47

tell Tibau to come back with the coffee in an hour or so?' he suggested.

'No, Jerome, really, we must start the day. I have to go back to the hotel and change. Mme Garzier will be wondering where I am.'

'She will not, of course,' he said with a smile.

'Not?' She stared at him. 'You mean, she'll guess that . . . this' – her little gesture took in the room – 'has happened?'

'My darling, she thought it had happened weeks ago.'

'What?'

'Everybody who has seen us took it for granted that you and I were lovers.'

'Jerome, that's awful!'

'Not at all. It's perfectly natural. You are a very pretty and charming girl and I am a predatory male. Why else would I have brought you to Paris?'

'But that wasn't why, Jerome.'

'Not entirely. But I must confess to you, my poor little girl, that I always meant to trap you into an affair. There, do you hate me now?'

She threw herself into his arms, laughing. 'Oh, yes, I hate you terribly.'

Tibau chose that moment to knock and come in with the silver tray of coffee. He set it down, tactfully looking elsewhere, went to the windows to draw back the curtains and open the shutters so that daylight came pouring in. He bowed without quite meeting anyone's eye, and went out. In the passage he smiled to himself. Really, Monsieur was always right. The girl was pretty, truly pretty – rosy and smiling and at ease with him. A good report to take back to the kitchens.

'After breakfast,' Jerome said, sitting cross-legged on the bed and drinking coffee, 'we'll go to the hotel and pack up your things. You can have the blue bedroom for them, although of course—'

But Gwen was shaking her head. 'No, Jerome, I don't think that's a good idea.'

'*Comment?* Why not?'

'I don't think I should move in with you—'

'But my dearest girl, it's only common sense—'

'Look here, darling, despite everything I am actually here to do a job. We do have a business arrangement.'

'Oh, *ça alors!*'

'No, I mean it. I must have some independence. I think I should keep my hotel room.'

'Gwen!'

She put a finger on his mouth to still the protests. 'I don't say I'm going to sleep there often,' she soothed. 'But I feel I must have a place of my own.'

It didn't occur to her that when she first woke she'd been vowing to do all she could to please him. Already her own nature was asserting itself. She was Jerome's lover, she was a lucky, happy, beloved girl – but she was also Gwen Whitchurch, a talented designer of furniture, who had work to do and needed some little nook where she could be alone to think.

Jerome's dark blue eyes were twinkling. 'I am after all a trained diplomat,' he said, 'so we must negotiate. I say you must bring your belongings here, you say no, you must leave them at the Saints-Pères. Now it's my turn to say, very well, I concede that you must keep the room there, if you insist. But at least bring some of your things here so that you needn't rush back in the mornings to change.'

'We-ell,' she said, entering into the game, 'that's a big concession . . .'

'Diplomats always have alternatives: I suggest that instead of fetching your clothes from the hotel we should go out and buy you some pretty things—'

'*Monsieur le diplomate*, negotiations are broken off! You know that in my country such a thing is thought very wrong! How dare you? Armed hostilities are about to break out—'

'I can't negotiate if you make me laugh. No, seriously, *mon amour*, we must buy you some clothes. Now that we are as we are, you'll be going about with me everywhere and your wardrobe . . .'

She smiled. 'Is it very awful?'

'Nothing about you is awful. But I have to admit, in the most diplomatic way, that your clothes lack a certain something.'

So after breakfast they went out, and this time Gwen let the money be spent without once troubling her head that it made her a 'kept woman'. Jerome for his part was content. The threat of being seen with her while she wore that awful pink satin was entirely done away with.

The weeks went by. Happiness seemed to cocoon her. She went out with Jerome to almost all his social engagements, was accepted everywhere without comment. Her world enlarged wonderfully – she met Derain, Cocteau, Stravinsky; she even met a few politicians. She began to feel completely at home in Paris, could find her way about with ease, arrange to meet a group of friends in the cafés of the Latin Quarter – La Coupole, le Pré aux Clercs, le Dôme.

Her mother noticed the change in Gwen's letters home. Instead of 'M. de Labasse' or 'the Count', it was 'Jerome' now. Part of Rhoda Baynes knew she ought to be writing awful warnings to her daughter but another part – the romantic Welsh part – murmured, 'Leave her alone, she's happy, she's growing up . . .' Now that the first shock of her running away had worn off, Rhoda couldn't help feeling a fond sympathy with what she thought of as her daughter's romance with an aristocrat.

The day came when the dining-room at the apartment in the Avenue Foch was ready to be shown to the world. Jerome invited a large group of friends to 'le cocktail' and asked a smaller group to stay on to dinner.

The room looked stunning. The pearly light from the lotus lamps glowed against the plain silk of the walls. The carpet, specially woven, was grey and gold and white in soft stripes. The colours of the curtains and blinds had just enough emphasis to draw the eye and allow it to glide on. But it was the furniture that drew the attention.

Gwen had found a cabinet-maker in the rue Notre Dame des Champs who, under her direction, had made the pieces. She had insisted on doing some of the finishing herself, to the astonishment of *le patron*.

The dining table and the chairs had turned out as she expected – softly elegant, faintly oriental yet not sultry, not alien. The sideboard had given her a lot of trouble until she hit on the idea of a breakfront in two sections. The two compartments weren't identical, so that the piece had the look of a wave advancing gently on a shore. To enforce the effect Gwen had inlaid the front panels with mother-of-pearl and green suede in soft whorls of movement. The top surface, on which dishes would be laid, was covered in hardwearing shagreen (called *galuchat* in French), dyed in shadowy green and blue.

She had also made occasional tables to hold lamps and sweet or cigarette boxes. Two taller pieces were for flowers only, and the flowers on that evening were large, open, yellow tulips that exactly echoed the colour scheme. On two of the walls, long narrow mirrors in sections edged with green and blue and yellow glass reflected back the scene.

When Tibau threw open the doors to let the cocktail-party guests see the room for the first time, a spattering of spontaneous applause broke out. People called out, as if they were at a theatre, 'Designer, designer!' and Jerome pushed Gwen forward.

Blushing, she acknowledged the congratulations. 'Thank you, I'm glad you like it . . .'

'Like it? I adore it!'

'For me, I'm glad to see a woman's touch in interior décor. The men, they are very adventurous, but you know sometimes . . .'

'Yes, so hard to live with . . .'

'Tell me, *ma chère*. When will you be free to make some things for me?'

'No, no,' Jerome admonished, 'for the present Gwen's work is exclusively for me. You must all wait patiently until September.'

'Very well, then, I put in a claim for September. Mlle Veetcha, I have a house near Haussmann . . . Would you . . . ?'

'No, no, me first! Gwen, I should like some furniture for my house at Juan-les-Pins – something *sportif* . . .'

It was clear her order book would be full for many months to come. Gwen's head was reeling from the clamour of enthusiasm. She was glad when the cocktail party broke up and they could at last settle down to dinner with the eight friends who remained.

To Gwen, this was the ultimate test. If the furniture didn't work when in actual use, she was a failure. But everyone was comfortable on the dining chairs, the servants were totally at ease with the long sideboard, the women (and some of the men) enjoyed glimpsing themselves in the narrow mirrors.

Later that night, Jerome took her in his arms and kissed her on the cheek. 'My dearest girl, I want to thank you for what you have done. You have given me a charming, charming room. What's more, you've justified the faith I had in you.'

Gwen was suffused with pleasure. Yesterday, when she had given the room over to the servants so that the table could be laid and the flowers arranged, she'd had a moment of absolute terror – that it would all look dreadful, that she'd be a laughing-stock. And, worse, that Jerome would be a laughing-stock for having believed in her.

It had been decided between them that she should take on two other rooms. Jerome had wanted her to take on the more intimate rooms – the small sitting-room which was most often in use, and his bedroom. The sitting-room she agreed to, but she shied away from the bedroom.

The reason was that she wouldn't be able to bear the thought of some other woman sharing it with him some day. She knew in some deep and wise part of her soul that the love affair between herself and Jerome wouldn't last for ever. She'd had that warning in the conversation she had overheard between Sybille and Toinette.

But more than that, she knew that Jerome wasn't deeply in love. He had great affection for her, she roused him physically, her talent pleased him, they shared the same sense of humour. But it wasn't an entire love.

For herself, she would have been happy to remain with him and never think of another man for the rest of her life. Whether that was a more sincere emotion than Jerome's, she wasn't sure. It was perhaps just tradition – she'd been brought up to think she'd fall in love and marry and 'settle down', and Jerome seemed to be the man that fate had sent her.

Yet Jerome wasn't the 'settling down' type. He wasn't thinking of marriage. He wasn't even thinking of a long-term commitment. How she knew this, she couldn't tell. But she knew that some day some other woman would take her place.

So, she refused to design anything for the bedroom. The thought of another woman lying languorously in a bed which she herself had brought forth from her own imagination was unbearable.

It was agreed that she would design for the sitting-room and the big drawing-room. Cocteau had agreed to suggest some ideas for the library, Clement Rousseau would do the bedroom. The whole thing must be costing a fortune.

Her sketchbook was full of ideas by this time. When

53

Jerome was off on some other engagement she would haunt the museums, art galleries, shopping streets, parks. The spirit of 1920s Paris wrapped her around.

She loved the way Parisians took all forms of art seriously and yet with a kind of intelligent amusement. Art Deco was somehow particularly Parisian. It was the art of cities and towns – she couldn't imagine it being successful in a rural setting. It was active, jazzy, sometimes bizarre and sometimes romantic. She gloried in the fact that she was now a part of it.

Cinemas, shops and cafés were influenced by the Art Deco fashion. Furniture became less heavy and much less dull. All kinds of new woods were being tried out. The French word for cabinet-maker was '*ébéniste*', which meant 'worker in ebony', which seemed to Gwen to symbolise the importance of the wood itself in any piece of furniture. She was one of the first to seek out and use timber recently found and brought back from the Far East, from Australia and New Guinea.

In the workshop in the rue Notre Dame des Champs, a corner had been set aside for her especial use. The men who worked there accepted her now as a *copain* – she wasn't some rich young lady playing at being a worker, she was a genuine cabinet-maker. Her hands bore those little scars from years past that told of a chisel slipping, a splinter piercing.

So she worked, and she dreamed, and she concentrated on the pieces for Jerome's apartment although it was clear she wasn't going to finish quite within the limits of their contract. But there – she wasn't bound to him by any piece of paper, she was doing the work for him because she loved him.

Yet in July, when she was deeply involved with a ticklish piece of carpentry at the workshop, Jerome said he thought he would go to Juan-les-Pins.

'I always do, you know,' he explained. 'July – Paris empties – that's the way it is.'

'I really couldn't come, darling.' She meant, Please stay – so as to be with me.

'Well, that's a pity. Laurent and Cecile are having about five or six people to their villa, and we'll be sailing a little – perhaps as far as Livorno. Sure you won't come?'

'I can't, Jerome. Edgar Brandt is making me some little wrought-iron pieces that have to be mounted at once into the woodwork . . .' She let the words die away, because Jerome wasn't listening.

She saw him off on the Blue Train. He kissed her fondly, urged her to join him if the work was finished sooner than she expected. But, as she walked out of the station, she was thinking, By the time I'm free to come, he'll be off on board the yacht – how could I possibly join him?

A few days later, dropping in at La Coupole, she came across Toinette Montanard sipping a Pernod. She and Toinette had struck up a friendship, perhaps because they were so apparently unalike. Toinette was tough, resilient, rather cruel, but honest.

'Ha, *l'anglaise*, I thought you were off cruising the Med?'

'No, I couldn't go.' Gwen explained about her ironwork at Brandt's studio. She ordered a glass of wine. Toinette was telling her of her own problems with a piece of costume jewellery she was making for a star of the Comédie Française.

'Don't you think so?' she ended.

'What?' Gwen jerked to attention. 'I'm sorry, Toinette, I was miles away.'

'That was evident. So, *mon amie*, the little clouds are appearing on the horizon, eh?'

'Not at all.' The waiter brought her wine, she took it and sipped it thankfully. It was a very hot evening, sultry, the air full of coming thunder.

'No clouds. Not even over the sea on the way to Livorno?'

Gwen gave a half smile. After a moment she said, hesitating, 'What does it mean, Toinette? I never thought he'd go without me.'

'Darling, a man like Jerome would rather die than stay in Paris in July. It simply isn't done. What is noticeable is that he didn't tie you hand and foot and take you with him.'

'He asked me to join him when I could.'

'Oh yes, yes, and how are you to get to him if he's twenty miles offshore?'

'Well, yes . . . So that seemed to mean he didn't care whether I came or not.'

Toinette turned her glass round and round on the cork mat. 'You take it better than I expected,' she remarked.

'Take what?'

'The . . . the loosening. The untying. You show no signs of making a fool of yourself by clinging and crying.'

I'm crying inside, thought Gwen. She sipped her wine. At length she said, 'I thought my heart would break when this moment came.'

'And is it broken?'

'Is it?' She considered. 'The fact that I can ask the question means that it isn't.'

'Good for you.'

'What should I do, Toinette?'

Toinette frowned but said nothing.

'Please tell me. You've seen this happening before, I think.'

'Well, yes.'

'Perhaps it even happened to you?'

'Not with Jerome. A couple of times, my heart's been broken. My way is pretty violent. Big rows, scenes where we threw things at each other. But Jerome would think that uncivilised.'

'Jerome would just walk away,' Gwen agreed. 'Besides, I'm not the sort of person who enjoys a row.'

Toinette leaned back in her chair, fanning herself with the menu card. 'Let me explain something to you,' she said. 'Jerome is a collector. He collects people of talent and pretty women. You happen to be both at the same time, so he values you very much. But if, as seems likely, he's not so attracted physically, there's nothing to be done about it. He's letting you know that the thing is ending, and he's hoping you pick up the clues.'

Gwen nodded. Slow as she was to sense such things, that much had come home to her.

'I understand that. What should *I* do?'

'Depends whether you want to stay friends or not.'

'Oh, I do. I'd hate not to be friends with Jerome.'

'Then everything is easy. You still have that room at the Saints-Pères?'

'Yes. I've been sleeping there since he went to Juan. I can't bear his great big bedroom without him.'

'Excellent. All you do is continue in the same way. He probably won't be back until September. You might arrange to be away somewhere at that time . . .'

'I could go to see M. Guinchy's house. He got first place in my order book for when I'd finished at the Avenue Foch.'

'Quite. Then when you come back you could tell Jerome it's more convenient, now that you've finished there, to work out of your own premises. It might even be a good idea to get a studio of your own. There are plenty of places to let in Montparnasse.'

'I could work out of the joinery in the rue Notre Dame des Champs. They've got a sort of loft that's only got old lumber in it, I could rent that.'

In a way it cheered her to be able to take these steps. She felt it restored her dignity. She wasn't any longer a mistress in the process of being discarded, she was a business-woman looking after her career.

The bill at the Saints-Pères had always been discreetly taken care of by Jerome. Gwen now had a little discussion with Mme Garzier. 'I think I ought to pay for my room myself, madame,' she suggested on Saturday, the traditional day for settling up.

'Really?' Madame said, her round pink face creasing up in distress. 'You and M. de Labasse are at an end?'

'Not precisely. But things do change, after all. I feel I ought to pay my own hotel bill.'

Madame made little shrugging movements, swaying her head. 'You and Monsieur are on bad terms?'

'Certainly not.'

'Ah, then . . . I think it would be . . . impolite to change the arrangement. Monsieur would be very hurt to think you refused this little . . . emolument.'

Despite the unhappiness that seemed to hang about her like a cloak these days, Gwen couldn't help a smile at this view. But Mme Garzier was very experienced in such matters and she might be right.

'All the same,' she insisted, 'I'd like to be independent.'

'This rage for independence,' mourned Madame. 'Well, I suppose that is your English nature. But I should choose a better moment. Perhaps, if you were to move out of here, when you went to your new hotel you could let Monsieur know that you prefer to pay the bill yourself. But in the meantime, if you stay on here, I should . . . I really should . . . allow things to remain as they are.'

Gwen bowed to this superior wisdom, vowing that as soon as she could she would find herself a room or an apartment of her own choice. The Saints-Pères was all right, and of course its name, meaning Holy Fathers, had been very reassuring to her mother. But it would always remind her of her arrival in Paris with Jerome.

With September, Jerome returned. He'd kept in touch with postcards and notes and a gift of roses from Grasse. Gwen had gone to Rambouillet to look at M. Guinchy's house. When she got back to Paris she found a message awaiting her at the Saints-Pères, saying

Jerome was very pleased indeed with the two finished rooms and when was he going to see her?

She rang him. 'Sorry not to be there when you got back,' she said, 'I was in the country. You enjoyed Juan?' Say you missed me, she was begging secretly.

'Very pleasant. You remember Robert wanted you to design some things for his villa at Juan? I looked the place over; you might enjoy the challenge.'

'He's next on my list after Georges Guinchy. Georges is planning a study and office from which he can work by telephone to his Paris business. It's going to take me a couple of months. Will you be in Paris now for a while?'

'Until the winter season at St Moritz. Although I might not go there this year – snow is rather boring after the first few days and I don't ski well.'

She waited. She wondered if he would ask her to go to St Moritz. If he did, she would put everything else aside and go.

The next thing he said was, 'I see you've taken away almost all your belongings from the apartment.'

'Well, it made sense, Jerome. Now I've finished there and I'm engaged on work elsewhere, I thought I ought to have a studio of my own. So I've got a corner of the workshop in rue Notre Dame.'

'Yes, of course, but . . . most of your personal things have gone too.'

She chose her words very carefully. 'I could always bring them back,' she said.

She knew almost as soon as the sentence was finished that he wasn't going to take her up on it. He said, with something like a sigh of relief, 'Perhaps it's more convenient the way it is.'

'You mean, just leave a few things?'

'You could use them if you happen to stay over.'

'Yes.' So they might make love again, one night, another night. But they wouldn't be lovers in the old way, which had been so precious to her.

'Well, so what are you doing with your spare time?' he demanded, starting on a fresh tack. 'I'm giving a sort of a party on Tuesday – dinner here and then we're going on to the theatre to see a costume rehearsal of Diaghilev's new ballet. Would you like to come?'

'To meet Diaghilev?'

'Of course.'

Serge Diaghilev was the impresario who had brought the Russian Ballet to Europe before the war. Since the Revolution in Russia, his company had regarded Paris as its base. He was a moving spirit in the artistic life of Paris, hiring great artists to design scenery and costumes for his productions. The mere thought of meeting him was enough to override any anxieties Gwen had about seeing Jerome again.

'I'd love to come,' she replied.

'Wear an informal after-six dress, because backstage at a theatre you won't be comfortable in a dinner frock. Eight o'clock, then.'

She noticed that he didn't say he would send the car for her. Those days were gone. She was no longer his special protegée. But she was at least still his friend.

The group who went to the Champs Elysées Theatre were friends already known to Gwen. Everyone was too tactful to take note of the fact that she was not regarded as hostess alongside Jerome. Conversation was mostly about matters artistic.

'I have a problem with Georges Guinchy's commission,' she confessed. 'He likes some ideas of mine for angular, black furniture – quite in keeping, it's a sort of private office, you see. But it absolutely *must* be lightened somehow and I'm hanged if I can see how to do it.'

'Trimming? Inlay?' someone suggested.

'He thinks that would look fussy. Well, never mind, something will suddenly strike me, I suppose.'

They were sitting in a ragged gathering in the stalls.

Everyone connected with the rehearsal was in work-clothes – the musicians in shirt-sleeves, the scene-painters in smocks and caps, Diaghilev himself in a silk shirt and heavy woollen cardigan. He was swearing in Russian at the lighting engineer.

Only the dancers were in costume. They wore gauzy loose robes, softly painted in flower designs.

'Those look like – you know, Jerome, they look like kimonos!'

'Very perceptive, my dear. That's just what they are. It's a Japanese ballet and the costumes and scenery are by Tamaki Hayakawa, a Japanese lacquerist I brought back with me when I came home from Tokyo.'

'Japanese!' The idea was still exotic enough to cause a murmur of astonishment among his friends.

'The costumes are lovely,' Yvonne Desarpes said, 'but a little subdued for a Diaghilev production, aren't they? We expect something more dramatic from him.'

'A Japanese ballet he decided to have, and Japanese art is what Tama has given him,' Jerome replied.

The rehearsal continued in fits and starts. The dancers were comfortable in their costumes but Diaghilev couldn't get the lighting to his satisfaction.

He came ambling over to speak to Jerome and his companions. They all rose as if he were royalty.

'Confounded things . . . It all looks so *dull*!'

Everyone assured him it looked charming. The verdict didn't seem to reassure him. Diaghilev, it seemed, didn't want charm, but theatrical effect. He beckoned to a figure who was sitting in silence and alone a few rows back, who rose and came to join him.

'Tama, can't you make the colours brighter?'

'Not on gauze. If you want bright heavy colour, you must have heavier cloth.'

The speaker replied in good French, but with an accent Gwen had never heard before. He seemed unable to pronounce the letter 'l'. He was a muscular man, quite short, though still taller than Gwen by a head. He wore a good European suit and a white shirt, above which his olive skin and dark slanted eyes looked strangely dramatic.

'Everyone, this is Tama,' Jerome said. 'He is a painter of lacquer, his family are famous for it in Japan. I was very pleased when he agreed to come to Paris with me two years ago.'

Introductions were performed. Tama bowed. Gwen saw him stare, almost in consternation, at her bronze-coloured hair. 'Forgive me,' he said when he realised she had noticed, 'but in my country, no one has hair that colour. It is very beautiful.'

'Ginger, we call it in my country,' she replied with a laugh.

She had no idea she had just met the man who was going to solve the problem of M. Guinchy's furniture for her.

The man who was going to change her life.

Chapter Four

Jerome thought it best to take his friends away after another quarter of an hour or so. Diaghilev was clearly in a bad mood. They certainly weren't helping by being there to witness his disappointment.

Tamaki Hayakawa went with them to the foyer as they left. 'Come with us, Tama,' Jerome suggested. 'We're going to the Chat Blanc. You know how you love to foxtrot.'

'Very kind, Jerome, but must stay here with Diaghilev until he is satisfied with the effect of costumes and scenery.'

'I'm sorry I got you into this, Tama. But if he wanted a paint-splash Japan for his ballet, he shouldn't have insisted on a real Japanese artist.'

'Quite so. Outsiders can see best what makes Japan seem Japanese. When asked to portray Japan, Japanese artist relies on his memory, not his invention.'

'I think the costumes are lovely,' Gwen insisted.

'True – lovely but not theatrical. My blame. I did not understand everything has to be twice as big and twice as bright for European theatre. Trouble comes from my profession. Lacquerist does not work on huge scale, you see.'

Someone murmured that it would be nice to see his work.

'Please come . . . Jerome knows my studio . . . Always pleased to entertain guests who are friends of M. de Labasse.'

An appointment was made for the afternoon of the

63

next day. Tama bowed, then left them to return to the displeasure of Serge Diaghilev.

'What's the story behind that?' Robert Marouis asked as they piled into taxis to be taken to the Chat Blanc. 'It's a long journey from Tokyo to Paris – what made him come?'

'Oh, the usual thing,' said Jerome. 'He had new ideas he wanted to express in the traditional art of lacquerwork. His father, who is a bit of a tyrant, wouldn't let him. Along I came with an offer to take him to Paris and introduce him into influential circles. He came like a shot.'

'His work must be interesting, if Diaghilev took him up.'

'Wait till you see it. Diaghilev went wild when I took him to look at it. He'd always had this idea for a Japanese ballet at the back of his mind and he'd got a young choreographer he thought could do the dances.'

'Ah,' said Robert wickedly, 'we know Diaghilev and his young choreographers.'

Jerome dismissed that with a negligent wave. 'He took too much for granted when he commissioned Tama to do this ballet décor. Tama may seem pretty Europeanised, but he knows very little about European theatre. In Japan, you know, the audience is much closer to the stage and there's almost no stage lighting. He just couldn't learn quickly enough how to make his designs work on that scale.'

'Well, I think it's awfully unfair,' Gwen said.

'True, true. But it's also pretty disastrous for Diaghilev. The ballet's supposed to be performed on Saturday night. Now I've seen the costumes I see that they don't really work. I hear the dances themselves are rather dull as well. It might be a very bad first night.'

Everyone expressed some slight sympathy for the impresario but it wasn't heartfelt. They forgot all about the matter at the Chat Blanc.

But as they broke up in the early hours of the

morning, Gwen reminded Jerome of the appointment at Tama's studio.

'You really want to go?' he asked in surprise.

'I do indeed. It struck me that lacquerwork may be just what I need for Georges Guinchy's study.'

'What a good idea! Very well then, we'll go. Who else wants to come?'

Only Yvonne Desarpes was interested enough to take it up. Jerome wrote down the address for each of them. They agreed to meet there at three in the afternoon.

The studio was in a little cul-de-sac off the Place Vendôme. Gwen arrived first, a fact which pleased her as it gave her a chance to examine the work on display in peace. A young Frenchman, scarcely more than a lad, waited on her.

'Is there anything particular you wish to look at, mademoiselle?' he inquired.

'I'm waiting for some friends,' she said. 'I'll just look around, if I may.'

'Of course.' He withdrew to the end of the small showroom. Gwen began to walk round the tables.

She had seen lacquerwork before, of course. Trays had always been in use in her home that had been 'japanned' – decorated usually in a glossy black with a design in gold and perhaps red. She'd always taken it for granted that these were produced in a factory in, say, Birmingham. And well they might have been, but they were a copy of something more valuable.

On antique furniture too, lacquerwork appeared. Buhl furniture – ornate, based on black enamelled or veneered wood – was heavily adorned with lacquer as well as inlays of ivory, tortoiseshell and brass.

In museums she had seen bowls and stands and cabinets. There was a Chinese cabinet in the Louvre, made in the twelfth century, a glory of gold and silver lacquer on black. She knew, from her own scant experience of working with decoration on wood, how difficult an art it could be.

The things on view in Tamaki Hayakawa's showroom were superb. Some were very small – cups for tea, cups for sake. Others were on a larger scale, such as screens and travel-boxes. Some were for modern use; there were vanity cases and cigarette cases, bracelets, shoe buckles.

The work was breathtakingly lovely. The finish and the gleam of the articles told of hours of work. But the design on which the lacquer was laid made the articles different from anything else. The design on each piece was unique, a master's hand drawing a heron, a chrysanthemum, a fish flashing through water, clouds and moonlight, little figures in a mountain landscape and, influenced by European ideas, a train disappearing into a tunnel.

A voice spoke at her elbow. 'Please forgive me. My apprentice didn't tell until a moment ago that you had arrived.'

She turned. 'That's all right, Mr Hayakawa. I've had a lovely time admiring your display.'

He was younger than he had seemed in the poor lighting of the theatre auditorium – perhaps twenty-five or twenty-six. He had straight black hair worn rather short and brushed plainly back. Today he was wearing a light-coloured suit which a Frenchman would have thought too pale for autumn fashion.

He bowed. 'You know of lacquer?' he asked. 'Very ancient art. You know perhaps, we use the juice of *Rhus vernicifera*, it is like the sumach tree you have here in Europe.'

He went on to deliver a little lecture, clearly often used, about how the lacquer was applied again and again over the original designs, thirty coats of clear lacquer, each meticulously dried and then smoothed to satin before the next coat was applied.

'A long process,' he remarked, picking up a cup and handing it to her. 'Very strong when finished, resists very hot tea, boiling water. You would think many coats of varnish would make cup heavy. But no, it is light to handle.'

'It's beautiful,' she said, turning it so that the sun caught it.

She so clearly meant it that his rather serious features broke into a smile; a glint of appreciation came into the black eyes.

'We have a saying, it is by Ogata Korin, a very famous *makie-shi*: the art of the lacquerist is to capture sunlight so that it can be a gleam of gold in the hand of a woman.'

'So it is,' she agreed softly. 'A gleam of gold.'

The *tête-à-tête* was ended by the arrival of Jerome and, a moment later, Yvonne. Yvonne went noisily round the room, admiring everything, picking things up and cooing over them.

'I absolutely must buy something,' she enthused. 'I'll have this vanity case with the lovely little train rushing into the tunnel. How much is it?'

When she heard the price, her mouth dropped open. 'My word,' she said, 'that's steep! How much for the clip-on shoe buckles?'

Jerome was urging Gwen to choose something. 'I'll have this little cup,' she said, holding up the article she'd been admiring when Yvonne came in.

'Please,' Tama said with a bow, 'accept it as a gift.'

Gwen knew that what he was offering was a very expensive item. Each of the pieces in the showroom was unique, a work of art. Each had taken many, many days to produce, with the final surface painted in gold and precious lustres by Tamaki Hayakawa himself, a master of his craft.

'Nonsense,' Jerome intervened with a wave of his hand, 'you've got a living to earn, you can't afford to give things away. I'll pay for Gwen's little sake cup.'

Yvonne wheeled about, pouting. 'Why does Gwen get hers paid for and not me?'

'Oh, dear, poor Yvonne . . . Very well, I shall pay

for both the things. There, Tama, send the bill to my house.'

Gwen knew, by some hitherto unknown sixth sense, that Tama was offended. She couldn't quite see how, because he was in business to make and sell lacquerware and had just sold two costly items. It was only much later she came to know that to the Japanese, the giving of gifts is an almost sacred act which ought not to be prevented.

Now Yvonne was examining the flower arrangement that stood alone on a pedestal at the far end near the desk. 'Flowers *are* expensive, of course,' she murmured, staring at the three small dahlias and the autumnal twig that made it up.

'No, no,' laughed the Count, 'that's the Japanese style. What's its name again, Tama?'

'*Ikebana.*'

'That's it, *ikebana* – you see things like that in every Japanese home. They think it's ostentatious to have great big bunches of flowers like our arrangements.'

'Ostentatious?' Tama repeated, struggling with the word. 'What does that mean?'

'Showy . . . rather vulgar . . .' Gwen suggested.

'Ah. No, it is not that, Jerome. We use few flowers because our rooms are not large. Besides, it is easier to achieve harmony with a few blossoms than with many.'

'Oh, harmony!' Jerome agreed. 'Everybody in Japan is always talking about harmony.'

'That is true. Here in Paris, harmony is less sought after.' Tama was smiling, the pained shadow of a moment ago gone from his features. 'Argument is the fashion here. When I first arrived and saw people talking in a café I thought a fight was about to break out but no – they were only arguing about Picasso.'

He paused. 'Please let me offer tea.'

Jerome began edging towards the door. 'No, sorry, it's very kind of you, Tama, but we're expected elsewhere.' His hand was on Gwen's elbow, urging her towards the exit. 'Mme Colbert invited us to *le five o'clock* to meet Sacha Guitry. Thanks a million for showing us your work – and good luck with the ballet.'

'Oh, the ballet,' Tama said, with a fatalistic shrug. 'The ballet is doomed.'

'Don't say that! These things always seem difficult at rehearsal but on the night, you'll see, it'll be a huge success.'

'Thank you,' Tama said without enthusiasm, and bowed them out.

'I wasn't invited to Mme Colbert's,' Gwen protested as they walked out of the cul-de-sac into the splendour of the Place Vendôme and Napoleon staring stonily up into a September sky.

'No, nor was I, but anything is better than Japanese tea,' Jerome laughed. 'You've no idea! It's bitter and usually half cold, and served without milk or sugar—'

'Good heavens,' said Yvonne, 'tea with milk and sugar is bad enough—!'

Jerome had hurried ahead to the corner of the rue de Castiglione and was waving at a taxi, which shrieked to a halt at his side. Directing the driver to take them to the Crillon, he bundled the two girls in.

'Why are we going to the Crillon?' Yvonne inquired as they whizzed past the statue of Joan of Arc at the rue des Pyramides.

'Why not?'

'We could have walked there in five minutes,' Gwen protested.

'We dared not linger!' Jerome said, holding up a finger in warning. 'He might have invited us to the ballet première.'

'You mean you're not going?'

'Certainly not! It will be a sure-fire flop.'

'I think that's mean,' Gwen said.

Jerome gazed at her with innocent dark blue eyes. *'Ma chère,'* he said, 'first of all, you know I don't care for ballet, I prefer satirical comedy. Secondly, Serge

Diaghilev is not agreeable when things go badly, and
he will blame it on me. And thirdly, I shouldn't know
what to say to Tama if the Paris audience booed him.'

'Well, I shall go,' said Gwen.

'But why?' Yvonne cried. 'Just because he was going
to give you that dinky litle cup?'

'My dear *girl*!' Jerome reproved. 'If we spent our time
rushing to the aid of unsuccessful artists—'

'But the costumes *are* successful. I think they're
lovely.'

'Well, that's true, they are, but they're not spectacular
enough for—'

'Too harmonious,' Gwen said, laughing.

'Right! Oh, poor old Tama. Perhaps we ought to go,
eh? And raise a cheer if others boo him.'

So, because Gwen had put her foot down, they went
the next Saturday with a party of friends to occupy
Jerome's box at the Champs Elysées Theatre.

Gwen knew very little about ballet: when in the past
month Jerome had taken her to the theatre it had been
to see a play, most of which passed her by because she
didn't understand French political jokes.

Ballet was a revelation to her. The programme opened
with 'Les Sylphides', a romantic ballet about nymphs
in a moonlit glade. The soft lines of the long muslin
skirts, the music by Chopin, the exquisite artistry of
the performers; they all cast a spell on her.

Next came a selection of purely 'classical' ballet, from
the dances of the 'Nutcracker Suite' by Tchaikovsky.
This was spellbinding in a different way – brilliant,
precise, full of a sweet charm.

She could understand that the Japanese ballet was
going to have a hard time, coming at the end of the
programme and changing the mood entirely.

'Chrysanthemum' was about a geisha who was beloved
by two samurai warriors. The curtain went up on a misty
Japanese scene showing a tea house in a garden. All
the colours were muted, people came and went softly,

the music (by a young protégé of Diaghilev's) sounded vaguely Oriental.

Chrysanthemum appeared in her gauzy kimono. She was on her points but the only step she ever used was a little tripping step called *pas de bourré*. This, Jerome whispered, was fairly authentic because Japanese women walked with little tripping steps, often on little wooden sandals. But the audience, accustomed to ballerinas leaping in the air to be caught in mid-flight by strong young men, grew restive.

When the two samurai lovers appeared, activity on the stage increased. There was a sword fight, very acrobatic, with much flashing of blades and tumbling to rise again. But the two dancers were clearly worried about getting hurt by the swords which, though of course not real, were whizzing about with such speed that they might inflict serious injury.

So the sword fight wasn't the dramatic climax that the choreographer intended. In fact, one wag in the audience called out above the bang of the cymbals and rattle of the drums, 'Afraid you'll cut your finger, Dmitri?' At which the audience laughed and applauded.

The ballet ended with Chrysanthemum in mourning for the lover who had lost the fight. She crossed the stage – still in *pas de bourré* but very slowly. A slow drumbeat was the only accompaniment. Someone – perhaps the wag who'd called out during the swordfight – began to chant Chopin's Funeral March, which unfortunately matched the drumbeat exactly. The gallery took it up. By the time Chrysanthemum reached the grave to throw herself upon it, the whole thing had reached the level of farce.

The curtain came down. It rose again to allow a view of Chrysanthemum still prone on the grave. The same voice called: 'Get up, get up, Ludmilla, we all want to go home.'

The curtain came down rapidly. After a slight pause

it went up to allow bows to be taken. The orchestral conductor joined the line on stage, looking worried. The obligatory first-night bouquet was handed to the ballerina, who seemed on the verge of tears. The choreographer came on, to be greeted with jeers and catcalls. The composer came on, with the same response. The two young men could have been eighteen-year-old twins.

'Well, they'll be shown the door tomorrow,' murmured Thomas Leclerc, one of Jerome's friends.

'Only the composer. You'll find the other one has a charmed life,' Jerome said.

'Oh, he's the current favourite, is he?'

'Sssh,' urged Gwen, for the designer was being brought on.

Tamaki Hayakawa looked neither happy nor unhappy. He came forward, bowed, and waited.

To Gwen's intense relief, a polite spatter of applause greeted him. The costumes and scenery had in fact been the best part of the ballet. She clapped vigorously, and after a glance of surprise the others in Jerome's box followed suit.

Tama glanced up towards the box. A flicker of expression came into his face – it might almost have been the beginnings of a smile of gratitude. But next moment his features were impassive. He bowed gravely and stood waiting for release from display.

The curtain came down, there was no demand from the audience for any further opportunities to show appreciation. The theatre began to empty.

'Well, that's that,' Jerome said. 'What shall we do now? Anyone want to join me for supper at the Bristol?'

'Aren't we going to go backstage to speak to Tama?'

'Tama doesn't want to be spoken to,' Jerome said. 'Besides, there's a party from the Japanese Embassy here tonight – I expect they'll be taking up his attention.'

72

'All the same, I think we ought to—'

'No, no, Gwen,' protested Sybille. 'We've suffered enough. Let's go and have supper.'

'All right, you go on. I'll join you later.'

Jerome, out in the corridor behind his box, half turned to stare over his shoulder at her. 'You really intend to go back?'

She nodded, picking up her evening bag from the box's velvet rim. 'See you later.'

'Oh, God,' groaned the Count. 'All right, we'll all go. But only for a moment!'

In the corridor leading to the dressing-rooms backstage there was none of the usual post-première noise and bustle. The dancers were probably crying into their make-up boxes, Diaghilev towering like a thundercloud over the composer.

A small group of Japanese were a little apart. Tama was being addressed by an elderly man in evening dress and the red ribbon of the Légion d'honneur. This was the ambassador. Tama was bowing deeply and saying nothing.

'What's going on?' Gwen asked Jerome.

'My Japanese isn't good, I've forgotten almost all I ever knew, but I think the ambassador is scolding Tama for allowing samurai to be held up to ridicule.'

'But that wasn't Tama's fault!' cried Gwen, her schoolgirl sense of fair play outraged.

'Tell that to the ambassador.'

'Very well, I will,' Gwen said.

Without ado, she pushed her way into the Japanese group. She interrupted the elderly gentleman in full flow.

'Tama,' she said, 'I just wanted you to know that I thought your designs were beautiful. It's a shame the others involved made such a mess of things.'

The ambassador said something in sharp inquiry to Tama. Tama said, in French: 'Mademoiselle Gwen Whitchurch, Monsieur l'ambassadeur. Mademoiselle,

73

allow me to present you to His Excellency Monsieur Kegara, the ambassador to France of His Imperial Majesty the Emperor.'

Gwen bowed, as she had seen was expected. But without waiting for His Excellency to speak, she rushed on. 'Monsieur l'ambassadeur, how pleased you must be at the authenticity of the costumes. The only part of the ballet, alas, that pleased the audience. Monsieur Hayakawa is to be congratulated, I feel.'

Kegara glared at her. But then, after a moment, his expression softened. He said something in Japanese to Tama, who smiled and bowed agreement.

'I was saying to my countryman that it is pleasant to meet someone with the heart to appreciate such things. Mademoiselle, thank you for your views.' Kegara glanced over his shoulder at his retinue. There were two men, younger than he and in full evening dress, and two Japanese ladies in marvellous, elaborate kimonos. Without speaking he conveyed to them that he wished to leave.

They all fell back. He walked through them as if they didn't exist, then they fell in behind him, the women walking with exactly the little steps that the ballerina had conveyed in the ballet.

Jerome drew in a breath. 'Gwen, you could have caused a diplomatic incident! Imagine breaking in on what the ambassador was saying!'

'Oh, nonsense,' Gwen said, although her own breath was coming rather fast. Monsieur Kegara wasn't the kind of man you treated lightly.

'Come and drown your sorrows with us at the Bristol, Tama,' invited Robert Soulent.

'No, I have to stay. Diaghilev is talking about alterations for the second performance.'

Yvonne patted him on the shoulder. 'No alterations can save it. It will come off after five performances, *mon ami*.'

'I hope you've got your money,' Toinette put in.

'Sure you won't join us? All right, everybody, come on.'

Gwen was borne away by the group. But all through the meal that followed her thoughts kept reverting to the picture of Tama waiting alone to be spoken to by the great Diaghilev.

Jerome sensed her preoccupation. He put himself out to coax her into a better mood, danced with her, and at the end of the night kept his arm about her as they broke up.

'Come home with me, darling,' he murmured.

She looked up, surprised. After a moment she said, 'Does that mean what I think it means?'

'Of course. We always said, didn't we, that it would be nice to have some of your things at my place in case you wanted to stay over occasionally.'

He bent his head to kiss her, and she felt herself melting to his mood.

So they went home and went to bed, and it was almost what it had been before – tender, passionate, exultant, rewarding. She gave herself up to it entirely, glorying in this upsurge of the flames of old.

But even as she exchanged with him kisses and caresses that gave delight, she knew something had changed. He had said, 'to stay over occasionally'. This was for tonight only. They were not resuming their old relationship.

She knew she had become one among the women who loved Jerome and whom he in his way loved. It wasn't the same, but it was something, and she was willing to settle for that.

Chapter Five

After breakfast next morning Gwen said, 'Do you have a telephone number for Tama Hayakawa?'

Jerome, still in his silk dressing-gown, looked up from the newspaper. 'Good lord, we did our duty last night! There's no need to commiserate with him over the reviews this morning.'

'It's not that. I just want to talk to him.'

'What about?'

'About undertaking some work for me on Georges Guinchy's furniture.'

Jerome's frown vanished. 'Oh, it's *business*!'

'Yes, of course, what else?'

'Ah . . . Well, you see . . . He has quite a lot of success with women. It's the charm of the mysterious East, I think.'

She studied him. 'Jerome, you were jealous! That was what last night was about, wasn't it?'

'Not at all! What an idea! I always find you attractive and delightful, you know that.'

'But you felt I was thinking too much about Tama and you wanted to take my mind off him.'

'I wouldn't do such a thing. You know I have a mind above such petty matters.' But he was laughing and she knew she'd guessed right.

She said with some sternness, 'Jerome, you mustn't act as if you own me. If I wanted to see someone else, that would be my own business – now wouldn't it?'

'Certainly. No strings on either side. Do you, as a matter of fact, find Tama attractive?'

'Well, he's very good looking . . .'

'In a Japanese sort of way.'

'Yes, those black eyes and that smooth olive skin . . . And he's something of a genius. That lacquerwork is exquisite.'

Jerome agreed that Tama was a master of his craft – that was, after all, why he'd brought him to Paris in the first place. 'And he's been a big success, although of course there isn't the same market for lacquer as there is for, let's say, painting.'

'You said he'd had a quarrel with his father?'

'Oh yes, quite a furore – Japanese sons don't argue with their fathers, particularly if the father is a master lacquerist. Tama had read that European lacquer-workers had found a way to put white into their work . . . I don't suppose you know enough about it yet, although,' he twinkled, 'I've a feeling you're going to learn a lot in the next few days. But white has never been seen in Chinese or Japanese lacquer—'

'Yes, it has, they do it with mother-of-pearl—'

'There, that's what I mean. Mother-of-pearl is silvery. But pure white, no. Jean Dunand here in Paris found out how to do it, it's some long process with crushed eggshell inlaid in the final coating. Anyhow, Tama wanted to try it and Papa went up in the air about it – going against tradition, foreign interference, and so on and so on.'

'Just because Tama wanted to put white into his lacquerwork?'

'Exactly. I came along at about that moment, just wanting to buy some of the work on show in the family studio, and got to know Tama. So, when I offered him the chance to come to Paris, and learn the technique from Dunand himself, he jumped at it. And Papa was furious and told him never to come back.'

'How awful.'

'I don't see how you mean, awful. He's doing pretty well, he's settled in Paris.'

'But he's so far away from home, Jerome. And there

are so few people for him to talk to in his own language in Paris.'

'What?'

'It's different for me,' Gwen said, reviewing her life since she came to France. 'There's a big English-speaking community here and when I feel desperate for a cup of old-fashioned English tea I can always run to the bookshop in the rue de l'Odéon. But how many Japanese are there in Paris?'

'Ha . . . Apart from the Embassy . . . Well, there's Foujita . . .' Foujita was an artist, who seemed to have abandoned all things Japanese to become more French than the Parisians. Try as he might, Jerome could only come up with about four names.

'There you are, you see?'

'See what? What are you trying to prove? That Tama's far from home, yes, I agree. But that he's lonely? I don't think so. Please don't get sentimental about Tama, my dear. He's well able to look after himself.'

'Good,' she said. 'In that case, he'll be easy to work with on Guinchy's furniture. Now, having gone all through that, may I have his telephone number?'

'In the book on the desk in my study,' Jerome laughed.

The call was answered by the French apprentice. Alas, M. Hayakawa had just gone out to the Théâtre des Champs Elysées and wasn't expected back for some time. Certainly he would take a message.

'Please tell him that Mlle Whitchurch would like to speak to him on a matter of business,' Gwen said, giving him the telephone number at the cabinet-making workshop.

Jerome was unwilling to let her go but she insisted she had work to do. She went to the rue de Notre Dame des Champs, where under the glass roof of the loft she had good light by which to work. She settled down with the diagram of M. Guinchy's study, to begin a scale model of the pieces she intended to make.

The men from the workshop had gone home and
Gwen was thinking of doing likewise when at last
the phone rang downstairs. She went down the steep
wooden staircase to answer it.

'Mlle Veetcha?'

She laughed. 'M. Hayakawa! Tell me, in your language,
can you make the sound "wa" as at the end of your
name?'

'Certainly.' He was at a loss.

'Well, my name is Whitchurch, not Veetcha. And I
hope you'll call me Gwen.'

Tamaki Hayakawa had had an utterly appalling day up
till now. He had gone to bed very late and slept very
badly, so that he'd woken with a headache and a feeling
that lead weights had been glued to his eyelids.

Then, as commanded the previous night, he'd presented himself at ten o'clock at the rehearsal room below
the theatre. Serge Diaghilev wasn't yet there, nor was
the young choreographer.

The composer and one or two others connected with
the production waited an hour. The composer spent it
assuring everyone that his musical score was excellent,
very authentic, truly Japanese. Tama, who knew for a
fact that this was untrue, held his tongue.

When Diaghilev arrived, he brought Yuri with him.
It then became clear to all assembled already that Yuri,
the choreographer, was not to be held to blame in any
way for last night's fiasco.

A long argument ensued. Diaghilev was insistent:
work would have to be done to improve 'Chrysanthemum'. The company couldn't afford to lose the
money already invested in it.

The conductor of the orchestra complained that the
score was almost unplayable. The composer, Lenya,
grew heated in his own defence. The lighting engineer,
a Frenchman and a member of the theatre staff rather
than of the Diaghilev company, refused to agree that

he had in any way fallen short and ended by shouting that he knew better than any stuck-up Russian émigré what would work in his own theatre.

When Diaghilev demanded that the costumes must be brightened up, Tama said he would do whatever was in his power but it meant asking the wardrobe mistress to buy new materials if heavier paints were to be employed.

The maître de ballet intervened to say that the girls in the corps do ballet would be unable to move if they had to wear long kimonos of heavier material. 'It's a blessing we haven't had any falls so far – couldn't we have *short* kimonos?'

Tama remained impenetrably polite. The choreographer answered for him, that short kimonos were unheard of for geisha, that it would destroy the authenticity, that the steps he'd given the girls to do depended on the gliding effect of a kimono that was floor-length when they were up on their points.

And so on and so on.

At about four o'clock they adjourned to the Ledoyen Restaurant among the autumnal trees of the Champs Elysées. Although Diaghilev had kept stressing the need to save money, he spent an enormous amount on buying a meal for everyone. The restaurateur, at first annoyed at having to provide lunch at four o'clock, beamed with pleasure when caviare was ordered.

Tama was unable to eat. The strain of wondering what would happen to his creations and of being polite to these incomprehensible people made food impossible to swallow.

It ended as he had foreseen – for he came from a nation who knew all about face-saving. The next performance of 'Chrysanthemum' was postponed indefinitely. Meanwhile the composer was to rethink his orchestral score, the choreographer was to review the plot of the ballet with a view to making it less gloomy (although of course his actual dance movements were accepted by all, under the warning eye of Diaghilev, as splendid).

The designer was to hold himself in readiness for new ideas on costume. His backdrop was considered to be perfect, not to be changed. Tama fully expected it to go straight into storage and never be seen again.

As Yvonne Desarpes had implied, he was lucky, in that he had received the fee for his work. But it wasn't for the money that he had accepted the commission. He had wanted to be associated with the great Diaghilev in a successful ballet. Tama was a ballet fan. From the first moment he saw the Diaghilev dancers, he had been entranced – there was nothing like it in Japan.

Perhaps, though, it was for the best that the ballet was being put on the shelf. His Excellency had not been pleased. And though Tama believed he had set himself free from the trammels of tradition, it was still difficult to be happy when a senior Japanese diplomat scolded him.

Home at his studio off the Place Vendôme, he found the note from the apprentice, in the strange European hand-writing which Tama thought ugly and difficult to read.

'Please ring Miss Whitchurch . . .'

It was the first good thing that had happened today.

And now she was asking him to call her by her first name – Gwen. Gwen Whitchurch, the fact that he could pronounce it with ease somehow gave him some claim on her.

'And so, Gwen Whitchurch, you left message to ring you.'

'You were at the theatre with the maestro? How did it go?'

'Let us not talk about it.'

'Poor man! Will you be forced to make big changes?'

'Ballet is being withdrawn.'

A pause. Then she said, 'Well, I can't say I'm surprised. It isn't very good – except for your designs.'

'Thank you.'

'You sound very depressed.

'I am not beaming with happiness.'

'I'm so sorry. But perhaps what I have to say will cheer you up a little. I wanted to ask if you would collaborate with me on some furniture for a client.'

'I beg your pardon?' he said, not sure he had heard her correctly. His French, after two years in Paris, was fairly good, but Gwen spoke it with an un-French accent and moreover the telephone was providing an accompaniment of whining and crackling.

'Some furniture I'm making. Georges Guinchy, do you know him? He's in this new business, radio sets – he has an office at his factory but he wants to work from home to some extent so he—'

'Excuse me. Did you say you are making furniture?'

'Yes.'

'You make furniture?' he repeated, astonished.

'Yes, didn't you know? That's why I came to Paris – to do the furniture for Jerome's apartment.'

'I had not heard of it.'

'Could we meet to discuss my idea?'

'Forgive, what idea is that?'

'That you and I should collaborate.'

'To do what?'

'Make furniture. I'll design the pieces and together we'll decide how they should be trimmed or decorated.' He heard her catch herself back. 'Excuse me. Perhaps it's beneath your dignity to decorate furniture.'

'Of course not. In Japan, in China, lacquer has always been used to decorate furniture. I am surprised, only. I did not know you were a designer. And then I did not expect to be asked to work on furniture. This is the first time, here in France.'

'You don't dislike the idea?'

'Of course not.'

'Could we get together to discuss it? I could show you some sketches—'

'Gwen, have you had dinner?'

'What? Well, no . . .'

'Neither have I. Could we talk about this over a meal?'

'Why . . . that would be lovely.'

'In an hour?'

'Yes, in an hour. Where?'

'Could we meet at the Café de la Paix?'

'Oh, that's too—' She stopped. She'd been going to say, That's too expensive. But she guessed it would offend him. Instead she said, 'Too noisy. Somewhere quieter, Tama.'

'Do you know La Déesse, in the rue Soufflot?'

'Near the Panthéon? Yes, I do.'

'I'll see you there at eight.'

'I'll be there.'

She hurried to her hotel room to change. She'd brought with her from Jerome's place the evening frock she'd worn last night but, after a moment's thought, she hung it in her wardrobe. Too dressy, and moreover if he remembered she'd worn it last night, too depressing.

She had a pale blue dress she'd bought from Chanel, a last year's model going cheap. It was straight and long-sleeved, in silk jersey, the waistline undefined, the hemline rather higher than mid-calf. The couturier had said it was an augury of things to come, that dress: 'Hemlines are going to go higher, the waist is going to become unimportant, everything is going to be softer and more pliant – and women are going to stop wearing corsets!'

While not quite able to believe all that, Gwen felt herself drawn to this new line. Tonight, she felt, was a chance to wear the dress for the first time and see how it succeeded.

She coiled her long bronze hair up into earphones above her ears. She put a little darkener on her brows and her lashes. She chose her finest silk stockings. She added a long rope of artificial pearls to the effect.

It was only as she was hurrying to the Métro that she

asked herself why she was making such a great effort to impress Tama Hayakawa.

He was already there. He rose from his table to signal to her. The waiter hurried to show her to her place. She gave up her short velvet jacket to him, accepted a menu.

'Something to drink?' Tama suggested.

'Sweet Martini, please.'

The waiter took the order. Tama smiled. 'How I love this of France – little drinks of many kinds. Always something to suit every mood.'

'You don't have that back home?'

'No, we have sake, which is quite strong, only taken in tiny cups like the one you bought from my studio. Although of course you can drink many cups, and get very drunk. For friendly drinks, we have tea.'

'Oh yes,' Gwen said, remembering Jerome's remarks about Japanese tea.

To her surprise, Tama laughed aloud. 'Oh, I know what Europeans think of Japanese tea. Bitter, gritty, unpleasant, no milk, no lemon, no sugar. Strong test of friendship, to offer tea to a European.'

When he laughed, his face was lit up. The black eyes glowed, the white teeth flashed, laugh-creases appeared about his mouth.

'If you offer it to me, I'll drink it without complaining,' she said.

'We shall see. I am not very traditional. I prefer French wine. And French food,' he ended, indicating the menu. 'So please let's order because I haven't eaten all day.'

When they'd made their choice Gwen produced the faithful old satchel from which she took some sheets of sketches. She handed them across the table without comment. Tama looked through them quickly once, and then once more, paying close attention to each sheet.

'Excuse me. I am not familiar with all furniture. What kind of room is this?'

'A study, a business room. M. Guinchy wishes to

conduct some of his business from out of town, by telephone. It's to show how modern he is, you understand – a manufacturer of this new thing, radio, so he must do business in a new way.'

'So this room has what? Desk, chairs, these tall pieces – what are they?'

'Filing cabinets. In the drawers one keeps documents, business papers, folders with information.'

'I see, so that is why the drawers are so many and so deep. Then these are cupboards . . .'

'Yes, ordinary cupboards, M. Guinchy would wish to have a drinks cabinet for visitors and also shelves for books and so forth. Then this . . .' she leaned across to point, 'this is the safe.'

'Safe?'

'Where important documents and money can be locked up.'

'Ah yes. Strong box, we call that.' He gave a little laugh. 'You can make furniture of iron?'

'No, no, only a cover for the safe. Safes are very ugly, you know. This one is going to be set in among the cabinets and bookshelves and have a door which will look just like the other cupboards.'

'Good. And the colour scheme?'

'M. Guinchy would like black and white. He wants the room to look very smart, very modern, not dull and cluttered like a traditional office. I'm going to persuade him to add gold to the colour scheme.'

'Ah,' said Tama.

'The point is, he – Georges Guinchy – wouldn't want traditional Japanese decoration with flowers or birds. He doesn't want anything . . . anything "pretty".' She waited, anxious in case he objected to the idea that his work was 'pretty'.

But he was nodding. 'I understand. And in fact . . . You know what these pieces look like?'

'What?'

'The skyscrapers we hear of in New York.'

She sat back, lips parted. 'Yes! Yes, that's exactly what they look like! Especially the tall filing cabinets.'

'So for decoration . . . What could be better than modern city scenes – a skyscraper skyline, cars, aeroplanes . . .'

'Radio – a radio transmitting tower . . .'

'Lightning motifs to show that it was transmitting—'

'Perhaps sunrise and sunset, to show that M. Guinchy's goods are always in use . . .'

The waiter arrived with the food. Unwillingly they set the papers aside to make room for plates. With a glance of apology, Tama began to eat the fish he had ordered, though still holding on with one hand to a sketch.

'Tell me, which way do the windows of this room face?'

'South-west. I thought of that – we don't want lacquerwork shining into his eyes distractingly during the day, but you see the sun doesn't flood in until late afternoon.'

'Excellent. Look . . .' he produced a pencil from his breast pocket, began sketching on the edge of the sheet of paper. 'I could make panels for the cupboard doors – the dimensions you give – almost square, yes, well, let us have sunrise on one end of the row of cupboards and sunset on the other, with a city waking up and a city going out for the evening. See, the clouds move away, the sun glints on the rectangles of the skyscrapers . . .'

He handed across a vivid few lines, the idea drawn in miniature. Gwen was already nodding in agreement.

The waiter wasn't pleased with them. They were inattentive to the food. However, they sat on for a long time buying more wine and coffee, and in the end the Japanese gentleman gave him a very substantial tip.

As they went out, Gwen said, 'I think you must see the room for yourself as soon as possible. I'll ring M. Guinchy first thing tomorrow and arrange for a visit. Are you free in the next day or two?'

'I have some pieces to finish for a patron – two days'

uninterrupted work.' He made a little illustrative gesture, to indicate fine work with a paint brush. 'Lacquer is a demanding craft: work is done, then there is a pause, then more work. Drying time is important, cannot be hurried.'

'You don't yourself do the first coats, the under-coats?'

'No, no, that is done by assistants. But I have to wait for the piece to be ready for its final coat, and then each material has to be applied separately – gold, or powered ivory, or whatever is to make the lustre . . . It cannot be hurried. And it must be done in proper sequence once it is begun. So for the next two days I am busy.'

'Of course. If I make an appointment with George Guinchy for three days ahead, that will suit you?'

'Perfectly.'

They reached the Métro, went down to the passage-ways, then paused before separating for their different journeys home. They shook hands.

'Good night, Tama.'

'Goodnight, Gwen. I am honoured that you should think of my work and wish to collaborate with me.'

She smiled and nodded. He watched her disappear on to her platform.

Perplexing, these European women.

When he first arrived in France, the women had shocked him very much, and in fact alarmed him. He thought there must be some mental illness among them. They were so assertive, so disrespectful, so careless of personal relationships – like, he thought, those who suffered from a madness of self-importance.

A Japanese male child, he had been first indulged and then respected by every woman with whom he came in contact. Even his mother had seldom raised her voice to him. Gentleness and obedience were the two greatest virtues of womankind.

In Paris, the women were not obedient. They were often noisy and demanding. They had opinions – well,

Japanese women had opinions too, but they never voiced them without being asked. Frenchwomen, however, joined in discussions, contradicted, laughed at their menfolk, and seemed to see nothing wrong in such disrespect.

It had taken him six months to get used to it. Then he began to find it exciting. They were so different, with their curvaceous bodies and long straight legs. He loved the way their silk-clad ankles flashed as they got in and out of cars; the way their hair floated in the breeze as they hurried through the summer streets; the way they threw themselves without inhibition into the jazz dances of the nightclubs.

To his surprise, he found they liked him. He enjoyed little affairs with various partners. They taught him the art of love in the European manner, although they said they found him thrilling for the different feeling he brought to the encounters.

Besides the personal and romantic aspects, there was that of business. An astonishing number of European women took part in business. Now that was not unknown. Many Japanese girls were employed in factories, offices, and the more modern style of shop in Tokyo.

But as far as he could recall, he had never met a Japanese woman in control of a business. He had never met a Japanese woman who had a career which she managed for herself. He had found the Frenchwomen in the fashion industry absolutely astounding, and the women artists, the women politicians, the women journalists, the women philosophers . . . Heaven and earth, there were even women aviators, women racing drivers.

Gwen Whitchurch and her career as a furniture designer shouldn't have surprised him. Yet he had taken it for granted when he met her that she was under the patronage of Jerome de Labasse for the usual reasons – because she was pretty, young, charming . . .

Not so, it seemed. She had a life of her own, quite

apart from that of Count de Labasse. And what was so pleasing was that her work brought her into contact with Tamaki Hayakawa.

He would be working with her on the furniture of M. Guinchy for weeks, perhaps months. Of course, if the truth were told, she needn't be brought into every process of making the lacquer decoration – once she had agreed on the designs and seen a sample or two, they need not meet again until the furniture was being finished.

Tama shook his head to himself. No, no. Constant consultation, that was what was needed. He pictured himself bending over the drawing-board with Gwen, her soft bronze hair against his cheek, her pale-skinned hands directing a pencil at some detail. His arm, perhaps, around her waist . . .

About mid-morning next day, she telephoned to say M. Guinchy would be delighted to see M. Hayakawa on Saturday for lunch at his house in Rambouillet.

'Will that suit you, Tama?'

'How do I get to Rambouillet?'

'We'll go together by train.'

M. Guinchy was delighted. Not only had he got this extremely talented girl to design his furniture but she had brought in a Japanese artist. To have both a young lady who was unique in the field and at the moment very fashionable, and an exotic creature from Japan . . . He knew he would be in the gossip columns of all the newspapers.

He hadn't the least idea how lacquerwork was done and, to tell the truth, he offended Tama more than once with his idea that he was going to be on his knees painting trimmings on the desk drawers, like a letterist putting a name on an office door. Yet in the end all was well. M. Guinchy didn't blink at the fee Tama named. He would have paid a lot more, just to be the talk of the business world in Paris.

He himself had an evening engagement in Paris. At the end of the day, he insisted on putting them in his car and driving them back. It then seemed a good idea to take them to the party he was going to, at the Ritz. He introduced them around: 'Mlle Whitchurch, who is making me some furniture in the new style for my study . . . she did those beautiful rooms for M. de Labasse, you probably saw them in *Maison Moderne*. And M. Hayakawa, who is going to decorate the furniture – goldwork, you know . . .'

This was a different milieu for both Gwen and Tama. Hitherto they had met the artists, the patrons of the artists, café society. Now they met the businessmen and their wives. They had a large table in the corner of the Ritz dining-room but the atmosphere was relaxed, the women in 'after-six' frocks so that Gwen didn't feel too out of place in her blue day dress.

The wives of the businessmen asked to be given some idea of what Georges' study would look like. Envy was expressed. 'Albert, why can't you do something like this with that dreary library of yours . . . ?'

In the next few days, the result of that evening became noticeable. The wives dropped in on Tama and on Gwen. Then there were suggestions: 'Couldn't you make me a little cabinet . . . I should so much like to have a needlework table . . .'

Commissions were agreed, to be undertaken as and when the work for M. Guinchy allowed. His filing cabinets and the desk were made. Guinchy agreed almost ecstatically to allow them to be on display in Tama's studio. They were photographed by many magazines, talked about in the newspapers. Somehow it became agreed the completed furnishings would be on display in the spring at the *Salon des Arts Décoratifs*.

Inevitably Gwen became involved in the making of the lacquerwork. She went with Tama to the workshop in the Marais where the first coats of varnish were applied to the wood.

'This finish is called *togi-dashu* in my country. It means, ground down – you see how soft and pure it is . . . ?'

'Like satin,' Gwen said, touching the surface with one finger. 'It's almost . . . unreal. You feel you could put your fingers right through it.'

'We call it the "dream world" surface – I shall use it for Mme Lefubure's needlework table, she is a very romantic lady.'

'You're right, she is. So you take that into account, do you?'

'Oh, of course. If I know the kind of person, I know the kind of design to offer, and if I know the kind of design, I know the kind of lacquer.'

The air in the old stables where the lac was applied and dried was very warm, although outside it was a cold December. Three middle-aged men sat at padded tables gently buffing different objects – a shallow bowl, a square box-lid, a long narrow panel. In a section at the back of the stables Gwen had seen the lac being prepared, colour being added – gamboge, cinnabar, ochre – beautiful, ancient names for lovely tints.

Although she'd heard Tama talk about the processes, she was surprised at how many there were. The work force here, numbering nine in all, applied a sealing agent, then size, then a first coat of lacquer. Then the object was dried in a sort of large slow stove, which Tama translated into French as 'une chambre tiède', a warm room.

After that it was rubbed down, polished, buffed. Another coat of lac was applied. The drying process was gone through again, the object was rubbed down, polished, buffed. And again. And again.

Only when the piece was coated with eighteen, twenty, thirty coats was it considered strong enough to receive the final artwork. Then it went to Tama's workbench.

His bench had an array of materials strange to Gwen.

There was white lead to make the outline of the design. There was lamp black, camphor, and liquid lac to build up edges for a relief design. There was gold dust in a lidded glass container. There was silver dust, ivory, oyster shell, tortoiseshell. There were modern oxides of metal, even one which would allow green to appear in the finished piece, a colour never before available in lacquerwork.

A panel for one of Georges Guinchy's cupboard doors lay on the bench, as yet without its design. Alongside lay the sketch – a geometric representation of a sunrise over a modernistic city. It owed something to European influence, to the artists who ruled in Paris – Picasso, Sert, Chagall; yet it was undeniably Oriental in some indefinable way.

'Are you going to start on that today?'

'No, for that I need much more gold. I clear my bench, take away all things I shall not use – no distraction, for gold is the most demanding. Also the most beautiful, in the end.'

'I've a furniture design here I'd like you to look at, Tama, it's for Mme Orjanu. She asked for a screen that would be completely different, and see . . . I've suggested this four-fold screen, each fold is a Japanese fan—'

'Difficult to make!' Tama exclaimed.

'Yes, very fine cabinet-work – the spokes of the fan must look just right. But I've tried it out on the lathe, it can be done. What I want to know is, will you make a lacquer design for it? When it's finished it must look like four traditional fans. What do you think?'

'It would look sensational!'

'Well, I think so. So does Mme Orjanu. But I can't start making the pieces until I know you will undertake the lacquering.'

'I will do it, of course I will! And Gwen . . . If it turns out as I hope, for the first time in this country, I shall sign my work.'

She could tell it was a great moment for him. Only later, when she came to know more about the Japanese, did she understand that until now Tama had not felt any of his work in Europe to be worthy of having his name in the corner.

Gwen knew she wasn't good at sensing nuances in other people. Partly it was because her attention was generally elsewhere, on the outside, looking at things, seeing proportions and shades, imagining how to use space and form. And Tama was more difficult to know than most. He was easily offended by the casual manners of the Parisian set, though he hid it well. His thought-processes were different, his basic assumptions gave him hurdles to overcome before he could be at ease.

Yet Gwen knew that they were close. They worked together without barriers. She could express rational criticism, he would take it without demur. In his turn he would comment on her designs, and she would take his suggestions. They were a partnership.

In the spring their work went on show at the *Salon des Arts Décoratifs*. It caused a furore, especially the folding screen. Commissions flooded in. Even if they had worked twenty-four hours a day, it would have been impossible to fulfil them all.

They met at Tama's studio to discuss which of the commissions they should accept and which postpone. Some they already had sketches for, some they stopped to discuss and set down ideas for, some they discarded. They were sitting in the room behind the showroom, amidst a sea of paper.

'It is getting late,' Tama said, stretching his compact body. 'We stop for a rest, I make some tea.'

Oh, said Gwen mentally.

'Don't worry, European tea. No milk, but you can have lemon.'

He put the kettle on the little spirit stove and lit it. From a cupboard he took a very ordinary packet of

Lipton's Tea. Seeing it, Gwen came to him and took it from him. 'Oh, this makes me think of home,' she said, smiling.

He turned towards her.

After a long moment he said, 'It is a great pity you belong to Jerome.'

She stared. 'Who told you that?'

'Everybody says so.'

'Everybody is wrong. I belong to myself.'

'But you and Jerome . . .'

'No. Not for a long time now.'

Once again there was a pause. He was thinking over what she had said, making sure he didn't get the wrong impression from it as he sometimes did.

'Will you belong to me?' he asked at length.

Grey-green eyes looked into black eyes.

'Yes, Tama, I will.'

He turned away from her. He put the tea packet back in the cupboard, turned off the spirit stove.

'Come,' he said, and taking her hand led her upstairs.

She had never seen his living quarters, and they were a surprise to her. An almost empty room, with a bench and drawing equipment under the tall Parisian windows. On the floor at the other side several rectangles of matting had been laid down, and on this rested a thin mattress, a futon.

He made a little gesture towards it. 'Here,' he said.

No power on earth could have stopped her from making love with him. It was nothing like when she had first gone to bed with Jerome, talking herself into it and being taught how to enjoy it.

This time her whole body seemed to flow towards Tama. And for him there was no coaxing, no sophisticated games. He took her with a total physical commitment that seemed to open the very gates of Paradise to her.

Little words of love, a strange mixture – English and

Japanese. Two bodies becoming one, two hearts beating strongly in unison.

'I love you, Tama, I'll always love you,' she told him with her voice, with her limbs, with every fibre of her being.

And from him she received the same promise, the same bonding of body and soul.

The night passed in learning the ways of one another. She asked if she pleased him, he asked if he had made her happy.

'I was so unsure, Gwen. I didn't know if it was right to want you in the way I did.'

'It was right, my darling. Nothing was ever more right.'

'So now you belong to me.'

'Yes.'

'I am serious, Gwen. You belong to me. No one else.'

'Of course, Tama. That's what I meant when I said yes. I love you.'

'And Jerome de Labasse?'

She hesitated, turning on the futon to lay her cheek against his.

'I shall always be friends with Jerome,' she said.

'No.'

'Darling, I can't stop liking Jerome just because we're in love.'

'In Japan, a woman does not have male friends.'

'But this is Paris, Tama. You know how things are here—'

'Yes,' he said rather fiercely, 'that does not make it right.'

'Tama, Tama, don't let it vex you. Jerome means nothing to me in that way.'

'Promise me. Promise me you will never be more than just a friend with him.'

'I promise, dearest.'

Next day Gwen went to Jerome's apartment in the

Avenue Foch. Jerome was experimenting with a new gramophone, a machine that played flat discs instead of wax cylinders.

'Listen, Gwen – isn't that lovely? That's Tetrazzini! Tibau, bring some coffee.' He switched off, smiling at Gwen. 'Long time since you were here, dear.'

'Yes, and I've come to say I shan't be here again, Jerome.'

'What?' he said in surprise.

'I've come to fetch my things from the bedroom.'

'Gwen! What an unkind thing to say! Have I offended you in some way?'

She found herself smiling at him. There was something so endearing about him.

'No, darling, not at all. But I'm moving in with Tama.'

Jerome sank down on the settee. 'Ah,' he sighed, 'the Japo.'

'Don't call him that,' she said rather sharply.

'You've let yourself be beguiled by the mysterious Orient, my dear—'

'Don't be silly, Jerome, there's nothing mysterious about falling in love with Tama.'

'I told you before, he has success—'

'This is different. It's serious, for both of us. So there will be no need to meet the bill at the hotel any more, Jerome.'

'I see that.'

'You and I had more or less come to an end, you know,' she said, trying to soften what seemed to be a blow to him.

'I suppose you might say that. I think I saw it coming with Tama.' He frowned at her. 'Are you sure you're doing the right thing?'

'Quite sure. I love Tama with all my heart.'

He studied her glowing eyes, her smiling lips, her air of having had a glimpse of Eden.

'Yes,' he said in sad acceptance, 'I can see you do.'

Chapter Six

Almost at once they became an established pair in Paris society. 'Let's ask Tama and Veetcha to the opening.' 'Did Tama and Veetcha take on the de Beche contract?' 'There was a feature on Tama and Veetcha in *Décor* this month.'

Veetcha was the 'trade' name Gwen had adopted; after the Parisians' mispronunciation of her surname. Once she and Tama began collaborating they set up a firm known as 'T&V', by which they signed their pieces – a signature much in demand as fashion took them to the top.

'Tama and Veetcha,' Toinette remarked to Gwen one afternoon in the studio. 'You notice who gets top billing. It's not Veetcha and Tama.'

'As if it matters, Toinette.'

'Oh, you're so slow to see subtle distinctions!' Toinette was impatient. 'Who discovered who? Tama was making an unspectacular living as a lacquerist until you thought of asking him to do the trims for Georges' furniture.'

'It was a bit more than trims, Toinette—'

'However much it was, he would never have been heard of to the same extent if you hadn't brought him forward. And what happens? A typical male trick – he puts himself ahead of you.'

'He doesn't put himself ahead—'

'All right, ask him to change the name of the firm to "V&T" – tell him you want first mention – you want to sign your pieces with your name first.'

Gwen couldn't quite see herself doing that. Besides,

in her opinion the situation was right just as it was. 'After all, Toinette, Tama *is* an artist. I'm only a furniture-maker.'

'How can you talk like that! Your things are lovely, and always have been. That beautiful table you made for Jerome . . . By the way, how is Jerome?'

'Quite well, I think. He's in Deauville.'

'Don't you see him?'

Gwen shook her head.

'That's rather hard, Gwen. He was a good friend to you.'

'He certainly was. But it's better not to see him.'

'Tama forbids it?'

'No, no,' she hastened to say, 'nothing like that.'

But it was something like that, and she grieved over it. She'd hoped that, by and by, Tama would come to accept Jerome as just another member of their circle. It hadn't worked out that way. Every time the two men were in the same room together, Tama would freeze up.

So it was better to avoid Jerome. She missed him, his easy affection, his encouragement and support – but if she was honest, it was time she stopped needing support. She was, after all, twenty years old, much in demand for her work, making a more than adequate living in this collaboration with Tama.

And she was very much in love. She ought to ask for nothing more. She had Tama – and if he wanted to mark out exclusive rights on her, who could blame him? He was so far from home, so much in exile, it was understandable that he didn't want to share her love with anyone else; he himself needed it so much.

They spent almost every day together and every night. Little by little she was learning more about him, though he was difficult to know. She was even learning some Japanese, partly to please him and partly because there was a special joy in being able to understand what he murmured as he made love to her.

Then there were the everyday phrases: *Ikaga desu kai?* – How are you? and *wafu* – Japanese style. *Wafu* figured often in their conversation – should a piece of lacquer decoration for a particular client be undertaken *wafu* or in the French manner?

He had several kimonos folded away in the *armoire*. One evening, to increase the *wafu* in their very Parisian way of living, she donned a kimono to surprise him.

He laughed so much she never did it again. '*Chérie*, you are too curvaceous for a kimono. Japanese women have almost no bosom, and they tie themselves around with the *obi*, which is a great flat sash. So they look like one slender stem, not a rosebush. And they have their hair done up very big and high, as if it were a flowerbud on the end of the stalk – they don't have strange lovely hair like a sunset.'

Kissing her, he began to undo the sash of the robe. 'And besides, that is a man's kimono, most improper, so please take it off at once.'

Which led to the kind of ending that she had perhaps had in mind all the time.

They were so happy they scarcely noticed the year speed by. France was as usual riven by political strife. Aristide Briand resigned, Raymond Poincaré came in in his stead. The wrangling over German reparations to France seemed to be settled in March. Tama and Veetcha made preparations to exhibit again at the Exhibition of Decorative Art for 1922.

And then a letter came for Tama from Tokyo.

Its arrival startled Gwen. Since she had come to live with him he'd never had a letter from Japan. She brought it upstairs from the letterbox on the door of the studio, staring at the name and address written in a carefully copied European script.

Tama was putting on his shoes when she came in. 'A letter, dear. From Tokyo.'

He straightened abruptly. Some emotion washed across his face and was gone. 'It will be bad news,' he said without apparent alarm, taking it from her.

When he opened it she saw that the paper inside the envelope was much finer than anything used in France, and was covered with vertical lines of Japanese script. How beautiful it is, she thought inconsequentially, although her attention was all on Tama.

When he had turned the last page, he glanced at her with a nod. 'My father has died.'

'Oh! Tama, I'm so sorry . . .'

He bowed in acceptance of her sympathy. For a moment he was almost a stranger. 'Thank you. My mother writes to say he died . . . let me see, it would be the equivalent of the 4th of February.'

'Was it expected?'

'In some ways, perhaps. He had stomach trouble but he would not obey the doctor's instructions about his eating habits.'

'It's so awful, to think of you being on the other side of the world when he perhaps wanted you there . . .'

He gave a little shrug then patted Gwen's hand. 'You see it from your point of view. You don't understand that to me he was a tyrant, an unbending man. He and I were not close.'

'All the same, Tama . . .'

'The problem now is, there are matters to attend to. Although I'm sure he intended to disinherit me, it seems he didn't actually do so, so Mother tells me I now own the family business and asks what I intend to do about it.'

'Oh dear! What *do* you intend to do with it?'

'Sell it, I suppose. But such things take time in Japan, and I should need to make sure it goes for a good price because my mother must be able to live on the proceeds.'

'And your sister?' He had mentioned his sister, Hanako, more than once.

102

'I don't have to provide for her in that way. But she is another problem. She was about to be married, but the bridegroom has withdrawn because of my father's death.'

'Withdrawn? How do you mean?'

'As far as I can gather, Nagahi-san was marrying Hanako in expectation of being adopted as my father's son after I was disinherited. Now, of course, since I have in fact become the legal owner of the lacquerworks, he's no longer interested.'

'Tama!'

Tama smiled. 'We are a very practical people,' he told her. 'Don't look so aghast. I shall see to Hanako's problem.'

'But how?'

'By finding her another husband, of course. But I really have to be there in person, to oversee what the go-between suggests.'

'Be there? You mean go to Tokyo?'

He sighed. 'I don't see how it can be avoided.'

'Oh, Tama, no!'

'I don't want to go. I've grown very settled here in Paris. But family honour is involved. Mother expects me to go home.'

She leaned her head against his shoulder. 'How long would you be gone?'

'I don't know. Six months at least. Perhaps a year, if negotiations over the business go on as long as they might.'

'A year! No, don't go, Tama, please don't! Send instructions to some lawyer in Tokyo to see to it all.'

'That wouldn't do honour to my father's memory.' He put an arm about her. 'For all that I didn't get on with him, I have to admit he was a great artist in his field. To sell his workshop as if it were a sandal-stall would be very unsuitable. I have to go to Tokyo, Gwen.'

She was shaking her head, unable to speak at the

thought of parting. Six months, a year without him!
How could she bear it?

He stroked her bright hair. 'Don't be unhappy. The
time will soon pass—'

'No it won't!'

'I can't help it, Gwen. I *must* go. My mother needs
me.'

Against that she could make no protest. His poor
mother . . . a widow . . . how dare Gwen push her own
claims against those of a bereaved woman?

Nevertheless the tears began to trickle down her
cheeks.

'There is one possibility,' Tama said, then paused.

'What?'

'You could come with me.'

'Come . . . ?'

'I hesitate to suggest it. It's so much to ask. You'd
be giving up your career in Paris just when everything is—'

'Oh, that doesn't matter!' She had straightened to
gaze up at him, eyes glowing through tears, with a
wide gesture sweeping away matters such as career or
Parisian ties. 'Come to Japan?'

'Would you?'

'Oh, of course, of course!' Japan, the fairyland
portrayed in his work, the land of elegant cranes
bending to see their reflection in pools, of cherry
blossom and chrysanthemums, of sunshine gleaming on
the snow-cape of Mount Fuji. She had often dreamed
of seeing it for herself, that land of beauty and harmony,
where those slender kimono-clad women tripped about
the streets under parasols shading them from the sun,
where the temples and palaces tilted their roofs to
heaven beyond vermilion gateways, where sparsely
furnished rooms were graced by simple flowers or
painted scrolls, where lacquerwork and porcelain and
water-colours were supreme works of art.

'Of course I'll come, Tama!'

'You will?' He was astonished at her immediate compliance, and grateful beyond words. He swept her up, kissing her, telling her again and again that he'd never for a moment imagined she'd say yes.

'How can you be so silly! I'd go to the ends of the earth to avoid being parted from you, darling. And going to Japan is such a wonderful idea. I don't suppose I'd ever have thought of it if this hadn't happened, but now it has, well, it seems almost as if it was meant.'

He nodded agreement. 'Yes, it is our fate. I believe in that. Our lives are set out for us and we must live them to the utmost as they unfold. So now it unfolds that we go to my homeland.' He broke off. 'Oh, good heavens, Gwen,' he cried in horror, 'think of the commissions we've undertaken!'

They were thrown into a flurry of business activity. For the next few days they telephoned and wrote to clients, explaining that as they were going to Japan they couldn't now carry out the work they had agreed to do. They returned cheques. They set about finding a tenant for the studio. They sold the lacquer workshop to a French lacquerist, who agreed to take on the staff though muttering, 'I don't want to turn out Chinesey stuff.'

They booked passage on the *Orient Pearl*, due to sail from Boulogne in ten days' time. Tama wrote to his mother to expect him in late March. Work in hand then began to take up his attention: he wanted to finish what he could before leaving.

Gwen was luckier in that some pieces she'd started could be finished by others. She spent time at the cabinet-maker's, going over the design plans and discussing what the intention had been for the finished effect.

She was explaining to Emile, the foreman, how to insert the shagreen 'leaves' on a panel when she heard a well-known voice calling.

'Jerome! I thought you were in Deauville.'

'I came back on purpose.' He threaded his way

between the workbenches to kiss her on the nose after flicking away a woodshaving that rested there among the freckles.

'Did you win any money at the casino?'

'Nobody ever wins money in a casino,' Jerome said in a gloomy tone.

He was looking well, yet there was an air of anxiety about him. 'Can we talk?' he said.

Certainly it was difficult to make themselves heard above the sound of the electric saw. She smiled, nodded, and led the way up to her studio in the loft. There, the sound was at least a little muted.

She gestured to the only chair. 'Please sit down, Jerome.' She herself perched on the edge of her desk. 'What's this about?'

'It's about you, of course. Is this true, what I hear? You're going to Japan?'

'Oh, the grapevine's been at work. Yes, it's true, why not?'

'Why not? Are you mad? You're leaving Paris just when you've got every interior decorator and room designer queuing up for your work?'

'Can't be helped, dear. Tama's father has died and he's needed at home.'

'So what? Why do *you* have to go?'

She gave him a look of reproach. 'Don't be silly, Jerome. He might be gone a whole year. I couldn't be parted from him for that long.'

Jerome bounded to his feet. 'Just what I would expect from him! Selfish dolt! So he's dragging you to Tokyo—'

'No, no, Jerome, calm down, don't say things like that.' She was taken aback at his anger and obvious concern. 'I want to go. He was uncertain about asking but I jumped at the chance.'

'Jumped at it. You must be out of your mind.'

'No, no, I'm right, I know I am. I couldn't endure it if he went without me. A whole year?' She threw out her arm to illustrate how long a year would be – a time stretching to infinity. 'I'd die.'

'No you wouldn't, and you're throwing your success straight down the drain. When you come back in twelve months, hardly anyone will remember you and you'll be right out of touch with new trends—'

'I'll bring back new ideas from Japan. Don't you see? A lot of Art Deco is inspired by the Orient. I'll have seen it at first hand—'

'You'll have been out of circulation for a year. Nothing changes so quickly as Paris fashion. By the time you get back someone else will be leading the field in furniture design. I absolutely forbid you to do this.'

She went up to him to put a kiss on his cheek. 'Don't be silly,' she reproved.

'Oh, Gwen . . .'

After a moment he jerked himself away, to pace up and down in the long low room, bending his head to avoid the stanchions that held up the glass roof.

'You're really determined to go?'

'Certainly. We've got our passage booked.'

'What are you doing with the business?'

She explained that they'd leased out the studio and were selling the workshop. 'Documents are being signed on that tomorrow. We'd taken space at the Exhibition of Decorative Art but we've had no difficulty selling that on to another exhibitor.'

'When do you sail?'

'Wednesday the 17th.'

He stared up at the sky through the grimy glass. 'Gwen, I don't think . . .'

'What?'

'I wonder if you really ought to go? Japan isn't an easy country to get to know.'

She frowned and smiled at him, shaking an admonitory finger. 'You always said it was a paradise.'

'Yes, for a man . . . But for a woman? I don't know . . .'

'What do you mean?'

'Well, you see . . . you've got to understand . . . Japan only opened itself up to the world about eighty years ago. Until then it was sealed away from Western influence, for reasons that go far back into its history. So they're very strong on tradition—'

'Oh, I know that, Tama's an example of that. He had to leave his own country to be free to do even a simple bit of experimenting with his craft.'

'It goes into every aspect of life. And none more deeply than the status of women.'

'Well, I know that too. Tama told me how shocked he was at the manners of the European women he encountered when he first arrived—'

'Please listen, Gwen. Don't keep telling me what Tama's told you. Listen to what *I'm* telling you. In Japan, they have a totally different way of looking at society. Their philosophy is based on different principles. Our idea of Liberty, Equality, Fraternity – they don't believe in any of that.'

He paused. Gwen nodded. She might have said that Japan wasn't the only country which didn't believe in those three things. But he had asked her to listen, and she would do so, because clearly her good friend Jerome de Labasse had something very important on his mind.

'I'm no expert,' Jerome resumed. 'I lived there for over four years and failed to learn enough to understand the Japanese.'

'But you liked it. You told me how much you liked it,' she said, unable to remain silent.

'Yes, in many ways, I loved it. But then I'm a man. I think a lot of European men fall in love with Japan becase possibly there's no country in the world where men are so venerated.'

'Venerated?'

'Whatever a man says in Japan is accepted by his womenfolk. It's not so long ago that if a man said to his wife, kill yourself, she would have had to do it—'

'Oh, yes, the samurai tradition – I know about that.'

'Gwen, will you listen? To some extent things have changed since the first Europeans came along. In fact, at first, there seemed to be a terrific change. European architecture, European tools and equipment, European clothes. But then there was a partial withdrawal. They felt they had gone too far, too fast. Especially as regards any change that might come to the condition of women. So when I got there, women were more or less back where they'd been before Commodore Perry sailed in in 1854.'

'Jerome, why are you giving me this history lesson?' Gwen exclaimed. 'I'm going to Japan, yes, but I'm a European – none of this about Japanese women affects me.'

Jerome was shaking his head. 'You're going with Tama. You're going to live in his family home, yes?'

'Yes, of course.'

'You don't know anyone else in Tokyo?'

'Of course not.'

'Gwen, your position would be very difficult. You'd feel very isolated. And under Japanese law you'd have no rights at all, because you'd in effect be a concubine.'

'What?'

'If you live with Tama without a marriage certificate, you're a nobody. If you should happen to be involved in any kind of difficulty, the law would pay almost no attention to you. You'd have no rights worth speaking of.'

'But . . . but . . . Why are you being so gloomy about it, Jerome? I'm not going to get into any difficulties! And if I do, Tama will look after me.'

Jerome paused in his perambulations. He sighed and shrugged and shook his head. 'Life isn't always a bed of roses, Gwen. Things can go wrong. Don't forget, you're going to a land where they've scarcely seen foreigners.

Tama's mother – she's going to have to accept a foreigner into her house. Moreover, a foreigner of very low status – a concubine.'

'Don't keep using that silly word! Tama and I—'

'Tama and you are lovers. Very romantic, and in Paris very well accepted. You try that out in Tokyo and see how you like it.'

'What are you saying, Jerome? I mean, really? Put it into words of one syllable for me.'

'If you insist on going to Tokyo with Tama – and I see your mind's made up – get him to marry you before you leave.'

She gaped at Jerome. 'Marry me?'

'Yes, marry you. Don't arrive in Japan without the status of a married woman. You simply can't even guess at how low your standing would be if you went as Tama's mistress.'

He came up to her, took both her hands, pressed them. 'Please, Gwen, I beg you, don't go to Tokyo without getting married first.'

'But . . . but . . . Tama and I have never talked about marriage.'

'Start talking about it now.'

'But Jerome . . . it's the man who proposes . . . How can I . . . ?'

He had to think about that. 'I see it's a problem. Not only from your side. In Japan marriages are arranged . . .'

'Yes, Tama was saying he had to go home to arrange a marriage for his sister.'

'It's done by a go-between – sometimes a friend of the family who interests himself in putting a suggestion forward, sometimes a professional who finds a husband – it's usually a husband, although some men do look around for a wife with money or good contacts in government . . . I quite see that Tama perhaps hasn't even thought about marriage because there's been no one to start the thing going.'

'I can't imagine anyone who could do that kind of thing here. It would seem laughable to ask anyone.'

Jerome sighed. 'You'll have to do it yourself.'

'But how? I mean, supposing I agreed that getting married is a good idea in the first place?'

'You could tell him that someone who knows Japan has suggested it would be better for you—'

'Don't be absurd, Jerome! The only person I know who knows anything about Japan, other than Tama—'

'Is me. Yes, of course. And he doesn't like me.'

'It's not that,' she protested. 'You make him feel . . . I don't know . . . insecure . . .'

'I wish I thought he had some reason for the feeling,' said Jerome ruefully. 'Well, you'll have to think of something. Because if you try to board that ship without a marriage certificate in your handbag, I'll carry you off it bodily.'

She laughed: 'What a drama.'

'Better still, don't go, Gwen. Really, I mean it. Don't throw away all you've gained here in Paris for a theoretical advantage in a year's time. Let Tama go alone.'

She shook her head with vehemence. 'I couldn't endure it. If I let him go, I'd only follow all by myself a couple of weeks later.'

'You fool.' He put his arms about her, hugged her, dropped a kiss on her hair. 'Well, I've done my best. Invite me to the wedding!'

With that he was gone.

Gwen took some moments before she returned to her discussions with Emile. She was thoughtful.

After all, if she and Tama were to go on a visit to her family in St Albans, it would raise eyebrows in that quiet little cathedral town. Living with a man to whom she wasn't married! Shameless! Hardly anyone would speak to her.

It was all right here in Paris, and particularly in the Latin Quarter where she circulated. There was a

tradition of tolerance about sexual matters, an easy
acceptance of relationships. Yet she knew that even in
France the provinces were less open-minded. Toinette
had said that in her home town of Tournon she'd
received open criticism for her 'laxity'.

She set the matter aside while she completed her day's
work. But as she at last took off her carpenter's apron
and put on her coat to go home, she knew she had made
an unconscious decision.

She would put the matter of marriage in front of
Tama. She would leave it to him to say yes or no.
Whatever he decided she would abide by.

But, to her own surprise, she found she wanted him
to agree to it. And so, like many another woman in
any continent – Europe, Asia, America – she prepared the
way by making sure that her man was in a good mood.

There was a restaurant not far as the crow flies from
where they lived, across the river near the Gare d'Orsay.
Tama was particularly fond of it because of its wine list,
and also because there was a little dance floor. He loved
to dance with Gwen to Western music: his particular
favourite was the foxtrot.

They liked to walk to it in the evening, spend an hour
or so dancing and sipping wine, and then dine on the
good peasant dishes on the menu.

Gwen suggested they should go there. 'You enjoy it
so much, and we might not have another chance before
we sail.'

'My word, how I shall miss things like that,' Tama
sighed.

They walked hand in hand to the Bouclier. The *patron*
hurried forward to welcome them. 'Is it true, what I
hear? You're going away?'

'Unfortunately, yes, monsieur.'

'I'm so sorry, M. Hayakawa. And you too, mademoiselle. We shall miss you.' He ushered them to their
favourite table, a little corner under a painting by Utrillo
of a lane in Montmartre. The *patron* had bought it for

a song before Utrillo became fashionable. The three-piece band was playing the American tune, 'I'm Going Back to the Shack', but no one was as yet dancing.

'When do you sail, if I may ask?'

'In a week's time.'

'You'll honour us again with your custom before you go?'

'Probably not, alas.'

'Then this evening, please allow me, the wine with your meal is a compliment of the house. Yes yes, I insist. But first, I know . . . the St Emilion.' He gave them the menu to study, bustled off, and came back with a bottle of the rich red wine.

Gwen and Tama always had a lot to say to each other, and now even more so – reporting back how the tying up of loose ends was proceeding, mentioning events of the day, reminding one another of things still to be done, deciding what to pack and what to leave.

They talked as they danced. Then they would sit twirling their wine glasses, consulting lists, making notes.

By and by it was time to order the food. Tama, who loved the flavoursome food of provincial France, chose *tripes à la mode de Caen*. Gwen chose a fish dish. With it came a bottle of white burgundy, compliments of the management.

Somewhere about ten o'clock, when they had accepted a special *charlotte aux pommes* and were feeling pleasantly replete, Gwen mentioned that she'd started a letter to her mother.

'Oh yes, of course,' said Tama. Gwen seldom spoke of her mother and stepfather, but then neither did he of his own mother and sister. Family ties, nevertheless, were important. 'This is to tell her you are leaving Europe?'

'Yes, and you know, Tama, I can't help thinking how much it's going to worry her.'

'Yes, true, a long, long way. The other side of the earth, in fact.'

'I'd go and see her, to try to reassure her, only there isn't time.'

Tama frowned, the smooth skin wrinkling up between his black brows. 'What a pity. Perhaps you could go, and I could finish up the business matters . . . ?'

'I'm still trying to explain to Emile what needs to be done with the cabinets for Mme Horneil. No, I think I'll just have to try to put it into the letter. I'll tell her that if anyone is unkind to me you'll stand up for me.'

'Unkind?' Tama was concerned. 'No one in Tokyo is going to be unkind. We are a very polite people.'

'No, I meant about the fact that you and I aren't married. I don't want to sound stupidly conventional or anything, but I don't think it would be very acceptable even in my home town if we turned up there—'

'Wait!' exclaimed Tama.

'How do they look on that kind of thing in Tokyo?' Gwen went on, ashamed of her own duplicity. 'They're pretty tolerant, are they?'

Tama slapped himself on the forehead, a gesture he'd learnt from the French, meaning, 'How could I have been so thoughtless?'

'Gwen, wait, of course – what a fool I am – you must think me terribly self-centred and uncaring . . . That's it, of course, that's it. We must get married before we sail!'

'What?' Gwen said, glad that her acting ability wasn't really being tested because Tama was so carried away with this thought he was hardly paying attention.

'Yes, good heavens . . . your mother . . . what would she have felt? And *my* mother . . . I can tell you it would have been a big mistake to arrive . . . Good gracious, how could I have *not* thought of it? Of course! I'll go to the prefecture tomorrow and get a special licence.'

'But, Tama, are you sure? It's a big step.'

Now he was brought up short. He stared at her, his olive skin coloured. 'Don't you want to?' he asked.

'Are you sure *you* want to?'

She had made him unsure. He hated to be caught wrong-footed. He studied her, trying to guess what he should be saying at this point. 'Ah,' he began at last, 'I think I've done this all wrong. Please forgive. You understand that I don't know how this is done in Europe. I never asked anyone to marry me before – not even in Japan, and there someone else would have done it for me. What should I say to you now?'

'You should say, "Gwen, I love you, will you marry me?"'

But she was laughing, and in fact he never said it. He seized her hands across the table, kissed first one then the other in the French manner.

'First thing tomorrow morning,' he said. 'As soon as the prefecture opens. And your mother, Gwen – you must send a telegram to your mother, telling her to come to the wedding.'

'Oh! Oh, she won't come. She never leaves home.'

'For a wedding, she'll come. Yes, yes, as soon as we've finished the meal we must go to the telegraph office and send a telegram.'

The telegram said: *Sailing for Tokyo 17th, getting married first, please come, reply urgent.*

The reply came next day. *Darling, congratulations, arriving Calais 3.30 Sunday.*

Neither Gwen nor Tama had time to spare for a welcome at Calais, so Gwen asked Toinette to go. Without telling Gwen, Toinette took Jerome with her. Rhoda Baynes was very reassured when she saw Jerome on the quayside.

'It's so good of you to come, M. de Labasse,' she said quaveringly. 'You met my husband, I think?'

'How do you do, M. Baynes,' Jerome said.

'Who's he?' Toinette muttered in French. 'An earthy type, that.'

'The stepfather,' Jerome told her. He had everything arranged to reassure Mrs Baynes – prior consultation with the dockside officials so that passport regulations were waived, a car to take them to Paris, a room reserved in the Hotel de la Concorde.

Gwen and Tama were waiting for them at the hotel. Gwen saw that her mother was immediately fascinated by Tama's good looks, his foreignness – everything about him appealed to her romantic heart.

Wally Baynes, on the other hand, was almost openly contemptuous. He towered over Tama when they were introduced and would have refused to shake hands. Tama, however, spoiled that ploy by bowing, as was his habit.

Conversation was difficult. Gwen had to translate everything her mother and Wally said into French for Tama.

'Can't he speak English, then?' Wally sneered.

'No. Can you speak Japanese?' Gwen said with sharpness. 'Or even French?'

He was silenced.

The wedding, a purely official ceremony, was on Tuesday. Gwen wore a new dress of blue crêpe, a mere slip of a dress after a new style by Coco Chanel. She carried a little bouquet of blue irises. Wally would have sneered even more if he had known that Tama himself had chosen them, explaining that flowers were of the utmost importance to the Japanese.

Despite himself, Gwen's stepfather had been captivated by Paris, by Gwen's ease in her life there. She spoke French with fluency, people seemed to respect her, the studio was in a very good situation in its nook off the Place Vendôme.

Then the food, the wine, the sparkle of the boulevards in the spring sunshine, the exuberance and naughtiness of the Folies Bergères, the elegance of the women . . . Ah, the women! To Wally's astonishment and delight Toinette had taken him to her apartment for an hour's 'relaxation' on Monday when Rhoda was shopping for a hat to wear to the wedding.

So he listened to the incomprehensible wedding ceremony and signed the register afterwards in a mood of amiability. A pair of gentlemen from the Japanese Embassy also signed as witnesses, then presented to Gwen what the prefect called a *'voir-dire'*, which seemed to mean a declaration for Japanese officials that the pair were legally married.

Any plans Wally had had for getting an arm around little Gwennie and giving her a good hug were abandoned. Anyhow, he didn't altogether fancy making an enemy of the new husband. Not a big powerful fellow, that Tama, but you could see he had a will of steel and would give a good account of himself if it came to a showdown.

And as for Gwen . . . well, you just had to look at her to see she was head over heels in love with the fellow. How her eyes shone when she looked at him. How they followed him when he moved away.

What could she *see* in him? Women were funny, thought Wally. Even Rhoda seemed to think he was great.

But Rhoda understood it all. Tama's spare, compact body, his fine olive skin and short black hair, the gleaming black eyes that seemed to light up from within . . . Oh, what a strange, wonderful creature! No wonder her daughter had fallen in love with him.

Next day they went to Calais in a party. Rhoda and Wally would see off Gwen and Tama and then board the ferry for England. Toinette, Sybille, Robert and others of Jerome's group had come and, greatly daring, Jerome himself. He was relieved to sense no antagonism from Tama.

'Probably knows it's too late for me to be any kind of a threat,' he muttered to himself.

His wedding present to Gwen had been a portable gramophone and a selection of records. Some were classical music but, as he'd pointed out to Tama, there were some of his favourite foxtrots: 'Oh, You Beautiful Doll' and 'Bye Bye Blackbird'.

'I expect the band at the Imperial Hotel plays those too. Give my regards to the bandleader when you go there.'

'Certainly,' Tama said with perfect good temper.

A steward of the *Orient Pearl* was going round sounding a hand gong and calling, 'Ashore, if you please, ashore those not sailing.'

Everyone kissed everyone else. Rhoda burst into tears. Toinette took charge of her to guide her down the gangplank, whilst exchanging a wicked wink with Wally over the bowed shoulders.

Jerome took advantage of the hubbub to kiss Gwen long and gently.

'Goodbye, Gwen. Write to me.'

'Yes, I will.'

'Goodbye, Tama.' He bowed in his best diplomatic-corps fashion.

'Goodbye,' said Tama, responding.

The shore party went down the gangplank. They stood watching as, very slowly and with siren going, the *Orient Pearl* moved away from the quay.

Gwen and Tama were at the rail, waving. Gradually their faces receded, and then the ship went out into the sea-way, to be masked from them by other vessels.

'Well, it will all turn out all right,' Toinette said in a hopeful tone.

'Of course it will,' agreed Jerome.

But she could see he didn't really think so.

Chapter Seven

Gwen had made a pact with herself not to be depressed by the docks at Yokohama. She knew from experience that seaports are no way to judge the rest of the country.

Her determination in this had been buoyed up by a sight of Mount Fuji as the *Orient Pearl* nosed her way across the coastal region known as the Black Current and into Tokyo Bay.

Viewed as it rose above distant cliffs, to Gwen the mountain seemed unreal. Twelve thousand feet of perfectly contoured splendour capped with glistening white, known to the Japanese, so Tama said, as *'O yama'*, meaning the 'Honourable Mountain', as if there were no other.

Gwen had been about to exclaim, 'It's so beautiful,' but as she turned with the words on her lips, she saw Tama's face. There was so much reverence and awe in it that she knew it would be wrong to speak. This was Tama's moment of home-coming.

Yokohama pier was different in one respect from Calais – there was far less rushing about and shouting. Little men in red caps, dark smocks, tight trousers and black shoes hurried on board almost in silence. At one or two gestures or sharp commands, they took up pieces of luggage then led the way ashore to the customs shed.

Gwen and Tama waited in line with their porters alongside. There was quite a lengthy display of officialdom being meted out to those ahead of them. But the name Hayakawa seemed to work some minor magic. Bows

119

were exchanged, the passports were returned, Gwen and Tama walked through.

There was a fair crowd gathered at the exit end of the customs shed, awaiting friends or relatives. Women and children in bright kimonos far outshone the men, who were mostly in dowdy European clothes. The crowd was not silent like the porters, but full of laughter and gaiety, fans fluttering, hands beckoning, the children calling out welcomes.

The transfer to the station was quickly made. Gwen was too busy keeping up with the fast trotting pace of the porters to be able to look around. The train for Tokyo was waiting at the platform. Their luggage was put on board – one trunk, two cases. They sank into the carriage, which seemed small and light compared with European rail cars. The engine gave a shrill toot, and they were off.

'How long is the journey to Tokyo?'

'An hour, if I remember rightly. Soon it won't be necessary to land at Yokohama, ships will be able to go into Tokyo itself when the channel's been dredged.' Tama laughed. 'Of course it was never necessary until now. We never had ocean liners sailing to Tokyo until the Americans came and woke us up.'

Once clear of Yokohama, the view improved greatly. The Japanese countryside rushed by. It seemed to Gwen just like a garden; trimmed, weeded, cultivated to the last inch. Often the terrain was steep, so into the hillside stones were laid to prevent precious soil washing away. And not just laid in dull straight lines – no, the Japanese laid their restraining walls in diamonds or chequered patterns.

Farms were very small, dotted with houses of wood and paper, frail looking, low built, tiled with wood shingles and finished off with a row of irises along the roof ridge. In the April day the green of the iris leaves seemed a fairy-like touch; all the more so where purple flowers were beginning to unfold.

People were about in the fields and the vegetable plots – both men and women with smocks girt up from bare legs, moving about bent double under mushroom hats. Some of the women had babies tied to their backs. Some had children at their heels, and the children too bent and worked – tending, weeding, picking, clearing.

There were children in the compartment in which they were travelling: tiny creatures with caps of shining black hair, brilliant short kimonos, and little wooden clogs over white cotton socks. Gwen looked at the children, and the children stared at Gwen: silent, amazed, concentrating all their attention on this strange, flame-headed female in her suit of beige flannel and blouse of silk – of unpatterned silk, plain silk, silk with no flowers or birds woven into it.

She smiled at them in delight. *'Hajimemashite,'* she said and, remembering her lessons, bowed a little from the waist.

Each little face broke out into a beam of pleasure. They bobbed their bows, repeated the polite phrases of greeting as they had been taught. The mothers relaxed a little. The fathers allowed themselves a bow.

Conversation began. But it was too fast for Gwen to follow. She'd helped while away the shipboard hours by improving her Japanese with Tama's help, but he always spoke so that she could understand him. This rapid exchange of chatter was beyond her.

She contented herself with nodding and smiling.

In what seemed less than an hour, the train steamed into Tokyo station. Everyone alighted, bows and polite farewells were exchanged. Porters arrived to take charge of their luggage. Unlike French porters they never seemed to haggle over a price, and always seemed pleased at what they were given.

Outside, Gwen paused to look. This was Tokyo, capital of Japan.

It might as well have been Toulon, or Twickenham. She saw a big open space, bounded mainly by wooden hoardings because of building operations. On the left was a Western building, three or four storeys high, concrete and stone, ugly and heavy. 'The Central Post Office,' murmured Tama. Across the way was a seven-storey building, flat faced, efficient. 'Business offices,' Tama said.

Gwen turned to look at the station they were leaving. Grandiose, French-style architecture of the worst kind, built of brick with contrast coping in stone, trimmed with various umbels and canopies of metal.

'Oh dear,' said Gwen.

'What's the matter?'

'It's not very Japanese, is it?'

Tama frowned at her. 'It's modern Japan. You couldn't very well build a railway station of bamboo and paper, could you?'

'No-o.' But why did the new architecture have to be in a style so aggressively out of keeping with what she'd seen in the countryide?

Well, it was their city – presumably they knew how they wanted it to look. Later she discovered that the real Tokyo, the Tokyo of the Imperial Palace, the Imperial Theatre, the Diet, was only a few minutes' walk away. A pity, though, that the traveller's first impression should be of this unpleasing European-type square.

There were *jinrickshas*, pony-carriages, and taxis waiting for hire. Because of the luggage, Tama chose a motor-driven taxi, although it would have been a new experience indeed for Gwen to ride in a vehicle pulled by a man.

She noted that Tama didn't attempt to give the driver an address. He gave a general direction, Higashi-Nakano, and as they neared the suburb in which the Hayakawa home was situated, gave specific route instructions.

Afterwards she learned to her cost that there was no such thing as a definite address in Japan. Addresses were given by wards and districts, not street and number as in Europe. As houses were often built on the site of a mansion once owned by a nobleman, there could be fourteen houses numbered 22 Shiba Park Road, and Shiba Park Road itself might not be near Shiba Park after the park had been sold off in land parcels. There were many roads that had no name at all: they existed, everyone knew they existed, but the only way to find a family living in them was to ask the ward policeman, who knew everything.

The taxi drew up with a rocking application of brakes in front of a roofed gateway. At one side a nameplate of lacquered metal announced in Japanese characters that this was the home of the Hayakawa family. Enclosed by a fence of red cedar, the house was visible: two storeys high, wood framed, and with wooden shingles for the roof.

The gate in the fence was solidly panelled. Let into it was another, lesser gate or door, which flew open at the sound of the taxi.

An old man in a dark smock and tight trousers was bowing almost to the ground. 'Welcome, welcome, Tamaki-san!'

Tama stepped through, giving a slight inclination of the head. Gwen followed, smiling and saying 'hajime-mashite'. The old man bowed and bowed, murmuring his welcome, hardly daring to look up at her.

A short paved path lay ahead, leading to a covered wooden porch one step up. On the porch stood two women, bowing with their hands on the fronts of their knees. All that Gwen could see at that first meeting was two elaborately dressed heads: one touched with grey, one jet black.

Tama stopped. He bowed deeply. 'Mother, I am glad to see you again.'

'Welcome home, my son.'

'Hanako, I am glad to see you.'

'Welcome, Tamaki-sama.'

'Here is my wife, Gwen-san.'

'Welcome, Gwen-san,' said Mrs Hayakawa, straightening a little so that her bow was much less deep and she could see her new daughter-in-law.

Her face had flooded with unguarded surprise. Gwen knew that her appearance must be a shock to her – taller than the older woman by more than a head, much more heavily built than a Japanese girl, and with bronze-coloured hair and eyebrows.

'*Hajimemashite*,' Gwen said, bowing, as she'd been taught. To Mirio-san, her mother-in-law, a deep bow. To Hanako-san, a lesser bow.

But she longed to be taken in the old woman's arms and kissed. She needed, at that moment more than almost any moment in her life, to be made to feel secure.

All around her were utterly alien things – a house of wood with paper windows, a gate with foreign writing upon it, people in clothes unlike any she had ever seen worn in real life before.

Even the sounds were alien: the clatter of the old man's clogs as he brought in the luggage, grunting and muttering in his own tongue; the murmur of welcome from the women. The scents were foreign – flowers and greenery new to her, something in the house being cooked with spices and herbs she couldn't name.

She looked in desperation at Tama for support. But Tama had his own problems. He was meeting again the mother on whom he'd turned his back four years ago, the widow of the man he had defied when he left Tokyo for France.

'Come in, come in,' said Mirio-san politely, moving aside to allow them to step up on to the porch. Her face showed nothing now after that one moment of complete surprise when Gwen was introduced.

Tama stooped to take off his shoes. Gwen, who had quite forgotten urgent instruction from Tama to do so, almost bumped into him. She too stooped and took off the court shoes she had worn on purpose so as to get them off easily before entering the house. No one in Japan ever entered a house with shoes on. It was to limit her range of footwear considerably in the immediate future.

They stepped up on the porch, Mirio-san bowed them into the house, into an almost empty room. Gwen learned later that it was an eight-mat room, quite large. Rooms in Japan were measured by the number of mats needed to cover the floor, each mat six feet long by three feet wide.

On the right-hand wall was an alcove floored by a dais about six inches high. In it stood a lacquered vase, gleaming lustrously in the light pouring in from the far end, the southern end, where the paper screens had been removed to let in the spring air and show the garden.

In the vase a slender branch of cherry blossom had been set, the flowers still in bud so that the deep pink seemed rich yet tender. With it were two long, sword-like leaves – nothing else.

Behind the flowers, on the wall, was the *kakemono*, a scroll which was changed less frequently than the flowers. Today it was a piece of beautiful Japanese calligraphy, which Gwen couldn't read. Hanako later told her it said, 'The crane folds its wings after its homeward flight.' This was an oblique reference to Tama's return to his homeland.

As soon as the newcomers entered the room, a partition at one side slid open. A woman in a plain kimono appeared, on her knees and bowing. She put into the room several thin cushions, then rose and hurried forward, still bowing, to set the cushions in the centre of the room. Bowing, she backed out, closing the sliding partition behind her.

'Shall we sit, Tamaki-san?' said his mother. She couldn't invite him to do so, he was the head of the house now and must give the invitation.

He took his place on one of the cushions. Gwen did

likewise, which seemed to cause a moment of consternation. When she knew more about the household she realised she should have waited for an invitation, and that she and Mirio-san should have seated themselves simultaneously. To sit down before her mother-in-law as she did on this first meeting was impolite.

Everyone was now seated. Mrs Hayakawa began what was obviously a rehearsed speech, some of which Gwen was able to follow without strain. There were the polite greetings she herself had learned, then inquiries after Tama's health, inquiries after Gwen's health, inquiries as to the discomforts of the sea journey. Tama replied in similar set phrases – he was well, his wife was well, the crossing had not been too unpleasant, how was the health of his honoured mother, how was the health of his sister?

The servant reappeared, followed by another. One offered *oshibari*, hand towels, for the travellers to wipe away the grime of the journey. The other brought tea on a lacquered tray. Gwen, sitting cross-legged on the thin cushion, reflected in the midst of her nervousness that it was a good thing there weren't the usual accoutrements of English afternoon tea, no saucers, no teaspoons, no plates for cakes and dainty napkins.

Mrs Hayakawa poured the tea. The first cup went to Tama, who put it to his lips in a ceremonious fashion then set it down. Gwen was then served. She looked at Tama for guidance. 'Sip it and set it down,' he told her, smiling. She obeyed.

Now tea could be poured for the hostess and for Hanako. After that, the members of the Hayakawa family seemed to relax a little. It seemed some first hurdle had been passed for them.

But not for Gwen. She still had to get to know her mother-in-law and sister-in-law. She sought in her mind for some phrase, among those she'd learned from Tama, to get a conversation started. The tea – she'd learned some sentences about taking tea.

But the tea was as awful as Jerome had prophesied. Rough on the tongue, bitter, made from green leaves and not brown, served with neither milk nor sugar, though in Gwen's opinion milk or sugar would only have made it worse. The words she was trying to frame died on her lips. It would be a complete lie to say, 'This tea is delicious.'

There was a pause in the rapid exchanges between Tama and his mother. He looked at Gwen expectantly. He wanted her to take part in the conversation.

She brought out one of the phrases she had learned: 'I hope all goes well with your household?'

This brought forth a flood of response, far too fast for her to make out a word. She glanced at her husband. Tama said, 'My mother is telling you about the death of my father. I won't translate, she says the doctor was incompetent.' He spoke in Japanese to her, then said to Gwen, 'I have told her we will pay a visit to the tomb tomorrow.'

'Oh, Tama!'

'It's expected.'

Hanako spoke. She had a very soft voice, so that Gwen had to lean close to hear what she was saying, but she spoke very slowly and distinctly. 'It is a great honour, Gwen-san, that you have learned so much of our language.'

'So much! Almost nothing.'

'I know nothing at all of your language. You are very dutiful, to learn to speak ours even if only a little.'

'I hope to speak more,' Gwen said. 'Better,' she amended.

Mirio-san said, 'On the whole, it is better if a daughter-in-law speaks little.' Her small face had an expression that Gwen couldn't read. It might have been disapproval, or disappointment.

Tama said in French, 'Daughters-in-law when they come to their new home speak very little. It is their

127

duty to listen rather than speak. So my mother is telling you that your silence is not offensive to her.'

It was an odd idea to Gwen. But if silence was agreeable in a daughter-in-law, she could provide that. She nodded and smiled at Mirio-san. Mirio-san gave her the very faintest of bows.

At a gesture from her mother, Hanako refilled their cups. The older of the maids brought little cakes of pounded rice dipped in soy flour and sugar. She offered them first to Tama, then to Gwen. As she did so she examined Gwen thoroughly and unashamedly. Gwen felt herself colouring up under the scrutiny. She said in English, 'You'll know me when you see me again!'

The maid drew back. She knew she had been reproved and was startled by the fact.

Tama said, 'You mustn't mind Kinie. She's been with the family since before I was born.'

'Oh, I see.' A family retainer, allowed certain liberties. 'I'm sorry I spoke sharply. I'm not used to being stared at.'

Tama said something in Japanese to Kinie, who gave a very translatable shrug, meaning, What's she upset about anyway? Tama spoke again, more sharply. Kinie bowed, glanced at Mirio-san with something like complicity, and backed out.

'You must forgive her. We don't think it impolite to stare, Gwen.'

She felt she'd been put completely in the wrong, making a fuss over nothing. Hanako, who seemed to be kindly disposed towards her, said in her soft voice, 'Please eat a cake. Cook made them specially for today. See, they are coloured red – a lucky colour.'

'Thank you.' She expected the cake to be as awful as the tea, but no, it was sweet and chewy and quite palatable. By means of nibbling a cake between sips, she was able to finish her second little cup of tea while Tama and his mother conversed. She caught very little of the conversation. Mrs Hayakawa made no attempt to slow her speech so that her new daughter-in-law might understand.

Presently Tama said, 'Mirio-san says she has business she needs to discuss with me. I expect you'd like to unpack and be shown the house. Hanako!'

At the mere utterance of her name, his sister came from her knees to her feet in one fluid movement. She stood ready, half-bowing to Gwen.

Gwen got up with more difficulty from her cross-legged position. In comparison with Hanako she felt like some lumbering cart-horse. Hanako was as tall as Gwen's shoulder, and was made in proportion – tiny, her height added to by an elaborate hairstyle decked with ivory pins. Under it her face was a very pale cream. She had small eyes, but almond-shaped and expressive. Gwen couldn't tell whether she was good looking by Japanese standards. Later she learned that Hanako was considered only average in looks, and not at all clever.

'This way,' Hanako said. She moved out of the room, not exactly backwards, but turned so that she was giving Gwen the place of honour ahead of her.

To Gwen's surprise they went out of the open doors at the far end of the room, into the garden. The garden was different from anything she'd seen in Europe – mostly paved, with trees and shrubs in among rocks. A pool with water trickling into and out of it along bamboo channels made a pleasant tinkling sound.

Hanako led the way on a path around the house. Here, under a flowering cherry tree, was what Gwen took to be a garden shelter. But, unlike the main house, this one seemed to be built of something more substantial than wood and paper. It had outside walls of plaster and was windowless. On the door, which was standing open, was a very efficient lock. Inside were various boxes and woven reed containers. Among them stood the luggage that had been brought from the taxi by the gardener.

'This is the *oshiire*, the storehouse,' Hanako explained. She drew the skirts of her flowered kimono close about her ankles to avoid snagging it on corners of boxes as they went in. 'I have seen pictures, in magazines,' she went on, speaking slowly and clearly, 'of Western rooms. Much furniture. Everything close at hand. Here we put most things in the storehouse, only have in rooms what is needed.'

'I see!' cried Gwen, enlightened. When she'd asked Tama how the sparsity, the emptiness of Japanese rooms was achieved he'd said, 'Things are put away.' She'd never been able to understand where.

'Please take out and put to one side what you need for everyday life,' Hanako said. She indicated a square of coloured cotton which had been laid out to accept the items. 'Kinie-san will bring them up to the room you will use. Do you understand?'

'*Hai, wakarimasu,*' Gwen said thankfully.

She unlocked the trunk and one suitcase, took out enough clothes for herself and Tama for the next few days. Toilet articles too, her drawing materials, and the presents she'd brought for the family.

And Jerome's wedding present to her, the gramophone with its records.

'I will carry these,' she ventured in Japanese, putting nightdress and dressing-gown over her arm.

'Good. I will also carry. This?' Hanako picked up the portable gramophone by the handle. Its unexpected weight made her lean over to one side. 'Oh!'

'Gramophone,' Gwen said, using the English word. She'd no idea what it might be in Japanese. She made gestures of the record going round and then put a cupped hand to her ear. Hanako stared at her. Gwen opened it up. Hanako put a finger on the turntable and moved it round, looking expectant. She thought the turntable would make the sound that Gwen had mimed.

Laughing, Gwen closed up the box. 'Later,' she said in Japanese.

They went into the main house, but by means of a wooden staircase at the side which led to the verandah along the first storey. The floor of the verandah formed the porch roof over the ground-floor windows. Tama had explained that in summer it was pleasant to sit in the shade of the porch to look at the garden, and likewise to sit on the verandah at night to 'view the full moon'. She only learned afterwards that one actually did this – one invited friends and went up to the verandah to view the full moon.

The room which was to be hers and Tama's opened on to the verandah by means of sliding screens. It seemed to be practically empty. No bed was visible, because the futons and covers were rolled up and stored in cupboards during the day. There seemed to be nowhere to put the clothes she was carrying.

Hanako crossed the room, slid aside an upper half-screen. Shelves for clothing. Smiling, Gwen laid her belongings on the shelves. She held up the toilet bag with its soapbox and toothbrush, its hairbrush and comb. 'Dressing-table?' she said in English.

Hanako raised her hands, palms upwards, meaning, 'What are you asking?'

Gwen took out her hairbrush, pantomimed brushing her hair then putting down the brush to examine the result in a mirror.

'Ah!' Hanako slid open the lower half-screen. The cupboard contained one shelf. On it stood a mirror in a lacquer frame. She made a gesture inviting Gwen to kneel and look in the mirror.

'What, down there?' Gwen cried.

Hanako looked at her in puzzlement.

'No, no,' said Gwen. She took out the mirror, set it on one of the shelves in the upper cupboard, and mimed doing her hair standing up. In fact, it would be better to do it sitting down. She glanced about. No chair.

'What do you look for?' Hanako asked.

'A chair?'

Hanako shook her head.

'No chairs?'

Once again the shake of the head.

'A stool?' But she didn't know the Japanese word for stool. She sketched it with her hands.

'Kitchen,' said Hanako. 'Bathroom.'

'I understand.' She would have to borrow a stool from one of these rooms if she wanted to sit down.

She and Hanako sorted out her belongings. Hanako made ironing movements – some of the clothes needed pressing. 'Yes, thank you, I'd like them pressed.' Gwen's reply prompted nodding and little approving claps of the hands.

So they conversed, in Gwen's few words of Japanese and Hanako's clear, slow speech, with gestures and miming, all interspersed with laughter.

Gwen felt a surge of confidence. She was going to get along fine. Hanako would help her.

They went down the inner staircase to the ground floor. It brought them to a passage on the far side of the house, where the kitchen was situated.

'Kitchen,' Hanako said. '*Nesan* – Kinie, Suzuki, Ota.' She pointed to the garden. 'Akira.' She made digging movements. 'Kazuo.' Sweeping movements.

'The gardener. Yes, I understand, Akira is the gardener. Kazuo does odd jobs. May I meet the servants?'

Hanako raised her eyebrows. But after a moment she bowed, before leading the way into the kitchen.

To Gwen's eye it was a cluttered place, all the more surprising in the Japanese setting. Cooking equipment stood on open shelves. The kitchen range was a shallow wooden box with a plaster top, in which there was a round aperture. On this a pot was simmering. Kneeling beside it was an elderly man in a grey kimono. He was tasting something from a steaming spoon.

At Gwen's entry he stood up. He stared at her. Behind him hovered a little woman of about thirty, in a rather plain striped kimono with a dark *obi*. A boy of about sixteen was kneeling to push charcoal into an opening at the side of the range. He leapt to his feet.

Consternation seemed to reign. They huddled together, gaping at Gwen.

'This is Gwen-san,' Hanako told them. 'She asked to meet you.' She pointed to each. The cook was Ota, the woman was Suzuki, the boy was Kazuo. Kinie was obviously elsewhere, and the gardener was in his own little hut in the garden. Five servants to look after a household of two women, Mirio and Hanako.

They all bowed very low, again and again.

'*Ikaga desu kai?*' Gwen inquired politely.

'Very well, thank you, Gwen-san,' they chorused. 'And you?'

'I am very well, thank you.'

They beamed at her. How very, very strange and wonderful. The new daughter-in-law, a light-skinned and copper-headed foreigner in peculiar clothes, had taken the trouble to come to the kitchen to ask how they were!

Ota bowed and ushered her towards the door which led out to the side entrance. She thought he was going to take her outdoors. But he pointed to an open box high up on the wall, under the skylight. There was a shelf, sheltered by a peaked wooden roof on the apex of which stood a shape, a sort of figure made of straw. It reminded Gwen of a corn dolly she'd once seen.

Ota bowed to it, clapped his hands twice, and intoned something. The others bowed and repeated the phrase.

'What is it?' Gwen asked Hanako. 'What are they doing?'

'They are asking the kitchen god to bless you, Gwen-san.'

'Oh! Oh, how kind of them!' Impulsively she held out her hand to Ota, but he merely gazed at it. She remembered she must bow her thanks. She did so.

Hanako took her out. When they had gone along the

133

passage a few steps she said, in her gentle way, 'It is not necessary to bow to servants, Gwen-san.'

'Oh dear,' said Gwen in English. 'Well, I won't do it again.' In Japanese she said, 'I understand.'

In the living-room she found Tama and her mother-in-law in deep conversation, with Kinie kneeling nearby and clearly a participant. Tama looked up as she came in.

'Have you unpacked, dear?'

'Yes, it's taken care of. I met the servants.'

His eyebrows went up. 'What on earth for?'

'Well . . . I thought they'd like to meet the new mistress.'

'Ah. Well, of course, my mother is the mistress of the house and will remain so, Gwen. I did explain that to you.'

'Yes, quite, but after all I'm the wife of the master—'

'You are the daughter-in-law, Gwen. Never mind, you'll get used to it. In any case you won't have to struggle with running a Japanese household.' He rose easily to his feet. 'I have to go to the police office now, to—'

'The police?' she echoed in alarm.

'Yes, to let them know we've arrived.'

'But what business is it of theirs?' She was not only alarmed now, but bewildered.

'Don't worry,' he said, laughing and giving her a pat on the shoulder. 'It doesn't mean we're criminals. A new wife must be registered as living in her husband's house, and I myself have to register as having come back here—'

'But why should the police want to know things like that?' She felt as if he was telling her they were under surveillance.

'It's all right, it's just regulations. You see, if this part of the city were to be destroyed in an earthquake, or if there were a fire—'

'Tama!'

He took her hand. 'Gwen, this is Tokyo. Earthquakes are quite frequent. That doesn't mean much, you feel tremors almost every day and only a few cause any damage. You remember, I explained – that's why the houses are made of wood and paper. If they fall down they don't hurt the people in them, and they can be easily rebuilt. Remember?'

'Oh . . . yes . . .'

'But if a house falls down in an earthquake it can easily catch alight because all our cooking and heating is from charcoal stoves. So fire too is a big hazard. And *so*,' he ended, raising a finger, 'the police need to know who lives in which house, to count the survivors after a fire or an earthquake, and look for anybody who is missing. Nothing sinister, you see?'

'Of course. I see. What a fool! I'm sorry, Tama, it just sounded so strange when you said it.'

'I'd better go now, so as to get back for supper. We'll eat about seven. Then after that, my dear, I think we'll have a bath and get to bed early. Do you agree?'

'Yes, Tama.'

He smiled, kissed her, bowed to his mother and sister, and went out.

As Gwen turned back to the others she glimpsed on the face of Mirio-san an expression of contempt and anger that made her blood run cold.

'What?' she gasped. 'What have I done?' But it was said in English, and Mirio-san was looking away.

Gwen had long outgrown any notion that everybody in the world must love her. Two years in the cut-throat world of Parisian art had done away with any such illusion. But she'd thought that Tama's mother would be as anxious to make things work between them as she was herself. After all, Gwen and Tama were only going to be with the family a short time. Surely it was in the interests of everyone that during her year with them they should get on well?

135

Hanako spoke quickly, as if to turn her attention from the moment that had just gone by. 'Let me show you the rest of the house,' she said. She led the way. They went into the room next door, which was just the same as the one they had left. Hanako stopped, looked earnestly at Gwen, then said something placatory.

'I don't understand,' Gwen said.

There was a long pause. Then Hanako took her hand and pressed it between her own two tiny ones. It was a way of saying, I am your friend.

The meal served when Tama returned was very strange. It was served in the living-room. The family sat on the floor. Trays were brought, one for each person. There was a fish stew, then a dish of mixed vegetables with sharp mixed pickles. Next came a platter of thinly sliced raw fish garnished with grated radish and a sauce that tasted something like ginger and something like mustard. Last came bowls of rice, rather sticky and glutinous. With the meal, more green tea was served.

The food was eaten with chopsticks. Gwen had practised during the voyage, under Tama's guidance, so she acquitted herself reasonably well. She felt all the time that Mirio-san's eagle eye was upon her. She tried to look appreciative of every dish, although she found the pickles too salty and too astringent, and the rice tasteless.

Conversation during the meal was mostly between Mirio and Tama. She's doing it to exclude me, thought Gwen, and then reproached herself – wasn't it natural that the older woman should have much to say to her son after an absence of four years?

At length the interminable meal was over. Gwen was so tired now she could hardly hold her head up. The strain of the day was overwhelming her. She sat in her uncomfortable posture on the floor, longing for an armchair in which she could lean back and relax.

About nine o'clock Kinie came in to announce something. 'The bath is ready,' said Tama. Gwen came to herself with a jerk. Her head had been nodding, she'd been about to fall asleep.

She clambered up. Kinie led the way. Tama went with Gwen out into the passage to a room next to the kitchen. Here stood a tall oval tub of cedar staves bound with iron bands. Clouds of steam rose from it.

The floor of the bathroom was stone, with across it a sort of duckboard of open slats, about a foot high. A box-like stool stood near the bath. Several cloth napkins and a wooden ladle lay on it.

Kinie indicated plain cotton towels folded on a shelf along one wall. She withdrew.

'Ah,' said Tama, breathing in, 'I've missed this!' The steam was faintly scented with herbs.

Now fully awake, Gwen looked about. 'This is the bathroom?'

'Yes, of course.'

'Are you going to go first, or shall I?'

'Don't be silly. We share it.'

'What?'

'This is a Japanese bath, darling. Come along, hand your clothes out to Kinie.'

Baffled, Gwen began to undress. Tama was naked first and handed his clothes out to the servant. He took Gwen's as she removed them, gave them to Kinie.

Gwen moved as if to get into the bath. Tama put a hand on her arm. 'No,' he said, 'this way.'

He dipped up a ladleful of hot water, gently poured it over her shoulders so that the hot water cascaded down her back. He mopped her back with one of the napkins, dipped the ladle again, and poured the water over her breasts. He smoothed away the trickles with the napkin.

'Now you,' he said. He handed the ladle to her.

Beginning to smile, she dipped up some hot water. She poured it over him, picked up a napkin, and dried it off. Then she refilled the ladle, poured again, and rubbed away the moisture.

'This is how it's done,' he murmured. 'We take turns, we pour the water, we wipe it away.'

'No soap, Tama?'

'We don't have soap.'

'What a shame, I've got some in my toilet bag. I could have brought it.'

'Next time.'

He took the ladle, plunged it into the tub to fill it with hot water. He poured it, smoothing it over her flanks and her belly with the wet cloth. Again he dipped the ladle, and the warm water streamed over her skin.

It was the most erotic thing she'd ever experienced. The warmth of the water, the strong hand moving the cotton cloth against her body, the soft stroking movements . . .

And his shoulders, broad and strong under her touch, shrugging and moving in pleasure . . . His chest, the rise and fall of his breathing, his black hair glistening in the steam, his teeth gleaming as he smiled . . .

When they had cleansed themselves of the day's grime, they climbed into the tub. The water came to neck level when they sat on a little bench against one side. It was very hot – not relaxing, stimulating.

Gwen reached out to take Tama's hand. She placed it against her breast.

'Yes,' he whispered, 'soon.' His lips curved faintly at the thought.

After a long soak they climbed out. With the rather hard cotton towels they dried each other off, sometimes in a tangle with them as they came closer, ever closer to each other.

Tama opened the door slightly. Two cotton garments lay on a tray outside. He handed one to her, shrugged into the other. This was the *yukata*, the sleeping kimono.

Gwen felt its folds cling to her damp skin. Her bronze hair was darkened by the moisture, tendrils hung in little curls against her cheeks.

Tama put his arm round her shoulders. They went out. Little wooden clogs, *gaeta*, stood waiting. Tama put his feet into one pair, Gwen followed suit.

Tama led her outside into the cool night air. Only a pearly light from beyond the paper windows lit the way. They went up the steps to the verandah. From there they stepped into their room. Someone had made up the bed, laid the futons on the floor and spread the covers over them.

They peeled off the *yukatas*. Clinging to each other, they knelt on the futons.

'Now you really belong to me,' Tama said. 'Now I have you all to myself.'

'Say you'll always love me, Tama.'

'Always, always.'

And those words beat like a refrain through the passion of that night, their first night as man and wife in Tama's homeland.

Chapter Eight

There was a bustling sound from somewhere, then a faint bang of wood against wood. That sound came again. Gwen woke up fully, opened her eyes. A milky-grey light was coming through the paper windows.

She felt for her wristwatch under her bran-filled bolster. She squinted at it. A few minutes before five. She put the watch to her ear – yes, it was going.

Ten minutes to five! But someone in the house was up and about. The noises she'd heard were the opening of the downstairs shutters and someone sweeping the floor.

She cuddled closer to her husband, trying to go back to sleep. But the sounds from downstairs kept rousing her each time she almost drifted off.

Now someone was sweeping the path from the house to the garden. A faint monotonous singing could be heard. Then a clang, as some metal pot or kettle struck stone. She learned later it was Kazuo setting down a pail on the well-rim. Water for the house came from the Hayakawas' own well.

She could hear the tock-tock-tock of *gaeta*. She gave up the attempt to sleep. It was quite pleasant to lie here, her arms around Tama, her cheek against his back, listening to the house come to life.

Then a strange thing happened. The futons on which they were lying seemed to sway. A tinge of nausea caught at Gwen's stomach. She stared up at the ceiling. It seemed to be tilting gently, first one way, then another. She heard a low rumbling, then creaks as the timbers of

141

the house moved and settled and were moved again. The mirror on the shelf in the lower cupboard toppled over, a curious sound from behind the closed screen.

Little cries from below told her that she wasn't the only one experiencing this peculiar event. She seized Tama by one bare shoulder, shook him awake.

'Tama! Tama! What's happening!'

He rolled over. His eyes focused on the swaying ceiling. He sat up. Creak-creak-creak went the house frame. Something fell in the room below, from shelf to floor perhaps.

He put his arm round his wife. The ceiling gave one last tilt then levelled off. The futons ceased to move below them. There was a moment of silence and then from the garden came the call of a bird.

'It's over, it's all right,' Tama said, giving her a hug and letting her go.

'But what was it?'

'An earth tremor, what else?'

'But Tama . . . Tama! The whole house moved.'

'Yes, and settled down again. Didn't it?'

'Yes, but . . . Tama . . . Was that an earthquake?'

He grinned, that sudden beguiling flash of white teeth. 'That was a room quake. You'll get used to it.'

'Used to it!'

'Yes, of course. They happen on average a dozen times a week, in some part or other of Japan. They always settle down again, although of course we have to be ready to dash outdoors if it looks like anything serious.'

Gwen huddled against him. She was really scared. She'd never felt so strange in her life as when the floor beneath her began to move – her sense of balance seemed to desert her, she couldn't tell what was up and what was down until the tremor stopped. Intolerable that Mother Earth, old reliable Mother Earth, should play such a trick on them.

'Truly, my love, it's nothing to worry about. Come now, don't be frightened.'

Tama stroked her hair, dropped little kisses on shoulders and cheek.

And very soon she relaxed, and kissed him in return, and they turned to each other in renewed desire. Perhaps it was a celebration of life that made them take joy in each other after that little threat of death.

When it was time to rise and dress for breakfast, Gwen donned her *yukata* to go out on the verandah and examine the day. Akira was at work among the stones by the pool, snipping withered leaves from little flowering plants. Birds with white-flecked grey wings fluttered among the dwarf blossom trees. She yawned and stretched. What a beautiful world . . .

Now she needed to visit what are generally called 'the usual offices'.

'Where's the *lavabo*, darling?'

'Ah. You have to go down the stairs, walk down the side path in the garden – not the main path, the one that goes to the left.'

An outdoor toilet? In the home of a master-craftsman in the capital city? Stifling her surprise, she obeyed his directions. Sure enough, she found a little outhouse masked from sight by azalea bushes, but had she been in any doubt she could have found it by the smell.

This was something Jerome had never mentioned, nor did she ever see it in any guidebook. But the fact was that, as far as sanitation was concerned, Japan was still back in the Middle Ages. Nightsoil was collected at regular intervals by horsedrawn enclosed carts, the contents of which were eventually used for agricultural purposes. In later conversation she heard Japanese ladies discuss the coming of Western drainage, but so far it only existed in the modern buildings in the city centre.

She grew accustomed to the situation. After all, it wasn't much worse than rural France or rural England of the 1920s. But it was the most disillusioning thing in her coming to terms with Japan.

When she returned indoors, Suzuki was waiting to usher her to the toilet room. This was not part of the bathroom. It was upstairs, on the opposite side of the staircase from their bedroom, and consisted of a low shelf on which stood a brass bowl with hot water for washing, another smaller bowl for teeth-cleaning. Suzuki brought fresh supplies of hot water. There was no soap, Gwen noticed, as she used her own supply brought from Paris.

A tortured session at the low dressing-table convinced her she could put her hair up without needing a mirror. Then she went downstairs for breakfast.

Two years in France had made her a fan of the *café complêt*. She'd not realised how much she had looked forward to and enjoyed that first cup of coffee and the flaky croissant that came with it until she saw the meal set before her on its tray.

In the left near corner of the tray was a small china bowl of rice. On the right was a wooden bowl of soup made with *miso*, a brown paste derived from soy-bean curd. A tiny plate of pickled vegetables occupied the far left corner, the far right corner held a flat dish of shrimps in soy sauce.

Kinie was hovering to pour tea. This was what Gwen learned to know as 'common tea', made from leaves already used. She found it easier to drink than the beverage made from new green tea.

She sampled everything with a distrustful spirit. The rice was palatable, she could swallow the soup once she'd eaten some rice. She ate a mouthful or two of the shrimp. But the pickled vegetables defeated her utterly. They were known to the Japanese as *konomono*, 'fragrant articles', but Gwen found the smell unbearable at first. She remembered that Tama said he'd felt the same way when he encountered French cheese for the first time – the smell to him was disgusting.

Yet Tama learned to enjoy French cheese, and in time Gwen came to eat Japanese pickles without having to nerve herself to it. But they never seemed right at breakfast. To her mind, the Almighty intended the human race to drink coffee and eat croissants and apricot jam first thing in the morning, just as he intended them to drink English tea at between four and five in the afternoon.

The plan for the day had already been discussed. First they must present the gifts they'd brought from France, then they must pay the visit of respect to the grave of Tama's father, then they must inspect the lacquer workshop.

Gwen went up to fetch the presents. They had been expensively wrapped in Paris; a special box for each, gilt paper, satin bows, a card with a border of embroidered silk flowers specially made for Tama by a friend in one of the couture houses. 'In Japan, presents are always wrapped beautifully. This is because we can't afford to give big things – presents are given so often that it would ruin you to keep buying expensive things. So we wrap them to look marvellous. And anything coming from France must be marvellous to my mother and sister.'

The cries of pleasure evoked by the appearance of the gifts bore him out. Hanako unwrapped hers with exquisite care, clearly intending to keep the paper, the ribbon and the card. Inside she found a French fan of cream Mechlin lace on red whalebone spokes. Fans were commonplace in Japan, but not a fan like this. She was enraptured, bowing again and again to Tama and Gwen.

Mirio's gift, less carefully unwrapped, was a filmy shawl of knitted wool, so fine that it could be drawn through a wedding ring. Gwen could see that Mirio wanted to be unimpressed, but despite herself she gave a little shiver of pleasure at the touch of its softness against her neck when she put it round her shoulders.

Next on the agenda was the visit to the grave. Gwen

didn't know whether to be worried about it or not. Before breakfast she'd seen Mrs Hayakawa perform morning worship. She went to an altar on a shelf just inside the front door, on which lay a rolled scroll. She bowed, clapping her hands three times. It took about five seconds.

Then she went to a shelf on the wall of the passage, facing east. Here sat a little statue of the Buddha. With a thin wooden rod Mirio-san struck a bell that stood on a padded cushion on the shelf. It made a little ching-ching sound. She murmured a few sentences as she bowed.

When Gwen asked Tama what it meant, he explained that Mirio-san was giving respect to the ancestors by bowing before the Shinto shrine, and to Buddha by saying prayers before him.

'But which religion does the family follow?' Gwen said in bewilderment.

'Religion? Well . . . I don't think it's much to do with religion. It's just tradition.'

So the visit to Shoji-san's tomb might not mean a long ceremony.

In fact it was extremely short. The family tomb was in the grounds of a temple reached by means of a short drive in a taxi.

A covered basket of woven reed was placed on the floor of the car. Mirio and Hanako shared the main seat with Gwen, Tama sat in the folding seat opposite. Tama was in his best European suit, a morning-dress suit, French tailored, with black tail-coat and pin-striped trousers. His silk hat had been lovingly brushed to a soft shine, his gloves were of grey kid. He looked like a young statesman.

His mother was in a dark kimono with an *obi* of black and gold brocade. His sister wore a pale kimono embroidered in blue and green, to give a watery effect. Her *obi* was stiffened green taffeta. Since this was a formal occasion neither wore the *haori*, an outer coat of black crêpe coming to the knees and bearing the family crest on the back.

The two women had spent some time doing each other's hair. Hanako's hairstyle had ivory pins from which dangled little strands of blue beads, Mirio had a plain brown pin carved like a flower. Each carried a fan. Gwen noted with an inner smile that, despite the fact it didn't match her costume, Hanako carried the French fan.

Gwen was wearing what she felt would have been suitable for such an occasion in England – a dress of dark blue wool, long-sleeved and trimmed with white. She wore a matching straw hat, navy court shoes, and carried a handbag. Hanako examined the handbag with interest after they got into the taxi.

'What?' she asked.

'Handbag.' Gwen snapped it open to show her the handkerchief, comb, coin-purse and wallet.

Hanako's eyebrows went up. 'Money?' she said, touching the purse.

'Yes.'

'You carry money?'

'Yes.'

'But your husband is with you. He will pay for anything you wish to buy.'

Gwen smiled. 'It's the custom in Europe for women to carry money.'

She heard Mirio-san make a sound like a sniff but when she glanced at her, Mirio-san was staring out of the window.

No vehicles were allowed in the temple grounds. They alighted to walk through the high gateway of red-painted wood. Tama carried the reed basket.

The path was uphill, smoothed by the passage of feet over centuries. At the top the temple engrossed the eye, tilted eaves, tiled roof, little shrines on the forecourt, dark cypress trees around. This was Asakusa, the most venerated temple in Tokyo.

Mirio led the way aside before they reached the building. They went between magnolia trees with opened blossoms upturned to the sun, along a path between graves.

She stopped, bowing, beside an upright square stone standing on a pedestal. Tama and his sister joined her, bowing likewise. Gwen hovered at the rear.

For a few moments all withdrew while the basket was opened. It contained a tray on which were laid out little covered containers of food. Tama lifted out the tray, took the lids off the dishes, then set the tray on the step of the grave while reciting some phrases in which the name of Shoji-san figured prominently.

Mirio and Hanako joined him. They too recited some phrases. Gwen took them to be prayers. After a moment the women fell back again. Tama took Gwen by the elbow to usher her forward. A few words were said – she felt sure she was being announced to Shoji-san as Tama's wife. When the words died away Tama pressed her elbow. She bowed in unison with the rest of the family.

That was the end of the ceremony. Gwen wanted to ask, 'What happens to the tray of food?' but didn't dare. Presumably someone came from the temple to take it away in due course – or perhaps it was left for the birds to eat and the dishes gathered up later.

They drove home without any sense of being depressed or subdued. Mirio-san seemed to have several things to point out as they passed – Tokyo had altered somewhat in the four years of Tama's absence. Since the conversation was in Mirio's rapid Japanese, Gwen played no part, but nevertheless enjoyed the sights: the narrow streets with their perpendicular flags as shop signs, the food products and clothes on display in the open-fronted booths, the brightly dressed crowds of shoppers. She longed to stop the car so as to walk among them. They seemed so cheerful, so brisk.

The midday meal was served soon after their return.

Vegetable soup with, thankfully, pottery spoons to eat it, steamed carrots and young burdock roots, dried herring in strips, and various sauces in small dishes. Gwen ate everything set before her because she was so hungry after taking almost no breakfast. The tea was once more 'common tea'.

Mirio-san went at once to speak to the servants about household matters. Hanako settled down to needlework. During her sojourn in Tokyo Gwen almost never saw Hanako without needlework in her hands, and couldn't help thinking that a better present to her would have been a set of ordinary French sewing needles. Those made in Japan were of poor steel, apt to suffer blunting from use and from the humidity of the summer climate.

In due course she and Tama set off for the lacquer workshop. Mirio-san looked astonished when she discovered that Gwen proposed to accompany Tama.

'Your wife goes too?'

'Yes, Mother, this is of great interest to Gwen-san.'

'In what way?'

'Gwen worked with me on pieces which we made for the rich people of Paris.'

'Gwen-san worked with you?'

'Yes, indeed. Gwen-san is a very talented designer.'

Mirio fell silent. She watched them leave the house with a look of frowning disapproval which she didn't trouble to hide.

They walked to the workshop, which was about a quarter of a mile away in a long low building behind a fence in an unnamed side-street running down to a stream. Gwen smelt the familiar smell of lac being melted, the odour of size and jute and colouring pigments, long before the gate was opened to Tama's knock.

The foreman of the workshop was tall for a Japanese, with his hair cut in the old-fashioned cue. He wore the two kimonos of everyday wear, a grey and white with a plain grey one. Over both was tied an apron of starched white cotton stained with vegetable dyes. He bowed in greeting, but not before his eyes had opened wide at the sight of the foreign woman with his master.

This was Minoru-san, longstanding employee. Behind him were ranged fifteen men whom Gwen came to know well as friends, all of them craftsmen of the first order. But at the moment they were gaping at her in amazement.

Long explanations were made by Tama. Gwen uttered her few words of Japanese greeting, to be rewarded with a flood of eager questions she couldn't understand. Tea was inevitably brought, Tama and Gwen were ushered to seats of honour on cushions in the showroom. A little maiden of about eleven seemed to be the workshop servant – later Gwen learned that she was Minoru's granddaughter.

While Minoru brought Tama up to date with the state of business, Gwen glanced about at the items on display. They were exquisitely beautiful, lacquer in the traditional *urushi* style, gold on a background of black or brown or dark red. When it was deemed polite to get up from the tea party, she pleased everyone by examining the pieces closely and complimenting everyone on their excellence.

She learned that all these had been decorated by Shoji-san. After his death, run-of-the-mill items sold to retail shops had been decorated by Minoru and Taro.

Minoru was regarded as deft but not a true artist. Taro was a young student who had been learning to decorate under Shoji but said diffidently that he lacked authority in his designs. Both said with apparent sincerity that they were glad to have Tamaki-san back, so that new work of first quality could be undertaken again.

Now wait, thought Gwen to herself, Tama isn't here to take up design and keep the place going, he's here to sell it at a good price. But it would have been the height

of bad manners to intrude on their evident delight at
seeing Tama again.

They spent a long time talking. Then there was a tour
of inspection. Gwen discovered why there was such a
large work-force – the jobs were divided up much more
than in Tama's workshop in France, where one man
would sometimes lay on lac and sometimes polish and
sometimes prepare ingredients. Here in the Tokyo shop,
one man did one job only – and indeed, sometimes two
men together did one job only.

When Gwen mentioned it on the way home, Tama
shrugged. 'Japan is full of people,' he said. 'Men need
work to keep their families going. It's a tradition, to
employ many people. If you'd looked at the train when
we first arrived, you'd have seen there are three men
in the driving cab instead of two, there are two train
guards instead of one. If you look at a delivery van
you'll see there's a driver, a porter, and another man to
help carry the packages or urge on the horse. When you
go shopping you'll notice that there are twice as many
assistants as in a French shop. In a restaurant there's
a waitress to take your shoes, a waitress to bring hot
towels, a waitress to bring the first course, and so on
and so on.'

She was touched by the idea. 'In a way it's making
work for them, isn't it? Giving them a living. How nice.'

'Well . . . It's prestige too. The more people you
employ, the more status it gives.'

'Oh.' A mistake to think she could understand the
Japanese so quickly and easily.

Next day Tama said he thought he had better visit
the family lawyer. It would be dull for Gwen, so the
proposition was that he should take her into the city
centre and leave her to look at the shops on Ginza. 'I'll
come to find you after I've finished with Nagai-san, and
we'll have lunch at the Imperial Hotel.'

'But how will you find me? Shall I wait in one
particular shop?'

Tama laughed. 'I'll find *you*. I'll only have to ask where is the European lady with the hair like dark flames.'

So it proved.

In the main shopping street it was possible to stop to gaze through a European-style shop window, but in the side-streets – which to Gwen were much more interesting – a salesman leapt out of an open booth as soon as she paused.

These shops had a 'signboard girl' sitting at the entrance, holding a placard announcing, presumably, the goods and their price. As soon as Gwen stopped the girl would block her way, then out would rush the owner, bowing and inviting her to sit on the floor to examine his wares.

She would resist, he would insist, bows would be exchanged with increasing determination – Gwen trying to get away, the shopman resolved that she shouldn't. After the fourth such encounter she discovered that if she made a gesture indicating that her clothes were inconvenient for kneeling on the matted floor, the salesman would give up.

Until the seventh encounter, by which time apparently word had gone on ahead. For when she made signs that her silk stockings would be ruined if she knelt, the shop owner triumphantly produced a stool.

Thus cornered, she went in, was bowed on to the stool, was brought tea and a folder full of black-and-white prints of which, in sheer admiration for the man's initiative, she bought two. They cost her the equivalent of fourpence. She couldn't feel she was wasting money by giving in.

But that victory encouraged the rest. Each time she paused, a stool was brought out. She began to think that perhaps it was the same stool, handed over the back fence from shop to shop. She hardened her heart. She didn't want to buy a length of *yukata* cotton, a carved toggle for her kimono, sweetmeats looking somewhat dusty in their floor-based glass case, socks with a separate division for the big toe, dry rice in a paper bag, pickles, scrolls, or a little statue of a local goddess.

From all this Tama rescued her at about noon. 'What have you bought?' he asked with his flashing grin at the rolled print cleverly wrapped in thin rice paper.

She unrolled it to show. He laughed. 'Jerome was just the same,' he said, 'he could never entirely resist the shopkeepers.'

It was the first time he had ever mentioned Jerome without something of a frown. Gwen smiled to herself. At last Tama felt confident enough to forgive her former lover.

The Imperial Hotel was almost totally Western, except that the standard of service was Japanese. They were bowed into it, bowed through the lobby into the restaurant, bowed to their table. The *maître d'hôtel* scarcely had to raise his hand to summon waiters, two sprang to his elbow at once.

The food was both Japanese and Western. The European dishes weren't up to the standard of Paris, but good. No strong pickles, no rice, excellent wine. Tama did the ordering in Japanese, although to Gwen's surprise one of the waiters spoke English.

It was the first time since her wedding day that she'd heard a word of English. The passengers and crew of the *Orient Pearl* had been French, Tama spoke to her in French, everyone else she'd met in Tokyo so far spoke only Japanese.

When the waiter said, 'Would Madame like more vegetables?' Gwen looked up in astonishment.

'You speak English?'

'Yes, madam.' He was delighted to be noticed.

'How did you know I was English?'

'You said "Oh dear" when your napkin slipped off your lap.'

'You speak it very well.'

'Thank you, madam. We have many, many English-speaking guests here at the Imperial.' He bowed himself away.

Gwen gazed after him. To her own surprise and dismay, she felt her eyes fill with tears.

'What's wrong?' Tama asked at once, alarmed.

'Nothing, dear. It's nothing.'

But a wave of poignant home-sickness had suddenly engulfed her.

She had to struggle with it more than once in the next two or three weeks, although Tama took her to occasional evening parties which included English-speakers, usually people connected with the university.

But in the daytime, if Tama had left her marooned in the house when he went out on business, she would seek refuge in the Imperial Hotel. It was easy to reach by trolley car. Here one could drop into a chair in the lounge and chat with English or American guests. Here one could get a cup of English tea with milk and sugar. Here one could order buttered toast.

At home she tried to settle in. She struggled valiantly to understand what Mrs Hayakawa said to her but the speed of her delivery was too fast, and she began to suspect this was deliberate.

Mrs Hayakawa was the *genro*, the dictator of the household. Tama was the head of the family, the leader in everything that had to do with business and honour, but Mirio-san ruled the house. Every order she gave must be obeyed.

But when she gave an order to Gwen, Gwen couldn't understand it. And if, after much trouble, Gwen learned what was being ordered, she found herself unable to carry it out.

'Supervise the laundry!'

With the best will in the world, Gwen couldn't do so. She had no idea how laundry was done in Japan. Who could have foreseen, for instance, that before a kimono was washed it had to be taken to pieces? That the pieces were afterwards starched and laid out on a starching board to dry in the sun? That under-kimonos, garments not to be starched, were threaded on poles and hoisted like sails between two posts?

Nor was Mrs Hayakawa pleased when Gwen prevented her from taking Tama's suit to pieces to wash. 'It must be dry-cleaned,' she explained, but in English of course, because she had no idea what the words were in Japanese. In fact, the idea of dry-cleaning was so new that it was unknown to Mrs Hayakawa.

A kind of climax was reached in the second week, when Hanako had asked to see how the gramophone worked. Upstairs in the room which Gwen thought of as her bedroom (although there was no such thing in Japan) the gramophone was brought out of the cuboard. Gwen selected a record of Caruso singing 'Your Tiny Hand is Frozen' from *La Bohème*, wound the handle, set the record spinning, and put the needle on the track.

After a moment of hissing, which Hanako listened to with great earnestness, the honey-tones of the great tenor rang out.

'Che gelida manina, se la lasci riscaldar . . .'

Hanako leapt back. She clapped her hands to her cheeks. A low sound of terror escaped her lips. She had gone pale.

'Oh, no,' cried Gwen. 'It's nothing to be afraid of. Hanako, don't – it's only a record.'

'No, no,' moaned Hanako, shrinking away from Gwen's reassuring hand.

'Look, Hanako, I can stop it at once. See?' Gwen took the soundbox off the record. The singing ceased at once, though the record continued to go round.

Hanako sank down to her knees. She stared at the gramophone. Her hands slowly slid away from pale cheeks.

'Man making noise?' she quavered, pointing to the case. 'Inside?'

'There's no one inside, Hanako. It's the record.'

155

Gwen took it off, held it on the splayed fingers of one hand, and with the other tried to demonstrate that the sound came from the grooves.

'From that?'

'Yes. Record,' said Gwen. 'Record.'

'Rekod,' said Hanako.

'Right! Record. Listen again. Now be ready.'

She put it back on the turntable and, with a glance of warning at her sister-in-law, put the needle back on track. Once again the hissing, but this time Hanako leaned forward, watching and listening with keen interest.

And once again Caruso told his beloved that her tiny hand was frozen. This time Hanako stayed firm, but shrugged up her shoulders protectively.

After a moment she swayed her head a little then pointed. 'What?'

'Singing,' said Gwen, who had learned the word by now.

'Singing?' To Hanako it was like no singing she'd ever heard. She put her hands over her ears.

'Oh, well, perhaps you're not an opera-lover,' Gwen laughed. 'Just a minute.'

She took off the soundbox, switched off, removed Caruso, and replaced him with a record of a tune she knew Tama had always liked, 'Valencia'. The recording had an introduction, a rumty-tum, rumty-tum of drums and muted trumpets, much more like the sounds of ordinary life than the opening of the operatic aria.

Hanako listened and nodded, and then when the orchestra joined in with the main tune, jumped a little but didn't object. Then the band's singer began the refrain – she frowned, leaned forward, listened, then said, 'Singing?'

'Yes. And we dance to it.' Gwen put out her arms as if she were being held by Tama, and began to quickstep about the room.

156

Hanako burst out laughing.

'Oh, you think it's funny? Well, let me tell you, your brother does this and he enjoys it very much.'

'Tama does it?'

'Yes.' Gwen got a suit jacket out of a cupboard, held it out by the sleeves as if Tama had it on, and continued to dance.

The door screen was pushed aside violently. Mirio-san stood in the opening.

'Stop! Stop at once!'

Hanako leapt up from her knees and in immediate obedience launched herself at the gramophone. The needle screeched across the record. There was silence, except for the hissing as the turntable went round. Hanako searched urgently for the switch to turn it off but failed to find it.

Gwen, thunderstruck, stood with the suit jacket in her hands.

'You!' cried Mirio-san. 'How dare you! How dare you make that terrible noise in my house! How dare you shake my house with your leaping about! I won't have it! You will behave yourself!'

'But Mirio-san, I was only—'

'I forbid it! You will not do it! And you, Hanako—'

'Mother, forgive me.'

'How dare you take part in this dreadful thing—'

'Mother, I'm sorry.'

'Hanako, explain to her that it's only Western music—'

'Yes, Western! Western, awful, terrible, without decency, without order, without respect! You have brought this to my house, this Western horror of noise and clumsiness and stupidity! You have brought shame to me!'

'Mirio-san, please don't talk so fast. You know I don't understand when you talk so fast—'

'Don't understand, don't understand. You understand *nothing*! Honour, decency, good manners, respect – you know nothing of them! Western woman, you have brought my son to shame – better if he had never been born than fall under your spell!'

With that she turned to go, with an imperious gesture beckoning her daughter to follow. Hanako, in floods of tears, obeyed with head bowed.

Gwen switched off the gramophone, which was in any case running down. She inspected the recording. It was wrecked, the skidding needle had gouged a great wound in it. To have brought it safely all the way from Paris to Tokyo and then have it ruined the first time it was played . . .

She sank down on the one stool the room contained, borrowed permanently from the kitchen.

She should have thought about what she was doing. Of course in this paper-walled house, every sound carried to every corner. The sound of the record playing must have startled everyone out of their wits.

She should have warned them first – better still, invited Mirio-san and Kinie to hear the gramophone alongside Hanako.

In sudden anger she threw down the damaged record. It bounced harmlessly on the matting.

How she hated this house, where every whisper could be heard! The lack of privacy was the worst trial she had to endure.

If Mirio-san scolded a servant, you could hear it in the upstairs rooms. If Hanako sang at her needlework in the living-room, the tune could be distinguished in the bathroom next to the kitchen.

Any time Gwen and Tama made love, one or other of the household would remark on it in a veiled compliment the next morning. Any disagreement or argument they might have could be overheard. Naturally no one understood what Tama and Gwen were saying, as they spoke in French. But a tone of voice could easily be recognised. Words of love could be understood even in a foreign tongue, as could words of anger.

And then, if Gwen asked Tama to coach her in some

special sentences she wished to say to Mrs Hayakawa, Mrs Hayakawa knew all about them before Gwen ever got a chance to utter them. If she painfully learned how to say, 'I want very much to take part in the running of the house under your direction, so please explain slowly,' Mirio-san turned away in contempt before she'd got past the first two words.

When Tama came home, Gwen could hear from the upstairs room how Mirio poured out to him her outrage at the incident of that morning. After about ten minutes Tama came upstairs. Gwen expected him to reproach her over her thoughtlessness but he said nothing. He took off his outdoor jacket, handed it to her to fold and put away, then went out on the verandah to sit in the sunshine of early May with a folder of business papers.

'Tama,' said Gwen. 'Aren't you going to ask my version?'

'Your version of what?'

'Of the row about the gramophone.'

He shrugged. 'It has nothing to do with me.'

'Tama!'

'What's the matter?'

'Your mother shouted at me for being thoughtless and noisy. I need your help in explaining I meant no harm.'

'But Gwen, it's nothing to do with me.'

'Tama, I need your help. I need you to sort things out. I want to please your mother, heaven knows I do, but I can't understand a word she says and no matter how often I ask her to speak more slowly, she never does. Please, *please* tell her that we aren't enemies, that if only she'll help me, I'll try to fit in.'

Tama closed the folder. 'Sit down, Gwen.'

She sank down cross-legged opposite him on the verandah.

'You must understand something. This is a woman's matter. I can take no part in it.'

'What?'

'My mother runs the house, she has authority over the servants and the womenfolk. I don't interfere.'

'But, Tama, I'm your *wife*!'

He sighed. 'Don't state the obvious, darling. Of course you're my wife. You're the wife of a Japanese man, living in a Japanese household. And so you must live by the rules of a Japanese family. I don't take any part in the business of the house. That's Mirio-san's domain. I can't interfere.'

'What do you mean, you can't? Why can't you?'

'It would be beneath my dignity. I can't get involved in a quarrel between women.'

Gwen felt as if she were stifling. She put up a hand to brush her hair back from her brow, which felt hot and sticky with angry disappointment, bafflement, dismay.

'Listen, Tama,' she said in a choked voice, 'I'm a foreigner. I'm alone here in a household where everyone lives by a set of rules I don't know. You're my only ally. You've *got* to help me.'

'I've explained, I don't interfere. In any case, what help do you need?' His tone was faintly irritated.

'I need you to make it clear to Mirio-san that I can't live by rules I don't even know. I need you to tell her not to be so impatient. You must tell her I meant no harm over the gramophone. I don't really understand why she was so terribly angry.'

He laughed. 'Oh, that's easy. She didn't regard the noise as music. You have to realise, Gwen, that Japanese music is quite different. It took me six months to recognise the sounds being played by a band of Frenchmen as music. In the end, of course, I came to like it very much – but Mirio-san had never heard a note of it before.'

'So what did she think I was doing?' Gwen asked in total perplexity.

'How do I know? She poured out some tale to me about a great noise and Hanako taking part in great

mischief, but I told her what I tell you – troubles between
women must be settled by the women themselves.'

'You really won't help me?'

'You don't need help. All you have to do is tell
Mirio-san you're sorry.'

'And will she tell me she's sorry she shouted at me
and called me a clumsy Westerner?'

'Of course not.' Tama laughed. 'A mother-in-law
never apologises to a daughter-in-law.'

'Tama!' Tears rose up within Gwen. Couldn't he see
she was very upset, needed his love and sympathy?
'Tama, I really don't understand any of this. I seem
to be in a position of total inferiority here—'

'Of course,' Tama agreed. 'That's it exactly. A
daughter-in-law must accept that.'

'Inferiority?'

'Yes,' he said, nodding.

'But I'm not Mirio's inferior, Tama,' Gwen insisted,
almost begging him by her tone to reassure her.

'From Mirio-san's point of view, you are. That's all
there is to it. There will never be peace in the house
until you accept that. Understand now?'

He smiled at her as if he'd made everything perfectly
plain and acceptable. She sat across from him, silenced.
He reopened his folder of papers and began to read.

Never, since she had first known him, had Tama
seemed more foreign to her.

Chapter Nine

Gwen apologised to Mirio-san over the episode with the gramophone. She could see no alternative if life in the house was to go on in comparative peace. Besides, she felt she'd been somewhat to blame in trying out the machine without first warning the others.

She rehearsed a few sentences with Tama. This time Mirio heard her out to the end.

'I apologise for startling you and the others in the house with the noise of my gramophone. I didn't mean to cause an upset.'

Mirio said, speaking for once slowly and with clarity: 'It is to be expected that you make mistakes because unfortunately you don't know our way of living. I accept your apology but you must not use the machine again.'

'Very well, Mirio-san.'

Later Hanako took an opportunity to speak to Gwen while they were out in the garden admiring the scarlet quince blossom beyond the pool.

'I express much gratitude for the way you spoke to Mirio-san. I know you really intended no wrong, and so it was very good of you to accept blame.'

'I think I was wrong, in a small way, Hanako-san. I ought to have realised that it would be completely strange and rather frightening.'

'Perhaps. And of course you are a daughter-in-law. Mirio-san was all the more angered at what she thought was disrespect.'

Tama had said that this was a wrangle among women and must be solved by the women. The only woman in

163

the house to whom Gwen could speak of her problems was Hanako. She said, 'Hanako, may I ask your advice?'

'Mine?' Her sister-in-law was startled. No one ever asked her, a junior member of the household, for advice. Of course, viewed in one way, Gwen-san was the most lowly member of the household, the new daughter-in-law, but all the same, Hanako had been self-effacing all her life, as was required. She was never asked for advice and would never have dreamed of giving it, especially to clever, educated Gwen-san.

'First of all, I need an opinion. You agree that there is a problem between myself and Mirio-san?'

Hanako said nothing. But a faint frown appeared on her white brow.

'Please, Hanako. Mirio-san and I don't get on. That's true, anyone can see it. So there's a problem.'

'Well,' said Hanako in a small voice, 'there is always a problem between mother-in-law and daughter-in-law.'

'I beg your pardon?'

'It is always so. Surely it's the same in your country, France?'

Gwen had long given up the attempt to explain to the family that though she had lived in France, she was English. She concentrated instead on what Hanako was saying about relationships.

'I suppose . . . In my country . . . The man's mother may think the girl isn't good enough for her son. Also the other way round—'

'What?' interjected Hanako, startled into impoliteness.

'What's the matter?'

'Did you say the wife's mother may think the son-in-law not good enough?'

'Surely that happens here too?'

'Well . . . Sometimes, when a family have no son, they marry a daughter to a man and adopt him as a son into the family. Sometimes they think that man isn't good enough, because he can't be as good as their own son.'

'I'm sorry?' Gwen said in mystification.

'The son-in-law – the adopted son – usually has problems . . . Do you have that in France?'

'No. I mean something different – that often a mother thinks the world of her daughter and so feels the man she marries isn't good enough.'

'But that's very strange! The marriage has been arranged by a good go-between, surely? The mother must be pleased to find a husband for her daughter?'

'Never mind,' sighed Gwen. 'Let's concentrate on our problem and keep it simple.' She thought it over. 'I think the main difference is, in my country the married couple don't as a rule live with the mother-in-law.'

'They don't?'

'No.'

'Where do they live, then?'

'In a house of their own. Or an apart.' 'Apart' was the Japanese term for an apartment, an entirely new idea just emerging as modern buildings, including blocks of flats, went up in the centre of Tokyo.

'The married couple go and live alone together?'

'Yes.'

'Then who advises them? Who is there when the babies are born?'

Gwen suppressed a smile. 'In general, young couples in Europe don't feel they need much advice. And as to babies, there's medical attention – doctors, midwives.'

'The grandmother plays no part?'

'Of course, yes – she spoils the children, I expect, but she only comes to visit. My mother had no trouble with her mother-in-law. My surviving grandmother lives many miles away from my mother; I only saw her about once a year.'

'Once a year!'

'So you see, Hanako, the situation here with Mirio-san is completely new to me. I don't know what's expected of me. Or at least, I can make guesses, but it's no use Mirio-san expecting me to live up to her expectations because I don't know how. I can't, for instance, supervise the laundry because I don't know how it's done here. I can't take part in sewing kimonos together because I don't sew well enough and I don't intend to learn. I can't sit for hours on my knees helping to arrange flowers or serve tea, because it hurts me very much to sit like that.'

'It hurts you?'

'It's agony.'

Hanako put a hand on Gwen's elbow. 'I'm so sorry, Gwen-san, I had no idea. Is that why you sit cross-legged?'

Gwen nodded her bronze head. 'It's a little more comfortable.'

'Ah . . .' It was a sigh.

'What's the matter?'

'Well . . . you see . . . for us, it's very wrong for a woman to sit cross-legged. Only men sit like that.'

Gwen had noticed the fact herself, but she hadn't realised there was any element of rightness or wrongness about it. 'You mean it's . . . it's . . .' She sought about in her Japanese vocabulary for the equivalent of 'immodest'.

'It's very unseemly,' Hanako said. 'My mother disapproves very much.'

'Oh,' Gwen exclaimed in exasperation, 'I can't do anything about that! I really can't! I simply can't sit on my heels the way you do, it gives me aches and pains in my legs and all up my back. Even sitting cross-legged for long is uncomfortable, although I think I'm getting used to that. Please, Hanako, tell your mother that I don't sit cross-legged on purpose to annoy her—'

Hanako gave a gasp of horror. 'I could never say such a thing to Mirio-san!'

'No, no,' Gwen said. 'I didn't really mean that. Of course you wouldn't say it quite like that. But could

166

you tell her . . . could you let her know that sitting for long on my heels is bad for me?' To say nothing of the damage it did to silk stockings, she added under her breath in English.

The other girl stood fingering a stem of quince blossom. They were out in the garden ostensibly to choose a spray for the vase under the *kakemono*.

'You have to understand,' Hanako said at length, 'that daughters do not give hints on behaviour to their mothers. I couldn't possibly suggest any change in manner to Mirio-san.'

'But how else am I to get her to understand that when I offend, as I seem often to do, it's because I was brought up differently? I've asked Tama to explain it to her but he says he can't interfere in the women's side of the house. I've got to sort things out somehow. I want Mirio-san to like me, Hanako. I want her to be a friend.'

Hanako was shaking her head.

'What is it? Why is it so impossible?'

'We have a saying, Gwen-san, that a husband should never fall in love with his wife. If he begins to cosset her, he'll only deprive his mother of her best servant.'

'Hanako!'

Hanako was nodding her head, avoiding Gwen's horrified gaze, looking intently at the quince blossom instead. She went on in a low voice, 'My brother is right, he can't interfere. But as to your idea of being friends with my mother, that is impossible. The best you could hope for if you were a Japanese wife would be to please your mother-in-law by your obedience and diligence. But you . . . you, Gwen-san, are a foreigner. My mother will never like you.'

Gwen felt as if she were slowly sinking into quicksand. She wrestled with the helplessness that was overwhelming her. 'Look here, Hanako, like it or not, Mirio-san must accept me. I'm Tama's wife.'

'No,' said Hanako, bending to study a spray of quince further down the bush.

Gwen put a hand on the kimono-clad shoulder, urging the other girl to stand up and face her. 'Hanako,' she said. 'I am Tama's wife. We were legally married in Paris.'

Unwillingly Hanako straightened. She kept her pale face downcast, though, so as to avoid meeting her sister-in-law's anxious gaze.

'Gwen-san,' she murmured, 'according to Japanese law, a man may not marry without the permission of his parents until he is thirty. In Mirio-san's eyes, you and my brother aren't really married because Tama never asked his father's agreement. The agreement of the mother isn't so important but as she's a widow and represents the wishes of Shoji-san and she *knows* he would never have agreed, her view is the legal view. She'll never accept you as his legal wife.'

It was the longest speech Hanako had ever made, and the most important, from Gwen's point of view.

It explained so many things. She'd always sensed that Mirio didn't like her, but there had been an undertone of contempt that puzzled her. Now she understood to some degree. Mirio thought of her as a foreign concubine, no matter what the piece of paper from Paris might say.

'Yet all the same,' Gwen said, taking a deep breath, 'she might be persuaded to live in harmony with me because Tama loves me. Because he does, Hanako. And I love him.'

'I see that. My mother sees it too. But, Gwen-san . . . She feels . . . I don't know how to explain this . . . She feels you make him less.'

Gwen stared at Hanako. 'What on earth—?'

'You speak to him carelessly. When you speak to him in French you seem to address him almost as if you were his equal. You don't use the respectful "you" when you speak to him in Japanese.'

'I speak to him in Japanese in the words he taught me, Hanako!'

'Well . . . That's the problem. You speak to him in "pillow-Japanese" – the language of lovers. It's unseemly to use it in public.'

'Oh, good God!' cried Gwen.

'But even when you don't speak . . . You see, you don't bow to him. You hug him and you kiss him when he comes in from a business visit.'

'But European women welcome their men home with a kiss—'

'They do?' Hanako looked startled. 'They go up to them and kiss them? On the mouth?'

'Yes, often. And they sit on their laps, on big cushiony chairs, with their arms around each other.'

'Gwen!' The other girl was inexpressibly shocked.

'There's nothing wrong in it, Hanako. When we feel love, we express it. Not too much in public, of course, but in our own homes we hold hands and exchange kisses and call each other pet names.'

Hanako said, 'My mother would never believe any of this.'

'What does she believe then? That I'm behaving oddly . . . ?'

'She feels you were badly brought up.' Some colour came up under Hanako's pale, clear skin. 'I'm sorry, Gwen, that is what she thinks. Or else, you are . . . a bad woman in your own country, who behaves in this way to flout convention.'

'Hanako, you must explain to her. I'm not in any way a bad woman. In fact, I was quite strictly brought up. My manners are just the same as those of most of the women in Paris. You say I treat Tama as if I were his equal. Well, that's true. I feel myself to be his equal.'

'Gwen-san! Think what you are saying!'

'But I am, Hanako. He and I came together because I invited him – *I* invited *him* – to work with me on some

169

furniture designs. We started a business together. We were equal partners.'

'That's impossible. No woman is the equal of a man.'

'Oh, Hanako,' groaned Gwen.

The gardener came trotting up on his wooden clogs. 'Well, ladies, have you chosen the flower for the *kakemono*?'

'This spray, Akira, please.'

'A good choice. What green leaves shall I cut?'

Hanako moved off to show him what she wanted. Gwen stood staring at the scarlet blossoms of the quince bush.

I hate this country, she found herself thinking. It looks so beautiful, but it's all a sham. Underneath, life is conducted in a strait-jacket, paralysed by tradition and passivity.

But it was Tama's country, and so long as they remained here while he tried to tie up the loose ends left by his father's death, so long must she attempt to live at peace in it.

She thought over what Hanako had said for the rest of the day. Tama was out, having a long lunch and a discussion with a marriage go-between, an old friend of his father's. Gwen ate the midday meal with Mirio and Hanako, scarcely speaking at all. When it was over she went out.

She walked towards the lacquer workshop. She often accompanied Tama there, and dropped in alone when he was busy elsewhere. The men had become accustomed to her; they would bow a welcome, offer tea, and then leave her to her own devices because they had work to do.

She sat in a corner of the screened shed where the student was putting a design on a handsome tray. Idly she watched his brush moving among the pigments.

In Paris she'd watched Tama doing just that. Paris! How long ago and far away it seemed! She would have given everything she possessed to be back there with Tama, in the upstairs room with its tall windows and its drawing board, quietly at work on some joint project for a client.

But she was here, in Tokyo. Trapped – the word forced itself into her mind.

How right Jerome had been! Only he hadn't known the half of it. Clearly he'd been unaware of the legal ban on marriage without parental consent up to the age of thirty, and why should he know it, since it would probably never have come up in connection with his work at the Embassy. But he'd witnessed the limitations of life for Japanese women and tried as best he could to prepare her for them.

What a man sees of the life of a woman is one thing. To experience it as a woman is quite another. Gwen knew she could never submit – never, never submit – to the rules that Mirio-san wanted to impose.

She knew, moreover, that whatever she did, she could never please her mother-in-law, never gain her friendship. It was hopeless, their view of life was totally at variance. Nor, now that she came to think about it, did she want Mirio's friendship. Now that she looked at her dispassionately – not as Tama's little Japanese mother, but as a woman she had just met – she saw that Mirio was narrow-minded, unbending, autocratic in her own small way, and unkind. Mirio had no thought for what it must be like to arrive in a foreign country with only a few words of the language; no wish to help her adjust and fit in. So no sympathy was offered, no patience or goodwill.

I understand why Tama felt he had to get away, Gwen thought. He must have felt stifled. Now she could sense what a battle must have ensued when he wanted to do something different with the art of decorating lacquer. What, change a method that had been good enough for his father and his father's father before him?

Things that had seemed relatively unimportant before

stood out now as important clues. Although electricity was widely available in Tokyo, as witness the trolley-cars that plied in the street, Shoji Hayakawa had refused to allow its use in his house or his work-shop. Lighting and heating in his home were by the old methods – oil-lamps and charcoal footwarmers. The kitchen, which could have had a gas stove, was still back in the Middle Ages. The laborious task of putting garments together after laundering could have been made light work by the purchase of a sewing machine.

The family had money enough for all these things. Other people in Tokyo enjoyed them. But not the members of the Hayakawa household. The dead Mr Hayakawa had not permitted them.

Tradition, tradition . . . And his wife held fast by those rules. It was useless to expect her to accept a modern European woman, whether as wife or mistress to her son.

Tama's sister was willing to be her friend; Hanako had fellow-feeling and kindness. The servants too, except for Kinie, who had come with Mirio when she first arrived as a bride in the household. Kinie and her lady Mirio-san would hold fast to the old ways. And, since they had authority, the household could never be a truly welcoming place to Gwen.

She shivered. She felt so alone, so friendless. Even Tama, whom she loved and who loved her . . . Tama would be no help because despite himself he was tied by tradition. He had made his own escape but couldn't bring himself to help in the escape of his wife from the rules of the past.

Gwen recalled what Jerome had said – that Japan was a paradise for men. Yes, but at what a cost to the women. And the women so sweetly, so meekly, bent their necks to the yoke . . .

Poor Hanako. Even now her brother was off with some old man, arranging which suitor she should marry.

He would be a man she would not meet until perhaps the day before the ceremony.

Thereafter he would be her master, just as her father and her brother had been before him. And she would be the daughter-in-law of some woman – not perhaps as difficult as Mirio, but a mother-in-law who would regard the young bride as her new servant. It seemed the women of Japan could not be allowed to live without strict rules, some of them self inflicted.

Perhaps, perhaps . . . Perhaps the twentieth century would catch up with them. There might be one or two brave souls, whom Gwen as yet knew nothing of, standing up for their rights. After all, it was only in the last few years that the women of the West had gained the vote. Japan would catch up. But not in time to make life in the Hayakawa household comfortable for Gwen.

Well, it was only for a few more months. She could bear it because by and by she would be free again.

In the meantime she must think of some way to live her life in face of the disapproval of Mirio-san. She had placated her once, over the gramophone incident, but never again. From now on Gwen would be polite, but she would not bow down to her, she would not apologise for being different.

One thing she could do was avoid Mirio. Mirio was tied, as most Japanese women seemed to be, to the house. They almost never went anywhere except to the shops, and even then nothing like as frequently as a European. Tradesmen called at the house, shopkeepers sent errand boys. So Mirio-san scarcely stirred beyond the boundary fence of the garden except for somewhat ceremonial occasions – the obligatory visits to her husband's grave, a trip to view the cherry blossom in the garden of the Imperial Arsenal.

So, to avoid Mirio was simple. Gwen would simply go out.

Tama would take her out on social occasions and, once

or twice, to a *thé dansant* at the Imperial Hotel. There were several outings she could make on her own. She could take the trolley into the city centre to look at the museums and art galleries, to read the English-language *Japan Advertiser* in the reading room of the library, or simply to explore and shop.

She could come to the workshop. The men would always welcome her, and sometimes Tama would be there, instructing the student Taro, checking on ordinary work with Minoru. They would spend an hour or two in the old way, she and Tama, in the old atmosphere of work and craftsmanship.

She could go to the Sunday service at the English church. She could take the train out of the city to some of the old temples whose gardens were famous. She could visit the sea coast and buy fresh fish.

Oh, yes, there were dozens of things she could do.

All the same, she found tears trickling down her cheeks at the thought of the lonely days she was going to fill with useless activity.

And she had forgotten to take the weather into account. Also the earth tremors. Japan was spoken of in Europe as the Land of the Rising Sun. Gwen began to think it ought to be known as the Land of the Falling Rain. All through the summer of 1922 rain fell, almost every day and almost all day. Moreover, the atmosphere itself was saturated, so that on a July day the body indoors was wet with perspiration that couldn't evaporate from the skin.

Then from time to time – sometimes as much as three times in a week – a tremor would shake the ground. Train stations would close. Trolley-cars would be unable to run because of subsidence in the streets or a breakdown in power. A shop she wanted to visit in Yurakucho had vanished into a hole in the ground when she eventually got there.

She struggled through the wet, uncertain summer until a day in August. She was trapped indoors by rain, incessant since dawn. The cicada made his see-saw call among the trees – me-mee, me-mee. All the shutters were open to let in any faint breeze, with awnings spread to keep out the rain. Gwen sat up in the room now accepted as the bedroom of the married couple – unusual in a Japanese home where beds could be, and were, spread anywhere.

She had read and reread every scrap of available literature in either English or French. She had tried to memorise her daily intake of *kana* characters, the simplified form of Japanese writing. She had nothing to do now. She ought to go downstairs and sit with the family, who were at work in the living-room on yet more needlework.

But if she did that, she would be expected to take part in the sewing. Her sewing was very poor, and though a kimono was put together in simple rectangles, she would be sure to do something to displease Mirio-san.

For a moment she was tempted to get the gramophone out of the cupboard. But that would be provocative. She had vowed that she would be always polite, always considerate. So she put that thought away. What was left for her to do to pass the next few hours until Tama came home?

She found her sketchbook in its folder, untouched since she arrived. First she had been too overwhelmed with the novelty of Tokyo life, and then too disheartened by the turn of events at home.

But today she felt a return of the urge to put something down on paper. Nothing serious, just an idea or two. She'd been watching the birds on the banks of the stream yesterday, in a pause in the day's rain. There was something about the way a crane stood, something about its legs, the joints . . .

A couple of happy hours went by as she sketched out her ideas. Tama came home; she could hear the welcome as they helped him get rid of his wet-weather gear –

European boots but elastic sided for ease of removal, a Japanese umbrella of double oiled paper, a French waterproof coat.

Would he like tea? Yes he would.

Gwen went to the screen door of their bedroom. 'Tama!' she called. 'Please have your tea brought upstairs. I want to show you something.'

'Very well, dear.' She heard him take the stairs two at a time. He came into the bedroom, wiping his brow. 'Hateful weather. It's at times like this I long for a glass of chilled French wine.'

'We-ell . . . There's no reason why we shouldn't have it.'

'What, dear? You know we have no wine—'

'But we could easily get some. Next time we go into the city, let's order some from one of the stores catering to the foreign residents.'

'I never thought of that!' he said, with a glance of admiration. Then his face fell. 'But we've no ice to chill it.'

'Darling, we can suspend a bottle down the well – the water is always cool.'

'What a great idea!' He gave her a big hug. 'You're a clever girl!'

'It's not my own idea, Tama, I saw it being done in a farmhouse in France when I was working there.' She had a moment of doubt. What would Mirio say? But then she thought, To the devil with Mirio. And then, more pacifically, If Tama commands it, it must be all right with Mirio.

While he was clearly in a good mood at her suggestion, she took advantage of it. 'Tama, I want to ask you for something.'

'Really? As a reward for being so clever? What shall it be? A new dress? An outing to the Imperial?'

She felt a tiny spasm of annoyance. She was no coquette, she didn't need to be showered with little gifts. She was a businesswoman.

'No, it's something much more interesting. I'd like to have a telephone installed.'

Her husband's mouth fell open. 'Here?'

'Yes, why not?'

'In the house?'

'And at the works too, of course. But primarily at the house.'

Tama was shaking his head.

'Why not, Tama?'

'My mother would hate it.'

'But darling, it would be so useful to you while you're trying to do all these complicated bits of business.'

This was undeniably true. Tama was enmeshed in a long series of negotiations, some of which he mentioned to Gwen, some of which she gleaned by things he avoided saying.

The selling of the lacquerworks was not going well. There were prospective buyers but when they heard that no one of the Hayakawa name would be connected with the venture in the future, their bids were very low. It was cheaper and easier to make lacquer of the ordinary kind by a factory system – why should anyone buy an old-fashioned lacquer shop unless a famous artist went with it?

Tama needed to make enough money by the sale of the business to invest for his mother. Mirio-san was not expected to live very much longer. In the somewhat brutal manner of the Japanese, life expectancy was thought of as fifty. At forty-seven, Mirio was in her last few years. But she might go over the expected limits – some women did, though not many men.

Therefore there must be an income capable of keeping her comfortably in this house, with its staff of servants, for at least ten years. No investment Tama could find would give a good enough income on the capital raised by the likely sale-price of the lacquerworks.

The other alternative with regard to the business was to put in a manager, who would be in the employ of

Tama's cousin, the next male relative in authority. But the male cousin, Moko-san, lived in Noshiro, about three hundred miles away, and moreover knew nothing about lacquer. Gwen guessed that Minoru the foreman was strongly resisting the notion of being bossed about by a man who would visit occasionally and who was an ignoramus.

When Gwen hinted that Minoru might make a good manager, the idea was met with incomprehension. Minoru couldn't manage. He was a workman, promoted through long years to the position of foreman. That was as high as he was entitled to rise.

Then there was the problem of Hanako's marriage. Two or three young men, and one not so young, had been contacted by the go-between. Hanako had to take property with her when she married – not money, but household goods and clothes, to a very considerable value. Moreover, the prospective husband expected to gain in prestige and business ties by the marriage.

But what advantage was there in marrying a girl with a widowed mother living on an investment which would yield only enough to support them? What was the good of marrying the daughter of Shoji Hayakawa if the Hayakawa lacquer business, Bright Omen, was no longer in the Hayakawa family?

The truth was, Tama had no real head for business. It had always been Gwen who handled contracts in their Paris days. He understood profit and loss – no use undertaking to make a beautiful lacquerwork panel if the price wasn't going to pay for the materials. But investment, looking to the future, balancing the pros and the cons – these things made him short-tempered. His mood when he came home these days was often touchy.

So, taking all this into account, anything that would really help him in long negotiations was a good thing. The telephone would be a boon. He had used it extensively in Paris, would be perfectly at home with it in Tokyo although the system was rather limited.

'You see, Tama, on a day like this there would be no need to go out and get wet and sticky. You could do a lot of business by telephone.'

'Yes, but—'

'And if we were going out for a meal in a hotel or a restaurant, there would be no need to send a runner with a note to reserve a table – we could ring up and book it.'

'Yes, but—'

'And if we were going to a theatre or a concert at the Imperial Theatre we could reserve seats.'

'But it's very difficult to get connected to the phone system unless you have friends in the telephone company.'

'Haven't you anyone you could ask among your business colleagues?'

Tama looked thoughtful. She knew he was going over the idea in his mind. Who owed a favour to the Hayakawa family? Who would be glad to speak for them to the telephone company in hopes of a return favour in the future?

'Mr Iwata wants me to make a box for the wedding of his youngest daughter,' he murmured after a moment's thought.

'Oh, is that the box I saw being dried?'

'He wants me to do it personally,' Tama went on, ignoring her interruption. 'I said I didn't have time because of other matters but, you know . . . He has a nephew who works in the offices of the telephone company.'

'Now that sounds—'

'And in any case,' he ended, 'it would be good to do some real work again. I'm sick of sitting in rooms with businessmen. I need something to act as a remedy – something to soothe me when they've made me angry. Yes, yes . . . It would be good to take to my brushes again.'

Gwen threw her arms around him. 'Tama! It would be lovely!'

179

If he turned back to the work in which he excelled, perhaps he would be more like the man she'd learned to love in Paris. The change in him since they arrived in Tokyo had come about so gradually that only now did she see it as a danger. Tama the lacquerist had been a confident, happy man. Tama the head of the household was worried and preoccupied – and his mood reflected on Gwen's so that she too was anxious, despite the fact that she could never be allowed to play any part in the marriage negotiations.

To have Tama thinking about taking up his brushes was an unexpected bonus. All she'd wanted to do, by suggesting a telephone, was to have him with her at home more often. But if in order to obtain the phone he went back to his proper work, that could only be a good thing. He was a creative artist. Lack of a creative role had had a bad effect on his moods.

They were so delighted with each other over this that Gwen quite forgot to show him the sketches she'd been working on, preliminary ideas for a little table with legs carved to look like the legs of the crane.

She forgot two other things. One was that it had never been part of the plan that Tama would set to work again for the Bright Omen lacquer workshop. The other was that Tama's mother would be very, very displeased about the telephone.

Mirio-san knew that Gwen was to blame, and made her displeasure known by subtle methods. Gwen's expensively made French silk evening dress was sent to the dry-cleaners without her instructions and came back ruined by inexpert work. One of her European overshoes, which she wore to protect her footwear from the all-pervading mud outdoors, vanished. The awning over her bedroom verandah pulled away from its moorings in a storm of wind and rain, so that sketches she'd left there were spoiled.

Gwen wasn't good at seeing into other people's minds, but she knew when one misfortune after another befell her that they couldn't all be accidents. Kinie, her mother-in-law's confidante, was arranging them.

In a way, she had her revenge. About three weeks later a team of workmen in dark smocks and tight trousers arrived, rigged up telephone lines, screwed a telephone to the framework of the inner passage, tested it with a chant of *'Hitotsu, futatsu, mitsu'*, bowed low to everyone, and left.

Almost immediately the phone rang. The entire household, who had gathered to watch the proceedings, leapt back in terror.

It was Gwen who picked up the receiver. 'Yes?'

'Gwen, is that you? This is Tama. They let me know the phone was connected, I thought I'd try it at once. Can you hear me?'

'Perfectly, Tama.'

'Tama?' whispered Mirio from behind her.

'Yes, it's Tama speaking,' Gwen said, turning to her. She held out the earpiece. 'Do you want to speak to him?'

Mirio backed away, her always white face tinged grey with fear. 'Never,' she whispered, 'never.'

'Please take it. It's only your son on the other end,' Gwen coaxed.

'Witchcraft,' muttered Mirio, and hurried away.

Later, when she'd recovered with tea and comfort from Kinie, Mirio-san gave orders that no one in the house was to respond to the ring of the devil-machine. When Tama heard this on coming home, he countermanded it at once.

'I have had the telephone installed to help me with business,' he said in loud anger. 'When it rings, whoever is closest will pick it up and politely say, "This is the house of Tamaki Hayakawa." If I am at home, I will come to take the call. If I am not at home, you will write down a message. Is that clear?'

'Yes, Tama-sama,' muttered Mirio in misery. She was being made to lose face. But she knew she deserved it for daring to tell her servants to ignore something her son wished them to use.

After that, there was something almost like wariness in Mirio's attitude to Gwen. Gwen understood the telephone. If Gwen understood this strange invention, she perhaps had some power.

Then there was the matter of the wine. A wooden box containing bottles with strange writing on the labels was brought to the house. The box was kept in the storehouse. From time to time, Gwen-san would have Ota put a bottle into a woven reed basket and suspend it on a rope in the well-water.

Then when Tama-sama came home, the bottle would be drawn up. It would be opened by Gwen-san with great care. The wine was poured into cups on stems, made of glass, which Gwen-san had brought home by taxi from a store in the centre of Tokyo. Strange wine cups, quite unlike the beautiful lacquerware or china used for sake. But Tama would hold the foreign wine up to the light in this clear glass cup, and admire it before he sipped it.

Once or twice he offered the glass to his mother, but she always refused. Hanako accepted a sip once, and said it was pleasant enough. Yet Tama seemed to take great pleasure in it, and shared this pleasure with Gwen-san.

She had never been like an ordinary daughter-in-law. She refused her share of the housework. She went out on her own whenever she felt like it. She understood about the telephone, she understood about the wine. She had sexual power – Mirio recognised this when she saw it, and knew her son was still deeply in love with his foreign woman.

Perhaps it would be wiser not to invent little disasters to her clothes or her silly sketches.

So, following the arrival of the telephone, a strange sort of peace emerged. Hanako was allowed to be friends again with her brother's new wife, and even went out with her sometimes to walk about Tokyo or visit Gwen's European friends. Hanako was astonished at the casual way these visits were arranged. Gwen-san simply picked up the phone, spoke to an English or American woman, said she would be dropping in, and off they went.

Hanako enjoyed these outings enormously. She was too shy to say anything at a coffee gathering, but she would move quietly about the room, examining the European furniture, tasting the European food, watching the European women talk and laugh and argue. The food of course was terrible, coffee undrinkable, but she couldn't deny that the European chairs were comfortable. And though the vigour and freedom of the women scared her, she couldn't help admiring them.

The telephone was also connected to the lacquer workshop. It was easy now for Gwen to get in touch with Tama, who was often there working on the box for Mr Iwata. It was easy, too, to get in touch with fellow-Europeans living in Tokyo.

Life seemed so much easier that the onset of the Tokyo winter hardly troubled Gwen. November was cold and bright, December even colder, but then there was Christmas to look forward to, and the Japanese New Year.

In mid-December the temperature began to go down. On Christmas Day, which Tama had declared a holiday for the household and for his workmen, there was a covering of snow on the ground. Indoors, the house was chilly. The only heating was the *hibachi* in each room, a low brazier with glowing charcoals.

Gwen went to church. Tama stayed at home to supervise the preparation of a Christmas dinner with foods delivered from one of the European stores. This was Christmas in the French style, however – no roast goose, no plum pudding. Instead there was *boeuf à la bourguignon* and a cake made from layers of meringue.

Dutifully Tama's mother and sister tried to enjoy the meal. But the casserole was too rich for them, and the meringue cake eluded their chopsticks. They didn't drink any of the wine. Gwen and Tama, on the other hand, enjoyed it all enormously, snoozed through the afternoon, took a long bath together in the bath house later, and went to bed to make love as an escape from the cold, draughty living-room.

The winter wind arrived. It blew through cracks in the old wooden frames, through chinks in the paper windows. These were lovingly mended by Hanako with artistic little patches, but as soon as one was closed up another opened. The evenings were spent around the *kokatsu*, a charcoal heater lowered into a pit in the living-room floor with space enough around it for the feet and legs. The top was covered with a quilt which rested on the knees. It was cosy, but it limited mobility severely. And the sitters' backs were still exposed to the icy draughts.

The New Year Festival came. A pine branch was planted at each side of the house gate. Over it, hanging on a scarlet cord, was a slender frond of fern; there was another exactly like it in the living-room. On the morning of New Year's Day the usual breakfast was replaced with a sacred beverage in special wooden goblets, and the rice was taken in the form of special cakes.

The postman brought dozens of cards from family, friends and business acquaintances. Neighbours arrived to offer greetings. The Hayakawa household went out to visit their neighbours. The entire day was spent in nibbling little sweetmeats and drinking either sake or green tea.

Next day, the shops reopened after the holiday. Brightly decorated horse-carts and pushcarts appeared bringing the first deliveries of goods in the New Year. Pedlars came to the door selling pictures of the good-fortune ship, on board which stood the seven deities of good luck. Everyone in the Hayakawa home received one from Tama, because they must be put under the pillow to bring lucky dreams. The luckiest dream, Gwen was told, was of Mount Fuji.

The holiday went on for six days, with first the shops reopening, then the government offices, then private businesses. There then came a day of rest and recovery. On the eighth day the Emperor reviewed his troops and the schools reopened.

'Now,' Tama said as he sat with Gwen in a taxi bringing them home from watching the parade, 'now we can say 1923 has really begun!'

Gwen sighed, looking back on the year that had gone. A strange mixture it had been, bringing her times of home-sickness and misery but also much that had opened her mind to new things. Her sketchbook was now full of ideas for furniture she might try out when they got back to Paris.

'I suppose we'd better start making plans about our journey home,' she said.

There was a little pause. The taxi skidded a little on the icy road, then righted itself as the driver crooned coaxingly, 'Travel, little lucky crane, travel.'

'We are home, Gwen,' said Tama.

'No, I meant Paris.'

'Paris isn't my home. It isn't yours either.'

'Well, you know what I mean.'

'No, Gwen, I don't.'

She twisted round to look at his face in the fading afternoon light of January.

'Tama, we always said we'd come to Tokyo and sort out the various difficulties caused by your father's death. And once that was done, which might take about a year, we'd go back to Paris.'

He was shaking his head.

'Tama, that was the arrangement!' she insisted.

He tilted his chin up. It was a movement she knew well: it meant he was going to be stubborn.

'I've changed my mind.'

'About what?'

'About leaving Tokyo. I've been thinking about it for some weeks now, ever since I began work again on my real job, the decorating of lacquer. I've decided we're going to stay, Gwen.'

Chapter Ten

Gwen was too full of anger and astonishment at Tama's pronouncement to say a single word in reply. She gripped the front of the armrest that separated her from Tama in the taxi. Her fingernails dug into the leather.

He couldn't mean it. He loved Paris as much as she did. He *must* want to go back.

Tama was watching her. She saw the gleam of the black eyes in the shadows. What was he waiting for? Her agreement, her compliance?

After a long interval he said, 'We couldn't possibly go soon, in any case. Things are improving about Hanako's wedding prospects, but you can't hurry these matters. And besides . . . in part . . . getting Hanako a good husband depends on my staying in Tokyo.'

'You're putting the responsibility on Hanako?' Gwen cried in scorn. 'I don't believe you.'

'I'm not going to get anyone very suitable for my sister if all we can offer in terms of family connections is a widow living on a pension. A bridegroom expects more.'

Gwen raised her clenched fists in the air and shook them. 'My God! You're talking about your sister as if she were a packet of tea or a length of cloth, to be handed about by other people. Why don't you let her choose her own husband, for God's sake? Someone who wants her for herself?'

'Don't be absurd, Gwen. You know that with us that's impossible.'

Now they were both angry. We're going to have a dreadful public quarrel, thought Gwen. We've got to think what we're saying to each other.

'Tama,' she said, struggling very hard to keep the bitterness out of her voice, 'when we first agreed to come to Tokyo, you said to me that arranging the family matters would take at most a year. I quite understand that you underestimated the difficulties. But that doesn't change the facts. We agreed we were going back to Paris at the end of it.'

'No we didn't.'

'We did, Tama. We let the studio on a one-year tenancy on the understanding we'd come back to it. We were planning to get back and do some new work.'

'The steps we took seemed reasonable at the time. But now that we're here I realise we can do better by staying here. Family matters make it necessary, business matters make it necessary, and my career as a lacquerist has more chance of success if we stay here.'

'How can you say that! Here you're one of many. In Paris you were unique – the only Japanese lacquerist working there!'

'But there weren't enough people to appreciate my work. Here in Tokyo I have my own reputation and my father's reputation too, as a basis for success. Already I've more commissions than I can handle. I don't want to throw all that away by going back to Paris.'

'I see. You're saying that even once you've sorted out all this absurd business of getting a husband for Hanako, you won't sell the workshop. You want to stay here and keep it going.'

'Yes, I do. I realise what a good foundation it makes, a foundation based on tradition and a loyal clientele.'

'Oh, tradition! But innovation, development? The new things you were achieving? Will your faithful Tokyo clientele encourage you in those?'

Tama made a little sound of dismissal. 'When I look back, I see the Parisians were mad on things just because

188

they were new. Whether they had any real value, I'm not so sure.'

'You mean you're content to stay here painting carps and chrysanthemums in gold on black lacquer boxes? You don't want to stretch yourself with—'

'Be careful what you're saying, Gwen. The traditions of my country have endured a long time. Not only in art – respect from a wife to her husband is one that has merit.'

'Oh, lovely, now you want me to bow and kneel on the floor behind you, I suppose! Tama, what's got into you?'

The taxi drew up before the gateway of the Hayakawa house. Tama got out and turned to pay the driver, leaving Gwen to get out by herself. It was only a little thing, but when they first came to Tokyo he wouldn't have dreamed of leaving her to cope on her own with the treacherous snowy surface under the running board.

The little gate in the main gateway sprang open. Kazuo was there, bowing them in. As they walked to the porch then took off their shoes, Gwen realised that for some months now her husband had slowly been growing more and more Japanese.

Not in all things. He still retained his pleasure in some of the frivolous ideas of the West. He still loved dancing, dance band music, French food, French wine – the trimmings of Europe. But in the basic things he was returning to the ways of his homeland.

Having servants at his beck and call was no doubt pleasant. Having womenfolk who thought him little less than a god was agreeable. Jerome de Labasse had said Japan was a paradise for a man, so why should it surprise Gwen if her husband wanted to stay in paradise?

In Paris he had been a success, even a great success after he teamed up with Gwen. But it would always be a struggle there, because there was continual criticism, restlessness, self-examination. Here Tama need face none of that. He could go back to the ways of his father, producing faultless lacquer in the old style with plenty of customers waiting to buy it. No one would tell him his work lacked energy, no one would compare him to some other innovator because there were no innovators.

At home his mother would run the household so that he need never trouble himself in any way over it. No irate concierge would ever complain to him that his friends made too much mess in her clean hallway, no tailor would be late with a new jacket, no lazy housemaid would sweep dirt under the carpet. Here, women would always seek to please him. Although the women of Europe had vivacity, wit, sexual boldness, they were a challenge. Here there was no challenge. Besides, he had the woman he wanted.

Gwen was sure he still loved her, just as she loved him. But not even for her would he give up the easy life that lay before him now, the life that seemed instinctively right for him.

When they were indoors Mirio and Hanako asked eagerly about the military parade. They asked for details over and over again. Then came the evening meal. Next should have been an evening in the living-room with the comfort of the *kokatsu* but instead they went up to the relative privacy of the bedroom. They settled by the *hibachi*, both on floor cushions, holding out their hands towards the glowing charcoal.

'Will you tell me exactly what you plan for the immediate future?' Gwen asked in a very level tone.

'The main thing is Hanako's marriage. If all goes well, it should take place about midsummer.'

'And meanwhile? You're not looking for a buyer for Bright Omen?'

'No. I don't think I'd get a good enough price, and any hint of a sale makes Hanako's prospects less good. If she has a brother with a flourishing lacquer business, the suitor is more likely to agree. There's a young man from a good family in Hamada, he's just got a promotion in the Customs Service – he sounds very good, Mr Inora recommends him.'

'So Hanako gets married in the summer. And then what?'

'She moves to her husband's family home.'

'I meant, about us?'

'What about us? We stay here in *my* family home. Bright Omen goes from strength to strength under my direction. Mother's taken care of, everything is simple.'

'Except for one thing. I want us to go back to Paris.'

'Don't be silly, Gwen. You know we'd have to start all over again if we went back after an absence of eighteen months. And I'm not going to sell the business. I've made up my mind about that. It's been in our family for generations.'

'You didn't feel like that about it when we sailed from France!'

'That was then. I've had time to think about it. I realise it would be wrong to sell it. It's my inheritance – artistic as well as financial.'

'But it's not my inheritance, Tama. I'm a European furniture-maker—'

'Now, now, first and foremost you're my wife.'

'You said that to me once, ages ago. You said I was the wife of a Japanese man living in a Japanese family. I accepted that then because I thought it was temporary. But I'm not going to go on for ever being treated like a second-rate daughter-in-law by your mother—'

'I told you before, Gwen. Daughters-in-law have to settle these things for themselves.'

'But your mother doesn't think of me as a daughter-in-law at all. She thinks we're not properly married.'

'Oh,' said Tama. 'How did you find that out?'

'Someone told me.'

'Who?'

'What does it matter? It's true, isn't it? We're not

191

really married according to Japanese law because you didn't get Mirio-san's consent and she'll never give it.'

'Gwen, I'll be thirty soon. We can get married according to Japanese law on my thirtieth birthday.' He was trying to coax her to laugh about it, and truth to tell the idea was faintly comic.

'Yes, well, I'll hold you to that, but in the meantime, Tama, what on earth am I supposed to do with my life? If we were back in Paris I'd be working with you and perhaps we'd be getting a proper home together. Here I'm no use at running the house, even if Mirio-san would let me. The days stretch ahead of me – it's just such a . . . such a waste of time . . .' Her uncertain spirits, inclined towards laughter a moment ago, turned towards tears. Her voice wavered. She felt lost.

'My poor Gwen,' Tama said, putting both arms round her and drawing her head down to his shoulder. 'Perhaps I'm wrong to think you can fill your days with all the little duties that make up the life of an ordinary Japanese lady.'

'Leaving aside the fact that I haven't got any little duties, because I wouldn't know how to carry them out in the first place.'

'You have your own talents.'

'But I'm not *using* them, Tama.'

'There's no reason why you shouldn't go back to designing, Gwen. If you come up with anything that looks worth developing, I expect I could find a cabinet-maker who might be able to follow plans drawn up by a European.'

She drew away from him to gaze up into his face. 'You mean that, Tama?'

'Of course. Why not?'

'But what about . . . ?' She'd been going to say that she'd been told she made him less by the manner in which she treated him, and perhaps having a wife who was a designer in her own right might not be a good thing for his public status. But in the first place it would mean telling him that Hanako had discussed it with her – and she sensed that it wouldn't please him. And then, why put objections in front of him? At the moment he was glad to give her the consolation of doing her own work. Let time show how he would feel when she took him at his word.

The charcoal was dying in the *hibachi*. Either they must clap hands to bring Suzuki with more charcoal, or they must move down to the living-room where it was a little warmer.

'Shall we go down and tell your mother we've decided to stay on?'

'Oh, she already knows.'

'You told her? Before you told me?' Gwen was so hurt that she jerked away from him, putting her hands up to hide the tears that filled her eyes.

'Of course, Gwen, I had to. It was a decision made partly to improve Hanako's marriage prospects. As Hanako's mother, Mirio-san had to be told.'

'I see.' But why had she to be told before he spoke of it to his own wife?

Because that was the Japanese way, she told herself wearily. Elders must be respected, the *genro* of the home must take precedence over a new young wife.

It seemed she had never really understood Tama. He had never been as Westernised as she imagined. But that couldn't be allowed to matter, because she loved him, and whatever happened she would stay with him.

In writing home, as she did every two or three weeks, she laid the groundwork for telling her mother she'd be staying permanently in Tokyo. She tried to paint a bright picture.

When she wrote to Jerome, however, she was more open. 'I have my own work to keep me going,' she wrote, 'but what use it can be here is difficult to see. The Japanese don't want furniture, except for small low pieces that can be put away in cupboards – and I don't think they'd want any alteration to the kind of thing they already use: they're such traditionalists. But I have one or two things I'm working on. At least it's something to do.'

Jerome replied at once. He didn't say, as he could well have done, 'I told you so.' Instead he urged her to send drawings of anything promising to him. 'I'll have the pieces made here in Paris, and if they look good I'll see if I can interest any of the leading cabinet-makers in using your designs. There's a growing interest in the Art Deco style – one or two things we thought quite *avant garde* are now being mass-produced.'

He ended, jokingly, 'For acting as your agent in this I shall expect the usual ten per cent.' And less jokingly, 'Don't be afraid to act for your own best interests, my dear. You are *not* a Japanese wife, but the wife of a Japanese. You can think for yourself.'

The dreary winter came to an end. Spring was heralded by the coming of the plum blossom in March. The Hayakawa family made a pilgrimage to see the Tree of the Sleeping Dragon, an old, old tree in a garden on the east side of the Sumida River. It was a day of snow, which seemed to make the plum tree's delicate blossoms all the more precious.

But despite the cups of warm sake drunk in toast to the tree, Gwen felt chilled to the bone and somehow more alien than ever when they got home. She tried to imagine a group of practical Anglo-Saxons or comfort-loving Frenchmen gathering on a snowy day to drink lukewarm spirits while gazing at a branch of plum blossom. To them it simply wouldn't have made sense.

That evening, her spirits plummeted further. The telephone rang about nine o'clock. Mrs Hayakawa tutted in annoyance at the sound. Kinie came to say that Mr Inora was asking for Tama-sama.

It was impossible not to overhear what was being said at this end. Gwen's understanding of Japanese was now very good, and amid the flowery exchanges the message was clear. Mr Inora was reporting that the prospective bridegroom for Hanako had not after all received the promotion in the Customs Service he'd expected.

The marriage could not now take place. The suitor was no longer good enough for Hanako Hayakawa. Mr Inora would start again with a very suitable young man who had recently been recommended to him, son of an importer of American tools.

No one thought of asking Hanako, who was clearly hurt. Mrs Hayakawa said, frowning, 'Really, this is most unfortunate.'

Tama shrugged. 'Mr Inora and I will have a meeting tomorrow to discuss this new man. He says he has his photograph.'

'Will you bring it home so that I may see it?' Hanako burst out.

'Hanako!' reproved her mother.

'Why not?' asked Gwen, annoyed on her sister-in-law's behalf. 'Is there any law against it?'

'There's no law against it,' Tama said. 'I just never heard of it being done.'

'Besides, what would be the point?' said Mirio-san. 'What has his photograph to do with it?'

'If it has nothing to do with it, why did Mr Inora mention it?'

'Oh, well, of course, it will give me an idea of whether the man is a smart type, likely to do well in life – that kind of thing.'

'Then Hanako-san would like to know that too.'

'Hanako will know that when her honourable elder brother tells her.'

'Could we please stop talking about Hanako as if she weren't here?' cried Gwen.

'Oh, please, Gwen-san, don't be troubled about me,' put in Hanako in distress.

'*Someone* ought to be troubled about you, it seems to me,' said Gwen, her green eyes sparkling with anger and her freckles glowing against colour that came up in her cheeks.

Really, thought Mirio, staring at her, what a strange-looking creature she was! How could Tama love her? And what right did she have to interfere in a matter which was the preserve of the head of the household and the head of the family?

'Gwen-san is very kind to be interested in Hanako,' said Mirio with frigid politeness, 'but she may rest assured that the future of her sister-in-law is being well taken care of.'

'In slow motion,' muttered Gwen in English.

'Gwen-san says?'

'I said it's taking a long time. It's painful for Hanako, having to wait like this.'

'How truly you speak, Gwen-san, but negotiations were interrupted and then broken off at the death of my husband, and then you know nothing could be done until Tama-sama came to take over as head of the family. Since then there have been issues to do with money. I agree this last alteration is a pity, but Gwen-san may be content in the knowledge that Mr Inora has arranged good marriages in fifty-two cases already, so all will be well.'

This was a long speech for Mirio, but in a way she was trying to reassure herself. The family had not been lucky since the illness of Shoji-san. Then at New Year, Mirio-san had had an unlucky dream. Usually when she put the picture of the seven deities under her pillow she had no dream, although she lied as most people did and said she had dreamed of, for instance, a goldfish or a covered bowl, both lucky signs.

This New Year she had had a short, vivid dream. She and Gwen-san were standing on a rock in the sea. The waves were washing up to their feet. Far away a sea-bird was calling. Gwen-san shaded her eyes to look for it. Mirio felt the waves cover her feet. Her feet were very cold. She woke to find she had pulled up the bed-cover too high and her exposed feet were indeed cold.

But the dream remained in her mind. Everyone

knew it was very unlucky to dream of the sea, or a sea-bird. To dream of both together could only mean great trouble.

Yet, as the year began, luck seemed good. Tama told her he intended to stay in Tokyo. That meant, Mirio was sure, that Gwen-san would go home on her own.

Alas, not so. Gwen-san, against all Mirio's expectations, decided to stay with Tama. Worse, Tama asked for Mirio's consent to a marriage according to Shinto rites. Mirio had refused; they had quarrelled seriously. Tama had said that on his thirtieth birthday or on the day after Mirio died, whichever came first, he would marry, according to Japanese law, his *geijin* woman.

Now there was this disappointment over Hanako's marriage.

It was all due to the foreign woman. She brought bad luck. Until she came to the house, Mirio had never had an unlucky New Year dream.

Tama was saying, 'Everything will be all right this time, Gwen. In fact, it will be better. The new man Mr Inora is suggesting lives in Tokyo. Hanako won't have to go to Hamada.'

'That was a bad idea, having to move to Hamada?' Gwen asked.

'Well, Tokyo's preferable.'

'Then why was it all so acceptable before? Why didn't anyone ask Hanako if she'd prefer to stay in Tokyo?'

'There was no need, Gwen-san,' Hanako said gently.

Gwen went surging on. 'Why can't Hanako be allowed to build up a relationship with a man, see if she likes him, and then think about marriage?'

'Hanako doesn't know any men,' Tama said with a laugh.

'Of course she does. At least she's met one or two—'

'In what way has she met one or two men?'

'When she goes out with me to visit my European

acquaintances. There are Japanese people there too, sometimes men, from the university or from government circles.'

'You're not suggesting that my daughter could become friendly with a man that her family haven't met?' Mirio put in.

'She might, if she was given the chance.'

'That would be most improper. Hanako, you are not to go with Gwen-san to any of these European gatherings.'

'Now wait a minute!' stormed Gwen. 'Let's ask Hanako what she would like to do!'

'Please, it's not important, Gwen,' said Hanako. There was entreaty in her voice. She was begging – don't make an issue of it, it will only cause bad feeling.

'My son's wife will excuse me if I say that the marriage of my daughter will be arranged satisfactorily without her help. Everyone knows that Gwen-san is fond of Hanako, but others are also fond of Hanako and know what is best. If you will excuse me, my son, I will go to bed now. Goodnight.'

With that Mirio-san rose in the fluid movement of the Japanese woman, went quietly to the screen, opened it, and slipped through. Before she could close it behind her, Tama went after her.

Gwen could hear him speaking in soothing tones to his mother. Mirio replied with muted anger. Among the words she distinguished were *'uchi no haji'* – 'She's a family disgrace!'

That's me, thought Gwen. The family disgrace.

She slept badly that night and woke next day disheartened and sick of life. Try as she might, she couldn't reconcile her view of what was right with what was going on in the Hayakawa family. It seemed to deprive Hanako of all human dignity.

I can't go on, thought Gwen as she wandered disconsolately among the new shoots of bamboo along the stream. I simply don't belong here. I've tried, I really have tried. But it's never going to work.

She decided to tell Tama she was going back to Europe. If they were going to break up, better to do it now, before more time had gone by and they had been married according to Japanese law. She had no desire to embarrass him any more than she had already.

She'd make one more attempt to persuade Tama to come too. After all, during his stay in Paris he'd been happy. He often spoke of it with fondness.

Whereas she was decidedly unhappy here in Tokyo. She couldn't bear the pretence of good manners and agreeable behaviour. It was shallow and insincere. She couldn't bear the waste of so much sweetness and goodness among the women, she couldn't bear the assumption that men must always be right.

If she gave Tama an ultimatum, he might agree to come. She didn't want to leave him – it was the last thing she wanted – but she couldn't go on making him the centre of her entire life, counting on him for almost every moment of happiness. She had to live in an atmosphere of freedom, of frankness, of camaraderie.

This difficult decision was even more difficult to put into action. She never seemed to find the right opportunity or, if she did, the words wouldn't come. She grew pale and tense, she lost weight, she felt ill all the time.

At the beginning of April she discovered the real reason behind this. She was pregnant.

Chapter Eleven

Gwen was suffused with joy. Tama's child . . .

She had never thought about children. She and Tama had always lived in the moment, the busy, stress-filled moment. First there had been the enduring thrill of their passion, then the pressure of working together, always in demand, always active.

Since coming to Tokyo there had been a different kind of pressure. Gwen had had to make tremendous efforts to understand how this society worked. She had had to struggle to understand and to make herself understood. She had had to face the antagonism of Mirio-san.

But now she was carrying Tama's child. Everything else faded into insignificance.

She'd been on her way to the tram stop to go into the city. She had stopped dead when realisation came to her. Now she began to walk on, her mind flying to the future. A little boy toddling about, clambering into her lap to be told a story. A little boy taller than most of the children she saw, because Tama was tall for a Japanese and she herself was much taller than any Japanese woman she had ever met.

But what was this little boy wearing? European clothes? Or a little Japanese smock?

Joy faded. Anxiety, alarm, flooded in. She must go now, now before anyone knew the secret. She must make sure her baby was born in Europe, so that he could have the benefit of proper medical care, the comfort of a European home, schooling . . .

No one could possibly guess as yet. She would

face Tama this evening when he came home, tell him that she had had more than enough of Japanese life, hated the climate, couldn't stand his mother, and was going home.

There. That was what she would tell him. And he would be aghast, and perhaps angry, and they would have a tremendous quarrel, and that would be that.

As she imagined the scene, her heart shrank from it. It was all wrong. Unfair, unkind, deceitful. She would hurt Tama just when she ought to be making him happy and proud.

She knew he would be overjoyed at the news of the baby. Although they had never discussed it, she knew he would want a son. Every Japanese she had ever met loved and adored children.

In this country of strange customs and tepid religions, the real gods and goddesses were the children. In all the time since she came to Tokyo, Gwen had never seen anyone slap a child. On the contrary – if a child fell and hurt himself, there was always someone to pick him up and comfort him: mother, servant, aunt, elder sister, even a passer-by.

She watched a couple of little girls playing in the street outside a little house. They trotted and toddled about, little black-eyed, doll-like creatures, laughing, throwing a ball of bright yellow felt to one another. They paused as she went by, looking up, staring at the strange foreign creature but breaking into laughter when she gave them a little smile and a wave.

Children were usually smiling, seldom unhappy. They greeted all the world as their friends. No one would ever harm a Japanese child.

Most of the holidays and festivals of Japan seemed to be instituted merely so that adults could give presents to children. Sewing-needle Day, Lunar New Year, Girls' Doll Festival, the Empress's Birthday, Kite-Flying Day, Iris Day for Boys, and on and on, national festivals added to by little family celebrations for first-cutting-the-hair or putting-on-*gaeta*. Perhaps this was to compensate them for the harshness of life to come. Whatever the reason, the Japanese treated their children with a loving wonder which Gwen had never seen elsewhere.

Not tell Tama he was to be a father? Could she really do that? Deprive him of what was the greatest joy of life for a Japanese?

She paused in her leisurely stroll. She was on a muddy street leading to the bigger road where the trams ran. She'd intended to go into the city centre to see if she could buy some *meruku shukuratu* for which she'd developed a sudden craving and which was the nearest the Japanese could get to the words 'milk chocolate'.

A craving for milk chocolate . . . Now she knew why. And she knew why the sharp smell of Japanese pickled vegetables had become nauseating, and why she'd been subject to stomach upsets for the last few days.

Mirio-san had been annoyed with her. She'd murmured under her breath about being 'ungrateful for good food'.

Gwen must go soon, or Mirio-san would guess.

But that would be such a wicked thing to do . . .

She knew it in her heart. To go away without telling Tama about the baby would be utterly, completely wrong. She must tell him, and then she must explain that she had to get home, to Europe, to England, to be with her mother when the baby was born. She wanted all the old-fashioned comforts for her baby: knitted shawls, a rocking cradle, a coral teething ring . . . She wanted her mother to hold her hand when the birth pains started; she wanted modern anaesthetics to ease the hurt.

Tama would understand that. He of all people knew the importance of family ties. He would let her go.

But if she went, would she ever come back . . . ?

Gwen knew she would not.

In the twelve months since her arrival, Gwen had

found much to admire in Japan. The goodness, the patience, the willingness of the people was very attractive. The scenery was full of charm – almost nothing was ugly to look at except for the imposition of European architecture on Japanese surroundings. The standard of service, the loyalty of servants – there was nothing like it in Europe.

But, and it was an important but, the people seemed to have bound themselves hand and foot by their customs. They seldom spoke out about their opinions – they would agree with almost anything you said because to disagree was impolite. As to the beauty of the surroundings . . . What pleasure was there in a house that looked charming if it was uncomfortable? The draughts when the wind blew, the lack of privacy, the problem of sitting comfortably where there were only two stools and one of those must stay in the bathroom . . .

And then the rigmarole when trying to do business, half an hour spent on formal greetings and good wishes before one could mention the real purpose of the meeting; the amazement when a woman was allowed to be present at a business meeting. The embarrassment when she went with Tama to a party at a tea-house, to find herself the only woman, utterly ignored by the *geisha* who cosseted and entertained the men . . .

Yes, the role of women in Japan . . . That was Gwen's greatest stumbling block. She had to get away, or she would become nothing but a cipher – the wife of Tamaki-san, not important except for her small part in making a man comfortable and happy.

Her own talents meant nothing. Tama had promised to find a cabinet-maker to produce the little table she'd designed, but so far little had come of it. Of course, he was busy – negotiations for Hanako's marriage were really going forward now, so much so that Hanako was attending bride-school. And Tama had work of his own to do; Bright Omen was flourishing.

She came to the tram stop. A tram came lurching up within a few minutes. She boarded it, gave her fare to the bowing conductor, took a seat. She watched the townscape of Tokyo pass the window – low-built wooden houses, some used as shops or business premises. A school, with a little line of children moving across the pavement in their school uniform, the boys in dark blue belted jackets with a white collar and matching trousers, the girls in smock-like dresses with white aprons.

When the trolley-car halted at the stop for Mitsu-Koshi, the department store, she automatically got down. The doors were immediately opened for her by two smiling boys. Inside, two young women, in dark kimonos bearing the store's insignia, bowed her onwards, murmuring the traditional greeting, *'Irrashai-mase'* – 'welcome to the shop'. Gwen walked on, so far away in her own thoughts that she didn't remember to smile a greeting as she usually did.

She had quite forgotten what she'd come for. She walked through the store, encountering bowing sales staff, fingering a length of Italian jersey presented for her inspection, shaking her head at a box of Swedish wine glasses.

By and by she came to the exit that would take her out near the Imperial Palace grounds. She could go out into the spring day, look at the blossom trees . . .

Something caught her eye. She was in the hardware department. Laid out on a counter was a display of American tools. The glint of a steel chisel, the dull gloss of a wooden plane-case . . . carpenter's tools.

She walked up to the display. As usual, a salesman was immediately at her side, bowing. But he couldn't disguise his puzzlement.

'The lady desire to inspect tools?'

'Yes, please.'

'A gift for husband?'

She didn't bother to contradict him. She took the box-plane which he was offering her. The wooden case

205

was hickory, the adjustable blade was of fine tempered steel. Holding it, she could imagine the smell of the wood shavings as they curled up under the tool.

How long it seemed since she'd smelt wood shavings! Months had gone by, and her hands had been without occupation, except for those sketches and one finished drawing for a table. A table never yet made.

She gave back the plane, picked up one of the chisels. It was a socket firmer chisel, the gummed label of the maker still on the leather-edged handle: Fulton Special, weight 6 ounces, blade 1/2 in. She hefted it in her palm, loving how it fitted there, as if it belonged.

She bought a set of chisels, a drill, a hacksaw with a set of blades, a plane, a spirit level. She asked for them to be sent, but took with her as a kind of amulet a little pair of pliers intended for taking out panel pins.

Where in Tokyo did you buy panel pins? Where did you buy screws, glue, sandpaper?

She would find out.

Next she went to the Imperial Hotel for morning coffee. She found she was ravenously hungry, having been unable to eat any of the usual family breakfast. She took a seat in the courtyard, where the bonsai trees in their ancient stone troughs were in tiny blossom. She ordered coffee with rolls and butter – rolls were specially baked each day in the kitchens of the Imperial by a cook who had been to Europe to learn how.

Out of her handbag she took the prettily wrapped package. She undid the paper and the string. A pair of pliers, fine American steel with handles enamelled blue.

Why had she bought them?

Because she was going to make something.

She needed a chair – a European chair with a back to support her, so that she could be comfortable during her pregnancy. Yet it had to be a chair that could be put away when she was not there actually using it, so as not to annoy Mirio-san by its mere presence in her house.

It had to be a foldable chair, slender in its proportions, the seat and back made of the kind of cotton used in Japan for awnings. There had to be points or knobs on the back so that a cushion could be hung from them as a comfortable back support. There had to be grooves in the sides of the seat so that cushions could be slid into them.

Take away the cushions, fold the chair sides-towards-middle to make a sort of sandwich, fold again so that the back came over to make a triple sandwich – and everything could be put away in one of the screened cupboards in the living-room.

She got out a pencil to sketch it on the back of an envelope. The envelope contained her mother's last letter, but she didn't even think of her mother as the pencil began to move quickly over the paper. Something like a safari chair that she'd seen in a book, the memoirs of a big-game hunter with lots of photographs . . . Yes, like a safari chair, only more delicate, more sophisticated.

When the waiter brought the food, she ate and drank hungrily. She propped her little sketch against the coffee-pot. She could make that in one day, two days at most.

She must ask Tama to find her a place to work. No problem there – a little shelter somewhere at the back of the works at Bright Omen. Or there might be some Japanese carpenter who would let her use his premises. She would need a workman, perhaps two, because some of the tools she'd need would be Japanese tools and she wouldn't be expert enough with those. A vice, for instance – the way the Japanese fastened wood for safe working was quite different from the metal clamps used in Europe.

When she'd paid and was going out to the fresh air, she smiled up at the sky. Life was good. She was going to have a baby, Tama's baby. She was going to get back to work.

Only when she was on the tram going home did she realise she'd made her decision. Her unconscious had done it for her.

She would tell Tama about the child. She would have the baby here in Tokyo. Perhaps after a few years, when he was of school age, she would go back to England so that he would have a European education. Perhaps Tama would come with her then.

In the meantime she would handle each day as it came. And today was the day she must tell her husband about their baby.

She wanted to do it, if she could, like a Japanese woman. The truth was, she'd no idea how to do it as a European. Everything to do with childbearing was lapped about with embarrassment in St Albans – no one had ever spoken about it. 'A certain condition', 'a delicate state' – these were the terms used to describe pregnancy.

But in the conversations when women friends came to visit Mirio, she'd heard quite a lot of talk about family matters. So when Tama came home that evening, she had rehearsed what she was going to say.

She was waiting for him in their room upstairs. She led him out to the balcony so that the sacred clouds of evening and the setting sun would be witness to the words. On the low table tea and rice cakes were set out. There was also a slender lacquer vase with two Japanese lilies, the same colour but one shorter than the other, symbolising mother and child.

She bowed – not as low as a Japanese woman, nor did it have the same effect, for she had no kimono-skirt on which to rest her hands. But it was a bow of love and acknowledgement, and it made Tama stop and stare.

Using the very respectful *anata* for the word 'you', and addressing him as Tamaki-sama, which was more respectful than Tamaki-san, she said: 'You are to be the father of our child, honourable husband.'

Tama's face broke into a smile, then a look of doubt

replaced it. 'Your Japanese is so limited, Gwen,' he said with a little preventative gesture of his hand. 'Say it in French.'

'Je suis enceinte,' Gwen said.

'Really?'

'Yes, really.'

He threw his arms around her in a very un-Japanese embrace. 'Darling! When did you find out?'

'Today.'

'Have you seen a doctor?'

'Good gracious, I don't need a doctor to tell me I'm expecting a baby!'

'But are you sure?'

'Yes, I'm sure.'

'Oh, Gwen!' He burst out into a flood of rapid Japanese, amongst which she could catch that he had longed for a son, that he was the happiest man in the world, that his family would now go on into the future, that his mother would be delighted, and that he had the most beautiful wife in the world.

'We must tell Mirio-san at once.'

'Yes.'

Mirio was seated on her heels in the living-room close to the opened screens at the back, looking out at the garden in the early evening light. A pair of spotted doves was perched on a branch of the dwarf cherry tree beyond the pool, the male cooing, the female preening herself. This pair was resident in the garden, something considered very lucky. Mirio watched them often.

'Mirio-san, I have something important to tell you.' Tama interrupted her reverie.

Mirio turned her head. Then, seeing this was a formal announcement, she moved so that she was facing into the room, managing it in that graceful way of the Japanese woman but which completely defeated Gwen.

'Mirio-san, you are to be grandmother to my son.'

Mirio stared at him wordlessly. Emotions sped across

her unguarded face – delight, alarm, anxiety. But then they were lost to sight as she bowed to the ground.

'Congratulations, Tamaki-sama. And to the mother of the son, congratulations.'

'Thank you. This good event comes in November, close to the Day of Meizi Setu.'

'A good day. A lucky omen.' Mirio came erect from her bow. 'We are blessed. This family will now continue into the years. We must visit your father's grave to tell him.'

'Yes, indeed.'

Before many minutes had passed the entire household staff had become aware of the news. Without anyone ordering it, Kinie brought in tea and cakes. Even Kinie was pleased, giving Gwen a special bow as she put the tray before Mirio. As for Hanako, Hanako was in seventh heaven at the thought of becoming an aunt.

In the ensuing weeks Gwen became almost the equal of Mirio-san in the household. She wasn't expected to take over direction of the household, and indeed couldn't have done it if it was asked, but in almost every other respect she was treated with deference.

Foreign foods, hitherto forbidden by Mirio, made their appearance. Coffee, that impossible drink, was made by Ota the cook – in two days he was a master of the art. *Meruku*, milk, that strange white fluid, was delivered every day for use with the coffee. Mirio couldn't understand it – all that trouble with perfectly boiling water and just the right amount of blackish-brown grit, and when the bitter brew had been produced it was then mixed with the white fluid to make it less bitter.

Coffee for breakfast! No croissants – that was beyond the command of even the special stores which stocked European goods. But bread was occasionally available, and certainly apricot preserves which came in tins from Switzerland.

Meat, too – lamb and beef – and potatoes, and flour

to make pastry for a pie-crust. When the heat of the Tokyo summer began to take hold, ices were brought from the stores in special containers. Anything Gwen desired was ordered by telephone and delivered – if it was obtainable in Tokyo.

More important, to humour his pregnant wife, Tama had a room built on at Bright Omen, where she could work. He hired two carpenters, father and son, to do the harder tasks such as sawing.

After three or four days of utter dismay at being given intructions by a woman, Yosu-san and his son Hayato began to enjoy themselves. The foreign lady had new tools to show them, tools unlike any they had had before. But she also encouraged them to use those they were accustomed to. She herself worked alongside. It was strange, it was unnerving – but it made a wonderful tale to tell the neighbours when they got home at night.

The folding chair was made, carried home by Hayato, and set up by Gwen in the living-room while no one was there. When the family came in from their various occupations – Hanako from bride-school, Mirio from a visit to lady friends, Tama from the lacquer-works, there stood the chair in the centre of the room.

Mirio-san could see it was beautiful. She had been brought up to appreciate visual beauty. But what use was it? Who in Japan wanted a *chair*?

Well, it seemed Gwen-san did. She sank into it with a sigh of relief, fanning herself in the warmth of the May evening. Hanako and Tama in turn tried it, declaring it very comfortable. Mirio-san sat on it gingerly, on the very edge, said some polite nothings, and then asked, 'Are we to walk round it from now on?'

'Not at all,' said her strange daughter-in-law. She whisked off the cotton-covered cushions, undid two little hooks that had been invisible up till then, pressed with her hands, and in a moment the chair lay on the matting, taking up as little room as a padded kimono. Smiling, Gwen opened a cupboard, put the

211

chair and cushions away, then looked round for their opinions.

'Oh, Gwen-san, how *clever*!' cried Hanako, clapping her hands.

'Thank you. I must say I too think it's clever.'

'I have a very clever wife,' said Tama, laughing.

So now this strange daughter-in-law had a chair to sit in. Perhaps at last she'd stop complaining about how difficult it was for her to sit on her heels as any respectable woman would, Mirio thought.

But something strange happened. Other people saw the chair or got to hear of it. Many people wanted to buy one just like it. It seemed that the Europeans of Tokyo had long been looking for a chair they could use in their Japanese lodgings without spoiling their look, and also some forward-thinking Japanese had been looking for a chair they could offer European guests without cluttering up their homes unnecessarily.

So the chair went into production. And then Gwen had her workforce increased, and electricity put in so that they could use some machinery of some kind to help work with the wood. And then she made a table – yes, another beautiful thing, slender and fragile-looking, a top and four thin legs like the legs of a bird but made in wood, easily taken to pieces. And people wanted to buy the table too.

A surge of creativity had seized Gwen. It was as if the coming of the baby were linked to the coming of new ideas. She sketched in the evenings, and next day would show the sketch to Yosu. They would discuss it, he would decide how to set about making the pieces from their strange mixture of tools and machinery. They produced the folding chair, the bird-like table, a screen of fretted wood through which coloured silk showed like a rainbow, items to hang from the window-frames so that tall Europeans could see to shave and do their hair.

Gwen sent the drawings to Jerome. He replied that he was offering them to Parisian cabinet-makers and had received some inquiries over the fretwork screen and the table but not, as yet, on the chair. The screen she had made before she left Paris, the one like four Japanese fans opened out, was now selling well. He ought to be able to send her a cheque soon. She should open an account with a Tokyo bank for her business receipts.

Her mother wrote in raptures over the coming baby. She longed to be with Gwen. 'Send me a snap of how you are – I'm so worried about you, all the way off on the other side of the world. And all this about working again – you ought to be getting plenty of rest, not pottering about with bits of wood.'

Summer came. Unlike last summer, which had been almost nothing but rain, this year there was the usual *tsu-yu* from mid-June to mid-July, several days of rain followed by several days of dry heat. Ground tremors seemed fewer than usual. The temperature in August was generally close to ninety degrees.

Gwen found she loved it. She'd never felt so well. She gloried in the heat, and the humidity seemed to bother her not at all. She piled her dark copper hair on the top of her head for coolness, wore loose silk dresses and flat-heeled shoes, moved slowly so as to avoid getting sticky with sweat, and was busy and content.

Contrarily, Mirio-san was torn between despair and delight. She wanted very much to be a grandmother – it was the next most important thing after being a mother. But what would her grandson look like? What if he inherited his mother's strange hair and green eyes? What if he had those odd brown specks on his skin which Gwen-san said were *furekuru*, freckles? What if he was as restless, as difficult to control?

At first Mirio-san had almost wished that her daughter-in-law would miscarry. But that was a wicked thing to hope for, and would be a bad omen for Hanako's marriage which was approaching fast now.

And here was another thing to think of. Once Hanako was married and gone to her husband's home, Mirio-san would be alone in the house with the foreign daughter-in-law, who would of course be even more important to Tamaki-sama once the baby arrived. How was Mirio-san to cope with this? Even Kinie, her faithful friend who had come with her as a bride, was now coming under the spell of the foreign woman, even to the extent of using soap provided by Gwen-san when she did the washing.

So she would be a party of one in a house where her daughter-in-law was liked by all – and loved, doted upon, by Tama. Mirio would be made to take second place. Already it was happening. Visitors came to the house, some Japanese but mostly Westerners, who conversed with Gwen-san. Mirio was unable to take any part unless Gwen-san or Tama translated. And when they did, the topic of conversation was almost always something she knew nothing about.

Art – yes, they talked about art, and Mirio knew something about art, because it was in her blood. But they talked about artists whose names were strange to her, Europeans it seemed. And they talked about furniture. Mostly about Gwen-san's furniture.

How could Mirio-san ever have imagined she would have a daughter-in-law who made furniture? Like some peasant woman, she worked with her hands, hammering and sawing and painting – like a fishergirl mending nets, like a farmer's servant-girl tending the bean-curd vat.

Sometimes Mirio felt she actually hated her son. It was he who had brought this creature to their house. How could he do it? How could he pay so much attention to her? How could he let her speak to him as he did?

Mirio had moments when she thought she was losing her mind. Her whole world seemed turned upside down. It would be better to be dead than have to live with this nightmare world. Sometimes Mirio-san thought longingly of her husband's ashes lying quietly under the stone of the family tomb.

But she couldn't die, not yet. Not until she had seen

her grandson. And that depended on the accursed *geijin*.

These tensions made Mirio's uncertain temper even more unpredictable. It became harder and harder to behave with the required decorum.

On the first day of September, Mirio rose with a headache. She watched her daughter-in-law accept the strange brew called *kofi*, watched her eat the slices of flat food called *buredu* and thought, I ought not to permit it! I ought to throw it all out!

As she often did, Gwen invited her mother-in-law to try some bread and butter.

'Unfit for any civilised person to eat,' Mirio said coldly.

'It's eaten over most of the world, *obaa-san*.'

Obaa-san was the title of respect now adopted for Mirio. It meant grandmother and had been deemed appropriate as soon as Gwen's pregnancy was well established. For some reason, Mirio took exception to it today.

'Don't call me *obaa-san*!'

'I'm sorry, Mirio-san. Is anything wrong?'

'What could be wrong? Hanako!' she called sharply to her daughter. 'You'll be late!'

'No, Mother, it's the flower-arranging class this morning. We were told to come in one hour later so as to give time to buy or gather the flowers.'

'What are you taking, Hanako?' Gwen asked.

'Never mind what she's taking! In fact, I think it would be better if she didn't go. The wind's rising very strongly; it means a rain storm from the sea before very long.'

'But Mother—'

'In any case, I want you to help get out the padded kimonos.'

'But, Mirio-san, we shan't be needing them for at least another six weeks—' Tama began.

'But they will need repairs, they always do. Give me

215

the keys of the storehouse, I'll get the kimonos out as soon as breakfast is over.'

Gwen had intended to stay at home today. She was working on an idea for a clock case that would fit into a Japanese room. European clocks looked odd in Japanese surroundings; her idea was to see if bamboo could be used somehow. The men at the carpentry-shop had plenty to keep them busy; she wasn't needed there. But these danger signals from Mirio foretold a morning of bad temper. Better to go out. She could go into the town to buy some fruit – cherries, perhaps. Strange to say, although cherry blossom was passionately adored in Japan, no one had ever thought of raising cherry trees that would bear edible fruit. Recently an orchard a few miles out of Tokyo had grown some European cherries and the fruit was, so she heard, newly on sale in the shops.

'Come with me, Tama,' she suggested. 'We could go into the Imperial and listen to the jazzband.'

'It doesn't come on until tea-time. Besides, I have a customer coming this morning. If you get any cherries, save some for me.' He kissed her absent-mindedly before he set out for Bright Omen.

When Mirio saw her daughter-in-law go into the porch with her waterproof coat and her shoes and overshoes, she checked her. 'Don't go out. There's going to be heavy rain.'

'I heard you say that, so I'm taking my rain gear.'

'If it rains typhoon rain, that coat won't be much use.'

'If it's as bad as that, I'll take a taxi home.'

'You'd better stay at home.' To a Japanese daughter-in-law, that would have been tantamount to an order.

But Gwen-san only said, 'No, I think I'll go out.'

It was, in fact, very windy outdoors. Gwen was glad she hadn't brought a paper umbrella, it would have blown inside out in a minute. There were no cherries to be had at the shops in the fruit market, so she bought persimmons and *nashi*, a sort of pear she'd come to like.

The rain began, a real downpour. People scrambled for shelter. Gwen tried to put on her raincoat but it was difficult with the wind blowing it first one way and then another. She spread it over her head for protection.

It was close to noon. She ought perhaps to get a taxi and go home. But, as always seems to be the case in the rain, there were no taxis.

The Imperial Hotel was not far off. She could reach it by hurrying through an alleyway where there was shelter of some sort from the rain. She ran into the lobby of the hotel, shedding her wet coat.

The best thing would be to have lunch here, wait for the weather to brighten, and go home later. But first she must go to the ladies' room to dry herself off and tidy her hair.

She walked across the hall towards the little passage where the sign directed her to the ladies' cloakroom. She put her hand out to open the room door.

It moved away from her.

Frowning, she leaned forward. The floor tilted up and sent her headfirst into the door panels.

'Earthquake!' cried the hall porter. 'Everyone outside, earthquake!'

Chapter Twelve

Gwen was on the floor, thrown there by her collision with the door. She scrambled up.

People began to come rushing into the foyer from all directions. The hall porter had wedged open the hotel doors. From beyond them screams and shouts came.

There was a strange rumbling, groaning sound. The lobby rocked. The light hangings swayed to and fro. A couple running down the stairs in the hotel were thrown to the bottom of the flight.

Gwen was clinging to the side of the doorway for support. Someone put an arm around her.

'Come on, ma'am, this is no time to hang around!'

She was thrust forward, towards the exit. The doorway tilted first one way, then another. A group of about a dozen people surged through it. A tramcar in the street beyond the hotel front court was slowly toppling sideways.

The ground shook under Gwen's feet. Her sense of balance had deserted her. She fell to her knees, felt herself sliding forward, threw out her hands and protected herself from falling heavily on her face.

Once more she staggered up. She was carried on by the group to the gateway of the courtyard. Out in the street, buildings were slithering about at crazy angles. She threw an arm across her eyes, for the sight made her dizzy. She couldn't tell how to stand up straight if the world fell apart.

'Hi, come on, get back – it's safer in the courtyard than out here!'

Those at the front collided with those trying to come out. For a moment there was a struggling muddle. Someone yelled something authoritative in a foreign language. Another voice translated: 'Yeah, right, the hotel's OK, get back!'

The group sorted itself out, staggered back into the courtyard. The bonsai troughs slowly glided across their low benches to fall to the paved court. The splintering of the ancient pottery containers was lost in the greater noise.

The angry groaning continued. It sounded as if the earth was giving up its very soul. Shrieks of terror, the crash of ruined buildings, the clanging of metal vehicles in collision . . .

An awful sound, a rush of wind and then a huge explosion.

'My God, what was that?'

'Gas,' said a crisp British voice. 'That was a gas main.'

The crowd that had retreated back into the courtyard stared at each other in dismay. They consisted of a score of Westerners, both men and women, three Japanese men in business suits, and a collection of perhaps ten Japanese in the hotel uniforms – waiters, the hall porter, a clerkess from the reception desk.

The earth shook with sudden violence. Everything shivered under the shock. People fell against each other, collapsed in a tangle to the ground. The uproar of the earthquake drowned for a moment the sound of falling masonry, the screams of crowds who had rushed outdoors to avoid being crushed.

A long, rolling shiver went through the earth. Gwen heard herself weeping with fear. She huddled down, covering her body with her arms. 'My baby, my baby,' she was sobbing.

Like an animal shaking its pelt, the earth settled itself

after its upheaval. The waves of movement died away, the awful rumbling sound became less and less until it was a vibration on the air.

One of the men heaved himself to his feet. He stood unsteadily, then threw out his hands to help up his neighbour. 'I think that's the worst over,' he said.

'For the moment,' someone added.

The hotel group got up, stricken to silence. But from the city itself the noise was tremendous.

Different now. No longer the sound of the earthquake but the sounds of the aftermath. A frightening, awesome crackling was making itself heard above the crash of wrecked buildings.

'Fire,' someone said.

'Yes. Inevitable.'

An elderly lady whose face was smeared with the blood of a cut forehead now stepped forward. 'Is everyone here all right? Anyone need first aid?'

They surveyed themselves and each other. Faces dirt-smudged, hair awry, dresses and suits soiled, cuts and bruises . . .

'Anyone in the hotel?' And then, in Japanese, 'This can't be all the staff?'

'No, madam, many go out other exits. Fire drill.'

'Yes, I see. Mr Melville, would you and some of the other gentlemen go in and see if anyone needs help?'

'Right you are, ma'am. Stewart, will you come?'

Two men headed back into the hotel, with the Japanese porter alongside. Gwen looked at the building. Glass gone from some windows, the doorway at a curious angle, but on the whole the Imperial Hotel seemed intact.

She turned on unsteady legs. Exactly the opposite was true of the rest of the city centre. Where before there had been a vista of office blocks, banks and buildings, now there was almost nothing. Clouds of grey dust were eddying up into the sky where once brick and stone had stood.

The noise was indescribable. Human voices screaming, shouting. The snap and roar of flames. Strange
rushing sounds, as air was sucked into the rising heat.
The crumbling, rending sound of walls going down,
whole floors of buildings cascading towards the earth.
The thuds and bangs of equipment, furniture, fitments, ricocheting on each level as they slid towards
the street.

Gwen looked at her wristwatch. A few minutes after
twelve noon. Her watch must have stopped. She shook
it, held it against her ear. No, it was still ticking.

Only ten minutes had elapsed since that first moment
when the door of the cloakroom swayed away from her.
Only ten minutes, and the world was wrecked.

Wrecked? Was the whole city wrecked? Was Higashi-
Nakano wrecked too? And the Hayakawa home?

She turned to head for the street. Before she'd gone
two steps her legs buckled under her. She fell, but was
helped up to a sitting position almost at once.

'Where d'you think you're going?' asked the elderly
lady.

'Home! I must get home! My husband—'

'Now keep still, my dear, let's look – you've grazed
your knees and one elbow. No, no, don't struggle to
get up – you've had a big shock. And you're not in the
best condition to cope with it, are you, dear?'

'I'm all right. Let me up. I *must* get home—'

'Where to?'

'Higashi – it's about two miles.'

'And how do you think you're going to get there?'

'A taxi.'

'My dear child, there are no taxis. There's probably
no road. Keep still, now, just be quiet and let yourself
recover from the fall. Tell me your name, dear, tell me
your name.'

Gwen ceased struggling to get up. She tried to
concentrate on the question. 'My name . . . I'm Gwen
Hayakawa.'

'Good. I'm Jane Bedale. I'm with the Methodist Mission at Ahasi, just in Tokyo for a few days on mission business. There now, feeling better?'

'Yes, thank you. Thank you, Miss Bedale. I think I can get up now.'

'No reason why you should. Just sit quiet.'

'But you don't understand! My husband and his family—'

'I understand, my dear, I understand perfectly. You don't know what's happened to them. But you can't get out to Higashi. You can't—'

The ground beneath them shivered violently. For a moment time stood still. But after a few seconds the shivering died away.

'There,' said Miss Bedale, shaking her grey head, 'you see, you can't even think of going anywhere. We don't know whether it's over or whether there's worse to come.'

'But—'

'What good will it do if you rush out there and get hit by a piece of falling masonry?'

'But—'

A sudden hot breeze struck them. It was like opening an oven door.

'What's that?' Gwen gasped.

'Fire, Mrs Hayakawa. It always happens after a quake. I was in one once in the East Indies – the fire was more devastating than the quake.'

Of course . . . All the wooden houses, the paper windows, the rooms with their charcoal braziers for heating, the city centre with its modern gas mains now set alight . . .

The house in Higashi with its charcoal stove in the kitchen – Ota had probably been in the midst of preparations for the midday meal. And at the workshop, Bright Omen, there were banked charcoal fires that fed heat to the drying chamber . . .

'I must get home!' Gwen cried. She got up on

trembling legs, supported but also held back by Miss
Bedale. The older woman was half dragged towards the
courtyard exit by Gwen's efforts to get away.

One of the men took two running steps to grab her by
the shoulder. 'Listen, ma'am, don't be foolish—' Gwen
collided against a tubby body clad in black jacket and
pinstripes.

'My husband . . . I've got to—'

'Don't you think others have folk they're scared
about?' said the American, pulling her back by force.
'But nobody better go out there.'

And one glimpse through the courtyard exit told her
he was right. A jumble of ruined buildings, some stone
and some wood, stood licked by orange and red flames
climbing among them. The roadway was blocked with
tumbled stone and brick, cars at drunken angles, two
trams with their wires in a tangle.

And people were everywhere, scrambling among the
wreckage, their clothes on fire from falling flinders;
people running, staggering, bowed in pain, dragging
themselves on injured limbs, calling for help, screaming
the name of a loved one . . .

At almost the moment that she understood the scene,
refugees began to scramble into the courtyard. The big
stone building with its paved entrance was safe, was not
likely to fall, was not on fire. People streamed into the
courtyard. Now it would be almost impossible to get out
because of the press of the crowd coming in.

Gwen was swayed off balance by the rush. Miss
Bedale and the tubby American man held her up. They
backed into the hotel, though unwillingly because it was
far safer to be outdoors. Falling ceilings and roofs were
a great danger indoors.

For a time Gwen lost track of what was happening. She was pushed one way and then another, half
protected by the two people who had taken her in
charge. By and by the press eased off a little. She
found she was in the entrance hall of the Imperial

Hotel, sitting on an upholstered bench, being urged to sip from a flask.

'I never go anywhere without a supply,' said the American with a grim twinkle. 'Good bourbon – it'll soon fix you up.'

She sipped. The smooth liquor slid down her throat. She suddenly realised she was parched with thirst. That was because of the dust – which was everywhere. She herself was covered with it, so was Miss Bedale, so was Frank Erander the owner of the bourbon, so were all the others in the lobby. They were caked with grey dust from the buildings that had fallen, from the earth that had dried in the searing heat, despite the soaking rainstorm earlier in the morning.

Thick smoke was flooding in from outside now, black and smelling strongly of burnt wood, burnt flesh.

'We must do something,' Gwen faltered.

'Sorry, ma'am, there's nothing to be done. I had a look outside, there's no way a fire engine can get to anything. Besides, I think the water supply's shot – all the pipes probably got busted in the first shake. Whoops,' he added, as the floor and walls of the lobby began to shiver again.

Gwen put her arms protectively across her body to defend the baby. Miss Bedale stooped over her as added protection. Chandeliers fell from the ceiling in a clang of metal rods and breaking glass. Screams and shouts told of injuries among people in the crowded lobby.

After what seemed like an aeon, the tremor eased off. There was a moment of intense, relieved silence. 'So much for that,' said Frank Erander. Then, raising his voice, 'Anybody hurt badly?'

One or two calls for help were made. Miss Bedale left Gwen to seek out the sufferers, and it seemed there was also a German doctor among the crowd helping out. The hotel manager had got into his office after levering off the door, which had jammed due to the tilting of the frame. He came back with first-aid kits.

Within an hour the lobby had sorted itself out into separate groups: those who had been badly hurt and needed attention from the doctor; those who had lesser injuries and needed Miss Bedale; those who were, like Gwen, in special circumstances. Almost everyone was suffering from shock.

For a time they were their own little world, trying to put things right within a small circumference. Gwen gave her attention to an elderly Frenchman who, it turned out, had a heart condition and had lost his medication. He grabbed her by the forearm when he discovered she could speak his language. 'Help me!' he begged. And, in helping him in his urgent need, for a time she was able to put away the thought of what had happened to the Hayakawa household.

There seemed to be no daylight, because the smoke had darkened the sky. And yet, by late afternoon, Gwen could tell night was coming on. The sun behind the clouds was going down. But worse, the clouds of black smoke were being illuminated from below by a red glare.

'The whole city's burning,' she whispered to Miss Bedale.

The missionary nodded with deep sadness. 'The Flowers of Yedo,' she said.

'What?'

'That's what they used to call the fires that sprang up in the old days, when the city was called Yedo. The flames looked like great orange and red blossoms among the wooden houses. But this must be the biggest garland of flowers the city has ever seen.'

The Japanese staff of the hotel, incredibly loyal and brave, had gone into the kitchens and managed to provide enough food for the throng in the lobby and courtyard. A little meat, a little soup, some rolls of bread, hot tea – because the hotel had its own water tank in the roof – eager hands received it, parched throats swallowed it down.

'You are very good,' Gwen said to the waiter who brought her a bowl of soup. 'To stay with us and serve us . . .'

'Lady, most of us live in the hotel, we come from other parts of Japan mostly. If Buddha is kind, our families are safe. So it is our duty to help those here. Especially those whose families are somewhere in the fire.'

Gwen's eyes filled with tears. She looked up at him through a mist. He said, with a tremor in his voice, 'The lady's family?'

'In Higashi.'

'Perhaps Higashi is all right.'

But it was hard to think so – the fires stretched way into the distance. When, slipping away, she toiled upstairs to look out of a second-floor window, all she could see was an ocean of flame. The sky overhead was orange, scarlet, vermilion. A strong wind caused by the fire had sprung up, spreading the conflagration forward in its path.

The earth tremors continued. Common sense told her to go back downstairs and out where she was safe from falling objects. Everyone went out with blankets and pillows brought from the bedrooms. They bedded down in the unseasonally warm courtyard, but few of them slept, and those that did were continually wakened by the crash of burning buildings – or by their own dreams.

Next morning there seemed to be no dawn. A pall of darkness hung over the city. Yet Gwen sensed something different. Now there was movement outside in the street.

She scrambled up, glad to be free of the pretence of sleeping. Stepping over huddled forms, she reached the entrance to the court.

People were going about outside, men in the kimono of the Tokyo Fire Brigade and in the uniform of the police. Stretcher teams were collecting up bodies. A big cart, meant to be horse-drawn but pulled by a team of men, was receiving the bodies and carrying them away.

Mingling with this rescue work were straggling individuals with bundles on their backs, making their toilsome way on the searingly hot roadway, out of the city, towards the country, towards relatives who might help them, towards air that could be breathed and trees that had not been burned to charcoal.

'Now, dear,' said a voice at Gwen's elbow.

'It's dreadful, Miss Bedale.'

'Come along back in. It's no use staring at it, it'll only make you feel worse.'

'But I've got to start out for—'

'My dear girl, even supposing you *are* going to start out for anywhere, you can't go without something inside you. Think of the little one – he needs nourishment.'

Gwen knew she was right. She allowed herself to be urged back to the courtyard, where life was beginning again as the others awoke.

The hotel staff had managed to get the storerooms open. There was tea, a biscuit each, and a piece of omelette. Later, perhaps about ten o'clock, the manager promised, there would be vegetable soup and pancakes. 'You understand, ladies and gentlemen, there is no gas and no electricity and only limited water. But we shall do our best.'

A vote of thanks was offered. The manager and his staff bowed in acknowledgement. Their black hair streaked with dust, their usually immaculate uniforms rumpled and stained, they nevertheless looked proud and efficient.

By mid-morning daylight had at last established itself through the huge overcast of black smoke. Although the heat from the burnt city was still intense, it was possible to walk in the roadway if one moved quickly and picked out spots where water had flowed from a burst water main.

Gwen was determined to set out after the meal of soup and pancake. Seeing she wasn't to be deterred, Frank Erender volunteered to go with her. 'I've got no one in Tokyo to look for,' he explained with a turn-down of his lips. 'I was here for a conference with the Tokyo Bank – I was going to meet the people for the first time at lunch yesterday. So I'm entirely at your service, ma'am.'

'But, Mr Erender, why should you—'

'Call me Frank. Look here, Mrs Hayakawa, I think you're being very foolish, but if you insist on going, you ought to have someone along to be foolish with you. And as I can't cook or do first aid, I'm no use here.'

Miss Bedale, who had appointed herself Gwen's keeper, gave grudging approval. Mr Erender was about fifty, in good health and sensible – if Mrs Hayakawa must really go in search of her family, he made a good guardian angel.

So they left the hotel, an incongruous pair – Gwen in her crumpled blue silk dress and leather court shoes, Frank in his banker's pinstripes.

'Now where's this place at, where we're heading?'

'It's about two miles out, a residential district.' She pointed. 'That way.'

The only way you could tell they were on a main road was by the heaps of wreckage, the derelict trams, and the stumps of the burnt telegraph poles still giving off little curls of smoke. Here and there, in the smouldering wilderness, the former inhabitants were trying to pull out a few belongings. Others crouched in the remains of their homes, grief like a mask on their features.

They walked along, stopped now and then by anxious people searching for relations. Many of them bore placards which they held out, the name painted or chalked in big characters. Some held out photographs.

Gwen and Frank shook their heads to the grieving inquiries.

'Let's go back,' Frank said, wiping tears away from his broad cheeks with the back of a grimy hand. 'This is tough to take.'

'I must keep going,' Gwen said. 'I'm like those people. I'm looking for my husband.' She put her hand on her middle where the baby swelled it out. 'I must find Tama,' she said.

So they trudged on. The sheer physical difficulty of keeping a foothold took up enormous energy, especially when yet another tremor caused the hot tiles of some collapsed house to slither under their shoes. Cracks would appear in the ground and then close again. Gwen could see where fissures had opened yesterday, and buildings had been half swallowed before yet another movement of the earth's crust caused the hole to fold together again.

Nothing looked familiar. After about an hour and a half Gwen began to think she had totally lost the way. By now she should have turned off to the left, down an unpaved road towards the more open aspect of Higashi. But who could tell which had been an unpaved road; who could tell where houses had stood and where there had been a trafficway?

'Were there any landmarks?' Frank asked, staring about as they paused yet again to take stock.

'Not really. There was a small temple in a garden, but that would have gone anyhow. And there was a stream . . .'

'A stream. With houses along it?'

'No, in fact, there were bamboos and a little bridge, where the path came down.'

'Well, let's look for the stream,' Frank suggested. 'Unless the earthquake's diverted or blocked it, that should still be there.'

The stream had run at the end of the path where stood the lacquer workshop, Bright Omen. Tama would have been at Bright Omen, offering tea to his important customer, when the quake began.

'Bright Omen Lacquerworks?' Gwen asked a group of men putting planks across a fissure to make a bridge.

They shook their heads. Whether they meant they didn't know or that it was gone, she couldn't be sure.

There was a building on fire a few yards along. Men were fighting to save it. As Gwen and Frank were about to give it a wide berth, she paused.

'They've got pails of water, Frank.'

'So I see. Look, why don't we—'

'But where are they getting the water?'

'Yes, by God,' said Frank. 'That's right.'

They used the chain of men passing buckets as a guide. They found a stream, full of mud and slow-moving, but still a stream.

'Kidu-ushi Stream?' Gwen asked the man scooping brown water into his pail.

He looked up for a moment, nodded, and went back to his task.

'This is the stream! Frank, we're in Higashi!'

'Well, good for us,' said Frank, taking off his black jacket and folding it over his arm. 'My word, I'm hot! I'd give anything for a glass of cold beer!'

She knew he was talking just to keep cheerful. She smiled at him, grateful for his stocky strength and his faithful company.

Following the stream was difficult. It disappeared now and again, where the movement of the earth's surface had toppled soil over it. But she could see the fronds and sometimes the roots of bamboo, so she could tell that they were on what had once been the banks of the brook.

By and by Frank pointed to some shards of brown wood. 'That looks like carpentered railing, Gwen.'

'It's the bridge!'

Frank stooped, trying to haul a piece out of the pile

of upended sheets of soil, reeds, bamboos, stones, tree-trunks. It was useless.

'Which way, if this really is the bridge you mentioned?'

'Up here, to the right.'

Part of the copse of trees was still standing. Beyond them should be a path between high banks and then the buildings of Bright Omen.

There was no path. They had to climb and clamber among new hillocks of black rock and earth. When at length the copse was well behind them, they stopped.

'Are we heading the right way?' he asked.

'I . . . I don't know. What do you think?'

'Ma'am, I'm no country boy to tell you about tracks and trails, I'm a Manhattan banker. Sorry.'

'We should be able to see the roof . . .'

If it's there – that was the thought in both their minds. But neither uttered it.

They stood staring about. Each turned a quarter circle, trying to sight a sprawling, one-storeyed building with a banner at its gate announcing 'Bright Omen'.

'There,' said Frank, pointing.

Gwen could see the corner of a frame of wooden beams which stood at a crazy angle. 'But that can't be the works . . .'

'We'd better take a look.'

They walked towards it. The surface of the earth had that strange appearance as if it had been gouged by a giant plough; great clods of earth on their sides, roots of plants showing instead of the growing stems. By now they knew what it meant – the ground had opened here, parts of the surface had caved in towards the opening, and then been left when it closed again.

The beams of wood stuck up like steepled fingers. Slates from the roof lay around in a scatter among the raw soil. There was a wheelbarrow a few yards off, and beyond that two or three wide reed baskets.

'Any of this look familiar?' Frank said quietly.

'Yes . . . Yes, the baskets . . . They use them to carry the lacquerware . . .'

Frank said nothing.

'This can't be Bright Omen,' Gwen whispered.

'It could be, Gwen.'

'No, no! There's nothing here!'

He shook his head.

There was no need to say it. They both knew what had happened. The earth had opened its maw, swallowed the workshop and everyone in it, and then closed over them.

Gwen put her hand up to her mouth in an uncertain gesture. She wanted to cry out that it wasn't true. It couldn't have happened.

But she had seen the same signs too often on their way here. And she had seen the grief-stricken figures kneeling by the few remaining scraps of building.

After a long moment Frank said, 'Look, my dear, maybe he wasn't here. Maybe he went home for lunch.'

She seized his shirtsleeve. 'Yes, that's it! It was nearly lunchtime when it happened, wasn't it? He's at home!'

'Whereabouts is home?'

'It's about ten minutes' walk away.' Normally, she should have added. For she wasn't even sure which way to go, now that the whole landscape had changed.

Were they standing in front of what had been the lacquer workshop, or at its side? And where was the blackish sandy path she used to follow? Everything was different. All she could do was trust her instinct.

They made their slow way over the churned earth. The smell of burnt wood told them they were coming to houses. Beyond a newly raised mound they came to the first of them, blackened ruins, with people moving about. Pathetic little heaps of belongings were piled here and there. Already mothers were trying to find cooking pots, fathers were trying to put up shelters.

Gwen went up to a woman with a child on her lap. 'Is this Higashi Ward, Tugu Street?'

'Tugu Street,' said the woman, pointing.

Gwen bowed her thanks, murmuring, 'Buddha's blessing on your family, mother.'

'And on yours,' said her informant with a sad smile at her swelling figure.

'This way,' Gwen said to Frank. She found she was almost unable to speak. Her throat seemed to have closed up, her teeth were clenched. Her whole body seemed chained up in fear.

Tugu Street hardly existed. All that remained were a few charred trees, an ornamental bronze dragon sundered in two by heat, red roof tiles and a stone lantern on its side.

About a hundred yards away a cart was stationed, covered by a tarpaulin. Men were moving to and fro with stretchers.

'Wait,' said Frank, 'I'll go and ask.'

'You can't speak the language.'

'I'll just say the name. Hayakawa, right?'

'Yes.'

He trudged on over the smouldering wreckage. Gwen went after him but slowly, trying with all her heart and strength to pick out something that would tell her which had been her home.

Nothing. Flinders, scraps, tatters. Metal objects had survived the fire – a ring of iron that had once held together a wooden tub, the lock from a door, some unrecognisable twisted lumps that might have been an angle, a lever.

Something flickered to and fro in the dull light. A fragment of pale blue brocade, singed at its edges.

Gwen knelt in the cinders of Tugu Street to pick up

the scrap of satin. She knew it at once. It was from the *obi* Hanako was to have worn with her bridal kimono.

Mirio-san had asked the bonze for an auspicious day for the ceremony. He had chosen 3 October 1923. A month and a day away.

In a month and a day Hanako would have been married. A married woman, gone to her new home, to live with a mother-in-law as Gwen had done. To be wife and mother, to fulfil her destiny, to spread that sweetness and gentleness through her new family.

Of that tender, loving spirit, this was all that was left, this little scrap of stiff blue brocade.

Kneeling in the dust, Gwen knew the truth. Hanako was gone. Mirio-san was gone. The household of the Hayakawa family were no more. The fire had engulfed them.

Tama was gone. The earth had eaten him up.

Nothing was left of her life. Nothing, nothing.

She was roused at last by Frank Erender's hand on her shoulder. She looked up. She read the answer in his grey face.

'They say if you like you can go and see if you recognise any of the bodies. But I wouldn't, Gwen. I wouldn't go.'

'No, all right.'

'They said no one survived in this street, Gwen.'

'I understand.'

'I'm so sorry, my dear.'

'Thank you.'

'It's only early afternoon but the light's going. Do you feel fit to start back? I don't reckon much to the idea of trying to walk on the sort of surfaces we've met up with, once it's dark.'

'We could see by the light of the fires,' Gwen said.

Frank looked at her with anxiety. 'You've had a big shock.'

'This was from a sash bought for my sister-in-law's wedding,' Gwen said, holding out the brocade.

'Gee,' he said, at a loss.

'There are some bits of metal there,' she said, throwing out a hand towards the black ruins. 'I think they're part of a gramophone. Mirio-san was so angry about the gramophone.'

'She was?'

'She liked the old ways. Tama was different, he was willing to try something new. But even Tama couldn't quite free himself from the old Japan.'

'Is that so?'

'And in the end it was the old Japan that killed him. The old Japan, the oldest part of old Japan . . . The earth turned on him as it's done a thousand times before.'

'Listen, Gwen,' Frank said, desperate to make her think of herself, 'maybe I could find a car or a cart or something.'

'I can manage on foot. I'm sorry, Frank. You must think I'm a fool to sit here maundering on.' A kind man, almost a stranger. She mustn't impose her memories on him. It would be better if she could blot them out of her mind, really. Then perhaps she could prevent the pain from growing. She could feel it inside her, growing – as her baby had grown, until it became the most important part of her.

Her baby. Tama's baby.

What had she said to herself a moment ago? That nothing was left of her life?

She had their baby to live for. When she bore his son, Tama would live on. She straightened her bowed shoulders.

'You OK now?'

'Yes, thank you.'

'Right then, ma'am, let's make a start.'

He helped her up.

She meant to hold on to the scrap of brocade but it

slipped through her fingers as she rose. A capricious breeze caught it as it fell.

A moment later it was gone, and though Gwen tried to see it, it was lost for ever among the rubble.

Chapter Thirteen

They set off. Gwen asked the burial detail for directions and was pointed towards the east. Strange to say, it was less difficult to find the way because Tokyo centre was still burning – all they had to do was walk towards the red glare reflected off the smoke-clouds.

But there were many detours. First there were the ground fissures, the piles of smoking debris, stretches of ruin impossible to cross because beneath them lay unsteady surfaces, welling water from the broken mains, hissing gas, hidden cracks that might trap them as they passed.

And as they came in exhaustion towards the Europeanised section, they found the army at work, blowing up houses to make fire breaks.

'Very sorry, no passage by this route. You must go round by De-ikiu Street.'

But where was De-ikiu Street? Vanished under piles of broken masonry.

At last, as the early dusk was deepening to night, they saw the damaged building of the main railway station. People were camped in groups in the big square before it. Tiny fires glowed where evening tea was being prepared. There were faint lights in the entrance hall of the building itself.

Now at last Gwen knew where she was. They had to cross the square and go left.

But she was incapable of going any further.

'I'm sorry,' she gasped, catching hold of the base of a fallen statue. 'I just can't . . .'

Everything was wheeling round her. This time it wasn't yet another earth tremor depriving her of her sense of balance. It was because of a fog that was invading her brain.

Her legs seemed to go from under her. She slid to the ground.

'Gwen!'

'I'm sorry, Frank. You go on. I'll be all right here.'

'Leave you here? Not a chance. Come on, up you get . . .'

But he couldn't lift her.

Kind Japanese hands restrained him. Two women, one elderly and one younger, were shaking their heads at him. They knelt beside Gwen. She felt something being slipped under her head to raise it from the uneven ground.

'Thank you,' she muttered.

'Our poor help is here. You are very pale, lady.'

'Yes. I'm . . . I'm . . . just too tired to go any further.'

'Lic still. Rest.' The elder looked up at Frank. 'Where were you going?'

'What are you saying?' he asked helplessly.

'To the Imperial Hotel,' Gwen said.

'Imperial Hotel, yes, all foreigners are going there. Good. Father-san should go on.'

'Father-san? Oh . . .' Through the haze Gwen felt a faint amusement. To Frank she said, 'They say . . . go on to the hotel. They're right. I just can't go any further . . . for the moment . . . Perhaps you could get . . . Miss Bedale?'

'But Gwen, where is the hotel from here?'

'Just . . . keep saying . . . "Imperial Hotel" . . . Everybody knows it . . .'

'Right. I'll fetch someone. I'll be back soon.'

He hurried off. The two women turned their attention to Gwen. One rose and disappeared among the groups around them. In a moment hot liquid was put to Gwen's lips. She sipped eagerly. She had had nothing since ten o'clock that morning, eight hours ago, except a little water from one of the broken mains.

When she had emptied the little cup, she was gently laid down on the folded kimono that formed her pillow. She tried to smile up at the anxious faces hovering above her but they slowly faded from view. Consciousness slipped away from her.

She was roused some time later by the sensation of being carried. She tried to sit up. A restraining hand was put on her shoulder and a voice said in English, 'All right, dear, lie still.'

She sank back on the stretcher.

Later there was a light. She focused on it. It was a candle flame. Alongside it a face was bending to study her. It was no one she knew, but the same voice said, 'Just rest, dear. You look as if you need it.'

Her forehead was gently wiped with a warm towel, a cover was tucked around her. The face and the candle flame withdrew. She looked up. There was a tent roof. But that too faded out. She slept.

The next waking was different. A terrible pain gripped her in the back. She heard herself moan. In defence she threw her arms around her body, her first thought that any pain might be damaging to her child. And then she was fully awake, understanding that the baby was coming.

Coming too early, into a world unfit to receive him.

'Help,' she gasped. 'Help, someone.'

At once the candle flame appeared, the same face beside it. Someone was kneeling by her makeshift bed. Another face joined it, this one a Japanese face.

'Ah, it's happening,' said the European voice. 'I hoped we could avoid that.'

'Who . . . who are you?'

'It's all right, dear, this is the Salvation Army medical post. You'll be all right—

'No – it's too soon—'

'How far on are you?'

'Seven months. Oh, please . . .'

'Now, don't be frightened. Seven months . . . Never mind . . . We'll manage . . . Mayo-san, please fetch my bag.'

The pains had rushed to the front of her body. They were coming fiercely. Gwen clenched her teeth against them. Everything was happening too fast.

'No, don't fight it, dear. Lie down. I need to examine you, to find out how Baby's lying.'

'Are you . . . a doctor?'

'No, love, but I've brought many a child into this world, so don't you fret. You're going to be fine.'

Efficiently the capable hands were feeling Gwen's body, the steady voice was chatting away as if there were nothing in the world to worry about. 'Well, you're right, Baby's only about seven months gone, but there's no problem about presentation. He's in a hurry, though, this one. Now, lovie, tell me your name and where to get in touch with your husband.'

'Gwen . . . Hayakawa . . . My husband . . . is dead . . .'

'Oh yes? Mrs Hayakawa? I've heard of you. Yes, yes, we hear a lot about everything, Tokyo's like a village in some ways. I'm Beth Fairford, I've been in Tokyo with the Salvation Army a long time. There, dear! I'm finished. I'm going to time the pains now. Mayo, where's that bag?'

Mayo appeared. Gwen heard the click of the medical bag being opened, but it was the last thing outside herself she could pay attention to for a long time afterwards.

The birth was an anguish, but it was quick. Tama's child was too eager to enter the world. She lay half-conscious, exhausted. She heard a thin cry. 'My baby?' she whispered, clinging on to reality with all her might.

'Yes, dear, a tiny little girl.'

'Is she all right?'

'Don't you worry, we'll see to her.'

A soothing voice was crooning to the baby. Gwen began to let her grip on the world relax. Anxious hands were at work trying to staunch a flow of blood. The flickering light, the tented roof – everything began to slip away.

Now and again she came back to a faint understanding of things. Daylight came, she made out the tented ceiling almost clearly. Then it went, and when next she looked there was instead a ceiling that swayed. Her mind half formed the thought; another tremor. Yet it wasn't that. She heard, but didn't recognise, the throb of a motor.

Her gaze later came to focus on brightness. Sunshine on white paint. She wanted to ask what room she was in, what building, but the sound came out slurred. A voice said, 'You're all right, Mrs Hayakawa, just rest.' She felt a little prick on her arm. She seemed to have no choice but to obey.

At length her awakening was different. She knew it as she opened her eyes almost lazily. Before, when she'd drifted into consciousness, it had been momentary. Now she was awake and aware. Her gaze came to rest on a Japanese nurse in a white uniform sitting by the bed.

'Am I in hospital, nurse-san?'

'Ah, Mrs Hayakawa,' said the nurse in sibilant English. 'So glad. This University Hospital. You know?'

'Oh, yes. University Hospital.' It seemed to take all the strength she had to repeat the words. She lay quiet a moment, summoning her resources for the next question. 'My baby?'

'In premature ward. We feed her through eye-dropper.'

'But . . . she's all right?'

'Make good fight.'

'How long?'

'Five day now. Each day better.'

Gwen closed her eyes and reopened them, to study the nurse. She knew only too well the propensity of the polite Japanese to tell you what they thought you wanted to hear.

She made an effort to frown with sternness. '*Ah so desuka?*' she demanded.

'*So desu,*' said the nurse, coming to her feet and bowing.

So it really was true. Her baby was all right.

The nurse took Gwen's wrist. After a moment she said, 'Pulse better. I go find doctor, who wishes know if you wake up. OK?'

'OK.' Then, as the girl moved almost out of range of her vision, 'Can I see my baby?'

'Ask doctor.'

When she had gone Gwen made a great effort to raise her head. She found she was in a little ward with about ten or a dozen beds pushed close together. A voice from the next bed said in Japanese, 'So glad you are better, Mrs Hayakawa.'

'Thank you. You know my name?'

'It was said quite often. Let me introduce myself: Miss Kanagoi, I am here with burns and a broken leg.'

'I'm so sorry,' Gwen said, remembering the constant need to be polite in Japanese conversation. It all took so much time, needed so much of her small store of strength. She had let herself sink back on her pillow – all she'd seen of the other patient was a bandaged head.

Now she was aware of other sounds around her, rustlings, low moans of pain, light footsteps as nurses moved to and fro, occasionally the trundling of wheels.

'We are fortunate,' said Miss Kanagoi. 'I mean, that the hospital was not destroyed.'

'Yes.'

'They say that as soon as we are well enough we must be moved out. Casualties are still being brought in.'

'Yes.' Gwen collected herself. 'What day is it?'

'Today is Saturday 8 September – exactly a week.'

She didn't have to say, a week from the earthquake.

For months to come, Tokyans would date things from that fatal day.

It was only polite to ask after Miss Kanagoi. 'How long have you been here, Miss Kanagoi?'

'Two days. Before, I was taken care of by office colleague. Our building collapsed, we were trapped two days and then in a tent.'

'I am glad you were cared for, Miss Kanagoi.'

'Thank you. I am glad for you, also. And your baby – they say she is doing well.'

'Thank you. I hope your family is safe?'

'They are with the Buddha,' said Miss Kanagoi.

They fell silent. A few moments later the nurse returned with a doctor at her side, a young Japanese in a white coat that had not been laundered for several days. He was grey with fatigue.

'Well, Mrs Hayakawa,' he said in English with an American accent, 'happy to see you are awake.' He took her wrist. 'Yes, your first question,' he went on as he counted her pulse, 'baby is quite well, weighs four pounds and four ounces, sleeps, takes milk through dropper, we are not worried over her. You, however, worried us much. How do you feel?'

'Groggy.'

'Groggy?' His black eyes closed as he frowned in concentration. 'Does that mean good or bad?' He relinquished her wrist, nodded at the nurse who produced a thermometer.

'A bit feeble.'

'Ah, feeble I understand. Well, you lost much blood. You will feel feeble for some time—'

'Can I see my baby?'

'That is not possible.'

'Something's wrong with her!'

'No, no,' he soothed, 'nothing except that she is two months premature. You cannot go to see her because you are too weak to be allowed up; we cannot bring her to you because she must be kept in warm temperature –

very difficult, electricity not yet dependable, she could not be carried here without perhaps danger and, of course, infection, the hospital is crowded, patients in corridors, you understand?'

'Yes,' Gwen said thankfully, and was prevented from further talk by having the thermometer slipped under her tongue.

Two days later they let her get up. They wrapped a borrowed kimono over her hospital-issue nightgown, put felt slippers on her feet. With a tiny Japanese nurse on either side of her she was walked through the ward, out to the hallway, along a passage to a room that had once been glass walled but now had paper screens. There was a charcoal brazier glowing softly in a corner, with a nurse on guard beside it.

A row of cots lined each wall. The ward sister led Gwen to one half-way along.

In it, wrapped in a cotton blanket, was a scrap of humanity crying angrily. This noisy little girl had a fuzz of bronze hair, almond-shaped eyes that glinted green through her tears, little fists that thrashed about a tiny, pointed face.

'Why is she crying?' whispered Gwen in alarm.

'Ten o'clock feed is due. She is hungry often. She gained an ounce yesterday, Mrs Hayakawa.'

Gwen was leaning over the cot. Her helpers had let go their protective grasp on her. She leaned in, picked up the wailing child. The two nurses and the ward sister gave a gasp of alarm. But almost at once the baby stopped crying. The nurses relaxed. Gwen held her daughter in her arms.

For the first time in many days, a wave of almost perfect happiness flowed over Gwen. For that one long moment, nothing else in the world mattered.

She had survived, she had borne Tama's child, and the child was safe. They would live on, the two of them, to keep Tama's memory alive.

The ward sister smiled at her. 'What name?' she

asked, laying a finger on the blanket that wrapped the baby.

Gwen had already thought about it. 'Tamara,' she said. It was as close to Tama's name as possible.

'Tamara,' echoed the sister, nodding.

Jane Bedale came to visit that afternoon. 'Sorry I couldn't come before. We had troubles of our own, as you know, and then we had a bit of a problem finding you. Poor Frank Erender was beside himself when we got to Station Square and you'd vanished. But Beth Fairford came and let us know.'

'She was so marvellous! And I didn't even really see her!'

'Once she'd turned up and reported you were safe in hospital, Frank agreed to sail.'

'Sail? Where?'

'The port of Kobe got going quite early, ships took foreigners off. They're being taken to California, which isn't too convenient for some, but the feeling was that this poor country had enough to do without having to look after foreign nationals.'

'So Frank's gone. I hope you have an address for him, I must write and thank him.'

'Yes, certainly. So what do you intend to do now? Doctor Igura tells me you'll be leaving tomorrow.'

'Yes, they need the bed. I'm not ill, you know, just terribly weak. But they're keeping Tamara for a few more days.'

'Tamara? That's nice. I hear she's doing well.'

'Yes, up to almost five pounds. If I could have fed her myself she might have done even better, but unfortunately—'

'Yes, I know, don't blame yourself, dear.' Jane patted her hand. 'Well, you'd better come back to the Imperial. The food situation is a tiny bit improved. Some of the fellows managed to get out to their own homes. Bill Sowden for instance, he has a house in Asahi, he came back with a handcart laden with tinned fruit and Camp

247

coffee.' She chuckled. 'It's a strange diet but we manage. I hear milk supplies are coming in from the country – should be all right for little Tamara. But what *you* need is iron tonic, and we don't have that.'

'I'll be all right. Will you come and fetch me, please Jane?'

'Surely. What time?'

'They say after doctor's rounds – that means some time around nine, I think.'

'Very well, dear.'

'And Jane . . .'

'Yes?'

'Could you borrow a dress and coat from someone? I've nothing to wear. These things I have on belong to the hospital. The clothes I had on are ruined, as you can imagine . . .'

'Good heavens, yes. Well, all right – one of the women at the hotel is sure to have something about your size. And relief supplies are coming in – people in other parts of the country have donated clothes and blankets and so forth. What about shoes?'

'It seems my shoes survived, thank heaven.'

The following day Jane arrived with Beth Fairford. Beth turned out to be a tall, rangy woman in a very worn Salvation Army uniform of blue and crimson, minus the bonnet. The bonnet, she confessed, had been lost somewhere in the earthquake.

They brought a bundle in a checked *furoshiki*, the all-purpose Japanese carrying cloth. When opened up, it contained a plain brown tweed skirt, a creased grey blouse, some underwear, a blue raincoat.

They helped her dress. 'It's lucky there's no mirror,' laughed Beth. 'You look a sight.'

'That doesn't matter.' And it was true. Who cared now what she looked like? Tama would never again exclaim with delight over her French finery, her shining hair, slender ankles.

She made a round of goodbyes. Miss Kanagoi had

already gone, but she went to each bed to bow and give good wishes. She thanked the nurses and sent a message of thanks to Dr Igura, who was too busy to see her off.

They went with her while she said a temporary goodbye to Tamara. They hovered outside the ward, refused entry by the sister for fear of infection. Gwen leaned over the cot to whisper to her daughter. 'I'll come and fetch you in a day or two, darling. Be good.'

Outside it was pouring with rain. The streets were a sea of muddy ash. And yet there was a resumption of activity, an attempt to get back to normal. Enough petrol had been found to get some motor vehicles going. Ambulances were bringing in casualties. Police vans were being used for public transport. Jane Bedale stepped into the street to flag one down.

About ten Japanese passengers squeezed up and made room for them. As the van made its lurching way into the city centre, Jane brought Gwen up to date with the news.

'The British chargé d'affaires has been to the Imperial every day for the past four days. I don't suppose you knew, the Ambassador was out at the summer residence in Chuzenji and they're staying there: the Embassy here was burnt down. Anyhow, Mr Gower comes with a list of people who've been in touch through a wireless link at Nagoya. Your mother – Mrs Baynes, right?'

'Yes,' muttered Gwen. She'd hardly thought of her mother since the earthquake. All her energy, physical and mental, had been devoted to surviving so that her baby might live.

'She's been enquiring for you. Mr Gower's sent word about everyone he's been able to trace so your mother knows you're alive and well. There was another enquiry passed on by the French Embassy – now, let me see, who was that?'

'Jerome de Labasse?'

'That's the one. Word's been passed on in that case too

– though mind you, the amount of traffic going through Nagoya is tremendous, so it'll take some time before you hear again from anyone.'

'What about you two?' Gwen asked. 'Have you been able to get in touch with relatives and friends?'

Beth Fairford shrugged. 'Friends know that a Salvation Army captain is always in the hands of God, dear.'

'And I've left it to the director of the mission to send out messages about me,' added Jane.

They swayed to a halt. They were in an expanse of dereliction that had once been Ayati Square. The two older women helped Gwen down. In silence they made their way to the hotel.

There Gwen found a sort of organised chaos. Shelters had been rigged from the walls of the court to keep off the autumn rain. Some of the Westerners had retreated back into the building, camping out in the lounge and the dining-room. Few, it emerged, were as yet willing to use the upstairs rooms, except on flying visits to grab clothing or toilet articles.

Everything was covered with a fine ash, black and grey. As soon as it was wiped off, it collected again. Everyone, Westerners and even the Japanese – usually so immaculate – looked crumpled and dirty.

The time was about eleven in the morning. Tea was being served out in a variety of bowls and cups. Tea was available five times in the day – early morning, mid-morning, midday, five in the afternoon, and eight o'clock. By now Gwen was well acquainted with 'common tea', the brew made from leaves already used at least once. The tea at the Imperial Hotel for the next few weeks was made from leaves that had been used at least a dozen times, but it was hot and wet, easing the constant thirst caused by the constant dust.

In other ways, life had improved. Electricity was almost totally reliable again, though gas was still cut off. Water was available in the hotel from three faucets in the lower part of the building – from the kitchen, from the ladies' cloakroom Gwen had been attempting to enter when the earthquake struck, and from a tap in the side of the building formerly used by the gardener to water the bonsai trees. In the morning the women used the ladies' cloakroom for ablutions, the men shaved by the garden tap.

'Now,' said Captain Fairford, 'our medical unit is handling the supplies of milk. When you're allowed to bring Tamara home . . . Well, at least, when you're allowed to bring her here, I mean . . .' She smiled and threw out broad, capable hands. 'It looks a mess but it works, dear. When you get your baby, be sure to have your name added to the list for special milk supplies. I'm hoping that in a day or two we'll have supplies of Ostermilk for babies – I'll let you have some.'

'Thank you,' Gwen said, struggling with the tears that seemed always ready to spring into her eyes. 'You've been so wonderful to me.'

'Nonsense, it was God's doing.' She kissed Gwen on the cheek and was gone.

'Bossy, isn't she?' Jane said, but with a smile. 'You know she and her team went patrolling round the city centre that night they found you, and though the little Japanese women told her someone was coming for you, they just scooped you up and carried you off. Never mind, it worked out for the best. Come on, Mr Gower's probably here now, he wants to talk to you.'

'Me?'

'Yes, there's been an inquiry from the town of Mikayo to the Tokyo police about the Hayakawa family. Mr Gower knew through the usual social grapevine that a Tamaki Hayakawa was married to a European so when he heard of you from us here at the hotel he thought he'd better have a word with you.'

Mikayo . . . It could only be an inquiry from Tama's cousin Moko.

She was led by Jane into the lobby of the hotel. Here

a corner had been set aside for officialdom. A member of the Tokyo police force was working his way through a queue of Japanese, some of them presumably trying to find out about relatives in other parts of the country. At a trestle table sat a tall European arguing with two elderly Westerners.

'But I assure you, Mr Sheldon, there *are* no passenger ships at Yokohama. The dock facilities all slid into the sea. The only way at present is via Kobe.'

'But you can't get a ship at Kobe going west! They're all going east to America!'

'I know that, sir, but if you'll just be patient, in a day or two—'

'I call it damned inefficient! Surely the shipping lines can sort themselves out better than this? I have urgent business in—'

'Excuse me, sir,' Gower interrupted, getting to his feet, 'this lady needs to sit down, I think.'

Gwen sank thankfuly into the chair he'd vacated. Mr and Mrs Sheldon eyed her with annoyance. She was interrupting something important.

'And how are we supposed to get to Kobe anyway?' Mrs Sheldon wanted to know. 'The railway's still—'

'If you go to Shibuma beach you can get ferried out to one of the small cargo steamers. That'll take you to Kobe within a few hours. Once there, you'd be better placed to get a ship to England.'

'What about the *Hawkins*? The British Navy . . .'

'The *Hawkins* is only taking injured people, Mr Sheldon. Really, your best chance is to get to Kobe and make inquiries there.'

'Very well,' said Mr Sheldon, without any sign of gratitude for the advice. 'If that's the best you can do . . .'

He and his wife sailed out, dishevelled, covered in dust, but still determined that nothing should interrupt their schedule of events, not even an earthquake.

'Sorry about that,' Gower said with a small smile at

Gwen. He was a tall, awkward young man with a soiled dress coat, a clean collar, and pince-nez. 'Now, first of all, are you all right? You're very pale.'

'I'm just out of hospital—'

'Oh, you're Gwen Hayakawa! How do you do?' He held out his hand, they shook politely. He called to a passing hotel employee, 'Waiter, if there's any tea left, could you bring some for Mrs Hayakawa?'

The waiter bowed and hurried off. In a moment he had returned with yet another cup of steaming tea.

'Miss Bedale said you had an inquiry after the Hayakawa family?'

'Just so.'

Gwen looked into her tea-cup. No words would come.

'I heard from Frank Erender – they're all gone. Is that right?' asked Gower.

'Yes, according to the stretcher party the house burnt down and there were no survivors. The people at the lacquer workshop were killed when the buildings slid into a ground fissure.'

'I'm so sorry, Mrs Hayakawa.'

'Thank you.' She took a deep breath, not a sigh but a way of fortifying herself for this unwanted conversation. 'The inquiry came from Mikayo, I understand?'

'Yes, from the family of Moko Hayakawa. He must be a relation, I take it.'

'A cousin, I think. My husband mentioned him now and again in connection with the wedding arangements for . . . for his sister.' Gwen had trouble stifling a sob. Every time she thought of Hanako, grief seemed to well up. 'Moko-san was to be invited to Tokyo for the wedding.'

'I see. You've met him?'

Gwen shook her head.

'I'll tell the Missing Persons Department of the Tokyo police to pass on your information. Is there any message you would like added?'

'Only . . . only the appropriate Japanese expressions of respect and mourning.'

'Of course.' He was nodding his head, making notes on the back of a handbill, the only writing paper he'd been able to get hold of for the morning's work. 'Now as to yourself, Mrs Hayakawa . . .'

'What about myself?'

'Have you any plans?'

Once again she shook her head. 'I can't make any until my baby's health is certain. She was born prematurely, you see.'

'Oh, I'm sorry, I'm afraid that bit of news . . . How is she?' Gower said with awkward kindness.

'She's doing well, gaining every day. They say I might be able to fetch her from hospital in about a week. They'd keep her longer but of course there are so many others needing hospital treatment . . .' She fell silent. There was no need to babble on to Mr Gower about her baby. He had enough to think about.

'Well, Mrs Hayakawa, I'm sure you understand that at the moment the power of the British Embassy to help is extremely limited. But things are improving all the time. One of the things we're trying to do is evacuate people out of Tokyo to more pleasant surroundings, unless they have important reasons for staying here. Would you like to be evacuated to the country?'

'Not until—'

'Yes, yes, of course – not until your little girl can go with you. Shall I put your name down provisionally for next week? I can't say exactly where you might be sent, but it would be somewhere less depressing than this. Better for the baby, I'd imagine.'

'Yes, thank you – please add my name to your list of evacuees.'

'Good. Now in the meantime, the hotel is supplying three small meals a day, for which the British authorities will pay. Clothing supplies are being distributed:

there's a makeshift wardrobe-centre in the billiard room; perhaps later you'd like to go and have a look. As to money . . . I can advance you the equivalent of ten pounds for day-to-day expenses, although really there's nothing to spend it on – transport, such as it is at the moment, is free, there are no supplies of food or anything much to buy, but you'd better have it just in case.'

He opened an old cigar box, counted out some yen notes, offered them to Gwen.

She hesitated. 'I have some money,' she said. 'In the British Overseas Mercantile. Is that still working?'

'Not in Tokyo, the building burned down. But most of the banks have opened branches in Asahi – in a day or two you should be able to get access to your account. In the meantime, use the loan from the Embassy purse.'

'Thank you.' She sat holding the notes in her hand. She had no handbag in which to put them.

Yet when Albert Gower shook hands and left, she felt that her life had begun to move forward again.

She slept a lot in the days that followed, and swallowed teaspoons of iron tonic provided by Jane from medical supplies to the Methodist Mission by American charities. She found a change of clothing among the piles of garments on the hotel's billiard table. Baby clothes there were none, but there were sheets and towels. She employed her time making shawls and baby napkins out of them.

On the daily visits to the hospital to see Tamara, she explained to her baby what she was doing.

'I'm trying to make everything ready for when we can be together, Tammy. Mr Gower says he thinks we can go to people at Nara, which is pretty, or at least it was . . . I don't know what it'll be like after an earthquake. But you'll like it, Tammy, because you'll be with me.'

At last the great day came. Gwen was allowed to take her baby, well wrapped up against a chill September day, out of the baby ward and into the world at large.

A dismal world. Sunshine glinted from behind clouds

255

on a flattened landscape. Hardly a tree had survived in the city centre, there was nothing to break the awful monotony of blackened heaps of burnt wood, of the grey wreckage of stone buildings.

Mr Gower had provided a car to take her to the Imperial Hotel, a privately owned Lagonda which had come in from the safety of the country. When she stepped out of it at the hotel entrance, a welcoming group was waiting.

'Let me see . . . Oh, isn't she pretty . . . Look, she's smiling . . . No, babies so young can't smile . . .'

Tamara Hayakawa rewarded the cooing interest of the womenfolk by giving vent to loud wails of hunger.

The hotel wasn't an ideal place to look after a baby. Gwen had moved indoors, to a room on the first floor reasonably intact after the shocks, but she was always uneasy, starting up out of sleep at the least sound or movement.

Feeding the baby was difficult. Because she was premature she had to have more frequent feeds than a normal child. Gwen was constantly asking for boiled water, mixing baby milk-powder, feeding her from the bottles supplied by the hospital, trying to sterilise them for the next feed. This in the face of continual interest from the Western women in the hotel, who found the baby a wonderful change from the monotony of waiting for life to return to normal. It was hard to give Tammy the rest and quiet she needed.

It was a relief to Gwen when Mr Gower came to say that the rail link to Nara had been restored and that she would be leaving the next day. She made a round of farewells, accepted names and addresses written on scraps of paper, promised to keep in touch. In the early morning of a Friday in October, a month or so after the Tokyo earthquake, she was helped aboard the train to Nara, about two hundred miles to the south.

At first the rail journey was slow and halting. Repairs had been made to the line but even so, long stops and delays were needed. But once they left the earthquake zone the train picked up speed. The other passengers, all Japanese, nodded and smiled at each other. They, like Gwen, were refugees from the earthquake. Soon they would see friendly faces, relatives waiting to receive them. Many of them left the train at intermediate stations – Sizuoka, Nagoya.

When the wooded hills of Nara began to hold the eye, Gwen gathered her belongings together. They were wrapped in the traditional *furoshiki* and consisted entirely of items for Tammy. Willing hands helped her alight. The station was old fashioned, made of wood – but the extraordinary thing about it was that it was standing up. She could see no earthquake damage. It was strange, almost unnerving.

An elderly Japanese couple were awaiting her, holding up a placard with her name written in Japanese characters. Gwen recognised it – it was one of the first set of Japanese characters she'd learnt. She set down her *furoshiki* to have a hand free with which to wave to them.

They stared at her, bowed politely, and turned away.

'Sir!' she called. 'Madam! I am Mrs Hayakawa.'

They turned back, almost in unison. They were still staring, but this time with consternation.

'Mrs Hayakawa?' the man said in surprise.

'Yes, sent by Mr Gower of the British Embassy.'

'*Hai*,' said the man, at last accepting the truth of it. 'Welcome to Nara. Forgive my poor welcome. Gower-san did not say that . . .'

'That I was European.' She sighed and shrugged. 'Does it make a difference?'

'No, truly, how could you ask, dear lady. We have several European guests at the hotel.'

'You're from a hotel?'

'I am Kenzo Jukoro, owner of the Green Prospect Hotel. This is my wife, Jitsuko.'

'*Ikaga desu ka?*' Gwen said, bowing.

'*Okagesama de genki desu,*' said Mrs Jukoro, bowing.

'*Domo arigato gozaimashita,*' said her husband, bowing.

Honour having been satisfied all round by the exchange of polite greetings and bows, Mrs Jukoro now felt free to do what she'd wanted to do all along, take a peek at the baby.

'Oh, how beautiful! Many congratulations on your lovely child, mother-of-the-baby.'

'Thank you.' Gwen was longing to say, Can we get on? It was chilly, she was tired, she had used up all the feeds she'd made ready for the journey, and she knew that Tammy would be wailing with hunger any moment now.

Sensing it, Jitsuko Jukoro gave her husband a meaningful look. At once he led the way out. There was a *basha*, a primitive one-horse bus with tiny wheels, waiting in the pebbly roadway. Gwen was helped aboard; Kenzo Jukoro oversaw the loading of her 'luggage', then climbed in; Mrs Jukoro clambered after; and with the driver's shout of '*Oi kudasai!*' they were off.

The hotel proved to be an inn in the traditional Japanese style. The wheels of the *basha* had scarcely stopped turning before a flock of servants ran out. While Gwen was still slipping off her shoes on the steps, two coolies came round the side of the buildings carrying a pole from which two huge buckets of hot water were suspended.

'Bath ready in a moment,' suggested Mr Jukoro.

'Baby needs feeding?' suggested his wife.

Gwen nodded. She was shown at once into an upstairs room, bare as all Japanese rooms but with tiny baby garments in the Japanese style laid out on a cushion. Gwen asked for hot water to mix the Ostermilk. In a moment a servant appeared with it.

In twenty minutes Tammy was bathed, fed, changed, and sleeping peacefully on a futon, under the watchful eye of a senior female servant. Gwen was glorying in the first bath she had had for three weeks, wallowing in a full tub of hot water, her back being scrubbed for her by a wrinkled old lady smoking a clay pipe.

She slept well that night. And for the first time, Tammy slept right through to early morning.

Everything seemed better, more optimistic, here in Nara. Here there were no buildings burnt to ashes, here there was no lowering cloud of dust, no smell of cinders and smoke. Nara, a tourist centre because of its ancient temples, had felt the shock that wrecked Tokyo, but only as a deep tremor.

The Jukoros were surprised that Gwen didn't want to go sightseeing. 'You don't wish to visit Todai-ji? You don't want to see the Great Buddha?'

'Later,' said Gwen. All she wanted to do for the present was sit in the rock garden of the inn with her daughter asleep in a basket at her side.

The beginning of November came with a blaze of colour in the dwarf maples on the hills. The other European guests, two married couples, one Scottish and one Danish, went for long walks up the steep slopes to wayside temples. Gwen took lesser walks among the streets of Nara, with Tammy in her arms.

She discovered a shop catering for European tourists and holding a stock of European clothes. At last she was able to buy a pair of new shoes, to find a dress that was in the right size. She even found some French soap. She began to feel part of the civilised world again.

A letter came from Albert Gower. 'I have had word from Moko Hayakawa, your late husband's cousin. He is very eager to meet you to discuss the future. I have replied suggesting that he travels to Nara to see you and have provisionally fixed a date for 8 November. If this is unsuitable to you perhaps you would be so good as to send a wire – the telegraph office of Nara

259

is functioning although I believe the telephone service is still out of action.'

The letter ended with good wishes and enclosed notes from one or two of the Imperial's inhabitants who wanted to let her know they were moving on.

Gwen knew that Japanese family feeling made it imperative for Moko-san to see her. She felt strong enough now to face a meeting with the new head of the Hayakawa family.

She sent a wire saying she was agreeable. Then, leaving Tammy in the care of a devoted maid, she went to Nagoya, which wasn't far off, the next main station on the electric railway. Here she found the British Overseas Mercantile Bank and ascertained that her account was still in existence.

The money in it had come from the sale of the furniture she'd made in her little workshop at the side of Bright Omen. There was quite a considerable sum. She drew out enough money to have her hair done and to enjoy her first European meal – soup, meat with vegetables, coffee with cream – for over a month.

Thus strengthening her morale, she awaited the arrival of Moko Hayakawa.

He proved to be about forty, and quite a different man from Tama. This was a provincial Japanese, set in his ways. Much smaller, grey haired, clad in the customary grey kimono of the mature Japanese male, he bowed only slightly when he was shown into her room at the hotel.

This was the clue she'd been waiting for. Moko-san's view of her was the traditional Japanese one – she was first of all a female and therefore not important, she was a widow and so even less important; she was the mother of a fatherless girl-child which made her something of a nuisance.

Hence the very slight bow. She returned him one of decent respect.

The servants scuttered round placing cushions for

him, bringing tea. When at last they had bowed themselves out, Gwen poured tea. 'Please accept this slight hospitality, Moko-san. I am honoured by your visit.'

'Thank you. It is of course my duty to visit the widow of my kinsman.'

'Thank you. Did you have a good journey?'

And so on through half an hour of civilities, until at last they came to the point of his visit.

'Have you any plans for the future, Gwen-san?' he asked.

'Not so far. I have lived only from day to day, Moko-san.'

'Of course. That is a good rule. Our lives are in the hands of the Buddha.' Having uttered the prescribed approval, he went on: 'You know certainly that it is my duty as head of the family to provide for you. You are welcome to my home in Mikayo, Gwen-san, where my mother and my wife will make you welcome.'

His tone told her that the last thing in the world he wanted was for her to come to stay with his family. In the first place, she was a foreigner, who amazed him by her uncouth appearance and casual manners. His wife would be very angry if she had to put up with this woman, and his mother – now over sixty and more imperious than ever – would make life unbearable.

In the second place, this foreign woman had no money. Everything belonging to the lacquer business was gone – the buildings had disappeared into the earth, with all the goods in the showrooms and all the equipment. The house in Higashi had burned to a cinder with all its contents. True, the two pieces of land would be worth something, but as heir to the Hayakawa estate those now belonged to Moko-san. If he sold them, it would take time, for Tokyo was full of people trying to sell ruined plots of land these days. And out of the poor purchase price, he would be expected to provide the bed and board of the widow.

Then there was the child. Moko-san had looked at

the child when he arrived, and as was his duty he had praised it. But truly, it was a hideous creature, with hair the same colour as its mother's and eyes that could only bring bad luck – green eyes, like a cat's.

All of this Gwen could guess. She had never been quick at understanding people, but living in Japan for eighteen months had taught her to pick up on certain unspoken clues. Moko-san didn't like her, wanted to have nothing to do with her, and had only come to Nara to deliver this message, all conveyed with a degree of politeness that told of Moko-san's true feelings.

Gwen had allowed a little silence to follow his polite invitation to make her life with his family in Mikayo. Now she bowed, a slight bow, the bow of not only an equal but of a superior. Moko-san's eyes went wide with astonishment at the effrontery.

'Thank you, Moko-san, for your cordial offer. I shall always remember it with gratitude.'

Moko relaxed. Something in the phraseology made him think she was not going to take him up on it.

'I have decided, however, to leave Japan.'

As she said it, an immense relief welled up within her. Leave this cruel land that had taken Tama from her – yes, it was what she must do.

She would go home, to start a new life with her daughter.

Chapter Fourteen

The SS *Malwa* was extremely comfortable. Determined to do the very best she could for her tiny daughter, Gwen spent a lot of her funds on a first-class cabin. The *Malwa* was the first ship on which she was able to book passage, but as she boarded the vessel at the end of November, she was pleased with her luck.

The British Embassy had issued her with a new passport to replace the one lost in the fire of her Tokyo home. She had written to her mother and to Jerome, explaining she would be on her way as soon as possible. So far she hadn't made up her mind where she would head for – she couldn't see herself ever settling down again in St Albans with her mother and stepfather, but the idea of plunging once more into the aggressive artistic world of Paris didn't appeal to her either.

Time would tell. She had the long voyage before her in which to let a plan form. She was still, as she'd told Moko-san, living from day to day. Strength would come to her by and by, sufficient strength to make the next decision.

She had written to Moko-san, enclosing money to pay for any ceremonies thought necessary for the spiritual well-being of those members of the family who had died in the earthquake. In due course, she knew, cakes and sake would be left at the family grave in the garden of the Asakusa temple.

And that, she felt, ended all duty she might owe to Japan. Part of her heart would always be there, and perhaps she would never be free from a feeling of guilt that she had survived while so many others had perished. But she must build spiritual strength so as to make a life for her daughter.

She spent most of the first few days in the cabin, making sure that Tammy wasn't suffering any ill-effects from the voyage. All seemed well. She herself had a hard time coming to terms with the comfort of the fitments. There were two single beds in her cabin, one of which she used for the rush basket in which Tammy slept. She herself used the other, and on the first night simply couldn't sleep – she was accustomed to the hard ground under a futon, not this luxury of a sprung mattress and soft pillows.

She was having her meals brought to her cabin. When the first tray arrived, she almost automatically expected it to be set down on the floor. But the steward expertly unfolded a small table, covered it with a snowy cloth, and she found herself sitting down to a full English breakfast – porridge, eggs and bacon, hot buttered toast, and a full pot of excellent coffee.

Next morning she ordered a French breakfast, wondering what she'd get. But when it came, there it was – a *café complêt*: croissants and brioches, apricot preserves in a pretty little blue pot, and once more excellent coffee.

But this time she found she couldn't eat. Her throat closed up with tears. She found herself remembering how Tama had tried to provide her with this after she had told him she was pregnant. The whims of pregnant women had to be tolerated – and so Ota had learned to make coffee. And now Ota was gone, and Tama . . .

By day three, she'd somewhat come to terms with the delights of running water both hot and cold from brass taps, and upholstered chairs to sit on. She decided to venture up to the public rooms, and to take her meals in the dining saloon. A willing stewardess kept an eye on her sleeping baby.

On day four, a fine sunny day, she took Tammy on

deck for an airing. As usual, a group of admiring women soon collected around her, to coo over the little flailing fists and the faint sounds from the rosebud mouth that might mean pleasure.

But there were other children aboard the *Malwa*: it was a passenger liner taking people home from tours of duty abroad – from Australia and the Pacific islands. So the novelty of this tiny baby soon wore off, although some of the little girls remained faithful, hanging around in hopes of being allowed to nurse this delightful living doll, so prettily dressed in a miniature Japanese kimono.

The *Malwa*'s next port of call was Hong Kong. Since there was cargo to load and unload, she would remain there for forty-eight hours. Gwen went ashore and there, in the plentifully stocked stores, she bought the basic items of a new wardrobe. She was even able to order the making of two new dresses which would be delivered to the ship before she sailed.

She'd felt the need of some respectable clothes. Even though she wasn't the only victim of the Tokyo earthquake aboard the *Malwa*, she felt awkward going into the dining-room or the recreation lounge in the ill-fitting items she'd managed to get together in Kobe before they sailed.

She bought European baby clothes for Tammy. The first time she dressed her in the traditional fine wool nightdress with silk embroidery, she felt her eyes brim once more with unwanted tears. Her mother had sent three just like it for the baby's layette – but they were cinders now, among all the rest at the house in Tokyo.

After Hong Kong the next port would be Singapore. She found she was looking forward to it. In Hong Kong there had been almost no time to look around because of the necessary shopping. But in Singapore she would be more at liberty. She would go to see some of the sights, drink in some of the atmosphere.

What kind of furniture, she wondered, did they have in Singapore?

But the day after they left Hong Kong, Tammy was sick after her morning feed.

Gwen's first reaction was something akin to horror. Her baby had seemed so eager for life, had always been hungry and quick to feed. She had gained well since that too-quick arrival into the world.

This was the first time she'd been sick apart from the dribbles that come after ordinary feedings. Gwen, holding the baby against her towel-clad shoulder and rubbing her back as she always did, was filled with utter consternation to feel the warm flow into the towel.

She waited until the bout was over. Tammy was crying in misery. Gwen laid her down on the bath sheet with which she always covered the bed. She mopped up the worst of the after-effects, then took Tammy into her arms to soothe her.

In about half an hour she was quiet. Gwen peeled off the soiled nightgown and, though usually she didn't bathe her until mid-morning, set about the task at once.

By and by a clean and apparently tranquil infant was returned to her Moses basket. Gwen put the back of her hand against the flushed cheek. Was there a slight rise in her temperature?

Her impulse was to summon the steward and ask for the ship's doctor. But she checked herself. She mustn't get in a panic just because her baby had been sick for once. Wait until the mid-morning feed, she told herself.

Tammy woke after about an hour, crying. Gwen rocked her and soothed her until it was time for the freshly prepared bottle.

As the baby took eager hold, Gwen's spirits lifted. Everything was all right. Tammy was hungry and eager again, as always.

But almost the moment she put her baby against her

shoulder to finish the ritual, Tammy was sick. And this time when Gwen cleaned her up, she found Tammy was also suffering from diarrhoea.

This time she didn't hesitate. She pressed the bell for the steward.

It seemed a long time before Dr Paldon arrived. He and his nurse had in fact been dealing with a heart attack, so he wasn't quite in the mood to be bothered with baby colic. Young, uncertain, boyish-looking, this was his first job after qualifying.

'Well, Mrs Hayakawa, you're quite right, your baby has a slight temperature and seems a bit under the weather. I think the little tummy needs a rest, don't you? So omit the next feed, although you can give boiled water instead. And then when you get to the tea-time feed, the milk-powder should be diluted to half strength. All right?'

'Yes,' Gwen said uncertainly.

He patted her hand. Now he recalled that the lady had been in the Tokyo earthquake and the baby, according to his records, had been born two months premature. Her anxiety was perhaps understandable.

'It's quite usual for babies to have these little upsets,' he assured her. 'Everything's all right.'

But everything was not all right. Tammy continued to have diarrhoea, fed poorly at tea-time, was sick again, and was now crying almost continually except when she fell into exhausted sleep.

Dr Paldon, summoned back, began to be worried. The baby was in a visibly worse condition than she had been this morning.

'Did you take her ashore in Hong Kong?' he inquired.

She shook her head. 'I went ashore. There were things I needed to buy. I asked one of the stewardesses to look after Tammy.'

The doctor didn't say aloud that he was very relieved to hear it. Hong Kong had its insalubrious areas, where it was easy to pick up a germ or two.

'Well, we'd better put Baby on a glucose solution. I'll have my nurse make it up and bring it to the cabin. I'll make arrangements for the soiled napkins to be taken away for a soak in lysol. If you need extra supplies, we have them in sick-bay stores.'

As far as he could tell there were no signs of any of the major infections, but he wanted to keep Tamara Hayakawa isolated here in the cabin, because there were about forty children of varying ages among the passengers. How very easy it would be to pass on the baby's ailment . . .

Gwen didn't even attempt to go to bed that night. She sat up rocking her daughter, who was crying weakly almost all the time. First thing in the morning Dr Paldon reappeared. Gwen watched his face as he examined Tammy. He, not yet adept at concealing his feelings, showed his concern. Baby Hayakawa was visibly losing weight. Losing what she couldn't afford to lose, because she was only now at about her proper birth-weight.

He began to fear this was a severe case of infantile diarrhoea. How it had been contracted he couldn't imagine, since that was a disease of insanitary conditions – and aboard the ship everything was spotlessly clean. Flies, of course, had come aboard at Hong Kong – it was just possible some part of the feeding equipment had been tainted.

Gwen could read in his anxious gaze that he didn't know how to help her baby. Something like despair rose like a tide within her. What had she done? In her eagerness to get away from Japan, had she brought her baby into a greater danger than the aftermath of the earthquake?

'Mrs Hayakawa,' said Dr Paldon at last, 'we get into Singapore tomorrow. I really think it would be better if your baby was taken to hospital there. I think she needs to be nursed in sterile surroundings and though I could set those up in the sick-bay, it would be difficult.' Not to mention the fact that I'm no paediatrician, he added to himself, and don't really know how to handle this.

Gwen agreed at once with the suggestion. A radio message was sent on ahead. When the SS *Malwa* docked at Singapore, an ambulance was waiting to take Gwen Hayakawa and her daughter to the Singapore Victoria Hospital. Gwen climbed in with the wailing child wrapped in a cot blanket.

The sister of the Children's Ward was ready for action. She took Tammy at once, carried her into an examination cubicle, unwrapped her gently, laid her on a rubber-covered table, and stepped aside for the doctor.

Dr McNair had seen many a case like this. 'It's all right, Mother,' he assured Gwen. 'She's very dehydrated and her temperature has got to be brought down, but we're used to it.'

'But what's wrong with her, doctor?' begged Gwen, who had been fearing awful things such as cholera.

'It's a severe case of infantile gastro-enteritis. Some bug or other has got into her intestinal system.' He nodded at Sister, who lifted the baby to put her on the scales. He frowned. 'She was how much premature?'

'Two months.'

'And weighed how much?'

'Four pounds four ounces. She was up to over six pounds—'

'Well, I'm afraid she's gone back quite a bit. Never mind, we can deal with it. In a week or two she'll be putting it back on again. Now, now,' he said, shaking his bald head at Gwen, 'no need to get tearful.'

'It's . . . r-relief,' sobbed Gwen. 'I thought . . . I thought . . .'

'Mothers are all the same. Always think the worst. No, no, your little girl will be all right, never fear. Now as to yourself – you look like a ghost. Have you friends here to stay with?'

'No, doctor, I just got off the ship because . . .'

'Yes, I see. Well, look, if you go down to the almoner, that's on the ground floor at the back of the building, you'll see the signs . . . I say, if you go to her, she'll give you the names of some hotels.'

'But can't I stay here, with Tammy?'

'Stay here?' cried the nursing sister, scandalised. 'Certainly not. Hospitals are for sick people, Mrs Hayakawa.'

'Yes, but Tammy and I . . .'

'I know, I know, you don't want to be parted from her,' said the doctor with a little glance of reproach at the ward sister. After all, he was thinking to himself, this poor soul has come two or three thousand miles on her way home and now she's stranded in a strange city. All the same, Sister was right. You couldn't have anxious parents cluttering up hospitals. 'You can visit every day, of course. The almoner will give you all the information. There are forms for you to fill up, too. So I think you'd best get on with that, and we'll start taking care of your baby, eh?'

There seemed no alternative. Already Sister and a nurse were closing her off from the child, while Dr McNair was shepherding her out of the ward.

A Malay hospital 'boy' in spotless white took her to the almoner's office. Miss Tooley had been alerted that Mrs Hayakawa was on her way to fill in the registration papers for the baby and seek help over accommodation. Miss Tooley spoke no Japanese and was debating whether to send out for an interpreter when the boy opened the office door and in walked a bronze-haired European girl in a crumpled blue silk dress.

'Yes?'

'My name is Gwen Hayakawa, my baby Tamara—'

'You're Mrs Hayakawa?'

'Yes, and Dr McNair said—'

'I was to give you some addresses—'

'No, first please give me details about visiting hours!'

With surprise and relief Miss Tooley set about dealing

with this strange girl. She supplied immediately a card on which were printed the visiting regulations of the Singapore Victoria Hospital. Mrs Hayakawa seized it as if it were a passport to heaven.

All the formalities were quickly carried out. Only as she was rising to leave did the matter of accommodation come up again, and it was Miss Tooley who raised it.

'I understand you need a list of hotels?'

'What? Oh, yes, I suppose I do . . . Yes, please, can you tell me a few that are near the hospital?'

'Well, in fact, Mrs Hayakawa, there are no hotels in the neighbourhood. However, if you'll give me an idea of the price you would like to pay . . . ?'

'Oh . . . Well, not expensive because you see . . .' How Gwen regretted the money spent in Hong Kong on fripperies. Silk dresses made in forty-eight hours, embroidered baby clothes. How could she have been so silly?

She'd expected, of course, to be aboard ship with almost no other expenses until she reached home. And there, she knew, she could rely on a loan from her mother to tide her over.

But now . . . Now the money withdrawn from the British Overseas Mercantile would have to be stretched out until she could resume the voyage with her baby restored to health.

Miss Tooley directed Gwen to a range of private hotels and boarding houses in what might have been called the Bloomsbury of Singapore. The region round River Valley Road where the great mansions of the merchant princes had been built was now a haven for those in search of comfortable, inexpensive rooms.

Gwen took a ricksha to River Valley. For the first time, she began to be aware of her surroundings. Tanglin Road, through which she was conveyed, seemed to be the European residential district – fine houses stood back from the road behind luxuriant gardens, with white boxes at the gates for the leaving of visiting cards. She passed the gates of the Botanical Gardens, startled to see monkeys swinging through the treescape.

The trees were splendid. The contrast with Japan was amazing. There, almost every tree in the urban landscape had somehow been miniaturised or dwarfed to fit in. Here, great sweeping branches arched overhead. Catalpas with broad bright leaves, Palmetto palms thirty feet tall with roundels of blades at the top, trees with small frills of foliage two-thirds of the way up a very tall trunk, trees with greyish-green stems whose roots stood out in flanges . . .

Colour, too, was much more vibrant here. Some of the trees had scarlet blossoms, some had scented yellow trumpet-blossoms, the pink and purple of bougainvillaea was everywhere. Beneath the trees, where in England small shy flowers would have sheltered, there were brilliant leaves – coleus, ameranthus, Joseph's Coat . . .

Even when buildings began to crowd in, trees and shrubs were everywhere along the pavements. Morning glories of an incredible blue climbed up the fronts of banks, jacobina grew in tubs at architectural gateways.

Presently the ricksha boy turned his turbaned head to say something in a pidgin English Gwen could scarcely catch. It sounded like 'Rattus Isoosoosha'. She later learned he was saying Raffles Institution, in reference to an imposing white stone building they were passing.

They were now in River Valley Road. Gwen directed him to draw up in front of a large house with, in its garden, a board-sign announcing in large letters 'Leonie Guest House'.

'Wait,' she said, getting down.

The door of the guest house opened as soon as she set foot on the front steps. A Chinese girl in loose blue trousers and a white jacket bowed her indoors. There was a reception desk with a little gong. The servant struck the gong, saying gently, 'Missie please wait.'

In a moment a thin, lantern-jawed lady emerged from a bead-curtained doorway. She wore horn-rim glasses, had a pencil behind one ear, and carried an old copy of *The Times* in her hand with the page folded to the crossword.

'Yes?'

'I was given your address by the almoner at the Singapore Victoria Hospital—'

'Oh, yes, that's Miss Tooley. What can I do for you?'

'I need a room for a week or so. My little girl is in the hospital; I need somewhere to stay.'

'Quite, quite, I see. You're Mrs . . . ?'

'Hayakawa.'

Eyebrows soared up so as to be visible above the horn-rims. 'And your husband?'

'I'm a widow.' How strange it seemed to say that. A widow. It had a sad sound, lonely, wistful. Yet at that moment Gwen didn't feel weighed down by grief. Tammy was safely in hospital, the kindly staff were quite sure she'd soon be better, she was in a city where she could communicate easily, where English was spoken, where she felt at home. At that moment her world seemed bright again.

'Er . . .' said the other woman. 'You've no luggage?'

'Oh, I see. It's still aboard the *Malwa*. If you're worried, I can pay for the room in advance—'

'No, no, that won't be necessary. I'm Mrs Targett, by the way, I own this place.' A faint lightening of her expression might have been interpreted as a smile. She fanned herself with *The Times*. The faint breeze stirred Gwen's coppery hair. 'Noonday . . . Always seems hotter around now. Care for a cup of tea or coffee?'

'Oh, I'd love a cup of tea! But my ricksha—'

'That's all right, I'll see to that. Nan-cho, fetch tea quick quick and send Omar to tell the boy that mem will be a little while.'

'Yes, mem.' The Chinese girl trotted off on bare feet.

'Come in, my dear. The verandah is cooler.'

She raised a flap in the reception counter to allow Gwen past. They went through the bead curtain, through a room with a desk and a stack of old newspapers on the arm of a cane chair, and out onto the verandah.

A great expanse of smooth lawn spread down from the verandah steps to a small swimming pool. In the shade of rain-trees, one or two hotel guests were lolling in steamer chairs.

'Residential, mostly,' said Mrs Targett. 'We're fairly free and easy here. Mr Hurden, down there in the blue shirt, he's a painter – does oil-colours of the sunsets and stuff, sells 'em to the people off the cruise liners. And Miss Luke, she's here on a long biology project, classifying butterflies. You'll meet 'em if you're here for dinner tonight?'

'Thank you . . . yes . . . visiting hours in the children's ward are from three to five . . .'

They sat down, the tea appeared as if by magic – fine porcelain, silver pot, both milk and lemon on offer, sugar in lumps with tongs to pick it up. It reminded Gwen of afternoon tea at her mother's, when her mother was trying to impress the neighbours.

It became clear that Mrs Targett was avid for news. Life in Singapore, it seemed, rolled on in a leisurely fashion from day to day. Nothing much happened, so that it was interesting to come across a newcomer.

The European community was quite small and arranged in tiers – civil servants and administrators at the top, rubber-growers, mine-owners and merchants next in importance, army and navy officers in their own niche, professional men such as doctors and lawyers next, and the 'bohemians – artists and writers and archaeologists and such', as Mrs Targett described them – somewhere near the bottom of the heap.

But that didn't mean they were belittled, she explained. It just meant they were to some extent free from the social constraints of the upper ranks. 'We're a jolly crew,' she remarked. 'Not so stuffy as the nobs, if you know what I mean.'

She plied Gwen with questions. Gwen was unwilling as yet to talk about her experiences. She merely said she'd been in Japan during the recent earthquake and was now on her way home to Europe. 'My baby picked up some germ or other, so the ship's doctor advised me to stop off in Singapore to get proper attention for her.'

'Poor little thing. How old is she?'

'Ten weeks.'

'Ten weeks? You're travelling with a ten-week-old baby? I wonder the shipping line allowed you to—'

'Believe me, Mrs Targett, all difficulties of that sort were put aside to help earthquake victims get home.'

'Oh, of course. Yes, I see. More tea?' asked Mrs Targett, peering into the teapot.

'No, thanks, I must get to the ship and pack up my belongings. If you'd let me look at the room now?'

'Right-o. This way.'

They went indoors and through the cluttered office, out into a hall at the back of the reception area, and up a handsome staircase of a dark tropical wood. Gwen looked about her in admiration. The woodwork was superb, the posts and banisters splendidly carved.

'Oh, yes, not bad, is it?' Mrs Targett said, seeing her wondering glance. 'Built in the time of old Sir Stamford Raffles, this was. For a mine-owner called Perchfold, made a fortune in tin, he did. Most of the houses around here are this sort of palatial thing. Sold off, you know, when the younger generation preferred something more like *Homes & Gardens* or wanted to get to London for the bright lights and all that.'

The room she offered Gwen was on the second floor, which had perhaps been the nursery floor of the old house. It was cool and airy, big-bladed fans lazily turning in the corridor, windows shaded by wide balconies, floors of some kind of local marble.

The furnishings weren't quite up to the same standard, being mostly of what Gwen came to recognise later as 'planter style' – rattan and cane, light, and easy to move and wash down as a guard against insects. A mosquito net was folded up on a long pole over the bed, which was covered with only a thin white spread.

Gwen found it pleasing. In some ways its simplicity reminded her of the house in Tokyo, yet there was a chair with chintz cushions and a full-length wardrobe. She agreed terms, then went out to the patiently waiting ricksha.

Before she parted from her in the hall, Mrs Targett said, 'Don't forget to get a refund on your ticket, dear – when you travel on, it might not be with the same line, you see.'

It was a point that might not have occurred to Gwen. But her first duty on board was to report to Dr Paldon.

'Well, that's fine,' he said when he heard the hospital verdict. He wondered if he need have been quite so eager to shuffle off the responsibility. All the same, a death aboard ship was at all costs to be avoided – and particularly the death of a child. Far better to get the Hayakawa child into a proper hospital.

Next Gwen went to the purser's office. She explained the situation and got a form by means of which she could claim a refund from the shipping office on Collyer Quay. It was for quite a substantial sum, because she was giving up a first-class cabin. She next packed up her belongings, few though they were, and had them taken ashore.

It was then she noticed for the first time the strange spicy smell that hung in the air. She paused at the top of the gangway, sniffing.

'Unique,' said the purser, who was seeing her off. 'That's the smell of Singapore. It comes from the warehouses where the spices are stored after they come in from the Indies and points east. Some folk hate it, some folk love it. No one ever forgets it, though.'

Gwen, looking out over the expanse of jungle green and white stone, thatched roof and pagoda eaves, minaret and palm tree, decided she might very well grow to love it. But of course she wasn't going to be here long enough for that.

Chapter Fifteen

By sheer coincidence, Gwen was allowed to take her baby home on New Year's Day. She felt there couldn't have been any better beginning to 1924.

There were problems, all the same. On the previous day she'd been invited to Dr McNair's office for a consultation.

'Now, Mrs Hayakawa, I want to say a few things to you,' he began with a grimace of concentration. He glanced at notes in a file. 'In the first place, your baby's had quite a setback. She lost a lot of weight, and though she's gaining again now in a very satisfactory way, it's a check, you understand? A decided check, to a baby who was premature to begin with.'

'Yes,' Gwen said submissively. She was still blaming herself for trying to make the journey home with such a young baby. She would never forgive herself for endangering Tammy.

'So she'll need extra care for quite some time. If I remember rightly, you stopped off en route for Europe?'

'Yes, doctor.'

'So what are your plans now?'

'Well . . . To go on.'

'I see.' He gave her a frowning glance. 'If you start now, you'll arrive in Europe in the middle of winter – won't you?'

'Well . . . I suppose so.'

'There could actually be snow on the ground.'

'I . . . suppose there could.'

'Do you think it's a good idea, Mrs Hayakawa, to expose your baby to a risk like that? She'll be about four months – in actual fact, she'll be two months in real age because of being a two months prem. And she's spent one of those two months in hospital recovering from infantile gastro-enteritis. Do you really think it's a good idea to take her to the cold winds and rain – or perhaps even snow – of England?'

Gwen herself had been worried about the immediate future. Not about the weather in England, but about the voyage. She couldn't any longer afford a first-class cabin. She dreaded the thought of caring for a young baby in a shared cabin.

Now this extra consideration. Of course Dr McNair was right. She ought not to risk Tammy's health again.

'What would you recommend, then, doctor?'

'Well, if you have urgent reasons for leaving Singapore, I should break your journey en route so that you arrive home when the warmer weather is well established. But if you have nothing against Singapore itself, I'd advise you to stay on here for another six months, and even better, for a year.'

He saw her green eyes widen with surprise. Really, she seemed extraordinarily young and vulnerable to be making these big decisions on her own. He was lecturing her like a father. But he gathered there was no one else to advise her – no relatives or friends in Singapore, no husband or travelling companion with her . . .

'I know,' the doctor went on, 'that there's a legend in Europe that Singapore is an unhealthy place. I think the plays by that fellow Somerset Maugham have given quite a wrong impression, confound it. Living in the tropics doesn't mean sitting around soaking up booze and sweating. Singapore is a hardworking city, with—'

'Oh yes, I've discovered that in the short time I've been staying here,' Gwen broke in.

The people at the Leonie Guest House didn't go in

for sitting about soaking up booze and sweating. They were almost all actively engaged in some occupation from dawn (which came around six) until four in the afternoon. No siesta was taken – the British felt a siesta was a lax, foreign idea.

Around four o'clock offices closed. But the office-workers then betook themselves to the various clubs, where they played tennis or golf, or they swam, or they visited friends for afternoon tea, or dropped in at the shops. Department stores stayed open till six, shops owned by Asians or Chinese remained open until well into the night. Markets flourished all over the city where goods could be bought at midnight.

There seemed to be social gatherings every evening – dinners, cocktail parties, dances. Hotels and nightclubs flourished. Cinemas and theatres were well patronised. At weekends there were beach picnics, outings up-country, concerts, fêtes.

Certainly it was hot. It was also humid. What Gwen had come to know as the 'north-east monsoon' had been blowing since she arrived. There were rainstorms, but the rain was carried away by ditches and canals that ran alongside the roads, so that traffic was never stalled by mud – as she had seen in Tokyo.

For Gwen, humidity was no problem. Summers in Tokyo had taught her the technique of dealing with it. The pale clear skin that went with her colouring was easily parched and dried by an arid heat. But in the moisture of Singapore she felt at ease, so long as she protected herself from the burning sun by staying in the shade and wearing a wide-brimmed hat. The temperature was high, naturally – what else would you expect of a place so close to the Equator? The newspapers published the previous day's temperatures, which had surprised Gwen by being mostly in the high eighties, which was scarcely more than a heat wave in England. It *felt* hotter.

She was told by Mrs Targett that it always felt hotter

because of the humidity. If one could learn to deal with that, one could deal with the heat.

And the way to deal with the heat was not to hurry – one functioned efficiently without dashing about in a hustle. And to drink plenty of fluids – though that didn't necessarily mean hard liquor. Mrs Targett's recommendation was plenty of tea and plenty of fruit juice. Gwen had found them very effective.

It was one thing, though, Gwen thought, for an adult to learn to cope. Would a young baby be happy in this sultry atmosphere?

At the query, Dr McNair grunted with laughter. 'The Malay children seem to like it.'

'But their health is not very—'

'The degree of health of the indigenous children is to do with sanitation, not the climate,' he snorted. 'Once we get modern drainage throughout the entire municipality and not only in the European quarter, the health of the children will be assured. Good heavens, Mrs Hayakawa, hundreds of children are born to European parents in Singapore and grow up to be perfectly fit and well.'

'But they get sent home,' Gwen put in.

'That's for educational reasons, not to do with their health. Let me tell you something, Mrs Hayakawa; Singapore was originally set up as a *health* station for the East India Company. Compared with cities in India and China, it's got a clean bill of health: pure water, a good vaccination system – an effective medical department sees to that.' He paused. 'I'm sorry, I've giving you a lecture like the one I give to new medical staff on arrival. All I wanted to say was that your baby would be in less danger here for a year or so than she would in Europe. She needs building up, you know.'

'I understand.'

'And if you keep her lightly clad – just a loose gown and her nappie – she can lie on a shady verandah and be quite happy in the heat.'

Gwen tried to picture Tammy at the Leonie Guest House. Kind though Mrs Targett was in her peremptory way, she was hardly likely to want a delicate baby on the premises for long.

'I might have to find a place to live . . .'

'In that case, if you aren't particularly settled where you are, I'd recommend you to go up to the Cameron Highlands in Pahang. That's the mountain ridge, you know – runs down the middle of the Malay Peninsula. The Highlands are really very pleasant. Six months or so in the Highlands would set your child up beautifully.'

'Yes, I see. Thank you.' She felt there was no point in telling him the idea was beyond her means. Her financial troubles weren't his concern. She would have to cable home and ask her mother – that was to say, her stepfather – for money.

Although the idea was distasteful to her, for Tammy's sake she would have to do it. Gwen went straight to the cable office from the hospital, for tomorrow – New Year's Day – it would be closed for the holiday.

She'd already sent her mother one cable, soon after she arrived, to say she was staying in Singapore for a short time. She'd followed that with a letter explaining that Tammy was ill.

She'd also written to Jerome and to Frank Erender and others of the friends she'd made at the time of the earthquake. Writing letters helped fill in the time while she wasn't at the hospital visiting Tammy. The visiting hours were rigidly adhered to, so only two hours each afternoon could be spent at the side of Tammy's cot. These were the only two hours of the day that really mattered to Gwen. The rest of the time she filled up somehow – writing letters, helping Mrs Targett with her crosswords, trying to learn a few words of Malay.

One of the things she'd done was to buy clothes for Tammy, to replace the fine woollen gowns that had been ruined by attempts to sterilise them. This time there was no thoughtless spree among the European shops.

Instead she went to the market in Exchange Alley, where cheap or second-hand goods were available. There she bought cotton gowns and a crocheted shawl.

My poor little girl, she thought as she took them back to the hotel. I'll make it up to you some day.

Mrs Targett had laid on a little celebration for New Year's Eve, nothing elaborate, just some drinks and snacks. She decided to extend it into New Year's Day, so that when Gwen arrived in a taxi carrying Tammy, she found the residents lined up round a buffet lunch, waiting to offer a toast.

'Happy New Year to the baby!' they cried, raising their glasses. 'Good health! Long life! Happy New Year to the mother too!'

And in response to this sudden outburst, they got a wail of alarm from Tamara Hayakawa that almost drowned them out.

In general, though, Tammy was a 'good' baby. Tiny though she was, she'd learned from her month in hospital that she would be picked up regularly, that her need for food and comfort would be cared for, that kind hands and gentle voices could be expected.

Just as quickly, she learned that in this new place, there were more voices, that shapes coming and going were no longer clad in white, and particularly that the woman with the hair of dark sunshine would always be close at hand. She now recognised the voice that went with the glowing halo of hair – she would turn her head to look for its owner.

Everyone at the Leonie admired Tammy. Bertie Hurden declared that when she was a couple of months older, he was going to paint her: 'You're just as beautiful as any old Singapore sunset, aren't you, my precious?' he said, hanging over her basket to tickle her under her chin. Tammy smiled up at the creased, badly shaven face. And Bertie Hurden was her slave for life.

Though there had been none of the social difficulties Gwen had expected from disturbed nights and constant

284

crying, there were problems. Money was rapidly running out, and still she hadn't had a reply from her mother about a loan. She hadn't any doubt that her stepfather was being difficult and her mother, though perhaps willing to send money from her own small resources, had no idea how to go about it.

She was sitting on her balcony with a pen and paper trying to see how she could economise further, when Bertie called up from the garden. 'Don't sit there moping on this lovely evening! Come out for a walk to clear the cobwebs!'

She put the pen down, not unwilling. 'Where are you going?'

'To Chinatown. I need to order some more frames for my paintings; there's a man there who makes 'em for me. Coming? – just time before dinner.'

The rapid Singapore dusk was falling. Tammy had been bathed and fed and settled down for the evening. Gwen decided to go out. There was never any difficulty finding a baby-sitter – all the servants and most of the guests were only too willing to keep an eye on her. Nan-cho was already on the stairs volunteering for the role as Gwen came down.

Gwen and Bertie walked slowly along the banks of the grimy Singapore River, past the woodyards, the air cool as the evening breeze blew from land to sea. The creeks off the little river were busy with sampans being poled from bank to bank. Palms rustled their leathery leaves. Singapore sparrows gathered for their evening roost.

Bertie, in his crumpled whites, was a familiar figure it seemed. Men looked out from the doorways of little shops to nod good evening. 'Painted him last year,' he observed, jerking his head at an ancient Malay sitting cross-legged under a tree with a tray of betel-nut for sale. 'Sold it for ten dollars – tourists thought he was "quaint".' He frowned and smiled. He was a short, plumpish man, not given to taking himself seriously as an artist but on the other hand well aware that his work was worth something.

By and by they came to Chinatown. Here the Chinese lived in a teeming, busy throng in the lanes running off New Bridge Road and off Tanjong Pagar.

Food stalls filled the air with savoury smells. Crowds sat at the tiny tables or on upturned boxes to eat with almost birdlike movements of their chopsticks. Naphtha flares dispelled the darkness that had already fallen. Streetboys barged about with piles of boxes or with laden wheelbarrows. Children tumbled among the legs of the customers, streaked with the mud from the latest rainfall, now drying.

'Fancy a snack of anything?' Bertie asked, pausing by a sugar-cane stall.

Gwen shook her head. She had little appetite these days. Partly it was the natural reaction to a hot climate, partly it was nerves. She was almost always tense and anxious, it seemed, except when she was playing with or nursing Tammy. Money worries were always in her mind. And somehow she found she couldn't trust Nature any more – it was as if the earthquake had caused her to be ultra-sensitive to the build-up of storm clouds, the rush of rain water in the gullies after a tropical downpour, the force of the wind off the sea.

They walked on, having to push their way past hard-bargaining Malay housewives at the vegetable and meat stalls.

'Where exactly are we heading?'

'The street of the woodworkers. Funny, isn't it, how craftsmen always seem to congregate in groups?' He turned off Eu Tong Street into an even narrower way. Here the crowd was a little less dense and the babble of voices didn't quite drown the tapping of hammers, the whirring of a drill.

'This alley is full of men who make small things in wood,' Bertie went on. 'I have a deal with Kam Toon – he makes frames for me a dozen at a time, all to one pattern, and then another dozen in a different style. That way I can ring the changes on the look of my display in the gallery.'

He had a corner in a curio shop off Raffles Square, the owner taking a commission. By the time Bertie had paid for his artist's materials and his frames and paid commission, he certainly wasn't making a fortune. But as he explained to Gwen, he was happy.

'And that's what really counts, don'tcha think?' he said with his nervous smile.

They stopped outside a tiny shop lit by a naked electric bulb. At Bertie's call, an elderly bearded Chinese came from behind a bamboo screen. 'Ah, tuan, honour for my poor dwelling. Take tea? Coffee?'

Bertie glanced at Gwen, she shook her head. She was already leaning over a bench at the side of the shop, looking at the special tools used in frame-making.

'You interested, mem?' asked Kam Toon. 'These the same tools my father used. See, this bradawl – I put new handle on four years ago, but steel shaft many years, mebbe fifty.' He handled it fondly, smiling at her with black, humorous eyes. He spoke in a rapid mixture of English and Malay, a sort of pidgin that Gwen had become accustomed to by now.

'You know those bamboo frames you made last month?' Bertie intervened. 'Can you do me another dozen right away? They look just right on the fishing scenes.'

'Give sizes, please,' said the frame-maker, holding out a scrap of paper. 'Narrow bamboo or thick, tuan?'

Left to her own devices while they discussed the details, Gwen drifted around the shop, picking up chisels and punches, laying them down. How lovely it felt to have them in her hands again. Old friends, they seemed, although they were different from those she was accustomed to, an Oriental version of carpenter's tools.

After a while, since a friendly haggle was going on

over a price, she sauntered out where it was cooler. She walked along the alley, led by a familiar sound – the whirring of a lathe. And by and by she found it, a simple, almost primitive device run from what looked like an old motorbike engine.

The man who was working at it glanced up as her shadow fell in his doorway. 'Mem wants?' he asked.

He was dressed in the usual dark blue of the Chinese worker and flecked with sawdust. His black hair was bound back out of his way with a rag. His feet were bare and dusty.

A nobody, one would say. But under his hands a beautiful stave of pale wood was turning into an intricately banded table leg.

'What are you making?' Gwen asked.

'Coffee table. Mem like?'

'The wood's lovely. What is it?'

'Grey palm. Much grow here.'

'What are you going to do about the foot? Are you going to fit the end into a block?'

'Huh?' grunted the workman. He straightened, switched off the lathe. 'You know furniture?'

'I . . . well . . . I used to make it.'

'Mem make furniture?' His black eyes opened in a stare of astonishment.

'Yes, I had a business . . . In Paris . . . Well, that's in the past. But I still like to look . . .'

'Please . . . come . . . This table, make for tuan but he waves hand . . .' He demonstrated a casual wave. 'Say table must be low, have carved legs he showed how, pretty to see, must have carved top for put under glass cover. If he likes, I make two matching chairs after. But legs of table too thick for legs of chairs so how matching?'

'What kind of chairs?'

'Tuan say, low chairs, not dining chairs – but what is low, mem? And if low, how will people see legs matching table?'

'Did the tuan say where he was going to use the furniture? Living-room? Bedroom?'

'He say "lou-u-unge", mem. What is "lou-u-unge"?'

Gwen laughed. 'Another way of saying living-room, probably. Look, it seems to me the tuan wants low easy chairs—

'But not covered cloth, only wood, mem – not easy chairs—'

'Yes, yes, wooden easy chairs for lounging in – I expect he's going to pad them out with separate cushions. Look, have you a piece of paper?'

'Yes, mem.' He darted to a box behind his bench, from which he produced an old handbill.

Gwen got out her fountain pen. On the back of the bill she sketched the table leg as she saw it on the lathe, sketched four more, put a table top on it that was proportional to the length of the legs, and by a simple scribble indicated its carving. Then with quick strokes she produced an idea of a big, low, sway-backed chair with short legs extending a little out from the seat and carved to match the table.

'Ah-h . . .' said the woodworker. He patted a low stool that stood nearby. 'Not very much high, like this?'

'I'll put in the measurements,' she said. Her practised eye gave the length of the table leg on the lathe – twelve inches. Using that as guide, she put measurements on the chair. After a moment's consideration she said, 'Those bars on the chairs mean a lot of work, so you ought to ask more for making them than for the table – oh no, you're going to carve the table top.'

He put his hands together in a momentary gesture of respect, then pushed the stool forward. 'Mem, please sit. My name Wo Joong.'

'I'm Gwen Hayakawa.

'Mem Japanese?' he said, surprised once more.

'My husband was. I'm English, as it happens.'

'Mem, tuan who orders the table and mebbe orders

chairs – he comes back next week, table finished I hope. I can show drawing of chairs?'

'Of course.'

'Mem, please have tea. Or fruit juice.' He clapped his hands. A tiny girl appeared from somewhere at the back. He gave orders in Chinese dialect, probably Hailam. She vanished, to return in a moment with a jug on a tray, and two plain but clean glasses. She put this on his bench, made the little prayer-like gesture of respect, and vanished once more.

'Your daughter?' Gwen asked.

'Lin. Six years old, very plain, very stupid.'

'She's lovely! I have a daughter too – five months.'

'Five months! Very little baby! I have son eight months, Tak-lam. He will make tables, chairs, carve wood.'

'It's in your family, Mr Wo?'

'Father and grandfather, many years back. Your family woodwork?'

'My father too.'

The little girl Lin reappeared with a tray on which steamed two cups of tea.

'Please,' she said, holding it before Gwen.

Smiling, Gwen took a cup. Then her eyes strayed to the tray. 'Was this made here?' she asked.

'What, here in shop? No, no can make lacquer. This made by Lee Pan Sum, in Mengar Alley. Give as present, congratulations on birth of son after three useless daughters.' He cuffed Lin gently on the head as he said it. She grinned.

'I'm . . . I'm interested in lacquer. My husband used to make it. In Tokyo and later in Paris . . .'

'Oh, please, take, look.' He picked the other cup of tea from the tray and nodded to Lin to hand it to the lady.

Gwen took it. It was good quality, but not in the same class as the work Tama used to do. She guessed that the gleam in the outlines wasn't from real gold but from some metallic substitute. Still, it was pretty, showing a pheasant with wings partly spread over its chicks.

'Are there many lacquer-workers in Singapore?'

'Many?' Wo Joong pondered, then held up two hands with fingers spread. 'About ten, twelve? One or two good as Lee Pan Sum, others do plain work. Singapore has all kinds – Chinese workman, Malay workman, Indian workman. Do work in ivory, sandalwood, silver, make jewellery from butterfly-wing, paint on silk, make baskets, do batik, emboss leather, block print, many thing. Women make dress, embroider, weave cloth, make fans, all kinds pretty thing.'

Suddenly aware he was getting carried away, he broke off, indicating that Gwen should drink.

She did so, marvelling at the store-house of wonders that made up Singapore. In Paris she'd had to search out people who could do the special work she wanted as a finish to her furniture. Here they were all around, ready to hand and with generations of skill behind them.

Bertie Hurden appeared, carrying a parcel. 'Oh, there you are, Gwen. Better be getting back if you want a shower before dinner.'

'I suppose so.' She set down her teacup, bent to tap Lin gently on the cheek with a finger, nodded to Wo Joong. 'Thank you for the tea.'

'Thank *you*, Mrs Gwen, for drawing. Please come back, Wo family very pleased.'

'I will, I promise.' With a wave she set off.

'What was that all about?' Bertie inquired.

'I was just having a chat. What's in the parcel?'

'Sample of a new picture frame. Kam Toon's used a blond wood, rather nice, though I wonder if my showy oils don't need a dark frame. I'll show you when we get home.'

It wasn't until after the meal that he remembered the frame. He unwrapped it, but the other guests weren't interested. Only Gwen sat with the frame in her hands, admiring the workmanship.

Kam Toon had contrived a perfect thing from slender slips of different woods, all pale in colour but with the palest on the inside of the finished frame and the darkest at the perimeter. Gwen, who understood such things, knew how much care had gone into making the mitre joints at the corners. Each layer of wood must have needed a different pressure of the saw, but the cuts had been made with such delicacy that it was impossible to see the diagonal join.

A master craftsman. One among many here in Singapore. Gwen asked Bertie how much Kam Toon had charged for the frame. Ten Singapore dollars. The equivalent of ten shillings, for the knowledge that went into the selection of these lovely slivers of wood, the putting of them together, the making of the actual frame.

She thought, To make furniture here would be cheap. Pieces that in Europe would cost the earth . . . But then, who would buy them? Here in Singapore?

Well, here in Singapore someone had commissioned Wo Joong to make an unusual coffee table and, perhaps, two matching chairs. Some tuan who had an idea in his head but didn't know how to draw plans to give to a carpenter. It was she, Gwen Hayakawa, who had sketched a chair for Wo Joong to offer to the tuan as basis for the actual construction.

There were furniture shops in Singapore. Mostly they sold rattan-work, or heavy, dark, Chinese-style pieces. Robinson's the department store had furniture imported from Europe – bedroom sets, living-room suites of settee and armchairs, dining tables and matching chairs in mock Jacobean or French Empire.

What if she, Gwen Hayakawa, were to design and make pieces that had real reference to the life-style here? It was a life lived mostly in the open air – on verandahs, by the side of swimming pools, under shade trees on the lawn, alongside tennis courts under awnings. Or in the evenings, if the Singaporeans dined indoors, they sat in low-ceilinged rooms with fans revolving, with french windows open to the sea breeze.

Some people wanted to recreate their home surroundings – to remind themselves of Basingstoke or Burnley. Yet there must be many who wanted something that looked 'right' – made in local woods, easy to care for, comfortable to sit in without being too hot in this humid climate.

Perhaps something along the lines of the safari chair she'd designed in Tokyo . . .

People who lived so much outdoors wanted something easy to carry into shelter when the rain began. Something that could be folded and stacked away for an hour or so, and then brought out again ready for use in a trice.

Her safari chair, made with a variety of brightly coloured heavy cotton for the seats and backs . . . Wo Joong could make half a dozen wooden frames in a week. While he was doing so, she could find the coloured cotton for the seats and backs. Wo Joong would know how to find the women workers to stitch it.

But of course it could cost money. Wo Joong couldn't be expected to do the work on credit. And the cotton must be of the very best quality, thick and reliable and *attractive* – difficult to find, perhaps, and expensive to buy.

Gwen knew only too well how limited were the funds in her handbag upstairs. She had enough for two more weeks at the Leonie and a little extra for day-to-day needs. If her mother cabled money, it would be needed for living expenses. There was no money for setting up a furniture-making business, even on a small scale.

She would have to borrow. But from whom? She only knew the people in the Leonie Guest House, and it was clear that they were only in the Leonie Guest House because they couldn't afford anything better. Mrs Targett herself was not well off. When Gwen had faltered that she was getting short of cash,

Mrs Targett had said with heartfelt sympathy, 'Aren't we all, dear!'

But, after all, banks had money. That was what banks were for – to accept the savings of one set of people and lend it out, at interest, to others.

Tomorrow she would go to a bank and borrow some money. With this optimistic thought, she went to the kitchen to warm Tammy's late-night bottle.

Gwen was still optimistic when next morning after breakfast she set out to borrow enough to restart the firm of Veetcha Furniture.

By late afternoon when the banks closed, all optimism was gone.

'It's an interesting proposition in its way, Mrs Hayakawa, and of course the Overseas Mercantile Bank would be happy to assist you. Have you anything to offer as security?'

'Security?'

'Against the loan. A piece of property, perhaps, either here or back home in England. A house? A shop?'

'Well, no . . .'

'Insurance policy? Shares?'

'No, I'm afraid not.'

'Have you business associates who could vouch for you?'

'Not here. In Paris . . . I have a friend who has been selling some of my work . . .'

'If you could bring us some proof of sales, perhaps . . . ?'

She held the same conversation five times before the day ended. Each bank manager welcomed her with a doubtful smile, which grew even more doubtful when he discovered that she, a woman, was thinking of starting a business. The situation was clear – the banks couldn't lend her any money because she had nothing to offer as evidence of business probity, no one to stand guarantor for her.

That evening she took Marion Targett aside and explained her situation. After a few moments of blank disbelief at the idea of little lonesome Gwen Hayakawa wanting to branch out into the furniture trade, her landlady tried to be helpful.

'You could go to the moneylenders,' she suggested, rubbing her gaunt jaw thoughtfully.

'Moneylenders?'

'The Chinese. You must have seen their advertisements in the *Straits Times*. They'll lend you money on no security at all, I believe. But they charge you the earth in interest. And I believe the interest goes up the minute you start falling behind in the payments. Shrewd businessmen, the Chinese.'

Gwen frowned. 'I don't want to get into a trap like that. I want to earn a living, that's all.'

'You don't really think you can run a furniture-making business, Gwen?'

'Why not? I've done it before.'

'Honest?'

'Yes, in Paris.'

'Oh, in *Paris* – that's different, mebbe. Women don't run businesses here, Gwen. I mean, this is a man's town – supervising the rubber estates, the tin mines, the shipping lines. There's a few like me, got a little hotel or a shop, but as to setting up a business to *make* things, I dunno . . .'

'But there's money here, Marion! You can see it in the big houses, the cars, the boats sailing about in the harbour—'

'Ho yes. Plenty of money – but who's gonna lend it to a woman?' Mrs Targett sighed. ''Less you've got any rich friends?'

'I haven't any friends in Singapore, Marion. Except you and the people here.'

'Too bad we ain't rich.'

'Except . . . Wait a minute . . .' She ran upstairs to her room. Tucked away in a drawer was a cable that had come from Frank Erender in New York.

To help pass the time while Tammy was first in

295

hospital, Gwen had written letters home, to Jerome de Labasse, and to those friends she'd made at the Imperial Hotel at the time of the earthquake. She'd received a quick response both from her mother and from Jerome. Later, letters had come from Jane Bedale and Captain Beth Fairford.

From Frank there had been nothing, but that was only to be expected, because he'd sailed from Kobe to San Francisco, then had to make the long journey across the United States to New York.

About two weeks ago, a cable had arrived. 'Your letter just caught up, very anxious about you and little one. Please write again to say you OK. If any problem, contact business acquaintance Sam Prosper, Singapore. Love Frank.'

In the excitement of bringing Tammy home, Gwen had quite forgotten the cable. Now she got it out, unfolded it, and took it down to Mrs Targett's untidy office. She held it out.

'Do you know a Sam Prosper?'

'Can't say as I do, dear. "Business acquaintance", it says. What kind of business?'

'I've no idea.'

'Let's have a dekko in the phone book.' She unearthed it from under a pile of bills. 'Prosper, Prosper . . . Why, here it is!'

She leaned back to let Gwen look over her shoulder. 'Prosper Enterprises (Pte) Ltd,' she read, 'Second Floor, Orient Bdg, Orchard Road.'

'Ummm,' said Marion Targett. 'Good address. Enterprises? What does "Enterprises" mean?'

'It could mean anything. But the Orient Building is quite high class, isn't it?'

'Sure thing. Ho, yes, he must have money, this Mr Prosper.'

A few hours ago it would never have crossed Gwen's mind to go begging for help from a stranger. But after the disheartening experience with the banks, she was ready to try anything so long as she didn't have to pay the rates of interest at the moneylenders'.

'I'll go to see him tomorrow,' she announced.

'Ummm,' said Marion. 'Better give your blue silk to Nan-cho to wash and iron. Got to look your best, ain't ya?'

The Singapore business day started early, but Gwen had to bath and feed Tammy before she changed. At last, clad in a silk dress made to measure in Hong Kong, a cheap straw hat, and sandals bought in the Tamil market, Gwen set forth in a state of nerves that had her stomach clenched in knots.

The Orient Building was known to her, she'd passed it several times. Its hall was floored in stone, there was a little waterfall dropping into a pool to make coolness, there were jungle ferns in pots in the shadowy corners.

The lift took her up to the second floor. Several doors were lettered in gold: Prosper Enterprises. One had beneath the name, 'Reception'. She opened it and went in.

A slender Chinese girl was typing at a desk. She looked up smiling. 'Yes?'

'I'd like to see Mr Prosper, please.'

'Yes? Your name, please?'

'Mrs Hayakawa.'

The girl consulted an appointment book. 'Mrs Hayakawa? I don't see your name.'

'I don't have an appointment. Would you ask Mr Prosper if he'd spare me a few minutes? It's very important.'

The Chinese girl was still smiling, but with less warmth. 'May I know what it is about?'

'It's a business matter.' She certainly wasn't going to say she intended to ask for help.

'I see. Please wait.'

She came out from behind her desk, went into an inner office. From behind the thick door it was impossible to hear anything, though Gwen unashamedly tried to eavesdrop.

After a moment she emerged. 'A business matter?'

'Yes, very important.'

The receptionist went back into the room. This time she didn't quite close the door. Gwen heard her say, 'A very important matter.'

A man's voice said, 'I didn't expect them to be brought by a woman . . . All right, show her in.'

Out came the receptionist. 'This way, mem.'

'Thank you.' Gwen went past her.

There was a tall man in a well-pressed white business suit sitting behind a desk. He watched Gwen come in. A look of astonishment came into his face. He half rose.

'Mrs Hayakawa?' he said, puzzled.

'Yes. Mr Prosper?'

'I'm sorry. I was expecting a Japanese woman.'

'My husband was Japanese.'

'I see. Well, it's new for Imyo-san to use a woman as a messenger but I suppose he thought a European woman could be trusted with business matters. Have you brought them with you?'

'I beg your pardon?'

'The pearls. Have you got them with you?'

'I don't have any pearls.'

He sat back, big hands spread out on the desk. 'Why the hell not?'

Gwen gasped.

Something in her manner must have alerted Prosper. He drew in a long breath, studying her. 'You're not from Imyo-san?'

'No, I'm not. My name is Gwen Hayakawa and I'm staying at the Leonie Guest House here in Singapore. I don't know any Imyo-san.'

'I see. We-ell, let's go back and start again. You asked to see me, Mrs Hayakawa? On important business? If it's to offer pearls, I have to tell you I have an exclusive arrangement with Takameki Imyo.'

'It's not about pearls, Mr Prosper. I came on the recommendation of Frank Erender.'

'Who?'

'Frank Erender. Of the Manhattan Exchange Bank.'

There was a pause. Then Sam Prosper said, 'Yeah . . . I sort of remember him.'

Gwen's state of nerves was now close to panic. Her introduction to Mr Prosper had gone all wrong. He probably thought she'd got in under false pretences, and now he was making it clear that his acquaintance with Frank Erender was slight. Taken together with his laconic American manner, the situation was quite different from the warm reception she'd hoped for.

But though her impulse was to apologise and go, she couldn't do that. Here was a man who might help her get the money she so desperately needed to give her baby daughter a year in Singapore to recover her health. She couldn't retreat now.

'I'm sorry, we seem to have got off to a bad start, Mr Prosper,' she said, wishing he would invite her to sit down.

But he was assessing her with cool blue eyes. It was plain he didn't feel any obligation to be polite to her.

'What was the name again?'

'Gwen Hayakawa.'

'And you're a friend of Frank Erender?'

'Yes, we met in Tokyo.'

'In Tokyo. I see. When was this?'

'Last September.'

'Mrs Hayakawa – if that's your name – Tokyo was in a mess last September and still is. Frank Erender wouldn't have been there.'

'You don't need to tell me Tokyo was in a mess. Frank and I were in the middle of it, in the Imperial Hotel.'

'What?'

Her statement had given Sam Prosper a jolt. Together at the Imperial Hotel? From what he remembered of Frank, he was the last man to go jaunting at foreign hotels, even with a girl as pretty as this so-called Mrs Hayakawa. If this was a scam, she'd chosen a poor method of offering credentials. She might claim she and Frank had been lovers, but Sam would need a lot of convincing.

He found her interesting, all the same. If she was working a confidence trick, she was certainly good at it – her air of total honesty, her fresh look, the nervous way her hands clutched her purse, even the freckles across her nose . . . Everything combined to give her the appearance of youthful sincerity.

Woa there! He'd always been a sucker for redheads. And this was a redhead of a particularly appealing kind; young and fresh and gentle looking.

Gwen had been a little startled at his exclamation when she said she'd met Frank at the Imperial. She sought for a way to get on, fairly quickly, to the matter of business. She felt that once they got to that, she could recover her confidence a little. She'd been thrown by his assumption that she came carrying pearls from Japan.

'Well, so you and Frank are old friends—'

'No, no,' she interrupted. 'We only knew each other a few hours – perhaps two days in all – I don't remember, the whole things was like a dream.'

A dream love affair. How corny can you get? thought Sam. 'And this idyll took place in Tokyo in September last year?'

'Idyll?' exclaimed Gwen. 'Idyll? What on earth are you talking about? It was a nightmare! The whole city was in flames!'

Now it was Sam's turn to be at a loss. So she'd mugged up on the situation. It wasn't a story about a love affair among the cherry blossom – it was going to be how they had met and clung together in the earthquake. Well, how did the rest go?

'You're quite right, Mrs Hayakawa, Tokyo was destroyed by an earthquake at the beginning of September. So what was Frank supposed to be doing there?'

'Well, I don't quite . . . Oh yes, he mentioned he was going to have meetings at the Bank of Tokyo. But the earthquake happened just before his first lunch appointment with the officials. I think that's right.'

She seemed to be searching in her memory for the facts. She was a good actress, he had to give her that.

'Swell! He was there on banking business. And you too happened to be staying at the Imperial—'

'No, no, I was going to have lunch. I liked to get away from my mother-in-law—'

'Your mother-in-law?' Sam echoed, baffled.

'Oh, that's not important now. It's all in the past. The point is, Mr Prosper, I'm staying in Singapore now and it's imperative that I provide an income for myself and my little girl for the next year or so.'

Here it comes, here's the sting, thought Sam. To show we trust each other, let's exchange wallets – or something like that.

'An income,' he said. 'In what way, if I may ask?'

'Well, you see, I want to set up a furniture-making business, because there are some marvellous craftsmen here. But I need a fairly substantial sum of money to buy the materials—'

'You want to set up a business.' Well, that was a new one, he thought. Usually they were offering shares in a diamond mine. 'Why don't you try the bank?'

'I did that, Mr Prosper. All day yesterday. But they want something as security, or a guarantor, and as I don't know anybody in Singapore and don't own any property—'

'That's tough,' Sam said. What a sob-story. A few more words and she'd have him bursting into tears. The funny thing was, it almost seemed like it might be true.

Come on, he thought, giving himself a mental shake, you haven't knocked around the world for thirty years to be taken in by a green-eyed copperknob.

'So as I'd had this cable from Frank mentioning your name—'

'What cable from Frank?' He held out his hand for it. Just in time. If it really existed, he could still retreat from his bad-mannered welcome without too much embarrassment.

'Oh, I . . . I didn't think to bring it.'

'You didn't?'

'No, or anyhow I was in too much of a fuss, what with getting the baby settled—'

'How old is this baby?'

'Five months.'

Shucks, honey, you're a real beginner, he thought. Alone in Singapore? A refugee from the Tokyo earthquake? And now a five-month-old baby! If his arithmetic was right, that supposed baby must have been born practically in the middle of the earthquake. Oh yeah? Didn't anybody tell you to get your story right before you start?

All the same, how did she get hold of Frank Erender's name? That was odd, when you came to think of it. And how had she found out that Frank and he had known each other in days gone by?

It looked as if she must actually have met Frank somewhere. But that it had been in Tokyo at the time of the September earthquake, Sam Prosper took leave to doubt. Well, better get to the point, then throw her out.

'What kind of a sum of money did you have in mind to borrow, Mrs Hayakawa?'

'Well, I need enough to buy the materials, pay the carpenters, and tide me over until I sell the chairs.'

'The chairs. I see. So that comes to how much?'

'A lot, I'm afraid. Twenty thousand Singapore dollars.'

Twenty thousand Singapore – that equalled about four thousand American. A nicely judged sum, enough to sound like a start-up for business but too little to frighten him off.

If she thought he was going to 'lend' her anything, she was out of her mind.

'Well, now, missy,' he said, 'I've listened to enough of this rubbish. You've had ten minutes of my time and that's all you're going to get. You'll find the door behind you.'

'What?' Gwen gasped.

'Good morning, Mrs Hayakawa, or whatever you call yourself.'

'But Mr Prosper—'

'If you really thought I'd hand over twenty thousand dollars—'

'But I didn't want *money*—'

'How did you happen to latch on to Frank Erender's name? He'll be fit to be tied when I let him know you—'

'I met him in Tokyo! What's the matter with you?'

'Yeah, yeah, and I met Mata Hari in Shanghai. On your way, lady.' He pressed the bell on his desk, so that Minla came in to usher out the visitor.

Gwen was still staring stupefied at the cold-eyed Mr Prosper. 'You must be mad!' she cried. 'Do you think I've been telling you lies? Why on earth should I do that?'

'For money, dear, for money—'

'I didn't want your stupid money! I wanted you to act as guarantor at the Overseas Mercantile Bank! All you had to do was pick up the phone and—'

'And get another side of this confidence trick you've set up – no thanks. Minla, see the lady out.'

Gwen shook off the girl's hand on her arm. 'You unspeakable barbarian! How Frank could ever have been friends with you I don't know! When I write and tell him what you've done, he'll never speak to you again!'

And with that, she turned and marched out, head high and with tears streaming down her cheeks.

She'd reached the Lawn Canal before her angry steps faltered. There was a stone bench under a coral tree. She sank down on it, the strength suddenly going out of her. Her tears were still flowing. She put her head down in her hands to hide them.

A gentle touch roused her. 'Mem not well?' A thin Tamil boy was looking at her with anxiety.

She shook her head. She couldn't speak.

'Fetch drink?'

'No.'

'Brandy? Coffee?' He gestured to one side. There was a restaurant a little further along, people already sitting under its awning to have a pre-tiffin drink.

Yes, she needed a drink. She tried to get up but her knees wouldn't straighten.

'I fetch,' said the boy, holding out his hand.

She gave him money, and the moment he was gone she knew she'd been a fool to part with even a coin or two of her scarce funds. She'd never see him again.

But a few minutes later he was back. With him came a turbaned waiter. 'Mem need help?' he asked, offering a brandy on a silver tray.

'Thank you.' She gulped the drink down. It made its fiery way down her gullet. After a moment she began to feel its effect. She drew a breath. 'Thank you, I'll be all right now.'

'Take you home?' said the boy, examining her with friendly concern.

'Call me a ricksha, please.'

'Good, mem.'

The waiter stood by until the ricksha came. He helped her aboard. He refused a tip. The small boy accepted a few coins. He was still watching her as she drove away.

So much kindness, she thought, leaning back. And a few moments ago, so much heartlessness.

At the guest house Nan-cho hurried out at the sound of the ricksha wheels. She clucked in concern at the sight of Gwen's face. It was she who paid the boy – Gwen walked blindly in and up to her room.

Mrs Target was sitting on the bedroom verandah

watching over Tammy. She rose in eagerness as Gwen came into the room. 'Well, my dear, did you settle—'

But then she broke off.

'Don't ask me about it, Marion. I can't speak about it yet. Could you just leave me alone for a bit?'

'But my dear! What happened?'

'I'll tell you later. Please, Marion.'

'Didn't you see Mr Prosper?'

'Oh, I saw him,' said Gwen.

About an hour later some lunch was brought up on a tray. Gwen sent it away. Then it was time for Tammy's two o'clock feed, so it was necessary to rouse herself. She went down to the kitchen to fetch it. As she returned through the hall, Marion came out of the office. 'Feeling better?'

'A bit.'

'Can I come up and talk while you give Tammy her bottle?'

'All right, Marion.'

She went out to the verandah, brought in a chuckling, waving baby, then settled down to give her the feed. Marion stood with arms folded, watching.

'I take it you didn't get Mr Prosper's help for the money.'

'No.'

'Why not?'

'I really don't know. We started off all wrong – he thought I was a Japanese woman coming from Japan with pearls.'

'Pearls?'

'Yes. That may be his business, importing pearls – I don't know, it was impossible to tell from the office what they do. Anyhow, after the muddle at the beginning it went from bad to worse.'

'I don't understand you, Gwen. How d'you mean, bad to worse? Once you told him about Mr Erender—'

'I don't think he believed me.'

'What?'

'He seemed to think I was telling him a pack of lies.'

'You're having me on!'

'Do I look as if I was? I had a dreadful morning, Marion. I've never been spoken to like that in my entire life.'

'Like what? Whatever do you mean, dear?'

'I don't *know*!' Gwen cried. 'All I know is that if Mr Prosper came to me on his knees and offered me a million tomorrow, I wouldn't even speak to him.'

Marion Targett hadn't quite believed that Gwen could start up a business of any kind, let alone one to do with making furniture. But now that the unknown Mr Prosper had treated her badly somehow, Marion became tremendously partisan. How dare Mr Prosper speak unkindly to Gwen, how dare he cast doubts on her honesty or her ability? Of course Gwen could make a success of whatever she undertook – Marion railed on angrily.

Gwen let the spate of unfocused enthusiasm flow over her. She scarcely heard it. All she could think of was the shock of that drawling voice telling her to get out, and the cold dislike on the angular face of the man behind the desk.

She thought she ought to write to Frank Erender about it. But somehow she couldn't settle to anything. She was too shaken, too much at a loss. Instead she slept for an hour or two in the afternoon, restlessly, without benefit, waking in a shiver over she knew not what.

At dinner she tried to eat. She'd had nothing all day, having been too nervous at breakfast and beyond thinking of food at lunch. But her appetite was gone.

After the meal she went up to her room. She couldn't face an evening with the other guests, the laughing competition of card games, the gramophone playing Marion's favourite, 'In a Monastery Garden'.

About nine o'clock Nan-cho tapped on her door. 'Mem, a gentleman to see you.'

Gwen frowned. 'It's a mistake, Nan-cho,' she called.

'No, mem.' Nan-cho opened the door, looked in. 'Ask special. He wait in Mrs Targett office.'

Unwillingly Gwen pulled herself up out of her chair. She went on listless feet down the stairs.

In Marion's office the tall man from the handsome office was standing next to the desk. As she drew back on seeing him, he held out a rectangle of paper.

'Please, Mrs Hayakawa,' he said. 'I cabled Frank Erender. This is his reply.'

She took it. 'Please give Gwen Hayakawa every assistance. Any loan repaid by me. Very anxious about her. For old times' sake, Frank.'

Gwen looked up.

'Seems I made a big mistake,' Sam Prosper said. 'Can we go back and start again?'

Chapter Sixteen

Her first impulse was to crumple up the cablegram and throw it at him.

Sensing her movement he said quickly, 'Hear me out first. I owe you an apology and I'm here to make it. And of course I want to do anything I can to make it up to you.'

'I accept your apology. Goodnight, Mr Prosper.'

'No, wait, Frank says in the cable he's anxious—'

'Why should you care what Frank says? You could hardly remember him when I mentioned his name.'

'Well, it came at me from left field. I haven't thought about Frank in four or five years.'

'Then whether he's anxious or not is no concern of yours.'

He sighed. 'Look, let's sit down.' He cleared old magazines off a chair and ushered her into it. He himself perched on the edge of Marion's cluttered desk. He took a moment to collect his thoughts.

Gwen let her eyes rest upon him in open appraisal. He was a tall, angular man, the facial bones sparely covered with the tanned skin that comes from years in the tropics. His nondescript brown hair was sunbleached at the front, there was a scar on his left cheekbone. He looked to be a little over thirty years old.

'I met Frank Erender in Rangoon,' he began. 'We buddied around for about a year. Frank hated it, couldn't wait to get home. He said nothing would ever get him out east again, so when you said you'd met him in Tokyo I didn't believe it.'

Gwen had let him seat her in the chair, and she was listening. But she had made up her mind not to believe in his explanations nor to be in any way beholden to him. She could never forgive him for his manner to her that morning.

'But it's true he was in Tokyo – I see that now.'

'His bank had sent him there.' She hadn't meant to respond. She just wanted to set the record straight, that was all.

'Poor old Frank,' he said. 'He's talked into going back to the Orient, and what does he get – an earthquake!'

He laughed. She said, 'It wasn't funny, Mr Prosper.'

'No. No, of course not. I'm sorry.' He was finding this hard going. There was something unexpectedly flinty in this gentle-looking girl.

'Well, see,' he struggled on, 'after you'd marched out I got to thinking about it. I couldn't understand how you knew Frank's name and, more interesting, how you knew he and I had been friends. It seemed only Frank could have told you. But that didn't mean any of the rest of your story was true.'

'Not true? How dare you! What did you take me for?'

'I thought you were a confidence trickster.'

'A confidence trickster?'

'Sure, Singapore's full of 'em. Confidence tricksters and cardsharps.'

'Not where I live,' Gwen said with indignant disbelief.

Sam looked around the shabby office, listened to the song from the guests' lounge – a scratchy recording of 'My Rosary' now.

'No, I guess you don't see too many around here,' he said, thinking privately there wasn't enough money here to tempt a conman. 'But they stream off the liners, hang around till they make a score and move on down the line. I could point out a couple right now, in the bar at Raffles.'

'Very well, if you say so, I have to believe that was your view of me. Now, may we call this matter closed?'

'Mrs Hayakawa,' he said in desperation, 'you and Frank somehow struck up a friendship. I understand that now. This was during the earthquake?'

'Just after. He helped me look for my husband.'

'But you didn't find him?'

She shook her head. 'The earth had opened and closed over him.'

'So you're alone here in Singapore?'

'Except for my little girl.'

'You really have a five-month-old baby?'

'Asleep upstairs in a Moses basket.'

'Gee,' he said, 'you make me feel like a real heel.'

He looked so shamefaced that it was almost comic. She felt the beginnings of a smile tug at her lips.

Sam was used to negotiating. He knew every signal, every hint of response. The angry girl was beginning to weaken.

'Well now look,' he said, 'I didn't really take in what it was you were saying this morning about the money. Twenty thousand Straits dollars, wasn't it? For what?'

'To start a business.'

'What kind of a business?'

'Making furniture.'

Making furniture. That was what he thought she'd said this morning.

'What kind of furniture?' he asked, at a loss.

She shook her head. 'Listen, Mr Prosper, I've had a rotten day. It's getting on for ten o'clock when I have to settle my baby down for the night. I'm tired, and worried, and a bit bewildered by your sudden appearance here. I don't think I've got the energy to explain to you about my furniture. So let's call it a day, shall we?'

'But, look, Frank says I'm to help you. Can we meet tomorrow to talk it over?'

'All right.' She was exhausted. She couldn't sit here trying to explain herself to this man, she hadn't the strength.

'Let's say I call for you about ten o'clock—'

'Eleven. Tammy gets bathed and fed at ten.'

Good God. She was going to start a business, and it had to be run to suit the bathing and feeding of a baby?

'Eleven o'clock, then. Then we'll talk about funds for your furniture firm. Can I ask if you have experience in that line of country?'

She looked up at him. There was something in her manner – dignity, self-assurance. 'Did you ever hear of Veetcha Furniture?'

'Well no . . . But I get other people to do my interior decorating for me, so I don't know that kind of thing.'

'I understand.' She rose. 'Well, I was Veetcha Furniture, and I took Paris by storm about three years ago. And now, if you don't mind, Mr Prosper, I've got matters to attend to upstairs.'

'OK. Right. Well, it's a date for tomorrow. Eleven o'clock. And in the meantime don't worry. Everything's going to be fine.'

He stood to accompany her to the hall. He held out his hand. After a moment she took it. She shook it without warmth. Then she turned and went wearily upstairs.

Sam Prosper lived in a big airy bungalow a long way up the Tanglin Road. When he got there he went to his study, looked up the number of the guy who had seen to the interior of the house, and was put through to him.

'Rupert? Rupert, I want to ask you about something to do with furniture—'

'Furniture? Dear heart, don't tell me you've taken against that cocktail cabinet. I assure you, it's the "in" thing.'

'Rupert, are you up on Paris furniture-makers?'

'Empire, you mean? Or Baroque? Look, Sam dear, you're not the Baroque type. Please don't start changing the furniture—'

'Rupert, shut up. I want to know about present-day furniture. Is Paris important at the moment?'

'Paris is *always* important. And at the moment? My dear *man*, where have you been? *Art Déco* is sweeping the world.'

'It is? Does the name Veetcha come into it anywhere?'

'Veetcha? Veetcha? Let me pause a moment, Sam. I seem to think . . . Wasn't he the man who did the escritoire in oyster-shell? No that was Joubert. Veetcha? It does ring a bell. Can you hold on?' There was the sound of the receiver being put down. After a pause Sam heard a rustling of pages.

'Yes, Veetcha – here it is. A business office done for a manufacturer of wireless sets . . . Lo-ovely . . . I have the illustration here in front of me, Sam, in *Les Salons Modernes*. Black lacquered in gold. Stunning, but stunning!'

'Anything else?'

'Let me see – yes, over the page – a screen in the shape of four Japanese fans. Now that I'm not so keen on. Sam, if you're thinking of getting anything from Paris, don't buy that screen – it would look absolutely wrong.'

'I'm not thinking of buying anything. I'm thinking of investing money.'

'You're going to start collecting furniture? Now, Sam, I don't know whether the value of Art Deco is going to go up or—'

'I'm going to invest in making it.'

'Making it? Furniture?'

'I've just been talking to Veetcha.'

'Eh?' said Rupert Freshford, startled out of his elegance of speech.

'Veetcha. She's a girl called Gwen Hayakawa—'

'Sam, have you had too many gin slings?'

'She's here in Singapore. I don't know the whole story yet, but she wants to start up a business—'

'I thought gemstones were your business, Sam?'

'Never mind what my business is. Do I take it you think Veetcha really is important in the furniture trade?'

'Trade? Well, trade isn't quite the word. These people – in *Les Salons Modernes* and so on – they design pieces, they lead the fashion but it's a bit of a gamble whether their ideas will be suitable for the market place.'

'I get you. High class, that's it? OK. I don't mind backing a high-class design business. There are enough rich women in Singapore who'd want specially designed furniture.'

'Veetcha?' said Rupert, suddenly waking up to it. 'Here in Singapore? Really? Sam, will you introduce me?'

'Aha. You can see an angle for yourself, eh? Telling your rich ladies, "I can get Veetcha to design something for you" – that's it, isn't it?'

'Well, after all, dear heart – business is business, isn't it?'

'It sure is.'

Sam had been willing to do anything he could to help the girl who, after all, turned out to have been friends with Frank Erender. If it cost him a couple of thousand bucks or so, he'd call it conscience money. But the way she'd given the name of her design firm, the quiet dignity of her manner . . . That had impressed him.

And now Rupert bore it out. The girl had been someone. And could be again, with a little help from Sam Prosper.

Yes indeedy. Very nice to be a good Samaritan at the request of Frank Erender. Even better to get some profit out of it.

The lady in whom he was going to invest slept well

that night. Partly it was from sheer exhaustion, partly it was the release from anxiety. Mr Prosper meant what he said. He would help her get the money for her furniture-making project.

When he called for her next day, his car turned out to be a splendid Sunbeam, the very latest fast touring roadster. He drove her out of the city.

'Where are we going?' she said in alarm.

'To have lunch in a hotel along on the beach. You'll like it. It's in the shade of the palms and open to the sea breeze.'

Gwen turned to look at his profile. He was smiling in satisfaction.

'Well,' she said in a cool tone, 'it had better not be far because I have to be back by two.'

'What?' He turned his head.

'For Tammy's afternoon feed.'

The smile had vanished. He looked put out.

'In fact,' she said, 'since we're going to be talking business, I'd rather we did it in your office, and as briefly as possible.'

It was on the verge of bad manners, and she saw that it startled him. She said: 'You must forgive me. A small baby can't be left for too long.'

'But somebody's keeping an eye on her? I mean, this thing at two – somebody else could see to it?'

'Mr Prosper, my baby's a little over five months old. Of those five months she's spent about two in hospital. I want to be with her every minute I can.'

'Sure,' he said, and at the next lay-by he turned the car to drive her back.

They drove back in almost complete silence. Gwen was busy with her thoughts.

That morning she'd awakened very early. She'd put back her mosquito net then gone out on the balcony to enjoy the freshness of the pre-dawn moments. Morning stars could still be glimpsed, pale behind the tumbling clouds blown by the sea breeze.

Imperceptibly the purple clouds had turned to oyster-grey, then to a soft peach as the first light of the sun lit them from beyond the horizon. Then, majestic, the rim of the sun had appeared. The clouds became masses of beaten gold.

It was the kind of scene Tama had loved to portray in his lacquerwork. It brought him back to her again, after weeks in which he'd receded behind the screen of anxiety over their baby's illness.

At his side she'd come all the way across the world. And now he was dead. There was no one here to care for her, to support her. Under this immense golden sky Gwen felt tiny, vulnerable, utterly without strength.

Yet on her depended the life and well-being of the child sleeping in the Moses basket. She was all that Tammy had as a defence against the world.

And the world could be cruel. Nature itself – the power that sent those clouds towering up into rainstorms that beat the ground into mud, that made torrents rush down the rain gullies. Nature, which had shaken Japan as an animal shakes its wet fur.

People, too, could be cruel. Her stepfather, trying to use her for his own pleasure. Mirio-san, her dead mother-in-law, a petty tyrant.

Sam Prosper yesterday morning – callous, suspicious, hard. She must be wary of him. He had come last night full of apology and she'd relented but now, looking back, she thought he'd been patronising.

The sound of the servants moving about in their compound across the garden had roused her. She had gone back into the bedroom. Tammy was clucking and chatting to herself. She had turned back the mosquito net, lifted her out.

'Good morning, my precious. This is the morning Mummy goes to see the Big Bad Wolf.'

With her mind made up to treat him with suspicion, she had dressed carefully for her appointment. She put on her other good dress, the green one from Hong

Kong. Gloves and hat borrowed from Mrs Targett –
plain white cotton gloves, a plain white straw. About
shoes she could do nothing – she had only the old court
shoes she'd retained from her Tokyo days and two pairs
of sandals bought from the market stalls.

But when she was ready to go down to the car, she felt
she looked more like a businesswoman; she felt more
able to deal on equal terms with this alarming man.

As he drove her back into the city, she wondered if
she was being unfair to him. He'd accepted her wishes
almost without question. But better to be safe than
sorry. Keep him at arm's length.

They stepped out of the lift facing the doors with the
firm's name. She said, 'Enterprises – what exactly are
these enterprises, Mr Prosper?'

'Oh, I have a finger in several pies.' He led her in,
nodding at the receptionist who looked up in astonishment. 'We changed our minds, Minla. Bring us in some
coffee, huh?'

Once in the inner office he carried on with what he'd
been telling her. 'My main business is buying and selling
gemstones.'

'You're a jeweller?'

'I'm a merchant. I buy rubies from Burma, sapphires
from Siam and China. I sell them on to the cutters –
mostly in Amsterdam.'

'And pearls?'

'Ah.' He grinned. 'They still haven't turned up. They
were supposed to be coming from Mindanao via a
Japanese dealer, but I guess he's sold them elsewhere.'

She looked around the handsome office. Rattan
shades outside to keep the sun off the windows cast
a beige light on dark wood floor, dark wood desk,
plain white walls with one or two photographs of sailing
yachts, orchids in pots on a corner table. The blade-like
leaves of the orchids stirred a little in the breeze from
the electric fan. There was a big, dark green safe against
one wall.

'Is that where you keep the jewels?'

'Gemstones. Yes, like to see some?'

'Oh, yes please.

He turned the safe dial, opened the heavy door, took out a tray on which several bags of chamois leather were lying. 'Sapphires,' he said. He pulled open the drawstring, poured out the contents of the bag.

Gwen was disappointed. Four or five small pieces of faintly coloured rock rolled out. 'Oh,' she said.

'Look like nothing, don't they? Asteriated sapphire. Once they're polished they look like heaven viewed from the Pearly Gates. But that's not my side of it, I just get the stones and send them on.' He scooped them up, rather in the manner of a man scooping dice back into a box, poured them into the chamois bag, and pulled the string tight. He opened another, dropped two stones on the tray – undistinguished, with a greyish tinge. 'Emeralds, from Canjurgam. The best emeralds come from South America – these are unusually good for this part of the world. Worth ten thousand pounds uncut – once cut and set, worth fifty thousand.'

'Good heavens!'

'Oh, sure. Little things like these – look like sugar crystals, eh?' He scooped up the two stones, put them back in their bag, and returned the whole thing to the safe just as Minla brought in the coffee.

At his nod, the girl poured it, handed cups, offered Gwen a pretty plate with a plain napkin, and Swiss sugar biscuits. She withdrew silently. Gwen sat sipping the hot, strong brew. Excellent coffee. But she already had an idea that this man liked the best in everything.

'Now,' he said, 'since your time is limited, let's get down to business. You want to make furniture here in Singapore with a native workforce?'

'Yes, it should be easy. I have a simple design I want them to make. Look.' She delved in her handbag, brought out a sketch of the safari chair which she'd done that morning in Marion's office before breakfast.

318

He took it eagerly, looked at it. She saw his face fall. 'But this is a kind of a deck chair,' he said.

'Yes, only more comfortable, with better support for the back.'

'But . . . but I thought you made beatuiful pieces, special pieces?'

'What made you think that?' she asked, surprised.

He looked down, frowning a little. 'I had someone look up that name you gave me last night. In a book. He said there were pictures of special furniture. Black and gold for some manufacturer.'

'Ah.' Gwen let her mind go back to that glorious room – the room she and Tama had made a work of art. 'But you only do work like that on commission, Mr Prosper.'

'Well, we could put out the word. No doubt someone in Singapore would want to hire Veetcha to make something special.'

So that was it. Someone had given him an idea of her former career and now he was impressed. Now she wasn't just some nuisance of a girl recommended by Frank Erender, she was someone he could introduce to his rich friends. And someone he could make money out of, perhaps.

'I can't wait around for commissions of the kind that Veetcha used to get in Paris,' she said. 'I need something that will give quick returns.'

He was clearly disappointed. He said in a grumbling tone, 'What kind of a name is that anyway, Veetcha?'

'It's the way the Parisians said my maiden name, Whitchurch. And come to that, what kind of a name is Prosper? Is it your real name?'

'It's the name on my passport.'

That was no answer. She had a feeling he'd led a somewhat turbulent life. Truly, she had to be careful in her dealings with him. He had been a friend of Frank Erender's, but that wasn't to say he made his money by anything as straightforward as banking.

'I want to put these chairs into limited production,' she said, nodding at the sketch. 'I'm going to offer them to the furniture buyer at Robinson's department stores, on an exclusive basis. There'll be a super-exclusive version for which I'll have cotton woven to any colour and design the customer likes, or I can have their name woven in if a club or a restaurant wants them.'

Sam Prosper was impressed. No beginner in the business world, this young lady, that was clear. He opened a drawer, got out his chequebook.

'How much was it you needed? Twenty thousand?'

She drew back at the sight of that bony hand picking up a pen. 'No, no, Mr Prosper, I don't want your money.'

'But I thought—'

'No, I want you, if you will, to give me a letter promising to stand guarantor for a loan at the Overseas Mercantile Bank.'

'But Mrs Hayakawa—'

'Don't worry, you won't be called on to make good any shortfall. I'll pay back the loan in good time.'

'But I'd rather lend you the money myself—'

'And I would rather you didn't.'

Ouch. He sat staring down at his chequebook. This lady was never going to forgive him for mistaking her for a hustler.

'All right.' He put the chequebook back in the drawer, pulled a sheet of paper towards him on the blotter. 'What would you like me to say to Jimmy Martingale?'

'You know the manager personally?'

'Sure. This is a small community. All the businessmen know one another. What'll I say? This is to introduce Mrs Gwen Hayakawa for whom I am willing to stand surety in the amount of twenty thousand Singapore dollars . . . ?' He was writing as he spoke.

He handed it across. She saw he had begun it with Dear Jimmy. How easy it was between men: they met in clubs and bars, played tennis or sailed together, were on first-name terms almost at once. It was a network from which women were excluded.

'Thank you,' she said. 'If you don't mind, I'll go straight there now and get the account opened. I'd like to tell Wo Joong this evening that I want to engage him.'

'You don't waste time, I'll say that for you.'

'Mr Prosper, when you have a baby who's going to need something more than milk five times a day in the not too distant future, you can't afford to waste time.'

She had risen and was holding out her hand. 'Thank you very much, Mr Prosper.'

He shook. 'Would you do one thing for me?'

'If I can.'

'Everybody calls me Sam.'

'I see. Very well, Sam.'

But she didn't invite him to call her Gwen.

When Minla had shown her out, he picked up the telephone and asked for the Overseas Mercantile.

'Hello, Jimmy? It's me – no, it's not about the regatta. It's business. Say, Jimmy, a girl's going to call in on you any minute now – a Mrs Hayakawa. Oh, you know her?'

'She came in a couple of days ago,' replied Jimmy Martingale. 'Some daft story about setting up a furniture shop.'

'You'll be surprised, Jimmy my boy. Listen, I'm guaranteeing her loan.'

'What?'

'Don't cause her any problems. Be nice. Read my letter, tell her it's jake, open an account for her, and let her go ahead. OK?'

'You're backing her? With your own money?' Jimmy said with open scepticism.

'Don't be a smart Alec. And say, if she goes a bit into an overdraft, don't get sore at her – I'm good for it.'

There was a silence. Then Jimmy said, with a chuckle

in his voice, 'Sam, you rogue! You're always thinking up new ways of catching 'em.'

Sam said goodbye and hung up. I should be so lucky, he thought.

Within two days Wo Joong and his brothers were at work making the safari-chair frames. His elder brother's two daughters sewed on the tough cotton backs and seats. Gwen had made an appointment with the buyer at Robinson's. She took the first sample in a taxi to show him.

It was a simple lightwood frame with a brilliant blue seat and back. He was enchanted with it. When she told him he could have exclusive rights in Singapore for the first two years, he couldn't sign a contract fast enough.

Within six weeks, Veetcha Orient (Pte) Ltd were in full swing. Chairs in all the hues of the rainbow began to appear under shade trees on Singapore lawns. Super-exclusive chairs were made to special order, with patterned cotton woven by the daughters of Wo Joong's married sister. Later Gwen made up the chair with Kelantan silk; these chairs became talking-points in Singapore's drawing-rooms. She sent photographs of the chairs to Jerome de Labasse, asking him to find someone who could offer them to Les Quatre Saisons or Printemps. Within six months she was exporting to Paris, to Liberty's of London, to Bloomingdales of New York.

Veetcha . . . Everyone thought it was her name. She became weary of correcting it after the first three months or so. 'In any case,' Sam told her, 'it's no advantage to you in Singapore to be called Mrs Hayakawa. This is a very European city and Veetcha sounds vaguely Hungarian, or Russian, or something. What I mean is, it doesn't sound Oriental.'

'But it seems so disloyal to Tama . . .'

'That part of your life is closed,' he admonished

her. 'You've got to think of yourself and your little girl now.'

Sam knew it always worked if you appealed to her feelings about Tammy. For himself, Sam could take or leave the kid. She was cute enough, staggering about in the grounds of the guest house clad in little frilly knickers and a shady hat. But he liked his womenfolk somewhat older and with more curves.

Like Gwen, for instance. As Gwen settled into the Singapore life-style and recovered from the after-effects of her Tokyo experience, she grew more and more attractive. Her hair for a start . . . Redheads always seemed to him to be something special, and her redheadedness was extra-special – a rich, amber-like shade. With it went grey-green eyes that looked at you directly and honestly – no simpering, no coquettishness. And the fine pale skin, and the freckles . . . Those freckles were really fetching.

But she was always cool towards him. It took him almost a year to get to call her by her first name. And that was the date she'd set for leaving Singapore – early summer 1925, when the kiddie would have gained the right number of pounds and inches for her age. Fine thing, to get on friendly terms just as she was leaving.

Sam was damned if he was going to let her go so easily. He had fingers in a number of pies, as he'd told her at the beginning of their acquaintance. So it was no hardship for him to arrange to hire Rupert Nicholson as interior decorator for the new hotel Sam and some colleagues were financing in the Cameron Highlands, and to urge Rupert to hire Mrs Veetcha as designer of the furniture.

Rupert needed no urging. He now knew chapter and verse about Gwen's career as a designer, had admired the folding chairs that established her reputation with the department stores, and had met her now and again at social gatherings.

'My dear Mrs Veetcha, it would be such an honour to

work with you! And this hotel, you know, is the first one in the mountains – I mean, as opposed to a government rest house. We can set a standard – goodness me, yes, be trail blazers!'

'But I was just on the verge of booking passage for Europe—'

'Dear Mrs Veetcha, please put it off for a bit. Say six months—'

'But if I put it off for six months it means we'd be travelling home for the British winter . . .'

'How true, yes, utterly annihilating, the British winter! Well then, put it off for a year, which would be all to the good, because this a prestige project, you see . . . You know how the rajahs like to go up into the mountains after tapir and so forth.'

'Mr Nicholson, a shooting-box doesn't need much furnishing . . .'

'Dear lady! The owners of the Pangkor Hotel are hoping to have the Sultan of Perak as a patron, and high-ranking government officials. There could be charity balls and all kinds of things there. I do truly think, Mrs Veetcha, you'd find it very interesting to do. At least come and have a look.'

Not entirely loth, Gwen allowed herself to be persuaded. She brought Tammy and her amah with her. They were driven by a grey-bearded Malay across the Causeway from Singapore Island to the mainland, thence up the Main Trunk Road to Tapah, and from there via a winding road that took them some five thousand feet up into the mountains.

On the plain there had been rubber, but all around on the slopes were tea plantations and orange groves. It was like a sea of dark green, with here and there a clearing where stood a Malay village and its vegetable gardens.

The air was sweet and cool; streams tumbled down the mountainside. There were government rest houses signposted along side roads, with an occasional small hotel run by the indefatigable Chinese for the benefit of commercial travellers and engineers.

At the Pangkor Hotel, accommodation was available in temporary quarters. Gwen thought it a bit like camping indoors. But the water and electricity supply had been connected and enough servants were already in position to provide cleaning and catering for the painters, decorators and gardeners.

Having seen Tammy happily entertained in a paddling pool under the watchful eye of the amah, Gwen went on a tour of inspection next morning.

'I'm sure you're thinking the hotel isn't going to be very large by European standards,' the manager remarked as he ushered Gwen and Rupert into the ballroom, 'but this is to have a sprung maple floor for dancing. We'll have a resident dance-band.'

The room was large and empty. So were the 'tea verandah', the bridge room, the restaurant with tables for thirty, the library and writing-room, the outdoors dressing-room for swimmers and tennis players, and the twenty bedroom suites.

Gwen fell in love with it. In essence the building was nothing but a large, three-storeyed stone box with many large balconied windows, but its setting was dramatically beautiful. If you looked out from any of the bedrooms you saw the pinkish new foliage of coral-shower trees, you could smell the intense fragrance of the pak-lans, and already the sand paper vines were putting tendrils along the balcony rails. A little egret perched on a swinging branch of a frangipani, its plumage a creamier white among the white of the blossom.

The manager wanted the place to be open for the season of 1926, the 'season' being the months of the south-west monsoon, from May to September, when it would be hot and sticky in the lowlands. That gave them a year in which to settle on a design scheme and plan the furnishing. Rupert began a discussion of colours and textures, produced paint samples, swatches of fabric, catalogues of electric fitments.

Gwen wandered off by herself. On the edge of the grounds she stood gazing out over the mountainside. A blue haze from village cooking fires rose to meet the blue of the sky. She could see the roofs of Malay houses, roofs thatched with the leafy branches of trees now turned a rich, almost tobacco brown.

Rich brown wood . . . Plain panelled walls in the writing-room, the desks of brown wood with brass trims, armchairs with wooden arms and big squab cushions of pale green and brown . . . Satinwood for the bedroom furniture, bedheads inlaid with pale pink quartz like the blossom of the coral-shower tree, built-in wardrobes, the doors decorated, the mirrors set into the walls, edged in pink quartz . . . The ballroom should have a cream silk ceiling with wall mirrors set in red frames and with red seating, a rich red timber suggesting the copperleaf plant that grew by the roadside lower down and the benches curving like the copperleaf itself . . . Blue for the dining-room, the chairs painted the blue of this smoke haze, the seats upholstered blue and grey, the backs a curving fretwork, with table linen and crockery in white edged with grey if Rupert would agree . . .

She was still standing there, her head full of visions, when Rupert came to find her. 'What do you think, dear heart? Does anything strike a spark for you?'

She was about to say, Oh yes, let me get to my sketchbook, I've got a thousand ideas. But she checked herself. She couldn't afford to give way to enthusiasm, not without fixing a fee. She had a baby to think of.

'Can we talk money?' she asked, keeping her voice very cool.

Rupert offered his arm. 'Very shrewd, dear,' he said. But he'd seen the light in her eye. She wanted this job. And he wanted it too, knowing it would make his name among the hotel-builders of Malaya. There were plenty of new hotels to come. Cruise passengers were asking to stay over for a few days before setting off on the next part of the voyage.

Once the money side was settled, Gwen went back to Singapore to start on the designs and find the necessary work force. She would have to find the premises where the work could be done.

No problem – the bank was only too eager to advance her any money she needed. And Wo Joong could find her as many skilled craftsmen as she needed.

So the idea of going home that year simply slipped away.

The following year the same, because the Sultan of Johore came to stay in the Pangkor Hotel with his wife, who immediately fell in love with the décor and wanted her apartments in the palace at Johore Bahru totally refurnished. She *must*, she simply *must* have the designer who had made the lovely bedroom furniture at the Pangkor.

For this important assignment, Gwen sought out the lacquerist, Lee Pan Sum. She could picture the salon in the Sultanah's quarters – a shimmer of mirror-work and lacquer in the dimness behind the shuttered windows. Pictures from Malay legend, portrayed in the gleam of gold and pearl on a dark crimson background . . . Mirrors that curved and seemed to sway like the palms outside . . .

The *Straits Times*, with the permission of their Highnesses the Sultan and Sultanah, published a long article about the work Gwen was doing in the palace at Johore Bahru. Now Gwen began to be invited to parties and dinners by the upper echelon of Singapore Society. Hitherto, she knew, she'd been somewhat questionable – a Bohemian, what? Or someone engaged in trade, not quite 'quite'? But now she was a protégée of the Sultan of Johore, Sir Ibrahim himself, someone to mention to one's friends. In some ways it reminded Gwen of her début in Paris. The difference here was that she felt in complete control of her future. In Paris, she had been tumbled along on the crest of a wave that took her by surprise.

Money was never lacking these days. She rented a house out to the east of the city, at Tanjong Katong, almost on the beach. There the breeze from the sea kept the rooms cool. There Tammy could run about as free as a sea-bird on the sands. There in the morning and the evening the skies were a blaze of apricot, turquoise and topaz. The Malayan priest would sing his call to prayer at the appointed hours. The lordly eagle would soar overhead watching for his prey among the jungle birds. The stars would come out like great beacons in the blue night-sky.

What was there to go back to in Europe? Her mother had never really understood Gwen's work, and as for her stepfather, he was useful for the reproduction of her designs for sale on commission in England but otherwise sent out no urgent invitations.

Jerome de Labasse in his last letter had been saying his family wanted him to marry and produce an heir, which seemed a reasonable thing now that he was into his mid-thirties – 'time to settle down,' he said, 'and really Claudine is very suitable'.

There was no one else there for Gwen to return to. The important things in her life were here, in Singapore – her little daughter thriving and happy, her career, her reputation, her circle of new friends.

Gwen realised she had come to think of Singapore as home. If there was anything lacking it was someone to turn to for physical love and comfort. Sam Prosper sometimes seemed to be offering that, yet there was a barrier between them, something that always prevented Gwen from warming to him.

Sam remained something of a mystery to her even though he was a frequent visitor to her home. He for his part had fallen victim to Tammy's charms from the moment she toddled up to him and grabbed his trouser legs. Looking down at the baby from the length of his lanky frame, he seemed enchanted. He got down in the sand beside her, his sun-faded hair on a level with her little copperknob, and at once began helping her with her sand-castle.

He and the child seemed to understand each other perfectly. The same couldn't be said for the mother. Gwen could see that everyone else thought Sam a 'character' – a law unto himself, peculiar because of course he was 'a Yank' – but to her he always carried the cold aura of that first encounter. And what had that been about? Smuggling pearls, she thought now. Something vaguely illegal, at any rate. She couldn't be at ease with him, no matter how he seemed to want her friendship. Though she longed for the warmth of human understanding, she couldn't seek it with Sam.

Rupert Nicholson was a good friend. But Rupert wasn't interested in women. That was all right, she appreciated his talents and left him alone to lead the kind of life he preferred.

There was Bertie Hurden at the Leonie, but he was a kind of a father-figure to her; kindly, helpful, devoted to Tammy.

She could even say that Wo Joong was a friend – but so was his wife, and so were his children.

Ah, she knew she was lucky. She had friends, and she had her daughter. Between herself and Tammy there was a strong, responsive love which never failed. When she came home at the end of the day, the little girl would rush to throw herself into her mother's arms, full of stories of what she'd done today, what she'd seen, what she'd heard on the wireless set. Those precious hours until it was time to put the little girl to bed were the best in the day.

It seemed greedy to want anything more.

Yet sometimes Gwen longed for someone who would send her flowers, who would ring her and ask if she'd enjoyed the party, someone to whom she could turn under the tropical moon and feel the flare of passion as they kissed.

Such things were not for her, it seemed . . . Until she met Terence O'Keefe.

Chapter Seventeen

It was the day of Tammy's fifth birthday. The little girl had been promised a party 'after dark' – the term was very impressive to her, implying a very grown-up status. All it amounted to was a gathering of children soon after the six o'clock sunset, in the garden, with Chinese lanterns strung between the trees, tables set out on the camomile lawn, and plenty of goodies to eat.

Gwen, busy with Wo Joong over the inlay for a macassar sideboard, was called to the telephone. It was Omar, her head boy. 'Mem, ice-cream delivered – only plain ice-cream, mem. You promised *anak-mem* many different – mango, pineapple, English strawberry, I forget which. Mem, I ring Cold Storage, they say sorry mistake, please choose other now. Which, mem, please?'

'Oh, lord, Omar . . . Why didn't you just tell them to send a selection?'

'Shall do now, mem? *Anak-mem* says must be chocolate too, Cold Storage ask, plain or milk?'

Gwen sighed. Omar was a faithful servant, had been with her ever since she moved into the house at Tanjong Katong. But he suffered from an inability to make decisions. Anything you told him to do would be done to the utmost perfection in his power, but knowing whether to order milk or plain chocolate ice-cream was beyond him.

'All right, Omar, leave it with me. I want to go out in a little while anyhow. I'll drop in at the Cold Storage and see about the ice-cream.'

'Thank you, mem,' cried Omar, relief clear in his voice.

'Everything else going all right? The cake's been iced?'

'Yes, mem, Sita now puts five little roses on. Pretty. New rubber swim-toys float now in pool. Chen and Mat now hang lanterns, all pretty.'

'And the *anak-mem* – what's she doing?'

'Play with new doll. Very pleased, sing songs to it. Says her name Goola.'

She laughed. *Goola* was pidgin Malay for sugar or sweet-thing. Her little girl was fluent in three languages – in English which she learnt from her mother, in Chinese which she learnt from her amah, and in pidgin Malay, the lingua franca of Singapore.

But not in Japanese. Sometimes Gwen felt guilty about the lack of any Japanese element in her daughter's upbringing. Sam Prosper always scoffed at this feeling because, in his words, the Japanese were a dead loss. But then Sam only respected those with whom he could do business, and he'd found the Japanese difficult to deal with.

'You don't want to bother about things like her Japanese heritage,' he admonished. 'It's more important to see she fits into European society. Which means, my good woman, that pretty soon you're going to have to send the kid to school.'

'School!'

He raised his thick eyebrows at her. 'What else? She can't run about on the beach with the Malay kids for ever.'

'Oh, Sam! I couldn't bear to be parted from Tammy like that!'

He had looked at her as if she'd taken leave of her senses. 'What d'you mean? You're parted from her every day from about six in the morning to about four in the afternoon – the school day fits in there quite easily.'

'Oh! You mean school here?'

'Yeah, school here. Infant school, I think they call it. There's a good one near the Botanic Gardens, they tell me.'

'Oh, I see! I thought you meant, send her home – like some people do – to England, you know.'

'You could do that too, I guess. But five's kinda young for that, I always think. As far as I can tell, lots of Europeans send their kids to Singapore schools. Mebbe they send them home later, to get a kind of a polish on them, or for university, or what-not. But you don't have to stand weeping on the quay while Tammy sails off for Southampton – not yet, at any rate.'

After the first shock Gwen had to agree that he was right. She'd been avoiding the matter of Tammy's education, thinking always of her little girl's health and well-being. At present Tammy ran free in the garden and on the shore, learning constantly by observation. She knew the times of the tides, which sea-birds thronged on the sands, which kinds of palm trees grew along the water's edge. She knew the family history of all her playmates. She could sing every song from the record collection in the living-room.

But now she'd reached five years old it was time to start thinking about formal education. And she was so strong and wiry that there was no danger in letting her attend school with other children. She might pick up the usual childhood infections, but she would shake them off as other children did.

So Tammy had been enrolled in the Napier Infant School for the beginning of the winter term. There was no winter in Singapore, the word simply meant the term beginning in mid-September and running until December.

Gwen had expected sobs and wails when she announced it. But no – Tammy regarded it as yet another fifth birthday present.

'Shall I have a proper desk, like in the picture-books?

And a teacher with a black gown and speckackles, and a dunce's cap if I'm naughty?'

'Not quite, darling,' Gwen laughed. From her inspection she'd learned that the Napier School was somewhat more liberal than the kind of thing depicted in Tammy's story-books.

She was relieved. And yet she was grieved. Tammy was growing away from her already, reaching out to a world other than that which Gwen had built around her.

With these thoughts running through her mind, she went in the late afternoon to the Cold Storage in Raffles Square to order the ice-cream. She could rely on its immediate delivery to her home by van in a large carton of ice.

The Cold Storage was the main food emporium of Singapore. Here expatriates could find such nostalgic items as Oxford marmalade, Huntley and Palmer's biscuits, haggis for Burns' Night, Gentlemen's Relish, or jars of English fish paste. Most people telephoned their orders or sent their 'boys' to hand in shopping lists, but there were always Europeans strolling among the displays.

Gwen sorted out the problem about ice-cream, ordering milk chocolate, strawberry, banana and coconut. Then, tempted as always by the sight of things she used to take home from the grocer's in St Albans, she moved among the counters.

At one of them a tall, dark man in crumpled whites was having an argument with the salesman. 'Of course I can see it says Full Cream. What I'm asking you is, what sort of cream? I come from a land where the farms produce the richest in the world – so don't be fobbing me off with something from a herd of Dutch Friesians!'

The salesman, a young Chinese in regulation white jacket and black trousers, looked bemused. 'Tuan, please read the label. Dutch Friesians . . . there is no mention of Dutch Friesians.'

'Ach, you wouldn't know a Dutch Friesian if it mooed in your face!'

Gwen, hearing this, laughed. The customer turned his head to look at her. She saw a pair of brilliantly blue eyes in a tanned face, black brows above, black hair showing under the panama, a wide smiling mouth with even white teeth.

'There, you see, even the lady thinks it's absurd,' he said to the salesman. He raised his hat. 'Pardon me, ma'am, do you yourself ever buy and use this tinned cream?'

'Quite often.'

'UK Produce, it says. Would you be knowing what part of the UK?'

'I'm afraid not. I should imagine it's Devon, though.'

'It's a fine thing when a man has to bother a kind lady for information he ought to get from the shopman. Is it your opinion, then, ma'am, that if I were to order this for my cook, it'd make a rich fruit fool as a dessert?'

'Yes, it would do perfectly.'

'You've earned the gratitude of Terence O'Keefe, ma'am. A thousand thanks.'

With a little bow and an admiring smile, he turned back to his purchases.

Gwen went on her way. It was time to head for home. But as she drove home under the shade trees on the Kalang Road and over the bridge to Tanjong Katong, she kept seeing little glimpses of that smiling face, heard the warm lilting voice.

Terence O'Keefe . . . New in Singapore, she thought, because she hadn't heard the name before and the European community knew each other to some degree. New, too, because he was in the Cold Storage doing his own shopping. Old Singapore hands soon learned how to use the catalogue and order by telephone. A bachelor, presumably, otherwise why would he be interesting himself in the dinner menu?

At home she found Tammy swimming about like a

tadpole among the new floating toys in the pool. She went indoors to don a swimsuit and join her. Half an hour of sheer pleasure followed, mother and daughter swimming and diving in the luxury of coolness.

Then it was time for afternoon tea, always served when Gwen was home. Tammy begged for sugar biscuits. 'You'll spoil your appetite for your birthday cake,' Gwen said, holding the plate out of reach.

'No I won't, Mummy,' was the sturdy reply. And it was only too true. The child ate like a horse and never seemed to put on any surplus weight.

Afterwards they went indoors to dress. Tammy had a new party dress in pale blue cotton muslin over blue batiste, blue socks, and white sandals. Her dark tawny hair was held back in a blue bow. Looking at her as May-may ushered her in for inspection, Gwen felt her heart contract.

What a pretty child! The slender, fragile bones, the tanned cream of the skin covering them, the glowing hair softly waving under the blue band, the slanting green eyes . . . It wasn't just motherly prejudice – Tammy Veetcha looked set to be a beauty when she grew up.

Gwen herself had put on a loose cotton dress and 'sensible' shoes. She'd run a birthday party last year, so she knew what hard work it could turn out to be even with a small army of servants to help. And this year the children were all one year older, one year more energetic and ready for mischief.

Sam dropped by just as the first of the guests were arriving. Tammy greeted him with a shriek of welcome, throwing her arms around him at about jacket-pocket level – for in his jacket pocket, she'd learned, goodies were to be found.

'What did you bring me, Uncle Sam? Did you bring me a special present? It's my birfday, I'm five today – did you know?'

'I think somebody told me,' he said, detaching her

hands and holding her off. 'As to bringing you a present, I have to be sure you deserve one first.'

'Oh I do, I do-o-o!' she cried. 'I can swim ten lengths of the pool, and dive off the first step.'

'All right, all right, you're the cleverest girl in Tanjong Katong, you're always telling me so, so it must be true. Here, let's see what we have here.' He pulled from his pocket a little parcel of gilt paper.

Tammy seized it. When she'd torn off the paper, a little block of glass was revealed with beads rolling about inside. 'If you're as clever as you think you are,' Sam said, 'you ought to be able to get those beads into the holes so that they spell your name.'

'They spell Tammy?' she asked in delight.

'If you get them in the right order. So off you go, ten minutes' peace and quiet with your friends while you work at it.'

Peace and quiet wasn't likely, as they were immediately squabbling over who should hold the precious block of glass. But they wandered off to a far part of the garden.

'Well, so the party's about to begin. Braced for the onslaught?'

'I hope so. Stay a while, Sam – at least until we bring in the birthday cake. Tammy would love you to be here.'

'Not me. Nope, I just dropped by to give the brat her present. You've got everything else organised, I'm sure.'

'Well, yes, although we nearly had a disappointment over the ice-cream. By the way, when I was in the Cold Storage this afternoon . . .'

'Yes?'

She conjured up the picture of the man with the brilliant blue eyes. 'I came across a newcomer, or at least I think he was. He said his name was O'Keefe – do you know him?'

Sam shrugged. 'Know of him. He's come in to replace Messinger at Greater Malay Freight.'

Messinger had been general manager of the freight shipping line until the previous month, when an accident while out after wild pig had caused him to be invalided home. GMF was a flourishing company with branches throughout Malaya and the islands, reaching out to the east as far as Hong Kong and west to Calcutta.

So the newcomer must be a man of some standing, because GMF didn't give away managerial posts on a whim.

'He's taking over Messinger's house too?'

'Goes with the job. You spoke to him, I gather?'

'He spoke to me. He asked advice about something he was buying. That was why I asked about the house – he doesn't seem to know the ropes about housekeeping in Singapore as yet.'

'Oh, the houseboys will soon put him right. You know how they hate to have the tuan interfering in their arrangements. What's he like then, this O'Keefe?'

'Good natured . . . Irish, I imagine.'

'You don't say so, with a name like that. Well, he's got his work cut out for him. GMF's schedules are all to hell and gone since Messinger went – I don't know what that assistant manager's been doing down on the docks.'

A shriek of triumph from the far side of the lawn announced that the children had made the glassed-in beads spell Tammy. Gwen laughed. 'There goes the peace and quiet. Stay and have a drink, Sam.'

'No fear, I'm off. What happened about the school, Gwen?'

'Oh, that's all arranged. Tammy starts next week.'

He nodded, waved, and left. He had known the answer to his question before he asked it. He had been in contact with the Napier School before ever he mentioned it to Gwen. Once matters were arranged, the headmistress and owner, Miss Franks, had rung him to thank him for the recommendation. Though he wasn't sentimental about Tammy, Sam took an interest in her. Or, more correctly, he took an interest in her mother. But it didn't do to let everybody know a thing like that.

Before Tammy started school, Gwen had to buy her the school uniform. This consisted of little cotton tunics in grey and blue check with the school's monogram embroidered on the breast, white socks, white sandals, and a white straw hat with a monogrammed ribbon. There had to be a supply of aprons for 'artwork' and a minute swimming costume for swimming and 'PT'.

While shopping for these, Gwen encountered Terence O'Keefe once more. This time it was in the restaurant at Robinson's. She'd spent a long two hours arranging to have name tags woven and sewn into the new garments, as per regulations. She was dying for a cup of tea by the time she'd finished.

'May I share your table?' said a voice at Gwen's elbow. She looked round. There he was, hat in hand, smiling, waiting.

'Oh, please do.' The restaurant wasn't exactly crowded, but it was true he might have had to look about to secure a table to himself.

He sat down, the waitress hurried up. 'Tea with milk and sugar,' he said. 'Strong tea, please, and fresh milk, not tinned.'

'Yes, tuan.'

'Can't get a decent cup unless you give them precise instructions,' he said. 'Too gentlemanly, the kind of English cup of tea they serve as a rule. And the other day it turned up with lemon instead of milk – ugh!'

'Did they make it to your requirements where you were stationed before?' she inquired, making an opening for him to talk about himself.

'Ah, so you know I'm a new boy, eh? Shows, I suppose. It's always the same – you have to learn the ways of every new set-up. I was in Macao until last month – do you know Macao?'

She shook her head.

339

'Ah, it's a darlin' spot! You never have to explain anything to the servants in Macao – the Dutch trained 'em before it got taken away from them. But coffee was the polite drink there. Well, now, you're the dear lady that helped me with the cream. May I know your name?'

Gwen introduced herself, giving the name she was known by in Singapore. 'And you told me last week, you're Terence O'Keefe.'

'Ah, you remember! That's flattering. You'll be pleased to hear the fruit fool turned out a triumph. Food's a bit of a hobby with me – I don't like cooking of course, but I take an interest in the preparation – I think I've a French chef somewhere in my ancestry, maybe.'

She laughed with him. He had a way of saying things, with a tilt of his head and a lilt of his voice, that made very small jokes seem charmingly amusing.

'And now yourself, ma'am . . .' His blue glance had fallen on her left hand. 'I see you're a married lady.'

'Widowed.'

'Ah, that's a sadness. My poor mother was widowed, brought me up, bless her, single-handed. Have you children, Mrs Veetcha?'

'A little girl, Tammy – short for Tamara. She starts school next week.'

'Another sadness, I'll be bound. The first day at school is probably worse for the mother than for the child, I'm thinking. So . . . You're settled here in Singapore?'

She knew she puzzled him. Women on their own were unusual in the colonies. He probably thought she'd been married to some planter or civil servant who had died here. But then, he was wondering, why didn't she go home? That was what usually happened. Very few women elected to stay on alone in the East – or, if they did, they were snapped up in marriage within a very few months.

'I run a business,' she said. 'I design furniture.'

'Indeed?' She could tell he was staggered. 'Now, don't be misunderstanding me, but you don't have the look of a businesswoman.'

'What does a businesswoman look like, Mr O'Keefe?'

The waitress arrived with the tray of tea. The conversation was suspended while she set out everything in front of him and poured a first cup. He sipped it. 'Ah, that's the true nectar,' he said. 'Thank you, dear.'

The waitress, blushing and surprised, withdrew.

'Myself, I'm in shipping,' Terence volunteered as he set down his teacup. 'Very dull compared with your work. I never thought of it before but sure, someone has to design the furniture I buy in the shops . . . Is that what you do, design for a shop?'

'No, it's my own business. But if you go into the furniture department here, you'll see some of my products. I sell to Robinson's here and to Liberty's in London and Les Quatre Saisons in Paris—'

'Do you now! So it's the big businesswoman you are, eh? Now it's for me to apologise for being a bit disbelieving at first. I'll look for your work in the furniture department next time I'm there, and I'll be there, it's certain, for poor Messinger and his wife had a spartan outlook judging by what's left in their bungalow.'

'Well, they shipped a lot home when they left. I'm afraid you only got the bare minimum supplied by the company when you moved in. Still, it's a good house in a lovely situation.'

'Oh, you know it? Of course you do – I daresay you and the Messingers were friends, so I shouldn't say anything rude about them, eh, now?'

'No, I didn't know them well. I live out at Tanjong Katong – a little bit out of the swim, you might say. Besides, I don't socialise much.'

'That's a loss to the rest of Singapore, I've no hesitation in saying.'

She smiled and rose. She had other things to do, and

besides, she felt she was getting too friendly too fast with this silk-tongued man.

'I have to go. Glad to have met you, Mr O'Keefe.'

He had got to his feet in politeness. 'Tanjong Katong, did you say? I might find myself out that way some time, Mrs Veetcha, and beg you for a cup of good strong tea.'

'I'll tell my houseboy you need special consideration, Mr O'Keefe.'

Outside, pulling down the brim of her shady hat against the strong sunlight, she allowed herself a little grin. What a charmer! And didn't he know it! Still, he was a pleasant companion to share a cup of tea with.

Sam dropped in one evening during the following week, to find out how Tammy had taken to school life.

'Oh, she loves it. She's full of ambition to get on with "joined-up writing". May-may says she talks non-stop all the way home in the car. Mind you, she's half asleep by the time she's put into her bath. Exhausting for her, even though it's such a short day.'

'She's asleep now, I take it.'

'Oh yes, dead to the world. Like a drink, Sam?'

'Gin and a lot of lime, please.'

She clapped for Omar, gave the order. She had a feeling there was something else Sam wanted to say. But they chatted about inconsequential things until the drinks were brought.

'You know that fellow O'Keefe?' Sam said.

'Yes?'

'Is that right, you had tea with him in Robinson's?'

'Oh, the Singapore grapevine's been at work, has it? Well, yes, we had tea at the same table in Robinson's, one day last week. Why do you ask?'

'Elsa Copeland says you seemed to be enjoying yourself.'

'Why not? He's a nice man.'

Sam sipped his gin sling. 'He's had quite a step up, from the career point of view.'

'How's that?'

'Well, his last post was Macao.'

'Yes, so he said.'

'Macao's a nothing post from the shipping point of view. All the big stuff goes via Hong Kong.'

'That's true, I suppose. How nice for Mr O'Keefe to get such a big step up.'

'Word in the club is that he got it because they had to fill the gap left by Messinger at short notice. He's sort of on probation here.'

'Really? Do they do that, in shipping? I'd have thought they couldn't afford the risk—'

'I didn't mean it literally,' Sam said with some irritation. 'I meant that they'd be keeping a sharp eye on him, since he's been in lesser ports before this.'

'Under the microscope, is he?'

'In a way. So you know, Gwen, it wouldn't do him too much good to be talked about as a flirt.'

'Good heavens, Sam.' She was annoyed. Why couldn't gossips mind their own business? Just because she and Mr O'Keefe had passed the time of day in a restaurant where the idle women of Singapore were likely to see them . . .

Sam said nothing. So after a moment she continued. 'You know, Sam, if Mr O'Keefe wants to chat with me, I can't see how anyone – even employers of the strictest kind – could object to it. I'm a single woman and he's a single man.'

'Not he,' said Sam.

She felt a chill catch at her so that the hair on her arms stood up. 'What?'

'He's married. His wife's name is Molly and she's a pillar of the Catholic Church.'

'Are you sure?'

'Didn't he mention it to you?'

'No-o,' she said slowly, 'it didn't come up.'

'Married six years. Now you know why Elsa Copeland was so interested.'

'Now look here,' Gwen said in real annoyance, 'the man happened to be in the same restaurant at the same time as I was. Because we'd exchanged a few words the previous week, he asked to sit down at my table. We chatted for about five minutes.' She stopped. 'Why am I defending myself? I've a right to chat with anyone I want to.'

'Sure thing. But you like him, eh?'

'There's no law against it, Sam. I like *you*.'

'Gee, thanks, sugar.' He swallowed the rest of his drink, then pulled himself to his feet.

He had made his point and didn't attempt to press it. She knew that the eyes of Singapore were always upon her. She was *different* – a career woman in a world where there were no other career women, a woman of artistic talent where talent was rare, a woman with a strange non-English name and a daughter of decidedly exotic appearance, a woman who had lived some odd sort of life in Paris, who had a longstanding friendship with that rather questionable Sam Prosper . . .

'Won't you stay for another drink?' she offered, feeling she had to make amends for showing her annoyance.

'Sorry, got business elsewhere – a little sea trip to one of the offshore islands; somebody wants to show me some Burmese stones.'

'Sam, sometimes I think you're doing business with pirates!'

'Sometimes I think so too. Well, yo-ho-ho and a bottle of rum. Give my regards to the young scholar.'

With that he stepped down from the verandah into the darkness of the drive. She heard his footsteps receding on the sandy surface, then the sound of his car.

Omar padded in to take away the dirty glasses. She nodded when he asked if she would be ready for dinner

344

in half an hour. Slowly she went in and upstairs to shower and change.

So Mr O'Keefe was a married man.

Well, so what? Most of the men in managerial posts were married.

Yet he hadn't mentioned it.

Why should he? That was the argumentative side of her nature, taking issue over it. Why should he begin confiding his marital status?

Because he had asked hers. 'I see you're a married lady,' he'd said. So when she'd told him she was a widow he should have responded with something about himself. But he had kept the conversation on Gwen and her daughter.

But then it had been such a short conversation. Absurd to put any importance on it one way or the other.

All the same, she recalled that she'd thought he knew just how much charm he had at his command. And he had been using it on her – oh yes, he had.

She found she was very sorry to discover that she ought to have stopped him.

At a party given by the Holcrofts, she came upon Terence O'Keefe again. Not only Terence, but his wife Molly.

The first question that came to mind on meeting Molly O'Keefe was why Terence had ever married her. She was tall – taller than her husband – thin, and had a wavering air, rather like a reed in the wind. Her features were regular but almost without expression. When introduced she offered a limp hand. A greater contrast to her husband could hardly be imagined.

'Either it's the attraction of opposites,' said Elsa Copeland arching a plucked eyebrow, 'or she's got money.'

'Oh, come, Elsa, that's rather harsh.'

'My dear Gwen, you know you're never any good

at reading character. Trust me, Molly O'Keefe must
have used witchcraft or a good bank balance to get
our Terence to the altar. And as I hear she goes to
early Mass every morning, it doesn't seem likely she
used witchcraft.'

Gwen was ashamed of listening to this kind of gossip.
She knew that when she wasn't present, Elsa would be
using her as a target for her barbs. All the same, it was
strange that a man as attractive as Terence should have
such a vapid wife.

Later, finding herself alongside Molly at the buffet,
she tried to chat. She remembered how she had felt
as a newcomer to Singapore and wanted to let Molly
O'Keefe know there were friends nearby if she wanted
them.

But it soon became clear that Mrs O'Keefe didn't
want friends – especially a friend who had a child.

'It's within God's power,' she said after Gwen had
mentioned Tammy, 'to bless even the unworthy with
children, and yet deny them to the most devoted of
his flock. He has His reasons for visiting this punish-
ment upon me, no doubt, and though I have tried
to expiate any sins by my devotion, I accept His
judgement.'

Later Elsa summed her up in one phrase. 'She's a
religious nut!' she declared. 'She ought to be in a
nunnery, if you ask me.'

'Poor soul . . .'

'Poor soul nothing! A woman like that has only herself
to blame if her husband develops a wandering eye –
and speaking for myself, I hope his eye wanders in my
direction!'

'Elsa!' shrieked her friends, knowing it was expected.
'You *are* a case!'

There were songs round the piano after supper.
Terence surprised them by having a wonderful tenor
voice. He sang 'I Will Take You Home, Kathleen' and
'It All Depends On You' with an effortlessness and an

expressive tenderness that caught at the heart – at least, at the hearts of the women.

Driving home late that night, Gwen heard the echoes of the last song. 'It All Depends On You . . .' And as he sang it, his glance seemed to rest on her for a moment.

Oh, nonsense, she said to herself.

And then, more sternly: It had better be nonsense. He's a married man.

All the same, what a life he must lead, married to a woman who thought she was under the displeasure of her God.

Gwen met Terence and his wife at other social occasions. She saw them about in Singapore in the ordinary way. She heard talk about them: Molly was thinking of making the trip to Lourdes; she had given money to help the campaign for the beatification of a Catholic priest recently dead; Terence had been in a fourteen-hour card game at the club and won a hundred and two pounds; he had been seen going into Elsa Copeland's house while Jack Copeland was up-country . . . The usual Singapore gossip.

One of the most persistent pieces of gossip was that Terence was a gambler. But then, most of the Singapore men were gamblers to some degree. It was in the air here. The Chinese and the Malays were notorious for it. They would queue up in the native markets to lay their bets with the local bookmaker, pushed out of the way by busy housewives buying fish or vegetables. So Terence was no different from anyone else.

Except, Sam Prosper said, that he was having to borrow to pay his gambling debts.

'He'd better watch out,' said Sam. 'If the directors of Greater Malay Freight get to hear of it, he'll be out on his ear.'

'But why, Sam? That's unfair.'

'Not a bit. He's in charge of a lot of money, down

there on the docks. What if he were to dip into the petty cash . . .'

'Now look here, there's not the slightest suggestion that Terence is dishonest!'

'I didn't say he was. But his bosses might worry about it if they heard he had to cadge off his friends to pay for the horses that come in last.'

'His wife's got money,' Gwen said. 'At least, that's what everybody says.'

'Sure, it's true, she's from a rich Irish family. The story is she paid off all his debts just after they got hitched. I'd imagine that by now—'

'Sam, how could anybody possibly know whether that story's true?'

'Well, it makes sense. Why else did he marry her, d'you suppose?'

'Because . . . Perhaps they were childhood sweethearts . . .'

'That woman was never a child,' Sam said, laughing. 'She was born tall and skinny and with a sour expression.'

'Who said only women are catty!' cried Gwen, trying to sound stern. 'She's probably very nice, if you could only get to know her.'

'I don't want to know her. And I certainly wouldn't want to be married to her. You can't help feeling sorry for the poor guy, even though he must have gone into it with his eyes open.'

Gwen gave him a hard glance. 'Have *you* lent him money?' she asked.

'Well! By what leap of intuition did you come to that?'

'Oh, I don't know, it was just the sort of "we-men-must-stick-together" tone when you said you were sorry for him.'

'Well, I am sorry for him. But that doesn't mean I don't see his faults. And I wish you wouldn't rush to his defence quite so fast, Gwen. He's the kind of guy who can spot a soft touch a mile off.'

'I'm not a soft touch. I'm a sensible businesswoman.'

'Oh, you've got a shrewd business head on your shoulders, I admit. It's not your head I'm worried about, it's your heart.'

'My heart is quite all right, thanks.'

'Yeah,' he grunted. 'Until he decides to serenade you one dark night.'

When at last Terence decided to turn to Gwen Veetcha for help and friendship, it wasn't one dark night. It was a hot Sunday on the beach, and Tammy was sitting in the shade of the palm trees making a necklace of orchid petals. Gwen was alongside with a sketchbook, pondering on the use of smoke-grey glass in the decoration of furniture.

Along the shore on the hard sand near the waves came a figure in white duck trousers and an open-necked shirt. His dark head was bared to the sun, he was fanning himself with his panama.

'Well now,' he exclaimed, 'so this is where you live, is it? A heavenly spot, indeed.'

'Good morning! What brings you out here?' Gwen asked, scrambling to her feet. She was aware that her coarse cotton skirt was creased and rumpled, that her bare feet were coated with sand.

'Why, I've come for that cup of good strong tea you promised me, Gwen.'

How long ago it was, that little conversation in the restaurant at Robinson's. Gwen couldn't help being flattered that he still remembered it.

He said he was on his way by car to Siglar, off which one of his company's ships had gone aground. 'I suddenly remembered you said you lived at Tanjong Katong. Hope you don't mind? It's so hot, and trying to find your way up little side roads to the rocks . . . It's so frustrating, I must have been mad to do it by land when I could have gone by boat.'

She led the way into the house, Tammy dancing alongside asking questions about the grounded ship.

'Will it float off by itself? Will it have to be pulled-ed off by tugs? Uncle Sam says the tides and things are very trech-em-us.'

'And so this is Tammy,' Terence said, letting the little girl seize him by the hand and swing him along. 'What a pretty girl!'

'Yes, and Miss Nore says I'm clever too,' Tammy told him.

Gwen chuckled. 'Please don't tell her she's pretty. She's vain enough as it is. Tammy, this is Mr O'Keefe. Say how do you do.'

'How do you do, Mr O'Keefe? I'm not vain really, that's only Mummy's joke.'

'Oh, you know Uncle Sam says when you grow up you'll want to live in a hall of mirrors.'

'Uncle Sam – that's Sam Prosper?' Terence asked.

'Yes, he's Tammy's adopted uncle.'

'I envy him,' Terence said. And as his eyes rested on the lively child skipping at his side, it seemed he was giving utterance to a secret regret.

Omar appeared as they came up the steps of the back verandah. 'Now, do you really want tea, or something stronger?' Gwen inquired.

'It's too early in the day for anything stronger, thanks. Whatever my failings, I'm not one for getting gin-sodden by midday.' They sank into chairs. 'I notice you're the same,' he went on. 'At parties, when people are getting a bit lit up, I notice you're still nursing the same drink you started with.'

She shrugged. 'I've got juvenile tastes,' she confessed. 'I really prefer fruit juice to wine, and most spirits taste like cough medicine to me.'

'Now I'd have thought you were very sophisticated and knew all about wine, having lived in Paris.'

'I lived in Tokyo too, but I never acquired a taste for sake.'

Tammy decided she had been excluded too long from the conversation. 'We've got a cat with four white socks,'

she announced. 'May-may says it means he's decided
from the Emperor's cat.'

'Descended, not decided, dear,' Gwen said.

'Oh yes. Well, anyhow, May-may says he's a royal
cat. Shall I show him to you, Mr O'Keefe?'

'I'd love to see him.'

Tammy dashed off, quick and bright as a Singapore
butterfly. Gwen looked somewhat questioningly at
Terence. She was wondering why he was really here.
All this nonsense about taking by-roads so as to be able
to view the ship from the point – she didn't believe it
for a moment. But what his real motive could be, she
couldn't imagine.

The truth was, Terence needed to borrow some
money. He had borrowed from most of the men with
whom he'd grown friendly over a twelve-month in the
port, and from some of the women. Looking about for
anyone he could touch for an urgent loan of fifty pounds,
his mind had turned to Gwen Veetcha.

Until now he'd always been unwilling to wheedle
money from her. Somehow she was different. The other
women had husbands; when they handed him banknotes
he could always tell himself it was the husband's money
he was taking.

But if he borrowed from Gwen, it was her own
hard-earned funds. And somehow that seemed wrong.

Seeing her now in the quiet of her own home and
with her pretty daughter, he was conscious of a strange
pang at his heart. If only he and Molly could have had
children . . .

It had soured a marriage already a little less sweet
than he had hoped. Molly had been such a willing,
quiet, loving girl. If he had to marry someone – and
for postings abroad a wife was always considered an
asset – Molly seemed ideal.

It had all gone wrong. No children, and Molly's growing religious obsession, and the feeling that he wasn't as
big a success in business as he ought to have been . . .

Not his fault. He worked as hard as the next man, he defied anyone to say the contrary. True, he liked a flutter at the cards or on the horses. Nothing wrong with that, surely? And if the women liked his company, he'd be a fool to complain.

It irked him when dull old fellows at the club frowned after him and muttered that he ought to 'put his shoulder to the wheel'. Or when Sam Prosper looked down his nose at him. Sam Prosper – who was he to act superior? Why, everyone knew he was only an inch or two above being a crook, with his peculiar business deals and his imports of gemstones from peculiar sources.

'Mr Prosper is a close friend of yours, I gather?' he ventured.

'Oh, I wouldn't say *close* – but we've known each other a considerable time.'

'They say he made his first big stake by gun-running in China in 1920.'

If he'd thought it would shock her, he was wrong. She merely smiled and said, shaking her head, 'Nothing about Sam would ever surprise me.'

Omar arrived with the tea, and then up ran Tammy with a black and white cat bundled in her arms. Gwen poured tea, Tammy and Terence had a conversation about the royalty of cats, and an hour floated agreeably away.

'I must be going,' Terence said, getting to his feet. 'Time's getting on.' He was thinking that he'd told Molly he had work to do at the docks, that he'd be back by the time she got home from church.

'Can I come with you in your car to see the ship?' Tammy asked.

'Darling, you mustn't be a nuisance to Mr O'Keefe, he's out on business, not for fun.'

'Yes, exactly,' he agreed. 'Some other time, Tammy.'

So he left, without ever broaching the subject that had brought him. All the same, as he drove back to the city he was happy. There was something so appealing about Gwen Veetcha, something so open and decent . . .

It would be nice to have her as a friend.

Friends they became. And friends they might have remained, except that Molly decided to make the pilgrimage to Lourdes.

Chapter Eighteen

The pilgrimage meant an absence of about a year. That's to say, it hardly seemed worthwhile just to make the voyage to France for a visit to Lourdes and then come straight back. Molly would take the opportunity to go to Rome in hopes of an audience with His Holiness, and then see her family in Ireland.

This plan filtered through to the rest of Singapore society. Quite why Molly wanted to go to Lourdes, no one understood. Molly said it was in response to a hint from her confessor. Terence avoided discussion of it. Privately Gwen thought it might be in hopes of being healed of whatever ailment it was that prevented her from having a child.

She sailed on the SS *Amelia* in the spring of 1930, towards a Europe in the throes of the Depression and so worried about the possibility of war that France was building a defensive wall called the Maginot Line.

For a member of their set, there had to be the usual farewell party aboard ship, despite the fact that Molly was unpopular and most folk couldn't care less whether she went or stayed. Quite a few people backed out, sending flowers instead. In a cabin that was like a bower of blossoms, Gwen and a few others made conversation over a glass of wine, longing for the purser to call sailing time.

Molly said little. When Gwen, out of politeness, said they would miss her, Molly shrugged. 'I don't think so. I'm not the sort to fit into the trivial round.'

One or two party-goers drifted out, so as to be

able to express their feelings at that remark outside in the corridor. Gwen valiantly pressed on with the conversation. 'Of course we'll miss you, and so will Terence.'

'Really?' said Molly. 'It's always seemed to me he's found plenty to occupy him.'

'Oh, yes, running the freight line takes up—'

'I wasn't thinking of his work. I was thinking about his amusements.' Molly touched her hand to the chain of the gold crucifix which was always tucked into the neck of her dress. 'But whatever or whoever he takes up with while I'm gone, the situation remains the same. We are children of the church and must live by its laws.'

Later, when the SS *Amelia* had disappeared over the horizon and Terence had gone home to begin his bachelorhood, the well-wishers resorted to the Seaview Hotel to restore their spirits. The remark about children of the church was taken out and examined.

'What she was saying, girls,' said Arthur Bushenby, 'is that no matter how hard you try, you'll never catch Terence because she'll never divorce him.'

'Divorce!' cried Elsa. 'Who's talking about divorce? Much too messy! No, no, she wasted her time with that bit of "No Trespassing". It would be quite enough to meet our Terence under the romantic moon without imagining he and I were each going to ask for a divorce.'

'Please stop talking like that,' Gwen implored. 'Molly is her own worst enemy, I agree, but after all, they *are* married and you can't talk about her husband as if he was Casanova.'

'I don't see why not. It's what he'd like to be.'

'It's what every man would like to be, girls,' Gerald Powers sighed. 'And any pretty lady who's waiting in line for Terence can pass the time by holding *my* hand.'

'You're a fine one to talk anyhow,' Elsa rebuked her, 'after your bohemian life in Paris.' Elsa had made it her business to find out through friends in France that

'Veetcha' had been known to have at least one lover, and perhaps more.

'But it's different here. In Paris, relationships between men and women were looked upon with tolerance. Here, everybody thinks the conventions are important.'

'Not to me,' Gerald said, putting a hand on his heart and looking at her with exaggerated longing. 'I'm willing to throw my cap over the windmill if you are, Gwen.'

'Oh, I wouldn't, if I were you,' said his wife. 'Sam Prosper will send one of his smugglers after you with a cutlass if you bother poor little Gwennie.'

'Perhaps I could hire a smuggler with a cutlass to bring Terence to a secret rendezvous,' mused Elsa. 'Any idea how much it would cost?'

'You're all impossible,' Gwen laughed, and went back to finish up some odd jobs at her workshop in Chinatown.

All the same, she found it troubled her to think of Terence in the arms of any of those careless women. If he must seek comfort, why shouldn't he turn to someone who really cared for him?

Herself, for instance.

But for the next few months they ran across each other only in the ordinary way. They were present in the crowd watching the cricket on the padang, they were in the same audience in the Capitol cinema that laughed over Charlie Chaplin in *The Circus*.

At last, in September, Terence came to Tanjong Katong to see Tammy – or so he said. But Tammy had been taken up-country to start as a weekly boarder at the Highlands School for Girls.

'Now am I not a fool to have got it wrong,' said Terence. 'I heard you talking about it the other day, but I thought she didn't leave until October.'

'I'm sure you heard me talking about it. Elsa said I was becoming a terrible bore, moaning about how much I was going to miss her.'

'Oh well, then, since I've missed Tammy, perhaps this can be a visit to cheer you up, eh?'

'It's kind of you, Terence.'

'Not at all. Nice to have a chat. It gets a bit lonesome on your own.'

'Don't I know it! But Miss Nore said Tammy needs more than she can provide at the Junior School – she's a very active child, you know, likes to dash about, and in the climate here she found the other children didn't keep up with her. Up in the hills where it's cooler there'll be team games and riding and so on . . .'

She heard herself chattering on. The atmosphere was fraught with tension between them. From the moment she saw him walking up the sandy drive towards the verandah, she'd known this would be a turning point for them.

She knew there was truth in his claim, that life at home was lonesome. Although his wife and he had very differing views of life, although she had left the running of the house to the Chinese servants, there was no one there to talk to now.

But Gwen knew he hadn't come here this afternoon for a chat. For many months now they'd been heading towards this meeting.

Try as she might to hide it, she knew he had sensed the physical attraction she felt for him. She loved his flashing smile, the cheerful glint of the blue eyes, the tuneful tenor voice . . .

She didn't blame him for being 'a ladies' man'. He couldn't help his instinctive charm. He exercised it almost without being aware of it. And the women who fell for him knew what they were doing, it wasn't as if he was setting traps for innocents.

Yet he had always avoided getting entangled with Gwen. She sometimes wondered if he knew that, should it happen, it would be serious. But she was always uneasy about trying to read the feelings of others – she knew she was no good at it, and so she always waited for others to take the initiative, except in business.

Now he was here. She was almost certain he had known quite well that Tammy had left. So he had sought her out when she was alone except for the servants – and the servants lived in their own quarters on the far side of the lawn. After dinner, if she dismissed them, they would wander off to their little houses and stay there until daybreak.

Of course they would know if the tuan and the mem spent the night together. Servants always knew everything that went on. But though they passed on gossip, it was only amongst themselves.

She offered Terence a drink. He accepted. When they had been brought they sat on the verandah watching the spectacular sunset.

'You'll stay to dinner?' she asked.

'That would be a great pleasure. I hate eating alone, don't you?'

She shrugged, 'It's something I've had to get used to.'

'Ah, of course. On your own a long time now, so I hear.'

'Seven years.'

'Do you think of him still, Gwen?' he asked softly.

'Sometimes. When I'm working. He and I worked together, you know, first in Paris . . . The strange thing is, though I sometimes feel him near when I'm busy in the workshop, I can hardly remember what he looked like now.'

'Tammy takes after him?'

'Hardly at all. And though I've tried to keep his memory alive for her, she's not the least bit interested.'

She'd felt it was only right to let Tammy have knowledge of her Japanese heritage. From time to time Gwen bought Japanese magazines, which were available in the small Japanese quarter around Middle

Road and Hailam Street. She would show Tammy the beautiful illustrations and trace out for her the words in Japanese characters, wondering if the child would want to learn more about her father's land. But no, Tammy wanted to be one hundred per cent European.

But she didn't explain any of this to Terence. They were only making conversation, not really speaking of deep matters. Feeling she ought to change the subject, she asked about the shipping industry.

'Ah, that's going to rack and ruin,' Terence mourned. 'This Depression in America, you see – it's causing the devil of a downturn in trade. I hear from the planters that far less rubber is being bought because, you see, there's far less need of it if factories are closing down. So there's less cargo to go out and less freight coming in.'

'I've noticed orders are falling off for my furniture. But on the whole I make luxury goods so I expected that.'

'And from the way you say it, it doesn't trouble you.'

She thought of what life had been like for her when she first arrived in Singapore – still reeling from the emotional shock of Tama's death, of the earthquake and all it had meant. She thought of the days and nights of anxiety over her sick baby. She thought of what it had been like to be down to her last few shillings, with the rent to pay and food to buy for Tammy.

No, a downturn in trade didn't trouble her. So long as Tammy was all right, so long as she herself was able to work, nothing could frighten her. If hard times were coming, well, she would live more simply, she would turn once more to practical furniture instead of the beautiful but costly things that had made her famous.

Omar appeared to say that dinner was served. She was suddenly a little uncertain – Terence had a reputation as a gourmet among the Singapore set. But Gowa the cook had been told by Omar that the mem's guest was Tuan O'Keefe, who often criticised the food even in the city's grand restaurants. So Gowa had made a special effort.

And besides, Gwen always had good wine. Jerome de Labasse sent her cases of it from France, wines he had himself picked out. Any defects in the food were masked by the charm of the vintage Quart de Chaume, which was followed by a glass of Calvados served with the coffee. Omar beamed when Tuan O'Keefe sat back in his chair, smiling and nodding as he turned the Calvados in the glass to admire the colour.

'Thank you, Omar, that will be all.'

'Mem wishes more coffee brought?'

'Just take this out to the verandah and leave it.'

He made the little gesture of agreement with his folded hands, bowed, and after carrying the lacquered tray out to the coolness of the verandah, withdrew.

For a long time Gwen and Terence sat in the soft beams of light that came from the house. Terence lit a cheroot. The red glow swelled and faded as he smoked, but after a time he let it die out. They had talked over dinner, more Singapore chat – shipping, rubber and tin prices, who had had a party, who was planning a boating expedition. Now they were silent.

From the coconut plantations that stretched behind the house, and from the beach, the sounds of the night poured out – the croaking of frogs, the song of the cicada, the beat of the waves on the shore.

Gwen's body was relaxed, indolent. Her limbs felt heavy. The cool night air seemed to lap her about like soft silk muslin.

In the darkness she heard Terence stir. His hand reached out to find hers on the armrest of the rattan chair.

'Do you want me to go, Gwen?'

For answer she rose, still holding his hand. She gave a little pull on it, so that he came to his feet, face to face. She could see his eyes gleaming in the reflected light, feel his breath on her cheeks, smell the masculine scent of tobacco, wine, coal-tar soap.

She went on tiptoe to press her lips momentarily against his. Then, turning, she led the way indoors and upstairs.

The house whispered as they passed – the creak of floorboards, clicking of bead curtains, tapping of shoes on stair-treads. Gwen's room was in darkness, the mosquito net over the bed a ghostly wedge of white in the gloom.

Her need and her longing carried her forward on an irresistible wave. So long, so long, since a man had held her in his arms . . . She had wanted this strength, this physical ardour, had wanted to merge herself and be lost in the passion of belonging utterly.

When at last they came to themselves again, they lay in the dark with hands gently linked.

'You're wonderful, Gwen . . .'

'Ssh . . .'

'I loved you from the very first minute I saw you.'

She rolled over to kiss his shoulder in acknowledgement of the confession.

'But you were always so wary . . .'

'Not wary. Uncertain.'

'Uncertain of what? That I cared about you?'

'Uncertain about where my place would be among the rest.'

'Rest? What rest?'

'Now don't deny it, Terence. You've conquered more than one heart since you got to Singapore.'

'Oh, that's only silly gossip . . .'

'Some of it, I suppose. But it doesn't matter.'

She heard him give a little intake of breath.

'What's wrong? Did you think I expected you to swear you'd never loved anyone but me and never would again?'

'Oh, Gwen . . . ! You're so *different*!'

She laughed. 'Different from the other six, is that it? I take it it's a compliment.'

In a way part of her charm for him was this difference – this acceptance of life as it was. In a way it made her seem experienced, worldly-wise. Convention didn't seem to trouble her. He put it down to the years she'd spent in Paris where, he imagined, lovers never had to trouble about what other people thought. Sometimes when he'd listened to her in conversation with others he'd felt himself to be shallow, almost trivial by comparison.

But if she loved him, he would change. He would do anything to please this wonderful girl who had opened a new world of physical pleasure to him tonight. Her eagerness, her hunger, had been a revelation to him. All the others – and there had been others, he didn't deny he'd been a bit of a Don Juan – paled into insignificance compared with the fierce glow of Gwen's love.

They spent the short tropic night in trying to learn a little about each other. She too had others with whom to compare her partner. He was more selfish than Jerome, less skilled in sensing her desires. He was instinctively kinder than Tama, more willing to let his heart beat in time with hers. But in the end he was himself; Terence of the bright smile and strong slender body, Terence of the light rich voice that whispered words of love.

He came again the following evening, and the next. But then they agreed that they must pay some attention to the social round of Singapore. Soon enough, whispers about their liaison would start to fly. They must at least preserve the conventions, not because they cared much what people said but because they had to live and work in a society where conventions were important to others.

On the whole, the love affair between Gwen Veetcha and Terence O'Keefe was only what they'd expected. 'It's a wonder to me she held out this long,' Kathy Price said to Elsa Copeland over tea. 'He always fancied her, you know.'

'Yes, but he had the good sense not to think it

would be a one-night stand where Gwen was concerned.'

'You think it's serious?'

'As far as our Terence can be serious about anything
– yes, I think so.'

'Oh, Elsa . . . That's not a good thing!'

'I don't see why not. Molly's away at present and when
she comes back Gwen won't expect him to confront
his wife and ask for a divorce. She knows it would be
pointless.'

'It doesn't sound much fun from Gwen's point of
view,' Kathy said. She was young and held strong views
on the rights of women.

'I don't know so much. She's been awfully lonely for
a long time.'

'Lonely? She's got loads of friends!'

'Lonely for a man, I meant, Kathy.'

'But she's got that marvellous Sam Prosper—'

'No she hasn't. She and Sam are just friends.'

'Oh yes . . .'

'I mean it, Kathy. I'd take a bet those two have never
been to bed together.'

Kathy sighed and stirred her tea. 'The more fool she,'
she said.

'It's never going to happen, now Sam knows about
Terence.'

'He knows? Are you sure? He doesn't give any
sign.'

'Well, we know, don't we? And we don't give any
sign. No, no,' Elsa said, fitting a cigarette into a
holder and signalling to the houseboy for a light,
'Sam knows and accepts it. This will settle down to
be one of those long-term faithful affairs where we
always invite the two of them together to our parties
and picnics, and everyone knows they're a pair but
nobody mentions it.'

'Ha!' said Kathy. 'You've forgotten Molly. Wait till
Molly gets back!'

Molly O'Keefe's absence stretched into eighteen

months, what with the visit to her family and a
retreat spent in an Irish convent. When word came
of her embarkation for the Far East, Gwen nerved
herself to speak of it to Terence.

'Everything will be difficult once Molly is back,' she
began. 'If you want to end it between us, I would quite
understand.'

'End it?' he cried, aghast. 'For God's sake, Gwen!'

'I just feel that—'

'You know how things are between Molly and me.
From her letters, it sounds as if she's even more wrapped
up in religion than she was before she left. She's always
known I don't feel like that about the Church – she goes
her way and I go mine.'

It hadn't occurred to him that Gwen's feelings about
his wife had some weight with Gwen herself. Gently she
said, 'I have a bad conscience about deceiving her.'

'But . . . in a way . . . we won't be . . . I mean,
Molly's always known . . . That's to say . . . She and
I . . . She understands, for heaven's sake, that I'm a
perfectly normal male animal and if I don't live a normal
married life I'm quite entitled to—'

Gwen held up a hand. She gave a little shiver. 'You
mean you and she don't sleep together?'

'She's been brought up to believe,' he said, shaking his
head, 'that marriage is for the procreation of children.
Since we can't have children, she thinks it's sheer
self-indulgence to want to have pleasure together. And
Molly's against self-indulgence.'

'Oh, Terence! I'm so sorry!'

'Oh, it's something I've had to accept. But you see,
it means that you and I don't have to feel any guilt.'

'I see that,' Gwen said slowly.

It was a salve to her conscience. She wasn't taking
from Molly anything she valued.

The discussion ended there. Terence was more relieved
than he could say. He couldn't face the world without
Gwen. The trade situation was steadily getting worse so

that he'd had to take a cut in salary in order to keep his job. With Molly reinstated in the house, home life would be no great fun. Without Gwen to turn to, everything would have been unbearable.

As for Molly, she sensed as soon as she was back that her husband had found a new lady-love. Within two days some kind friend had hinted to her that the lady in question was Gwen Veetcha.

Molly thought it over: Gwen wasn't the kind of woman to cause her any trouble. On the contrary, she might even be an improvement on the others. She wouldn't expect Terence to make long and difficult journeys to up-country rubber plantations in a husband's absence; she wouldn't demand expensive presents . . .

Having told her confessor about it and received the advice to suffer patiently, Molly did just that. She thought Gwen a strange girl, different from the others, less of a pleasure-lover, busy with a business of her own, and with that strange Eurasian child to bring up.

The child, in Molly's view, was the important point. Gwen Veetcha would want a quiet life for the sake of the child.

Tammy flourished at the Highland School for Girls. She was clever enough to hold her own in class but not a 'swot'. She was good at games, earning a place in the junior basketball team and making a good beginning with tennis. But her great enthusiasm was horse-riding.

Like many another little girl, Tammy fell in love with horses. She spent all her spare time in the stables with the Malay grooms, helping to clean out the stalls and fork hay. She began to enter for junior gymkhanas, did well.

Strangely enough, it was at this point that trouble began.

Until then, the other girls at the school had accepted Tammy as one of themselves. She was pretty, but they weren't at the stage where prettiness and the ability to attract boys had entered into their lives. She was clever, but not as clever as Amy Wilkins or Dorothy Dark. She was developing a good backhand, but she wasn't a match for Lenora Sillerby.

But in the gymkhanas Tammy shone. She outdid even Rose Matthews, who was more than a year older.

Rose Matthews was the daughter of parents who liked her to succeed. When she came second in two jumping events one after the other, they looked at the winner and remarked that she was an odd-looking creature. 'Touch of chi-chi there, it's easy to see.'

Chi-chi? Rose was startled. It meant Tammy Veetcha was a half-caste.

But of course – that strange name, not English, probably Siamese or something funny like that. And those slanty eyes! Why hadn't it occurred to her before that her schoolmate was a half-breed?

Any stick to beat her with would have been welcome. But this one was a good, thick stick. Life was hard for Eurasians in Malaya unless they knew their place. And their place certainly wasn't at an expensive girls' school, nor on the back of the pony first over the winning fence.

Gwen became aware of the problem only gradually. First Tammy wasn't eager to go back after the weekend break, then she began to mutter that she hated school up in the mountains, why couldn't she go to school in Singapore?

Gwen went to see the principal. Yes, alas, there was some prejudice, hard to say how it had come about because until a few months ago Tammy had been well accepted. Yes, perhaps it would be better if Mrs Veetcha took her elsewhere.

Tammy started at a school in the Tanglin area of Singapore. But because she was nervous now, she didn't make friends. The other girls thought she was stuck-up because she was pretty. They invented a name for her

– Chinky. Tammy grew nervy, suffered stomach upsets when it was time for her to be driven to school each morning. Gwen was immediately alarmed.

'Now, now, Mrs Veetcha, there's nothing wrong with the child,' the doctor soothed. 'She's a bit tense, but that may be due to anything – settling into a new school, or the weather . . . I always think people get edgy just before the monsoon breaks.'

'But as a baby she had enteric fever—'

'Yes, yes, I'm aware of that. Believe me, it's nothing of that kind. It's just some little phase – part of growing up, perhaps.'

Gwen was extremely anxious. Why couldn't this fool of a man see that something was seriously wrong with Tammy? From a bright, confident child she'd turned into a sickly little ghost in a few months.

'How old is the child?' Dr Clandon inquired.

'She's ten, doctor.'

'I wonder if perhaps . . . It sometimes happens, you know, that as the child leaves babyhood in this climate, the body grows less comfortable. It may be putting a strain on Tammy, the heat and the humidity . . .'

'But she always seemed perfectly happy.'

'You say you brought her down recently from an upland school?'

'Yes, two months ago.'

'It may be that. She may be a child who thrives better in a cooler temperature.'

'But she's lived here all her life and—'

'In fact, Mrs Veetcha, I wonder if you'd consider a suggestion?'

'Of course, anything!'

'I wonder if she wouldn't be better off with a spell at home?'

By 'home' Dr Clandon meant England, of course. No matter how long one lived and worked in Singapore, 'home' was always England.

The thought of parting with Tammy made Gwen

gasp as if cold water had been dashed over her. 'Oh no!'

'I don't say it's absolutely necessary, but it's something to consider. If she's having problems with her schooling, perhaps a good English girls' school is just what she needs?'

'But she and I have never been parted—'

'Come, come, dear lady. You've been parted from her for the major part of each week while she boarded up-country.'

'But that's different.'

'Yes, of course it is, I quite understand. But think it over, Mrs Veetcha. A lot of people find it worthwhile sending their children home at about that age.'

Gwen thought it over and decided against it. She talked about it to Terence and got little help. So she turned to Sam Prosper, who could be relied on for a dispassionate opinion.

'Seems to me it's worth a try,' he said when he'd heard her out. 'The kid's losing weight, you can see that – there's no more meat on her than a sparrow's elbow. Something's getting her down, and if it's the half-breed jibe, she'd be better off at an English school.'

'Are you saying people in England don't make nasty remarks about slanty eyes?' Gwen countered, thinking of her stepfather when he first met her husband Tama.

'Mebbe they do, mebbe they don't. The point is, in England they don't see them doing menial tasks and being ordered about the way they are here. There's not the same bad example.'

'It's so far away, Sam . . . I don't think it would be right.'

'Have you asked the kid?'

'What?' She stared. 'Ask a ten-year-old child?'

'Well, she's the one that's going to do it, right? Doesn't she deserve a say?'

Put that way, it did seem wrong not to ask Tammy's opinion.

To Gwen's astonishment and dismay, Tammy voted to go to school in England.

England had been the setting of most of her story-books. Children in England had a lovely time at boarding school. She pictured herself making friends with 'Felicity of the Fourth Form'.

Moreover, there were bigger and better gymkhanas in England, riding-stables everywhere, open fields and moors to gallop over.

Yes, she wanted to go to school in England.

Chapter Nineteen

Because of the Depression, fewer people were travelling, so Gwen was able to book passage on the *Marchioness*. That would allow them plenty of time to settle Tammy in England before she started school.

Gwen had several reasons for travelling with her daughter rather than entrusting her – as some people did – to the ship's 'governess'. First was her unwillingness to part from her. Travelling with her to Southampton was a way of postponing the separation.

Then there was the chance to visit her mother. Twelve years had gone by since Rhoda Baynes last saw her daughter. Her granddaughter was known to her only through photographs. Rapturous cables came back from St Albans, saying that Rhoda and Wally were dying to see them, would do anything they could to help with the school situation.

Disregarding that, Gwen went to an agency in Singapore from whom she got brochures about girls' boarding schools in England. She picked out one or two, sent cables asking if it would be convenient for her to make a visit of inspection in June and saying that correspondence could be sent to await her at her mother's house in St Albans.

There was also a chance on this visit home to look at the economic situation from a wider standpoint. In Singapore it was difficult to tell whether the down-turn in the furniture trade was going to affect her more seriously. There were still some very rich people in the Straits, who were still ordering her work, but the orders from London, Paris and New York had been diminishing. She would have a chance to walk about the big cities of Britain, look in the windows of the furniture stores, get some idea of what the future might hold.

She might hop across to Paris. She would like a face-to-face discussion with the buyer at Les Quatres Saisons. Moreover, she would have the chance to see Jerome de Labasse. He was a happily married man now, his letters told her, with a small son and daughter. It would be good to see Jerome again.

The usual on-board party was arranged for their sailing. Terence was noticeably absent. He'd begged Gwen not to go. 'How am I going to get on without you? Don't go, Gwen, please, I need you.'

If she'd been leaving for any other reason, Gwen would have given in. But for Tammy, she hardened her heart to Terence. 'Tammy needs me too, darling.'

'Oh, I know, of course, I see that – but you'll be gone so *long*.'

'Six months. It'll be past before you know it. Besides, you'll be so busy you won't notice I'm away.' This was a reference to the bridge tournament, in which he was to take part. A noted card-player, he was expected to win the bridge trophy.

He refused to be comforted. 'Write to me every day.'

'Of course.'

'And from every port en route.'

'Yes, I promise.'

'Children,' he muttered morosely, 'I know they have to take first place but . . .'

'This is a big change for my little girl. You wouldn't want me to neglect her at a time like this?'

But, truth to tell, Tammy seemed to need her mother a lot less than her mother needed Tammy. Excited by the idea of the voyage, of the adventure of going to England, of starting at a 'proper' boarding school (the Highland School having been only weekly boarding), above all at starring in this drama of travel and change, Tammy was in better spirits than she had been for months.

Gwen couldn't help being secretly hurt at the eagerness with which Tammy had made the decision to be parted from her. She tried to remember whether, at ten years old, she would have been so happy to be sent away from home. The answer was no – but then she'd had a much more ordinary home than Tammy's, a very ordinary schooling, no prejudice to fight against . . .

Sam Prosper said, on listening to her murmurs on the subject, 'Tammy's self-centred. Fundamentally all children are, I guess. They see grown-ups as adjuncts to their own lives, not as real people with emotions and needs. So Tammy has no idea you're broken up about being parted.'

'Yes, I see that, but I thought she might realise she'll miss me . . .'

'Would you prefer that? Want to have her hanging round your neck crying?'

'Of course not.'

'Then count your blessings.'

Sam was at the going-away party. He came on board followed by two of his houseboys carrying a huge tin bath of ice, in which nestled six bottles of the best champagne. Sam seemed to have even more money these days, despite the Depression. People said that it was because he'd been gun-running to the resistance forces in Manchuria ever since the Japanese invaded it eighteen months ago.

He let Tammy have two or three sips of champagne. She giggled and soon after fell asleep. 'Dead drunk,' he commented, putting cushions round her so that she could nap in comfort while the party continued.

On parting he found a moment to talk to Gwen in private. 'Chin up, babe. You're doing the right thing.'

'Oh, Sam, it's awful! Do you know, I feel all trembly . . . I don't *feel* that I'm going home, I feel I'm leaving it.'

'It'll still be here when you come back.' He grinned. 'The people too.'

She knew he meant Terence. She almost said, Keep an eye on him, Sam. But that would be asking far too much, even from such a tolerant friend.

He said, wrinkling his nose, 'I only came to this party because I get the chance to give you a big hug and a kiss.' He suited the actions to the words. 'Be good, kiddo. And tell your drunken daughter goodbye when she wakes up.'

But when Tammy woke up she was so eager to go on a tour of the ship that she couldn't wait for descriptions of the farewells.

Throughout the voyage she enjoyed herself hugely, joining in the ship's sports, eating large meals, going ashore for sightseeing trips with her mother at ports of call. She endured the boring passage through the Suez Canal with fortitude. At Port Said, taken to see some antiquities in the museum, she spent a long time staring at a reproduction of the head of Queen Nefertiti.

'Ah,' said the guide, 'you are admiring our great beauty. She is famous, deservedly so.'

Afterwards Tammay said to Gwen, 'That queen – is she really beautiful?'

'Yes, wonderful. Didn't you think so?'

Tammy shrugged, looking thoughtful. After a long moment she said, 'She had slanty eyes, like me.'

'So she had,' Gwen agreed, puzzled.

'If *I* had black hair too, I'd look like her.'

'Oh, I hardly think so,' her mother said, and the matter was dropped. But if she could have seen into the future she might have realised that this was the moment when Tammy understood she was going to be a beauty, despite the taunts about her slanty eyes.

England was a disappointment to Tammy at first. Southampton Docks were awful, and the weather was so *cold*. But then Granny swept her up into her arms, welcoming gifts of sweets and toys were thrust upon her,

they had tea in front of a real fire with real flames in a real
hotel lounge with upholstered furniture like in the story-
books, and then they were on a train passing through
green countryside, with real sheep and real cows grazing
in fields, and a farm cart with bundles of real hay waiting
at a level crossing, the big shire horses with plaited manes
and plumes of creamy hair around their hooves . . .

Heaven!

It took Tammy two days, perhaps three, to understand
instinctively that she could twist her grandmother around
her little finger. Her grandfather – step-grandfather,
Mummy had said at first, but that didn't seem to mean
anything – was less soft hearted but not difficult to
handle. They spent a week 'getting their land legs', as
Granny kept saying, which puzzled Tammy until it was
explained to her.

Then she and her mother went to inspect the schools.
There were three, all in former mansions, with playing
fields around them and a village or small town nearby.
There seemed little to choose between them academi-
cally. What Gwen was looking for was a caring, efficient
headmistress, and what Tammy was looking for was
riding stables.

Stanton School in Wiltshire pleased them both. Miss
Powers was kindly, intelligent, and calm. Gwen had
written originally under her married name but explaining
that she herself was English: Miss Powers took both her
names – Hayakawa and Veetcha – in her stride and
seemed unperturbed by the Eurasian features of the
daughter.

The school had no horses but there was a livery
stable almost next door. Because many of the girls were
daughters of military families with relatives serving in or
retired from the cavalry, riding was an optional part of
the curriculum.

It was arranged that Tammy would join at the beginning of the school year in September and, it so happened,
a few days after her eleventh birthday.

Meanwhile there were several weeks of freedom ahead. She was taken by her doting grandmother to London Zoo, to Madame Tussaud's, to Harrods to buy her school uniform. Seeing her daughter totally engrossed in these new experiences, Gwen went about her own business.

It became clear that the Depression was serious. In the big cities many shops had 'For Sale' or 'To Let' signs outside. There was a look of despondency about those which were open – prices marked down, sales for spurious reasons. People in the streets seemed lacklustre, their clothes rather shabby. There were many street-singers and street-musicians trying to earn an honest penny before the constable moved them on for obstructing the traffic.

On the other hand, there was great activity in some of the amusement industries. Picture palaces and dance-halls – called Palais de Danse – were being put up in the main streets. And it was from the managers of these that Gwen received very lucrative commissions.

The buyer at Liberty's put her on to it. 'A friend of mine has money in the new cinema going up in Manchester, Mrs Veetcha. I wonder if you'd be interested in taking part in the interior decoration?'

Gwen at once began to shake her head. 'I'm not an interior decorator, Mr Restham, I'm a furniture-maker.'

'Quite, quite, I understand that, but you know, there *is* furniture in a cinema, even though you might not think so at first. There are chairs and benches for the foyer, and counters for the selling of sweets and ice-cream. And then it seems they're going to have boxes, like a theatre, and they want special chairs and I think door-panelling . . .' He paused, pulling at his grey moustache and eyeing Gwen with hidden amusement. 'I daresay you know that many of these big modern cinemas have what they call a "theme" – from the decoration point of view, I mean. Some are

Spanish, some are Moorish, some are New Orleans. The one in Manchester is to be called the Emperor, and it's got a Japanese theme.'

Now Gwen was looking at him with an amusement that matched his own. 'Springs to mind, doesn't it?' she said. 'My name, I mean.'

'Indeed, indeed! Who else has so much ability in the Japanese and Chinese style? You're the outstanding Orientalist in the world of furniture, Mrs Veetcha. So I wonder . . . may I mention your presence in England to my friend Arthur Grant?'

Arthur Grant hired her almost on sight. Moreover, he introduced her to a colleague who wanted a 'Chinese look' to a new Palais de Danse. From sketches she did on a first view of the hall, she was commissioned to design the chairs and tables, also screens and trellises for the booths which would run along three sides and frame the bandstand.

The money was very good. 'No expense spared,' Arthur Grant assured her in his bluff North country accent.

Greatly heartened, Gwen took time off to whirl Tammy away on a trip to the seaside. The little girl was of course quite accustomed to beaches and the sea, but Brighton was an utterly new experience. Rides on the dodgems, sticky rock with the name all through it, crowds of people queuing up for trays of tea to take on the pebbly beach, Punch and Judy shows . . .

By now it was August. Gwen had spoken to Jerome de Labasse on the telephone. He had begged her to come to see him in Paris and now, it seemed, she had time to spare for the trip. Tammy was happy to be left in the care of her grandmother, the more so as she had made friends with the owner of a small riding stable on the outskirts of St Albans.

So Gwen went to Paris.

Jerome was waiting for her at Calais. As before they drove to Paris in a handsome car, but this time there was no chauffeur. 'One must make economies, no?' Jerome said with a shrug as he took his place behind the wheel.

He had changed very little. He was now just past forty, still slim and trim in his lightweight blue suit, though perhaps a little fuller in the face and neck. He felt her studying him as they drove. 'Approve or disapprove?'

'What a question! It's just that I'm so glad to see you, I can't stop looking at you.'

'And I you, my dear. Good lord, what a beauty you've become! I like the short hair.'

'You do? It's coolness, of course. You wouldn't approve of the way I look in Singapore – very unsmart.'

'So you say. I'm sure you look charming, you always did, even in a carpenter's apron. How is it that you still have the same pale, fine skin despite living in the sun?'

'I stay out of the sun.'

'Working, always working, no doubt. It was the only fault I could find in you – you were wrapped up in your work.'

'Yes, I still am.'

'What, no one in Singapore to brighten up your leisure hours? No one with whom you can admire the tropical moon?'

'You ask too many questions,' she said, laughing and colouring up.

'Aha.'

'Aha to you. Tell me about your children – they're how old?'

'Armand is five and Julie is three. Lovely children. I shall get out my pocket-book at the next traffic light and make you look at their photos, like any other adoring father.'

'And your wife? How is she?'

'Claudine is very well, thank you.'

'Shall I meet her?'

'She's in Cannes, of course. This is August, Gwen.'

She turned her gaze away from him, to stare through the windscreen. Of course. No one of consequence was in Paris during August.

After a moment she said, 'Shouldn't you be in Cannes too?'

'I am. At least, I've only come to Paris for a short stay.'

She couldn't understand how she could have been so silly. When she rang his Paris apartment the phone had been answered, as usual, by his manservant Tibau. As soon as she had announced herself, Tibau had said eagerly, 'Of course, Mme Veetcha. M. de Labasse was hoping you would ring. I'm instructed to take a message.' And when she had given him the date and time of her arrival he had said, 'Monsieur will be in touch.'

It hadn't occurred to her when Jerome rang back that he was calling from his villa on the Cote d'Azur.

'You just came back to meet me?'

'Of course, Gwen! I would have come back from the middle of the Sahara to spend some time with you again.'

This was more serious than she'd intended. She'd thought they would have a happy two or three days of reunion, of visiting the old haunts, looking up old friends. But the tone of his voice told her his view was entirely different.

She said nothing for a long time. Then she began in a manner she hoped would come across as friendly but not too friendly.

'I've looked forward so much to seeing you, Jerome. You were important in my life – in fact if it hadn't been for you I'd never have left St Albans, never have met Tama . . .'

He understood very well what she was trying to say. 'But Tama is dead,' he replied.

'But that doesn't mean . . .'

'You haven't remarried.'

'No, I never thought of it at first, and now . . .'

'Now you have a lover but you don't marry him. Which means, at a guess, that's he's married already.'

'Jerome, all I'm trying to tell you is that we can't expect to go back to the way things were a dozen years ago.'

'Why not?' It was said with good humour but there was an undernote of seriousness. 'My dear Gwen, I never cease to regret letting you go! I should have married you when I had the chance.'

'Oh yes. And your family would have been delighted, no doubt.'

'Oh, the family . . .' He in his turn fell silent. They drove along the straight French motor-road.

Finally he said: 'My family wanted me to marry and, as the saying goes, settle down. That meant having children to inherit the estate. Well, that's been arranged—'

'Arranged!'

'Don't be shocked. You remember quite well, I'm sure, that these things are given due attention, but once attended to, a certain tolerance comes in.'

'Now you want me to say, tolerance of what? But I know what you mean, Jerome. All the same, I have to ask, what does Claudine say to the way you use that "tolerance"?'

'Claudine is an intelligent woman. Besides . . . she too makes use of that "tolerance".'

Gwen shook her head. 'An ideal marriage, clearly.'

'You can joke, but it's true. Claudine and I rub along quite well together. The children are nice. It's more fun being a father than I expected – but all the same, one can't be a father *all* the time.'

'I don't like the way this conversation is going, Jerome. I came to Paris to look up old friends and perhaps make some new business contacts. There was nothing in my plan about French tolerance or anything like that—'

'Oh, come now, Gwen . . . You're surely not saying you thought we could be mere friends—'

'Yes, that's just what I thought.'

'How naïve. I always intended to get you into bed—'

'Oh, really?' She was laughing. 'And if when I got off the boat you'd seen a skinny sun-dried woman with wrinkles and stringy hair, you'd still have longed to make love?'

'Ha!' He smiled and shook his head. 'You forget, you sent me photos – what you call them, snapshots – and there you were, alas only in black and white but smiling at me from under glamorous palm trees . . . I knew you would still have that strange attractiveness, only a hundred times more so because I've missed you so much.'

'It's flattering—'

'Say you missed me, Gwen.'

She measured her words. 'No. I'm being honest, Jerome. I was so overwhelmed by Japan when I first got there that I scarcely ever thought of you. And then after the earthquake, when I got to Singapore, I had such a struggle – I missed you then, perhaps, but only as a friend, my dear, only as a friend.'

For answer he grimaced and took both hands off the wheel to gesture in dismay. 'It's going to be a harder task than I thought!'

'What is? And for God's sake pay attention to your driving.'

'Persuading you.'

'Give it up now, Jerome dear. Give it up now.'

In amicable disagreement they entered the outskirts of Paris. Gwen said, 'Where are you heading?'

'To the apartment, of course.'

'You expect me to leap straight into bed with you?'

'No, of course not, but we'll leave your luggage—'

'I'm booked in at the Lutetia.'

'What?'

'I made a telephone booking. Of course I did, Jerome. It never for a moment entered my head you'd expect me to stay in your apartment.'

'Oh, well, we can cancel the booking—'

'Not at all. I want to stay at the Lutetia. I've given the address to one or two businessmen who want to make appointments.'

'We can tell the hotel to pass on the messages—'

'Jerome, I am staying at the Lutetia. My mother has the number to ring me if Tammy wants me or anything. If you don't mind, take the next turning to the right.'

'Gwen, you're being very stubborn.'

'Yes. The next turning to the right.'

Clearly put out, Jerome obeyed. Almost in silence he took her to the Hotel Lutetia on the Boulevard Raspail. He would have gone in with her but she prevented him, offering her hand and a polite leavetaking.

'Gwen,' he protested. He looked like a little boy who's been denied an ice-cream.

'We can see each other this evening if you like.'

'You're sure one of your precious business contacts isn't going to invite you out to dinner?'

'If he does I'll refuse. Come, dear, don't sulk. Either we have a nice friendly dinner this evening or we say goodbye now and that's an end of it.'

He sighed and shrugged, kissed her hand, then straightened. 'An end of it indeed! Who was it who said, I have not yet begun to fight? Some mad American, I believe. Nevertheless, I quote him, so beware.'

Gwen watched him drive off. Then, shaking her head, she went into the hotel.

There were messages for her at the hotel desk. Once in her room she ordered afternoon tea, drank it while she unpacked, then sat down to answer the business calls. She'd only just dialled the first one when there was a knock on her door.

She opened it. A huge bouquet of roses behind which was a small bellboy. 'For you, madame.'

The card said, 'I have now begun to fight.'

Thirty minutes later, when she'd finished her business calls and was running a bath, another knock. This time a huge bouquet of carnations. 'Still fighting,' said the card.

The next offering was a big spray of gardenias. 'The fight goes on,' the card told her.

The bellboy's smile grew broader with every visit; the room began to look like a florist shop. So it went every half-hour until eight-thirty, when Jerome himself arrived with a spray of orchids. 'All is fair in love and war,' he said as he held out the flowers.

'Jerome, you're quite mad.'

'Love is a divine madness, I read somewhere. My dear, you look beautiful.'

She was wearing a black satin evening gown with a square neckline and a long clinging skirt. She pinned Jerome's orchids to the narrow shoulder-band. The orchids, carefully chosen, were a tawny brown, a shade lighter than her hair.

Jerome glanced about the room. 'I believe I made a mistake. There's hardly room left among the blossoms to take you in my arms.'

'You're here to take me out to dinner.'

'If I take you to eat duck at the Tour d'Argent, will that help to soften your heart?'

'No, but it will improve my temper. I get cross when I'm hungry.'

'*Zut alors*, let us hurry to the restaurant. I could easily fall out of love with a bad-tempered woman.'

They were expected at the restaurant. There were special flowers on their table, the food had been chosen in advance. The wine, to which Gwen was rather indifferent though she had the tact not to say so, was exquisite.

They came out under a light August midnight. All

Paris was twinkling around them. Depression or no Depression, this was still a city of luxury and light. They strolled to Jerome's car, parked on the Quai de la Tournelle near the bridge.

He helped her in. 'Now,' he said, 'we drive to the Avenue Foch, no?'

'We drive to the Boulevard Raspail.'

'What, after all the money I've spent on flowers, on food, on wine? What ingratitude.'

'Oh, if I'd known you were trying to bribe me I'd have asked for emeralds.'

'Emeralds? Is that what will persuade you? Very well, first thing tomorrow, you shall have emeralds.'

'Jerome, be serious.'

He sighed. It wasn't a pretence, it was a deep sigh of bewilderment. 'Please, Gwen,' he said. 'I *am* serious. It's not really a game, though that seemed a good defence at the time. I need to make you understand . . . I want you so much, I can't think straight. Darling, please don't keep up the pretence. Let things go back to what they were between us.'

He had taken both her hands in his, was holding them against his chest as if to make her feel the beating of his heart. She freed them gently, then put one against his cheek.

'I do love you, Jerome,' she said. 'But not in a physical way. I can't help it, that's just how it is.'

'Oh, if it's only that!' he cried, hope springing in his voice. 'I can make you want me, Gwen. I can make you feel it through your blood and your bones.'

Yes, in the way he had that first time. It came back into her mind as if it was all happening again – herself, impelled by gratitude and a feeling that she ought not to put up a defence against his certainty, he determined to be her lover, to be her *first* lover.

She would always be grateful to him. He had taught her things about her own body that she might never have appreciated without such a teacher. At the thought she

384

gave a little sigh. He put his arms about her and she felt herself melt towards him.

But she wanted to be a faithful lover. At the other side of the world, perhaps under a soft midnight sky, someone longed for her, depended on her.

She stiffened in Jerome's embrace. 'No, my dear, it wouldn't be fair.'

'To whom? To me? I can think for myself, Gwen. Or to you? Why shouldn't you have love and joy—'

'I was thinking it wouldn't be fair to someone who's waiting for me.'

'Ah.' He sank back into his place behind the wheel. 'Ah, I see.'

There was a long moment of quiet. Then Jerome said, 'Boulevard de Raspail, I think Madame said?' and set the car in motion.

He accompanied her into the foyer but didn't ask to come up. She gave him a goodnight kiss on the cheek. He submitted without demur.

Next morning she was about to go out at nine o'clock for her first business appointment when the desk rang to say M. de Labasse was below and would like a word with her.

'Please tell M. de Labasse that I am just on my way down and will see him in the foyer.'

With a last glance in the mirror at her appearance – businesslike white silk suit, black courts, black handbag and straw hat – she went down in the lift. Jerome was hovering. An awful idea struck her.

'Jerome, if you have actually brought emeralds, I'll take you to be certified!'

'No. No, Gwen, I'm serious. Please may we talk? I want to explain myself to you.'

'Jerome dear, I haven't time. I'm due at the office of Lesgosts Frères in fifteen minutes.'

'Please telephone and postpone it.'

'Not at all, Jerome. It's important business.'

'*This* is important.'

She could see that it was. All the same, she couldn't stop to hear it. In correspondence with Lesgosts it had been suggested she might make a design for the furniture of a block of *appartements meublés* going up near the Bois. These were to be let to foreign diplomats and were to be of a very high standard. If she got the contract for the furniture it meant working with some of the best interior decorators of France and earning a lot of money.

'I can't put them off dear, really I can't. You must believe me.'

'Then we must meet after your appointment.'

'I'm having lunch with the manager of Caradon.'

'This afternoon, then—'

'No, honestly, Jerome – I filled the whole day with business appointments, on purpose, because I knew I would be in Paris only a short time.'

'Only a short time!' he echoed with bitterness. 'Only a short time for me—'

'Jerome,' she intervened, 'I have a ten-year-old daughter in England.'

He was brought up short, jerked out of his own self-involvement. 'Of course, I'm sorry – you must think me selfish and uncaring. Of course, you can't stay long, you want to get back to – how is she called? – Tammy. But what I want to say to you might change things—'

'I must go, Jerome.'

'Come to the Avenue Foch this evening.'

'No, no . . .'

'Just for drinks and a talk, Gwen. I promise.'

'I don't want to go there. Can't we meet for dinner again?'

'But this is important, personal – our future – we can't talk about it in a restaurant.'

She glanced at her watch. She was already late for her appointment. The taxi was ticking away outside the hotel doors.

'Very well, at the apartment. What time?'

'Whenever your day is over, Gwen. I'll be there.'

She dashed out, fell into the taxi, gave the address of Lesgosts Frères, and only then understood she'd been a fool to agree.

Well, she would telephone later to say she couldn't make it after all.

But the day rushed on – congenial talks with men in the furniture business, with a director of the property company, with their interior decorators. The contract for the furnished-apartment block was hers, and more, the decorator had in mind many details of lacquer, wanted her to make sketches and, even better, wanted the work to be carried out in Singapore. 'I've seen some of the work you've sent back,' he said, 'and I want the pieces you do for me to be as good.'

So she would be taking back work for Wo Joong and Lee Pan Sum, even work for Bertie Hurden, whose paintings of Oriental lagoons seemed to be exactly what was wanted for the lacquer-work. She felt exhilarated: times weren't easy in Singapore, it was good to think she would be improving the income of her friends.

At length, about mid-afternoon, she had a few minutes before her next appointment. She went into a bar near the Opéra and asked for a *jeton* for the telephone. But as she was about to dial Jerome's number, she hesitated.

What had he said? 'Important – personal – our future.' Our future? What future?

He couldn't – he couldn't surely – be thinking of breaking up his marriage for her?

She retrieved the *jeton*, put it in her handbag for some other occasion, then went out to walk to her appointment in the Place Vendôme.

She had to give her mind to it because it involved putting business in the way of her stepfather at the St Albans' works. Wally Baynes had the exclusive rights to reproduce Gwen's designs in Europe, and as a consequence was doing rather better than some furniture-makers in these times of recession. But any extra orders would be welcomed, and the French furniture chain of Petouche were about to ask her to design a dining suite exclusively for them.

Soon after five she got back to the Lutetia. Her room was full of the scent of Jerome's flowers. She had a bath, changed into the only other evening dress she'd brought with her, a plain after-six dress of blue georgette. She tried last night's orchids with it, decided they looked awful, tried one of the gardenias and then, thinking she was trying to be 'fetching' and ought not to, went out without them.

Tibau opened the door of the apartment. He had gone very grey but otherwise seemed just the same. He accepted the georgette wrap that went with the dress, and ushered her into the small sitting-room.

It was one of the rooms she'd helped to redecorate. He had kept it just as it was when she'd finished it except that there was a new silk wallpaper. How well she remembered her sketches for the sofas, the occasional tables . . .

Jerome was standing by the window. He crossed the room to greet her with a kiss and an embrace. 'Darling, how tired you must be! What will you have to drink?'

'Campari-soda, please, Jerome. Yes, I'm tired, it's been a long day.'

'Successful?'

'Very.'

'I congratulate you.' He smiled, genuinely pleased. 'It must seem strange to be doing business again in Paris?'

'Yes, the language has changed a lot since I was here – more slang, less formality.'

'Ah, the American influence. Do you have Americans in Singapore?'

'A few,' she said. Suddenly she saw Sam Prosper in her mind's eye, sitting behind his dark-wood desk in his office full of growing orchids. She wished she had Sam with her now. That shrewd brain, that ironic eye . . . He would have been a great help in the discussion that was about to take place. For, she sensed, this was going to be important.

Jerome brought her her drink. She sipped it gratefully. The heat of the Parisian summer hadn't troubled her, but the rush of the traffic, the noise, the long hours in stuffy offices . . .

'I wanted to explain myself better,' Jerome said. 'I think I've given you a wrong impression.'

'No,' she said with a smile, 'you were perfectly frank in your intentions.'

'But that was only half the truth. Of course I want to make love to you, Gwen, I've been consumed with the idea ever since I heard your voice again on the telephone. But it isn't just that – it's not a foolish nostalgia for the past—' He broke off. 'Although, when I look back, I see that I was never honest enough with you.'

'Jerome dear, there's no need to—'

'Yes, I want to make you understand. Of course I wanted to go to bed with you from the first. You were very pretty, very talented, very trusting. I felt I owned you – not in a bad way but you know, as your patron . . . It didn't occur to me that I loved you. Not until you went to live with Tama.'

Gwen set down her glass, rose from her chair. She didn't want to talk to her former lover about her dead husband.

'I was jealous when I saw how much he meant to you. I should have tried to get you back but I didn't know how. I have a reputation for being able to end an affair with good humour, I felt I had to live up to it. But I was wrong.'

'What's the good of going over all this, Jerome?'

'Then you went away. I expected you back in a year or so, and then I was going to get you back, somehow,

I don't know how. But you didn't come, and you didn't come, and then you wrote to say you were having a baby. At that, I suppose, I thought it was really over.'

She nodded. 'And so it was.'

'I met Claudine and we went through the usual courting-dance . . .' He smiled with irony, his thin lips nevertheless drooping a little. 'Well, then of course I married and "settled down" and we had the children and it's all very well – I know I'm lucky. But there's an emptiness, Gwen.' He touched his evening jacket at the breast. 'Here, where there used to be contentment.'

'Darling, we all have to face loss. In every heart there must be emptiness at certain memories.'

'Of course I understand, you lost your husband, you know what it is to feel like this. I don't pretend I've suffered as you have – it's just that something's been missing. Until now.'

'Now is no different.'

'Yes, it is, my love. We've got a second chance. I could hardly believe my luck when you said you wanted to see me. It meant, you see, that you still felt something for me—'

'But I explained that, Jerome—'

'Yes, yes, I know, friendship – but it's a special kind of friendship, you can't deny it. Last night you came into my arms, and for a moment I felt everything was back the way it used to be.'

'But it wasn't. I told you . . .'

'That it wouldn't be fair to this lover in Singapore. Of course. Honour demands you remain faithful to him if you can. And for just a night or two of pleasure, it would be letting him down, as you English say. But that's the point. I should have explained that to you from the first. It isn't just for a night or two. I want you to stay here with me, Gwen.'

She picked up her glass, turned it round a time or two, set it down. 'What put this into your head?'

'It makes sense. It's the only thing that makes sense.

Claudine and I don't really love one another. She would understand that I had always really loved you. And don't you see, Gwen, if you decided to stay in Paris, it's a new start. That man, whoever he is, he would have to face the fact that your relationship is over. And in any case, Paris is where you belong. Your artistic reputation was founded here. This is the centre, the world centre, of Art Deco. You could re-establish yourself here—'

'Wait, Jerome, wait!' The tirade had buffeted her so that she could hardly think. 'Let's get things straight. Leave out all the bit about my career – I can handle my career, don't trouble yourself about that. The first thing is, what do you mean about us?'

'I want us to be together for the rest of our lives!'

'But Jerome—'

'I know – your daughter – but she could be brought to Paris, the education for girls is much better here than in England. She would soon settle down.'

'I wasn't thinking about Tammy – I haven't got that far yet. I want to know about us.'

'We'd pick up where we left off. I'd show you that I know how silly I was to let you go!'

'Jerome, calm down. Please calm down.' She sat down beside him on the sofa. They sat facing each other. She took his hand. 'Now, slowly, clearly . . . Tell me . . . Are you saying you would leave Claudine for me?'

'What?'

She paused. 'Are you talking about a divorce?'

'Divorce?'

'You're not talking about a divorce.' It was a statement, not a question.

'There's never been a divorce in my family,' he said, bewildered.

'So, what you're offering is that I should come to Paris and live as your mistress.'

'Oh, Gwen, you know how permanent that can be. We can go to the lawyers, make a contract—'

'Jerome!' She drew back to stare at him. 'Is that what

all this emotion has been about? You want to settle me in an apartment with an income and a poodle dog.'

He took her by the shoulders and shook her. 'That's not what I mean! You know very well it's not! I want us to have a life together that would be the same as marriage without the ceremony. You would be free – good God, you can't seriously think I want to set you up like a *cocotte* – you'd have your work, your little girl would be with you, I swear I'd be like a father to her, Gwen.'

She wrenched herself free. 'That's enough.' She got to her feet, moved away. He too rose but when he tried to take her by the shoulder she shrugged him off. 'I think I was expecting an offer of marriage. But if that's what it had been, I was going to say no.'

'Don't decide now, Gwen. I can see I've handled it badly, I've made you angry—'

'I'm not angry, I'm dismayed. I keep misunderstanding people, I'm just no good at reading their feelings . . . Jerome, I was a fool to come here tonight. But I thought it was only fair to you, because I thought you were about to break up your marriage for me.'

He frowned. His face, tanned by the Riviera sun, had lost colour. 'Oh no. I couldn't do that.'

And all at once she wanted to laugh. He was so much the aristocrat, so sure that what he wanted must be acceptable to everybody else. Poor, darling Jerome . . .

She loved him, she would always love him. He had been one of the most important men in her life. But she didn't understand him, and he certainly didn't understand her.

'Listen to me,' she said. 'I'm here for two more days, then I have to go back to England to settle Tammy in her school. Soon after that I go back Singapore—'

'No, Gwen, don't go!'

'I must. I have a business there, a workforce that depends on me—'

'And not only the workforce,' Jerome interrupted angrily.

'No, that's true, there's someone there who loves me and needs me.'

'*I* need you, Gwen.'

She shook her head. 'Not in the way that Terence does.' No, Terence had no assured standing in society, no inherited money. He had a job that was growing more and more shaky every day. He had a wife who couldn't give him children, who hardly seemed to know anything existed outside the Church. Terence, for all his charm, was vulnerable and unsure these days.

'What I'm trying to say,' she went on, 'is that if you want us to go on being friends, I'll be here until the day after tomorrow, then on that afternoon I head for home. And now I'm going back to the hotel for a meal and an early night.'

'I don't see why you can't stay here and discuss this with me like an adult.'

'I have discussed it, dear. I've said all I have to say on the matter. Goodnight, Jerome.'

She went out while he was still trying to think of a way to detain her. Down in the hall, Tibau appeared to put her wrap round her shoulders. 'Madame is leaving without dinner?' he asked in perplexity.

'I'm afraid I can't stay, Tibau.'

'Then if Madame will sit down, I will ring for a taxi.'

'No, thank you, I'm sure to find one on the Avenue.'

'Madame, isn't there some mistake?'

'No, Tibau,' she said, stepping past him through the open doorway, 'no mistake.'

Chapter Twenty

The commissions Gwen brought back from Europe kept Veetcha Furniture going through the following year. This was as well, for the down-turn in trade had become serious. Up-country rubber plantations in Malaya were allowed to go back to jungle, tin mines were allowed to fall idle, shipping fell off.

Everyone had to economise. Gwen dispensed with her gardener-chauffeur and one of the amahs, and then started seriously thinking she might have to lay off some of her furniture craftsmen.

But she was lucky enough to become fashionable with the Hollywood film producers, who hired her to make furniture for their grandiose mansions in Beverly Hills, entailing a voyage to California and back. The money thus earned helped her to keep all her workforce employed. It also helped to subsidise the furniture works in St Albans where her mother and stepfather were only just making ends meet, and to pay Tammy's school fees, which were high.

The first summer vacation, Tammy came back to Singapore. The following year Gwen went to England. According to this routine, Tammy should have come to Singapore in 1936, but wrote to say she would like to go to her friend Rosemary's family for the holidays. They were both entering junior show-jumping events, it would be fun, please say yes, Mummy . . .

To tell the truth, Gwen was relieved. She would have been hard-pressed to find the money for the passage this year. All the same, the thought of not seeing her daughter for another year grieved her, so that for weeks she felt there was nothing to look forward to.

If she was having her problems, so was Terence O'Keefe. At the beginning of 1937 he was summoned by Greater Malayan Freight to a conference in Hong Kong, where the managers from all the Far East ports were asked to report on the state of trade and give a forecast for the coming year.

Terence was scared. 'It means the sack, I can see it coming,' he told Gwen the night before he sailed. 'They're cutting down staff, from their point of view it makes good sense.'

'But they must have shipping managers in the main ports, Terence—'

'I've already taken a cut in salary – if they ask me to take another, I'm going to resign!'

'Don't meet trouble half-way, dear. Just have all the facts at your fingertips and speak up for yourself.'

'Oh, I'm going to, don't you worry. I'll give them a piece of my mind if they start any funny business.'

Gwen guessed that for some time now the household expenses of the O'Keefes had been met from Molly's private income. So they would never starve. Yet if GMF dispensed with Terence, it was almost certain he would go home to Ireland. Although he himself loved the Far East and the status enjoyed by Europeans there, his wife often spoke about 'home'.

So added to Gwen's depression over not having seen Tammy was the fear that Terence might have to pack up and go.

Sam Prosper told her to cheer up: 'Sure, GMF are going to economise on staff. But if that nitwit had the least understanding of business he'd see that it's the assistant managers who're going to get the boot.'

'You think so, Sam?' Gwen asked, brightening at the idea and then feeling ashamed because it seemed heartless to the junior managers.

She was at a party given by Sam. He said it was his

birthday, but she was almost sure it was untrue. He gave parties seldom but when he did they were always special. Everyone angled for an invitation, even those who rather looked down on him because of his odd business pursuits.

One of the attractions was the great collection of gramophone records he'd acquired. He was a jazz fan from way back, had records of 'King' Oliver and 'Jellyroll' Morton. Couples loved the long, slow beat of the blues, ideal music in a climate where energetic dancing was too much trouble in the evening.

As they talked now, from behind them in the big living-room a jazz clarinet was weaving a mournful silvery net around the song 'Blue Moon'. There was a little laughter, a little lazy conversation. The air was full of the scent of Sam's orchids. It was late, past two in the morning.

'Tell you what,' Sam said, lolling back in his rattan chair, 'everybody can soon stop worrying about the financial situation.'

'What makes you say that?'

'Because "prosperity is just around the corner".'

'Oh, the politicians keep trotting that out but it must be a corner that's turned into a circle.'

'No, it's true. Money's going to come pouring into Singapore any minute now.'

'Sam! What do you mean?'

He touched a hanging lantern so that it swayed gently to and fro, putting his long narrow face into light then shadow. 'Maybe I shouldn't say this because you used to be married to a Jap, but have you noticed what his countrymen have been up to in China the last couple of months?'

'Oh, that . . .' She had certainly noticed.

The Japanese magazines and newspapers she bought from time to time in the shops around Hailam Road had gradually grown more and more strident in tone. So much so that she would have given up trying to keep in touch with things Japanese, except that she felt she owed it to Tammy. Although her daughter insisted she didn't care about her Japanese inheritance, the day might come when she would want to visit the home of her father – who these days was spoken about in Japan as one of the last great lacquerists.

Gwen had read of Tama's fame as she tried to keep up her knowledge of Japanese, reading it painstakingly in the evenings when she had nothing else to do, speaking it when she could with the shopkeepers.

It was hard to think of these little, smiling, affable men as related to the Japanese troops now 'carrying out manoeuvres' in China. What they could be up to, Gwen couldn't imagine.

'It'll all die down,' she said in answer to Sam's remark.

'Didn't die down in Manchuria, did it? They're still there, holding a piece of China that doesn't belong to them.'

'You're not saying they're going to take Peking?'

'Sure.'

'Oh, nonsense, Sam! That would mean war.'

'No, it's just the extension of their . . . what do they call it?'

'The Co-Prosperity Zone – at least that's what they call it in their newspapers.'

'What else do you gather from what you read? D'you get the impression they're going to hand back Manchuria to its rightful owners?'

'Well . . . no . . . I don't understand it . . . The way I remember them, they were very inward-looking people, not much interested in things outside their own country.'

'That was fifteen years ago, Gwen. Since then they've got a far bigger population, and it's going to get bigger still.'

'Oh yes. The Land of the Children – that's Japan.'

'All those new mouths to feed, and only a couple of

little islands to do it on. And no mineral resources, no oil of their own. The Co-Prosperity Zone is a great idea for them, if they can co-prosperity themselves into coal-fields and tin mines and oil-wells. See what I mean?'

'Either it's too late at night or I'm just stupid, but I don't really understand, Sam.'

He laughed. 'If you don't, some of the Army and Navy guys do. They're beginning to worry about Japan. That's what I mean when I say money's going to pour into Singapore. They're going to build it up as a naval base.'

'There's no possible way you could know that for sure.'

'Not for sure. But the Chinese merchants here are saying it's going to happen. And they have their finger on the pulse.'

Sam's contacts among the Chinese merchants were legendary. She felt disinclined to argue with him when he quoted their views. She was silent.

Then he startled her by saying, 'I'd be careful what you say to those Japs around Hailam and Middle Road. One or two of them are probably spies.'

'What?'

'There are about half a dozen in Singapore, so I'm told.'

'If that's a joke, I don't think it's funny!'

'Still feel some loyalty to them, do you?' He got up to stretch and yawn. 'Gee, I love this time of day. You can feel the dawn sort of sneaking up beyond the horizon, waiting to turn everything soft and pearly before the sun gets up.'

'Sam, forget the word pictures and tell me what proof you have for saying Mr Akamata or Mr Namura is a spy.'

'No proof. But that's what the Chinese say.'

'And you believe them?'

'Honey, I do business with the Chinese every day of my life practically. I know when to trust them and when to rub my rabbit's foot. About the Jap spies, I think they're telling the truth.'

'But why, Sam? Why should the Japanese government send spies to Singapore?'

'So that they'd know what to attack when they decide to move on Singapore.'

'Sam, you're out of your mind! Take on the British Empire? They'd never do it!'

'You're probably right.' And with that he shrugged and dropped the subject.

The conversation came back to her two months later when the news came through over the wireless: Japanese troops near Peking had clashed with Chinese forces. By the end of July the Japanese army had taken Peking and then Tientsin.

Everybody in Singapore might have been talking about it if something much more important to them hadn't occupied their minds: the Prince of Wales had married the love of his life, Mrs Simpson. There had been a pro-Prince of Wales faction and an anti-Prince of Wales faction all through the time of the abdication, but these had died down during plans for celebrating the Coronation of his brother. Now they started into life again.

So perhaps only a few in the city thought much about the Japanese in China. Gwen was perturbed enough to speak of it to Wo Joong.

'Do you think they mean to stay in China, Joong?'

'Certain, mem. Never bother to take Peking if not stay.'

'I don't understand it . . .'

Her foreman gave her a calm glance. 'Easy to understand. Japanese have strange feeling for China. China give Japan writing, painting, tea-making, all important things. Sometimes, mem, want to teach lesson to people you owe much to.'

'Why, that's philosophy, Joong!' she said, smiling.

'Chinese famous for philosophy.' He picked up the blueprint they'd been studying and prepared to put it in the file-cabinet.

'Joong . . .'

'Mem?'

'Are there Japanese spies in Singapore?'

He stood still with the plans half-way into the cabinet. Then he said, 'Why does mem ask?'

'I buy things at those shops along Middle Road, chat to them a bit. I'd hate to think I was chatting with a spy.'

Joong smiled. 'More philosophy: spy only listen to useful information.'

'That's true, I suppose.'

But it troubled her, all the same.

Sam had persuaded her to try air travel for her summer journey to England. 'It's the only way to go,' he told her.

'No fear. Nobody's going to get me into a machine that leaves the ground.'

'Come on, don't be a fuddy-duddy. Flying's the modern way. Think of the time you'll save. Singapore to London in four days.'

Put like that, hurtling through the air at a hundred and thirty miles an hour might have its advantages. She allowed him to talk her into it, the more so as he knew someone at Imperial Airways who could give her a discounted ticket.

So, off she went from Singapore Harbour in a Short's flying-boat with ten other passengers on the first leg to Rangoon. From Rangoon they flew to Chittagong, then the next morning to the Hooghly River, thence by Atalanta flying mail-carrier in two hops to Bombay, by flying-boat once more to the Gulf of Oman, to the Red Sea, to Rome, and then overland to Calais and across by ferry to Dover. All in five days, if you didn't count overnight stays.

Tammy and her friends were greatly impressed. 'Fancy! Flying! Was it very scary, Mrs Veetcha?'

'Very,' Gwen confessed. 'Especially at first. I don't think it'll catch on.'

She was in England to see Tammy compete in show-jumping. She had progressed from junior-class to intermediate. There were four events for which she was entered along with her bosom-friend Rosemary Collingworth – two in Wiltshire, one in Worcestershire and one in Gloucestershire.

That summer of 1937 was exceptionally fine and hot. Gwen sat in the stands with other proud parents, revelling in the scene – green grass, white barred fences, gleaming horses, young men in pink coats and girls in black or dark green jackets and cream jodhpurs.

Tammy looked especially good with her Titian hair shining under her black velvet cap and her slender hands holding the reins in the regulation posture. She did well in two of the shows, gaining second in one match and third in another. In the other two she was outshone by better riders, but to Gwen's surprise didn't seem unduly put out about it.

'I think you can make too much of it,' she said over a consolation tea in Gloucester's best hotel. 'John says it doesn't do to get too horsey.'

'And who's John, if one may inquire?'

'Oh, he's just a man I know.'

'From where? Near the school? Or home at St Albans?'

Tammy made circles on the table-cloth with the tines of a fork. 'He's assistant to the vet at Stanton.'

'Oh, that's who John is,' Gwen said, hiding a smile. 'And he doesn't approve of horsey women?'

'Well, who could? There are other things in life besides horses.'

Gwen was pleased to hear it. For the last six or seven years, all her daughter seemed to think or dream about was horses. On the other hand, what about John who assisted the vet at Stanton . . . ?

'What's he like?'

'Who?'

'John.'

'Oh, him. John Singleton. Well, he's . . . he's very nice. But awfully conceited, you know.'

'No, really?'

'Thinks he knows everything.'

'Well, maybe he does – about veterinary things.'

'Oh ye-es, nobody could argue on that point. But he treats me as if I were a child.'

'Oh dear. That's not very polite.'

'No, it isn't, is it, considering that I'll be fourteen in a month's time.'

Gwen looked suitably sympathetic. Tea was brought, together with scones and clotted cream and raspberry jam. Tammy ate three scones one after another then said, 'Do you think marriages between young women and older men are all right?'

'Ah . . . Older men,' her mother ventured. 'How old is "older"?'

'A lot. Perhaps as much as twelve years or so.'

From this Gwen deduced that the young vet was about twenty-six. Newly qualified, probably, and much too busy learning his profession to be bothered with an adoring fourteen-year-old.

All the same, it was something to think about. Tammy was turning into a young woman – a very lovely young woman; slender at the waist, with soft curves above and below, olive skin, rich flame of hair, and eyes the colour of new leaves under rain.

They celebrated Tammy's birthday with a family party at the old house in St Albans. Then it was time to see her back to school. Gwen took the trouble to drop in at the surgery of the veterinary surgeon in Stanton – only to learn that John Singleton had moved on to a job with a farming syndicate in Norfolk.

So much for Tammy's romance.

But a fourteen-year-old girl is always going to find

someone to be in love with. When she wrote to Gwen in Singapore, it seemed she'd given her heart to the tennis champion Fred Perry. Soon after Christmas it was the film star Robert Taylor who was her idol, and soon after that it was Leslie Howard.

'All quite normal,' Terence remarked as he chuckled over her latest letter. 'Do you think she's really going to give up horse events?'

'I sincerely hope so! It costs the earth. Rosemary wants to buy out the horse – you understand they shared one, kept it in a paddock at Rosemary's home. Tammy seems to think she ought to have it so I'll just ask a nominal price.'

'And what's Tammy going to do? To fill the gap, I mean?'

'There won't be much of a gap. Matriculation is looming – she has to have that if she wants to go on to university.'

'And does she?'

'Shouldn't think so,' Gwen said. 'She told me she thought university girls were terribly stuffy, and mostly wore glasses.'

Terence laughed. 'What then? Finishing school? Secretarial college?'

'What would be your advice?'

'Me? Darling, what do I know about teenage girls?'

'What does anybody know?' she said, sighing. 'We'll just have to see, I suppose.'

She hadn't really expected to get any advice from Terence. He was busy these days. The job crisis at Greater Malay Freight had turned out quite well for him: junior managers had to be given notice, European shipping clerks were replaced with Chinese who would take lower wages, but shipping office managers had been left in place.

Terence had come particularly well out of the reorganisation because he'd made a friend among the directors at the Hong Kong conference. A fellow bridge-fan, he and Terence and a couple of others had played late into the night.

'Pays to have friends in high places, you see,' he said with satisfaction as he told Gwen about it. She could only nod and smile but on the whole liked it better when Terence didn't play cards. He often lost money he could ill afford, in all-night poker games.

The building-up of Singapore as a base for British forces, foretold by Sam, was taking place. Naval engineers began to be seen about on the waterfront. Work began on extending the airfield at Kallang. Oil-supply depots were installed. Barracks were put up along the Bukit Timor Road.

As a result, trade in the city picked up. There were orders enough to keep Veetcha Furniture going. Yet for Gwen something had changed in her view of her work. The month she'd spent in England had given her the chance to look at what was on offer in the best stores, and it confirmed something she herself had been feeling for some time: the high-decoration style was falling out of favour.

Gone was the wish for exuberance, for mother-of-pearl inlay, for lacquerwork or filigree silver edging. An urge towards simplicity seemed to be taking over. The Bauhaus style with its tendency towards neatness and functionalism was winning the day – especially in America.

Gwen had been feeling a kind of boredom with her own designs. They had begun to seem fussy, overdone. Now and again she'd found herself sketching something very simple, very cool.

When she saw the displays in Heal's and Harrods, they seemed to be saying, 'Yes, you were right.'

Many of the pieces she saw were made from metal, tubular metal. She felt she could never come to terms with making furniture from metal tubes. But when she looked at the pieces made from wood, she saw something that chimed in with her own thoughts. The designers *used* the wood, not just as a material of strength to support the human form or rows of clothes or stacks of dishes, but as a source of beauty in itself. The grain of the wood was displayed, the tone of the wood was enhanced, the gleam, the surface interest, the natural properties . . .

In Singapore, timber was available in vast variety. There was teak, ebony, cedar, sandalwood, upland pine, locust, sumac, mahogany, grey palm, even the tough wood from the great rhododendron that grew up-country. There were more whose names were known only to the Malay or the Chinese.

Using those, with all the skill that Wo Joong and his colleagues could bring to bear, using their knowledge of old ways to polish and display the sheen . . . The day would come, she told herself, when she would bring out a new collection, furniture to bring to the world's notice the glory of the timber that grew in Malaya.

She was happy. She had found a new inspiration for her work. Everything in Singapore was pleasant; Terence was safe in his job, the recession was dying away. At the end of July, Tammy would come for her summer visit. The only cloud on the horizon was the political situation in Europe.

'Do you think there's going to be a war?' she asked Terence as they strolled in the cool of the early morning in the coconut plantation behind her house.

He wrinkled his brow. 'Could be, I suppose. That little tyke Hitler seems to be asking for it. Not to worry, though, it won't affect us here in Singapore.'

'I've got a daughter in England, Terence!' she reminded him.

'Oh, Lord, yes, I forgot that. Oh, she'll be all right even if it happens. Where is she? Wiltshire? Nothing's going to happen in Wiltshire.'

'No, probably not.'

In late June Terence was summoned to Hong Kong again. This time the conference was about how to re-expand the shipping line in view of the demand for rubber and tin caused by rearmament in Europe. It was probably just coincidence that there was a bridge tournament in Hong Kong at the same time.

Gwen always felt bereft when Terence went away. So when Tammy arrived in July she was all the more delighted to see her. She had all kinds of things planned for them to do together. But this year beach picnics and outings in Uncle Sam's cabin cruiser seemed not to appeal.

'You can't blame her,' Sam soothed when Gwen worried about it. 'It's natural she should have the boys flocking round her. She's a knockout for looks, isn't she?'

She certainly was. Two young men gave up membership of the Singapore Club when Tammy was refused admittance on the grounds that she was a Eurasian. Bertie Hurden asked if he might paint her, Mrs Targett gave a 'Bohemian' party for her at the Leonie Hotel. The fashion buyer at Robinson's Department Store offered her swimsuits at cut-price if when she wore them she'd just mention where she got them.

'I hope it doesn't all go to her head,' Gwen fretted. 'The sooner she's back at school, the better!'

But over the wireless came the news that a big crisis was looming in Europe. Adolf Hitler was laying claim to part of Czechoslovakia. It was said that bomb shelters were being dug in the London parks. 'You're not going back to that,' Gwen announced. 'You'll stay here with me.'

'Oh, *Mummy*!' sighed Tammy in the tone that daughters use when mothers are overreacting.

And it turned out she was right, for Mr Chamberlain went to Munich, settled it all with Mr Hitler, peace was assured, and everything could go back to normal.

'So I'm going back to school, I suppose?' Tammy said.

'A bit late, but yes, thank goodness, it's all turned out for the best. With your exams coming up next year, it would have been terribly upsetting for you to change to a Singapore school.'

Tammy shrugged. She didn't really want to go back to Stanton School and take exams, but on the other hand she didn't want to go to some mid-Victorian establishment up-country and have them sneer at her for having slanty eyes.

Gwen missed her when she'd gone. She felt she hadn't seen enough of her on this holiday. But as Sam said, it was only natural Tammy should want to be with youngsters of her own age. Although the young men who had taken her dancing had been somewhat older . . . But that was all right, there was such a shortage of women in Singapore that girls 'came out' rather earlier than they would have at home in England.

The New Year came and work on the British base seemed to gather momentum. Gwen's Japanese newspapers rejoiced in a very arrogant way over the Emperor's troops entering Hainan in China. War clouds seemed to be gathering in Europe – but then Mr Chamberlain had declared last year that peace was assured so all the anxiety was probably over nothing.

Tammy sat her exams in June. When the results were posted, it proved that she'd scraped through. Her headmistress wrote recommending that she should take two subjects again and try to do better. It would mean working through the summer holidays but it would be worth it.

Gwen, greatly troubled but trusting in Miss Powers' opinion, cabled her agreement. Perhaps she should make the trip to England – but she'd been expecting Tammy here, so had made no arrangements for an absence. And besides, wouldn't it fluster her daughter if she arrived looking worried?

So Tammy stayed at Stanton School, stifling rebellious

thoughts and working for half of each day on the subjects that had let her down, mathematics and economics. Around her the whole of Britain waited with bated breath for the final act of the drama that had been unfolding in Europe over the last two years, but Tammy was untouched.

The school was to reopen for general classes on 18 September. Only Tammy and one other girl, Cicely Myers, were in residence. 'You know,' said Tammy as September began, 'it's my sixteenth birthday on Sunday. Generally I have a party at my Granny's.'

'Shall you go there on Sunday?' inquired Cicely, looking doleful at the idea of being left alone.

'Miss Powers says it's better if people who don't need to travel stay at home. Don't know why – something to do with the government, I think.'

'Ooh, then let's have a party of our own, Tammy! We'll get Cook to make some little sausage-rolls and we can buy a cake . . .'

Cook was quite amenable. Supplies were bought on the afternoon of the day before.

And then on the morning of Tammy's birthday, 3 September, Mr Chamberlain announced in a choked voice over the wireless that Britain was at war with Germany.

It seemed to put the staff at Stanton School into a state of shock. At first Tammy and Cicely couldn't understand why, because although of course they knew war was a terrible thing and they'd been in to Salisbury to get fitted with gas-masks, all the fighting was going to be in Poland, which was a long way off.

But then it became clear that Miss Powers was expecting all the girls back to school almost at once. And, what was more, she was expecting an influx of girls from other schools, London schools, and it would mean Cicely and Tammy and a lot of Stanton girls were going to have to double up with complete strangers.

That was bad enough, but then Granny and Grandad arrived and began arguing with Miss Powers about whether Tammy ought to go to stay with them in St Albans, which was most decidedly *not* what Tammy wanted, because Grandad was a bit inclined to hug you and plant slobbery kisses on you when you didn't feel at all like it.

Tammy wrote by airmail to her mother, suggesting that it might be a good idea if she came back to Singapore. Her letter crossed with one which arrived from her mother saying she'd asked Miss Powers to arrange for her to leave as soon as possible.

Gwen, half across the world in Singapore, was beside herself. 'I should never have let her go back last year,' she wailed to Terence, who patted her shoulder and tried to be a comfort.

'How could anyone possibly know that fool Hitler was actually going to send the balloon up?' he sighed. 'Never mind, darling, your little girl will soon be safe and sound with us.'

Not so. There was a long queue of people waiting for passage on ships, and most of the ships were needed for the transport of war materials. It wasn't as if Tamara Veetcha had any special claim – she had relatives in England, she was at a good school safe in Wiltshire, she wasn't needed by her mother to act as wage-earner or nurse. No, no, said the officials at the Ministry of Transport, Miss Tammy Veetcha must wait her turn, and in any case she was really Tamara Hayakawa and only half-British to begin with.

Gwen was beside herself. She avidly devoured the newspapers, she tuned in to the BBC. And gradually her anxiety abated. There were no mass air raids, no attacks with poison gas, no fighting along the Maginot Line in France, nothing . . . It was the period known as the Phoney War, and it went on well into 1940.

But in March of that year something happened that was much more terrifying to Gwen than any

German air attack. She received a cable from Miss Powers . . .

'Regret to tell you Tammy has run away. Letter left on her bed says not to worry but am greatly perturbed. All efforts being made, will inform as soon as possible.'

Chapter Twenty-one

Gwen didn't wait to be 'informed'. In floods of tears she rang Sam Prosper. She read the cable to him. He said, 'Oh hell.'

'Sam, I want to fly home immediately.'

'I understand that. But it's not so easy now, what with the war . . .'

'Could you try your friend at Imperial Airways?'

'Leave it to me, babe.' He sounded grim. 'I'll get you on a plane. There's guys in Singapore who owe me favours.'

Whatever debts he called in, they resulted in a seat on the Catalina due to fly out at first light next day. She spent the intervening hours giving instructions to Wo Joong, sending cables home, and trying to think what to pack for the journey. She left in the middle of a typical monsoon rainstorm.

The flying-boat soon climbed above the weather. Soon they were zooming through cloudless skies. She was the only non-government employee in the passenger list of fourteen; all the rest were naval, military or civil servants. They eyed this pretty, anxious woman with interest but had the good sense not to try to make conversation with her.

The route this time was different due to wartime exigencies. Gwen made no overnight stops for rest, but within an hour – sometimes within minutes – transferred to the next plane for the next leg of the flight.

She slept fitfully in her seat, watching dawns and sunsets above the clouds and hardly knowing which was which. She couldn't this time make the last part of the journey by the overland route from Rome because Italy was now Britain's enemy. She transferred at Malta to a four-engined propeller aeroplane.

The landing at Croydon Aerodrome was bumpy. Though it was the middle of March, there were heaps of snow along the runway. Outside the temperature was arctic. In the thin waterproof which had seemed too hot in Singapore, Gwen was frozen.

The Immigration officials kept her a long time. They looked at her passport, conferred together, regarded her with dubiety. Her husband was no longer living? She was a resident of Singapore? Where would she be staying? What reason did she have for visiting Britain? Her daughter – she was a British resident?

Customs officers went through her overnight case very thoroughly. Everything – soap-box, toilet bag, pockets of her dressing-gown – was carefully examined.

Finally they let her go. She'd been given a temporary Identity Card and told she must report at the registration office in St Albans to get her visitor's ration card.

In the visitors' lounge her mother and stepfather were sitting on the edge of their seats waiting for her. Rhoda, immediately on seeing her, burst into tears. 'Oh, Gwennie, Gwennie, how ill you look! It's all too dreadful! Oh, precious, how can you ever forgive me?'

'Now, now, Rhoda,' Wally said, with his arm around her and a large handkerchief at the ready. Over her head he said to Gwen, 'She's been like this ever since Miss Powers rang us. I tell her it's not our fault.'

'Why? What happened?' Gwen demanded, drawing back from her mother's attempts to weep on her shoulder.

'I'll tell you as we go. I've got the car in the car park – come on. Good God, girl, is that the only coat you've brought?'

'Oh, never mind that!' she cried, and hurried out

through a door where an arrow pointed to the car park.

Wally had brought, not his handsome Lanchester, but a serviceable little Austin. He explained as they got in that it was because of petrol problems. He got a special allowance for furniture deliveries and it was some of this he had 'borrowed' to make the trip to fetch her home.

'Home? To St Albans, you mean? I want to go straight to Stanton—'

'No, no, dear,' Rhoda protested, taking her daughter's hand. 'You look so exhausted, you must have a night's sleep . . . And a coat, I should have brought you a coat – you'll have to borrow one of mine.'

'Anyhow,' said Wally, 'I don't have enough in the tank to drive to Wiltshire.'

'I never expected to be driven there. I'm going by train.' She insisted that Wally drive her to the Strand Hotel where she had cabled for a room, so that she could tidy up, have a meal, and ring Miss Powers for the latest news.

'What was this about "your fault"?' she asked as they drove away from the aerodrome.

Wally grunted. 'It was quite an ordinary conversation,' he said over his shoulder. 'How were we to know it was going to put ideas into her head?'

'What? What are you talking about?'

'Well,' Rhoda said, swallowing back sobs, 'as you know she came to us for Christmas. Miss Powers was quite glad to let any of the girls go who had safe homes to go to – she kept those who came from London or the big towns because of possible air raids, you see. Though thank heavens there's been absolutely nothing since that first siren.'

'That was a trick to make us all sit up,' Wally said. 'Just after old Neville finished his piece that first Sunday. Never was a bomber coming over, at least that's what everybody says.'

'But about Tammy,' Gwen urged.

'Yes, well, Tammy was with us for Christmas. She went out a lot – quite a gad-about, your little gal—'

'Wally, she had every right to want to go dancing and to the cinema,' his wife put in. 'After all, she's sixteen years old. And life at Stanton can't be much fun these days with nearly three hundred girls where there used to be a hundred and two.'

'Oh, please, Mother,' Gwen begged, beside herself with anxiety to know what had prompted her daughter to run away.

'See, Tammy was saying what a dull life it all was, how having a mother in the furniture trade was as boring as you could find, and Rhoda here laughed and said "You don't know the half of it".'

'And then I told her about you running away, dear,' sobbed Rhoda, 'I wanted to make her see how romantic and different you were.'

'Oh, yes, really piled it on, didn't you?' Wally said, with a little shrug. Sitting in the back, Gwen couldn't see his face, but something about his tone told her he was rather enjoying himself. Perhaps it pleased him to see Gwen brought low over her darling daughter.

'Gwen dear, I meant no harm. If I'd ever imagined . . . But she listened with such a lot of attention and asked questions and seemed . . . you know . . . impressed, so I thought it was a good thing to have done.'

Gwen clenched and unclenched her fists. 'Even if she suddenly found out I'd run off years ago . . . I mean, I had somewhere to go to . . .'

'Someone to go *with*, you mean,' said her stepfather. 'And it turns out, so had Tammy.'

'Tammy? You mean, a man?'

'Seems so.'

'Oh, Gwen,' her mother wailed, 'we had no idea she was meeting him—'

'Meeting him where? How?'

'She'd go out, you see, travel up to London by train,

meet a school-chum of hers, Annette Willis. They went to the Corner House, to the Lyceum dance hall – no harm in it, we thought. But it seems she'd met a feller . . . Reggie something.'

'Reggie something. You don't know his last name?'

'Annette says she never heard it, or if she did she can't recall. The two of them palled up with two young men, Reggie and Michael. Michael's a soldier, he's been tracked down, knows nothing, never met Reggie before they asked the girls to dance at the Lyceum. What I'm saying is, they weren't friends, the only reason they got to know each other was that the two girls were together so the men got to know each other. Anyhow Michael fades out of the picture, he's at Aldershot, only up in London on a pass.'

'How was Michael found? By the police?'

'Yes, Miss Powers called 'em in as soon as she'd questioned Tammy's friends and found out from Annette about this Reggie.'

Wally had the best grip on the story. When his wife intervened with her recollections it was usually some side issue that lost the thread of the narrative. It seemed that Reggie and Tammy had kept in touch by letter after she went back to school at the end of the Christmas holidays.

Annette, much shocked and frightened, confessed that Tammy and Reggie had planned to meet again for the Easter break which this year would be over the weekend of 23 March. But then Miss Powers had announced that, in view of the bad weather and the difficulties of travel, it would be better if the girls stayed at school. Concerts and sing-songs were to be arranged to make up for the loss of the holiday, and a longer break promised for Whitsun.

So Tammy had decided to run off to meet Reggie. When asked where, Annette could only weep and say she thought they were in London. Where in London? She had no idea.

The Wiltshire constabulary had learned that a girl meeting Tammy's description had taken a late-evening train from Salisbury to London. They had done well to get this far. Now they had to hand it over to the Metropolitan police, who had a lot more important things to do than track down a pair of young lovers. And London, since the exodus at the beginning of the war, was full of empty houses and flats that made a good hide-out.

The drive to the Strand Hotel was completed in the dark. Gwen was so cold she could hardly bend her fingers. Her mother insisted on coming in with her to see her settled in her room, stayed to make sure she drank the tea she ordered, begged her to lie down till train time. But Gwen couldn't rest until she had put through a call to Stanton.

'Mrs Veetcha? I'm very sorry, there's no further news at this end,' said an anxious Miss Powers.

'Has anyone any idea whether they planned to go to Gretna?'

'The police looked into that. It seems not.'

'I'm coming as soon as I can. There's a train at ten. I should get there by early morning—'

'Oh, Mrs Veetcha, I do advise you to wait until daylight. The train service is in a dreadful state because of the weather and the war – it might take you eight or nine hours to get to Salisbury.'

'I'll be there in the morning,' Gwen said, and hung up.

Next she rang Scotland Yard, to ask if the sergeant handling the London end of the case had any news. He wasn't available but a constable looked up the file and said sorry, nothing to report.

It took Gwen half an hour to get rid of her mother, for whom Wally was waiting downstairs in the bar. As soon as she'd gone, Gwen hurried through the black-out to the Army and Navy Stores down the road, where just as they were closing she bought a thick cardigan and a tweed coat. Neither was very attractive but, the saleswoman said in all seriousness, 'They'll see you through the war.'

When she got back to the hotel, she saw from a notice on the bathroom door that hot water would be available from six to ten. She therefore had a hot bath, which to some extent relaxed her and at least warmed her. She ate a passable dinner in the restaurant.

After explaining that she wouldn't actually occupy the room tonight but wanted it kept while she went down to Wiltshire, she was advised to take sandwiches for the journey.

'Sandwiches? I'll get breakfast on the train.'

'Dear me, no, madam. No restaurant service these days. There's a war on, you know.'

She accepted the sandwiches made up for her in the hotel kitchens, also a flask of coffee. She thought the precautions rather absurd, but they proved highly necessary. The train she boarded was not well cleaned, the black-out blinds and the very low-wattage lamp gave it an air of misery and, true enough, there was no food available.

Soon after six she stepped out at Salisbury into a dark morning with a powdery snow falling. There were no taxis. But after inquiry she learned there was a bus that passed the end of the station road, which would drop her off in the market square in Stanton. From there it was a ten-minute walk to the school.

Miss Powers was up and waiting for her though the rest of the school was only just stirring. The old mansion had a blank-eyed look, with sticky tape criss-crossing its windows as a precaution against shattering glass in an air raid, and heavy black-out curtains still closed. When she was ushered into the headmistress's study, Gwen felt it was much colder than formerly: fuel restrictions, of course.

419

'Mrs Veetcha, I can't tell you how sorry I am about this business.'

'Has there been anything further since last night?'

'I'm afraid not. We don't expect anything further at this end, you know. May I take your coat? And can I offer you anything? Tea, coffee, something to eat? Breakfast isn't until seven-thirty but—'

'I'd like some tea, if I may. Please show me the letter Tammy left.'

Miss Powers rang a bell on her desk. 'The police took it. But I remember what it said. Ah, Nancy, please bring tea for two at once and – perhaps some toast, Mrs Veetcha? No? Then just tea, Nancy.'

There was a small fire in the grate, emitting more smoke than flame. Miss Powers put Gwen in a chair at one side of it, sat down opposite. She took off her glasses, began to clean them to give her nervousness some escape.

'The letter, Miss Powers?'

'It said: Dear Miss Powers, I am going away to make a good future. Don't worry about me, I know what I'm doing.'

Gwen stifled a gasp. 'That was all?'

'Yes.'

'No message for me?'

'No.'

It took Gwen a moment to get her voice under control. 'Don't you think that's a strange letter?'

'Strange?'

'Well, no announcement that she's going to get married, no reference about going with "the man I love".'

The headmistress put her glasses back on, pushed at them to settle them. 'I . . . er . . . I would say that Tammy isn't the sort of girl to give much of herself away – especially not to her headmistress.'

'But are you sure you've got it right? It sounds almost . . . business-like.'

'In what way?'

'"Going away to make a good future." Not "going away to be married" or "going away because I can't bear the life I'm leading" – it's not emotional, it's businesslike.'

'You may be right.' The maid came in with the tea. They waited until she'd gone. Then Miss Powers said, 'It seems quite certain that she went to meet this man called Reggie.'

'Who says so? Annette Willis?'

'Yes, and Rosemary Collingworth. She's still close to Tammy even though they don't do show-jumping any more. Tammy and Annette Willis are friendly enough but it was only because they both were allowed home for Christmas that they shared their outings in London. Annette went up to town from Surrey, Tammy from Hertfordshire. They met at the Corner House.'

'I'd like to speak to the girls, if I may.'

'Certainly. But the police have already questioned them both, and several others.'

The two girls had been told last night that Tammy's mother was coming. They were both very subdued when, as the rest of the school filed into the dining-room for breakfast, they were brought to the headmistress's study. They were dressed in the navy skirt, navy sweater and white blouse of the sixth form.

'Now, Annette, I want you to tell Mrs Veetcha what you told me about Tammy and this young man.'

'Yes, Miss Powers.' Annette was a small, cuddly girl with thick brown hair and a high colour. 'We met him at the Lyceum dance hall. He asked Tammy to dance. Soon after that Michael came up and invited me, and then at the interval we went and had a milkshake together.' She paused.

'Go on,' said Miss Powers.

'We danced mostly with them that evening. I danced one dance with Reggie and one with another boy but mostly with Michael. Tammy did the same with Reggie. We made a date to meet them the next evening. I quite liked Michael but we didn't stick with each other, though Reggie and Tammy did. I said to Tammy, "He's really keen on you." And she said she thought he was.'

'Yes?'

'Well, Michael had to go back to Aldershot. But Reggie wasn't going in the Forces – he had bad eyesight.'

'Wore glasses?'

'Yes, I told that to the sergeant,' muttered Annette. 'Glasses with thick rims, and a dark suit and a brown tie, and an awfully good dancer.'

'What did he do for a living?'

'I don't know. I wasn't all that much interested.'

'Did Tammy see Reggie every day of the Christmas holidays?'

'Probably. She and I didn't see each other every day. But she mentioned Reggie when we did.'

Gwen knew her mother had the impression that the two girls had been going out with each other, and only with each other. She sighed inwardly. Would some preventive step have been taken if Tammy had mentioned the acquisition of a boyfriend?

Annette had nothing more to tell. Miss Powers turned to Rosemary Collingworth. 'It's your turn now, Rosemary.'

'I didn't meet him. I don't really know anything about him.'

'But you know what Tammy told you.'

'Oh, I didn't listen to half of it. She mooned on and on about him, as if he was Clark Gable or somebody.'

'Did she tell you she was going to go away with him?'

There was indeed something faintly horsey about Rosemary, for she moved now like a restless colt.

Tall, thin, rather weather-beaten, her looks might have influenced Tammy to give up competitive riding.

'She didn't exactly say she was going away with him. She said they had plans. I got the impression she meant plans that would mean they'd be together but . . . I mean, really . . . who would ever have thought she'd dash off like that?'

'Please try to remember anything helpful. Please, Rosemary. I'm dreadfully worried about her.'

Tammy's best friend blushed and looked down at her shoes. Then out of the corner of her eye she looked at Miss Powers. Gwen thought: she doesn't want to talk openly in front of the headmistress. The Powers, the girls called her. She was a good teacher, expecting hard work and good behaviour. To have to confess something that would make her think less of you might be difficult.

'I expect you want your breakfast,' Gwen said. 'May we have a little chat afterwards, Rosemary?'

Rosemary nodded without speaking. Both girls made a dash for the door.

'Rosemary knows something,' said Miss Powers.

'That's what I thought.'

'Then why doesn't she tell?'

'I expect Tammy made her promise not to.'

Miss Powers sighed. 'Do you remember when you were that age? It was easy to think that you were in a sort of pact to keep grown-ups out of things . . .'

'If you'd let me speak to her alone, after breakfast?'

'Of course. And speaking of that, won't you have something now? We can have it here, no need to run the gauntlet in the dining-room.'

They ate scrambled eggs and drank fresh tea. By and by a bell rang to warn that classes would begin in ten minutes. Miss Powers rose. 'I'll let you have this room for your chat. Don't worry about Rosemary's class, I'll tell Miss Jordan that she won't be there.'

The maid came in to remove the breakfast tray and to stir up the fire. By and by Rosemary reappeared. She moved to the fireplace, to stand like a penitent before Gwen.

'I've made up my mind to tell you. I promised Tammy to say nothing for a week at least. But I had no idea you'd come flying back from Singapore . . . I feel rotten about it.'

'Yes,' Gwen said. 'I suppose you do. So what is it you weren't to tell?'

'Tammy's gone off to be a model.'

Whatever Gwen had expected it wasn't this. She was struck dumb.

'Like those girls on magazine covers. Reggie is a photographer. He told her he could make her famous.'

'Oh, no . . .'

'It wasn't anything to do with love. I mean, I think she likes him and from what she says he's dotty about *her* – but when I heard Miss Powers talking to the sergeant about Gretna Green and all that I knew she'd got the wrong idea.'

'Do you know where they are?' Gwen demanded.

'He's got a studio in London. She didn't say where but I think it's Marylebone because she once said something about Madame Tussaud's being near.' She hesitated, and her lips quivered. 'I'm really sorry, Mrs Veetcha. I didn't think it would feel like this. I thought it would be exciting but seeing everybody so worried . . . and now you . . . I just have to break my promise.'

'Thank you,' Gwen sighed. 'I'm very grateful.'

Rosemary gave what information she could. Reggie had said he would make Tammy famous, that he was going to take pictures and offer them to the magazines in time for their summer issues. That meant, she said, that the pictures had to be taken and sent out in the spring – Tammy had expected to go to his studio during the Easter break. She had been forced into alternative action when the Easter break was withheld.

'And what was to happen after that?'

'Reggie was going to manage Tammy's career. Models get all kinds of engagements, you see – it's a tremendously busy life and she said she'd need someone like Reggie to take care of the business side.'

'But, Rosemary . . . she's only sixteen!'

'But she looks older in a photograph. She showed me some Reggie'd already taken – you couldn't tell she was a schoolgirl, really you couldn't.' She broke off, looking very unhappy. 'Are you going to send the police after them?'

'Yes . . . no . . . I don't know . . .' If she could find her daughter and get her away, perhaps there need be no further police involvement. She couldn't bear the thought of Tammy being dragged off like a criminal.

Having heard all that Rosemary knew, Gwen passed on the news to Miss Powers. She left at once for the London train. She reached her hotel by mid-afternoon. She had a meal, washed and changed, then rang to ask if the hotel office had a directory.

'A telephone directory, madam?'

'No, a London business directory.'

'I'm afraid not. But there's sure to be one in the reference library at the top of Kingsway.'

She went there by bus. She turned to the section dealing with Marylebone and made a note of all the photographers. She had no surname, but knew his first name was Reginald, though that might be limited to the initial R.

Unfortunately many of the photographers had trade names such as Sunray Photographers or Portraits by Patrick. And for all she knew, Reggie might only be employed, he might not own his studio. All the same, Rosemary had said, 'He's got a studio.'

There were two with addresses not far from Madame Tussaud's. One had the initial R. Knowing it was far too much to hope for that her first effort would find Tammy, she went out, found a taxi, and was driven there through the icy, blacked-out streets.

At the address there was no light to be seen, no way of reading the name-plates in the doorway. 'You new to London, missus?' said the taxi driver. 'Never go anywhere without a torch.' He got out and shone a pencil-ray on the name plates to show her that R. Hartfield, Photographer, had a studio on the second floor.

She rewarded him with an extra tip. He opened the street door for her to reveal a very dim hall light and a steep flight of stairs. 'Mind how you go,' he said cheerfully as he left her to it.

There was adequate lighting inside. On the second floor she found two doors, one with an upper half of reeded glass with black lettering: Reginald Hartfield, Photographer. The door was closed, but there were lights within.

She tapped on the glass. No response. She knocked harder, with her knuckles. She could distinguish a shape coming towards the door.

'I fixed the black-out, warden,' said a male voice.

'It's not about the black-out. Are you Mr Hartfield?'

'Yes, but I'm closed. You'll have to come back in the morning.'

'I don't want a photograph. Please may I speak to you?'

'What about?'

'Please open the door so we can talk. It's important.'

She could see an arm come towards the door; she heard the lock turn.

She was looking at a young man in shirtsleeves and waterproof apron. He was of medium height, had darkish hair and glasses with thick rims and side-pieces. He was eyeing her doubtfully.

'Mr Hartfield?'

'Yes, what is it?'

'My name is Gwen Veetcha. Does that mean anything to you?'

The question was needless. His mouth fell open at the name. 'Oh,' he gasped.

She pushed past him. The reception area consisted of a desk with a phone, a couple of small armchairs, and a low table with an album of sample photographs. On the walls enlargements of his work. There was an archway with a set of heavy dark blue curtains. Beyond the arch, bright lights were shining.

'Is my daughter here, Mr Hartfield?'

'No – what d'you mean . . . Who—?'

She walked on, through the curtains. There was a large plate camera on a tripod facing a dais on which was a gilt sofa backed by some potted palms. Spotlights were trained so that the rest of the room seemed utterly black. A fan lay half open on the sofa.

'Look here, you've no business – I'm in the middle of a session—'

A door in darkness behind the sofa opened. 'I've taken the plate out of the rinsing-tank – is that all right, Reggie?' called a voice.

Gwen drew in a breath.

'Tammy?' she called. 'Tammy?'

There was a muffled scream, something made of glass fell to the floor and was broken.

Into the light surrounding the sofa walked Tammy. She was wearing a wool dressing gown over a sort of sarong of blue silk, and over all this a waterproof apron like the one worn by Reggie Hartfield.

'Mummy!' she exclaimed.

'You silly, selfish girl!' Gwen cried. 'We've all been out of our heads with worry!'

'Now wait a minute, Mrs Veetcha, there's no need to take that tone—'

'You keep out of it,' Gwen said through her teeth.

'I'll deal with you later, perhaps by handing you over to the police for abduction!'

'I didn't abduct—! You can't say that! Tell her, Tammy.' The photographer was scared to death.

'It's all right, Reggie,' Tammy said. She had recovered almost at once from the shock of seeing her mother. 'I'll explain it to her in a minute. In the meantime, I'm afraid I just dropped the last plate. We'll have to do that pose all over again.'

'I . . . I . . . It doesn't matter about the plate—'

'You're absolutely right. There will be no more posing.' Gwen took her daughter by the arm. 'Come along, put your clothes on. We're leaving.'

'No we're not,' said Tammy, trying to pull herself free. 'You don't understand. I'm making a start on my career. I'm going to be a model girl.'

'You're coming with me this minute.'

'No I'm not! Let go of me! Who do you think you are, coming in here ordering us about? I've a life of my own—'

'You'll do as I tell you.'

'Oh, you always think you can order me about and send me here and there like a parcel! Well, not this time. This time you can just clear off.'

Gwen's hand flew out. Her palm smacked across Tammy's left cheek. The sound of the blow seemed to fill the brightly lit room.

'Oh, I say!' cried Reggie, starting forward.

'You stay out of it!' Gwen cried, rounding on him. 'You inconsiderate fool, filling her head with nonsense! Tammy, go and put your outdoor things on.'

Tammy was standing with one hand against her cheek. Tears had welled up and were pouring over her fingers. She lowered her head, then covered her face with both hands.

'Oh, Mummy . . .' she wept.

'Crying isn't going to do you any good. Go and get dressed.'

'You never . . . you never hit me before . . .'

'No, and perhaps that was my mistake. *Go and put your clothes on.*'

It was a tone Tammy had never heard from her mother. Whimpering with the pain of the blow and the shock of the act, she went with bowed shoulders to obey.

Chapter Twenty-two

Reggie Hartfield went out to flag down a taxi. Tammy packed her belongings. Reggie actually carried her case downstairs, bleating that he hoped Mrs Veetcha wasn't going to see all this the wrong way.

As Tammy was about to go into the taxi, she turned to him, as if expecting a kiss or an embrace. Gwen put herself between them. Tammy flinched away, they both got in and, in stony silence, were carried to the Strand Hotel.

The receptionist was able to transfer Gwen's belongings to a double room. Tammy was registered, they went upstairs. Still in her coat, Gwen went to the telephone.

First she rang her mother in St Albans. Cries of joy, sobs, tears . . .

'I assure you, Mother, she's perfectly all right. I'll tell you all about it when I see you. Tomorrow, some time, I think. No, we'll catch the train—'

'I'm not going back to St Albans!' Tammy interrupted, dragging at her mother's arm as if to get the instrument away from her.

'What?' Gwen said. She covered the mouthpiece. 'What did you say?

'I'm not going to Granny's, to have Grandad sniggering over me!'

Gwen stared at her daughter. 'What's that about Grandad?'

But Tammy had turned away, to throw herself into a chair and glare at the ceiling.

Gwen turned back to the phone, where Rhoda was anxiously begging to be told what was going on.

'It's all right, just a tantrum. I think perhaps we'll stay on at the hotel for a bit. No . . . No . . . Well, you can come here . . . All right, tomorrow.'

As soon as she'd disconnected she rang Scotland Yard. Once more she was told that Sergeant Turner was off duty and put on to a constable, who looked up the file.

'Safely home? I'll leave word for Mr Turner, he'll get it first thing in the morning. In the meantime, can I have some details?'

'Of course. What do you want to know?'

'At what address was your daughter found?' Gwen spelled it out. The next question was: 'With whom was she found?

'A photographer – Reginald Hartfield.'

'Mummy!' Tammy exclaimed, sitting up straight and throwing out a hand in entreaty.

'Be quiet. The police have got to know.'

'But I don't see why.'

'Good God, child, don't you understand? Miss Powers sent for the police the minute she read your note.'

'No,' gasped Tammy. 'No, there was no need . . .'

'I'm sorry, constable, that was my daughter interrupting. What else do you need to know?'

'May I ask how you got on to the chap?'

Gwen explained that a schoolfellow had confessed to some slight knowledge of Tammy's whereabouts and that she herself had followed it up. 'I'm hoping, constable, that not too much need be made of it . . .'

'That remains to be seen, madam. May I ask if you've had a doctor's examination?'

'What?' cried Gwen, aghast.

'You haven't. Well, up to you, of course. I'll leave all this for Mr Turner. He'll probably want to see you. Will you be at home tomorrow morning?'

'Constable,' Gwen said in exhaustion, 'the way I feel,

I couldn't go another step for the next ten days.'

By now it was going on for ten o'clock. Gwen was working now almost on automatic reaction. Nothing but anger seemed to keep her going. She ordered her daughter to take a bath and get ready for bed. She rang reception to ask if she could have some food sent up and after some persuasion succeeded in getting hot soup, rolls, the remains of the fish dish which had been the chef's speciality for dinner, and some coffee.

Tammy refused to eat. Whether distress and disappointment had taken away her appetite, or whether it was a protest, Gwen couldn't tell. She herself ate heartily. Almost at once she was overcome with fatigue.

She undressed in a dream. As she came out of the bathroom after brushing her teeth and washing her face, she glimpsed her daughter watching her. Tammy was calculating that her mother was too tired to stay awake.

Alerted, Gwen went ostentatiously to the room door, locked it, and put the key under the pillow on her bed. 'Goodnight, Tammy,' she said as she got in.

Tammy sat on the side of the other bed, wide awake.

'You can sit there all night if you like,' said her mother with weary grimness, 'but if you do, put the light out first.'

With that she turned over on her side, pulled up the covers, and was at once deeply asleep.

Tammy shook her awake next morning. 'Mummy, the maid's knocking, asking if she can make the beds.'

Gwen returned as if from a drugged state. 'What?' she asked groggily.

'The maid's at the door.'

'Tell her to go away.'

'But it's nine o'clock and—'

Gwen dragged herself out of bed, began to go to the door, remembered she had the key under her pillow, and went back to get it. She unlocked the door. An elderly maid was glaring at her in disapproval.

'Come back later.'

'Can't do that, we're short-staffed.'

'All right, we'll make the beds ourselves. Go away.'

Grunting with annoyance, the maid pushed her linen trolley along towards the service lift. Gwen closed the door. She felt stiff, heavy, unrefreshed. But she had to start the day. The police sergeant might be here soon.

She bathed and dressed. It was too late for breakfast in the hotel.

'We'll go out to a Lyon's.'

'I'll stay here. I never eat breakfast.'

'You're coming with me.'

Sullenly Tammy put on her nappa coat and her pale blue beret, Stanton school uniform for sixth formers. They went to a Lyon's near Waterloo Bridge. There Gwen ate toast with terrible margarine but with marmalade left over from some pre-war store. She drank several cups of very strong tea.

She felt better, but Tammy's sulky face across the table depressed her. So did the tea-room. It had been a cheerful enough place prior to the war, walled with mirrors and with windows on the Strand giving a lively view of passers-by. Now the mirrors had been taken down for safety reasons leaving huge expanses of beige wall, and the windows on the Strand were closed off by a permanenet black-out. Wartime London was certainly no fun, even if the expected raids and gas attacks had never arrived.

Gwen had left word at the desk that they would be back in half an hour. When they walked into the vestibule, a very large man in his late forties rose from a chair.

'Mrs Veetcha? I'm Sergeant Turner.'

'Yes, sergeant, sorry we had to go out, we missed breakfast.'

'Quite all right, madam. Is there somewhere we could talk?'

'Upstairs would be best, I think.'

They went up to the bedroom. There was something dishevelled about it, though Gwen had hastily made the beds before they went out – with no help from Tammy. Tammy went in now like a prisoner in handcuffs, sat on her bed, and stared at her shoes.

'Glad to see the young lady safe and sound,' said the sergeant.

Tammy said nothing.

'As to this Hartfield . . .' He took out a notebook, opened it.

Tammy stiffened.

'I went there first thing this morning. He says it was all above board. I looked at the pictures he'd done – true enough, fashion shots, quite respectable. Well, anyhow, those that I could find – he may have done away with the naughty ones. Is that what he's done, miss?'

Tammy made no response.

'What was your impression last night, Mrs Veetcha?'

Gwen hesitated. 'He was in the middle of processing a photographic plate, I think. My daughter was helping him.'

'Voluntarily?'

'Oh, yes, voluntarily. The story was that she'd gone with him to start on a career as a photographic model. They had to get pictures done to send round to the magazines.'

'Tut tut,' said the sergeant. 'The tales these fellers tell.'

Tammy made a sound that might have been the beginnings of a protest – something like: 'It was true!' But she stopped herself at once.

'See, Mrs Veetcha, the chap tells me he thought she was eighteen. She told him she was.'

'Tammy?'

Tammy turned her face away, stubbornly silent.

Gwen sighed. 'I think that's probably true,' she said. 'I gather she was extremely keen to be a model.'

'Wanted her picture on the magazine covers, eh? A lot of girls have that notion. Not many of them run off from school, though.'

'What comes next, sergeant?'

He rubbed his forehead with the end of his pencil. 'That's up to you, madam. Fact is, there's no evidence of taking against the will, no evidence of immoral purposes, nothing of that kind. As to the other aspect, the young lady is over the age of consent so you see . . . I suppose you could bring a case of taking away without the consent of the parent—'

'No, no. I would prefer . . . I daresay it's weakminded of me, but I'd rather the whole thing was put aside, if it's possible.'

'Well, Mrs Veetcha, to tell the truth, the police have a lot to do these days without bringing a prosecution that might get thrown out . . .'

'Exactly. Can we just leave it, then?'

'If that's your own feeling. I don't want to persuade you against your wish.'

'No, I would prefer . . .'

The sergeant rose from his chair, put away his note-book, and made for the door. A slight jerk of his head let Gwen know he wanted a word in private. She went out with him to the corridor.

'If I was you, madam, I'd keep a strict eye. Seen a few rebellious youngsters in my time, and she's just waiting for the chance to slip off back to him. Not that he'd have her, mind – I put the fear of God in him.'

Gwen summoned a smile of gratitude. 'Yes, I can see she's angry with me. But to tell the truth, I'm angry with *her*.'

'Only natural. Best thing is, back to school and get her busy on exams and that sort of thing.'

'I don't think so. I shall take her home to Singapore.'

'Ah,' said the sergeant. 'Probably best. Good morning to you, then.'

Gwen's mother arrived just before lunch. She fell

436

adoringly upon Tammy, who bore it in cold silence. They ate in the hotel, then Gwen went out to send cables and to start on the matter of making travel arrangements.

She cabled to Sam: 'Tammy found safe and well. Returning with her as soon as poss. Tell friends and staff. Gwen.'

By 'tell friends' she meant, 'tell Terence'. She knew he would do so, and also alert her chief houseboy Omar that she was coming back.

But travel was difficult. The Home Office agreed that she had come as a visitor and was entitled to go. She was also entitled to take her daughter, who was a minor. The problem was the long waiting list for berths. As to air travel, the mere notion was laughed at. 'Oh, it may have been possible to fit you in from Singapore, madam, but there are a great many more people wanting air passage here in London – most of them official.'

Then, at the end of a week, the Transport Department at the Home Office rang her. 'Mrs Veetcha, I'm very pleased to tell you that we've had word from the shipping line American Eagle that they can offer you a double berth on the *Beulah* sailing on Wednesday for Tokyo via Singapore and the East Indies.'

'How did that come about?' Gwen gasped.

'I'm afraid I've no idea, madam. The passenger manager rang this morning to say they had this vacancy. Shall I give you the number so that you can ring him?'

'Please. And do I take it my daughter and I have clearance to go?'

'Certainly madam. If you call in on Tuesday the permits will be ready.'

Gwen had no doubt that Sam Prosper had pulled strings with the shipping line. It was a merchant line which plied between New York and the Far East, calling at European and Asian ports en route to Japan.

Rhoda was stricken when she heard the news. 'I thought you'd be with me for quite a while, darling,' she mourned. 'And as for taking Tammy back with you

. . . I feel so badly about that . . . I know you feel you can't trust me to look after her any more . . .'

'Nothing like that, Mother,' Gwen soothed.

But it was something like that. And with that went an uneasiness about her stepfather's attitude to Tammy. She recalled her own anxiety years ago – the reason she herself had left home. Perhaps Tammy had felt the same threat, and it was partly for this reason that she'd gone out all day every day during the Christmas holidays – simply to be out of Wally's range.

Wally came with Rhoda to Southampton to see them off. Gwen noticed how her daughter stayed safely the other side of the group from Wally. Yes, it was best to take her to the safety of Singapore, safe from anything that might threaten her within the family, safe from romantic foolishness, safe from the hardship of the war in Europe.

The SS *Beulah* was a cargo ship with berths for eighteen passengers. Being American, it touched at ports en route that would have been closed to British shipping. Food was plentiful, the weather once they got to Egypt was fine. Gwen, knowing that Tammy was safely held within the ship's confines, relaxed.

In fact, though she didn't confess it, she felt quite ill for the first part of the voyage. She knew it was sheer reaction. But as her daughter had made it quite clear she was in no mood to sympathise, Gwen kept her miseries to herself.

Between them there was an armed truce. Gwen tried to treat her daughter with firm kindness, Tammy refused to respond in any way. She hardly spoke, she ate as little as she could, she wouldn't take any part in discussions about her future, she mooned about the ship causing the first and second mate to lose track of their duties.

'Going through a difficult phase, I expect,' said a kindly American matron, Mrs Attwood, when Tammy had once more got up from table after a silent meal.

'I only hope it isn't going to last much longer,' Gwen said.

'Oh, my dear, you'll look back on it in a year or two and laugh.'

Gwen certainly didn't feel like laughing now. In fact, she often found herself on the verge of tears for no specific reason. But it wouldn't do to let Tammy know how much her behaviour was hurting her.

They reached Singapore in mid-May. It wasn't the best time to bring Tammy home because the wearisome southerly wind, known as the 'Java breeze', was blowing. This was a strong current of air from the East Indies which blew during May and June, and which strangely enough had no refreshment in it. May and June were always the season of colds and minor fevers. Tammy immediately went down with one.

'It's only influenza,' said the doctor. 'Keep her in bed, plenty of rest, plenty of fluids. You look as if you could do with the same treatment yourself, Mrs Veetcha.'

'Thank you, doctor, but I'm quite all right.'

Sam was not of that opinion. He had met them off the ship and called next day, to find Tammy ordered to bed by the doctor.

He said to Gwen, 'You look beat. Look, let the servants take care of the kid – they can take her lime-juice or tea just as easily as you can.'

'You don't understand, Sam! I feel so responsible . . .'

'Because you brought her home and she went down with flu? Don't be silly.'

They were in the shade of the dombeya at the far side of the lawn. The strong yet sultry breeze moved the heavy foliage and the masses of dried flower-heads that was all that remained of the winter's glory of soft pink blossom.

'I feel responsible because I've brought her back and I've no idea what to *do*!'

It was a wail of misery. Sam, about to light a cheroot, paused to stare at her.

'Come on now, honey, this isn't like you. You're not the kind that gives way.'

Gwen shook her head, gazing beyond him towards the sea. There it was, turquoise blue capped with white, and beyond it, far off in Europe which she'd been so glad to leave, dreadful things were happening. The Nazis had invaded Belgium and Holland, were pouring into France. The reports on the wireless grew more and more frightening with every hour.

Omar appeared bringing pitchers of fruit juice and ice. He poured lime for Sam, pineapple for Gwen. 'Missy sleep,' he announced.

'Thank you, Omar.'

'Tuan stay for lunch?'

'No, Omar, I got to get back to the office.' When Omar had bowed himself away Sam went on, 'See? He and Lala can take care of Tammy OK. And as for what to do about her – she ought to go back to school. There's a good day school in Tanglin.'

'I suggested that. She says she doesn't want to.'

'Does that come into it, what she wants? I mean, she's kinda put her foot in it, she ought to be trying to put herself right with you.'

'It's the other way round. She thinks I ought to be apologising to her.'

'What, she runs off and gives you a heart attack, and it's all your fault?'

'No, but I handled it badly. I lost my temper. I . . . I hit her.'

Sam sipped his lime juice. 'We-ell . . . I got a few tannings when I was a kid. I never expected my Pop to apologise.'

'No, but don't you see . . . I mean, she thought she was in love . . .'

'Was she?'

'I don't know. She won't discuss it. I think she and the man were lovers, but whether there was any real love on her side . . .'

'Run that past me again? You think she went to bed with him but didn't love him?'

'I have an awful feeling that . . . perhaps . . . it was ambition that made her go with him.'

'Ambition? With a two-bit photographer?'

'She thought he was going to open the way to a great career for her.'

'My, my. Of course she's known for a long time that she's got looks worth a string of Burma rubies.'

'What am I to do, Sam? I can't just let her kick her heels around Singapore.'

'No, not with all these eager young men around . . .' He thought it over. Picking up his cheroot from the ashtray, he waved it in inspiration. 'Give her a job in your firm.'

'Doing what? She thinks furniture is dull, and the office work is only enough for Gan Toy and Lim. Besides, she and I don't get on together any more.'

'Yeah,' said Sam. He smoked for a moment in silence. His brownish eyes were watching a chestnut bulbul struggling to stay on course against the wind in its flight to a neighbouring palm.

'OK,' he said. 'I'll give her a job.'

'You? Doing what?'

'Oh, I can use bright intelligent girls in my office. Let's say she does three days a week, and the other two days she goes to college to learn typing and shorthand.'

Gwen sat up in her chair. Something like a light seemed to have appeared at the end of her particular tunnel. Yet she had doubts.

'You'll be soft-hearted with her, Sam. If she takes a day off you would never scold her.'

'Sure would. You know she's never been able to twist me round her little finger the way she does with others. And if you doubt me, I'll put her in the charge of Minla. You know Minla's never soft-hearted with anybody, not even herself.'

441

They sat in silence considering it. 'I wonder if it would really work?' murmured Gwen.

'Try it and find out.'

'Oh, Sam, I just don't know . . .'

'Well, wait till she gets over the flu. See how it goes.'

'Yes. Thank you, Sam.'

'You're welcome.'

'Sam . . .'

'What?'

'I haven't had time to sort myself out because Tammy fell sick the minute we got back . . . What's the gossip these days?'

'On what?' he asked, although he knew.

'Oh, everything. Elsa rang to say welcome home and went on about troubles among our friends . . .'

'You know Elsa. Always keen to tell the worst. I bet by now she's told everybody in town that Tammy's got the spotted palsy never mind flu.'

'Heard from Terence lately?'

That meant that Terence hadn't rung to say welcome home, nor sent any message or flowers. Well, that figured. Terence had worries of his own these days. The word was that he owed two hundred in a Chinese gambling house and didn't have the money. Moreover, Molly O'Keefe had refused to pay up for him, on the grounds that her priest had told her it was a sin to encourage a gambler.

The trouble with owing money to the *tongs* was that the interest ran so high. The longer he didn't pay, the more he owed. And there was a cut-off point at which the *tong* leaders usually decided a little encouragement was needed: encouragement like an ear sliced off, or a finger going missing.

Sam had long accepted the fact that he wasn't going to win Gwen Veetcha. The mistake he'd made at their initial meeting had sent their relationship off on the wrong path. He wasn't the kind to grieve over what he

couldn't get, and besides there were consolations . . .
Yet they never quite consoled him in the way he hoped,
never came up to what he might have had with Gwen.

What really browned him off was that she should have
fallen for a self-satisfied Donovan like O'Keefe. He had
realised from the first that there was passion in her –
oh yes, she'd shown that in the way she flared up at
him when he accused her of trying to run a con-trick
on him. But why should she waste it all on Terence?

Well, that's the way the feathers moult, he would tell
himself with rueful resignation.

So now here she was back home with a wayward
daughter and an extreme case of the blues, and that
cheap dish didn't show. With any luck, the *tai pan* of
the gangs would get really miffed with him and hang
him out on a palm tree to dry in the sun.

But you couldn't exactly say that to Gwen when she
looked at you with anxious grey-green eyes out of a
pale face.

'Oh, Terence is pretty busy. His firm got contracts
for shipping machinery to construct the airfield and
so forth.' And bad cess to him, he added under his
breath.

'I see. I just wondered. More lime juice?'

He rose, shaking his head. 'I got a guy coming in
from Padang. Don't forget about Tammy's job. And
for pete's sake stop worrying.'

'I hear and obey,' she said with a tremulous smile.

As he got into his car he thought, Gwen would be
devastated if Terence O'Keefe was found with a fatal
red necktie in some alley. So when he got to his office he
asked Minla for an outside line, dialled a certain number,
and had a brief conversation with a friend. The result
was that a certain worried card-player got an extension
on his IOU.

After a couple of weeks in bed Tammy was well
enough to go and lie under the palms on the beach.
On a portable radio she listened to dance music. Now

and again she took in the gist of the news bulletins: things were going very badly in Europe, British forces were being pushed into the sea at Dunkirk. Bombs, long promised, were at last raining down on London.

How strange it all sounded to her. Grannie and Grandad were presumably in danger but it seemed unreal. Her mind was taken up with her own affairs: the shame of being slapped, of being dragged away in disgrace, of losing her chance of a successful career, of having to obey her mother who had suddenly become a tyrant, a gaoler.

I'll show her, she thought. But how wasn't clear.

To Sam's surprise she accepted the offer of a job. She began work in June. She was given a desk in the general office at the far end of the passage in the Orient Building. There was a small staff: two fast typists, a book-keeper, and a boy to run the errands. Tammy's title was 'Correspondence Clerk': she opened the post and bought the stamps from the Post Office.

At Sam's instruction she enrolled for the course at the secretarial college. The summer term had only a month to go, impossible to start on the shorthand course at that point. But she could begin to learn to type, he said, and so she did. She wasn't to call him Uncle Sam in the office. He was Mr Prosper. Yes, sir, she said, thinking her mother had put him up to it. All part of the plot to keep her in her 'proper place'.

Weekends were of course free. Going out early one Sunday morning for a swim, she was startled to see a figure slipping away from the back of the house and around by the beach.

The first orange tints of light caught his dark hair, his crumpled white suit. Terence O'Keefe!

She stood stricken to a statue. Terence and her mother! Until that moment such an idea had never occurred to her. Her mother in love? In the arms of a man? Her mother and Terence O'Keefe?

But Terence O'Keefe was a married man . . .

Then all kinds of chatter and gossip among the girls at school came back to her. Of course married people strayed off the straight and narrow. Hadn't the Prince of Wales's sweetheart, Mrs Simpson, been married when he first knew her? And film stars – film stars were always in the papers for their love affairs.

She was shaken with a sudden rage. How dare her mother come to the studio and drag her away from Reggie! How dare she treat her as if it was wrong to go with a man! Why, she – *she* – was having an affair. Had been having an affair, probably, for years – yes, because now she recalled how Terence was often at the house, often seemed to be around for no reason, and Mummy would go to the phone whenever he rang as if it was important . . .

For some long moments she stood in the shadows, twisting her swimming cap in angry hands. At last she pulled it on and plunged in among the waves. The initial chill of the water sobered her. The anger ebbed away.

In its place came a train of thought.

Terence O'Keefe . . . Handsome, vain, rather foolish . . . And Mummy loved him. What a fool to love a man like that. You see, it made her vulnerable . . .

When it first dawned on Terence that Tammy Veetcha seemed to like him, he couldn't quite believe it. After all, he was more than twice her age, and heaven knew, what with all these construction engineers and forces personnel, there were enough young men to catch her attention.

But no, she seemed to like him, really like him. At parties when he was invited to sing, she was always one of the first to make a request. Her favourite songs were 'Love is the Sweetest Thing' and 'Have You Ever Been Lonely?'

One day he came across her sheltering under a canopy at going-home time. Her mother's car had failed to turn up. He offered her a lift, she said she was hot and sticky, wouldn't it be nice to stop for a drink somewhere before he drove her home?

'Ah, me love, you're too young to go into a bar,' he said.

'We could go into Raffles – you could have a whisky and I could have lemonade. Do say yes, Terence, it's such a stuffy day.'

Well then, wasn't it true that the Java breeze made you feel under the weather? He took her to Raffles, no harm in it.

Of course Elsa Copeland got to hear of it. Not long after, someone murmured it to Gwen.

She asked Terence about it next time she saw him. 'Yes, I found her the day before yesterday when your car didn't come for her. We only had a short stop at Raffles Hotel before I dropped her at your road-end.'

'You should have come in, Terence,' she said.

'I hadn't the time, we were having guests for dinner so I had to get back.'

'I see.'

Yet Tammy had never mentioned it.

Gwen's workshop was busy at the moment. The influx of construction men and top-ranking civil servants meant the refurbishing of bungalows for their use. Nothing adventurous was ordered, but that was just as well for Gwen seemed to have lost all impetus towards original work. The state of the world around them was so depressing. People said poor old Britain was in a bad way but never mind, the colonies would come to her aid and everything would be all right.

'Ha!' grunted Sam when he heard these optimistic views at the club. 'Doesn't it strike anyone that the colonies are going to have their own troubles?'

'What, India? Australia? Don't be silly, old man.'

'Didn't any of you notice that Japan has signed a ten-year military pact with Germany and Italy?'

'So what? You're not suggesting Japan will try anything on against *us*?'

He could see they thought him crazy, so he stopped trying to argue. Besides, there was an atmosphere of stability and comfort in Singapore that was difficult to disturb. It was a kind of Never-Never Land in which nothing bad could happen.

Christmas came with the usual festivities. And with it came Jane Bedale.

Gwen had kept up a desultory correspondence with the kind Methodist missionary who had befriended her in the Tokyo earthquake. Latterly it had narrowed down to Christmas greetings and occasional postcards when either of them went somewhere interesting – Gwen sent cards from England or France, Miss Bedale from Nara or from one of Japan's outer islands.

She turned up in Singapore, unannounced and more or less a refugee. Gwen heard her voice on the telephone with astonishment.

'It's me, Jane Bedale – I looked you up in the phone book. Gwen, how are you?'

'I'm fine – but what are you doing here?'

She heard some of the tale then, and some when she went to visit Miss Bedale in her new post at an orphanage in the Malay quarter. It seemed that the Japanese had become more and more antagonistic to the work the Methodist mission was doing.

'You see, we had one or two children of mixed parentage in our orphanage, and recently they've become awfully strong against the mixing of races—'

'Yes, I gathered that from the *Shimbun*—'

'You keep up with their newspapers?'

'Yes, for Tammy's sake. I feel I ought to keep some link going . . .'

First there was surprise on Jane's square features, then approval. Her once grey hair had now gone a perfect white, below which her piercing eyes looked bluer than ever.

'Well, we suffered harassment – there's no other word for it. I think they organised gangs to come and jeer at us and throw stones. So Mr McAllister went to protest.'

Mr McAllister had been the minister at the Nagasaki church to which the mission was attached. He hadn't minced words with the local police chief, had been told to be more respectful, had told the police officer he couldn't respect a man who encouraged attacks on innocent children, and was thrown in gaol.

Of course he was let out in a few hours. The British consul had hurried to his aid. 'But we were made to feel terribly unwelcome. Things were raked up against us – Mr McAllister, for instance, had preached against the invasion of China.'

'Yes, that's so *awful* – they seem to be doing such terrible things. I don't understand it, they seemed so kind and patient.'

'They've changed, Gwen. You wouldn't recognise it now if you were to go back. Tokyo, naturally . . . they rebuilt it, as of course they've done many times, but now . . . It's full of statues to warriors, it's the same in other cities. They've become so militaristic . . .'

Gwen nodded. 'In the magazines I buy, there are lots of colour photos of army parades . . .'

'Well, one way or another it was made clear we were only bringing trouble on the kids, so we transferred them to other schools and got out. And here I am, starting all over again with a new set of kids and a new language.'

'Malay is easy,' Gwen said in encouragement. 'Especially the pidgin Malay we all speak here.'

'God will help me,' Jane said simply. 'He won't let me down in these last few years. I'm close to retirement now, you know, Gwen. I thought I'd end my days in Japan, but it wasn't to be.'

Gwen took Tammy to meet her. She hoped that the wholesome, open friendship of a woman like Jane Bedale might bring some warmth into her daughter's world. But Tammy was unimpressed with the mission and irritated when, in moments of crisis, Jane broke out in Japanese.

'I think it's absurd to stay abroad so long that you practically forget the English language,' she said when Gwen ventured to ask what she thought of Miss Bedale. 'Speaking Japanese isn't going to get her anywhere.'

'But Tammy, there's a rich culture behind it—'

'So you keep saying,' her daughter replied with a shrug, and walked out of the room.

As the year progressed, the news of the war grew somewhat better. Allied forces were doing well in North Africa and the US signed a Lend-Lease Bill with Britain.

'Good old US of A!' cried Sam. 'I knew they couldn't just stand back and see the Nazis clobber everybody!'

For her part Gwen had little to cheer her. Heavy air raids had resumed on England. She worried for her mother. She waited for every postal delivery: these had become less regular than formerly as mail-carrying ships were sunk and civilian airlines came under attack.

But more than anything, she worried about Tammy. Her daughter had become a student at the secretarial college for two days a week. Gwen would have been pleased to have any evidence that Tammy actually went there on the said two days. The car was always sent to meet her at first, but then she claimed that it felt restrictive, that she would like to go with some of the other students for a coffee or an ice-cream. And it was difficult to refuse this small freedom.

For her daughter's seventeenth birthday, Gwen gave a party. It followed the usual pattern – open house, tables and lanterns on the lawn, plenty to eat and plenty to drink, records from one's own collection and borrowed from friends for dancing that went on into the small hours.

As the party was breaking up about three in the morning, it struck Gwen that she hadn't seen her daughter for some time. In the role of hostess she'd been a little too busy to keep an eye on her. Well, so what – gone off with some of her friends for a swim, perhaps, or to watch the sunrise . . .

Gwen went to bed. But she couldn't sleep. She tossed and turned, getting tangled in her mosquito net. At length she got up on an elbow to look at her clock.

Four a.m. She got out of bed, tiptoed along the landing to peep in at her daughter's door. And found the bed empty, undisturbed. Tammy had not yet come home.

When at last she came in at five, Gwen was sitting waiting for her in the living-room. 'Where have you been?' she demanded.

'Out.'

'Where? Who with?'

'Wouldn't you like to know!'

'Tammy, this behaviour of yours is just getting to be too much to bear. I'm your mother and I have a right to know where you've been till this hour in the morning!'

'Right? What do you mean, right? Don't think I don't know what you've been up to all these years! Packing me off to school in the Cameron Highlands so you wouldn't have me in the way—'

'Tammy!'

'Sending me to England – oh, that kept me off your back for a whole year at a time! And now you have the cheek to ask me where I've been when I don't show up for an hour or two—'

'Tammy, I never sent you away so as to get rid of you! How can you even suggest such a thing?'

Tammy, a thing of perfection in her dance dress of green voile, clenched her fist and shook it.

'So you could be with Terence O'Keefe! Don't think I don't know – everybody knows! You think you've been so discreet, but you're a laughing-stock!'

Gwen stiffened in her chair. 'Tammy! What are you saying!'

'Hurts you, does it? Good, I'm glad. Now you know

what it's like to be made to look a fool over someone you care about.'

Gwen felt as if she were drowning in a sea of bitter confusion. 'Wait – listen – Tammy, don't shout at me like this! Let's be calm . . . Please, dear . . . I don't understand.'

'You understand well enough. Oh yes, well enough to be jealous! What does it feel like to lose out, eh? I hope it hurts like hell!'

Her daughter seemed to have lost all control of herself. She was half laughing, half crying. A flush of triumph was burning under her olive skin, her green eyes sparkled through tears.

'He's so easy, so easy! It's hardly worth the trouble, he falls into the net like a stunned fish! And you love him, that's what's so rich . . .'

There was a moment's silence. Gwen put her arms around herself. She was shivering. She said in a low voice, 'You're paying me out, is that it?'

'Got it in one.'

'You loved Reggie so much?'

'Reggie? Reggie, yes, I wanted Reggie, but I wanted my career more – and you snatched it away from me. You didn't even believe me when I told you it was important. You knew best, oh yes, you knew best. But then it dawned on me that this all-knowing mother was stupid enough to make a fool of herself over Terence O'Keefe. Do you know that everybody in Singapore knows he's your lover?'

'Tammy . . . Tammy . . . That's all right. Nobody cares about that. Terence and I . . . If people laugh, it's with kindness in it. You're too young to understand.'

'Too young, am I? Too young to understand, too young to do what I want in the world. But not too young to take him from under your nose!'

'I don't know what good you . . . It's so *ugly*, Tammy. He's old enough to be your father.'

'He's forty-one. In any case, I prefer older men,'

Tammy said in a tone of contempt, 'so distinguished, that touch of grey at the temples, don't you think?' She produced a little laugh. 'You know Freud says that if you fall for older men it's because you're looking for a father figure. That's what I'm doing – looking for a father figure to replace that mythical Jap you couldn't wait to get away from.'

'No! No, I won't let you say things like that!' Gwen sprang up, seized her by the shoulders.

Tammy stared into her mother's eyes. 'Go on, what are you going to do? Hit me again?'

Shocked, Gwen unclasped her hands from the creamy shoulders. She struggled for words. 'I can't imagine what you've been thinking. I loved your father – I loved him dearly.'

'Oh yes, never forgot him for the rest of your life; big show of keeping up with his memory.' Her fingers flicked out to twitch the silk kimono her mother had on. 'Wearing Jap silk, reading those tacky newspapers, chatting with the Japs in Middle Road . . . You're such a *hypocrite*: all the time you're supposed to be "remembering" my father you're having it off with darling Terence.'

'How can you possibly understand . . . ? Do you think I ought to go through the rest of my life completely alone?' Gwen whispered, broken.

'Well,' sneered Tammy, 'looks like you'll have to, because I've got him now.'

'Oh God . . . poor child . . . You don't know what you're doing.'

'Don't *patronise* me! I know just what I'm doing. I set out to get Terence and I've got him.'

'And what now?' Gwen asked, putting a hand up to her eyes so as to hide her tears from that angry gaze. 'What comes next?'

Her daughter shrugged and walked towards the staircase. 'I'm happy with the way things are at the moment,' she said, pretending to yawn with sleepiness.

'I'll leave it to simmer for a while. By the way, I'll be taking tomorrow off from work – don't let the servants waken me. Night-night, Mummy dear.'

Her light footsteps went up the staircase. Her room door opened and closed.

Gwen heard the sounds as if from a long way off. Then, stiffly, she pulled her dressing-gown around her and walked out of the house.

Out under the soft sky, she felt the morning sea-breeze caress her cheeks. She raised her face to stare up into the gleam of gold that was the sun's early rays.

She raised her arms to it in supplication. 'What am I going to do?' she cried.

Chapter Twenty-three

There was in fact nothing she could do.

For the first few days after that bitter scene, Gwen was too shaken to be able to think, let alone make any constructive move. In any case Tammy avoided her, going out by a side door when she left in the morning, going straight up to her room when she came home at night.

Then, just as her mother was recovering a little from the shock of their quarrel, there was a new problem. She came home one afternoon to collect some plans she needed at the workshop, and found Omar loading Tammy's suitcase into a taxi.

'What's going on?' Gwen cried.

'Missy tell Lala to pack things. Taxi take to Missy Gordon's flat. All right?'

'Where is Missy?'

Omar spread his hands. 'Ring from office.'

Gwen ran back to her own car, got in, and drove back into Singapore much too fast. She hurried into the Orient Building, went up in the slow lift, and dashed into the General Office looking almost wild. The office boy sprang up from his seat as she threw open the door.

'Miss Veetcha – I must speak to Miss Veetcha at once.'

'One moment,' said the boy in some alarm. He went into the main office. After a moment Tammy came out, frowning and looking rather white.

'What's the meaning of having your things moved?' Gwen demanded, and immediately regretted it. Her tone was all wrong, authoritarian when it should have been concerned.

The office boy looked startled, and almost said, 'Ssh . . .' at this intrusion on office routine. Tammy said, 'We can't talk here.' She walked out without taking the trouble to invite her mother to follow.

They went down to the cool hall, where there were some cane chairs and a low table with magazines. Neither sat down. Tammy gave a little shrug and a movement of the head that sent her coppery hair swinging.

'I'm not running off to a love-nest with Terence, if that's what you're afraid of. He wouldn't want the scandal, now would he? I'm just going to share Betty Gordon's flat.'

'Without even consulting me?'

'What would you have said? No, I forbid it? That would be pointless. We both know it's best if I move out—'

'No, Tammy, I don't know that! You're only just seventeen, and this Betty Gordon, I don't even know her!'

'She's one of the students at the college – she and I have a lot in common, she's a half-caste too—'

'Tammy!'

'Don't you like me to use that term? It's what I am, after all. Though Betty's better off than I am for her father at least is a Brit, which you must admit makes a big difference.'

'How can you speak like this! Where did you learn to think in this way? Your father—'

'Never mind about him, he's just something I have to live with. But I don't have to live with a woman who's trying to think of a way to punish me for what I did.'

'That's nonsense! I just want to make you see how wrong—'

'Oh yes, I'm always the one who's wrong. You're the one who's in the right, though you've let me think you were so pure and good and hard-working while all the time—'

'Tammy, the fact that I was in love with someone was never your business until you started on this stupid vendetta.'

'It's not stupid to me. Nobody makes a fool of me and gets away with it.'

At that moment the outer door was opened by the Tamil commissionaire to admit Sam Prosper. He paused on seeing them, took off his hat and said, 'Afternoon, ladies.'

Neither made any reply. Tammy was staring coldly at her mother, Gwen made a little helpless gesture with her hands.

'Sorry, private chat . . .' Sam went past them and, instead of waiting for the lift, walked up the stairs so as to leave them to their tête-à-tête.

But Gwen didn't know what more to say. She shook her head helplessly. 'Tammy, you may say "Never mind about your father", but you're a lot like him in some ways. You can't bear to lose face.'

Her daughter raised her eyebrows. 'So you know better than to "forbid" me to move out.'

'No, you're right. Perhaps it's better we stay apart for a while. Just let me ask one thing – Betty Gordon, how old is she? I can't just let you go to—'

'She's twenty if it's any of your business, and her father works on the railway up in Johore Bahru. She's getting up her shorthand and typing, God help her, because she wants to land a good job in the Civil Service.'

That was at least a little reassuring. Gwen nodded, feeling herself dazed with the confusion and hopelessness that besieged her.

'Please keep in touch,' she begged as she turned to go. 'Please, Tammy.'

'Keep in touch!' It was said in a tone of irritation. 'How can I avoid it in this town? If I don't let you know what I'm doing, there's sure to be some busybody who will.'

With that her daughter ran upstairs fast, as if to work out some of her anger.

And Gwen went out into the late afternoon sun, wondering how she could have so totally mis-handled a relationship that ought to have been sweet, strong and precious to both of them.

After dinner that evening, as she was reading the papers, Omar came in to say Tuan Prosper was here asking for her.

'Show him in, Omar. Bring drinks.'

When Sam had settled himself in the chair he usually chose, under the ceiling fan, he said: 'I'm not going to beat about the bush. It dawned on me this afternoon when I saw the two of you in the middle of a fight – it's true what they're saying about Tammy and O'Keefe?'

Gwen groaned. 'Does everybody know?'

He frowned. 'I didn't believe it, it sounded so crazy. How could a girl like Tammy fall for a man she must think of as middle-aged?'

'She hasn't fallen for him.' Haltingly she told him the real story. He sat silent and, she could see, growing angrier and angrier with each word.

'What a rotten thing to do,' he grunted when she came to an end.

'It certainly isn't pretty.'

'And Terence – what's he saying?'

'I can't get in touch with him. When I ring him at the shipping office he's always out or engaged – and you can imagine I wouldn't want to go to his office or to his house myself.'

'I'll see him all right,' Sam said. 'I'll wring his neck!'

'It's not his fault, really it isn't, Sam. She set out to get him and he . . . he . . .'

'He was easy game. Yeah. Well, what happens next?'

'God knows. You know I'm no good at this kind of thing. I never seem able to sense what people are thinking or feeling. I had no idea Tammy's resentment ran so deep. And I never thought she would turn her attention to Terence.'

'I'll wring *her* neck,' Sam said.

Omar came in with Sam's drink. He took it, sipped a moment, then said, 'Seriously, what would you like me to do?'

'For instance what?'

'Talk to Tammy.'

'Do you think it would do any good?'

'Frankly, no. She's always been sure of herself, ever since she was a kiddie. Sure she was right, sure the world turned around her!'

'You're saying I spoiled her.'

He smiled. 'We all did. Such a pretty little thing. And now, such a beauty – you feel you ought not to do anything that might upset her because she's so perfect, at least to look at.' He held his ice-laden glass against his forehead for coolness. 'No use looking back and saying we should have beaten her six times a day and sent her to a convent. She'll have to grow up one day, find out she can't have the world the way she wants it just because she's pretty.'

'What kind of damage is she going to do to herself in the meantime?'

'Search me,' he sighed. 'But if it's worth anything, I'll help pick up the pieces when the time comes.' He studied her a moment. 'You look beat, kiddo. Like to come out on the *Dimestore* on Sunday – get a breath of sea air? I'm taking Peter and Susanne and a couple others, do some fishing and swimming.'

'Thank you, Sam, I'd like that.' Anything to help fill the days that she couldn't drown in work.

Gwen saw Tammy fairly often, out and about in Singapore. They would pass each other in the doorway of a shop, be at the same concert in the Municipal Hall. Now and again Gwen went to the Orient Building at four o'clock just so as to see her come out and head for home. The flat she shared with Betty Gordon was in New Bridge Road, within walking distance of the office.

Once Gwen rang the flat, impelled by a need to hear her daughter's voice. The call was answered by a young woman whose accent was a mixture of Scottish and Singapore-Malay.

'Tammy's not here, who's calling?'

'This . . . this is her mother.'

'Oh, the Wicked Witch of the North, eh? How are you, Mrs Veetcha?'

'Never mind that, how's Tammy?'

'She's all right, angling for a job as a part-time model for Robinson's fashion parades.'

'She is? Do you think she'll get it?'

'Why not? She's got the figure for it. They're going to put on their usual "Party-time" show for Christmas and she hopes to be included in that.'

Gwen immediately planned to get tickets for the evening show of dresses for the festive season. 'Thank you for telling me,' she said. 'Is there anything she needs? Are you all right for money?'

'We manage quite well, thank you. And the question you don't know how to ask – yes, she's still seeing Terence, but not so often.'

'Oh.' The girl's open manner came as a surprise to her. She'd somehow expected partisanship from her. 'Do you think she . . . they . . .'

'Oh, the Lord knows,' said Betty Gordon. 'I think she despises herself for keeping him on a string, if you want to know the truth. But you know Tammy – she's determined not to look silly by ending the thing too soon. She's one who thinks about her image, isn't she – doesn't like to lose.'

'That's true.'

'I've got to hang up, Mrs Veetcha, I'm dressing to go out.'

'Yes. Thank you for talking to me. If ever you . . . if there's any problem . . . would you . . . ?'

'Surely. I'll not let her drown without trace if I can help it. Night-night.'

This conversation helped to buoy her up through the last days of November. On the first Monday of December, she had tickets for the fashion show. She saw her daughter appear and reappear in first one beautiful dress then another. She looked well – thinner, somehow taller with her Titian hair swept up in a French plait at the back, moving with ease and grace, turning and swaying to let the women see the gowns.

Six days later, on the night of Sunday 7 December 1941, Singapore was bombed.

Gwen woke up, as if out of a bad dream caused by a thunderstorm. She found herself momentarily tangled in her mosquito net. She heard a thin, high-pitched whine, and then the ground shook under the house. There was an explosion, loud enough to frighten, but not too close.

She ran to the window in her silk nightdress. High above the sea, caught in the crossed beam of two searchlights, a plane was diving. Tracer bullets sped up, red and bright, towards it. Guns were barking – bofors fire, she later learned.

Gwen stared, fascinated. The plane escaped the searchlights, which found, followed, and then lost another. She felt the ground shake again and again. Explosions followed. She thought they sounded as if they came from the west, along by the docks.

She ran back to look at her bedside clock. A quarter past four in the morning.

She switched on her radio. Soft dance music. She stared at it, unable to believe it. Dance music? And the city was under air attack?

She was startled when her phone rang. She snatched up the receiver.

'Gwen? Are you OK?' It was Sam.

461

'Yes, I'm all right. Sam, what's going on?'

'The Japs have bombed Pearl Harbor and targets all over the British territories here – Malaya, Hong Kong. I heard it on Radio Hawaii.'

'Where are you, at home?'

'No, at the office, the bombing here has hit the business centre—'

'Tammy!'

'She's okay, I hoofed it up the road to have a look; nothing's hit New Bridge Road. Look, Gwen, take shelter, huh?'

'In what?'

'Under a table's better than nothing.'

'They won't attack Tanjong Katong—'

'You've got Kallang airfield not too far behind you. So watch out, babe, will you?'

'Yes, all right.'

'I better get off the line, don't want to tie up services. See you later, Gwen.'

'Yes, see you later.'

Wails of terror from across the compound told her the servants were out of their quarters, watching the attack over the city. Despite Sam's advice, she joined them on the shore, staring at the flashes and the leap of flames that meant hits on the proud settlement of Singapore. The city was so unprepared that the street lights were still on: there had been no expectation of a black-out.

At six o'clock her radio, which she had left playing, told her that the British Commonwealth was at war with Japan. There was confirmation of attacks on the American base at Pearl Harbor with many battleships sunk. Japanese troops were said to be in Siam, the state to the north-east of the Malay Peninsula.

The citizens of Singapore – British, Malay, Chinese and Tamil – emerged stunned from their homes. The unthinkable had happened.

And their only reaction was to go to their shops and offices to see what could be done. The 'Passive

Defence Service', never taken seriously, set to work to look for survivors in the rubble. Fires, particularly in the wooden-built Chinese quarter, were soon put out.

Gwen saw the crews at work as she made the two-mile drive into the city. Her plan was simple: she intended to fetch her daughter away from her flat to the comparative safety of Tanjong Katong. But the plan, like much else in Singapore that morning, didn't work.

She met with big bomb craters in her road. Then she was waved off on detours to the right by auxiliary policemen. There was a strong smell of burning, smoke stung her eyes. Eventually she came along Waterloo Street, heading towards the Singapore River. It was then that she saw most of the hits last night had been on the Chinese quarter.

At once she gave up the idea of getting to Tammy. First she had to know what had happened to Wo Joong and his family. She made her slow way past Bras Basah and Stamford Street, all the time feeling the growing heat of charred houses, hearing the sound of motor-pumps forcing water on embers. Rescue teams were digging in the rubble.

She got to the end of the North Boat Quay. There was a crowd there, Chinese mostly, watching with frightened eyes. Gwen parked, got out, forced her way through.

The timber yards were now a charred heap. Behind that the house roofs could no longer be seen. Stretchers were being carried past, the forms wrapped in blankets that covered the face.

At last she reached the spot where her own workshop, and Joong's house, should have stood. There was nothing there but a tent-like collection of smoking beams. Nearby stood Chiang, Joong's second eldest son, in ash-streaked blue jacket and trousers.

'Chiang!'

He turned, stared for a moment as if he didn't know who she was. Then his palms came together in the traditional greeting. 'Mem Veetcha—'

'Chiang, what's happened? Is Wo Joong . . . ?' But her voice trailed off. His face told her what she needed to know.

'Your mother?'

'Also taken to the ancestors. Two younger brothers, youngest sister.'

'Oh, Chiang, I . . . I don't know what to say . . .' Her throat closed up on the words. Her friend for so many years . . . His little round-cheeked wife, the smallest child with the straight-cut fringe across her forehead . . .

'Mem unhurt?'

'Yes, yes, never mind about me. Where are the rest of your family?'

'Eldest brother take them to cousin, Shoy Street, early morning. Now arranges funeral. Mem . . .' He looked at her and away again.

For a moment she was at a loss, then understood he was asking for wages due to him and his family, so that he could arrange a proper Buddhist funeral.

'Of course, Chiang. Only, I haven't any money with me – can you come with me to the bank?'

No European in Singapore ever carried money; everything was signed for by 'chits'. But today she would need cash, because Chiang wasn't the only workman who would have to be paid. Her workshop was gone and with it all the made pieces, all the special timber supplies, all the design plans, all the tools and equipment . . . She would have to pay them all up to this day, and add a customary parting present.

There was a queue at the bank. Once she had the cash, she turned it over to Chiang, who bowed in acknowledgement and promised to pay off the rest of the workforce. On the kerb outside, under the growing heat of the sun, they said goodbye.

'What will you do, Chiang?'

'Ancestors will show the way, mem. And you?'

'Why . . . I don't know . . .'

She got into the car, once more intending to get to New Bridge Road. But now the road was jammed with ambulances. Gwen was hailed as she followed behind. 'Mem please take these two people? Bad burns, need hospital.'

A Tamil police auxiliary was ushering forward an Indian woman with a little girl of about five clinging to her sari skirts. The woman's arm and shoulder were loosely wrapped in a piece of gauze. The child had burns on her face. Neither was bad enough to need an ambulance, but the sooner the wounds were treated the better.

At the hospital Gwen had to queue up. To her astonishment she found Elsa Copeland, in a white, wrap-around apron, shepherding new arrivals to one side or another.

'Good heavens, I didn't know you were a nurse,' Gwen exclaimed.

'Not me, dear – I'm just acting usherette, it just happened. I see you've been pressed into service too.'

'Yes, but I didn't mean to—'

'Neither did I, but you see how it goes. We can use all the help we can get, Gwen. Last night was only the beginning.'

'I don't understand it,' Gwen cried. 'Why did they do it?'

Impatient horns warned her others were waiting to deposit casualties. She nodded at Elsa and drove on through the turn-around and out again.

By the time she reached the flat in New Bridge Road it was midday. At her ring the door was opened by a sturdy Eurasian girl with black hair and grey eyes. 'Oh, Mrs Veetcha.'

'You know me?'

'It's an easy guess, you're so like Tammy. I'm Betty, of course.'

'Is Tammy here?'

'No, she went to work.'

465

'To work!'

'I did too. I think everybody felt the need to gather together – for reassurance, or something. Anyhow, she's not come back. Myself, I'm packing to go. My dad rang me at the office to order me home to Johore Bahru.'

'How are you going? Are the trains running?'

'Och, yes, a bit out of schedule but not too bad. I'm going while the going's good.'

'Do you think it's wise? Going north?'

'Better to be out of the city, my dad says.'

'I suppose so . . .'

But after she had shaken hands and left, Gwen was by no means so sure. North to Johore Bahru meant a few miles nearer Siam. And there were Japanese forces in Siam. Though that might not mean anything, because of course there was jungle between the Japanese in Siam and the Malay States – so perhaps Betty's father was right in believing that Johore would be safe.

The Orient Building was intact. The uniformed commissionaire was on duty, immaculate in white cotton suit and white peaked cap. The lift worked. If you had been dropped from Mars on the pavement outside the Orient Building you would never have guessed there had been an air raid in the early hours of the morning – everything was so much 'Business as Usual'.

In Sam's offices there was a slight difference. The office boy wasn't there to intercept her. She walked in to find the staff about to leave for lunch. Tammy was locking the stamp-book away. She straightened as she saw her mother enter.

'Tammy, I've been to your flat – Betty's packing to leave.'

Tammy frowned. 'Running like a scared rabbit, eh?'

'Listen, it'll be a lot safer for you at home with me.'

Tammy was already shaking her head. 'Oh no. I'm not having people say that I was scared witless like any other half-caste—'

'Tammy! Nobody would say such a thing! It's only sense to take what precautions—'

'I'm not coming out to Tanjong Katong.'

'But you can't stay on your own in New Bridge Road'

'Why not? All the more room for me – and all the freedom to do what I like.'

'Tammy, this is *serious*! We're at war!'

'Yes, and guess who with? That precious bunch you kept asking me to get interested in, my father's sacred race with its long and honourable traditions of art and family loyalty. Ha, ha.'

Gwen stared at her daughter in dismay. Then she whirled, hurried into the reception office. Minla's desk was empty. She rushed straight on into Sam's room.

He was on the telephone. He raised sun-bleached brows, waved at her to sit down and wait.

He listened to his caller, then spoke in Chinese. Gwen understood enough to know he was trying to persuade someone not to do something. In the end he hung up, looking vexed.

'That was Minla's eldest brother. They're going to head up-country; her uncle has a pineapple plantation near Kalang Pontiang. Well, there goes the best secretary I ever had. So, Gwen . . . how did it go last night?'

'We're all right. Sam, I want you to talk to Tammy – she's got to come home with me—'

He held up a hand to stop her. 'I gather she doesn't want to?'

'It's absurd. Her flatmate is leaving – like Minla. Anybody who has family up-country is moving out. I won't have Tammy on her own there. She's got to come home with me.'

Sam shook his head. 'It's not my business, Gwen.'

'Come on, Sam, you've always been like an adopted uncle. If you tell her to move out of that flat and come home, she will.'

'I'm not so sure. And anyhow, I'm not sure you're right in wanting her home.'

'But *Sam* . . .'

'She came in this morning all full of determination to show she wasn't just another scared Eurasian. I tried to tell her I didn't think the Eurasians were any more scared than the rest of us but she doesn't believe it. She doesn't want to be seen to "run away".'

'Look here, nobody can foresee how long it's going to be before we sort out this Japanese attack.'

'That's right, nobody can foresee a thing. Nobody foresaw that they'd come flying in and drop bombs on us without an ultimatum or a diplomatic breakdown . . . Sixty people killed, over a hundred injured badly. And from what I can gather, they sank half the American navy—'

'Oh . . . Sam . . . I quite forgot you'd said . . . Oh, I'm so sorry . . . Your country's at war now, too . . .' Her eyes filled with tears. She sank down on the chair that faced his desk. She bowed her head while she searched for a handkerchief.

'Yeah, I feel kind of low about it myself,' he said with irony. 'So I understand how Tammy feels. Let her alone, Gwen.'

'But . . . but . . . the city centre is likely to be attacked again—'

'Sure, but so is everywhere else. This is a small island, Gwen. No place on it is going to be safe. That's why I think if Tammy goes anywhere, she should go on a ship that's leaving Singapore.'

'Leave?' Gwen said, aghast.

'Yeah, leave. The sooner the better.'

'But that would mean being parted from her again.'

'No, you should go too.'

'No!' she said, sitting up straight. The tears on her

cheeks were forgotten. 'I'm not going to run away either—'

'Honey, don't be stupid, this is going to be a tough deal.'

'Singapore is my home! I'm not going to be driven out!'

'You don't know what you're talking about. I was in China while they were taking one or two of the lesser towns, and believe me, Japanese invaders mean business.'

'I don't care! I'm not going!'

They argued for almost a quarter of an hour. In the end Gwen stalked out in a temper. Nothing was going to make her leave the city she had learned to call home.

Sometimes in the days that ensued she wondered if she had made a right decision. The *Tribune* published the dreadful news that the *Prince of Wales* and the *Repulse*, warships which had only recently been in harbour showing themselves off to the Singaporeans, had been sunk in the Malacca Straits. The depression that followed was severe.

And the bombing attacks continued, right through into January when they reached an intensity that was unbearable. There seemed to be no British planes to intercept the bombers. They flew over, formations of sometimes as many as eighty bombers in majestic array and with an escort of fighters. They dropped their loads with impunity.

Gwen had enlisted as a hospital auxiliary, using her car to ferry ambulant casualties. It was gruelling work, as every day more of the city was reduced to rubble. Streets were blocked by ruins and by shell-holes. Delayed-action incendiaries were likely to go up under her wheels at any moment. Falling buildings would crash just as she had gone by.

She tried to see her daughter at least once every day. Tammy had taken a job in the Cold Storage, which was often besieged by customers desperate for food supplies after their houses were reduced to smithereens.

Sam had closed up his business, though he used his office as a base from which to help in the work of trying to keep the docks going for there were valuable cargoes of tin and rubber there, needed in Britain for the war effort and likely to be sent up in flames in the next raid if they couldn't get them loaded and away.

All Singapore's defences were based on the presumption that an attack, if it came, would be from the sea. The news that the Japanese were coming by land, from Siam, down the Malay Peninsula, through what everyone had always assumed was 'impenetrable' jungle, struck terror into their hearts.

The city was full of refugees who had fled before that attack up-country. The Leonie Hotel was full to bursting with bewildered women who had left their husbands up-country. Miss Bedale's orphanage was one of many crammed with orphaned and lost children. Gwen went there when she could with any food supplies or clothing that she could cadge for them. Some of the well-off donated their own children's cast-offs. Sam Prosper turned up at the door with a hundred dollars'-worth he'd bought new in Robinson's.

The *Tribune* and the *Straits Times* could give little news of what was really going on. Mainly they provided information about where to go for milk supplies for young children or where new bomb-shelters were available. In late January they published an announcement that European women and children were to be evacuated by sea.

The effect on morale was disastrous. Until then the official line had been that the Japanese were being held, that reinforcements were coming, that everything was well in hand. But truly dreadful reports of events in Hong Kong had been circulating. Hong Kong had fallen on Christmas Day. A few refugees who had got away by sea told their story of murder and rape, of drunken soldiers bayoneting patients in hospital beds.

Gwen felt all hope leave her. It was like a nightmare, with no prospect of awakening to a more cheerful reality.

I'm going to get a passage for Tammy on one of the ships, she told herself.

But the queues at the Agency House at Cluny were enormous. As Gwen approached in her car, the long uphill drive was already crammed with people, cars were parked nose to tail on the road verges, everything seemed disorganised and chaotic under a thunderous sky.

Gwen joined the long queue. She had progressed about fifty yards when the warnings sounded and Japanese Zeros swept over, machine-gunning the crowd. Everyone rushed for shelter. Gwen was toppled into the big concrete storm-drain at the roadside. When, ten minutes later, she clambered out with grazed knees and elbows, she had lost her place in the queue.

At last she was allowed into the house – formerly the private bungalow of the P&O district manager. There were two tables, one for those hoping to head for Colombo, one for Britain. Gwen headed for the one labelled 'Britain'. The clerk in charge was a man she'd seen around at social gatherings; his name was Gerald Printan.

'Name?' he inquired without looking up.

'Gwen Veetcha.'

'Oh yes.' There was a half-smile of recognition. 'Self only?'

'No, not for me, it's for my daughter aged seventeen.'

'Passports?'

'This is mine. I don't have my daughter's.'

Printan opened the passport. After a moment he looked up in surprise. 'This passport is in the name of Hayakawa.'

'Yes, Veetcha is my business name.'

'It's a Japanese name, isn't it? Is your business in the Japanese quarter where we rounded up all those informers?'

'No, in the Chinese quarter—'

'In the Chinese quarter? That's a bit odd. A British national in the Chinese quarter?'

'Yes, but I make – I made furniture.'

'Your daughter's name is also Hayakawa?'

'Yes, but we don't—'

'Does she claim British nationality?'

'Of course,' Gwen said in vexation.

'I don't know what's "of course" about it. She might be on a Japanese passport for all I know. And she isn't here. And you don't have any *British* documents for her.'

'Well, no, I didn't quite know what the rules would be.'

'I'm sorry, Mrs Hayakawa, we have British women and children here who need my attention. Next please.'

'But just a minute, I'm British and so is my daughter.'

'I'm afraid I can't spare time to handle your problems—'

'I don't have any problems, I want my daughter's name included on the—'

'Excuse me, Mrs Hayakawa—'

'My name is Veetcha! Everybody calls me Veetcha.'

'I wonder how many of us knew that Mrs Veetcha had Japanese connections?' Gerald Printan asked in a tone of anger and resentment. 'Please step out of the way, I've a lot of others to see to.'

'Mr Printan—'

'If you don't make way for the next applicant, Mrs Hayakawa, I'll be forced to have you taken out by the guard.'

Shocked into silence, Gwen backed away. In a moment her place at the table was taken by an anxious Englishwoman with two small children huddled at her side.

Gwen came out to another air raid warning. She took cover in a garden shed. When she got out to the road, she found her car riddled with machine-gun bullets through the engine.

In a sudden fury she beat her fists against the metal bonnet. And then snatched them away as the sun-heated metal burned her. Fool, she said to herself, it's no use losing your temper with the car . . .

She was lucky enough to get a lift back into the city centre. The man who picked her up said, 'Shan't be giving many more lifts in this old girl – once this tank of petrol's gone, there'll be no refills.'

'What?' she cried, startled.

'Oh yes, haven't you heard? They're burning the oil depots so the Japs won't get them.'

'Then they think . . . they really think . . . the Japs are coming?'

'What's to stop 'em?' he said wearily.

She went in search of Tammy at the Cold Storage. By now it was a case of giving away the stocks, merely so they wouldn't spoil as the freezing machinery broke down due to the lack of a steady electrical supply.

'Tammy, I need to talk to you.'

'Can't you see I'm busy?' her daughter replied over the heads of a surging crowd of customers.

'But this is important—'

'So is this, madam,' an elderly man intervened. 'I've got eighteen wounded men in my bungalow and nothing to give them to eat!'

It was hopeless. Gwen withdrew, making a vow to mount guard outside the door of Tammy's flat until she saw her come home tonight.

Out in the city, cars had been left abandoned just as they were when the petrol ran out. The smell of burning rubber and burning oil hung heavy in the hot air. Gwen longed to get home, to have a shower and to change into clean clothes, but there seemed to be no taxis, no transport of any kind that she could hail.

And then, unexpectedly, a van drew up alongside. It was driven by a Malay, with Molly O'Keefe, Terence's wife, sitting alongside. 'Good afternoon, Gwen,' Molly said.

'Molly! What are you doing there?'

'I'm out scouting for food for the Catholic Welfare Centre. We thought of going to the Cold Storage but I see the crowd's out to the pavement.'

'Yes, it's a mob . . . What kind of food?'

'Anything, but particularly fruit and vegetables – we've got six or seven families from up-country and the children are getting quite poorly from lack of fresh fruit.'

'There are vegetables in my garden,' offered Gwen, 'and a coconut plantation behind my house—'

'Hop in, we'll give you a lift home.'

She clambered in the back. Instead of an hour's walk in the heat, she was transported home in ten minutes. Once there, they picked pumpkins and sweet potatoes, while the Malay went to knock coconuts down from the palms in the deserted plantation.

'How are things going with you?' Gwen asked, rather nervous of conversation with Molly given their circumstances.

Molly's thin sallow face lit up with pleasure. 'I feel I'm called to a hard service in the name of the Lord,' she said.

Aren't we all, thought Gwen. Still more nervous, she asked, 'How's Terence?'

'I hardly see him. He's on the docks till all hours. You know the government was so stupid, it refused danger money for the Malay and Tamil dock-workers, so naturally they all disappeared. Terence and some of the other managers have been organising squads of loaders, paying them out of their office funds at whatever rate they can fix – and goodness knows it's not worth bothering about because Singapore dollars haven't any value now.'

'No,' agreed Gwen with a bitter sigh.

'What about you?'

'Oh, I spent the entire morning trying to get a passage for my daughter—' she broke off, rather expecting Molly to say she didn't want to talk about Tammy, but Molly held her peace. 'There's a tremendous queue. I was turned away.' She paused. 'Are you going to try for a berth?'

'Leave my husband and the work God has called me to?' said Molly. 'Never!'

In a way it was admirable.

Gwen helped fill all the baskets she could find with garden produce and coconuts, loaded them into the van, and waved them off.

She went in to take a shower, and was grateful when the water gushed out. The water supply had been intermittent for some days, as mains were severed by bomb damage and then more or less repaired. She put on a change of clothing: a loose shirt, cotton slacks and ankle boots – her usual garb these days for long hours at the wheel and for picking her way through rubble.

That night there were six raids. The airfield a few miles behind Gwen's house was torn up and all its hangars set on fire. In terror the house servants ran off into the coconut plantation. It was the last she ever saw of Omar and Lala and the rest.

She had to give up her plan to wait for Tammy at her flat. It would be madness to try to walk to the city in the dark.

Next morning she found a bicycle in the servants' quarters, one that Omar sometimes used when he wanted to visit his parents in Paya Lebar. In the grey light of dawn she cycled into Singapore. It was Sunday 1 February. Gwen went to church for the first time in many years.

St Andrew's Cathedral was being used as a casualty station. Nevertheless, among the stretchers and the makeshift beds, there was room for a congregation

475

to stand. There was a short service, with prayers for courage and for endurance, a few unaccompanied hymns, and a homily urging Singaporeans to put their trust in God.

Instead of being comforted, Gwen felt besieged by doubts and fears. Things had gone so terribly badly, almost unbelievably so. This once-beautiful city was nothing now but a dirty heap of rubbish and smashed buildings, its streets littered with blasted trees, old cars, and shattered glass.

She came out to find a group of people talking anxiously on the Padang. She heard the word 'Causeway'.

'What is it?' she demanded in a surge of panic. 'What about the Causeway?'

A man with a grey, tired face turned to her. 'The Japs crossed it last night.'

Crossed the Causeway!

The Causeway was the narrow roadway which joined the island of Singapore to the mainland at Johore Bahru. Until now it had always been possible to say, 'They'll never get across the Causeway,' or, 'Our troops will hold the Causeway.' But now that last barrier was gone.

She didn't for a moment doubt it. Besides, there was the sound of the guns. For some days Singaporeans had been growing accustomed to long-range guns trained on them from across the Straits. Now the sound had changed. The Japanese attack artillery was on the island of Singapore itself.

Gwen walked away from the arguing group on the grass of the Padang. Never in her life had she felt so lonely, so afraid. Seeking what comfort she could, she walked through Raffles Square and on to the Orient Building. There was just a chance Sam might be there.

There was no commissionaire on duty outside. She went in. The hall was cool and dim, but there was no sound of activity. She stood on the first step of the stone staircase, looking up.

'Hello?' she called. 'Hello? Anybody there?'

A door banged above. Then a few quick steps and a voice. 'Gwen? That you?'

'Sam!'

She heard him running downstairs. He appeared, taking the last steps four at a time. 'Gwen, I tried to ring you last night but the exchange has packed up. Were you there?'

'Yes, I got a lift home from Molly O'Keefe.'

'From Molly?' he said, taken aback. 'What happened to your car?'

'Got shot up while I was queuing for a ticket to get Tammy out on a ship.'

'Which one's she going on?'

'I didn't get it, Sam. I was turned down.'

'Turned down? On whose say-so, for God's sake?'

'Oh, let's not go into it. Besides, when I saw those poor women with little children, I felt it was more important for them—'

'Don't you believe it!' he replied sharply. 'Tammy's going to be in real trouble when the Japs take over. I saw them, I tell you – in Genchan, in Ma-ho – they're very strong on racial purity, they come down hard on anybody of mixed race. Tammy's just the kind of girl they'll put through hell.'

'No, Sam!' She drew back in revulsion.

'I hoped you'd both get a passage on a boat.'

'It's no use, you've only to look at the hordes of people queuing—'

'Well, I'll tell you this! I'm not staying here to have my head chopped off with a Samurai sword.'

'You? Why should you—' She broke off, her mind beginning to pick up on clues she already had. 'You mean, when people said you'd been running guns into China, it was really true?'

'I refuse to answer on the grounds it might incriminate me. But if they've got a little list, I reckon I'll be on it. So listen, babe – go home, pack a few things, collect up Tammy and be ready when it gets dark tonight.'

'Why? What are we going to do?'

'We're leaving Singapore, honey. On my boat.'

'The *Dimestore*?'

'Yeah, on the *Dimestore* – you, me, Tammy, and as many of Miss Bedale's orphans as I can cram aboard.'

Chapter Twenty-four

The first problem was, where could they board the boat?

At the outset of hostilities, Sam had taken the *Dimestore*, his forty-foot cabin-cruiser, out to the lee of one of the myriad rocky islets beyond the harbour. There, camouflaged with some old timber, it had remained.

He could bring it in to shore. But the waterfront at Singapore was now mostly wreckage. The area still usable was now under guard, and only those with authorised tickets for the evacuee ships were allowed on the quay.

'We could board at the Geylang River,' Gwen suggested.

The Geylang River, a small watercourse, ran some distance behind Gwen's house at Tanjong Katong, to come out inside a spit of land called Tanjong Rhu. There was a fairly good road running from near Gwen's house to the mouth of the inlet.

'How would we get the kids aboard? Is there a jetty?'

'No, but there are sampans and houseboats moored edge to edge in the rivermouth. We could walk across those and board from the last one.'

'Right. The next question is, how do we get the kids to the Geylang?'

That gave them pause. Some of Miss Bedale's children were mere toddlers. It was impossible for them to walk the two difficult miles through the waterfront of Singapore to the Geylang.

Sam had a car, but it was now immobilised because the tank was empty. But the Chinese, always quick to see a business opportunity, had petrol. They got it by issuing out after dark, finding cars which had been abandoned due to damage or breakdown, and syphoning off what was left in the tanks.

Among Sam's friends there were those who knew the petrol-merchants. Within an hour a man had arrived on a motorbike with a can strapped to the carrier. Sam paid for it not with money but with the gold pen from his desk set. The petrol was decanted into the tank of Sam's Packard. Gwen was given the task of ferrying the children.

'I'll pick up Tammy en route. She'll need to dash home and pack some clothes.'

'OK, but if she argues don't let it be in public. We don't want everybody to know about this.'

'Sam . . . I feel awful about this. It really is like running away.'

'Running away from what? This burg is finished, Gwen. There's no defence worth speaking of, the Japanese are on the outskirts, and let me tell you this – in a day or two there won't be any water.'

'What?' she gasped.

'Water's pouring away out of the burst mains. Macritchie Reservoir will soon be empty. So you see, either the city dies of thirst, burns up under incendiary bombs – or it surrenders.'

She nodded, unable to speak.

'You'll have to make about three trips for the kids, Gwen. Last I heard, which was yesterday, she had fourteen. Where the heck are you going to park them?'

'They can go to my house. There's no electricity and perhaps the water's packed up by now, but there's food there.'

'Yeah, good, that'll be the holding point then. I'll go out and fetch the *Dimestore* as soon as it gets dark.'

'Do you think you'll be able to get out to it?'

'Sure, why not, I'll go in a sampan, it'll look like just another Malay going out to visit his grandma on some little island. I'll come in to the Geylang at about nine o'clock, if there isn't an air raid under way.'

'I'll have them there by then.' She hesitated. 'Sam, where are we going? I mean, apart from out of Singapore? The *Dimestore* can't take us far.'

The cabin-cruiser was essentially a pleasure boat. Sam had it fitted up with two double-berth cabins, so that if he took out a party of friends on a fishing trip they could overnight in comfort. For fourteen children and four adults, it was going to be a very tight squeeze. The range was limited by the capacity of the fuel tanks and would be further reduced by carrying so many passengers. Gwen's question was a valid one.

'We're going to Sumatra,' Sam said. 'So far as I know, the Japanese haven't bothered with the Dutch East Indies. Once we get to Sumatra, we can get a steamer from one of the west-coast ports – Padang or Benkulen.'

'I see.'

'Don't be scared, sugar. I've done worse trips than this in my time.'

'But not with a cargo of women and children.'

'We-ell, no, but you have to try new things now and again or you get stuck in a rut. OK, honey? Think you can face it?'

'Of course. I'm sorry to seem shaky. It's just . . . it's just . . . I've been through all this before. In Tokyo, during the earthquake. Everything was coming to pieces then – no water, no electricity, smoke and flames everywhere . . . I've got this awful feeling that my life's gone round in a useless circle.'

'Well then, you got out of that OK, didn't you?' he urged. 'You'll get out of this too. Off you go, collect up the others. See you later.'

She turned to leave the office. Then suddenly she came back, put her arms about him, and hugged him.

'What would we do without you?' she murmured, and fled.

Tammy was off-duty on a short lunch-break when Gwen got back to the Cold Storage. She was in the staff canteen, sitting at a cluttered table, eating a fast-melting ice-cream out of a paper box. She looked up, frowning, as her mother approached.

'What now?' she said in unwelcoming tones.

Gwen glanced about the basement room. Two young Chinese assistants were playing a version of *fan-tan*. At another table, an elderly woman assistant was asleep with her head on her arms. No one was paying any attention.

'Tammy, we're leaving.'

'Oh no we're not.'

'Yes, we are. Sam is taking us out tonight on the *Dimestore* with the children from Jane Bedale's orphanage—'

'I'm not going!'

'Please, Tammy. Sam wants *me* to go.'

'Go, if you want to. Who's stopping you?'

'You are. I'm certainly not going without you.'

Tammy looked down, her mouth in a mutinous line. She gave her attention to pursuing the last of the ice-cream around the waxed paper.

'Listen, dear, Sam says it's only a matter of days before Singapore has to give in.' Quickly she gave her daughter the gist of what Sam had told her. 'Sam has to go – he's likely to be executed if he's still here when the enemy march in.'

'Well, that gives Sam a good excuse. But we haven't got one.'

'Tammy, you've heard what happened in Hong Kong. Girls like you were specially targeted because of their mixed parentage.'

'But why should you and I escape? Why should we be the only ones?'

'Don't be absurd! There's a shipload of evacuees going

out this very day – Mrs Targett and all the women at the Leonie are on it. And if you think Sam is the only one making escape plans, you're more idealistic than I thought you were. Uncle Bertie Burden left two days ago on a sampan. Anybody who can get out should go, unless they're doing some vital war-work – and would you say we're doing that?'

'Well, you're working for the hospital—'

'Not any more. My car was wrecked yesterday. And it seems to me a lot more useful to go with Miss Bedale and help with those children than hang around here.'

'Has Miss Bedale said she needs help?' Tammy challenged.

'I don't need to ask her. There are fourteen children in that shelter of hers – I think she'll have her hands full on a trip to Sumatra in cramped conditions, don't you?'

'All the same . . .'

'Look,' said Gwen with some impatience, 'I can't waste time here. I've got to get those children out to our house at Tanjong Katong and it's going to take me all afternoon. I'll drop by at your flat on the last trip. If you're packed and ready to go, I take you along. If you've decided to stay, I take the children and come back to stay with you.'

'I don't want you to come back.'

'Then come with me to board the *Dimestore*.'

Tammy hesitated. 'I can't just walk out. They're expecting me back behind the counter in ten minutes.'

'Oh, good heavens, they'll find somebody else to dole out the stores!'

'But it will look so odd. What excuse could I give?'

'Well,' said Gwen, 'after all you're only seventeen. Tell them that your mother says you're not to work here any more.'

For the first time in many months, her daughter actually smiled at her. 'True, too,' she said.

At the mission home Miss Bedale was trying to spoon gruel between the lips of a wailing baby girl. 'She's hungry,' she said as Gwen leaned over to watch. 'But it's milk she needs. She's not ready for solids yet.'

'I've got some tinned milk at my house, I think.'

'Could you bring it, Gwen?'

'No, you come and get it. I want you all to come.' Gwen explained the plan. Jane pushed a grimy hand through her tangled white hair while she heard her out.

'There are such a lot of us,' she muttered.

'We'll manage. Pack up and let's get going.'

'You're right. God must mean me to take them or He wouldn't have made it possible. All right, I'll get the first batch ready.'

Gwen helped to pack eight children into the car. There were two Eurasian girls of about eight and eleven, who took charge of the crying baby and a toddler. Two other small children sat at their feet in the back. The rest went in the front with Gwen.

The drive out to Tanjong Katong was slow and difficult. So many fires were burning that many of the streets were impassable. Sometimes Gwen drove over piles of rubble that had once been shops or dwellings. Once out past Whampoa the going was a little better, but the Japanese were bombing the airfield again: she had to draw in at the side of the road and lead the children to shelter under a bridge at the Kallang River.

Her house had been hit in the raid, but not badly. There were holes due to shrapnel in the roof, some craters in the once-perfect driveway, and the front verandah had slipped forward into the garden. Already, since the servants' going, the garden was returning to jungle.

But the stores in the kitchen quarters were still intact. She got out a tin of milk, showed one of the girls how to open it so as to feed the baby.

To the other she said, 'What's your name?'

'Selina.'

'All right, Selina, you're to look after the children until

I get back. Keep them indoors in case there's another attack. There's biscuits if they're hungry and bottles of soda water and lemonade. Don't drink the water from the tap – it may be dirty.'

'Yes, mem.'

'Good girl.'

She hurried back to the Packard, got in, and with a wave drove off. Without passengers who needed care and attention, she was able to make better time. But when she got back to the orphanage she found the road blocked – during another air attack buildings at the end of the street had collapsed. The children would have to walk out to meet the car where it stood at the corner.

Miss Bedale had them ready. With two children on Jane's lap, two jammed in beside her on the back seat, one on the floor and one in front with Gwen, the last six were carried away towards Tanjong Katong.

As close as she could get to New Bridge Road, Gwen drew up. 'I'm just going to collect Tammy,' she said.

'My dear! Where is she going to sit?'

'She's going to take those two on her lap,' Gwen said with a shrug and a smile.

Tammy was ready and waiting, clad in a serviceable linen skirt and blouse, knee socks and tennis shoes. She carried a small hold-all.

The journey this time took them longer. Light was failing – early, due to the overhang of smoke that was like a canopy above the city. When at last they trundled into the drive of Gwen's house, darkness was almost upon them.

In the half-light the house looked derelict. 'It's all changed,' Tammy said in a wondering tone.

'Everything's changed, dear,' Jane Bedale agreed. 'Come along now, let's get indoors and get some sort of meal together.'

Some water came out of the taps. They boiled it in a big saucepan over a primus stove in the servants' compound. They made a stew with some vegetables from the overgrown garden and a tin of corned beef. To wash it down Jane and Gwen had bottled water, Tammy had wine from her mother's special store. 'Might as well use some,' she observed, 'we certainly can't take it with us.'

At about seven-thirty, Gwen began on the task of getting the group along the shore to the mouth of the Geylang River. There were no stars, no moon – they were blotted out by the clouds. But from the clouds light was reflected, the red glare of fires in Singapore City. The air was very still, very hot. There were only faint sounds from the Malay township, the surge and grind of the waves coming into shore and receding, the whine of insects, the boom of bullfrogs.

By eight-thirty they were on the edge of the river, on a roadway with shuttered shops and houses on the landward side. Sampans, skiffs and some houseboats lined the shore. Tiny chinks of light escaped from the houseboats, along with the smell of cooking.

The others huddled around Gwen. The youngest children were asleep, one in the arms of Jane Bedale, one in Selina's and one in Tammy's. The eldest girl, Liu, was trying to comfort the rest, who were quiet and scared.

Gwen had arranged to signal with a torch every five minutes from nine o'clock on – short, long, short, short, which Sam said meant 'Stop, I have a message.'

But she was just getting the torch out of her pocket when a hand touched her shoulder. She jumped.

'It's all right, it's me,' said Sam in her ear.

'How did you find us?'

'Came ashore, walked down-stream on the sand. You're all wearing lightish clothes, stands out against the houses.'

'Is everything all right, Sam?'

'Well, yes. *Dimestore*'s up-stream a bit, in a deepish channel. This way.'

She turned at his touch and followed him, murmuring

to the others to do likewise. In about five minutes Sam stopped. 'Across the boats here,' he said. 'Try not to make too much noise – it should be OK, though, the boat-people know you're coming, I dropped them a few dollars.'

In single file they went after him, on to the deck of a houseboat, then on to another, then down into a sampan, then in a clamber over two more. Then, in the pinkish-grey half-light, Gwen could see the cabin-cruiser, her white wheelhouse gleaming but riding without lights.

Sam called in a low voice, 'Give a hand there.'

'Someone's aboard?' Gwen said in surprise.

'Yeah. Mr and Mrs O'Keefe.'

'What?'

Sam made no response. He was handing up the smallest of the children. One of them made a sleepy wail of protest. He said, 'Shh, now, shh.'

In a few minutes all the children were aboard. Jane scrambled up, then Tammy, then Gwen. 'Take the kids below,' Sam said. 'You know where the bunks are, Tammy, and there are cushions and blankets in the saloon.'

'I know where,' Tammy agreed, and vanished into the cabin-cruiser.

Sam said softly, 'Cast off.'

'Right you are.' It was the voice of Terence O'Keefe,

Gently *Dimestore* was pushed off from the sampans to which she'd been moored fore and aft. She drifted into mid-channel. The slow current of the Geylang River took her so that she edged seaward without help from her engines. Dim shapes of houseboats and houses fell away. The sound of the sea at the river mouth greeted them. They felt the heavier surge of the Straits' waters.

Still they floated forward. Then, when at last eddies began to turn the boat by the stern, Sam switched on the engines. They throbbed into life with perfect efficiency. He throttled back – he only wanted enough power to steer.

They went slowly on, out into the expanse of Singapore Harbour. To their right they could see the hulks of disabled ships, the toppled machinery of the docks. Then, inch by inch, these fell behind. The sound of the waves at the estuary was lost. A faint breeze touched their faces.

They were heading out into the Malacca Straits.

Sam was at the wheel. Jane and Tammy were with the children. Gwen could sense the presence of the O'Keefes on the seats behind her, watching Singapore fade from view.

'How do they come to be aboard?' she asked in a low voice.

'Terence walked up to me at the docks while I was bargaining to be taken out in a sampan to get *Dimestore*. He was going to ask me something or other but heard what I was saying. So he begged me to take him.'

'Begged you?'

'Said he wanted to get Molly away but she refused to go unless he came too and of course they wouldn't take a man on the evacuation ship. I had no choice, Gwen, he was getting noisy about it and I didn't want to attract too much attention.'

'I see that.'

'And then you know, it seemed not a bad idea to have another man along, to help handle the boat.'

'Yes.' She hesitated. 'What Tammy's going to say I can't imagine.'

'It's a hell of a set-up, isn't it? But with luck they'll only be boxed up together for twenty-four hours or so.'

Gwen shrugged in the darkness. 'I'd better go below and warn her.'

'Yeah, and tell her if she misbehaves I'll put her over the side to swim for it.'

She couldn't summon even the glimmer of a smile at this sally. She went down the steps into the saloon. The bigger children had been bedded down on the benches with cushions for pillows, but they weren't asleep. They were whispering together. One of them, a boy of about five who said his name was Petie, caught at Gwen's skirt as she went past.

'Are we going home to England, lady?' he asked, frightened yet eager.

'No, dear, we're going to Sumatra.'

'Is that on the way to England?'

'Yes, but there's a lot further to go even then.'

'Mummy said we were going to England, but we didn't, we stopped in Singapore and she died.'

'I'm sorry, Petie. It'll be all right, we'll look after you now.'

'Will you? All the way to England?'

'All the way to England. Go to sleep now, dear.'

Obediently he closed his eyes. Gwen went past him to her daughter, who was stroking the hair of one of the little dark-skinned boys, Malay or Tamil, it was impossible to know.

'Tammy.'

'Ssh, he's just dropping off.'

Gwen touched her arm, nodded towards the galley. They went into the neat little room in the darkness.

'Tammy, did you notice other people aboard?'

'Yes, someone who helped take the children on.'

'That was Terence.'

'Terence?'

'He and Molly are with us.'

She heard Tammy's hissing intake of breath.

'I know it's a surprise, darling. It gave me a shock too.'

'You didn't know?'

'Sam himself didn't know – Terence got himself included at the last moment.'

'He must feel some embarrassment,' Tammy said with bitter amusement. 'He's got his wife, his present mistress and his discarded mistress altogether in the same place with him. I'd have thought he'd rather have faced the Japs than that!'

'It's rotten for you, I know . . .'

'Don't worry about me. What can't be cured must be endured, as the saying goes.'

The cabin-cruiser forged on through the waters of the Malacca Straits on a bearing for Jambi, an unimportant little town on the east coast of Sumatra. Sam's plan was to land there and travel across land by rail to a port on the west side where steamers plied to and from Colombo. But the sea was proving choppy as the wind rose, and with its heavy load *Dimestore* was making only a little over six knots instead of ten. The island of Lingga was still visible off the port side when a grey dawn broke.

With it came the Zeros, winging across the waters looking for prey. Terence was taking a turn at the wheel, Sam was dozing on the seats of the wheelhouse. The first of the squadron swept down to look at the little cruiser and zoomed off.

'Take cover!' Sam shouted, starting into wakefulness.

The children screamed as the next plane flew over almost at sea level, its guns hammering. Then the next, and the next. There was a splintering of wood as the bullets buried themselves in the teak decking. The pram dinghy hoisted over the stern disintegrated in shards of spruce.

Gwen could feel the *Dimestore* begin to list. The oil from an unlit riding lamp caught fire as a bullet zipped through it. Flames began to spread along the coping.

Sam was struggling to launch the wooden life-raft. 'Jump!' he shouted. 'Jump! The fuel tanks will go!' He threw himself down the steps to the saloon, picked up the first child inside, grabbed another by the arm to drag him on deck.

Jane Bedale was in the stern sleeping cabin with the babies. She came at a staggering run with a child in each arm. Gwen dived through the saloon to the forward cabin to fetch the children held there. Tammy came after her, picking up a toddler by his upflung arms. Molly O'Keefe was in the saloon handing the older children out to Terence.

The raft was bobbing on the waves. 'Jump!' commanded Sam, giving Molly a shove. She leapt into the water with a boy in her arms, came up gulping and spluttering, pushed the boy on the wooden fretwork then turned to the boat. 'I'll catch them – quickly!'

Sam sent a child sprawling into the water. Another jumped of his own free will. Molly grabbed them the moment they came up for air, hauled them on the raft. Jane Bedale jumped, holding on to her two babies like grim death. She put them on the raft, clung on herself, looked round to grab another child as Tammy put him over the side.

The fighters came winging around on the turn. Machine gun bullets ruffled the water. Gwen jumped with Petie in her arms. Cold salty water closed over her, she heard him scream in terror. They came up, the little boy coughing and gasping. She put him on the raft, swam towards *Dimestore*. Tammy helped one of the older girls to push herself off into the sea. Gwen grabbed her clothing as she surfaced.

The wooden canopy of *Dimestore* and all one side was ablaze now. The attack planes ripped the burning wood with their machine guns.

'Get away,' shouted Sam, 'paddle the raft away!'

'No,' Jane cried. But then she realised that *Dimestore* was going down, and the swirl of the water was dragging the raft towards it.

Tammy came sailing into the water with the last of the small children. The older ones had jumped. They were either on the raft, holding it, or holding the clothing of the women.

The two men dived. As soon as they reached the raft they pushed off, swimming hard to put distance between themselves and *Dimestore*. The women pushed too, while keeping the children on board with one hand.

There was a hard blow, as if a fist had struck the water. A shaft of heat. Gwen turned her head. *Dimestore* had gone up in a sheet of flame. Spars of wood were going lazily up into the air from it.

The fighter planes swept low over them. The sound of the machine guns was loud, a hard chattering. Molly O'Keefe gave a cry and let go.

'No!' Terence shouted, lunging after her.

The little life-raft dipped under their movement. 'Hold on,' grunted Sam. He dived under. A moment later he and Terence came up, Molly supported between them.

'Molly! Molly!' Terence cried.

Back came the Zeros. 'Dive!' shouted Sam. The older children obeyed, hiding under the water from the bullets. Jane Bedale threw herself over the little ones on the raft to protect them. The planes executed a quick swooping turn, then zoomed up and away. The sound of their engines died.

A sort of awful silence followed, broken by the crackling of wood and the sizzling as heated metal met sea-water. Gasping, coughing, choking, the survivors clung to the bobbing raft. Gwen began a count. Six children on the raft, seven in the water clinging to it or to the grown-ups. One child was missing.

Gwen dived under, searching. But the water was dark and green, and within the surrounding six or seven yards she could find nothing. Sam tried, tried again. It was no use.

Terence was trying to get Molly to open her eyes.

'She's all right, she's just fainted,' he insisted. 'Put her up on the raft.'

But when they tried to do so, his arm came away from her shoulders covered in blood. Gwen put her head against her breast. There was no heartbeat.

Jane Bedale was still lying on the raft, causing it

to veer over as the little ones struggled to sit up. Tammy helped free them then dragged Jane into a sitting position. She had a wound to her arm; blood ran down over her fingers.

It was a dreadful roll call. One child and one woman dead, one badly wounded.

The sun began to rise behind Lingga. The white edges to the waves were tinged with pink and coral.

'Oh God,' sobbed Terence. 'Oh God!'

'What are we to do now?' Gwen said.

'We head towards that rock. It's not far, if we all push and paddle, we should make it in an hour—

'But it's just a *rock*, Sam,' Tammy cried.

'But the fishermen of Lingga probably come out to set their traps there. Come on, we must do it – come *on*!'

He was right. They had to do it. There was nowhere else close enough, no ship or fishing boat in sight.

'Molly!' begged Terence.

'We have to let her go, Terence.'

'No! No, Sam, we'll take her to the island . . .'

He tried to hold on to her as clumsily, lopsidedly, they set out to steer their raft to the rocky islet they could see about a mile away across the waters. But after about twenty minutes, without a word, he slowly let her body go. It seemed for a moment to sway beside him, then it sank out of sight.

The islet was just that, an islet. There was almost no shore, the rocks rose straight out of the sea. Perhaps if they had been in a boat, with oars, they could have rowed round to find a landing place. As it was they had to crash ashore as best they might. Tammy spread-eagled herself on the raft to hold the tiny ones safe. The rest fell among the sharp stones, cutting and gashing themselves.

The adults floundered in among the boulders, stumbling and falling. Sam had the rope of the raft in his hand, to drag it out before it was seized by the waves and taken away. The women pulled themselves to their feet to save the babies. Tammy knelt up, the raft at an angle, but the children held safe to be handed ashore.

For a while all they could do was sag among the stones, letting relief flow through them, letting strength ebb back. Then there was the task of getting the wet clothes off the children, spreading them out to dry in the hot sun. Gwen bound up Jane's wounds with strips from her blouse.

Sam said, 'I'll go and take a look around.'

'This is no time to go exploring!' Terence objected.

'I'm going to see if there's any signs that the fishermen come out here. And to look for fresh water.'

'Oh. Yes. Sorry, old man. I'm . . . I'm upset.'

'I know, Terence. I'm damned sorry.'

'Not your fault . . . my fault . . . I made you take us.'

Sam trudged away, taking a route parallel to the shore about three yards from the water's edge. He had to make detours round dark volcanic boulders. Soon he had disappeared round the sharp contours of the shore.

The sun was climbing high. The children, especially the younger ones, had to be moved into shade. Despite the fact that some of the rocks were six feet high or more, shade was hard to find.

In about half an hour Sam returned. 'There are fishing traps,' he reported, 'but they haven't been emptied for days. There's a narrow beach on the eastward side, just a shelf of sand that runs out about a dozen yards. There's no fresh water except in pools where the rain's collected.'

They stared at him in dismay. 'No houses or huts?'

'No. A derelict sampan with its bottom stove in, caught between two rocks round the next headland, that's all. The island's only about sixty yards across from this side to the other; there's no level ground to build a house.'

'Oh, God,' groaned Terence.

'What do you think we should do?' asked Jane Bedale.

Sam shook his head. 'We'd be marginally better off in the inlet where there's sand – it would at least be better to sit on until the tide comes up and covers it. The fish traps are accessible from there – we could pull them up and have something to eat.'

'But how would we cook it?' Terence asked. 'There's no wood for a fire.'

'There's bits of flotsam – we could find enough. What we need is matches. Anybody got any?'

A search through pockets revealed no matches, but Sam had a case filled with thin cheroots and a gold lighter. He flicked the wheel of the lighter, but it refused to work.

'Flint's still wet,' he said. 'And probably sea-water got in among the lighter fuel. We'll lay it out to dry and mebbe in an hour or two it'll work.'

They decided to transfer to the sandy beach. Revitalised by having something to do, they set off, each of the fit adults and the two older girls carrying a child, Miss Bedale guiding another with her good hand, and the rest scrambling along after them.

They went over the top of the islet instead of round the edge, because it was faster and because it gave them a chance to look out from the highest point. But no ship, no vessel of any kind could be seen. En route they paused to scoop up water in their hands from the rain-pools. To give the babies a drink, they used Sam's cheroot case.

It was possible to find shade on the little eastward beach. The sand was already being covered by the tide which meant they still had to sit among the rocks, but a little sand had blown into crevices so that enough comfortable spots were found for the toddlers.

While Sam's lighter was dismantled and spread out to dry, Gwen and Tammy waded out to the fish traps. These were signalled by long stakes driven into the sea-bed. Nets were spread between the stakes. They went down in a jump to look at the catch. Many fish were caught in the nets, some had been nibbled by other fish. They untangled half a dozen of the largest to take back. By the time they waded ashore, the tide had covered the beach.

The older children had collected wood. With a dried-out envelope from Terence's pocket and some tiny shards, they got a fire going in a sheltered spot among the rocks. Carefully they set larger pieces of wood in a tent over it. To their delight, the wood caught.

'Don't let that go out,' Sam ordered. 'Until we get off this rock, that fire is the only way we can keep warm at night, cook our food, and signal if a ship goes by.'

They roasted the fish by holding it over the fire on a stick. The first they ate was still only half-cooked, but they were so hungry it tasted like manna. The second fell into the fire and got half-burned but still tasted good. The third was treated with great care, was allowed to cool properly before they tried to eat it, and was the real easing of their hunger.

Except for the baby. They had nothing to give the baby girl except water. They had had tinned milk for her aboard the *Dimestore* and had given her two feeds during the night, but she was hungry now, wailing with hunger pains, her black eyes filled with tears.

Clouds rolled up, the monsoon wind blew, rain came lashing down. They tried to keep out of it among the rocks but there was little overhang and so most of them got soaked again. The sun came out to dry them out but nightfall was coming.

Sam suggested that they should try to get parts of the wrecked sampan along the shore to make a shelter. 'If it rains during the night and we all get wet again we'll end up with pneumonia.'

'But how are you going to get a sampan over the rocks?' Terence objected. 'It's heavy . . .'

'Swim bits of it along round the shore. OK?'

'Isn't that a bit risky? We could end up hacked to pieces if the sea washes us inland—'

'I'll go with you,' said Tammy, getting to her feet.

'No, you stay with the children.'

'The children are all right.'

'Don't go, Tammy,' begged Petie. 'You'll get killed like my mummy.'

'No, I won't, Petie. I'm just going a few yards out.'

'I'll go,' Terence said with an angry sigh. 'You stay with Petie, I'll go.'

The two men set off along the rocks. A long time seemed to go by. The sun was slipping down into the westward horizon when at last bobbing heads could be made out perhaps a dozen yards off-shore. Gwen leapt up and waded out, followed by Tammy and the two girls, Selina and Liu.

The men had been towing a shaped piece of the sampan behind them by means of what had once been its mooring rope. The women seized the broken edges, heaved and pulled, lost their footing on the sand, went under but came up still pulling and tugging. They brought the curved wreckage ashore, all of them holding it up so it wouldn't snag on sharp rocks and be damaged further.

For ten minutes afterwards they sat gasping and getting their breath back. Then, with a concerted effort, they picked up the shell of wood and carried it up among the rocks. By balancing it across two of the largest, they made a sort of triangular shed, open on one side, protected by rock on the other two.

There was room under it for perhaps five people. Miss Bedale was put in the place of best protection, with the baby in her good arm. Tammy and Gwen sat beside her, each with a child on her lap. Petie was next to Tammy, with his arm around her. Selina and Liu both had a smaller child to care for. The rest crowded in between the shelter and the fire.

Terence and Sam stretched out beside the fire. They

had a pile of sticks with which to tend it during the night.

The abrupt tropic dusk fell. They clung to each other, afraid. They heard planes go over high, bombers, heading for Singapore. The baby had ceased her loud crying but was whining miserably now, losing hope of food.

Twice during the night they heard planes. There was a fighter patrol at dawn, perhaps the same one that had strafed the *Dimestore*. But they went past without spotting the castaways on the rock.

The tide was out, the beach was clear. They went down to wash, to get fish from the fish traps, to spread out in comfort on the sand. Selina and one of the other children gathered wood. Terence cooked the fish. They sat out on the sand in the early sun, eating the first meal of the day.

Sam went up to the top of the rock to see if there was anything moving on the sea. When he came back he said he'd seen a junk's sail far out, but nothing within signalling distance. The older children were organised into a look-out team, turn and turn about.

The day wore on. The baby stopped crying. She lay listless, her black eyes dulled, no tears now.

'She's going to die,' Jane Bedale said, bending over her to wash her drawn little face with rain water.

'Somebody'll come,' Gwen said. 'The fishermen who own the traps . . .'

'Not in time,' said Jane.

They ate three meals of fish, drank rain water from the pools. Terence and Sam and Gwen brought back the rest of the sampan, so that they could enlarge the shelter. That night was a little more comfortable, though it rained torrentially and they had to build a little shelter over their precious fire.

The planes went over in the night, and at dawn the fighters roared by. Terence went up to the look-out rock after breakfast. He came back at a stumbling run, shouting.

'There's a boat! There's a boat!'

At once everyone rushed towards him. They all went back with him to the look-out point. Sure enough, coming out of a sea-mist about half a mile away, a boat . . .

Its shape was uncertain in the haze. But now they could hear, faintly, the labouring of an engine.

'Hi!' they shouted. 'Help! Hi, out there! Help!'

'Go down and pile wood on the fire,' Sam ordered Liu. She turned and leapt down the slope. A moment later they could hear the crackling as she added their precious store of wood to the flames. Then smoke went up – Liu had had the sense to add some wet sand.

The boat edged along, heading south. Its outline became clearer. It was a motor launch, of the kind used perhaps as a ferry across a river, for seated passengers and of shallow draught. It was riding low in the water, its engine sounded uncertain.

'Altogether now,' Gwen said. They shouted in unison. 'Help! Help!'

And to their delighted relief, the boat's prow turned towards the island.

As the mist dropped away from it they could see it was crowded. Built to carry eighteen seated passengers for short trips, it now held something like twenty-eight people. They were wet, dishevelled, clutching boxes and suitcases. The man at the wheel was a bearded white man.

He let the motor idle, cupped his hands to shout. No one could make out what he was saying.

'Hallo on the boat!' shouted Sam. 'We need help!'

'Hallo on the shore!' came the reply. 'English, are you?

'It's a Dutch boat!' Sam grunted. 'Captain, can you take us off?'

'How did you get there, my friend?'

'Heading for Sumatra out of Singapore. Jap fighters attacked us. Where are you headed?'

'Heading for Palembang out of Lingga . . .'

'Lingga! Is Lingga under attack?'

'Yes, my friend, the Japs are landing, we had to run for it in the middle of the night. Look, I am sorry, we cannot possibly take you. As you see, we are almost under water as it is.'

'You've got to take us,' shouted Terence. 'We can't stay here!'

'How many of you are there?'

'Thirteen children, five adults.'

'Out of the question! Look at my boat—'

'Captain, we've got an eight-week-old baby here dying of starvation,' Jane shouted. 'You've got to take her, at least!'

There was a pause. The captain appeared to have a consultation with his passengers.

'We will take the baby!' he yelled.

'Come on, captain!' Sam urged through his cupped hands. 'Take the kids! They're at the end of their rope. And we've got an injured woman – she needs medical treatment.'

Another conference. 'I'm sorry, my friend, we cannot take so many.'

'If you throw overboard some of that luggage . . .'

There were cries of protest from the people in the boat. One old man, standing in the prow, was hugging to his chest a fine French clock. He put his jacket over it protectively.

'Wait!' shouted the Dutchman.

They held another conference, longer this time. Some of the people were clearly urging that they should lighten the boat so as to take as many of the castaways as possible. One man, to set an example, threw his suitcase into the sea. It floated off, eddying here and there in the tide.

The captain of the launch waved his arm for attention. 'We are agreed to take the children and the injured lady. I am sorry, we cannot take anyone else. We will come as far in as we can and then lighten ship. Then you must wade out to us with the children.'

'You've got to take us all!' yelled Terence.

'Have some sense, man, the boat'll go under if we all try to get aboard,' Sam sighed.

Cautiously the launch edged closer inshore. Most of the passengers let down into the water some case or package or bag. The containers bobbed about between boat and shore.

'Now,' called the Dutchman.

Jane looked at Gwen and Tammy. 'I won't go,' she said.

'Yes, you will. You have to take the baby and look after her.' Gwen picked up the little girl, a rickle of bones now in her soiled baby clothes, and put her in Jane's good arm. Then she helped her walk down the steep little beach and into the sea.

The water was at neck level by the time the grown-ups had waded out with the smaller children on their shoulders. Selina and Liu and the bigger children swam the last few yards. Jane was helped aboard, the others were handed up.

When it was time for the last batch to be taken out, Petie refused to go. 'No, don't make me, let me stay,' he begged, clutching Tammy's skirt.

'But you *must* go, Petie—'

'No, I want to be with you,' he wailed, screwing his eyes shut and clenching his fists on the linen skirt.

'Good friends, please hurry up,' called the captain. 'I must get to the Sumatra coast before dark – I don't know how to steer by the stars.'

'Just a minute, captain!'

But Petie refused to be persuaded. In the end Tammy said, 'Let him stay. I'll look after him.'

'We don't want a kid hanging around if we can pack him off.'

'I told you, Terence, I'll look after him.'

'OK,' agreed Sam.

The other four children were carried out to the launch. As they were handed aboard Sam said, 'Got any food to spare? Any matches?'

A woman who had helped take Jane into the boat searched in her handbag, produced a box of Dutch matches. A string bag containing some fruit and a slab of chocolate was passed across.

'Thanks a lot,' Sam said. 'What's your name, captain?'

'Piet Janstra. Yours?'

'Sam Prosper. I wish you all the best.'

'Yes, my friend, and I wish you another boat coming by – but I must warn you, it isn't likely, the enemy has got Lingga under control and nothing is getting out to sea.'

'Thanks for the word. Any news of Singapore?'

Janstra shook his head. 'Hard to find out the truth. Japanese propaganda was all we could get on our radios so you mustn't take it as truth, but they say the Singapore government is asking for surrender terms.'

'How about Sumatra? Lingga is Dutch East Indies and if the Japs have landed there, have they landed in Sumatra?'

'No, I think not. So that's where we go. Goodbye, Sam Prosper.'

'Goodbye, Piet.'

The launch engine throbbed into life, the boat began to gather way. Its passengers waved and called in Dutch or Malay, 'Goodbye, good luck.'

The others backed off to let them go. Soon the launch was receding out of hearing. They swam back to shore, Sam holding the matches clear of the water.

Petie was sitting in a huddle waiting for them. He grabbed Gwen's hand. 'Am I staying with you?'

'Yes, love, of course you are. And look, we've got some chocolate for you!'

They sat on the beach, sharing out to each a cube of Dutch chocolate. The delight of its sweetness was like heaven.

'Now, let's catch that stuff before it floats away,' Sam commanded, heading back into the water.

'What stuff – oh, from the launch.' They plunged after him, catching a floating suitcase, a reed basket about to be swamped. Between them they hauled in two cases, three baskets, a small trunk, and a box with a handle. All the rest had sunk before they could reach it.

One of the cases had a man's suit, several changes of underwear, and three pairs of boots. The other contained fine towels and sheets and pillow-cases. The baskets had a miscellaneous collection of combs, shaving tackle, tin mugs, books with the pages glued together with sea-water, an embroidery tambour. The small trunk had a set of bone china. The box with the handle was a plate camera.

'Damn,' said Sam, 'I grabbed that box because I thought maybe it had tins of food in it. A camera! It's not even as if we're fit to be photographed.'

'That's the truth,' Gwen said, feeling herself smile for the first time in days.

They looked at each other. Gwen was a reasonable sight in twill slacks and a blouse shortened at the hem to make bandages. Tammy's linen skirt had shrunk and was stained with sea-water. Her blouse was torn, she'd discarded the knee socks. Sam's clothes had taken many a knock on the boulders in the past couple of days – buttons had gone from his shirt and he had a tear in the knee of his trousers. Terence had no tears as yet but his once-white suit was a sickly yellow-beige and he was shoeless. Little Petie's knitted shirt had shrunk up so that his middle was exposed, though his shorts were still respectable.

They spread out the contents of the luggage to dry. The sun was well up now, the day was hot. They tended the fire, grilled some fish, had a meal and then a rest. Then Sam got up.

'Come on, Terence, we're going to get *Dimestore*'s raft from the rocks where we left it.'

Terence frowned at him. 'What on earth for?'

'Because we're going to Sumatra on it.'

'Are you mad?'

'No, quite the reverse. The Japs are on Lingga, right? How long before they start sending out patrol boats to scout the outlying islands? We want to be gone from here when they come—'

'But Sumatra! How do you propose to get there by raft?'

'Paddle, of course.'

'Paddle! You mean like when we were wrecked, pushing along in the water? How far?'

'It's about fifty miles and no, we won't push the raft along in the water. We'll sit on it and paddle with spars of wood taken from the sampan. And if I can find a pole long enough among the flotsam, we can even make a sail from one of those sheets we've inherited.'

'The idea's absurd—'

'Why do you say that?' Gwen put in with indignation. 'What would you prefer? That we just sit here and do nothing?'

'Another boat will come along—'

'Bringing a Japanese landing party. You heard what that Dutchman said.'

Terence hesitated. 'Well . . . even if it did . . . Wouldn't it be better to be taken to Lingga and interned?'

'Not on your life!' Sam exclaimed. 'I'm not going to be taken prisoner, and you can take that as gospel.'

'But it's so dangerous . . . .'

'Sure it's dangerous. You stay here if you want to, wait for the Japs. Me, I'm going to get that raft and set out for Sumatra with anybody else that wants to go.'

So saying he marched off along the shore.

'Go and help him,' said Tammy. 'He can't handle the raft by himself.'

'It's simply not sensible—'

'All right, I'll go,' said Gwen.

'No, Mummy,' said her daughter. 'It's a man's job.'

Shamefaced, Terence reluctantly got up to follow Sam.

Because the tide was going out, it took the two men some time to swim back with the raft. They dragged it up the beach and up into the rocks. Then they lay down, exhausted. Gwen brought them water heated in a tin mug with some chocolate dissolved in it – a weak, strange drink but it seemed to revive them.

Later they collected up all the things from the luggage and took them under cover for fear of a rainstorm. They made a meal and, after sundown, sat by the fire making a plan.

'We'll take the empty suitcase and the trunk and tie them to the raft – that'll give extra buoyancy. I couldn't find a pole to make a mast, so we'll have to paddle – we'll select bits of this shelter,' he nodded overhead at the sampan, 'tomorrow.'

'We'd better pick out something by way of a change of clothing from those things,' Gwen suggested. 'Terence, have you tried on the boots?'

'Yes, they're too big—'

'Well, pad them out with two pairs of socks. It's better not to be barefoot, we've no idea what the coast may be like when we get to Sumatra.'

'We'd better take the sheets with us, as a protection against the sun.' Tammy stroked Petie's hair; he was asleep in her lap. 'Poor little mite, he's burnt enough already.'

'Are you really going to do this?' Terence said in dismay.

'Of course we are, Terence.'

'We're going to paddle fifty miles?'

'The current will help us. Haven't you noticed,' said Sam, 'that the current off this rock sets towards the south-west?'

Terence's face in the glimmer of the firelight reflected

only uncertainty. 'I don't think we should do it,' he muttered.

But when, soon after midday the next day, they pushed the raft out from the beach and got aboard, he clambered on it too.

'Sumatra here we come,' said Sam, and dipped his plank of wood in the water.

Sure enough, the raft wheeled gently, then set out towards the south-west.

Chapter Twenty-five

They sighted Sumatra about an hour before nightfall next day.

Sam had said they were doing about two knots, with the help of the current. He had also said that Sumatra was about fifty miles off. His calculations weren't far wrong.

They had all been at work at the paddles. One would rest while the other three paddled. It meant you got half an hour's rest every two hours. While you rested, you ate and sipped water, or dozed.

They had taken with them all the cooked fish they could prepare and the remainder of the fruit and chocolate given them by the passengers in the Dutch launch. Petie, sitting in the middle of the life-raft, had the job of catching fresh water when it rained. When the sun shone he had to make sure the sheets were spread over the paddlers so as to save them from sunburn. He was proud of his usefulness.

They paddled through the night. Sam corrected their direction from the stars. They preferred paddling at night, the air was cool, it was less wearisome when you couldn't see a vast expanse of empty ocean stretching away from you.

Two or three times in daylight they sighted fishing-boats – two under sail, one pulling in nets. But they were too far off to hail. They sighted an island too, larger than the rock on which they'd been living and with signs of habitation. But current and tide combined were too strong, they couldn't put in to it.

Planes came over at intervals, sometimes bombers, sometimes a smaller flight of fighters. Each time they huddled low, but if the fighters could see them they paid no heed. At night the bombers were high over the sea in the moonlight.

The first land that hove into view on the horizon was actually, so Sam said, the large island of Banka. He ordered them to let up on the right-hand side, to paddle harder on the left. That would take them in towards Sumatra. Then they felt a push, a strong current sending them off-shore. 'A river,' said Sam in a worried tone.

They put their backs into it. Little by little they edged towards the great mass of land to the west. Then the tide turned in their favour, sweeping into the river mouth. They heard surf, saw green vegetation – trees, mangrove swamps, the masts of fishing boats.

A sampan coming out of the delta was approaching. It was poled by a tall, thin Malay. At sight of them he drew out the pole, held it as a brake on the water, stood staring.

'What river is this, tungku?' Sam called, giving him a very polite title.

'Tuan, you don't know? This is the Indragiri.'

'We are very tired. Will you tow us to shore?'

'Willingly, willingly, tuan.'

He pushed with his pole on the river bottom. The sampan sped towards them, glided alongside. He threw a rope. Terence caught it, tied it to the raft. Grinning, the oarsman bowed, then turned about to face the other way. He pushed off with his pole, made a slight jar, and then with his next stroke sent them speeding up-river to a landing area on the muddy beach.

The raft grounded, stuck, almost up-ended at the shock. They staggered off on to the mud. Their limbs were cramped from twenty-four hours crouched on the raft. Their skins were chafed and rubbed by sea-water, by wet clothes. Their hair was matted with salt. Their fingers were like claws, their wrists had seized up after so much paddling.

Fishermen on the mudflats mending nets got up to hurry forward. People came running down the walkways from the stilted huts. A chattering crowd gathered.

The sudden access of noise after so much sea-silence was overpowering. They stood, dazed.

Then a way was opened in the crowd. A very old man was coming down the beach, an old man in a long, worn sarong and an embroidered felt cap. This was indeed the tungku, the headman of the village.

'Tuan,' he said, placing his hands together to bow. 'Mem.' Another bow. 'We are honoured by your presence. Please come to our home.'

He led the way to the largest of the huts. Gwen took Petie by the hand. They followed in the wake of the tungku, the people making way. They went up a plank walk, into a house on stilts, with windows open to the air but shaded by reed mats, with rushes on the floor and sleeping benches along the walls.

'I offer you food, drink, bath, what you need, tuan,' the tungku said in grave and formal Malay. 'This is the law of Allah towards visitors.'

'We thank you, tungku. May we bathe and make ourselves clean? And much to drink – we have been more than a day at sea with only rain water.'

'It shall be.'

Two hours later, bathed, changed into clean clothes, fed, and with jugs of hot coffee at hand, they sat down to talk with the tungku.

'From Singapore?' he said in surprise. 'Others have come, from Lingga and Banka. You are the first from Singapore.'

'From Banka?' Terence cried. 'Wasn't that the big island you steered us away from?'

'Yes, but only because I thought we ought to try for the mainland.' He turned to the tungku. 'The Japanese are in Banka?'

'Oh yes. Here also.'

'*Here?*'

'Yes, armed boats with troops came, two days, three days ago. I hear they are in Lampong, but I do not know how true this is.'

'Many Japanese? Or scouting parties?'

'Not many, but I think many will come.'

'Dear God,' groaned Terence. 'Out of the frying-pan . . .'

'Tuan,' the tungku said, 'if you wish to keep out of the way of the Japanese, it is not hard. I think perhaps a week, two weeks, before they can have troops in all places. Is it your wish to keep away from the Japanese?'

'And how,' Sam said in English. In Malay he said, 'It is our sincere wish. We hoped to get to Padang, on the west coast, to board a ship going across the big sea to Colombo.'

'A good plan. The Japanese are not yet on the west coast, I think. Well, eat, drink, sleep. In the morning we will talk again.'

The tungku laid his hand on Petie's light brown hair. The boy was asleep, cuddled against Tammy. 'Your son?' he asked her.

She blushed. 'Oh, no, tungku, I am not married.'

'No? What a waste. Well, when you are ready to sleep, my wife will show where the women and the child can lie. The tuans will sleep here.'

'Thank you, tungku.'

That was a night of blissful sleep. Straw pallets on bamboo benches seemed so soft in comparison with the rocks on the island or the cramped seat on the raft. In the morning Gwen rose, stretched, and tottered out of the hut. She was stiff in every limb. But when the village women had shown her the bathing pool behind the huts, she stretched out in the water, letting it soothe and lull her limbs.

Breakfast was flat rice cakes, fruit, and fish stew.

Gwen ate heartily. She had seen her reflection in the pool – all skin and bone, no flesh on her body after almost a week on starvation rations and, before that, sketchy meals in Singapore.

The tungku summoned them to talk after the meal. He addressed himself to Sam, as if to the headman of another village. 'You still wish to make for the west coast?'

'Unless you advise against it,' Sam replied.

'No, I think it a good plan. Have you any idea of how you will go there?'

'The railway?'

'It is a journey to the railway town. And no doubt the Japanese would be there.'

'You are right, headman.'

'There is a road across country, but the Japanese commandeered trucks and cars – they will be using the roads, I think.'

'Yes.' Sam looked at the others, his face a picture of concern.

'But there is a way to travel most of the way across country, tuan.'

'Yes?'

'By boat.'

'Oh God,' cried Terence, 'don't say we have to take to the sea again!'

'The sea? Tuan is not thinking what he is saying, the sea is behind him. But to reach the west coast there is a waterway – the river Indragiri.'

'It's possible to go up the river by boat?'

'Surely, tuan. By sampan.'

'Are we going to have to learn to use those long poles? I thought we'd finished with all that kind of thing—'

'Be quiet, Terence. Let the tungku finish. Excuse my friend, tungku. We have had hard days lately.'

'Truly. But it will not be necessary for the tuan and his friend to pole the boats.' The tungku looked offended. 'We have skilled men here, who know the river.'

'We may hire them, tungku?'

'Of course. You understand, they must be paid. If they take time off from fishing, their time must not be thrown away.'

'We understand, elder of the village. We are willing to pay. Tell us what the price would be.'

'Not British Singapore dollars. They have no value now.'

'We have no dollars, tungku.'

'What do you offer instead?'

Before they had left the rock they had looked through the luggage from the people on the launch and taken from it what they could easily put in their pockets. Ivory combs, mirrors, gold-rimmed spectacles, pencils, a powder compact, needles and embroidery threads, a tiny silver photo frame. Then there were the tin mugs, two china dishes in which they'd carried the cooked fish, and the fine percale sheets they'd used for shelter.

Strangely enough it was the sheets that the sampan owners seemed to hanker after. Perhaps they had been prompted by their wives, who wanted them for sarongs or the long jackets that went over them. So a bargain was struck: the four sheets from the raft, and Sam's gold cheroot case, for the services of two sampans and their oarsmen.

They were to rest today. Tomorrow they would start out, in the cool of the dawn.

'When you get to the headwater of the Indragiri,' warned the tungku, 'you will have to leave the boats and climb through a pass in the mountains to reach the coast. I have never done this but I have heard of it. It is said that it is very cold, so be ready to buy warm clothes when you get there.'

'Thank you, tungku.'

The rest of the day went by like a dream. They lay in the shade of the palms, they dozed or watched the fishermen put out to sea. The women washed their clothes in the stream, laughing and teasing each other. Children ran about in play, or walked solemnly carrying baskets of rice or eggs, or throwing grain for the chickens. It was a scene of perfect peace. Singapore and its horrors, the attack on the *Dimestore* – it all seemed a million miles away.

As daylight waned Terence asked if, now that they were safe, they could have a little ceremony in memory of Molly. They at once agreed. No one knew what to say. Only Tammy, with more recent memories of morning prayer at school, was able to summon up a few words that seemed to fit the occasion.

'Oh God . . . author of peace and lover of concord . . . defend us thy humble servants in all assaults of our enemy . . . And grant peace to our dear friend departed . . .'

They all said 'Amen'. Afterwards Gwen said to her daughter, 'You did well.' Tammy looked embarrassed and turned away.

Gwen was worried for fear Tammy might go to comfort Terence, who was off by himself staring at the river, hands in trouser pockets, shoulders hunched, cloaked in melancholy. But she was waylaid by Petie, demanding help in plaiting a lead and a collar for one of the village puppies.

Sam joined Gwen as she sank down on a fallen log. 'The little feller takes her back towards her childhood,' he said, nodding at the two bent in concentration over a knot in the straw rope.

'Yes. She leaped into being grown-up too fast, like a steeple-chaser heading for a fall.'

'I feel bad about landing her in all this.'

'You couldn't possibly foresee this, Sam. I never dreamed that they – my husband's people, I keep reminding myself – would shoot at children in the water.'

'The awful thing,' Sam said, his voice shaking, 'the awful thing is I didn't even know the name of the kid that drowned.'

'Beni. His name was Beni, his mother was a Malay, his father was European, we thought.'

'He might still be alive if I hadn't pushed Miss Bedale into leaving.'

'She wanted to. She said God had put the chance in her way.'

'Damn funny thing to do to her, if you ask me,' Sam said with a grimace of anger on his long, tired face. 'And to the boy.'

'I thought about him when Tammy was saying those words for Molly. I sort of said them for him too.'

'"Defend us in all assaults of our enemy". You could say them for us – for to tell the truth, Gwen, I'm not certain Sumatra is as safe as I'd hoped.'

She touched his arm. 'It'll be all right, Sam.'

'Sure.'

That night they turned in early, for they were to start before dawn next day. They would be going up-river against the current, so the work of the pole-men would be hard, and impossible to carry on through the heat of the day. Therefore they would travel early, then rest, then travel until sundown.

When they asked if they should take provisions, the tungku waved away the idea. 'You may get European food if the tuans are still on the palm-oil and rubber plantations, and if not, you can get rice and tapioca from the *kampongs*.'

They gave him the little silver photo-frame as a gift of gratitude. Though he clearly had no idea of its use, he took it with a smile and a bow.

The sampans lay by the long jetty leading across the mud to the shallows. In a procession the villagers came to see them off. The travellers climbed into the sampans, the pole-men took up their stance, and with a cry of 'Peace attend your going!' they were off.

Within an hour Gwen understood the discomfort of being a passenger in a sampan. It was impossible to sit comfortably. Either you had to have your legs extended straight, or you knelt, or you crouched. Either way, within ten minutes you longed to move. But to move was to set the boat rocking and break the oarsman's smooth rhythm.

The river seemed alive with flying insects. They had tried to cover exposed skin as best they could, but there was no way of keeping them off their faces or their hands.

Gwen, her daughter and Petie were in one sampan. The two men were in the other. They were making about two miles an hour against the current. Gwen felt it would have been quicker to walk – except that on either side of the river was first mangrove and later thick jungle.

As to the tuans on the palm-oil plantations, during the whole of that first day they saw no Europeans and very few Sumatrans. Planes went by overhead, sometimes swooping low as if on observation patrol, but there was never any machine-gun attack. They slept at midday in the thick green shade of the riverbank, ate some wild bananas, and set out again. By late afternoon they were at a wide, shallow bend, and here they found a settlement.

'Keremu,' they were told. The sampans slid in by the bank. People came out of the houses.

They were given a polite welcome, offered food and shelter. But clearly the villagers didn't want them there. Their dialect was unfamiliar but Sam gathered a Japanese motor patrol had been by on the road about a mile inland.

'We understand, tungku,' he said. 'We'll be gone before morning light.'

But after they had gone two or three miles the next day, the boatmen began to grow anxious. 'Mem, it would not be good if the Japanese saw white mems in the boat. You must lie down.'

Gwen was about to argue but saw real fear in the man's eyes. There was a path along the riverbank – it was just possible a party of Japanese might march along it.

'Very well, Ali,' she agreed.

He held the boat steady while they changed position. There wasn't really room for two European-size women to lie down, and Petie was an added awkwardness. All three squirmed with discomfort in the heat of their own bodies.

When the undergrowth came down to the water's edge they could sit up. Otherwise they had to be prone in the boat. It was a blessed relief when mid-day approached and they were able to disembark for the boatmen to rest. Any potentially threatening foot patrols would be resting themselves for an hour or so.

That night they were to have tied up at Tana, but as they glided towards it in the tree-shadow, they saw it had been burned out. Stillness, and the smell of charred wood, hung in the air.

The two boatmen stopped the boats midstream. They stood staring at the hamlet. Nothing moved there. They came in to the shore. The Sumatrans stepped ashore. Nothing happened except that a skinny dog appeared from among the ruins to watch them.

Sam scrambled to his feet and got out.

'No, tuan!' whispered Ali.

'Someone must go to look – will you go?'

'Oh, no, tuan.'

'Then I'll go. Stay here.' He walked quietly across the riverbank path, in among the half-dozen houses, and was lost to view. In about five minutes he reappeared. 'Deserted. Come on.'

They disembarked, hearts beating heavily at what they could see. 'The Japanese have been here,' Tammy suggested.

'But why burn the village? The villagers wouldn't put up any resistance?'

Sam was looking sad and angry. 'By the looks of it this was a Chinese village. I guess they tried to fight off the troops—'

'Fight them off?' said Terence. 'You mean they had arms?'

'Mebbe not. But they knew what it means to be taken by—' He broke off. He didn't want to say what he thought of the Japanese style of warfare in front of Gwen and Tammy.

'What are we going to do?' Gwen asked, understanding what he had left unsaid. 'Is it safe to stay?'

'Reckon so. The troops have gone by. Anyhow, looks as if it was only a small party that came here – tyre-marks of one truck. They've probably rejoined the main body.'

'The main body? Look here, Sam, does that mean we're following along behind a Japanese *army*?'

'Your guess is as good as mine, Terence. I'd say not an army – but a strong penetration force, mebbe three or four companies—'

'Then we ought to turn back!'

'Back? What would be the good of that?' cried Tammy. 'They're there too – the tungku at the mouth of the river said so.'

'That's right!' Terence exclaimed, throwing up his hands. 'That's right! We're right in the middle of them!'

This conversation had been taking place in English. The Sumatrans watched with anxiety. 'Tuan, what is to be done?' asked Ali, who was the elder and leader.

'My brother, you and Kemal are free to leave us. This is more dangerous than you expected—'

'Free to leave us?' Terence interrupted. 'Are you mad? They'll go back and tell the Japs—'

'Shut up, Terence. Forgive my friend,' Sam went on to Ali, 'he has worries.'

'We all have worries. But as to leaving, that we cannot do, because our wives have taken the goods you gave for the price of this journey. So we go on, and with the help of Allah we go well.'

'With the help of Allah,' Sam agreed.

After some discussion it was agreed to spend the night here then go on as usual in the morning. There were no obvious sleeping quarters, but there was shelter of a kind among the charred bamboo beams. After a search they found a storage basket containing some dried fish, which they cooked with tapioca roots pulled up from the village gardens.

Petie curled up to sleep that night as close to Gwen and Tammy as he could manage. While he didn't quite understand what danger they were in, he was infected by the anxiety they all felt.

Gwen couldn't sleep. Some time after midnight she heard someone rise and go stealthily out of the wrecked village. She pulled herself up on an elbow. A figure in white shirt and trousers – either Sam or Terence, not one of the Sumatrans.

Could it be Terence, leaving them, looking for the road so as to turn back, or to hand himself over to the Japanese troops to be interned?

No, no, how could you think such a thing? she said to herself in horror.

But even as she discarded the idea she realised how much her opinion of Terence must have changed if she could even think him capable of such actions.

When, about an hour later, the figure reappeared, Gwen squirmed herself free from Petie's embrace. In the starlight she went to meet him. It was Sam.

'Where have you been?'

'Taking a look-see along the road. It's a good road, leads past a palm-oil plantation. There's the glimmer of a light about a mile back, must be a village, maybe big enough to have a postal collection office. Nothing moving, neither Japs nor Sumatrans.'

'What do you think, Sam? Should we go on to the west coast?'

'Gwen, it's a hell of a question! If the troops have made landings only on the east coast then they've got to penetrate across country and through the mountains to take the rest of the country. In that case, we might make it to the west coast before they do – they have to fight their way, after all.'

'But we've heard no fighting, Sam.'

She heard him sigh in the darkness. 'That only means we haven't been within earshot, honey. There's been fighting – the plantation's got the marks of machine-gun fire along the tree-trunks. And that may mean, you see, that there are Dutch troops around. If we could just join up with them . . .'

They sat down with their backs against a clump of hibiscus bushes. Presently they went to sleep leaning towards each other, Sam's arm about her shoulder.

In the morning as they were preparing to set out, there was a rustle among the bushes. They wheeled in alarm. A boy stepped out, about twelve or thirteen, in the local Sumatran sarong.

The two boatmen grabbed him, shook him in anger for the fright he'd caused them. He talked to them rapidly in a Sumatran dialect the others couldn't follow.

'What's he saying?' Terence asked in panicky concern.

'He says, tuan, Japun were here two days. Tuans on plantations stay and fight, all die or go as prisoner. Mems drive away perhaps three days ago, head west. He says Japun very bad, kill many many, burn many many, take all things, radio, watch, ring, chicken, pig . . .'

'Dutch tuans,' Sam said. 'Dutch troops?'

Ali interpreted the question into the local dialect. He reported that most of the Dutch troops in Sumatra had been sent to stations round the main ports as protection. Only rearguard parties had remained in the area and they were now gone, fighting to delay the Japanese take-over as long as they could.

'Why's he here?' Terence asked with suspicion. 'Spying on us for the Japs?'

It turned out the boy had come to fetch the dog they'd seen when they first landed. Ali and Kemal thanked him

519

for his information, warned him not to speak of seeing them, and let him go.

'We better not land at any more villages,' Terence said as they made for their boats. 'We might find the Japs already there.'

'Could be,' Sam allowed. They discussed it with the boatmen, who agreed. The plan now was that they would draw into the bank some distance upstream of a village and one of the Sumatrans would walk back to find out how the land lay.

It saved them from steering straight into captivity that noon. They heard the sound of shouting and occasional gunshots as they approached the settlement. Ali at once poled his boat to the opposite bank, followed by Kemal, where in the shelter of overhanging trees they inched their way past. When they had gone perhaps a quarter of a mile at a snail's pace, he set out with extra vigour.

They laid up in the undergrowth on the far bank, until the sun had gone down from its height. By about four-thirty they were approaching a village, signalled to them by the scent of cooking fires and the barking of dogs. As they had planned, they went past it, unnoticed. After they had tied up, Kemal, being the younger, with more courage and curiosity than his compatriot, went sauntering down the bank.

He came back looking shaken. 'Japun in village!'

The others could only stare at him in silent dismay.

'Has there been fighting there?' Sam asked at last.

'No, tuan, all is peaceful except that Japuns are very happy, sing, shout, wave guns in air.'

'Happy?' echoed Tammy in scorn. 'At taking a little village like that?'

It puzzled them. They sat down on the riverbank to try to think what to do. Night came as it did under the trees of the river, sudden, black, a cloak of safety. They were hungry, and it was too early to sleep.

'Will you go back to the village, see if you can buy some food?' Terence asked Kemal.

'No, tuan.' Kemal shook his head vigorously.

'I'll go,' Sam said.

'Don't be silly – a white man?'

'Look, Terence, it's dark. I'm not going to leap about inviting the Japs to see me, I'm going to find a nice quiet little old Sumatran and buy some grub.'

'Don't do it, Sam,' Gwen said.

'No, don't,' urged Petie. 'My daddy went to speak to the villagers and he didn't come back.'

'Look, we've got to have food. We had almost nothing yesterday and the boatmen can't work without food. Besides, I'd like to get some idea what they're so happy about.'

'That's a stupid idea – how could you possibly know even if you watched one dancing the gavotte! You don't speak their lingo.'

'But I do,' said Gwen.

There was a moment of silence.

'No, Mummy,' said Tammy.

'No, Gwen,' said Terence.

They looked at Sam for his agreement. Somehow it had become a rule that Sam made the decisions.

'I dunno . . .' he said, rubbing his chin.

'Good lord, Sam, you can't possibly—'

'We wouldn't attract their attention. If we just filtered in and got some idea of what's up—'

'Uncle Sam, you must be mad!'

'He's right, Tammy,' Gwen said. 'We need food and it would help us to find out what's been going on.'

The argument lasted for almost an hour. By then it was completely dark, and hunger pangs were beginning to trouble them all.

So Sam and Gwen set off along the narrow riverside path that would take them to the village.

The Sumatrans had gone indoors. Chickens were cooped up, pigs were penned, cooking fires were damped down. The largest hut, the headman's, had its door open. Lamplight poured out from it. There was the sound of singing, a Japanese song Gwen recognised from her days in Tokyo, one that Kazuo the gardener had loved: 'Winds blow, petals flutter before it, How strong is the wind, strong as a young man . . .'

'They certainly seem happy,' Sam whispered in her ear.

'Also quite drunk,' she returned.

'You know what?' Sam said. 'They're celebrating.'

'But what?'

'Emperor's birthday?'

'No, that's gone by.'

They crept nearer. Gwen could hear a rattle of guttural conversation, the scrape of spoons or knives on tin plates, a hissing in the background which she couldn't recognise.

'What's that sound, Sam?'

'I hear it . . .' A long pause. 'I've got it, it's a radio set – they're trying to tune in the station!'

They knelt outside the hut, out of the beam of light from the open door.

'What are they saying?' Sam asked quietly.

'Boasting about something . . . one of them said he's going to write to his wife . . . they're enjoying the food, they've got river fish and yams, I think . . . Now that was somebody giving an order!' A louder voice had rung out. There was the unmistakable stamp of a group of men leaping to their feet.

It was impossible to see into the hut without going into the beam of light, because the windows had their rattan shades lowered. Sam lay down, wriggled along the ground, raised his head a moment to look in the doorway, then backed to Gwen's side.

'They're standing to attention – about eight men. One of 'em's fiddling with a radio.'

There was a howl of static, and then a voice, untuned at first but quickly pinpointed on the radio dial. An authoritative Japanese voice, reading a prepared statement.

For about five minutes the official announcement went on. Then a command. The men in the hut shouted. *'Banzai! Banzai! Banzai!'*

'Oh, hell,' groaned Sam.

Stooped over so as to hide among the bushes, they crept back to the very edge of the village.

'What was the radio saying, Gwen?'

She could hardly speak. Her throat was choked with sobs.

'He said . . . He said . . . Singapore fell today, British Malaya has surrendered.'

Chapter Twenty-six

That was the night of 15 February. It took them another twenty-two days to reach the headwaters of the Indragiri river. Or rather, twenty-two nights.

Gwen and Sam had stayed on the edge of the village after hearing the news of the surrender until silence fell. The troops settled down to sleep. Some time after midnight Sam roused a man in one of the smaller huts, nearly scaring him to death. A whispered conference led to the provision of rice wrapped in leaves, a gourd with curried pork and sweet potato, and a handful of jack-fruit. For this Sam paid with the cheroots from his one-time cheroot case.

They took the food back. After the meal Sam said, 'I'm going back to buy a boat.'

'A boat?'

'You must have noticed, the river's getting narrower and deeper as we go up-stream. We need a boat with paddles or oars.' When this was translated into Malay for the boatmen, they nodded agreement. Sam and Kemal went back; Sam reawakened the old man who'd sold him the food. He had to go away and consult someone else, but by and by they stole down to the water's edge.

In the magnificent tropical starlight Sam could see the village water-craft pulled up or moored. Nothing was big enough to take all of them. He bought a keeled boat with two paddles, together with a shallow dug-out, long and narrow but light, with six paddles. Sam asked for and was given four extra paddles. For all this he paid with the gold chain from Terence's pocket-watch.

He and Kemal pushed the boat out into the stream, pulling the dug-out after them by rope. They used their hands to paddle softly away from the hamlet, then, when they felt at a safe distance, used the paddles. They had made arrangements for the villager to come up the river bank next day and bring back the sampans by water, to moor them unnoticed among the village craft.

It was better to put as much distance between them and the Japanese patrol as they could. They set out at once, Kemal and the two women with Petie in the dug-out, the two men and Ali in the boat. Everyone paddled, except of course Petie who remained sound asleep all through the first night.

They found it quite feasible to travel by night. Experience had already told them it was less exhausting than in the heat of the day, and the river was easy to navigate. Now and again they would strike unexpected sandbanks, and then they would have to get out and do a portage. But they found they could keep going quite well through the hours of darkness so long as they could get food to keep up their strength.

They bartered some needles and embroidery thread for the following day's food, then decided it would be better to buy several days' supply at one go. Thus for almost a week they never had to enter a village. When next they did, it was to hear that the Japanese were behind them again, but on the road making forays to either side.

Nevertheless, they were still ahead of the enemy when they reached Taluk, at the head of the river.

Taluk was a sizeable town by the standards they'd come to accept. There was a main street with shophouses and a government rest-house and a post office, though the post office was closed. Sumatrans and Chinese inhabitants were going about their business. There were no Europeans, so their arrival caused a stir, but they were assured that the road to Golok and the mountains was still open.

Here they said goodbye to Ali and Kemal. As the traditional gift of gratitude they gave them Terence's pocket-watch. It hadn't worked since he dived off the *Dimestore*, but the case was made of gold. With many good wishes, the Sumatran boatmen turned their boats and headed down-stream for home, leaving the Europeans to make their own way henceforth.

Since there was no motor transport in Taluk, they bought themselves a lift on a bullock-cart heading up into Golok. It was the utmost luxury to lie among the produce and be carried along the road. They slept to its rocking motion. They were very tired physically but their spirits had been raised by the prospect of a good road through the mountains.

From time to time they would kneel to look at the countryside. The mountains could be seen ahead – high, clad in dark green jungle, with cloud wreaths round their heads. Beyond that lay the west coast and a port where they might get a steamer to Colombo.

In Golok there were more shop-houses, another closed post office, a small government office also closed and, remarkably, a café. They approached it expecting it to disappear like all mirages, but no, the proprietor came out, a middle-aged Eurasian with an apron round his waist.

'Coffee?' he asked.

Coffee! And sugar to go in it. And cakes made from rice and the local fruits. Petie's eyes lit up for the first time in days.

They sat on wooden benches in the atap shelter in front of the café, sipping their coffee and chatting; four battered, ragged Europeans and a child. Gwen felt exhilarated, almost triumphant. They had come this far – they would go the rest of the way.

'Colombo here we come!' cried Sam, lifting his coffee-cup in salute.

They slept overnight in Golok on the floor of the government office. But first the men went to the local

527

barber to have a proper shave and a much needed haircut. Gwen and Tammy went shopping for soap, insect repellent, aspirin, dried fruit. Later they all went in search of clothing – jackets and rubberised capes to keep out the mountain cold, slacks for Tammy to replace the torn skirt, rubber shoes for Petie whose leather sandals had given way.

In the morning they set out on the road over the mountain. They had their cold-weather clothes in an old sack together with boiled sweets and fruit, which they'd bought in exchange for one of the ivory combs.

Gwen found it wonderful to walk again on a good road surface, to walk and talk as if out for a day's ramble. Underfoot the going was easy enough. But the gradient was steep – they climbed a thousand feet in seven miles the first day. Soon Gwen found she had no breath for chatting as they toiled upward along the zig-zag road.

The distance from Golok to the far side of the mountains, as the crow flies, was about fifty miles. But on foot along the terraced gradients it was perhaps three times the distance. They did twelve miles the first day, fourteen the next. Now and again a Sumatran on a bike would pass them, free-wheeling down from the other direction, and they were passed by two groups of seasoned foot travellers with bundles on their backs.

'This is going to take us forever,' groaned Terence.

'Another ten days.'

'Aren't there any short cuts?'

'Straight up the mountainside, if you want to try it through the jungle. Myself, I don't fancy it without a compass.'

'All right, sorry I mentioned it!'

There were hamlets in clearings on the mountainsides. They were usually able to buy cold rice and curried vegetables. They preferred not to stay overnight in the settlements for fear of Japanese motorised patrols coming up the road.

They slept under the jungle trees – high, high above

them like a cathedral roof. When it rained, they sheltered under their rubberised capes. Monkeys would swing along in the tree-tops, calling to each other with strange hooting sounds. To Gwen's surprise there were few birds to be seen – an occasional hornbill, but most of the smaller, prettier birds must be up in the canopy. Few flowers except ground orchids, because the light in the jungle was too poor.

Each morning they would wash in a stream, clean their teeth with a frayed twig, eat some food saved from the previous day. As they ascended, the water in the streams grew colder and colder to Gwen's legs as she plunged in.

They needed their jackets and their sweaters as they reached the pass at the mountain's shoulder. They were about three thousand feet up. Through windows in the jungle vegetation they could see superb views of Sumatra – dark green valleys shading into brown shadow, clouds sailing over the narrow glint of rivers, a strange grey ribbon they recognised as a railway line. Away to the east there were vapour trails of aircraft. But, as they stood shading their eyes and staring, they saw a great lake to the north and then, directly west, the ocean . . .

Going down was of course much easier. The ascent had taken them eleven days, the descent took them three. On a day towards the end of March, they entered a large village in the foothills.

By selling the gold-rimmed spectacles they'd brought from the luggage from the launch, they obtained a large hot meal, the first in over two weeks. They got lodgings in village huts. Gwen begged a big kettle of hot water and a tin bath, so that she could bathe Petie and put him in newly washed clothes. He sat contentedly chewing sugar cane outside the hut while she and Tammy washed from head toe.

Outside the village, they were told, a Dutch planter was organising resistance against the Japanese. They were given a big welcome by Freddi van Skuys when they were conducted to his estate. They saw Sumatrans drilling, weapons being cleaned.

Van Skuys was a square-built figure in a semi-military outfit, with a big grey moustache and protruding teeth.

'English, eh? Where from?'

'Well, to get it straight, I'm American and O'Keefe here is Irish. But we're from Singapore.'

'Ah . . . Singapore . . . A bad business. How long since you left?'

'We know it surrendered, if that's what's bothering you. We heard it on somebody's wireless.'

'*Ja, ja*, bad news you always get, right? And there is more too, because the Dutch troops are not doing so good and Batavia has fallen. Well, if they have Java, Sumatra still holds out, *ja*?'

'We saw a lot of Japs on our way here—'

'Ach, I know they are in Siak and Jambi. And I hear their spotter planes have been over the mountains. I am ready for them,' van Skuys said, picking up a hunting rifle and shaking it in defiance.

'Any news from the west coast?' Terence asked with apprehension.

'So far, nothing happens there, God be thanked. Now, come, you will have a drink – whisky, gin?'

They sat in rattan chairs, over drinks served by a Sumatran servant in white sarong and tunic. All around the green trees of the plantation smiled in the sun. The war might have been a figment of some fevered imagination.

'You want of course to get to the coast for a ship. Understood. Tomorrow morning, I send you on my truck as far as Petamei. This is sixty miles. Then you have not far to go to the coast. Padang would be best, there goes a bus to Padang. Steamers for Colombo come in there. That is where I sended my sister.'

'Your sister went out via Padang? How long ago?' Sam inquired.

'What is today – Thursday? One week ago, she went. By now she is probably halfway to Ceylon.'

It was heartening to hear. They accepted van Skuys's offer of overnight hospitality. For the first time in weeks, Gwen slept in a bed again. It was so comfortable that she stayed awake half the night savouring the enjoyment of a cool sheet, a mosquito net, a pillow.

They were served a hearty breakfast somewhat in the Dutch style, with fruit and cheese and home-cured ham and coffee. Van Skuys shook hands warmly, telling them they must come to see him in a few months when they'd got the better of these *'verroten Japannes'*.

Immensely cheered, they rocked off in the estate's truck driven by a Sumatran in a white drill jacket.

In Petamei they were set down in the main street. There was an office with a board at the side of the door announcing the times of buses to Padang. They climbed down, thanking the driver, who beamed at them before driving off up a side track on estate business.

They went into the bus office. It was empty. They stood about, waiting for the bus company employee to come. After ten minutes they went outside. A little group of Sumatrans was standing in the street, watching them with curiosity.

'When is the bus for Padang?' Sam asked.

Although his Malay was curious to their ear, they caught the name Padang. They broke out in a torrent of explanation. It all went by too fast for Sam and his party to understand, accustomed as they were to the pidgin Malay of Singapore.

At length a Chinese girl stepped forward. She addressed them in Dutch. They shook their heads at her but Sam said, in Cantonese, 'We want to take the bus to Padang.'

She smiled as she recognised the language but the smile was instantly chased away. 'The bus didn't come back from Padang yesterday.'

'Didn't come back?'

'No, it should have come in at about six in the evening but it didn't come.'

'Why not?'

'We're not sure.'

'Have you rung up to inquire?'

'Oh, no, sir, there's no telephone. And the telegraph has been out of action for two days.'

'Oh, lord,' breathed Terence.

'Has anyone been to the coast to find out what's happening?'

'Sir, we are afraid to go. We've heard rumours that the Japanese have taken Padang.'

'They've come all the way across country from Jambi?' Sam exclaimed, astonished.

'We hear . . .' She hesitated. 'We hear they landed from the sea, sir. Do you think it's true?'

It was only too likely. While poor Freddi van Skuys was making preparations to fight them as they came overland through the mountains to the east, the Japanese had sailed round in warships to the west and sent in landing craft.

After all, why not? They had come down through the jungle from the north when everyone in Singapore had been expecting a sea-borne attack from the south. They had planned to surprise their enemies – and surprise them they had

'Well, that's that,' said Terence, sitting down on a wooden box waiting to be loaded on the bus that would now probably never run.

'What's what?' challenged Tammy, going red with annoyance.

'Well, it stands to reason, what's the use of going to Padang? Is it not a pointless thing to be doing? They're there ahead of us.'

'Only just ahead of us,' Gwen pointed out, trying to think clearly. 'If they *have* landed, they can't have complete control in only a couple of days.'

'What are you saying? That we should go down into a town that's in enemy hands?'

'What do you suggest, Terence?' Tammy asked in a hard tone. 'Sit here and wait for them to drive up the road?'

'There's no need to take that tone with me, Tammy. I'm only looking at it from a commonsense point of view.'

'Gwen's right,' said Sam all at once. 'Think back – we got out of Singapore when the Japs were on the outskirts. Mebbe we could get out of Padang in the same way. There must be docks and jetties stretching along the waterfront. All we've got to do is get down to them—'

'And be taken prisoner. Wouldn't it make more sense to hand ourselves over—'

'Not me!' Tammy cried. 'You can do what you like, Terence, but I'm never going to walk into a prison camp.'

'She speaks for me too,' Gwen agreed.

'I think you're outvoted, Terence.'

'Outvoted on what? What would you be thinking of doing?'

'We'll head for Padang, find out if we can get on a ship, and if not . . .'

'If not what?'

'We'll sort that out when we come to it.'

'You're all mad,' Terence said, flustered and unwilling. 'And in the first place, how are we to get to Padang?'

'It can't have escaped your attention,' Sam said, with an ironic grin, 'that there's a river running the other side of the houses. Let's hire a boat.'

'Oh, not another boat,' groaned Terence.

But no one was listening to him.

This river running to the west from the mountains had a swift, deep current. They made good time in a boat with two oarsmen. By late afternoon they could

see the glint of the sea and smell the smells of a port
– spices, salt, coal-smoke, harbour-weed.

They put in at a wooden jetty at a bend with a
store and two or three houses. The boatmen smiled
uncertainly, accepted some Dutch money supplied by
van Skuys, and made off back where they came from.

The people in the little settlement came hurrying
to greet them. There was the usual problem with the
language, but by and by a man came forward who spoke
a version of Malay that they could understand.

'Tuan, the Japanese have control of the port. You
would be unwise to go into the town. We have seen
soldiers along all the main road and most of the
side roads.'

'I told you so,' said Terence.

'Will you be quiet!' Tammy cried, whirling on him in
fury. 'If you can't say anything more helpful, just hold
your tongue!'

'Young lady, that's no way to speak to—'

'Oh, shut up!' she said, and walked away.

And this conversational tussle between lovers was
the last for some days. Tammy simply refused to speak
to him.

After a few minutes' consultation, the Malay-speaker
said he could lead them to a hide-out where some of the
locals, mostly Chinese, had set up a resistance group.

'I think there are Europeans with them, I'm not sure.
Shall I show the way?'

'What good is this going to do?' Terence inquired as
they set off after him along a jungle path.

'Dunno till we get there.'

Gwen began to feel very tired after they'd been
walking a while. Partly it was physical fatigue, partly
it was the disappointment. To have come so far, with
– only a short time ago – such high hopes, and now to
be brought up short . . .

She found Sam at her elbow, giving her a hand.
'Got the blues? Me too. I never was so knocked

out as when this guy said the Japs have got the port.'

She nodded, her gaze on the ground in front of her, watching her feet make one weary step after another.

'We'll think of something,' he urged.

Once more she nodded. Then suddenly she felt ashamed. He must be tired too. Yet here he was wasting energy on cheering her up.

Struggling to produce a smile, she looked up at him. 'Sam, I just want to say . . .'

'What?'

'Whatever happens, thank you.'

'For what? For getting you into this mess?' Bitterness had crept into his voice.

'For making the effort, for *trying* – for not giving up.'

'Ha,' he snorted. But she saw his expression lighten.

The hide-out was a hut and a cave in a hillside above the river. There was a man on watch, who held up a sharp-looking *parang* as they approached through the bushes. Their guide called, there was a grunt of acceptance. Then others appeared: coolies who had escaped from the docks in their wide blue pants and jackets; Sumatrans in tunics and duck trousers and in the uniform of the Dutch East Indies Regiment. And then, astonishingly, a fair-haired woman in a linen skirt and jacket came out of the cave.

Gwen only had to look at her to know she must be the sister of Freddi van Skuys. She had the same rather prominent teeth, though in her case contained between wide smiling lips, and the same square shoulders only atop a curvaceous figure.

'Miss van Skuys?' ventured Gwen.

'*Ja. Hoe gaat het u?*'

'Excuse me, I don't speak Dutch—'

'Oh, English! How do you know my name?'

'We left your brother this morning, Miss van Skuys.'

'My name is Klar. What are the English doing here, I am wondering?'

'We were hoping to catch a steamer to Ceylon.'

'Yes, and I too. But two days ago came in patrol boats of the Japanese and yesterday, much fighting for the docks, so I had to come out of the town and here I am with other good friends, who have been in fights for three days now. *Kom binnen* – you would like drink of tea, perhaps?'

It seemed she'd taken on the role of housekeeper. They went into the cave, where panniers and haversacks held supplies. A small fire was burning, with a tin slung over it to boil water. Within minutes the new arrivals were sipping hot tea and trying to talk to the resistance group in some version of Malay.

The news about Padang was not entirely bad. There had been hard fighting and the Japanese control wasn't complete. But there was no possibility of a steamer leaving for Colombo, though there were two ships in the port. Both had a Japanese guard aboard whereas the captains and crews had been imprisoned ashore.

The chief of the resistance group appeared to be a Sumatran sergeant. 'It would be good if you could go,' he said bluntly. 'We here wish to go on fighting but it is not good to have women with us.'

'I agree,' Klar said, nodding. 'My brother told me, go home, you do better there to help than here.'

Terence agreed. 'Do you think we want to stay?' he said. 'We came tramping here over a mountain, and before that . . . Well, what else would we be wanting except to get on a boat and get away!'

'It is possible,' said Sergeant Gerak.

They all looked at him. 'How?' asked Gwen.

'There is a yacht. It is tied up at a jetty on the waterfront in the fishing village perhaps a mile along from Padang.'

'A yacht. Now that I like,' Sam said. 'What kind of yacht?'

'A five-ton ketch. It was owned by Major Maartens. The major was killed in the attack on Padang.'

'Are you saying we can just go down to the quay and board her?'

'Ah,' said the sergeant. 'That is the difficulty. The yacht is under guard.'

'Well, that's that,' said Terence.

'Not necessarily,' said Sam, watching the sergeant.

'No, not necessarily. We might make a night attack . . .'

An argument began. Some of the group felt it was wrong to risk men's lives simply to get a boat they themselves wouldn't be using. Others asserted that if they *could* get the boat, they ought to use it for their own purposes. But Sergeant Gerak simply waited them out.

'Who among our unit can sail a ketch?'

No response. Having known the answer, the sergeant smiled with grim satisfaction. 'Very well. Tuan, you can sail a ketch?'

'Sure can. Raised on sail by my New England fore-fathers.'

'Then it seems right, doesn't it? We help the tuan to take the yacht and he sails away with the women and the boy. Then we can get down to the real fight.'

His chief opponent, a young Sumatran, sneered. 'And how do you suggest we can take it without losing half our men?'

'We'll think of something . . . Those Japanese uni-forms, for instance. If we put those on and march to the jetty, we might—'

'And if we're challenged? You'll say, "We are the crew" – in Sumatran?'

There was a pause. They sat staring at the empty tea mugs.

Then Gwen said, 'I could teach you how to say "We are the crew" in Japanese.'

A hubbub ensued. Sergeant Gerak dived into the

recesses at the back of the cave, returning with a uniform. From its pocket he produced some papers.

'What does that say?' he asked.

She opened the paper book. 'It says,' she began, 'that this is Captain Iraki Komatani, and gives his enlistment number and unit. I can't translate the unit but it's the 3rd Battalion something or other.' She looked up. 'Where did you get this?'

'We took it off a patrol we ambushed last night.' He looked about him. 'There were seven men. We have seven uniforms.'

'You'll never get away with it,' Terence said.

'It's worth a try, Terence. After dark . . .'

'I'm not putting on any Japanese uniform and marching down a jetty—'

'That's not necessary. I could put the ketch in at some rendezvous point to collect you and the girls.'

Sergeant Gerak said, 'We could steal the yacht and then Tuan Prosper could put us ashore at some good place along the coast. The Europeans could go aboard while we make our way inland to Nanag – there are Dutch army stores there, we ought to get to them before the enemy does.'

The rest of the uniforms were brought out. Gwen shuddered when she saw them – some were heavily bloodstained. It was easy to imagine how the stains got there when she remembered the glint of the *parangs*.

Gerak called for volunteers. He looked in expectation at the Sumatran who kept challenging his authority. 'Kerim?' Kerim shook his head. Three of the Chinese nodded acceptance.

Sam looked over the uniforms, trying to find one that he could get into. He had to be one of the party, of course, because he was to pilot the ketch. After some discussion two others, both Sumatrans, volunteered.

They went off to the dimness at the back of the cave to kit themselves out. When they returned they all looked reasonably Japanese except for Sam. His long legs looked absurd in any of the trousers, so he had retained his own, which were made of white duck. He'd used puttees – long strips of khaki cloth wound from ankle to knee – to disguise them. They had seen Japanese soldiers in similar outfits: in fact, quite a few of the enemy seemed to discard their official kit for anything they thought more comfortable for jungle fighting.

'Nobody would ever mistake you for a Japanese,' Terence said in scorn. 'You're far too tall.'

'Well, all right, I'll stoop! And don't forget it's going to be dark.'

It certainly was. The day had been broken up by thundery showers of very heavy rain, and even when the rain wasn't actually falling the clouds roiled overhead. So long as the wind remained in the same quarter the clouds would ensure a thoroughly black night.

'Now,' asked Sam, 'what's Sergeant Gerak got to say to the guard?'

'Let me think. You'll march on to the jetty – someone ought to be calling out "left, right" – that's easy. Well, the guard will challenge. I suppose he'll say the equivalent of "Who goes there?" . . .'

'To which Gerak answers what? I mean, if he's expecting a password—'

'Gerak must shout him down from the outset. Japanese men tend to be very short with their inferiors. You must hold out the captain's papers, Gerak – and as soon as he takes them start barking orders. You've got instructions to move the boat—'

'Surely he'd have written orders?' Terence put in.

'Written orders . . . I suppose he would,' Sam said. 'But it doesn't matter what the guard says. As soon as Gerak's close enough he's going to clobber him. That right, Gerak?'

'Tuan?'

Sam made an expressive gesture, finger drawn across his throat.

'Yes, tuan,' said Gerak with a grin.

Gwen was given a piece of paper and a stub of pencil. She wrote down phonetically the words they would have to use and then rehearsed them in how to say them.

The trouble was, Gerak was hopeless. Although they went over the few words again and again, he produced, 'Here are your orders!' when he was supposed to be saying, 'I am Captain Komatani'. And all the time he sounded like a Sumatran.

'Try to produce the words from the back of your throat,' Gwen urged. 'All in one shout, with the accent on the last word, and sounding very impatient.'

He tried again and again. It was no use.

'I'll take on the part of the captain,' Sam said at last. 'I think I know how it should sound – I heard them often enough when they were shoving people around in China.'

'Tuan, it is my duty—'

'I know, Gerak, but it will not work if you do it.'

Sam huddled himself down into his jacket, thrust his head forward, and shouted: *'Oi, kora! Gunso! Kudasai, kudasai!'* He looked at Gwen. 'How's that?'

Gwen nodded. 'Much better! Just keep on like that – high and mighty, very short-tempered.'

'Uchi no haji!' snarled Sam. *'Chigau, chigau!'* – There, what am I saying?'

'"You're a disgrace to your mother",' Gwen said, laughing, '"wrong, wrong again!" Where did you hear that?'

'Oh, some goon drilling a squad in Tientsin. I thought if I were one of the soldiers I'd kick his teeth in.'

'That's just the tone,' she agreed.

Time was getting on. The Sumatrans held a last whispered consultation.

Sam took Gwen outside the cave, to a point in the shelter of the atap hut. 'I want to give you something,' he said.

He took from the inside of his shirt a leather pouch

540

which he had been wearing on a thong round his neck ever since they left Singapore. He lifted it over his head, hanging it instead round Gwen's neck. 'This is just in case I don't make it—'

'Sam!'

'It's OK, we're going to do it, but you never know. Inside the pouch there's enough gemstones to buy your way out of almost anywhere.'

'No, listen, Sam—'

'Let me finish. If this doesn't work, go back into the mountains. The Sumatrans will help you. Just hide up until you hear word of the Dutch troops and join up with them. OK?'

'But you're talking as if—'

'I'm talking as if we're taking a risk. Yup, we are, though I think it'll work. All the same, I just wanted you to . . . to . . .' He hesitated. 'I wanted you to know I love you, Gwen. I always have.'

She stared at him.

'Surprises you, huh?' He coloured under the tan of days spent on the run. 'I never meant to tell you. But now . . . it just seems . . .'

She threw her arms round him. 'Darling, you're going to get the boat and we're going to be together for always!'

He gasped, 'Gwen!' then held her tight. 'Oh, damn, this is a fine time to find out—'

'Never mind – any time's a good time! Oh, my darling, my dearest, why didn't I understand until now?' Her heart was beating like a drum. She felt as if the heavens had suddenly opened to allow all the sunshine in the world to fall upon her, a gleam of gold more wondrous than any she had ever seen.

'Too busy over Terence,' he said, his voice full of regret and tinged with anger.

'Yes, what a fool! Please don't hate me for being so silly, darling. You know I'm hopeless at understanding people . . .'

She stood on tiptoe to kiss him. Their lips had just touched when there came a call from the cave-mouth. 'Tuan? We are going.'

'A moment, sergeant!' Sam caught Gwen up close and kissed her with ferocity. 'You're my girl now, right?'

'Yes. Yes, Sam.'

'Well, don't forget it. See you soon.'

He let her go, turning on his heel so as not to be held back by the tears in her eyes.

Night was falling with its usual suddenness. The attack group had to get to the quayside of a fishing village, Kampong Selamak. The escape party had to reach a point a little further up the coast but cut off by a swift stream. Once there, they were to wait until they saw a signal by torch from the ketch. After returning the signal they were to put off to board it in a skiff. The sergeant and his men would then come ashore in it.

Gwen, Tammy, Klar and Terence set off with Kerim as guide. Gwen carried Petie, hugging him to her as if in holding him she could hold the happiness that had suddenly come to her, perhaps even pass on a little of it to the anxious child. Two helpers came along with baskets of food – fruit, cooked rice in a gourd, a flask of the local rice spirit. There was no knowing if there were any stores aboard the ketch.

An hour and a half's hard walking by jungle paths brought them across the stream at a narrow point. They reached the coast on the side of the stream north of Padang. A further half-hour on a rocky coast track found them at Ujong Buru, a small headland about a mile inside the bay next after Kampong Selamak.

Kerim went down to the beach to make sure there were boats to be borrowed. The rest sat down among the rocks to wait. Kerim returned, whispering, 'Many fishing boats, no guards that I can see.'

A tremendous rainstorm drenched them. After it was over, their cold wet clothes clung to them.

All at once Gwen was shivering – and not from cold. Terrible doubt had seized her.

'What have I done? What have I done?' she cried. 'They'll all be killed! I should never have helped them—'

'Ssh!' commanded Kerim, grabbing her arm. 'There may be patrols.'

Gwen put her hand over her mouth to stifle her sobs. As if it was happening before her eyes she could see it: the men marching along the jetty, halting on command; Sam approaching the guard; the levelling of the guard's rifle, the shots bringing down that long, angular body. And his shots, raising the alarm, bringing other soldiers running. And a fight; bayonets flashing, rifle butts clubbing down on them . . .

Petie, sensing her distress, began to whimper. 'Ssh, darling,' whispered Tammy, taking him out of her mother's arms to comfort him. 'It's all right, everything's going to be all right.'

Klar said quietly to Gwen, 'I think perhaps all goes well. That bad rainstorm . . . No soldier will surely look close at papers in a rainstorm, and then, you know, it's all over if they're close with him.'

'Do you think so, Klar?' Gwen could hardly keep her voice steady.

'I think so, *ja*, I think it goes well.'

'Then where *are* they?'

They all stared out over the black waters. No light winked at them.

'They've been taken prisoner,' Gwen moaned.

'Ha . . .' Kerim cleared his throat. 'We will wait one hour more and then we must take cover, because if they were taken prisoner and questioned . . .'

'They would never tell!' Tammy declared.

'I think they would tell,' Kerim said. 'We cannot risk it, I think.'

You've got to be sensible, Gwen told herself. Sam wouldn't like you making a fool of yourself. And besides, that scene I imagined – that was all happening in daylight – and it's night-time, really dark, and so perhaps . . . perhaps . . .

But where are they? her heart demanded.

'There!' Terence exclaimed.

'What?'

'A light!' In the darkness he was pointing. Kerim felt along the arm to find out the direction and then said: 'Yes, the signal.'

'Who has the torch?'

'Me, it is in my pocket.' Klar dragged it out, handed it to Kerim, who returned the signal.

They clambered down to the beach. The men picked up a shallow boat, trudged down the sand with it, and launched it in among the waves. The others waded after them, piled into the long shallow boat.

It seemed a long paddle out to the light. But then, in the almost complete darkness, Gwen could sense a lighter patch. It was the mainsail of the ketch, half-lowered so that she would make very little way but ready to be raised so that they could take off into the breeze.

As they reached the side of the boat, hands were waiting to haul them aboard. There was a chatter among the Sumatrans. Gwen sensed something panicky in their talk. Kerim grunted: 'I told you so!'

'What?' demanded Terence. 'What's happened? Did the guard—'

'The guard was no trouble,' Gerak's voice said in the darkness. 'But we didn't understand how to get the sails up and some fool called out in Chinese—'

'And a searchlight was trained on us,' interrupted another voice. 'Luckily the tuan sped out of the beam—'

'Sam?' called Gwen. 'Sam, are you all right?'

'It's OK, it's OK, everybody keep it down,' Sam replied from somewhere aft. He sounded short-tempered. 'We got spattered with machine-gun fire – some of the men jumped overboard. Gerak's sore because I had to leave them but I *had* to get out of range of those damned guns—'

'I have lost two men, tuan,' Gerak said stiffly.

'Look, is it a good thing to be sitting here in the water arguing?' Terence wanted to know. 'They know the boat's been taken, won't they be sending out search boats?'

'You bet. So let's get going. Who's going ashore?'

Three of the Chinese elected to stay aboard with the Europeans. Everyone else climbed down into the skiff.

'Goodbye, tuan,' Gerak said. 'Allah go with you.'

'And with you.'

A moment later the skiff had glided away. Within seconds it was lost in the darkness, and even the sound of the paddles was gone.

Gwen felt her way along the deck and down into the cabin. Tammy followed, bringing Petie. The cabin curtains were drawn, it was pitch dark, but by feeling about they found matches and a lamp on gimbels. By its light they took stock. Petie was sitting cross-legged on a padded bench, white-faced, exhausted.

'Bed for you, young man,' said Gwen.

They found the main cabin aft. There were two bunks. Petie was tucked up. 'Don't go,' he begged as Tammy turned to leave him.

'All right, Petie, I'll be here.' She sat down on the edge of the bunk.

Klar said she would try to get a meal going. She went to examine the galley. Terence elected to help her.

Left to herself, Gwen went in search of Sam. He was at the wheel in the darkness, watching the faint light of the compass.

'Where are we headed, Sam?'

'North-west,' he said, 'towards Ceylon.'

'That's a long way, darling. Can we make it in this boat?'

'Sure thing. Might take a while.' He drew in a breath and sighed.

She sensed weariness, irritation. She felt she understood. A successful stratagem had been ruined when someone foolishly called out as they were getting away.

She put her arm around him. 'I think you did marvels,' she began.

And then stopped. There was something sticky on the back of Sam's shirt.

She drew her hand away. Now her hand was sticky too. In the dark it was impossible to see what it was.

'Sam?' she said.

'Yeah, right. I got hit during the get-away.' The tone of his voice wasn't after all conveying irritation – it was anxiety that was edging it. 'Soon as you can, get somebody to come here and take the wheel, because . . . because . . .'

He didn't finish the sentence. He slid to the deck unconscious.

Chapter Twenty-seven

Lam was the strongest and the least intelligent of the three Chinese dock-workers. The *tuan besar* had told him to pull on certain ropes, and that was what he had been doing.

He spoke Cantonese, the Sumatran dialect of Malay, and a little Dutch. He knew no English.

But the cry of distress needed no translation. He let go the rope he was grasping, ran aft in the darkness to the sound of the mem's voice.

He didn't know what she was saying. When he asked in Sumatran, she switched to the strange Malay she spoke. He could hardly understand her. But he heard *'tuan berluka'* and knew that the tuan was hurt.

He knelt on the deck. The tuan lay there motionless. He felt the length of his body, found a wet patch on his shirt. He attempted to lift him. The tuan was too heavy.

Then Sen Chuen arrived. Together they picked up the tuan and took him below. There in the weak lamplight the expanse of bloodstain was clear.

'Dear God!' sobbed the mem with the bronze hair. The other Europeans crowded to see. The little European boy woke from his sleep, saw the fright in the faces of the grown-ups, and drew back in dismay.

The *mem balenda* took charge. Gladly the Chinese relinquished responsibility to the mem from the plantation.

547

'Lay him on the bench,' she commanded.

When that was done she unbuttoned Sam's shirt. With water and a cloth brought from the galley she bathed the wounds. There were two gashes in his chest. No one spoke.

'I think,' said Klar after a moment, 'these are what you call it when the bullet comes out . . . ?'

'Exit wounds?' Gwen suggested, white lipped.

'I have to turn him over.' Klar gave instructions in Sumatran. Sen Chuen and Kee helped her. They got Sam's shirt off. She bathed the wounds again.

There were two round, angry holes in the back muscles.

'So . . .' Klar said. 'The bullets go in his back and they come out in his chest. One cannot know what they hit on the way. And, *luister* – that was what? Five hours ago? He has lost much blood.'

She looked round at the others. They looked back at her in horror.

'I know a little,' she ventured. 'From the plantation – men get hurt, there are accidents. Shall I . . . ?'

'Oh, please,' begged Gwen, 'please, help him!'

'First we must clean the wounds then stop the bleeding. That means disinfectant, a pressure pad, good bandage.'

Tammy had been opening the cupboards that lined the saloon. She found the first-aid box – plasters, bandages, iodine, aspirin – the usual amateur's kit.

With Gwen's help Klar bathed the entry and exit wounds with iodine. She made pads of gauze. Then with firm movements of her strong square hands she bandaged his chest.

When they had laid him down on the bench again he made a sound of something like protest. Klar looked up. 'Brandy?' she asked. 'Whisky?'

Terence found the bottle of rice spirits provided by

the guerrilla band. She poured some into a spoon, put it to Sam's lips while Tammy supported his back.

To Gwen's enormous relief Sam sipped once, twice, then coughed. His eyelids fluttered. He opened his eyes.

For a long moment he looked up at her as if he didn't recognise her. Then his gaze focused.

'Hi, babe,' he said.

The laughter of relief leapt to Gwen's lips. 'Oh, Sam! Oh, thank God! I thought you were . . . I thought . . .'

Sam surveyed the room: Tammy at his shoulder holding him up, Klar beside him with Gwen, behind them Terence's head, and in the doorway the Chinese waiting to be told how things were going.

'So who's steering the ship?' he asked.

'Damnation!' Terence cried. 'Someone should be at the wheel!'

'How about you, buster?'

'Me? I don't know how to—'

'No big deal,' Sam said in a tired voice. 'North-east monsoon's still blowing? Get her back on west-north-west—'

'But it's not my—'

'Want her to veer right round and take us back to Sumatra?'

'Wouldn't that be best?' countered Terence. 'The way things are – without you to pilot the boat – we're sunk.'

Tammy moved over to stare into his face. 'Hold your tongue!' she said in a low voice. 'You're talking as if he's dying!'

'Well, look at him. What's the use of pretending? He's had it.'

In the weak light Gwen saw Sam's face colour up. 'Who says so?' he demanded. 'Just gimme a couple of hours, I'll be OK. But in the meantime, somebody's got to head her into the wind—'

'I'll do it,' said Tammy, moving towards the door. 'What do I have to do?'

'9The compass has a luminous dial. Move the wheel until the pointer's showing west-north-west. You'll feel the pull on the wheel. And somebody should be ready to take over in an hour. And to get the spanker up on the mizzen – if the wind hasn't picked up by daylight.'

Tammy went out, taking one of the Chinese with her as relief.

'Now,' said Klar, 'I fetch you some soup. And then you rest good?'

She bustled off. Sam reached for Gwen's hand.

'Hush-a-bye-baby,' he said, and was asleep.

She sat with his hand in hers all through that night. Once she heard planes drone past overhead, but they were high, up above the cloud cover, unaware of the *Lelie* spinning along below on the dark ocean. Once she heard a ship's engines, and Sam roused, but they went by a long way off.

When the sun's rays came in at an angle through the cabin windows, Sam came slowly awake. He squinted at the sun. 'We're heading too far east,' he said.

'Kee's at the wheel – I'll tell—'

'No,' Sam said, 'help me up.' He made efforts to sit up.

'No, Sam!'

'Come on, baby, I've got to get up on deck—'

'No, you'll start bleeding again!'

He paused. He met her eyes in a level gaze. 'Look, Gwen,' he said, 'it's no good if we keep drifting off east. We've got to get into the shipping lanes, perhaps get picked up by a ship, something coming from Australia mebbe. But we'll never meet anything if we're too far east. I've got to get up there, keep an eye on the course.'

Since it was clear he'd try to do it under his own

steam, she went for Sen Chuen and Lam. They carried him up on deck. There they made a bed for him from spare canvas, propped him up with cushions from the saloon, and rigged a sun awning. He watched Kee struggling with the wheel, and gave instructions in crisp Cantonese.

Next he called the rest of the men and explained that they had to get the spanker on the mizzen so as to make best use of the wind. There was a lot of floundering and flapping. The *Lelie* tottered about in the water as the breeze caught her sails one way then another. Sam shouted instructions. Gwen tried to make him stop because he was tiring. She saw him close his eyes in vexation at their unhandiness.

But at last the spanker was up and bellying with the breeze. The *Lelie* spurted noticeably faster.

He sent them to check the ship's stores. The result was not very encouraging because the owner had never intended a long sea voyage, only short coastal trips. There were tight-lidded tins of dry stores – beans, rice, biscuits. There were two tins of sweetened condensed milk and some tea and coffee, though not in large quantities. There were beef essence cubes, spices, a string of onions, some dried fruit.

The most worrying point was that the water tanks were only half full. A law was instantly promulgated: no fresh water except for drinking – washing and cooking must be done in sea-water. Luckily there was salt-water soap in the toilet-room.

They gathered round him at his invitation, crouched or sitting about the binnacle. 'It's this way,' he said. 'We've probably done about eighty, eighty-five miles. We're well out of Sumatran coastal waters and there's been no pursuit.'

He translated this into Cantonese. Kee, who had become the leader of the three Chinese, said: 'When we were attacked we headed straight out to sea. Now,

I think we have turned more north, tuan – is that so? I think they have lost us.'

'I think so too, Kee.' To the others he went on: 'The first idea was to head for Colombo under our own power. But the way things are, that's not too practical. I think now we have to get into the shipping lanes, try to get picked up. From now on there's to be a constant look-out in daylight hours, OK? One at the wheel, one on look-out, and if you see a ship, sing out. If she's a merchant vessel, we head for her. If she's a warship—'

'A *warship*?' Terence said, horrified.

'Sure, they make war at sea, didn't you know? If she's a warship, we steer away – she might be Japanese and we don't want that, do we?'

'No, not at all,' Klar said with a shudder.

'We have to have strict food rationing – Klar, will you take that on?'

'Of course. But I think we could help the food by catching fishes.'

'I'm thinking there's little chance of catching anything at this speed,' Terence said.

'No, but could we not reduce speed, perhaps even stop and lower the anchor for an hour or so, when it's dark? I think fishes get caught best in the dark, is that right?'

'Could we stop, Sam?' Tammy asked.

'We could, but I'd rather not while this monsoon is blowing. Don't forget, the monsoon dies off at the end of April. We want to cover as much sea as we can while we have it.'

He looked at Klar. 'Could you translate that into Sumatran, Klar, I kind of don't feel like going over it again.' He lay back on his pillows. 'I think I'll catch a wink.'

It was so unlike him to admit he was tired that Gwen was at once anxious. And later, in the early afternoon, he began to mutter in his sleep. Gwen asked him if anything was wrong, but he wouldn't rouse.

She went for Klar, who felt his forehead then fetched the thermometer from the first-aid box. When she withdrew it from between his lips she frowned.

'He has much temperature. This may be infection. You see, when bullets go in, they take with them little shreds of his shirt, powder, who knows what? These things are in the wound. I don't know enough to probe for them, we don't have the medical tools . . .'

'What must we do, Klar?'

'We must help him to fight the high temperature, so I think we take him below – this canopy keeps off not enough sun, I think.'

The Chinese carried him down, this time into the aft sleeping cabin. They put him on one of the bunks. Gwen fetched a basin of sea-water, wrung out cloths, and bathed his head and face and arms. His skin was fiery to her touch.

By nightfall he was in high delirium, tossing and turning, muttering in anger and anxiety. Gwen and Klar took turns trying to cool him, to soothe him. By and by Klar lay down for some rest. Gwen sat beside Sam, watching, watching.

No one had cared to suggest they stop for a fishing attempt. No one wanted to try decreasing sail without Sam to supervise. No one knew how to lower and raise the anchor. Without him they were helpless, at the mercy of a hostile ocean.

Above on deck, Gwen could hear the coming and going of footsteps as the wheel watch was changed. She could hear the drumming of the wind in the sails, the creak of ropes in cleats, the murmur of the Chinese in the forward sleeping cabin. So far the *Lelie* was heading on across the waves but there was no captain, no one to let her know she was being firmly handled.

Dawn came. The sun streamed in. Sam was shivering in his fever. Gwen pulled the blanket around him, thinking how much weight he had lost since they left Singapore. They were all thin and exhausted after six weeks of deprivation, stress, endless effort.

Had he strength enough to fight the poison that had entered his body with the bullets? To make up for the loss of blood, the physical shock?

He had to get better. If he died, Gwen wanted to die too. There would be nothing worth living for without him. Nothing but an emptiness as vast as the sea if Sam wasn't there.

Klar roused herself and got to her feet from the other bunk. She went into the galley, where by and by Gwen could sense food was being prepared. When Klar came back she put an arm round Gwen's shoulder.

'Go up on deck, get some fresh air. I sit with him.'

'I don't want to leave him.'

'I understand. But you should go. You have eaten only two mouthfuls since Sumatra, *ja*? Sam would want you to look after yourself. Go, stretch the limbs, eat.'

Gwen looked at Sam. He was unconscious, shivering. He would not wake soon, she somehow knew it. If his spirit had been returning to him, she would have sensed it.

She went into the toilet-room, undressed with weary languor, washed all over with cold sea-water, combed her hair. She put on her clothes again, then went through into the galley.

Tammy was sitting by the narrow table, eating a little meal of beans and rice. As her mother came in she looked up and shook her head. 'You look like a ghost,' she said.

Gwen nodded and sighed. There was weak tea in the pot. She poured some.

'Try to eat some food, Mummy. It's not bad.' Tammy put a little of the *pilau* on another plate, but when Gwen tried to swallow it her throat closed against it.

They sat in silence. Then Tammy said, 'I'm glad we've got this moment alone together. I wanted to say something to you . . . I'm sorry for the way I acted.'

'What?' Gwen said, at a loss.

'I was so rotten to you over Terence.'

'Oh, that,' said her mother. It seemed a million years ago, in another life.

'That's just it. It seems so trivial, so mean and stupid, compared to what we're going through now. I must have been out of my mind to behave like that.'

Gwen tried to summon up an interest. 'Perhaps it was my fault,' she murmured. 'I didn't realise he . . . that man . . . meant so much to you.'

'Reggie,' Tammy supplied. 'You'd forgotten his name. I almost have myself. I didn't care all that much about him. I was just angry with you. I thought you'd made me look a fool.'

'Ah,' said Gwen, with a faint smile, 'I told you before – there's something of your father in you. You don't like to lose face.'

'Something Japanese. That's hard to live with, Mummy. They're the enemy. That means I'm partly an enemy to myself.'

Gwen shook her head. 'Darling, I'm too tired to understand that. All I know is that you've your life before you. I want you to get to safety so you can live it.'

'I want that for you, too, Mummy – for you and Sam. It's going to happen, too, I know it is.'

'Yes, dear,' said Gwen, without really believing it.

She went to look in on Sam before going on deck. Kee was sitting with him now, throwing dice on the other bunk to while away the time. She said to him in very slow Malay, 'Call me if Tuan wakes.'

He nodded. She went above. Clouds were wheeling overhead, letting the sun show and disappear. She saw dishes set out to catch the rain that was clearly going to come. At the wheel Sen Chuen was watching the compass with earnest concentration. Klar was doing some laundry in a bucket of sea-water. Terence was on look-out while he ate a plate of *pilau*.

Gwen stood with Sen Chuen, learning the basics of how to steer. When his two hours were up she took over. It was harder than she had thought. She could feel the movement of the ship through the wheel, trembling with the power given to her by the sails.

By and by Klar came to her. 'Sam would like to speak to you.'

'He's awake?'

'Yes.'

'How is he?'

'I don't know. Better – the temperature goes down by three points but not normal, you know? We need some of these wonderful new medicines to fight the infection . . .'

Gwen went down into the cabin. Sam was sitting up, in control of himself though there was still the glitter of fever in his eyes.

She went over and kissed him. His skin felt hot, dry. He needed a shave. He looked gaunt and sick.

'How're you feeling?'

'Peculiar. My chest hurts when I breathe.'

'Shall I get you a drink? What about a—'

'Lay off,' he said in irritation, 'I've had all that from Klar. I may be a bit under the weather but I'm not in my second childhood yet.'

'You *are* in a bad mood,' she said, smiling.

'Why shouldn't I be! Klar keeps telling me to lie quiet and rest – she can't seem to understand there are things I need to know.'

'Such as what?'

'Such as where we are exactly. I need to get a fix by the sun. I asked Klar to go and look for the ship's instruments but she patted my shoulder and told me not to worry.'

'Ship's instruments,' said Gwen. 'What should I look for?'

'A box or a case. It ought to have a sextant and a log—'

'A book, you mean?'

'That too, mebbe, but I meant another kind of log – you tow it alongside on a cord and it tells you what speed the boat's doing.'

'I'll see,' said Gwen.

She looked in all the cupboards and table drawers. She tried everywhere. In the end she went back to the patient, who was fretting in anxiety.

'I can't find anything.'

'Oh great! That means they were probably taken ashore when the yacht was put under guard. Is there a rocket pistol – for firing distress signals? Did you see a set of flags?'

'Nothing like that.'

'I guess they were all confiscated. No instruments . . . I'll have to do it by dead reckoning then. I need to get on deck to look at the compass.'

'Not now, Sam.'

'Look here—'

'I really don't want to sound like Klar, but you ought to take it easy, at least for today. You were really very sick all last night, my love.'

He grunted in annoyance. 'If I didn't feel as weak as a kitten I'd pin your ears back.'

'Temper, temper.'

'At least you're keeping a good look-out, just in case a vessel comes into sight?'

'Petie's on duty. He loves it. So far he's reported a school of dolphins and an old oil drum.'

'He's a good kid but I'm serious, Gwen – have one of the adults keep an eye out too.'

'Yes, of course.'

She sat talking with him for about half an hour. He began to look drowsy. He made almost no complaint when she settled him down.

Next day his condition was more or less the same. He insisted on being helped on deck. Once again they made a couch for him. Sometimes he dozed. Sometimes he made calculations, ordered slight changes in the course.

Kee elected himself Sam's special guardian. He helped him on deck each morning, took him below each night, besides playing his part in the ship's rota. He took on the task of doing Sam's laundry, shaved him, even tried to give him a haircut with a pair of nail scissors.

Despite Sam's misgivings, Petie was a good look-out: once he reported and described what could only have been a periscope, which alarmed them all. Some days later he pointed out a plume of smoke on the horizon on the port bow. They all watched it with eagerness but it faded.

'Oh, hell,' groaned Sam, and ordered a one-degree alteration in steering. He was obsessed with the idea they might miss the chance of a merchant ship.

The *Lelie* slipped through the waters before the wind. Rain poured off her decks two or three times in the day, so drinking water was so far no problem, but the food supply was running low.

'Should we think about Klar's idea – try fishing?' Gwen asked.

'Not yet. Honey, I'm a little out of my head, I know that – how many days have we been at sea?'

She herself had no real notion. 'I think about nineteen, twenty,' she ventured.

'So let's say we got to Padang in March, we were two days there – is that right? Yes, and came aboard, and let's say we've been at sea twenty days. So we're in mid-April, is that right?'

'I think so, Sam.'

He nodded and let it go. She had no idea what was

bothering him until, a few days later, the wind suddenly dropped. One day it was there, the next the morning watch came on deck to a dead calm.

'What's happened?' they asked each other.

Sam smiled with some grimness. 'Monsoon's dying. Dog days coming.'

'Dog days – that means high summer, I thought?' Terence suggested.

'Well, in the northern hemisphere – July, more or less. It's just a phrase. Means calm weather.' Sam breathed lightly two or three times, as if his chest were hurting him. 'See, a sailing ship can't move without wind.'

They looked in dismay at the limp sails.

'Now's the time to try fishing,' Sam said.

There was no ship's dinghy – that was another item that had been taken ashore when the yacht was confiscated by the Japanese. So they cast their lines from the ship's rail. They had some success, were crowing with triumph at landing a sailfish, until Petie gave a cry and pointed.

A triangular fin was gliding parallel with their side.

'Shark!' Terence gasped.

'It's OK,' Sam said. 'He'll circle around – he's seen the smaller fish snapping at the bait, it's made him curious. Just don't go in swimming, anybody.'

No one had any such intention.

At nightfall a breeze sprang up. The sails filled, the helmsman got the ship on course, they heeled off again. Through the night the wind dropped and resumed, played cat and mouse, blew for an hour, then dropped.

They had only made a few sea miles. Next day they were becalmed again. The sun beat down from a cloudless sky. It was hot aboard the *Lelie*, because first there was no breeze, and second there wasn't the passage of air that blew through the cabins when she was underway.

Now they had fresh fish, but the water was getting

low. There was no rain. The stifling atmosphere made them thirsty but the water ration was reduced.

They became listless, weak, slack-limbed. It was hard to keep look-out through the heat haze of the morning and against the glare of full daylight. The *Lelie* was swayed by the waves, drifted a little in a northerly current. They slept on deck at night because the cabins were so airless.

How many nightfalls they had greeted in this dreary way Gwen didn't know. She only knew she was suddenly awake, with Petie clutching at her shoulder.

'Auntie Gwen! Listen!'

Ship's engines. A steady churning, off in the darkness.

'A warship?' Terence's voice asked.

'It must be a Japanese destroyer,' Tammy said fearfully.

'I don't care! We can't go on like this!' Terence cried. 'I'm going to signal it!'

'No,' Klar protested, 'we could end up in a camp!'

There was a momentary flicker of the electric torch. Then Tammy flung herself on him, sending him sprawling in the dark. The lighted torch rolled along the deck. 'No! No, we're not going to be taken prisoner!'

'Good God, Tammy, we'll die out here—'

'I'd rather! I won't let you.'

Gwen heard Sam heave himself up from his sleeping place. There was a scuffle, impossible to discern. Then the torch was winking: SOS, SOS.

'Uncle Sam!' shrieked Tammy, grabbing his arm. 'How could you!'

Gwen could see her beating at him with her fists. Sam was holding her off with one hand, waving the lighted torch with the other.

Gwen thrust herself between them. 'Tammy! Tammy, don't—'

'But he's *giving in*!'

She heard Sam's weak chuckle.

'Bunch of landlubbers! No Japanese warship has engines like that! Can't you tell an old tramp when you hear her?'

Chapter Twenty-eight

As the SS *Drago* chuntered in towards Trincomalee on the north-east coast of Ceylon, RAF planes came out to monitor her. Next came a coastguard cutter to inspect her papers. The officer in charge of the boarding party took one look at Sam and had him taken ashore in a fast launch.

With plentiful food and water, the six-day voyage had allowed the others to pick up somewhat in health. Sam had grown steadily worse. Gwen could only be glad that he was being rushed to hospital, although ideally she would have wanted to go with him. This the coastguard lieutenant wouldn't allow.

He kept all the Europeans isolated for a few hours while he listened to their tale of escape. Satisfied at length that they really were refugees and not some sort of fifth column, he had them taken to the port infirmary.

Gwen's first question was, 'How is Mr Prosper?'

'Who?' asked the naval doctor who was about to examine her.

'Mr Prosper – the man who was brought ashore first.'

'Oh yes. Difficult to say. We had him flown to Colombo – needed tricky surgery, they have better facilities there.'

'Surgery? Is he very bad?'

'He's not good. Your husband?'

'No. No, Sam's . . . well . . .'

'I see,' said the doctor. 'Well, he should be all right,

they'll dose him with M&B . . . sulphanilamide. Now about you, my dear . . . You look as if you've been to Timbuctoo and back . . .'

They were all kept in overnight but given a clean bill of health – that's to say, no infectious diseases, although they were all suffering from vitamin deficiencies and anaemia. Petie was a little unwell, due mostly to nerves – it was months since he'd been in a town, among a crowd of people.

Overnight their clothes had been washed and ironed, but nothing could disguise the fact that they had seen very hard wear. Terence was disgruntled that he had to be interviewed by an official from the Colonial Office in such a state.

When it was Gwen's turn to go into the office to see Mr Gunter, she took Petie in with her.

'Well now, Mrs Veetcha, is it?' he said, peering at his list through lenses so thick they might have been made from the bottoms of lemonade bottles. 'Is that Hungarian? Polish?'

'Neither, Mr Gunter, it's the way the Parisians said my maiden name, Whitchurch.'

'The Parisians? You know Paris? I spent all my leave there when I was at the London office . . . Do you know the Café de Garonne near the university?'

'Oh, very well. I lived in Montparnasse.'

They sent some time recalling favourite spots. Then Mr Gunter said, 'Well, *revenons à nos moutons*. I don't quite see . . . er . . . why you kept on the name the Parisians happened to use?'

'It's just for business. Easier than Hayakawa, which is my real name.'

There was a pause. Mr Gunter took a deep breath which made his embonpoint push against the desk.

'That name appears on my list. Miss Tamara Hayakawa.'

'My daughter.'

'That's . . . er . . . a Japanese name?'

'Yes. My husband was Japanese.'

'Your husband . . . What, exactly, is the situation between you and him?'

'He was killed in the Tokyo earthquake of 1923.'

'Ah.' Mr Gunter looked relieved. A Japanese husband dead so many years posed no problem after all. 'You retained British citizenship?'

'Certainly.'

'You don't have any documents, I suppose?'

'They went down with the *Dimestore*.'

'The *Dimestore*?'

'The cabin-cruiser in which we escaped from Singapore.'

'You were residing in Singapore?'

'It was my home for nearly twenty years.'

'Er . . . In Singapore . . . I never served there but I understood . . . British women were usually the wives of British businessmen or officials . . . What I mean is, were you staying with a relative? A brother, perhaps?'

'I was running a business.'

Mr Gunter looked perplexed. 'What kind of business?'

'I made furniture.'

'Dear me.'

She had a feeling he found her distinctly odd. He consulted some documents, cleared his throat, and went on. 'Shall you wish to be repatriated? That is of course your right, but I ought to warn you that there is a long wait because any civilian transport ship would have to go in a convoy—'

'If you mean repatriated to Britain,' Gwen said, 'I don't wish that.'

'You don't.'

'No.'

'What do you intend to do?'

'Stay here.'

'And your daughter?'

'She will stay too. I don't intend letting her make the journey back to England in the middle of a war.'

565

'Quite so.' He shuffled his papers. 'I imagine the business you had in Singapore is now utterly defunct. Have you any other source of income?'

'Don't worry about it, Mr Gunter,' Gwen said with some irritation. 'If I can be allowed to send a cable, I can get funds from home – some of my furniture designs are in production in Britain and there should be money owing to me.' It had never once occurred to her to use the gemstones in the chamois pouch Sam had put around her neck. That was her talisman, to be handed over only to him.

'Oh, that simplifies matters. Would you be supporting Miss Hayakawa?'

'Of course.'

He made a note on his documents. 'I think you should have identity cards issued to you within a day or two. Until then, I'm afraid you'll have to stay in the infirmary grounds – this is a naval base, we can't have unidentified persons wandering about.'

Gwen shrugged. 'I've no objections to that so long as I can use the telephone.'

'Indeed?' he said, surprised. 'You know people in Trincomalee?'

'I want to telephone a hospital in Colombo. My greatest friend is there, seriously ill.'

'I see. I imagine there should be no problem about that.' He put away the top document, riffled through, and produced another. He studied Petie through his glasses.

'Now, young man. What's your name?'

'Petie.'

'Petie what?'

Petie looked up at Gwen. Gwen said, 'We don't know his last name. He was in an orphanage in Singapore.'

'Mummy was in Singapore,' Petie volunteered. 'She was killed with the bombs.'

'Ah yes,' Gunter said as gently as he could. 'What was Mummy's name?'

Petie gave him a glance of scorn. 'Mummy, of course.'

'Er . . . yes . . . Well, what was Daddy's name?'

'Daddy.'

'But what I mean, Petie, is this: didn't Mummy sometimes call him something else?'

'She called him darling sometimes.'

'She did. Yes. Well, what did the servants call him?'

'Tuan,' said Petie simply.

Mr Gunter had been brought up in Birmingham, where little boys knew their names and addresses. He persevered.

'But Petie . . . in case you ever got lost, didn't Mummy teach you what to say to people?'

'Get lost? You mean like Hansel and Gretel? But *they* didn't have an amah,' Petie pointed out. 'If they'd had an amah to look after them they wouldn't have got lost.' His mouth trembled. 'I wonder where Nunah is? She wouldn't leave her village. Did the bad soldiers get her?'

'Never mind Nunah. Suppose she wasn't there and you'd wandered away – could you tell people where you lived?'

'But they *know* that!' cried Petie, losing patience. 'Everybody on the estate knows the *tuan kechil*.'

'Who's that?'

'Me, of course. Don't you know anything? It means "the little tuan", I thought everybody knew that!'

'What you're saying,' Mr Gunter muttered, labouring to understand the situation, 'is that you never learned your name and address because there was no need to . . . Until, I suppose, the time came to send you away to school.'

'Send me away?' Petie echoed, with a glance of terror at Gwen. 'Are you going to send me away?'

'Of course not!' Quickly she put an arm round him.

'Voyons,' she said in a cold tone, *'ce pauvre enfant a beaucoup souffert. Faut-il souffrir de plus?'*

Mr Gunter blushed. 'But I have to ascertain, Mrs

567

Veetcha . . . You see . . . who's going to look after him?'

'I am, of course.'

'Well, that . . . That can only be temporary. We ought to find some relative.'

'I quite understand it must be temporary.' She patted Petie lightly on the head. 'One day perhaps we'll find your father again, won't we, Petie?'

'Daddy went out to help the soldiers fight the nennemy,' said the little boy, 'but he didn't come back.'

Gunter shook his head. 'Mrs Veetcha, it may be some years before we can retake Malaya . . .'

'I've learned to take things as they come,' Gwen said. 'For the present, it's enough to have Petie here safe and sound, and to take care of him and see he gets three square meals a day. If that's all, Mr Gunter?'

He rose as she did. 'I feel there's really no need to see Miss Hayakawa,' he remarked as he opened the door for her. 'And as to the Chinese you brought with you, we're waiting for an interpreter for them. Good morning, Mrs Veetcha.'

The welfare officer at the infirmary put through a call to the Royal Victoria Hospital in Colombo. The response was that there could be no report as yet on Mr Prosper as he was now in surgery. A call in about four hours might be better.

Later that day, a Red Cross worker came to the infirmary with a selection of clothes garnered from the well-to-do of Colombo. As Tammy, Klar and Gwen looked through them, Gwen remarked, 'This is the second time in my life I've had to wear charity clothes.'

'Really?' said Miss Dwyer. 'When was the other?'

Gwen explained about the time in Tokyo after the earthquake. Meanwhile Tammy and Klar were turning over the garments. 'It's easy to see why the owners gave them away,' Tammy laughed. 'They're mostly awful.'

'Now now, be thankful you've got them. All the same,

as soon as Granny sends some money, we'll go out and buy something that fits!'

The Red Cross worker offered a sum from their emergency funds. Delighted, the three women went to the shop in the hall of the infirmary where they bought combs and hairpins and lipsticks. But Gwen kept back a fund of coins so as to use the telephone in the foyer.

Alas, when after inquiry she'd been put through to the right ward, Sister asked if she was a relation.

'No, not exactly . . .'

'I'm afraid I can't give out information except to relations.'

'But at least tell me if the operation has been—'

'Mr Prosper is out of theatre and is as well as can be expected.'

'Is he conscious?'

'He's recovering from the anaesthetic.'

'When he comes to, will you tell him Gwen sends her love?'

'I'll see he gets the message.' And the phone was firmly put down.

So it went on. No information could be divulged except to a relation. For four days Gwen kept inquiring, and at last was told that Mr Prosper was off the critical list. 'Did you give him my message?' Gwen asked.

'Message?'

'I sent him my love.'

'Oh, I'm sure he was told.'

'Did he give you a message for me?'

'Not that I'm aware of.' And once again the phone was put down.

Gwen was beside herself with anxiety. But without documents, without money, there was no way to get to Colombo.

At the end of a week identity papers were issued to them all. Two days later a cable came from her mother: 'Darling, so relieved to hear from you at last. Money transferred in your name to Colombo

Branch of Overseas Commercial. Love from Walter and me.'

The bank had not as yet received confirmation of the transfer but on the strength of the cable agreed to advance her a fair sum. At once Gwen announced to the others that she was off to Colombo by train as soon as she could buy the tickets. 'Do you want to come?'

It seemed best. Gwen sought out the three Chinese who had come with them from Sumatra, but only Kee wanted to travel on – Sen Chuen and Lam had been offered jobs at the naval base in Trincomalee.

So the others set out on the one hundred and twenty-mile journey. It was hot and sticky and uncomfortable – once they would have complained loudly at the discomfort. But after recent hardships, to them it seemed almost luxury.

They arrived in Colombo in the middle of May, to a handsome, busy city sweltering in a temperature of about eighty-eight degrees. It was a little over three months since they had set out in the *Dimestore* from Singapore.

They had arranged accommodation at a government hotel not far from The Fort, the business section of the port. Gwen and Tammy shared a room. Petie had a little truckle bed in an alcove. Klar was next door, Terence was on the floor above. Kee had sauntered off almost at once, announcing he had cousins in the Chinese quarters with whom he could find shelter.

Gwen's first action was to buy a pot of orchids to take to the hospital. When she arrived there at the correct visiting hour, she was told that Mr Prosper wasn't allowed visitors.

'No visitors?' she said, appalled.

'Mr Prosper isn't well enough to receive visitors.'

'I was told he was off the critical list!'

'I'm afraid there's been a set-back.'

'Please – what's wrong – I must know!'

'Are you a relation?'

'No, I'm a close friend, he may have mentioned me – Mrs Veetcha.'

'I'm sorry, Mrs Veetcha, we can't discuss the patient except with a relation.'

'But I've come all the way from Trincomalee . . .'

'I'm sorry, it's a hospital regulation.'

Trying not to cry, Gwen handed over the pot of vanda orchids. 'Will you give him this, please, and tell him it's from Gwen?'

'I'll do that,' Sister said with a faint relaxation of her starchy presence. 'Perhaps you'd like to write a note?'

'Oh – may I? Oh, please – can you lend me a pen? And a piece of paper?'

Sister's office provided both. Gwen wrote, 'Darling, I'm just outside the ward doors but they won't let me in. Please get well enough for visitors! All my love, Gwen.' She was ashamed to see that tears had caused blots over some of the words.

She telephoned next day to inquire whether she could visit. The answer was no. She sent flowers with a card pinned to the wrapping. She came back to the hotel from the market where she'd bought the flowers feeling depressed, disheartened, anxious.

Tammy was on the hotel verandah with Petie, both of them sipping orangeade through two straws in one glass. One look at her mother's face was enough to tell her how she felt. 'It'll be all right,' she urged, clapping her hands for the 'boy'. 'They'll let you see him tomorrow.'

'But Tammy – he must be very, very ill . . .'

'Uncle Sam's tough. He'll be all right,' Tammy said with conviction.

'I think Uncle Sam is as tough as anything,' Petie agreed, taking Gwen's hand and squeezing it hard.

When she had ordered iced tea for her mother Tammy said, 'I've something to tell you, Mummy.'

'Yes, dear?'

'Terence has asked me to marry him.'

'Oh!' An icy hand clutched Gwen's heart. Please,

God, she said inwardly, don't let her make such a terrible mistake! 'And what did you say?'

'I said no, of course,' Tammy said with scorn.

'Oh, thank heaven!' gasped Gwen.

'Wait till I tell you the rest. Klar told me I'd been very unkind to him, and they've gone out for a long drive in a gharry so she can console him.'

'Tammy!'

'Auntie Klar was ever so cross with Tammy,' Petie remarked. 'Auntie Klar said she was a very unkind girl – but I don't think she is, do you, Auntie Gwen?'

'My hero,' said Tammy, pushing Petie down on the boards and tickling him. 'I'm going to wait till you grow up and then I'll marry *you.*'

'Ow, ow!' he giggled, rolling about. 'I'll tell Auntie Klar you're a very *naughty* girl.'

'Poor Klar,' Gwen said, drinking a welcome mouthful of tea. 'I wonder if she knows what she's doing.'

'She's the mothering type. Perhaps he's just what she needs – someone to look after.'

There was a coolness that evening between the two sets of people. It was clear to Gwen that Klar liked comforting Terence and that Terence liked being comforted. Later it emerged that he had been inquiring after employment with the Transport Authority and there was the possibility of a post on the docks at Trincomalee.

'I shall certainly take it if it's offered,' he said. 'I'm grateful to you, Gwen, for lending me money – and Klar feels the same – but a man ought to look after his own responsibilities.'

'Oh, of course,' murmured Gwen, noticing that Klar now seemed to be included among his responsibilities. But she didn't really care what Terence and Klar did. All she cared about was getting in to see Sam.

At last, at the end of her third week in Colombo, she was shown into a day ward that was in fact a long shady verandah opening on to a garden bordered with broad-leaf trees. Sam, clad in terrible striped pyjamas and a faded cotton robe, was reclining on a padded lounger at the far end.

She could hardly restrain herself from running wildly up the ward. She reached the side of the recliner. Sam looked at her.

'Hi, sugar. I thought you'd ditched me.'

'Ditched you? I've been trying to see you for weeks! Why didn't you reply to any of my messages?'

He smiled. 'You don't know these nurses. They're worse than Klar. Try to have a conversation with them, they pop a pill into you and next thing you know you're asleep.'

She was studying him. He was pale and thin, but the shiny glitter of fever was gone from his face. His voice didn't have its usual strength but there was humour in his tone again.

'Oh, darling, I've been so worried about you!' she cried, and kneeling beside the lounger, threw her arms around him. She felt him gather her against him. For a long time they stayed bound together in that first embrace.

'Come on,' he said at length, 'let me go or you'll have me bawling like a baby.'

It was true, his troubled breathing told her so. Reluctantly she released him, but instead caught up one of his hands to hold in both of hers. Along the ward, other patients looked studiously at the view.

'So . . .' Sam said. 'How've they been treating you, babe?'

'All right. The Colonial Office was a bit stuffy at first but they've accepted us now.'

'Who all is with you? Tammy? Terence?'

'Tammy and Petie, yes. Terence and Klar may be going back to Trincomalee – Terence is getting a job there.'

'Terence and Klar?'

She nodded.

'It figures,' he said with a wry smile.

573

'Kee is outside, hoping he'll be allowed to see you for a minute.'

'He is? Well, jiminy-jee! Good old Kee . . . I'd like to see him. I owe him a lot.' He was silent a moment. 'All seems like a dream, doesn't it? Here it's so peaceful, it's hard to remember what we went through.'

'We should put it behind us,' Gwen said, out of the experience in her own life, of starting again after Tama's death. 'We're going to think about the future from now on. And the first thing is, when do you think you'll be up and about again?'

'Oh, I'm up and about now,' he protested, pretending annoyance. 'I'm a big boy, they let me go to the bathroom on my own.'

'So when can you come home?'

'Ah. That's a problem. Where is home, in this case?'

'With me, of course,' she said. 'Don't ask foolish questions.'

'But listen, Gwen, you can't just say it in that casual way.' His brows came together as he sought for the words. 'It's likely to be kind of a long business, getting back into action. They sort of pussyfoot around but I gather I've had an embolism, whatever that may be, and it's caused a part of one of my lungs to pack up.'

'But you can get better,' she insisted.

'Oh, sure. They say scar tissue – great stuff, scar tissue – it'll form and in time I'll compensate for the cavity: at least that's what I think they say.'

'That's all right then.'

'Honey, have you been listening to what I say? It could take months and months. I don't see myself saddling you with an invalid—'

'Oh!' cried Gwen, experiencing a sudden enlightenment. It was a rare experience for her – she felt she could see through Sam's behaviour, understand what lay beneath.

'Is that what it was all about?' she surged on. 'Not

letting me come to see you, not answering my notes? You thought you were going to be a liability?'

'Well, see, it's easy to say, "Of course I can manage", but honey, you'd get fed up, looking after a—'

'Don't talk nonsense,' she said, giving his hand an angry little shake. 'You remember, that night at Padang? You asked me if I was your girl and I said yes. Well, that's the way it is, until you can look me in the eye and say honestly that it's over.'

She sat watching him, waiting.

He lay back against his cushions, his eyes half-closed, 'You know I'm never going to say that.'

There was nothing that needed saying after that. They sat thinking.

Businesslike, Sam resumed. 'Where you putting up now?'

'The Regency Hotel. Small, inexpensive, not suitable for convalescence.'

'Inexpensive? Why the economy? Didn't you use the gemstones?'

'Of course not,' she said. 'And that reminds me . . .' She began to pull on the thong around her neck, intending to get the pouch out from the neck of her dress and hand it over.

'No,' he said, catching her wrist. 'Don't give it to me. I've nowhere to keep it here. Besides, you're going to use it.'

'Me?'

'Yes, you. When you get back to the hotel, spread a handkerchief, tip out the stones. You'll see one, about the size of a pea, kind of brownish-red – nothing much to look at. When it's polished it'll be worth a small fortune. I want you to take it to an honest merchant—'

'But, Sam, I don't know anyone in Colombo! As to honesty—'

'It's OK, I'll talk to Kee about it.'

'But Kee's only a—'

'Only a coolie, right. But his fourth or fifth cousin

will know somebody who works for somebody who knows . . . And so on. The guy his clan recommends will be OK; he'll have money. He'll want the stone, for investment – he can't send anything to Amsterdam to be cut until the war's over and it's too good to give to an Indian cutter. So we're dealing with big money here, and he'll make a good offer. You tell him you have to ask your principal and come back and tell me.'

A gleam had come into Sam's eyes, his colour had improved. Gwen looked at him with love. 'You absolutely adore this kind of thing,' she challenged.

'Well, it beats lying in bed with tubes sticking in you,' he said.

Gwen visited Sam every day. Every day he seemed better. He said the doctors thought he could go home at the beginning of June. 'So we've got to have a home for me to go to. Kee tells me he thinks he's got the right business name at last.'

Kee came to Gwen next day, looking important. He gave her a piece of paper with a name and address painstakingly written out in European script. At that address lived a very rich silk merchant.

After that it all went as Sam had foretold. An agreement was reached, money was deposited in an account in the local branch of the American Maritime Bank. Gwen was sent out to find a bungalow for them to live in.

'I leave it to you, sugar. If you like it I'll like it. It's got to have enough rooms so that Tammy won't feel she's under our eye – she hates not having freedom. Petie will want to be near you, I suppose. My only other thought is it can't have many stairs – I get out of breath doing stairs at the moment,' Sam said.

The bungalow was on the western outskirts of Colombo, in a garden still being carefully tended by a crew of servants. The previous occupant had been an RAF Wing-Commander. Included in the rent was the hire of the staff – cook, head and under-houseboy, an amah for the memsahib and three gardeners, one of whom acted as chauffeur.

They hired an amah for Petie. 'We have to have Kee as well,' Sam said. 'I don't speak any of the local lingo so if I want to curse somebody out it's got to be in Chinese.'

They moved in at the end of the first week in June, leaving Klar and Terence at the Regency Hotel. Terence looked a little put out on his first visit to the bungalow. 'Well,' he remarked, 'well . . . You must have friends in high places, Sam.'

'Only at the bank,' Sam replied cheerfully.

'When we are in Trincomalee,' said Klar, 'perhaps we shall find a good bungalow too.'

'That's going to happen? You've landed a job?'

'Oh, there is no question of *that*! They are only too anxious, *ja*? to have Terence on the staff. And for me too there is work, because, you know, there is a contingent of the Nederlands Navy at Trincomalee and they suggest that I make for them a club-house, you know?'

Klar beamed at them, her arm through Terence's, the fair head and the dark close together . . .

They left ten days later, promising to write, to keep in touch. But Gwen had a feeling they would lose contact. She wasn't unhappy at the thought. Terence belonged to a part of her life that was now totally and completely over.

She settled down to be ruler of her own little kingdom. A nearby doctor had taken over the care of Sam's health, and from him there were to be regular visits for the next six months, together with regular trips to the hospital for check-ups. She had to learn some of the local language, Sinhalese. She had to find a school for Petie.

'And I'm going to get a job,' announced Tammy.

'Doing what?'

'Don't know yet. I've been asking around. There's

some pressure towards joining the WRNS or the WAAF but I don't think I'm cut out for that.'

Sam chuckled. 'You don't think the uniform would suit you, tootsie.'

'There is that. Besides, you have to train, do drill – terrible stuff. All the same . . . I'm going on for eighteen. They might call me up.'

'A fate worse than death? Better find yourself some important war work before they get to you.'

'Sam,' Gwen reproached him later that night when Tammy had gone out to a party at the naval base, 'don't encourage Tammy to shirk her responsibilities.'

Sam was drinking egg-nog, part of the regimen to build up his physical strength. He detested the stuff, it always took him half an hour to get the drink down. 'Listen, sweetness, Tammy's been through enough for the present. The last thing she needs is to be pushed into a barracks with fifty other girls.'

'Would that be so bad? They seem a nice lot, those you see out and about in the town.'

'Oh, sure, they're great girls, but Tammy . . . Tammy's special, she's a beauty, she's got a great sense of her own importance and a will of iron. I don't think she'd take orders too well.'

'Really?' Gwen said, surprised. 'You think she's wilful?'

'Oh, Gwen! Your own daughter and you don't know that?'

Gwen sat down beside him on the verandah sofa. She swung it to and fro gently. 'You know me,' she sighed. 'I've never really learned to size people up.'

The days went by, peaceful, hopeful. Sam's health improved, to her deep satisfaction, but as yet they had never made love. She sometimes wondered if she should ask Dr Thinaburan about it, but it seemed too personal a topic to enter into even with someone so gentle and tolerant.

Petie settled down to school life. It appeared he was

happy with sand boxes and plasticine but didn't like 'letters'. 'Not a scholar,' Sam remarked. 'I sympathise. I never cared much for "letters" either – always playing hookey to go out in a boat.'

'Which was where, Sam? I mean, you claimed New England forefathers.'

'Yup, my father ran a ship's chandlery. Prosper's Stores, Everything for the Mariner. That was in Mystic Harbour – couldn't get out of it fast enough!'

'My father made furniture,' Gwen said. She looked back at that distant figure, busy at his bench, his dexterous hands busy with a drill. She thought, I'd like to make something . . . Something that smells of the spicy wood you can buy here . . .

Perhaps, in a month or two. When Sam was really better, when she had more time. She was busy, busy and happy. Her world had its own stability.

But suddenly that stability was shattered. Tammy came to her room late one night after an evening with some of her new friends.

'Mummy,' she said without preamble, 'I want to go to Delhi.'

Chapter Twenty-nine

Gwen was creaming her face. These days her skin seemed to drink up all the moisture she gave it. She met her daughter's serious gaze in her mirror. She picked up a piece of cotton wool, wiped cream off her cheeks, then said quite calmly, 'Why Delhi?'

'Because they're going to make a film there.'

'Who are?'

'The COI – that's the Central Office of Information.'

'And why are you needed there?'

'They've offered me a part in the film.'

Gwen was taken aback. Tammy, she knew, had met all sorts of people since they arrived in Colombo, but this was the first time she'd mentioned film-makers.

'Who exactly has offered you a part, Tammy?'

'His name's Norman Pickering. He's a producer in the department for developing propaganda for the Indian sub-continent. James Lovatt can vouch for him, and Mrs Watts.'

James Lovatt was in the city government. Mrs Watts was a patron of the arts, wife of one of the wealthy tea-planters.

'My word. That makes him entirely respectable. But I don't quite see why you should be offered a part in a film, dear. You've no training as an actress.'

'I don't think you need much training for films,' Tammy said in all innocence. 'I think you do little bits at a time so it's not like learning the whole of *Romeo and Juliet*. And anyhow, it's my appearance they want.'

'Your appearance. You mean your good looks?'

'I mean the fact that I'm Eurasian.'

'How does that come into it?' Gwen asked, startled.

'Well, I gather the film's to be about how everyone is pulling together for the war effort, and there's to be a bit with the Hindus and a bit with the Moslems and a bit with the business community and I'm to represent the Eurasians. I think I'm going to be in an office and have lines about how important my war work is.'

'But you're not doing any war work.'

'I will be,' said Tammy, 'if I have a part in this film.'

This was such a neat argument that Gwen had to laugh. Her daughter flung an arm around her shoulders and put her cheek against hers. 'Say yes, Mummy. They say they can't take me without your consent, because I'm still a minor.'

'It's a bit of a surprise, darling,' Gwen returned. 'Let me talk it over with Sam.'

Tammy pouted. 'He'll say no.'

'Why should he?'

'Because he'll guess you'd rather I stayed here. And I want to go, Mummy. It may lead on to other things.'

Next morning Gwen stopped Kee as he was carrying the breakfast tray towards Sam's room. Sam was still supposed to be having plenty of rest, taking breakfast in bed, lounging about on the swing sofa on the verandah.

'Would you ask Tuan Prosper if I could speak to him for a few minutes, Kee?'

'Yes, mem.'

He didn't close the door. She heard the quick exchange in Cantonese. A moment later Kee came out, ushered her in, closed the door after him.

Sam was sitting up in bed, the mosquito nets folded back, his morning paper half opened. The louvred shutters were still half closed; bars of sunlight lay across his bed.

'Well, it must be important. Petie's got measles?'

'No, it's about Tammy.'

'I'm sure Tammy's already had measles.' He dropped the banter. 'What is it, Gwen? You look troubled.'

She gave him a resumé of the previous night's conversation. He pulled at his lower lip, then sipped orange juice from his breakfast tray.

'It's not like that Reggie-Who'sit lark? It's genuine?'

'Well, it's too early to ring Mrs Watts, but I'll do that later. I think it must be all right or Mrs Watts wouldn't be mentioned at all.'

'I'm with you on that. Films for the Central Office of Information, huh?'

'I feel I ought to say yes because it's "in a good cause". But Delhi . . . It's so far away.'

'Nice safe place, though. I'd have balked at it if they'd suggested taking her to London.'

'Yes, you're right, it's safe. But she's safe here.'

'But getting bored.'

'Is she? I thought she was happy with the parties and outings and things.'

Sam stared thoughtfully at the coffee pot. 'Can we talk to her about it? I mean, is she carried away, or will she listen sensibly?'

'Oh, she seems very level-headed. I think she sees it as the start of some kind of career.'

It always took Sam quite a while to get up and get dressed. Whether he'd always been like that, Gwen had no means of knowing. But certainly in Colombo Sam couldn't seem to get going in the mornings, although the rest of the world was up and about by six.

It was after ten by the time he came into the shady living-room where Gwen and Tammy were now having coffee. Gwen had rung Mrs Watts and been reassured as to the bona fides of Norman Pickering. It appeared he'd just finished a short documentary about Sinhalese members of the British Navy.

'Now,' said Sam to Tammy, sinking into an armchair, 'once again from the top. Norman Pickering offers you a part in a film to be made in Delhi. He needs your mother's consent. Do you get paid? Do you get a contract? Is this a one-off affair? Do you get left stranded in Delhi when it's over? What?'

'I get paid,' Tammy said quietly, 'there's a standard rate for bit-players. I get a contract but it's only for this one film. There will be other COI films but I shouldn't think I'll get a part in any of those. However, there are commercial film-makers in Delhi . . .'

'Indian film-makers. They make those incredible epics they put on at the Sumhali Cinema.'

'No, there's a commercial American unit making a film from a novel by somebody famous, about an airman.'

'But are they based there? I mean, are they going to make other films?'

'I don't know,' Tammy confessed. 'But I'd have the chance to talk to them.'

'Yeah,' said Sam. 'Talk's cheap. It amounts to this – you really don't know what would happen after this propaganda film is made.'

Tammy frowned at him. 'Don't make it out to be worse than it is. I'm not going to be *stranded* in Delhi – I can always come back to Colombo if I don't land any other acting parts.' Her expression lightened, she glinted at him. 'You'd send me the money to come back, wouldn't you, Uncle Sam?'

Sam exchanged a glance with Gwen. 'Not bad,' he said. 'She sounds quite sensible.'

'Oh, Uncle Sam, this is the chance of a lifetime for me!' Tammy burst out. 'It was heaven-sent luck that I happened to meet Mr Pickering at the Lovatts?'

'Why, exactly, does he want you for this film?'

'I explained that. It's because I'm Eurasian.'

'You with your slanty eyes and everything, you mean?'

A year ago – even only a few months ago – a taunt like that would have sent her into a fury. Now she shrugged and said, 'Mr Pickering says there are almond-eyed beauties by the score in Delhi. What makes me important is my colouring. If people sit up and look at me, they'll perhaps pay attention to what I say about the war.'

'Doesn't worry you, having your half-caste status exploited?'

'Mr Pickering says I ought to capitalise on it. He says the "exotic" look is the coming thing. The war's made everybody more open-minded, he says.'

'Gee, he sounds impressive,' Sam said with irony.

'Well, he is. He's been in films for nearly twenty years and never been out of a job.'

'He says.'

'The rest of his team say it too. They respect him. Mrs Watts respects him.'

'So much for Mr Pickering,' said Sam, nodding. 'Well, something else. No qualms about urging everybody to help fight against your father's people?'

An angry gleam came into Tammy's eyes. 'They tried to kill me,' she said. 'I don't feel I owe them anything.'

'That's straight enough, at any rate. When are you supposed to leave?'

'Next Tuesday – Mr Pickering and his crew have got permits to travel on an RAF transport plane to Bangalore.'

A pause.

'You think she should go?' Gwen asked.

'I think so, honey.'

In a way Gwen had known the outcome was inevitable. It seemed to her that Fate had intended her beautiful daughter for something more exciting than an office job in Colombo.

When Petie heard the news, he let out a wail of dismay. 'You can't go, Tammy! You can't go away!'

Gwen saw her daughter's green eyes fill with tears. 'I want to go, Petie,' she told him. 'And I'll come back, of course.'

'Take me with you! I want to go too!'

'I can't, darling. I'll be too busy to look after you in Delhi.'

'What are you going to do in Delhi, anyway?' he demanded, clenching his fists as if to beat her.

'I'm going to be in a film.'

'A film?' The upraised fists began to fall. 'Like "The Wizard of Oz"?'

'Perhaps not in colour, Petie. And I don't think there'll be any songs.'

'Shall I be able to see you in the film? Will it come to the Star Cinema?'

'I'm sure it will,' Gwen put in, seeing a way to make it seem better for him. 'And you'll be able to tell your school friends about it.'

'I'll take them to see you at the Star Cinema. Will your name be on a big board outside, Tammy?'

'Perhaps,' she said, hugging him.

He seemed satisfied for the present. But there was an underlying anxiety in him. And why not? Everyone he loved and needed had been taken from him: his father, his mother, and then Miss Bedale, thought Gwen.

Miss Bedale . . . Nothing had been heard of her, although they had made enquiries through the Red Cross. She had vanished, like so many others, lost in the octopus embrace of Japanese power – China, Burma, Malaya, the Philippines, the Dutch East Indies. Lost, she and the children she had sworn to care for. Piet Janstra and all the refugees on his boat, no word of them.

There was no word either of Bertie Hurden who had set off with a companion by sampan from Singapore. Of Marion Targett there was news – the Red Cross reported she was in Portugal. But Gwen could get no information about Petie's father, because she had no idea of his name.

She tried not to let Petie see how upset she herself was about parting from Tammy. When they talked about it, it was always in cheerful tones. Sam was best at this. He teased Tammy about becoming a film star.

The small but pretty collection of clothes bought for her by Sam was quickly packed. A little farewell party was given for her on the Monday night. It had been agreed that Gwen and Petie wouldn't go to the airfield to see her off on Tuesday morning; they were afraid it would distress Petie at the last moment.

Gwen and her daughter sat for a long time in the perfumed darkness of the garden after the guests had left and Sam had gone exhausted to bed.

'I'll write,' Tammy promised. 'I'll try to get through on the telephone – but you know how difficult that is.'

'I expect you'll be busy,' Gwen said. 'Still, I've got the name of the hostel in Delhi – I'll write to *you*.'

'I feel funny. This isn't like when I used to say goodbye before leaving for school in England.'

'No. This time it's open-ended. You might go on from this film to something else. It might mean a career.'

'I'm not building up any hopes.'

'No, better not.'

Tammy suddenly clutched Gwen's hands. 'Perhaps I don't really want to go at all,' she cried. 'I'm not sure. Mummy, do you think I'm doing the right thing?'

It was a cry from the heart . . . For the first time since her babyhood, Tammy was saying she needed her mother.

Though she reproached herself for it, Gwen felt a surge of joy. That precious bond which meant so much to her was restored. Through pain, through hardship and loss, they had come together at last. Nothing was of more value to her – not the gems locked in Sam's bureau drawer, not the gold with which Tama used to paint shining surfaces.

She took her daughter into her arms, stroked her coppery hair. 'You have to go, dear,' she murmured. 'You'd always regret it if you let this chance slip by.

And after all, if you don't like it, you can always come back to me.'

'To you and Sam.'

'Yes.'

Tammy sat up, blowing her nose and wiping her eyes. Even in floods of tears and the uncertain light of the swinging paper lanterns, she was still pretty. 'Are you and Sam going to get married?'

'That's like your journey, darling. Open-ended.'

'Hasn't he asked you?'

'No.'

'But why not? He thinks the world of you, anyone can see that.'

'He's not the marrying kind, perhaps.'

'You ought to take the initiative, Mummy. "Make an honest woman of me or else!"'

'Or else what?'

'Or else you'll leave him.'

'Don't be silly, dear. I couldn't leave him. I love him.'

'Yes,' sighed Tammy. 'I hope some day I'll find someone I can love like that.' She kissed Gwen softly. 'I've got to get to bed, otherwise I'll be red-eyed as well as red-haired in the morning.'

'Sleep well, my precious. And all my love and good wishes go with you tomorrow.'

For a week or so after Tammy's departure, Gwen felt disorientated, bereft. Petie on the other hand was fine for the first two days but then, as it dawned on him Tammy was not going to be around again for a long time, he began to seem very unsure of life.

He refused to be driven to school unless Gwen promised to be there when he came back. He would run into the bungalow on coming home calling, 'Auntie Gwen? Are you there?' Sometimes at night she would wake to find him standing by her bed, wordlessly feeling for her hand. She would take him in beside her, stroking his hair and soothing him until he fell asleep.

When Dr Thinaburan came on his next regular visit to Sam, she asked him to look at the boy.

'He is quite well physically,' he told her, 'though rather thin, but that will improve. His trouble is that he is full of fear, poor child.'

'I understand that. He has reason enough . . .' She sat with her hands over her lips, holding back the words that would describe what Petie had been through. She knew by now that people didn't really want to hear your 'escape story'. 'What's the best way to help him?'

'Love him,' the doctor said with a kindly smile. 'That is the cure for so many things, dear Mrs Veetcha. Look at Mr Prosper: he has improved beyond all our expectations, and it is not through medicines, but because he is loved.'

Gwen was taken aback. She'd never heard an English doctor speak in these emotional terms. But the Sinhalese were different – open about their feelings, whether joy or sorrow.

'You really think Mr Prosper is doing well?'

'Certainly. Perhaps he will take a year or two to be fully himself again but he is well – well enough to enjoy life.'

'Then, I wonder . . .'

'What, dear lady?'

She wanted to ask if 'enjoying life' included physical passion. She tried to phrase the question. But her inhibitions, her upbringing, prevented the simple question – can Sam and I go to bed together? Besides, her own misery over the loss of her daughter and her anxiety over Petie overpowered her for the present.

She kept it hidden from Sam. She took to going for drives by herself in the trusty Austin, out along the shore road to watch the Tamils fishing in the shallows, their nets making butterfly wings over the water. She bought some wood samples in a timber yard, ran her fingers along the grain, sat with them on the arm of her chair under the flamboyant trees. She drew lines on paper, then screwed up the paper and threw it away.

One afternoon she came home from a stroll. Petie would be home soon. A storm was building up, the clouds like a grey silk sari shot with coral and beige and tangerine, the sea like pewter over which there lay a gleam of gold.

From the bungalow came the beat of music. 'I hate to see that evening sun go down . . . 'Cos my baby, he done left this town.'

'St Louis' Blues'. She picked up her step and went quickly up the verandah and through the french windows.

Sam was beating time to the record on the turntable. He caught her up with an arm around her and began to do a slow foxtrot round the sofas and the coffee table.

'What's all this?' Gwen laughed.

'I found a shop in the Tamil quarter that sells secondhand records. Isn't that marvellous? That's Duke Ellington's band. "Feelin' tomorrow, jus' like I feel today . . ."' he sang.

She swayed to the rhythm. It was wonderful to have Sam's arms around her. This was the comfort she needed but had never asked for because he must have no extra burdens – he had to concentrate on getting fit and whole again. He held her loosely, but she felt his arm across her back, she could smell the tang of the soap he used.

She thought, Maybe it would be all right, just to steal a kiss. She looked up at him, lips parted, smiling, inviting. He looked down at her and something tensed in him.

The car drove up and came to a halt outside. Petie came running in. 'Auntie Gwen? Auntie Gwen?'

'I'm here, darling.'

He rushed into the living-room holding out a painting on a sheet of card. 'Look, I did a pitcher of you! Look, you can tell it's you, it's got the right hair! Do you like it, Auntie Gwen?'

'It's marvellous. Isn't it, Sam?'

'Just like you,' Sam said, grinning at the matchstick figure with a mop of reddish-brown hair. 'You need a haircut, though.'

Petie raised his head to listen to the music. 'What's that funny noise?'

'Funny noise? Funny noise? When you say that, stranger, smile!' warned Sam, pretending to shoot Petie with his thumb and forefinger.

'Is this the beginning of a new jazz collection?' Gwen asked.

'Could be, could be. The guy in the shop said he might have some by Muddy Waters. I'm going back in a couple of days. So . . . Where've you been all day? Taking tea in the Palm Court? Ordering new dresses?'

'I went for a walk around the timber yards,' she said.

'Gee! You certainly know how to enjoy yourself.'

'Petie, Cook's bringing you milk and biscuits—'

'Could we have a puppy?' Petie asked. 'There was nice puppies in that place by the river, where Tammy helped me make a leash . . .' He stopped, startled by the fact that he'd said the name. His mouth trembled. It was the first time he'd spoken of Tammy since she went away, and the first time he'd voluntarily recalled memories of their escape.

Was it a good sign? Gwen didn't know. She looked with uncertainty at Sam.

'Sure you can have a puppy,' Sam said, stooping to put a hand on the little boy's shoulder. 'We'll ask around for anyone who's got one for sale.'

'Tomorrow?' Petie asked, brightening. 'After school?'

'Not tomorrow, I've got a business appointment tomorrow. We'll go puppy-hunting on Saturday.'

'Promise?'

'I promise.'

When he had gone to get his snack, Sam said, 'It just takes time, I suppose.'

'Yes.'

'You too. You won't miss her so much by and by.'

'I'll feel better once I get a letter from her.'

'That reminds me – there was a phone call.'

'From Tammy?' she said in astonishment. There hadn't been time yet for her daughter to reach Delhi.

'No, no – sorry, I mean an ordinary phone call. Some guy in the Social Services Department wants to talk to you.'

'Did you take a number?'

'Yes, but they'll all have gone home by now. Anyhow, he said if he didn't hear from you, he'd take it as a favour if you'd drop in tomorrow, any time between two and three. A Mr Croyde.'

'What's it about?'

'Search me.'

'I'd better go and see Petie's drinking his milk.'

'A puppy, huh? There's a blues called "Hound-Dog Blues",' Sam said with a grin, and turned his record to play the other side. Smiling to herself, and somehow greatly cheered by his good spirits, she went her way.

Next day she confirmed the appointment with a secretary in the Social Services Department. She had little tasks to occupy her until after lunch. She was prompt at the office in Silversmith Street and was shown into Mr Croyde's room without delay.

He proved to be a middle-aged man in the usual white ducks, with a beard and moustache that seemed to take him back to a previous era.

'Mrs Veetcha, glad to meet you,' he said, holding out his hand across his desk. 'Tea? Coffee?'

'No, thank you, I'm fine. What is this about, Mr Croyde?'

'Well, it's about the little boy.'

'Petie?'

'Petie. We've got him registered as Petie Veetcha, but in fact that is not his name, is it?'

'No, we don't know his last name. I explained that when we applied for identity papers.'

'Yes, I understand his mother was killed in Singapore and his father is listed as missing.'

'Yes.'

'And you have undertaken to care for him.'

'Yes.'

'We have some other children in Colombo from refugee ships. The usual thing is to foster them out to citizens of Colombo or find them a place in a children's home.'

'Petie doesn't want to go into a children's home,' Gwen said quickly. 'He's happy with me.'

Mr Croyde picked up a pen, which he proceeded to balance on his forefinger. 'The question is, is it best for him to be with you?'

She sat up straight. 'Best? What do you mean, best? He's happy, he's with people he knows and loves.'

'But we have to consider the boy's moral welfare—'

Gwen was startled. 'What on earth does that mean?'

'Well, Mrs Veetcha,' Mr Croyde replied, colouring a little, 'it's been brought to the attention of this department that you are living with a man called Samuel Prosper, an American citizen, and that you and he are not married.'

'That's quite true. We're not married. What business is it of yours?'

'Anything to do with the welfare of children is our business, Mrs Veetcha. And by the way, I'm right in thinking that in fact your name is not Veetcha, but Hayakawa?'

Oh, thought Gwen with a groan, they're not going to hold that against me after all . . . ? 'Yes, my name is Hayakawa. My husband was Japanese. He died twenty years ago. I use the name Veetcha for business reasons.'

'Business reasons? You're in business?'

'Not at present, but I'm thinking of starting again. I design furniture.'

Croyde looked at her as if he thought she'd gone out

of her mind. 'Mrs Hayakawa, if you start up in business in Colombo that of course is your own affair, though I can't see the point of it myself. But the little boy Petie is my concern, and I must tell you that the department cannot allow him to remain in a household where . . . where . . . you are living with a man who isn't your husband.'

Gwen stood up. 'If you imagine we've been living in sin you can just think again. Sam Prosper is still recovering from the wounds he received helping us – my daughter and Petie and me – to escape from Singapore. And my daughter has been a member of the household.'

'My information is that your daughter has now left Colombo.'

'Is that all you find to do? Snoop on people's private affairs?'

'Mrs Hayakawa, I'll let that pass because I can see you are upset. The departure of your teenage daughter now leaves us with a situation where you're under the same roof with a man who is not your husband.'

'All right, I'll move out and take Petie with me.'

'Forgive me for being frank, but there are better homes for an orphan child than with a single woman who seems to have no reliable income. We couldn't allow you to keep Petie under those circumstances.'

'Surely if Petie would be happy with me, that's all that matters?' Gwen cried.

'Petie's happiness is of course important. But we have to take notice of the fact that if he stays with you and you stay with Mr Prosper, that is not a moral situation.'

'Good God, is that all you have to bother about?' Gwen's voice was loud and angry. 'People are being killed and maimed all over the world and all you can think about is whether Sam and I are lovers? It's bureaucracy gone mad!'

She stamped out, past the startled secretary. She threw herself into the car and drove home in a temper.

594

Luckily traffic was light. She jammed on the brakes outside the bungalow, calling to Miran to put the car away.

In the sitting-room Sam was just about to have afternoon tea.

'Fools!' stormed Gwen, throwing her hat and gloves on to a table. 'Utter imbeciles!'

Sam leaned back in his chair. 'I heard that red-headed women had fiery tempers,' he observed.

'Oh, shut up, Sam!'

'Do you want to tell me about it?'

'That fool,' she raged, 'that nincompoop . . .' And out it all spilled. 'Bureaucratic idiots, all they can think about is the letter of the law! Blinkered minds, that's what they've got. Don't they understand we're all the family Petie has now?'

'Right,' said Sam. He got up, put his arms round her, and patted her back. 'Calm down, honey.'

'But he made me so *angry*—'

'Gwen, stop wasting energy on him. Come on now, calm down.'

She drooped against him, her head on his shoulder. 'I could have hit him, Sam.'

'That would have been a relief to you, but no help to Petie.'

'I'm not going to let them take Petie!'

'No, darling, of course not.' They stood together under the slow turn of the ceiling fan, locked in each other's arms.

'There's a simple solution.'

'What?'

'Let's get married.'

She leaned back to look up into his eyes. 'Sam?'

'What do you say?'

'Yes,' she said simply.

He kissed her, a long kiss that grew longer and longer until at last her head began to spin. She dragged herself away enough to aim a mock punch at his chin with her knuckles.

'So, all of a sudden, you want to get married?' she asked.

'I've wanted to for a long time. Only I thought I was going to be a semi-invalid for the rest of my life. Couldn't wish that on you.'

'Oh, you fool,' she whispered.

He frowned at her. 'So you say. But a guy doesn't like to be a burden to somebody he loves.'

'You'd never be a burden to me, darling. Never.'

'Seems not, the way things are going. The doc gives me hopes of a more or less normal life.'

'He said that to me too.'

'I've been feeling pretty good this last two or three weeks. Sorted out a few business contacts, thought up a few ideas.'

'Yesterday, you were out walking around the markets – you bought that record . . .'

'Yup, covered about two miles. I'm not saying I can make business trips the way I used to, but I can still wheel and deal from an office.'

'That's wonderful! Oh, I remember now, you mentioned a business appointment, I should have noticed.'

'You had enough to think about,' he soothed. 'And now you know, so it's all come together, hasn't it? Sorts out this problem over Petie.'

'They will let us keep him, won't they?' she asked, touched by a faint doubt.

'Let 'em try to take him away from us,' he said, looking fierce. 'I'll call in the United States Marines!'

They applied for a special licence next day. The day after was Saturday. Petie woke in a fever of excitement over the idea of looking for a puppy. Good advice from James Lovatt brought them to a Tamil family with what seemed like a whole tribe of tubby, yellowish dogs with wavy tails.

'That one,' said Petie, running after a lively little fellow with a white spot. 'Please, that one!'

In the end the puppy stopped cavorting by himself

and came to sniff Petie's hand. 'He wants to be my friend,' Petie claimed. 'His name's Spot.' The puppy seemed to agree. He went amicably home in the car with Petie and the syce.

'Don't let him chew my slippers!' Sam called after them as they drove off.

The next stop was a jeweller's to choose a wedding ring. Gwen had always worn the simple jade band that Tama had given her but now she took it off. As she wrapped it in a handkerchief and put it in her handbag, she knew that this was another part of her life that was over. When she said the word 'husband' now, she would mean Sam, not Tama.

Sam bought her a plain broad golden band. She thought, This is the gleam of gold I'll have with me for the rest of my life.

They were married three days later. Petie was given the day off school to attend the wedding. He had very little idea what was actually going on and didn't care for the white jacket and trousers he was made to wear, but he was pleased about the holiday.

He was the only person present who knew them. The witnesses were two clerks from the registrar's office. Gwen couldn't help thinking how her mother would grieve when she learned that once more her only daughter had been through a workaday ceremony in a government office. No bridal dress, no confetti, no orange blossom.

Ordinary, businesslike . . . So it appeared. But Gwen felt like a bride in a cloud of tulle – eager, happy, triumphant. Her heart was beating hard under her cool blue dress, her eyes were shining as Sam slipped the ring over her finger. Now she belonged to him, as he belonged to her.

But that had been so for a long time now. This was only the outward show. The true marriage had been in their hearts that evening in Padang when he had been about to leave her to capture the yacht. He had said it then: I love you Gwen, I always have. And she had said: I'm your girl.

'Where are we going now?' Petie asked in the car as Sam drove away from the registrar's office.

'To have a celebration, chicken.'

'What's a celebration?'

'It's where you have a great time and feel good.'

'Am I having a celebration too?'

'You sure are.'

'Can I have it at the cricket ground? John and Peter Lovatt are there watching their daddy playing cricket. Can I go there for my celebration?'

'Cricket?' groaned Sam. As an American, he could never understand cricket.

However, he delivered Petie at the club grounds, where the child was taken in charge by the Lovatts. 'I've got a dog,' Petie told the elder Lovatt boy importantly, 'his name's Spot, you can come and see him after if you want to.'

'We'll see he gets home after the match,' Mrs Lovatt said. 'And by the way' – her lively eye had spotted Gwen's new wedding ring – 'I gather congratulations are in order.'

Gwen smiled. Sam shrugged and nodded. He was not about to enter into a conversation on the topic.

He led Gwen out to where the car was parked in the shade of a group of palms. He handed her in, got in at the wheel, and stared through the windscreen.

'Right,' he said. '"Alone at last". Let's go home and go to bed.'

'Sam!'

'Well, can you think of a better celebration?'

'But – wait – are you sure you're well enough, darling?'

He turned to her with a smile that made her bones melt.

'Let's go home and find out,' he said.

TESSA BARCLAY

THE FINAL PATTERN

'Tessa Barclay always spins a fine yarn . . .
gripping and entertaining'
Wendy Craig

Jenny Armstrong, mistress of the thriving Corvill and Son
weaving business, returns to her native Scotland
determined to achieve prosperity and comfort for her
reunited family. But the death of her brother Ned brings
disruption and harm . . .

Once again young Heather Armstrong is caught up in her
widowed Aunt Lucy's machinations; Jenny's rekindled love
affair with her husband Ronald is threatened and
strangers lurk in doorways to spy on the Armstrongs and
their friends. Jenny uncovers a terrible secret in Lucy's past
that still demands vengeance, and there is an unknown
enemy to be reckoned with . . .

THE FINAL PATTERN is the compelling sequel to
A WEB OF DREAMS and BROKEN THREADS –
'Just what a historical novel should be' Elizabeth Longford
'Filled with fascinating historical detail and teeming with
human passions' Marie Joseph
– also available from Headline.

FICTION/SAGA   0 7472 3542 2

More Compelling Fiction from Headline:

TESSA BARCLAY

BROKEN THREADS

'Filled with fascinating
historical detail and
teeming with human
passions' Marie Joseph

Jenny Corvill, mistress of the Waterside Mill in Galashiels
and driving force behind the prosperous weaving concern
of Corvill & Son, is determined to relinquish the reins of
the business to her new husband and enjoy life as a young
bride. But no sooner is the honeymoon over than her plans
are disrupted – and by her own sister-in-law, Lucy.

For the pretty and frivolous Lucy the delights of life in the
Scottish Borders are severely limited and she leaps at the
chance to set up a second home in fashionable London.
Seduced by a smooth-talking playboy and headstrong
under the spell of love she plunges the Corvill family into
disaster. As a result Jenny is forced to undertake a
heartrending journey into the dens of the Victorian
underworld.

'Just what a historical novel ought to be' Elizabeth
Longford

'Tessa Barclay always spins a fine yarn. Her novels are
gripping and entertaining' Wendy Craig

From the bestselling author of the Craigallan and
Champagne series, BROKEN THREADS is a charming and
engrossing companion to A WEB OF DREAMS – also
available from Headline.

FICTION/SAGA   0 7472 3554 6

A selection of bestsellers from Headline

FICTION

DANCING ON THE RAINBOW	Frances Brown	£4.99 □
NEVER PICK UP HITCH-HIKERS!	Ellis Peters	£4.50 □
THE WOMEN'S CLUB	Margaret Bard	£5.99 □
A WOMAN SCORNED	M. R. O'Donnell	£4.99 □
THE FALL OF HYPERION	Dan Simmons	£5.99 □
SIRO	David Ignatius	£4.99 □
DARKNESS, TELL US	Richard Laymon	£4.99 □
THE BOTTOM LINE	John Harman	£5.99 □

NON-FICTION

ROD STEWART	Tim Ewbank & Stafford Hildred	£4.99 □
JOHN MAJOR	Bruce Anderson	£6.99 □
WHITE HEAT	Marco Pierre White	£5.99 □

SCIENCE FICTION AND FANTASY

LENS OF THE WORLD	R. A. MacAvoy	£4.50 □
DREAM FINDER	Roger Taylor	£5.99 □
VENGEANCE FOR A LONELY MAN	Simon R. Green	£4.50 □

All Headline books are available at your local bookshop or newsagent, or can be ordered direct from the publisher. Just tick the titles you want and fill in the form below. Prices and availability subject to change without notice.

Headline Book Publishing PLC, Cash Sales Department, PO Box 11, Falmouth, Cornwall, TR10 9EN, England.

Please enclose a cheque or postal order to the value of the cover price and allow the following for postage and packing:
UK & BFPO: £1.00 for the first book, 50p for the second book and 30p for each additional book ordered up to a maximum charge of £3.00.
OVERSEAS & EIRE: £2.00 for the first book, £1.00 for the second book and 50p for each additional book.

Name ....

Address ....

....

....